I0593377

THE KING MUST FALL

A GRIMDARK MAGAZINE ANTHOLOGY

edited by

ADRIAN COLLINS
MIKE MYERS
& SARAH CHORN

GdM

For Bradley P. Beaulieu, who trusted us to turn his idea into a book.

For the Grimdark Magazine *team past and present, whose efforts over the last eight years have built this tiny publishing house.*

For the authors, who created so many amazing stories to bring this theme to life.

For the grimdark and dark fantasy community who backed this project.

For Andy, who I wish I could publish just one more time.

For Fiona.

CONTENTS

Grimdark Magazine has chosen to maintain the authors'
original languages (eg. Australian English, American English,
Canadian English, UK English) for each story.

THAT SHOULD BE ME UP THERE

RICHARD K. MORGAN

Running things, says hapless mob boss Johnny Caspar, in the Coen brothers' magisterial black comic gangster movie *Miller's Crossing.* Caspar looks small and squashed behind his desk as he says the words, and his expression is all doubt and dyspeptic misery. He's in too deep. Truth is, he never really wanted to be *running things,* he's not much good at it, and - no real spoiler - he won't be doing it very much longer. Rarely in fiction has a king looked so ill at ease on his throne. Rarely has a fall from power come so clearly foretold. Despite his mafioso excesses, you can't help feeling sorry for the guy.

What goes for Prohibition-era America is just as true for any other context, real or imagined. Kings or Queens, Capos or Captains, it's an eternal human truth that *someone* has to run things, and just as eternally true that someone *else* will think the incumbent isn't up to the job. *That, they will say, should be me up there.* Roll these two human verities together like antique ivory dice—like soothsayer's rune-bones whose origins it's better not to know—and watch as the combinations come up. Brutality and betrayal, death and departure, the endless struggle for power or revenge. Gaius of the Julii, called Caesar; Mac Bethad mac Findlaich; His Highness Oliver Cromwell; Vladimir Ilyich Ulyanov. The bloody outcomes of the game stalk the corridors of our history, haunt our myths and legends, stretch back into prehistory and beyond. Right now, back on the African Savannah where we first rose to power, that self-same psychodrama is still playing out in some mangy baboon troupe who, at least, have the excuse that they don't yet know any better.

We don't have that excuse. We *do* know better. But we just can't seem to help ourselves. It's who we are. It's who we have been since time immemorial; it's in our gene code, it's in our blood, and the blood we spill, time and time again.

No wonder we cleave to these tales so hard.

Truth is, as you'll see in the stories that follow, there are a whole lot of reasons to bring down a king, some of them good, some not so much. Maybe it's a family affair - a scuffle between rival brothers as in Luke Scull's *The Dark Son*, or murdered kin too numerous to count, as in Matt Ward's *The Varcolac*. Maybe, like a number of the rulers you'll encounter in these pages, the King has too much blood on his hands, has inflicted too much wholesale slaughter and misery, as Kings are wont to do, and you simply want him gone. Or maybe, as in Deborah A. Wolf's myth-inflected *On Wings Of Music*, the wrong you were done is something far more intricate and intimate and arcane.

Or maybe there is no actual wrong at all. Just a wrong time, wrong place, and Fate—these three old women who met you on the road, planted the seed in your mind, and then stood back to see what you'd do.

Whatever the impulse, whatever the rationale, whatever the path, you'll do what you think is best—for you at any rate, maybe for others too—and then, when you're in deep and bloodied, and with no way back, you'll doubtless tell yourself you had no choice. If the King must fall, then it follows that someone—or something!—must bring him down. Like the implacable workings of vengeance in Adrian Tchaikovsky's *The Face of the King*, the tale must be told, the mechanism set in motion, the coded pattern enacted. To each their allocated role, to the sticking place the courage or desperation each will need, and to the victor the spoils. Only don't be surprised if those spoils turn out less than wholly satisfactory when all is done. For in this grim collection of tales—no real spoiler here either—the reward for regicide is rarely sweet.

In fact, when the crunch comes, not all the Kings in this volume will even be obliging enough to Fall. Assassins can miss their mark, conspirators can misunderstand the stakes, thrones can be prisons after all. Contrary to what Disney likes to tell us, there are no Rightful Rulers, no Lion Kings—only operators and opportunists and the sharp-toothed mammalian intrigue between. *Running things* turns out to be a bit of a zero-sum game, and what you gain in friends and grateful subjects on one side, you'll inevitably lose in support somewhere else. Everyone makes mistakes, but the mistakes of a King affect thousands of lives, and even what look like *good* choices from a seat on the throne can make you enemies in the thousands too. A good king minimises that shit, a bad one, whether through lack of acumen or interest or maybe just manoeuvring room, lets it slide.

The rest is luck and timing. And one way or another, blood will follow.

So we take our seats and the age-old drama kicks in. Maybe we want this particular King to fall, or maybe we'd quite like him to repel all boarders and hang onto his throne after all. (Because, make no mistake, regardless of how bad, or merely bad at the job, they are, some of these guys can be charming as fuck.) Maybe the fall is deserved, maybe not, and maybe, just maybe—as drunken killer William Munny tells the toppled sheriff in the western *Unforgiven*—*deserve's got nothing to do with it.*

It doesn't matter.

We're in deep now, captivated by the same primal rhythms we've carried with us since our African Savannah days. Perhaps we'll learn something here, something true. Failing that, we can still bear witness. That, and thrill to the precarious high wire performance of loss and gain, the clash of steel and cries of battle, the gut-swooping horror of the cost.

Hush now—the curtain rises. The stage is set. Settle back in your seat, sink into the grim, dark, free-fall brutality and human desperation of it all.

And thank whatever gods you own that this story isn't yours.

Richard K Morgan
Riven Kingdom of Brexit
October 2021

WHAT YOU WISH FOR

DEVIN MADSON

The king stood before the window, shoulder to the glass. Through the throne room's dusty panes, the city was all crumbling walls crisscrossing blackened buildings, each one filthy and scorched. Fires were unusual in Vircena, the daily heat quite enough to contend with, but today, it seemed, was not a normal day. From his vantage point, the king already counted ten separate blazes—each a pool of rage amid the clustered crowd.

An explosion shook the floor, setting the glass plates rattling in their frames. The king pressed his hand to the nearest pane's smooth surface, steadying it, but the rest went on rattling, mocking him. In a few hours, the sun would set leaving the fires to brighten the usually lightless night.

Eleven blazes now. They seemed to spread every time he blinked, leaping up all over the city, not just outside the palace walls where the people stood thickest. Where the shouting rose, visceral and raw.

Thumps reverberated through the floor, giving the cloudy old marble a heartbeat that lived in time with the king's pulse, like he stood within the bleached and withered remains of his own chest. Thump. Thump. Thump. But the sound wasn't life, wasn't reassuring. Anger never was.

The king sighed. His head ached and it really was too hot for insurgence.

Footsteps approached, soft and wary. Without looking around, the king said, "I'm too tired for this, Doraan."

"Aren't we all, Your Majesty. It's been a long few years."

His old friend joined him at the window, a stale waft of sweat and oil hanging about him. For a long time, he didn't say anything, just stood looking, as the king did, upon the mass of people in the square. They seemed to heave and swell like the stormiest sea, crashing against the walls in a determined and inevitable effort of destruction.

"Who is it this time?" the king said. "Cassen? Rosel?"

"We aren't entirely sure, Your Majesty, flags of both have been spotted in the crowd. Sharbelle, too."

"The woman whose followers set themselves alight outside the gates last month?"

"Yes, Your Majesty."

The king looked back at the seething crowd, twisting his ring around and around his finger. A mark of his responsibility, a responsibility that felt impossibly heavy on such days. If only people would listen. If only they would think. "Fools!" he snapped. "Damned fools, the lot of them."

"By all accounts, Sharbelle is a scientist of the old school and is very well regarded."

"That doesn't stop her being a damned fool. All the more shameful that she leads them astray when she ought to know better. That bastard Rosel, too."

"They're fighting for their freedom, Majesty."

The king laughed, waving his hand in the direction of the chaos. "Freedom? Bah! This *is* freedom."

His long-time friend turned a reproachful gaze on him. Even out of the corner of his vision, Doraan was insufferable. Of course, Doraan knew. He'd always known, but there was knowing and there was speaking—manifesting implacable truth with their words.

In the hollow silence, the king kept twisting his ring around his finger. The action saved him from breaking away to pace about the room, displaying the fear he should keep close. Confident. Proud. Upright and sure and dependable to the end—that was a king's most important role. To maintain the people's confidence in their ruler's protection at all costs. To give them no reason to doubt. To worry. To want freedom. They were the lessons, the laws his father had instilled in him—in them both—at a young age.

"What is freedom?" the king huffed.

Chancellor Doraan glanced down at the king's hands, speeding in their simple act of distraction. "Freedom for them or for us?" he said, before turning back to the window. "Sometimes the things that work for a long time stop working. Keep an animal in a cage long enough and they will eventually see the bars."

"Very philosophical. Maybe you should be wearing this instead." The king lifted his crown and held it out—a bitter show because not even the most ambitious of men would take it now. Doraan flinched, but the theatrical moment had been worth it to be free of the crown's weight. Free from the way it seemed to tighten around his skull more and more each day, refusing to let him forget it was there. The weight. The restriction. The endless responsibility he couldn't escape, the bars around his life, the same bars that trapped the people outside, if only they could see it.

"Fools!" he spat again, spinning away from the window to seethe at the emptiness around him. Long ago the throne room of Vircena had been a fine space, hung with decorative silks and gems and the rich spoils of conquest. Now the king only had history's word for it, ghosts of grandeur surrounding him and choking the city with false hopes. What a time that must have been, when Vircena had been the centre of the world.

The city had been dead for a long time.

"Selfish, selfish shits," he said, the twisting of his ring no longer keeping him from pacing. His bare feet made hollow thuds upon the floor. "They should be happy with what they have. Happy they are alive. Happy they have food and shelter. All this ridiculous shouting and setting buildings on fire only makes things worse for them."

"Rosel has been preaching the histories. Is it any surprise they want more? Want their freedom and glory back?"

"I thought we put a stop to that?"

"We raided his known meeting places and arrested and hung a number of conspirators, but without catching Rosel himself there's only so much we can do to dissuade him." Doraan cleared his throat. "And … there are members of the leading council who have voiced fears that the move was unwise."

"Unwise?" The king halted his pacing to glare at Doraan. "They think it best to just let them go on spreading dangerous ideas? Who said so? It was Elder Loren, wasn't it? We will never live down my father's folly in raising a dangerous renegade to the council."

"Not Loren. At least, he wasn't first though I understand he agrees. It was Elder Rootherta."

"May the gods save us." The king pressed his hands together a moment in prayer before demanding, "What did she expect me to do instead?"

"I'm unsure, Your Majesty. I don't think she's claiming to have had a better plan, merely that cracking down so hard on Rosel's followers only encourages them. They see themselves as martyrs to a noble cause. They say they're just learning their history."

The king touched a hand to his forehead. His headache had grown worse, and by the way things were going, the day was unlikely to improve. "And leaving such dangerous dissent to fester discourages them?"

Expecting no answer, he strode back to the windows. More fires had sprung up, smoke rising to touch the barrier. Most was drifting through it, into the Unseen Sky, but some got trapped against the thin film of magic and hung overhead like a fluffy blanket. It gathered in swirls at the vertex, where the crackling column of magic hit the reflective silver disc that spread the barrier over the city. Up there it blended in, both smoke and magic a gloomy grey, misty and opaque, but the barrier thinned as it spread toward the ground, grey becoming pale white and, where it met the ground, an opalescent sheen through which distant fields of bright red poppies danced in the breeze.

The king touched the poppies embroidered onto his sash, all had faded, their loose threads unravelling.

He squeezed his eyes shut and stood listening to the distant roar of the crowd, trying to imagine it was no more than the battering of a strong wind or the rush of the river that, back in his youth, had filled every winter.

"We'll get through this," Chancellor Doraan said, touching the king's shoulder. "There's always a way."

"I wish I had your optimism. Necessity is not the same as possibility."

An authoritative knock sounded upon the doorframe and the king turned. Captain Carcrista bowed, her expression grim, or rather grimmer than usual. The captain of the palace guard rarely had reason to smile. "Your Majesty."

"Spit it out, Captain," the king said, his heart sinking. The noises from outside pecked at him like hungry birds. "What is it?"

"The mob has breached the outer gate."

Chancellor Doraan paled. "What? How?"

"They seem to have used some sort of acid, Chancellor, but we're still trying to find out more. Although right now *how* is less important than what's next. If they breach the inner gate as well, we won't be able to hold them back." She drew a deep breath and let it go in a huff. "Permission to send out the chargers, Your Majesty."

"The chargers?" The chancellor shook his head. "With people crammed so tightly into the square, there are sure to be many causalities."

"Necessity is not the same as possibility," the king repeated, setting his aching forehead to the cool window. "If we want to end this before it ends us, we have to create the possibility, not expect it to fall in our laps at the last minute." He turned to the captain. "Do it, Captain. Send out the chargers."

Rosel leaned against the bricks, his shoulder scraping loose dark flakes of dust. "Still no sign of Tak?"

"The bastard probably ran off," Sharbelle said, picking grit from between her teeth. "He never did like a fight."

Cassen looked up from his place crouched near the edge of the balcony overlooking the square. "All of you are talky-talk and no action. Pompous twats."

Sharbelle's look could have cut glass. "If you don't think you need us, then by all means, go slam your head against those gates and see how far you get on your own."

"A damn sight farther than you'd get without me."

Cracking his fingers one at a time, Rosel watched them argue. He disliked both of them, but at least Sharbelle was bright and Cassen was honest. Tak was a self-important jerk he'd rather not have to talk to let alone be associated with. It pissed him off to no end that he had to worry the man wasn't going to show up.

From the balcony, the gathered crowd in the square was more seething mass than individuals, all noise and movement and *life*. It filled the space between the inner and outer walls of the old palace, while still more pushed through the broken gates. One of Sharbelle's great ideas, the acid. If the king played the right cards, they'd get a chance to try out another of her plans.

"If we have to wait much longer, we going to lose the crowd," Cassen said, rising to stalk the length of the balcony and back. "I want to be right at the front. I want to be able to tell my children and my grandchildren about the look on the old king's face when he finally realised power lies in numbers not dented old crowns."

"You'll get your chance," Rosel said, trying to hide his fidgeting. He was the wise one, the historian, but there was something intoxicating about so huge a movement of humanity that made him itch to be down there. He cursed Tak anew for keeping them waiting.

"We have to wait for the chargers anyway." Sharbelle's words were matter-of-fact, no glimmer of excitement in her eyes, and Rosel tried to conceal his quickening heartbeat.

"Chargers?" Cassen said. "Too risky. They could kill hundreds, no *thousands*, with those, and even our bloody-handed king won't do that. He knows he's lost."

"Too much risk for a man who killed his own daughter?"

Cassen sneered, and Rosel wished Tak would hurry the fuck up. "You still think the king is some wicked mastermind making blood sacrifices to the gods," Cassen jeered, all but spitting in Sharbelle's stony face. "We'd have not gotten this far if that were true. He's not evil, he's just a coward."

"Then where's Princess Grace?" Sharbelle said.

Cassen shrugged one scar-rippled shoulder. "I don't care. She might be dead, but there's no reason for him to have killed her, and no," he added as Sharbelle parted her lips to retort, "don't give me any of that conspiracy blood magic bullshit. I don't want to hear it."

"Says the man standing beneath a magical barrier and fighting to have it taken down," Sharbelle murmured. Her tone was always so superior. It annoyed Rosel, even when he agreed with her.

"That's totally—"

"All right, that's enough!" Rosel stepped between them. "There's a pattern, Cassen, as you would know if you paid attention. Princess Grace wasn't the first member of the royal family to go missing. No body, no grave, nothing, just a piss-weak announcement and they all moved on with their lives like she'd never existed. He might not have killed her, but if you don't think that's suspicious, you're even denser than Tak."

"Who's denser than me?"

"Fucking finally," Rosel said, eying Tak's double layer of armour. A chest plate from the First Era; mail from the Fourth. Both were well-preserved, but he looked ridiculous and Rosel doubted the arsehole would be able to manage more than a few swings in it.

Rosel swallowed his disdain. Unity would only remain while there was respect, the great General Shuane had always said, and when there could be no true respect, only a false veneer of politeness could maintain alliances. Until allies were no longer needed and you could stab each other—politely—in the back.

Seeing Rosel's stare for something it wasn't, Tak grinned ear to ear like a mad man. "So, are we doing this?" he said. "Are we taking back our freedom?"

Cassen rolled his eyes. "No, we're just here having a picnic. What does it look like? Where's Vorn?"

Tak's grin twitched. "He was disappeared last night. The townies said he shouldn't have been walking so close to the barrier and that the *monsters* got him. Threatened me when I called them on their bullshit and demanded to see him." Tak laughed, high and manic. "Idiots might have chosen differently if they'd known what was coming, eh?"

"It's too bad we can't get a message to him," Sharbelle said. "Having someone we trust on the inside would be invaluable."

"Oh, we might not be able to get instructions to him," Tak said, "but you can be sure whatever prison cell they have him locked in, he'll—"

Loud cracks echoed across the crowded space between the inner and outer wall, stilling the sea of people. Before the old palace, the tall, rusting inner gates were moving, pushing people back. "They're opening the gates!" he shouted. "Ha! Didn't we tell you, Cassen? They're throwing everything at us."

"Well, I'll be damned," Cassen said. "We're fucked."

As the gates slowly opened, people surged forward only to fall back just as fast, before finding themselves trapped by the wall of people behind them. Screams erupted over their chanting.

"Chargers!" Tak gasped. "What the fuck? I thought those were all destroyed?"

Six chargers emerged through the gate, pressed so close together that their metal sides scraped and squealed over the screaming crowd. The chargers were built like battering rams, long enough to contain a dozen soldiers beneath their metal carapaces. At the front was a flat plate to hit structures and crush people who got in the way, while a line of portholes dotted each side.

Rosel had only ever seen pictures of the chargers. He'd only stood at the front of a room and described them to those curious about Vircena's history. While Sharbelle and Tak and Cassen shouted at one another, he watched in awe as the chargers fanned out, slowly speeding up as the soldiers running beneath the metal shells gained momentum—an insect with two dozen legs and as many arms. Not the arms of men, but arms of steel, blades that jutted from the portholes and spun as the charger rolled. It was, Rosel thought, a beautiful sight.

Panic gripped the crowd, the people in the front pushing and shoving to escape the chargers' blades. Though they spun slowly at first, the blades were sharp, and blood spat into the air as they slashed through the mob, crushing all who could not escape their path.

"You think I don't have a plan for this too?" Sharbelle snapped at the two big men. "Stop catastrophising and just listen!" She rolled her eyes. "Men! May I never have to work with another one again after this shit."

Tak glared at her. "You're the one being all dramatic and secretive."

"You could have just fucking said so," Cassen added.

Sharbelle folded her arms and waited for them to shut up. "You done?" she said when at last Cassen and Tak fell silent, Cassen grinding his teeth. "We've got devices ready to—"

"Who's we?" Cassen glared at Rosel. "Did you know about this?"

"I knew she had a plan for the chargers, but no details. This isn't on me."

Sharbelle snorted. "Trust you to distance yourself."

"Can we stop fucking arguing and get to the point?" Tak said, likely the wisest words to ever form on his tongue. "I didn't join you dicks to hang around at the back looking like a coward."

"Don't worry, you'll get your chance at glory." Sharbelle glared at each of them in turn. "Tak, your job is to draw the chargers' attention, so rally your people at the back of the crowd and make a lot of noise. You're good at that."

"Noise? That's—?"

"Meanwhile," Sharbelle went on, turning to Cassen. "Cassen, I need you and your Brutes to do what you're good at and cut my girls a path to the side of each charger. Doesn't matter where along the side, but it needs to be the side, not the front or the back."

"You want to go where all the pointy spinning bits of metal are, then?"

"That's the place."

Cassen shrugged. "Your funeral. What's Rosel doing?"

"What he always does—lighting the way."

"Seek the truth, find the road," Rosel said, pressing his fist to his heart.

"Seek the truth, find the road," the others repeated, amid the overwhelming noise of the screaming crowd. Rosel shivered with excitement. All his life he'd read about glorious battles and conquests, clever ruses and political backstabbing. Now he was going to be part of it. He was going to make history.

They climbed down from the rooftop, each going their own way. Tak hurried ahead despite the weight of his mismatched armour. The man had a manic energy Rosel always distrusted, but individually they'd been getting nowhere for years.

When Rosel dropped from the railing, he found Cris leaning against the wall, watching the slaughter. "They really did it, huh," she said, eyeing the scene as one might assess a work of art. "I saw Sharbelle bustling off. Does that mean we're ready to move?"

"That's the plan." Rosel wrapped his arms around her, drawing her close, his hammering heart pressed to hers. "We're finally going to end this. The girls will have a free life."

"And that's all we ever wanted," she replied, speaking into his shoulder. "No one needed to die for it, but I will tear apart anyone who stands in my way."

Rosel laughed and kissed the top of her head. "I knew there was a reason I married you, you blood-thirsty mama bear."

She pulled out of his hold and grinned up at him. "Part mama bear, part lion bringing kills back to my lazy husband who's been lying in the shade philosophising."

"Hey! I do things." Rosel hooked his arm through hers and together they strode toward the heaving crowd. People were still pressing in, others breaking free, the shouts and screams rising like a storm. With the smoke billowing overhead, all they lacked for a real storm was the bite of rain on skin and the hiss of it burning hair and cloth.

As they walked toward the palace, the crowd thickened, pressing in from all sides. There, Rosel took a deep breath and started to sing. It was an old song, one upon which the foundations of Vircena had been built. Its low notes thrummed like a heartbeat while its melody soared upon a tide of hope. Around them others joined in, faces turning to him like flowers to their sun, like disciples to a god, swelling Rosel's confidence as he pushed forward.

At the back of the crowd, Tak and his followers made their own noise, chanting and shouting as they thrust banners into the sky. They climbed on one another's shoulders and waved lit torches, drawing the chargers straight down the line. The man had done his part after all.

On, Rosel walked, Cris at his back. Catching his song, most people tried to make space for them. Some, however, just wanted to escape, screaming as the chargers rumbled by, cutting people down. The only people pushing toward the war machines were Cassen's Brutes, recognisable by their broad shoulders and closely shaved heads. They thrust their shoulders into every gap, levering them wide to forge a path. Those panicking and trying to escape were throwing others into the people behind them. Some fell, gargling and screaming as they disappeared beneath the heaving mass. When people pushed back, Brutes slammed fists into noses and jaws and temples—one even had a kitchen knife already covered in blood. A few more deaths wouldn't be noticed among so many people falling to the king's chargers, but it wasn't how Rosel would have done it. That was the value of having Cassen on your side.

"Watch out!" Cris yanked Rosel sideways as the crowd pushed them toward another Brute driving a path for one of Sharbelle's acolytes—a fierce woman with her hair and brows singed off. People fell around the mismatched pair, grasping at their arms and legs and clothing, only to be pulled under by the raging current of bodies.

Just beyond the spinning blades, the Brute halted, but Sharbelle's acolyte sped on, dropped to her knees, and slid beneath the charger's carapace, disappearing into the tangle of soldier's legs.

A shout. Thumps echoed. Rosel needed to keep moving but couldn't tear his gaze away from the scene. Momentum carried the charger on, jolting and stuttering, spitting insurgents, guards, and Sharbelle's acolyte out behind it.

Cris's grip tightened on Rosel's arm, and he held his breath. The charger was still moving, still ploughing into people and cutting them down—this wasn't the turn Sharbelle had promised.

A deep boom, more vibration than sound, rumbled beneath the panicking crowd. Smoke billowed from beneath the charger's carapace, and all nearby began coughing and gasping for breath. The charger slowed. Stuttered. A soldier dropped from beneath it, followed by another gripping his throat and gasping for breath. Nearby, another charger spewed smoke and started to slow.

"She did it!" Cris cried, but there was no time for celebration. Not yet.

The song had faded from Rosel's lips, but he began anew, louder and stronger, lifting each word to the crowd in a call for unity. People nearby surged to join him, while others tore the blades from the becalmed chargers and began to turn them around. They could break down the gates with the fool's own defences—a fitting end, Rosel thought as he strode on, one that would long be remembered.

They were so close. Soon there would be no more barrier. No more stories of false dangers, just freedom from their leader's tyranny.

Monsters, Rosel thought as the inner gates loomed. A poor bastardisation of *Lamonsor*, Vircena's oldest enemy, twisted into tales to keep the rabble in line. Monsters were always waiting around every corner to attack those who wandered too close to the barrier, who were out too late, alone at night, or who spoke out too loudly about the king's lies. Rosel had expected them to come for him many times for daring to preach Vircena's history.

"We never used to be prisoners," he would say, standing on a table and shouting his truth to the rafters. *"We were warriors. Now we're imprisoned, kept docile and afraid."*

Rosel gripped the hands of a dead woman missing both her legs and sang on as he hauled her out of the way, clearing the path to the gates. Seek the truth, find the road.

"We ruled an empire, but when we were defeated in battle our leaders didn't rally, they ran. King Lojan—" Here his students would always shout "Mad King Lojan!" Rosel smiled at the memory, even as he sorted through the dead and the dying, slipping and sliding on thick globs of blood.

"Help us clear the way!" Cris cried, but Rosel was floating now, soaring upon his song and his destiny. Each body shifted was another step closer to freedom, each note he sang was another assurance that he would be the one they all remembered—the man who'd used the past to save the future.

"We knew how to live then. How to fight then. They were our greatest years, and we ought to look back and learn from that wisdom, ought to—"

"Out of the way!"

With their blades dislodged and discarded, the chargers were speeding back toward the gates, cheered on by a crowd turned ferocious, caring nothing for the wounded and dead that lay crushed beneath their stamping feet. This was it. This was everything they had fought so long for. How sweet freedom would taste.

The first charger slammed into the gate, followed by another, the deep, reverberant clang of metal hitting metal a cry to war.

The palace seemed to shake around them. The king pressed his hand to the wall, as much in an attempt to steady the building—the world—as to steady himself. Beside him, Chancellor Doraan breathed out in a low hiss. "I …" Doraan cleared his throat. "I … I'm not sure … what we do now."

He'd been so calm back in the throne room, sure that this time, as with every other in their lifetime, the protections would prevail, the people would give up and peace would return, dissatisfaction sliding back beneath the surface to simmer on. But not this time.

"I have to talk to them," the king said.

"What?" Doraan turned, a tremor in his voice. "Ba—Your Majesty, you can't. They'll tear you apart."

"And if I don't? If we can't turn them back and they get through? Pull down the barrier?"

The chancellor blanched. Swallowed. Nodded. His hand trembled as he gripped the king's shoulder. "I could—"

"No, you know that wouldn't work. It's me they want. Me they hate. Perhaps if I can speak to one of the ringleaders, one on one, we might have a chance. Something I ought to have done a long time ago, perhaps. Now I go to Grace." The king touched his sash, picked at the threads pulling loose from its faded poppies. "At least that is a fitting end."

Chancellor Doraan's jaw opened and closed, but the king was glad he swallowed both his hopes and his fears—neither of any use now. Instead, Doraan pulled him close, and they held one another tightly, as they had the day their fathers died. Beneath them, the floor shuddered again. History was pressing in, insisting on change, the distant clamour and roar like an oncoming storm.

The king stepped back, sure that if he didn't go now, he never would. "Goodbye, old friend."

Doraan bowed. "Goodbye, Your Majesty."

Neither of them looked back.

The king shouted orders as he hurried through the palace—to his guards to make their final stand, to his council to exert what influence they could, and to his servants to run and hide and hope. It wasn't much, but making plans helped him not think about his destination.

Heavy doors blocked the way to the barrier chamber—a stone room set deep in the heart of the palace foundation, as though those who had built Vircena had known what was coming.

In a kingdom eternally scorched by the sun, the barrier chamber was the coldest place in the whole city. Each stone emanated its own chill. At the last door, the guard saluted but said nothing, his lips pressed tight as though to keep himself from asking for a truth he didn't want to hear.

The door creaked as the guard hauled it open for him, gaze averted from its interior. "Thank you for your service," the king said, and stepped in without looking back.

The barrier room was circular, built from banks of stone steps and benches leading down to a central dais, while overhead the roof curved up into a funnel. Like the room sat at the bottom of a well, weak light filtered down from a skylight high above. And there, sitting in the light upon the dais, was a young girl, her arms spread wide. Raw magic crackled around her, hissing and spitting as it tore toward the hole in the roof. And in the glow that fell around her, dozens of hazy red poppies seemed to sprout from the stones.

"Grace," the king whispered.

She didn't move, didn't seem to hear him, not even the echo of his steps bouncing around the roughhewn walls. Every step brought him closer to her until he could see each detail of her face, unchanged in the years since she'd stepped into the circle.

"It's all right, Papa. I'm not really going anywhere after all."

The king closed his eyes for a long moment, trying to hold in tears. He rarely came down here anymore. His wife had visited Grace every day while she'd been alive, but each moment with their daughter had been like a cut to her soul, slowly bleeding her dry. They had all sacrificed so much for the city's safety, but Grace more than anyone. She had given her life to protect the people who should have taken care of her.

"I'm sorry," he said, lowering himself onto the stones beside her with a groan of aching joints. "I should have done better, have been out there with my people instead of hiding."

No answer beyond the crackling of magic. Her expression didn't so much as flicker, though around her the poppies swayed in an absent breeze.

There on the dais the king sat and waited, hoping every distant sound was Doraan coming to tell him they'd turned back the tide. Minutes, hours, days—he couldn't tell how long he'd been there when at last the door opened. He spun and half rose to his feet, heart pounding, but it was not Doraan.

"Good afternoon, Your Majesty," Rosel said, limping slightly as he strode in, a woman splattered in blood walking at his side. "No doubt you were hoping for someone else. I'm afraid none of your council will be joining us."

"Ah, Rosel, I should have known. What did you do to them?" the king said, watching shadows shift in the hallway behind the man.

A small smile lightened Rosel's features, as more people poured into the room—shadowy figures spreading out along the wall. "I'm a kind man," Rosel said, starting down the steps. "So I won't answer that question."

Whispers hissed through the gathering audience as people pointed at Grace.

"I thought she was dead," one man said.

"By the looks of it, she may as well be." Rosel halted before the central dais, forcing the king to look up in order to meet his gaze. "What did you do to her?"

The king had known he would have to talk to these people eventually, yet the sharp, disrespectful question set up his hackles. "You will address me as Your—"

"The hell I will. Tell me what happened to her."

"She gave her life to maintain the barrier."

Soft jeers and laughter echoed around the room, but Rosel, at least, didn't sneer. "A high price for our captivity," he said. "I hope you feel it was worthwhile."

"Captivity? Is that how you see your safety."

"Safety? From what?"

Something in the man's faint smile made the king uneasy. "There are monsters beyond the barrier," he said, repeating the simple knowledge all children learned in their cradles. *Don't walk near the barrier or the monsters will get you!* "Without the barrier, we would all be dead."

The same soft laughter passed around their audience and the woman behind Rosel rolled her eyes. "Always the same old lies," she muttered.

"Lies? That's what you think them?"

"That's what they are," she snapped. "Lies and manipulation. There're no monsters. There never were any monsters. Your ancestors created the barrier because they were cowards, and they passed those lies and their power down from king to king while we suffered. Stagnated. Starved. Well, your time is over, old man. We've seen through you. We know the truth."

Murmurs of agreement circled them, and panic rose in the king's chest. How could he convince them? What could he say? The truth was simple—so simple every child knew it. The monsters had come and together the people and their leaders had hidden themselves away in safety, the barrier was all that stood between Vircena and destruction. Until now. Now that the very people they'd sought to protect had become their own worst enemies.

"Please," he said, looking Rosel in the eye. "You have to believe me. The monsters are real. I wish as much as you do that I could leave this city, that there were no dangers outside, that I could have my daughter back, but it's this life or none. Is that a decision you can make for everyone?"

Rosel paused, eyes narrowing.

"You are a historian?" the king pressed on. "A man of learning? Then you know about the battle of Lamonsor. You know about the final march. The little—"

"I know what your doctored history books say," Rosel said with biting superiority. "I know what you tried to hide from us all. I've seen your great grandfather's diaries—"

"My great grandfather wrote no diary! What nonsense is this?"

"Nonsense?" the woman with Rosel stepped forward. "You call the truth nonsense? Why are we standing here talking? Did we come this far, spill this much blood, to waste time on *him*?"

Him. Like he was the dirt beneath their feet, like his sacrifices were nothing. Worse than nothing. A conniving tyrant.

Hunger filled the agreement that whipped around the room. Behind him, Grace hadn't moved from her spot, couldn't, though he wished he could shout at her to run and save herself.

Rosel stepped forward. "You're very right, my dear," he said, his eyes bright. "It's time to end this once and for all."

He pulled a long blade from his belt and drove it into the king's stomach, yanking it out before the king even realised what had happened. Pain spread through his gut like cold fingers no matter how hard he pressed upon the wound. The room twisted and turned, the people around him blurring. Except for Grace. Never Grace.

♛

Rosel watched the king bleed out. His blood was the same colour as everyone else's, his body no different from the lumps of flesh that littered the palace square, yet it still felt strange to have killed a king.

In the centre of the dais, the young girl sat in the same pose she'd held since they'd entered, her eyes closed and her arms spread, palms flat, seeming to direct the magic crackling up and out through the distant hole in the roof. Princess Grace, not dead, but close enough.

Behind Rosel, Cris hissed, "Do it. Stop her. Open the way."

Seek the truth. Find the road. Freedom and truth were all the people of Vircena had wanted. All this death was the fault of those who had stood in the way.

Rosel reached out, warily, toward the princess. The barrier around the city was gaseous yet solid, constantly shifting and softening and swirling, but what emerged from Princess Grace was an electrical storm.

Rosel edged closer, reaching for the closest poppy as he'd once tried to reach through the barrier as a child, wanting to smell the flowers.

Sharp pain ripped through his fingers and up his arm and Rosel jerked back, cradling his hand. "Shit!" He looked around at his wife, only to find her scowling, hands on her hips. "I'm not sure how to get through," he said.

"No, you just don't want to," Cris said. "Look if you can't do it then I will." She stomped over to Cassen. "Give me that spear."

He shrugged and handed it over. Cris didn't so much as glance at Rosel as she strode up to the princess caught within her magic cage.

She was wrong. He did want this. He wasn't a coward, but the serenity of the princess's expression twisted his heart. His daughters looked like that while they slept. Thankfully, they were safe at home, away from all this.

"For freedom," Cris said and thrust the spear through the magic and into the young girl's neck. Giving it a vicious twist, she ripped it out again, the spear crackling and smoking.

Princess Grace's eyes flew open. Blood poured from her throat. Stiffly, she reached for the wound while around her, magic flickered and spat. Sparks flew, burning black spots onto stone and skin. Cris fell back, shrieking as she patted furiously at her clothes.

With a final angry hiss, the magic died leaving behind a silence that made Rosel's every breath as loud as Cris's cries. Upon the dais, Princess Grace crumpled. Her skin began to wrinkle, shallow lines deepening to thick creases around her eyes, her body shrivelling even as it grew to adulthood. The poppies around her winked out leaving only her splattered blood in their wake.

"The barrier," Rosel whispered and reached for Cris's hand. "Come on! I have to see it!"

Excitement shivered through Rosel's body, his heart racing as he sped up the stairs into the palace. Dead guards and rebels lay lined up along the floor and propped against walls, heads hanging lifeless—all necessary sacrifices to the cause he told himself to silence the flicker of guilt.

With Cris hard on his heels, Rosel took one flight of stairs after another, Sharbelle and Cassen shouting behind them. From the depths of the palace, he at last burst out onto the tallest wall, finally stopping as he hit the parapet, his fingers scraping upon the rough stones.

The light had changed. Where once it had been pale grey like the hazy barrier, it was now a deep, hot red, baking his skin like he'd stepped into an oven. The sun roiled angry overhead, seeming to spit at them with the same hate as Princess Grace's dying magic.

Cris gasped. "No," she whispered. "No, no, no. It can't be."

Sharbelle cried out and Cassen fell to his knees, both staring out beyond the city. Where once there had been fields of dancing poppies there were now rocky crags and dry riverbeds, swirling clouds of red dust, and the hollowed-out husks of dead trees. And, approaching cautiously, a loose gathering of twisted creatures all claws and teeth and bones. One tested the barrier as Rosel once had, but where he'd been forced back, the creature stepped right through. Gargled cries rose from hundreds of throaty howls and the creatures sped forward.

Rosel froze, his mind untethering from his body as the mob below screamed, pushing and shoving toward the palace entrance. Sharbelle and Cassen began to sob. Cris shouted, "we have to get home!" yet he did not move. Behind him, someone begged forgiveness from the gods, begged to be given their time over to make different choices, but Rosel could not make his mind work at all. He could only stand there as the creatures kept coming, hundreds and then thousands of them, all slick greenish skins and transparent wings of peculiar beauty.

When teeth nipped at his arms and his legs, Rosel did not fight. He let their long, clawed fingers yank his hair, tearing clumps loose, let them slice deep gouges in his skin, and pull him slowly to pieces like a divine meal. Perhaps his last thought ought to have been regret or sorrow, have been of his wife or his children, or the city he and his companions had doomed, yet it was the king he saw, the king he thought about. Of the fear in his eyes when he'd realised the people of Vircena had doomed themselves.

THE DARK SON

LUKE SCULL

Prince Salidar Karakian narrowed his eyes and rubbed distractedly at the scar around his neck. Far below, coiled in the basin between three hills and the endless emerald depths of the southern jungles, the city of his birth sweltered in the late afternoon sun.

Shar the Golden. Jewel of the Sun Lands. Capital of Shamaath. Salidar's gloved hand fell away from his scarred neck and curled into a fist. *A pit of vipers. None more venomous than my own dear family.*

How long had it been since he'd last gazed up at the gilded spires of the Palace of Prosperity Everlasting? How many years since he'd sat beside the burbling fountains in the grand atrium of his family's royal residence, birdsong fluttering around him while he closed his eyes and meditated on the day's lessons, the sweetness of the papaya fruit on his tongue?

He licked his parched lips. No sweetness there, only sour sweat. A decade and a half in cooler climes had caused him to forget just how damned hot it was in the South. As for lessons, he carried the most important one he'd ever learn around his neck. An essay etched deep in his heart. The priestesses sang of seven virtues, seven sins—yet none of the Pantheon's gifts to humanity were greater than the gift of hatred.

Prince Salidar turned and frowned at the army of mercenaries encamped on the hill behind him. A whole company of Sumnians, a thousand fighting men, under the command of the monstrous general now sneering at the city below. The merciless sun glinted off his teeth as he raised his spear and pointed the bladed tip at Shar. "We attack at dawn," he rumbled, his voice like thunder rippling down the hills. "I long to see what riches she holds."

"Unimaginable riches, I assure you," replied the prince. The ruined whisper the noose had made of his voice couldn't quite hide the weariness in his words. This was at least the fourth time General Zahn had questioned the veracity of Salidar's claims. The general was not a man given to trusting anything he couldn't see with his own eyes or hold in his giant hands. "Shar's coffers overflow with gold. The jungle's riches are without end, and though to venture there is death for most, Shamaath has successfully mined its resources for centuries."

"Huh." Zahn rolled his shoulders and tensed, eight feet of scarred muscle shining with sweat. He wore no armour above the waist, opting instead to display his godlike physique for the world to marvel upon, a ridiculous affectation or a measure of supreme confidence, depending on where one stood. Given Zahn's army and siege weapons were the means with which he intended to take the city, Salidar had resisted the urge to comment on the general's sartorial choices. "Shar the Golden. We will see how well the name is earned. I will fashion a golden sceptre from your city's riches and a vest from the bones of your kin."

Prince Salidar grimaced. "If you wish to make a fashion statement,

I will be happy to introduce you to the best tailors in the city once I sit upon the serpent throne."

Zahn flashed him a smile, a knowing look in his dark eyes. For all his monstrous strength and predilection for acting the savage, he knew a sharp mind whirred beneath that hulking exterior. Zahn was an educated man. A very *dangerous* man. "You fear for the fate of your treacherous family? Do not tell me you begin to waver now that you stand on the precipice of vengeance."

"I am here to claim the throne that is my birthright. The city will be seized, and my family made to answer for what they did to me. But this is a liberation, not an invasion. I want no more violence than is necessary."

Zahn chuckled then. "*The Dark Son.* An assassin without peer. A man who has killed and betrayed and stabbed countless other men in the back … urging restraint?"

Prince Salidar winced at the gentle mockery. Once, he had been the great shining hope of Shamaath. The Gentle Prince, they had called him. A man more interested in books and history and the cataloguing of the Great Green Sea's unimaginably diverse flora and fauna than the endless political intrigues of which the royalty and nobility were so enamoured

But then the royal family renounced him. Lies, betrayal, murder— these things were expected, encouraged even, within the unspoken rules that defined the upper echelons of Shamaathan society. Prince Salidar had been accused of nothing so banal as the usual machinations of his venomously ambitious kin. His crime was far worse. He had been guilty of loving with an unguarded heart.

"I left that name in the North,' he whispered. "The Dark Son. I am a prince, and soon I shall be a king. My face is the last thing my brother will see before I take his crown."

General Zahn chuckled again and turned to regard his company. Catapults and ballistae were being tortuously manoeuvred over uneven ground by sweating, cursing Sumnians. Behind them marched lines of the southern mercenaries, bristling with spears and scimitars, brown faces hungry for violence and the promise of riches beyond their wildest dreams. Zahn gave an approving nod, turned back to Salidar, and winked. "They call your country the Kingdom of Snakes," he said, one huge hand reaching down towards his crotch, eyes dancing with mischief.

"They do," rasped the prince, his own gaze narrowing. He had a terrible feeling he knew what was coming.

"Witness!" bellowed Zahn, pulling his monstrous cock out with a practiced flourish. "A Sumnian has no need of poisons and other coward's weapons! We fight like men, and we die like men! Kingdom of Snakes— meet the king of snakes!" The general proceeded to shake his cock at the city below while his mercenaries roared with laughter, thumping their weapons against their shields, white grins splitting brown faces.

Prince Salidar wisely said nothing. Barely a day seemed to go by without Zahn displaying his prick for one reason or another. As far as unfortunate character traits were concerned, he supposed it wasn't the worst. He had seen things in the North, in the Trine and beyond, that would haunt him the rest of his days. Had done things that would haunt him. He recalled his final conversation with his student.

"I wanted to give you something."

The young man looked at him, face filled with eagerness. Guileless. Trusting. "Of course, master. What is it?"

"This." He thrust the blade forward. Felt skin part, the dagger sinking deep. Heard a shocked gasp. Warm blood pattering against the cobbles.

"But ... why?" The question was wet and sticky, but it didn't disguise his student's shock. The hideous note of betrayal.

Strange how another's crimes become your own. In the years since he'd escaped Shamaath, Prince Salidar had become every bit the kind of man he'd once despised. Was vengeance just another lie he told himself to justify what was his in his nature?

He sighed. Maybe the Sumnians had it right after all.

The city of Shar was old, older by far than the northern cities where Salidar Karakian had sold his services for the last fifteen years. Legend had it the first king of Shamaath had founded Shar on the site of a triumphant victory over a savage race of lizardfolk that had ruled the lands north of the great jungle for time immemorial. *Saurons*, the ancient texts had named them. The retreat of the Saurons from the Sun Lands subsequently unlocked the vast resources of the Great Green Sea to prospectors, and the riches those early explorers had recovered from the jungle literally paved the streets of Shar with gold. Isolated from its neighbours by the Singing Sands Hills and bulwarked by the jungle to the south, the Kingdom of Snakes grew prosperous far beyond the scarce bounty its wind-scratched deserts and prickly grasslands provided.

Not long ago, the royal family of Shar had almost half the mercenary companies in Sumnia on its payroll. Zahn's influence and the apparent decline in fortunes of house Karakian had ended those contracts, save one; Salidar hoped Zolta would prove as pragmatic as his reputation suggested once the Third Circle was breached.

The prince adjusted his hood as he entered Shar though the city gates—or at least, what remained of them. The once magnificent, gilded arches were a mangled ruin, the adjacent walls a smoking pile of rubble. The trebuchet loads had descended in flaming arcs and left utter devastation in the Golden City. Already Shar's Serpent Guard had fallen back to the Fourth Circle, leaving the fifth, outermost sector of the city undefended.

Just ahead of Salidar, the gigantic figure of Zahn seemed to cast a shadow over half the city. Red-eyed faces peered through the smoky haze at the colossus striding at the head of the foreign army. Screams cut through the crackle of burning wood and smouldering stone; the laughter of the mercenaries behind him. The prince rasped at the Sharians within earshot to get inside their homes and lock their doors. He trusted the mercenaries to rein in their savagery as much as he would trust a starving jackal with a lame rabbit. He'd seen them unleashed before—in Dorminia, some years back. A different land, a different conflict, but the same wolfish grins and menacing swagger that promised things would get much worse before they got better ... if they got better.

The entire city was divided into five concentric circles: The royal palace was the decadent heart at its centre. The nobles and richest merchants lived in opulence in the First Circle. The Second and Third were where most of the city's tradespeople lived and where the bulk of its commerce took place. The Fourth was the military heart of Shar. The Serpent Guard served the city as both watch and standing army, answering to the Council of the Seven and ultimately to the king, though its loyalties had changed several times over the centuries—usually with the current incumbent of the Serpent Throne. The Karakians had themselves climbed to prominence over the poison-bloated corpses of the previous royal line, whose entire household had been rounded up in the Royal Concourse and slaughtered before the impassive gaze of the Serpent Guard.

A slice of history I ought to have heeded. Ruthlessness and naked ambition are our family heirlooms. The blood of our line runs as cold as that of the snakes we so proudly display on our flag. Salidar stopped a stone's throw from the gate leading to the Fourth Circle. Flags displaying the royal insignia of house Karakian hung lifeless in the still air from both sides of the gatehouse. *An auspicious sign, perhaps.*

As they neared the wall dividing the Fourth Circle from the Fifth, Salidar heard a sudden commotion from behind the gate, the bark of orders issued and rattle of weapons readied. The gates swung open and Prince Salidar's hands went to the daggers under his robe. Serpent Guards began filing through six abreast, snake helms obscuring their faces, double-ended spears raised and mirror shields held high to reflect the rising sun into the eyes of the foreign mercenaries. Behind him, Salidar heard the Sumnians shifting into an offensive position with angry curses. He pulled his hood further down to shade his eyes and readied himself for action, but a commanding voice stopped the city's defenders dead. A guard wearing the frilled cobra helm of a captain stormed forward, hesitating only a little at the sight of General Zahn. He removed his helm and tossed it at his feet, hefted his spear and levelled it at the monster among men.

"Sumnian bastard," he spat. "This is an act of war! Turn around now and leave. Take your men and leave the city by nightfall, and on my word as Captain Ansell of the Serpent Guard, we will forget this ever happened."

Zahn raised an eyebrow. "You would overlook the deaths of your kin in this section of the city? The damage our weapons wrought?"

Captain Ansell stared at the ruins of what were formerly the city gates and shrugged. "The Fifth Circle is of little consequence. The peasants can bury their dead and rebuild. Some pruning of the poor may even be good for them. Fewer mouths to feed. Now, unless you wish to invite Shamaath's wrath down upon you, leave here immediately. Tell whatever fool sent you that Shar cannot be conquered. Not by any light-skinned Sumnian goat-fucker with delusions of grandeur."

Prince Salidar Karakian slowly pulled back his hood and took a step towards the captain. Though it strained his damaged throat, he raised his voice to carry his next words beyond Ansell to the Serpent Guard silently watching on. "I am no Sumnian," he declared, turning his head slightly so all could see his finer, darker features. "I am Salidar Karakian, eldest son of Daramus Karakian. I was born in the four-hundred and sixtieth year of this age and anointed crown prince by the Prophet himself. My brother Malik—my *younger* brother Malik—has sat the serpent throne on a falsehood since our father passed. I am the true king of Shamaath … and I am here to claim my throne."

A moment of stunned silence greeted his words. Then Captain Ansell gave a humourless laugh and spat at Salidar's feet. "Lying dog," he grated, jabbing the glistening spear tip at Salidar. The Serpent Guard were infamous for their use of poisons extracted from the snakes and more fantastic beasts that roamed the Great Green Sea. "The crown prince perished in a hunting expedition before half of my men could hold a spear. Your words are piss to me. I will deliver your lying tongue to King Malik myself."

Zahn turned to his own men. One of them immediately handed him his monstrous spear, single-bladed, unlike those of the Serpent Guard, but so long and thick it made their weapons look like children's toys. "You call your rightful king a liar? Let us decide who speaks truth with a test of strength! It is a Sumnian tradition. Best me, and my comrades shall leave this country peacefully. You have my word." He smiled broadly, his golden teeth glittering.

Captain Ansell craned his neck and stared doubtfully up at the human behemoth. Zahn was a giant of a man, but he was half-naked and vulnerable to the poison-coated polearm the captain wielded. Salidar could see the question in his eyes: *What kind of man carries himself so nonchalantly in the Kingdom of Snakes?*

The captain turned back to his waiting guards and took an inconspicuous step away from the general. "Men," he shouted, his voice a fraction higher than before. "Kill them all. Mount the corpse of this giant savage on your spears so his body may serve as a warning to any Sumnians lurking outside the city."

In one smooth motion, Prince Salidar drew his favoured curved dagger with his left hand and flicked a throwing knife from his right, hitting the nearest guard in the throat and dropping him dead. He spun away, into the cover of the advancing mercenaries as they crashed into the Serpent Guard, the two sides stabbing and hacking each other with spear, sword, and wicked curved scimitar. Salidar drew another dagger with his right hand and he stabbed with twin talons of death, one coated in manticore venom, the other the poison of the stormbringer toad, so called because a sighting of the rare creature heralded the arrival of the great storms that would batter the Sun Lands for weeks.

The Serpent Guard were Shar's elite fighting force, trained from childhood to defend the city without fear. They were experts in hand-to-hand combat and specialised in swift, deadly strikes. Before they were sworn into the Guard, each was required to bite the head off a live snake to prove their devotion and fearlessness. They were a formidable force—more than a match for most enemies that would dare take up arms against the city.

They were a formidable force but still died in their dozens when faced by the ruthless invaders from neighbouring Sumnia and the returning prince. The thousand men who made up General Zahn's company were veterans of countless conflicts, survivors of fights and skirmishes across the breadth of the continent. They were born of war, forged in battle, forbidden to marry until they had slain at least one man in combat. Each was a finely honed weapon, a lion unleashed in a city of lambs made complacent by wealth.

Salidar ducked an arcing spear and dashed forwards, striking out, one-two, puncturing flesh and finding the gaps under snake helm or between plates of armour. General Zahn stood like an island among a circle of broken bodies. His towering form was covered in blood, the wicked blade of his mighty spear trailing crimson droplets as it skewered the city's defenders and swept them into the path of the cringing guards behind them. One guardswoman tried to strike while Zahn's back was turned. He spun around and deflected the tip with his iron bracer. She tried to pull away, but Zahn swept his spear around, knocking her feet from under her. He lifted one absurdly large boot and stamped down on her chest, shattering her ribs, the boot grinding down until she screamed in agony. Captain Ansell yelled for reinforcements, urging more guards through the gate. A flash and an explosion rattled Salidar's eardrums, and suddenly the gate, guard tower, and most of the surrounding wall were gone. Shattered stone and tangled limbs lay all around. The obscene bulk of a trebuchet load the size of a house crowned the ruin of what had once been the city's strongest defensive position. The Sumnians were the quicker to recover, clambering over the wreckage into the city's Fourth Circle and slaying stunned and fallen guards where they lay.

Salidar sheathed his daggers and shook dust from his robe. His hearing was returning, bringing with it the screams and groans of the wounded guards. He ghosted over the debris, pausing a moment to watch with fascinated horror as General Zahn and two of his men lifted the wounded Ansell to his feet. While his men held the captain in position, Zahn grabbed Ansell's spear and with agonising slowness pushed it straight up between his legs. The captain screamed, an awful sound that seemed to last forever. When it was done, Zahn picked up the captain's corpse, stuck the butt end of the spear into a crevice in the rubble of the wall, and propped him up to face the palace.

"A warning," Zahn said grimly. "We are coming, and we cannot be stopped. A lion does not cower before a snake. Let your fate demonstrate the folly of resisting the inevitable."

Salidar swallowed his nausea and stared at the palace looming high in the distance. He had brought hell to the Golden City and blackened its streets with the blood of its guards. He hoped his people would forgive him.

When he was twelve, Salidar Karakian was sent to the Temple of Seven Songs to learn the scriptures of the Book of Aya and assist the priests with their duties. The great temple to Shar's patron deity had long been the religious heart of the Kingdom of Snakes. The Deniers claimed the gods were gone, murdered centuries ago, but they had been chased out or executed and those that remained were driven underground. Salidar had seen enough evidence in the North to suggest the Deniers may have a point—but as far as he was concerned the existence of the gods was a question for scholars and theologists. His only god for the past fifteen years had been gold: the one power to unite all faiths, and the omnipotence of which was never in question.

Salidar remembered his last encounter with the Prophet. He had been helping catalogue the holy texts in the scriptorium when the strangely hairless mystic had appeared at the top of the stairs, simple white robes with the golden sun of Aya trailing behind him, accompanied by his chaperones: an albino woman and a dusky-skinned male. The former was as pale as snow. The latter was of the South but not as dark as the people of Sumnia and certainly not of Shamaath.

Despite his bald scalp, the Prophet—Chosen of Aya and spiritual leader of Shar—was eight years old and had been for as long as anyone in the city could remember. As the priest who Salidar had been assisting fell to his knees in reverence, the Prophet stared at the prince with eyes far older than those of any child. "*The Dark Son,*" he had said, in the high-pitched lilt of the curious youth, but with an undercurrent of something ancient and terribly wise. "That is what they shall call you. The eldest, the rightful, the wronged, the wrathful. Your heart will carry you far from Shar, and your return shall herald a storm that will feed the seeds of rebirth. You are the Dark Son, accursed of the sun, beloved of the shadow. The next time we meet, the king will die." With those words the Prophet had turned and left, his strange guardians following behind.

As Salidar stepped over the rubble and the torn and ragged corpses of the city guard across the Grand Plaza of Shar's First Circle towards the Palace of Prosperity Everlasting, he glanced at the Temple of Seven Songs. The Prophet's words had haunted him for years, first as a warning and later as a promise. Now he stood on the precipice of his destiny. The city would indeed be reborn, the cancer at its heart cut out. As king, he would put an end to the plotting and corruption and endless coup attempts. He would demand the wealthy and the nobles shift their priorities. Perhaps he'd even begin sowing the seeds of a fairer society. It sounded absurd, a man who had killed countless people and betrayed trusted allies suddenly advocating on behalf of the common folk. Fifteen years in the crucible of the North had taught him that life was rarely simple and, as it happened, quite often nothing short of absurd.

The golden spires rose before him, not quite as impressive as he remembered after his time in Thelassa, but nonetheless a sight that pulled at the strings of his weary heart. That brief song of longing struck a discordant note of apprehension as he saw what awaited him. At the top of the stairs leading to the entrance of the palace was the welcoming party he had been expecting and dreading in equal measure.

General Zolta was wider than he was tall, and he wasn't a particularly short man. It was unclear who would prove the weightier if he and Zahn were somehow placed on opposite sides of a giant set of scales, but whereas Zahn was a chiselled giant, Zolta was a waddling mountain of flab. He grinned a white smile as Salidar stopped at the foot of the stairs. To either side of the gross general, Sumnian mercenaries held crossbows cocked and readied.

"The Dark Son!" Zolta exclaimed happily, his jowls wobbling. "I could scarcely believe it when my employers told me who was leading this army. How long has it been since Dorminia, my friend? I still remember the look on your apprentice's face the night you took his life."

Salidar flinched. "Some of us were forced to bloody our knives, Zolta. The knack for getting very rich while doing nothing seems to have eluded me."

"Nothing? I am wounded! One cannot underestimate the boost to morale having a stalwart ally at one's back can provide."

Salidar felt the giant presence of Zahn beside him. He too had been a participant in that short war. Unlike Zolta, Zahn had more than earned his share of the White Lady's coin.

"Do my family have a stalwart ally at their back?" the prince rasped, his voice a scratchy whisper.

There was a tense moment of silence. With General Zolta's company defending the palace, taking the throne would be a bloody and drawn-out battle. The Serpent Guard would have time to regroup. There was even the risk that reinforcements would arrive from elsewhere in the kingdom. If that happened, it was by no means certain Salidar's force wouldn't be routed and his plans scattered to the winds. The two mercenary companies stared at each other, the fate of the kingdom balancing on a knife's edge.

Suddenly, Zolta grinned and spread his arms wide. "A stalwart ally must sometimes be a pragmatist. The king has not been forthcoming with our latest stipend, and I fear our commission has run its natural course. With some … encouragement … I believe my men can be persuaded to take an early vacation. Anywhere but Shar should suffice."

Salidar winced at the mention of *encouragement*. He knew the general's definition of the word, and it generally involved piles of gold large enough to rival his gigantic stomach. The prince promised himself this would be the last time he dealt with Zolta. "I will see you appropriately compensated," he hissed through gritted teeth. "You agree to stand down?"

The general nodded happily and turned to issue orders to his mercenaries. Moments later, they began filtering out of the palace. Most were carrying valuables looted at the last minute: costly urns, portraits, silk curtains, anything they could quickly carry away. Salidar swallowed the urge to protest and watched General Zolta waddle off with the last of his men. The sun began to set in the eastern sky, bathing the city a bloody red. It was time for the family reunion.

♛

The entrance halls of the Palace of Prosperity Everlasting were much as Prince Salidar Karakian remembered them. He stalked through winding corridors and circular rooms in which he had played and laughed and studied, the regal countenances of dead ancestors staring down at him from the gilded walls. Everything was gold and ornate, carved white marble, a breath-taking display of excess that would shame even the White Lady's palace in distant Thelassa. Salidar moved through the serpentine opulence of his former home as though he were a ghost: half present, half a spectre from the past reliving memories of a time when the mention of family had not triggered a shudder of revulsion.

Servants fled from the returning prince as he led General Zahn and his men deeper into the palace quarters. He hesitated a moment outside a pair of wooden doors etched with the carving of a striking viper, then shoved them open and took a step into the training hall. So much of his life had been defined by the things he had learned within that small courtyard under the strict tutelage of Master Savaras, a man with a face like stone and all the warmth of a winter blizzard. Savaras had trained the young prince in the arts of war, in various forms of unarmed combat as well as swordsmanship and the secrets of the hidden blade. Despite his gentle, bookish nature, Salidar has excelled during these practices. All Shamaathan princes were expected to be able to handle themselves in a fight as well as in the shadowy world of Sharian politics. The two often went hand in hand.

Salidar's younger brother Malik had not been so adept in the training hall. Many an evening had passed with the two brothers recounting horror stories of the day's training and their master's seemingly unquenchable quest for perfection in his students—often with Malik nursing a bruise or two. He'd had a ready smile, Malik. A ready smile and a charming nature, quick to win friends while Salidar often struggled even to greet visiting royalty. Despite their differences, Salidar had truly loved Malik. He had trusted him like he had trusted only one other person.

As Salidar stood facing the training dummies and other apparatus, staring but not seeing and rubbing absently at his scarred neck, he considered how flawed perception could prove. He gazed at the long, vertical pole in the centre of the hall, its wooden length nicked by countless blades. Steel blades, spears, and target boards of differing shapes and sizes could be raised or lowered at various points down the length of the pole, which could be made to rotate at speed via a spring-based mechanism in the corner of the hall. He had been practicing his throwing knives the day his father had stormed in with a contingent of Serpent Guards. The conversation had been short and furious.

"When I heard you were courting, I was elated at first," the king growled. "My reclusive older son, a constant disappointment to me, finally summoning the courage to spread his seed? I began to dream you would produce a fitting heir! Then your brother told me the sickening truth."

"Father—" Salidar tried to say, but the king was in no mood to listen.

"Silence!" he roared. "I could tolerate your meekness and lack of princely mien while you were young. I believed I could mould you into a king fit to rule, given sufficient time. But this … dalliance of yours … it is an abomination! No son of mine will lay with another man. You profane us all before Aya. There can be

only one fitting response to such wickedness."

"What have you done?" Salidar whispered. But just then two more guards arrived carrying a body between them and he knew instantly.

The sudden numbness in his chest had made him feel like he was dying even before the guards restrained him, placed a noose around his neck, and tied it around the topmost spear, leaving him to dangle helplessly, gasping for breath. They tied the corpse of his beloved to his feet, steaming innards spilling out onto the dirt-packed earth, pulling him down, strangling him. His father simply watched, a portrait of grim fury.

And then Master Savaras had appeared and took in the scene with an unreadable expression. He cut the rope with a single hurled knife and then set about the Serpent Guard with his practice sword, cracking limbs and sending bodies flying. The young prince had caught a single, growled word, *"Run"* while he was disentangling himself from the snaking intestines of his murdered lover and tangled rope and desperately sucking air through the burning agony in his neck. He had fled the palace and soon after Shar, understanding that to remain within his family's reach was to die.

"No place like home," said Zahn beside him, snapping Salidar from his bitter reminiscence. The enormous general was grinning, as though he knew exactly what had taken place in this hall. Salidar doubted any rope could restrain *him*. More likely he'd have broken the wooden pole in two and murdered the king and his entire retinue of guards with his bare hands.

"Home is where the heart is," Salidar replied coldly. "Best left in the past."

They left the training hall and continued through the palace until they reached the grand atrium. Sunlight spilled through the open roof, bathing the benches and fountains in its warm radiance, turning the burbling water into liquid gold. The birds were all gone, their cages empty; the absence of their song stirred a strange feeling of emptiness inside the prince. He dipped a finger into the largest of the fountains, disturbing a school of tiny angelfish the colour of brilliant aquamarine. He remembered the sound of laughter, a soft hand in his. Soft lips and the taste of papaya. They'd often sit here and talk for hours. The profane stickiness of bloody entrails in his hands jumped unbidden to his thoughts and he stiffened. "The throne room is just ahead," he rasped. "Be ready."

As it happened, the throne room was all but abandoned. The Serpent Throne stood empty. An attendant was weeping on his knees beside the dais as the prince and his mercenary allies swept in. The aide immediately plead for his life, face wet with tears, a trail of snot hanging from his weak chin. "Where is my brother?" Salidar whispered. "Where is the king?"

The attendant swallowed hard, terrified gaze shooting to General Zahn and beyond to the Sumnians gathering with their weapons readied. "He … the king is in his chambers," he stammered.

"Does the king have any guards with him?"

"Only a few Serpent Guards. Let me live, please! I have a wife and daughter!"

Salidar stared hard at the pathetic figure grovelling on the floor. A part of him wanted to cut the man down, but the bloodthirsty expressions on the faces of the mercenaries stayed his hand. "I hope you are more loyal to your family than you are to the throne," he frowned. "Consider yourself unemployed. Now get out."

As the attendant scampered away, jeered by the onlooking Sumnians, Salidar nodded at the stairwell behind the throne leading up to the royal quarters. "My younger brother is up there," he said. "Deal with his bodyguards but leave him to me." His hand went to his favourite dagger, the curved blade that his beloved had presented him on his eighteenth birthday. A fitting way to repay the ultimate betrayal, he reckoned.

The Serpent Guard were waiting for them just outside the top of the stairwell, double-sided spears to one side and short bows ready to fire. The first wave of Sumnians took the arrows on their shields and then waded forwards with scimitars flashing, driving the guards back along the corridor. Prince Salidar ducked around a corner as the Serpent Guard fought a helpless retreat, ghosting down a side corridor with ruthless purpose towards the king's bedchamber. A pair of guards were waiting outside the ornate wooden doors and charged him, their spears poised to strike. All the anger inside him seemed to explode and Salidar leapt to meet them, joining the deadly dance with a rage he hadn't felt in many years. He was so close now.

He turned aside one thrust, dodged another, and punched his blade through the throat of the closest guard. He tried to jerk his dagger free, but it caught on the rim of the snake helm and the other guard gashed his thigh with his spear blade. Salidar wheeled away, warm blood trickling down his leg, and silently cursed. Of course, the spear tip was poisoned! He had an antidote stashed in his robes, but the guard stabbed at him again and he was forced to retreat. A monstrous shadow appeared, and Zahn's massive hand closed around the guard's neck, lifting him a foot off the ground. There was a sickening *crack* as his other hand twisted the man's head at a grotesque angle, dropping the corpse on the blood-slick marble floor.

Salidar uncorked and downed the antidote, grimacing at the intense bitterness. Then he limped over to the door to the king's bedchambers, only to find it locked and most probably barricaded. Zahn waved him aside and threw all his monumental weight and strength behind it. Door, lock, and hinges all exploded from the frame, sending an upended chest of drawers and armoire crashing into the room in a splintered ruin.

Malik sat on the bed, crying, lips trembling.

He had changed greatly in the fifteen years since Salidar had seen him. His handsome face was creased with worry lines. His once-athletic frame had seemingly given way to kingly excess, and his black hair was receding and thinning at the crown. His actual crown rested on the bed, and in his trembling hands, he pointed a crossbow at Salidar.

Before either brother could say a word, Zahn stormed forward. The crossbow clicked and suddenly the bolt was sticking out of the general's chest, but he hardly seemed to notice. He smashed his giant fist into the king's face. The king's nose crunched, the bone between his eyes snapping.

Blood and teeth spewed onto the richly carpeted floor.

"General, *enough*," Salidar hissed. He crossed the chamber to his fallen brother while Zahn casually plucked the bolt from his chest and broke it between his fingers. "Malik," Salidar said, tasting the word. He had imagined it would sound triumphant, infused with all the power of righteous vengeance duly claimed, but it didn't. "Fifteen years ago, you betrayed my trust to our father. You stood by and watched while he had me hanged. I loved you, brother, as well as anyone in our accursed family can love another. Tell me, Malik. Why?"

Malik stared up at him, one eye a red mess, the other wide with pain and terror. "You … committed heresy in the eyes of mighty Aya. To love as you did, a union between two men … it is forbidden."

Salidar stared for a moment, fury rising again. "You mean to say you sentenced me to death because of your devotion to Aya? The same god you honoured by *fucking your way around every whore house in the Fifth Circle and snorting moon dust until your nose started to rot?*"

Malik spat up some more blood. "It was not just Najam, brother," Malik managed to say. "You were unfit to be king. A leader … must inspire his people. We are beset by threats you cannot begin to understand. You … you are a deviant … a disgrace."

"Father had Najam killed," Salidar said coldly. "Master Savaras died to save me or else I too would have returned to Aya that day. You stole my throne. You stole my life."

"Brother …" Malik began, but his words fell on deaf ears. Salidar bent down and placed his dagger to his brother's breast and pushed the blade between his ribs. Malik gasped and blood gushed over Salidar's fist. Moments later, it was over. Salidar laid his brother's body down with a gentleness that surprised him and rose slowly, wincing at the pain in his thigh. The Serpent Crown waited for him. He reached for it, but movement from under the bed stopped him. A young boy climbed out from beneath the bed skirt and knelt over Malik's corpse.

"Father," the child cried, and something in Salidar turned as cold as the bitterest winter in the far north. General Zahn grinned and put his bloody fist to his mouth to stifle a chuckle.

"My brother … this man … was your father?" Salidar asked.

"You killed him!" the boy screamed, wrapping his little arms around the man who had, until very recently, been the king of Shamaath.

"The crown prince must die," said a voice that couldn't have belonged to someone much older than the sobbing youth huddling on the bloodstained carpet. The chosen of Aya stood in the doorway to the bedchamber, flanked by his ever-present guardians, the albino woman and the dusky-skinned man. Salidar Karakian stared at the hairless, youthful head of the Prophet.

A thousand thoughts whirled through his head. Why was the Prophet here? Why had he allowed this to happen? *This child stands between me and the throne.*

"My job here is done," boomed Zahn, nodding to the Prophet. "I have done as we agreed. My men must be paid."

"You shall be," said the Prophet. He turned to Salidar and regarded him with black, ageless eyes. "Well, elder Karakian? Kill the boy. Claim your throne."

Salidar stared from Zahn to the Prophet and back again. "You arranged this? This was *my* vengeance to take!"

"And you have it," the Prophet said. "Did you not think it odd you were able to bring an army across Shamaath without meeting any organised resistance? The Great Green Sea stirs yet Shar has grown weak. Your brother had lost his nerve. It was … time for a change. First, however, your nephew must die." Salidar stared at the crown prince—his nephew—sobbing and shivering over his dead father. The boy looked up at Salidar. "Please … please no."

Salidar glared at the Prophet. "Fuck you," he whispered.

The Prophet blinked. "General Zahn, it appears the Dark Son is unwilling to get his hands dirty. If you'll do the honours …"

Zahn reached down and plucked the boy from the carpet.

Prince Salidar Karakian drew his second dagger and spat at the Sumnian warlord. "You called yourself a lion," he grated. "Yet you would kill an innocent child?"

"I take no joy in it," Zahn rumbled. "He will die quickly and painlessly."

"Hurt him and *you* will die."

The world seemed to stop for a moment, everyone staring at everyone else. Then the Prophet sighed and waved a hand in Salidar's direction. "Snow, Sand … restrain the prince. I fear he requires further education in the sacrifices necessary to rule."

The two guards stepped towards Salidar, hands on hilts, as calm and implacable as death.

The situation was hopeless. Salidar was outnumbered, wounded, and at the mercy of forces he didn't understand. He did the only thing he could.

"You need a prince to put on the throne," he rasped, backing away until he felt a slight breeze caress his shoulders. Fifty feet separated the king's bedchamber from the ground. "Kill the boy and you have nothing. Do you know what I told Najam the day he was murdered?"

"Tell us, Your Highness," said the Prophet in that maddeningly unflappable child's voice.

"I told him that if a snake could shed its skin and start afresh, perhaps my family can too. It is never too late to begin again. To break the pattern. Sometimes all it takes is to love with an unguarded heart. And to die free of regrets."

Prince Salidar Karakian spun and jumped through the open window to the palace grounds far, far, below.

GLORY TO
THE KING!

ANNA SMITH SPARK

She opened her eyes that were crusted shut. It was very dark. A low hump of light.

'Lidae. Gods, Lidae. I thought you were dead.'

She rubbed dirt from her face. The dirt was ashes. The ground beneath her was black and cracked. Very dry: like flaking skin. It sounded as it moved under her weight. There would be bones beneath her stripped away, breaking beneath her weight. Like the skeletons of leaves. A torch flickered, a face bending over her, black against the black sky. She got to her feet slowly. Wiped ashes from her face.

'Lidae!' Emmas. Tall and strong and kind. A kind man. Black skin and golden hair, golden eyes. His hair and his eyes rippled in the torch light. He looked alive and clean.

'I thought you were dead,' Emmas said. They looked around together at the dead around them, piled up in mounds and valleys, towers and palaces of the dead.

Emmas handed her the torch. Her hand felt hot and dry, holding it. She held the flames very close to her face, felt the heat of them. The smell of them. Watched them move.

Emmas was bending down scrabbling. 'Look!' He held up a flat disc of bronze crusted with black like her eyes. Fretted, filigree at its edge, lacework to adorn the queen's gowns. So thin and delicate he snapped it off in half, gave her a piece. Breaking and giving bread.

'I was out here searching for stuff,' Emmas said. 'Saw you lying there. Thought you were dead. Then you moved.'

'Thank you.' Her voice had a dried pain to it. Rattle. Like a stone hung around her throat.

'Nothing to thank me for.' He said, 'If you'd have been dead, I'd have taken your sword.'

'So … I'm sorry, then?'

'That's more like it.'

She wiped human ashes from her face.

'You want a drink?'

'Yes.' Gods, yes. The piece of bronze she has holding rubbed against the waterskin. New-cast bronze, she thought. Like new-baked bread. It still had some heat in it. The water tasted rank. Metal-meat-sweet-shit-rot. She said, 'They got trapped, then, in the river? Like the plan?' She said in fear, 'Or we did? We won? We did win?'

'Course we won. They got trapped. Thousands of them. The river ran red. Their corpses dammed the river edge to edge.'

'And … the …?'

Awed voice: 'The King killed it.'

'I saw it.'

'I thought it had killed you.'

'It was made of fire, reaching up into the sky. It had teeth of fire, and a crown of fire, and wings like sheets of white flame. I saw it. I thought it had killed me.'

'The King killed it. We won.'

She drank water soiled with men's dying. Rubbed human ashes off her face.

Lidae said, fervent: 'Praise the King.'

The squad were camped around a fire on the other side of a ridge of corpses. Dry crunch of bones underfoot. Could have been here a thousand years already. Burned and hacked and dried. Brown and old. Odd light: dust and smoke covering the stars, the sky down so close; dark as closed eyes when she had been buried in corpses; little lights flickering green and red and pale, corpses still burning, little torch mounds; the hump of light on the horizon, scab red, that was the town as it burned. The ground flashed in places, rippled, dim lights on dark water. Lidae stared and stared at it, and realized it was sand melted and fused into black glass.

'Take care.' She slipped on death filth and Emmas put out a hand to steady her.

'I'm fine.' She drank some more water. Her boots pushed down into a woman's face screaming up white. Eyes still open. Tears dried to steam.

'Another good one.' Emmas bent, retrieved another disc of bronze from near the woman's out-stretched hand. Thin as birch bark. The liquid bronze had flowed around an iron arrow head, trapped it there in the very centre, the black iron bleeding out into the golden bronze. 'Look at that,' Emmas said. 'That's a fine one.'

Death-cast, the soldiers called the bronze discs. Death-bronze. Some curious trick of mage-fires on bronze arms, bronze armour. Molten bronze floating and sinking in melted fat, melted bones, melted skin. Luck charms. Sacred things.

'How long was I out here?' Lidae asked.

Pause. 'A day.'

The sun had been rising, when they went in. A day sleeping in the sun on a soft bed of corpses. Through the fish-reek of her body, she felt almost rested. Warmed by the fire, soothed by her sleep.

'You're not wounded?' Emmas said suddenly.

'Bleeding to death, can't you see? No, I'm not wounded.' Scraped and bruised and sore and scalded. Luxurious heavy sleep warmth in her limbs.

'You're missing most of your hair,' Emmas said.

'It will grow back, I expect.'

A young woman of twenty. Tall, strong like her sword. Skin white and smooth as new-fallen snow. The blood was good for the complexion, it was sure knowledge, all the soldiers in the Army of Amrath had skin like fresh silk. Dark red hair, thick and silky also, they ate a better diet in the Army of Amrath than the peasants or the city folk did. Grey eyes, smoke grey, dove grey, very bright. She would be red, in the dawn tomorrow, if the sun rose through the smoke and the flies and the dust. Burned red by the god fires. Red and bald as a screaming baby, she thought.

The camp was rising out of the dark before them. They held the killing ground, they would camp here, squat on its borders, pile up the dead in walls and towers, surround themselves with the glory of what they had done. Severed heads on spears to watch their victory dance. A man groaned on a spear, still just living. The horse heads of the beasts the enemy had brought against them, horses with sharp fanged biting teeth, horned and winged. A row of them, raised up on sarris points. Their jaws moved, mouthed hungrily, as Lidae walked past. Beyond the wall of spears the tents had been raised, greased canvass or badly cured leather, small crude things vile to sleep in, and in the centre … Lidae's eyes stared, searching it out … there, on a distant rise, lifted up on a mound of corpses, the King's Tent, red, blazing, huge. So vast the circuit of the camp, so great the army squatted within it, that the King's Tent looked tiny it was so far off. The smoke of cook fires hung low in the air. The red tent blazed through it like a ruby. She had heard some of the men say it looked like a human heart.

Emmas said, 'This way.' The camp had shifted since she left it the previous night, marched off with Emmas and the rest to battle. Its fabric changed even, new tents and new equipment looted from the enemy, a wailing shrieking of women looted to accompany the tents. A new smell of women's blood. 'Makes me think of the sea, the camp does,' Emmas had once said. 'Always the same, always different.' Emmas led her past a squad of cavalry, proud big men lounging in the firelight on their beds of bones, watching their slaves polish and repolish their horses' trappings. Fine smell of meat cooking, plump cuts on a spit over the fire. A slave woman looked up from her work preparing the meal with hopeless red-rimmed eyes.

'They're too cruel,' said Emmas. 'Gods.'

'I wouldn't say that any louder,' said Lidae. When they were well out of earshot she said, 'It might not have been her child.'

'It was. It amuses them,' said Emmas.

'That's cavalry.' The smell of the meat was making her mouth water. A day is a long time to lie sleeping in the sun without meat or bread.

By their own camp, the spear shafts were adorned with long red ribbons streaming in the wind. A full panoply of enemy armour was set up on stakes beside their cookfire, helmet and chest-plate adorned with gold. The helmet crest was a wolf, teeth bared, crouched and snarling; beneath the crest, all along the left side from the temple to nape of the neck, the helmet was cracked open in a great ragged break. A flaw in the bronze, in the casting, and a sword or an axe had got in. At the base of the panoply Marcras was kneeling, offering up a cut of meat and a crust. 'Thank you, gods, life-stealers, you have kept me safe, left my life my own, I begged the luck and the luck came.' Marcras was still such a boy, Lidae thought, the way he begged.

'Lidae!' Marcras saw her. Leapt up. Bright happiness in his face. Golden hair, bright tanned skin, glowing with happiness, his pretty boy's blue eyes smiling. 'I knew you'd survive! Be out there somewhere! We won we won we won!'

'We certainly did win.' Sammik, lounging by the fire, smiling at Marcras indulgently like she smiled at her little children.

There was fresh good meat roasting at their fire also, bottles of ale, a basket of bread. Emmas saw her looking, frowned at Marcras. 'Get Lidae some food. Woman's been lying out with the dead all day.'

'Yes, yes, yes, of course! I knew you'd survive, Lidae! And the King! Did you hear, did Emmas tell you? The King killed every single one of them!'

'I heard.' She said with a smile like Sammik: 'You didn't expect anything else, did you?'

'No! No, but …' The boy's first battle. Eager as a puppy. Gods, I suppose we were all that dazed with new love for the King, once.

Sammik said, 'Food for Lidae, Marcras? Now, maybe, would be good?'

'Oh. Oh, yes, yes, sorry, Sammik, sorry, Lidae!' He was off almost running. 'But the King … gods!'

Sammik shook her head. 'How old is he? Someone remind me?'

'Here's your sword, Lidae,' said Emmas. It was wrapped in a cloth bundle, like a baby swaddled up, at Cana's feet.

'I saw you fall,' Cana said. 'I took up your sword. Because it's beautiful. If you had been dead, it would have been a victory offering to the King.'

She said to Emmas, 'I thought you said you were going to keep it?'

Emmas laughed. 'Look around you, Cana. Breathe in the air, eat your meat. The King doesn't need another victory offering.'

Lidae unwrapped the sword. Ran her hand down the blade that was still crusted dark red. The red glass set in the hilt like a jewel flashed up at her. Dirty with blood and filth. The red glass was chipped. 'Thank you, Cana, for recovering it. Thank you, Emmas, for not taking it. Thank you, my King, for not yet having received it.'

'Welcome,' said Emmas.

A trumpet sounded. Silver music. Three notes, ringing. Urgent. A joyous sound, a dance in the heart, a call like a love song. Made them laugh and weep. And a drum to pound out a rhythm of feet marching, ready them and time them. A man's skin stretched tight over a man's yellow bones, struck with a sharp bronze knife.

'To arms!' Emmas shouted. 'Men of Amrath! Up now, ready yourselves to fight!'

'We won?' Confusion. Lidae's hand clutching at her sword, her heart beating like the drums beat. They were all armed and waiting. But the city had fallen, the god was dead, the battle should be done.

Emmas said, 'We won this morning, yes. Now we have to win again.'

Lidae looked down at her filthy armour. 'I've lost my helmet.'

'Too late,' said Emmas. 'Have to hope you find another one.'

The trumpets rang, more desperate, more joyous. They are coming! The enemy is come again! Men of Amrath, Army of the God King, Army of Ruin, prepare yourself, get up, the enemy is come and their blood must run red. The killing ground calls us, yearning. The air is heavy with the scent of death. The sky shall rain blood, the earth shall bleed, the world shall be rent open by their dying. Men of Amrath, Army of Amrath: plague they call you, ruin, pestilence, murder and grief and famine and flood. Rise up now. Show them the truth of it, beyond any human speech. Kill them. Lidae on her feet, her sword screaming. Emmas, Cana, Marcras, their swords hungry, their faces lit. We will conquer the world. We will destroy it all, for after us there is only death.

They drew up in their files. Swordsmen, cavalrymen, sarriss. Wait. Wait. Wait. Lidae with her sword: tight in ranks, lined up close with the rest. Cana beside her, tall, a good man, she found, to be drawn up beside when the enemy came. Marcras on the other side of her champing his lips, sweating. Emmas fumbling with his armour straps.

Marcras's voice, muttering: 'King Amrath. God Amrath. King Amrath. God Amrath. King Amrath. God Amrath.' Marcras had breadcrumbs on his armour. She thought: you never got me that bread and meat, Marcras, you arse.

Swordsmen, cavalrymen, sarriss. Drums. Heart beats. Hard heavy eager breathing. Champing hungry teeth.

Wait. Wait. Wait.

Then the trumpet. Marching forwards. Dark, so dark and blinding, feet trampling on the landscape of the dead. Two days this battle has been raging. Now, here, in the night, in the dark, on the bodies of our victims, let us finish it. The city is falling and the very last of them are come to meet us. Thus in the dark we turn and march to embrace them. Lidae's eyes fixed ahead, and Cana's eyes; Marcras's eyes wide as platters. They could not see where they were going, the dark a hand closing over them. Didn't matter. Never mattered. They had fought before in the bright summer daylight and in the fighting their eyes had been blank and blind.

Acol the squad captain shouted, 'In the dawn's sweet light this morning we fell upon them, we crushed them. Yet even now, when the King has won a great victory over them, they will not bow down and accept their defeat.'

Marcras, voice shaking love fear: 'King Amrath. God Amrath. King Amrath. God Amrath. King Amrath. God Amrath.'

Acol, like a starving man seeing food and water: 'Thus now we must finish them. Kill them.'

Sammik, Emmas, Lidae, Cana: 'We will kill them.'

And the trumpets and the drums and the sound of men marching towards them. The sounds in the dark of metal and bone, of men dying. Distant. Very close.

'They are coming. They still think that they can harm us.'

'King Amrath. God Amrath. King Amrath. God Amrath. King Amrath. God Amrath.'

'We will kill them.'

Staring out into the dark, watching the dead heaped thick around them. Pools of torchlight, and the low hump of light in the distance that was the town they had destroyed. The sound of the enemy coming towards them.

'King Amrath. God Amrath. King Amrath. God Amrath. King Amrath. God Amrath.'

'Kill them!'

Feet crunching on bones. Closer. Close now. We killed them this morning. March forward, hold spears, wait.

Darkness. Smell of their metal. Fear-piss, fear-sweat. Rasp of metal blades. Hear them quaking.

'Where are they?' Emmas screamed out.

The sky was torn open. The King's green dragon swept shrieking overhead. The battleground on which they stood illuminated, green and cool like the light in woodland, the enemy there so few, so few, barely armed, marching through their comrades' deaths onwards, half-dead, already dead. The dragon howled. Darkness again, eyes blinking. Wait for them. Wait for them.

The enemy met them, few pitiful ranks, waiting, longing. Those who fled in the dawn when the Army of Amrath broke over them, knowing they had failed, the Army of Amrath had come down upon them, swept them away into ruin, the few last of them that had despaired and run screaming, fled from death, hoped as fools hope to live. In the charnel house of their defeat that had gathered themselves, seen the futility of living; now in the dark they came to be devoured, throw themselves upon their conquerors' blades and beg for death. They came on as men already dead and rotten, their eyes were dead, their hands were cold where they held their swords. They moved with the stiff pain of the sick and dying. They did not bleed, where the Army of Amrath cut them.

'Kill them!' Acol screamed. Lidae, Marcras, Sammik, Cana screamed together: 'Kill them!'

They fell away in dust, where Lidae stabbed them. They fell apart beneath her sword that was filthy with their comrades' blood. They were dry as stones. The corpses upon which they walked were dried to scabs. They sucked the moisture from the earth, left it grey and barren. The King's dragon came down from the depths of the sky and consumed them.

The greatest army that ever walked the face of the earth. Men and women and children march in its ranks. The sick, the old, the dying. The diseased and the wounded and the broken in heart and in mind and in body, limping, crawling, dragging themselves across the earth on the rotting, pus-filled stumps of their limbs. Maggots, the poets liken them to. Blight in the crops. Murrain in the fields. 'That's us!' the squad captain shouts in joy, as the poets sing of them. *The pestilence that devours a city's children, the people weep and scream for mercy but there is no mercy, the people of the city die in bloody shitting sweating pain.* 'That's us, lads! We kill … everything!' Two years ago the Army of Amrath came out of the north with a howl that brought a thousand women to miscarry, came down and soaked the world in blood. The earth behind them is slicked with human ruin. A trail spreading behind them, blood and fat and offal. The salt of sweat and tears and semen. Ashes. The sky above their columns is black with flies when they march. Countless legions: the stars in the winter sky, the poets compare them to in their praise songs, the grains of sand on a beach, the drops of cold rain when the storms come. They cannot be counted, they cannot be reckoned, no man on earth not their King Himself can number them. At their head, the point of their sword thrust, rides their King Amrath. He is their glory, their wonder, their beloved; He is the wonder of all the world of Irlast. Ith, He has conquered. Illyr. Immier. The Wastes, the northern deserts where the sand is grey. He will make Himself King of the World, conqueror of all that lives. Everything that turns its face to the sun, He will make kneel before Him. He will slaughter them, butcher them, revel in the shadows of their deaths. War, famine, rape, pillage, plague, heart's grief: these things sweep across the world sweet and bloodied, familiar to us now as breath. None can be spared, not through wealth or poverty, not through kindness, not through love not through hate. In Malth Elelane the Tower of Joy and Despair, He was crowned King and Lord. In Ethalden the Tower of Life and Death, He was crowned a god on earth, King of Ruin, King of Shadows, King of Dust, King of Death. Pain is His handmaiden. Grief is His handmaiden.

Glory is His shield. Triumph is the bloodied cloak He wears as other men wear their hair and skin.

He shines in men's very souls, fills them surrounds them with His wonder and His love. Of all that a man dreams, of all hopes and choices, the greatest dream of the human heart is to fight for Him.

Glorious. All-powerful. All-conquering. Like Him.

When it's all over he sits in his tent with his sword on his knees all bloodstained. It should, he thinks, it should make him happy. He turns the sword over and over in his hands, watching the way the lamplight moves on the blade. Fresh blood and well-polished metal, in the clear lamplight he can see his face reflected in the blade, his hair and his eyes and the silver crown on his head. He screws his eyes closed at that, pushes the sword away. It falls heavily at his feet with a soft thud. His hand aches where he was holding it, his fingers gripping the hilt so tightly, for so long. His whole body is stiff from battle. On every part of his body there are wounds that ache him. He pours himself a cup of wine, and he can see his reflection for a moment in the dark liquid, the lamplight catches on his silver crown and makes it flash. A star, in his winecup. He puts the cup down undrunk, shudders, snatches it up, drains it.

The sword is so close, he thinks. And on his belt a dagger, unused and sharp as a cold wind. There's a crease of skin on his wrist where the blood hasn't marked him. If he twists his hand back it's like a line painted there white, like a word, and he could put his sword blade there or his knife blade, like a word written there on his skin saying to do it.

Gods and demons, just look at yourself. Look at yourself, Marith.

Filth, you are. Worthless.

You really are a waste of fucking space, Marith. Disease, you are. Walking talking bloody disease, boy. You know that. You've wanted to die your whole life, haven't you? Every single day, boy, that's right, yes? But you can't won't do it.

You can kill innocent men, Marith. And women. And children. Babies.

Fucking dogs. But the one thing that deserves to die—you're too much of a coward to kill.

Kill yourself, Marith, you pitiful little shit. Do it.

He bends forward and vomits. Blood and firewine running down his chin. Two days ago—three days? one? four?—he put his sword blade on his wrist after he had been dressed for battle, pressed the blade down until it hurt. Then he was afraid. He went out into battle and killed and killed, and no one could harm him.

He's vomiting up his enemies' blood.

He tears off his silver crown, throws it down to lie with his sword at his feet. He kicks them both across the floor, screams, throws down a cloak over them to hide them.

They came back to their camp tired and happy. Lidae felt herself ringing with tiredness, her body aching and the world heavy in her head. Gods, food and drink and sleep. It must be dawn soon, the sky was ebbing to the rich deep blue of the last breath of night. The people of the Yellow Empire, they feared the dawn, if she remembered. A strange people, as everyone said. She had seen the way it grew so slowly here in the wilds from night to golden daylight, darkness and then a light with no shadows, and then the true light and the shadows came: beautiful, huge clear skies changing. Filthy and exhausted, she stretched her hands into it, breathed in drawing it into herself.

She said, 'I will never stop being grateful.'

Emmas said, 'What? We're alive, yeah. Yeah, let's drink to that.'

Cana the artist who valued her sword for its beauty was dead. After thinking all day that she was dead.

Somewhere in the distance to the south there was still the sound of fighting, the cavalry cutting down a few last stragglers off in the burned hills. Hunting, not war. They sank down by the remnants of their campfire, Emmas said to Marcras, 'Get the tea on.'

Marcras was walking away from the fire. 'Marcras. Get the tea on.'

'I need to make an offering for our survival.'

'Gods, Marcras.'

'I'll do it,' said Lidae. Stirred up the embers. From their packs they dug out tea and bread and salt meat.

'We need to get another camp slave,' said Emmas.

'Treat her better,' said Lidae. 'Yes?'

The tea had an iron taste to it from the water. There was a way to hold your food that Lidae had been taught and taught Marcras in turn so that the bread and meat they ate was not fouled with the blood on them.

'That must be the end of them,' said Emmas. 'The battle must be won.'

Marcras came to sit by the fire, wiping his hand where he had dedicated a hacked lump of something before the panoply to the King. Lidae passed him a cup of tea.

'We're finished here,' he said. 'We are, we must be. The horsemen are starting to come back. We'll be in Gaeth tomorrow, the city will fall or open its gates to us.'

'If there's anyone left,' said Lidae, 'to open them.'

'And the treasures there ... It's not a big city—' Lidae thought, the poor sweet boy, so ignorant, knows less of the world even than I do '— it's not a big city but it's rich.' Marcras's hands and eyes sketching out things in the air in front of him that a rich city might hold if he only could imagine it.

'We'll get a camp slave there, then,' said Acol. 'The king of Geath: he's got twenty virgin daughters, they say.'

Emmas's eyes bulged.

'And twenty virgin sons.'

The sun was coming up now golden. Cloud in the east on the horizon stained by the morning, Lidae could pretend in her heart that they were the peaks of the great snow-capped mountains. They finished their meal, bedded down as they were filthy and sticky, curled into sleep in the warm rising sun. Lidae dreamed of something sweet and peaceful, soft as flowers, woke to the ringing of more silver trumpets to find the evening drawing in. All day she had slept warm in the gentle sun. Stiff from sleeping in her armour. Clotted black with stench and ashes. Her hair was matted to her face with blood. The rest of them struggling up to their feet stretching, rubbing their eyes, 'what's up, what's up, what's going on?'

'We're marching.'

Marcras said happily, 'See?'

'Gods, you stink,' Emmas said to Lidae. 'You absolutely stink.'

She felt like she must smell. 'So do you, Emmas.' Another time, a long time ago now, when she had lain all day in a pile of corpses, sticky with her family's blood. The same weariness the ache the stench the dirt feel, heavy clogged limbs and head. The smell of survival. Beautiful.

From the pale of dawn the sky now flamed with sunset, long gold shadows and the sky red and black. All over the corpse-plain soldiers were stumbling gathering themselves. The aftermath of battle. The preparations for new dizzying battles to come. In the centre there, far off, looming, shining, the King's tent was being dismantled. Ox carts stamped and puffed to receive it. Sweetwood poles and furnishings, the trappings of a royal court the heart of an empire. The generals' tents, the tents of the generals' women; servants, kitchen tents, sick wagons loaded with living corpses to be carted pointlessly on. In the dark we will be marching, west into the sunset where the sun falls away to be devoured by the night; we fought in the darkness and we were blind to all but killing; we march in the darkness staring as if lit by a thousand suns. The clean efficiency of an army long practised, men and women who have lived all their lives in the columns of the march. Lidae gathered her things together quickly. Her one change of dress, her change of boots, her cookpot, her tea mug. At her waist she wore a purse filled with gold coins, her sword, her knife. That was all that she owned to carry. Somewhere far behind the baggage train would come bringing her wealth from all the cities she had butchered, a cart drawn by a looted packhorse weighed down with looted goods. The man who drove it had been looted also. The one time she had gone to look at her possessions he had been kneeling in the dirt on shaking legs praying, spittle white around his mouth.

'Right lads. Up and marching,' Acol the squad commander said.

'Up and marching,' Emmas shouted to Lidae and Sammik and Marcras. The trumpets rang again. The drums began to beat out the rhythm of their marching feet.

'Gaeth,' said Marcras. 'Gaeth, small and rich and waiting.' His face was bright with happiness. They marched for long hours through the darkness. Torches ahead of them, lighting all the long columns like a winter feast. They sang as they went, loud and tuneless, the paean, the war song of the King Amrath, bawled out into the dry night. It was very clear, warm almost to sweating; the air had a strange smell to it, inviting. Stirred memories, feelings: they cannot be true memories, thought Lidae, but they feel so real and true, it makes me feel sad. They went five abreast, she was marching on the far edge of the column, she turned her head to look out away from the bronze helmet of the man ahead of her, out into the night. With the torches, the dark beyond was total, a flat blankness stretching away from her, the stars above vast.

'Look!' She pointed, Emmas beside her turned.

'What?'

'A shooting star.'

He sighed. 'I never see these things.'

'Perhaps there'll be another.' Last year, she thought, do you remember, just after I joined, we all saw them, ten, twenty shooting stars over the course of three nights' marching, we all knew what they meant.

After another hour the trumpets rang, the order came back that they were to make camp here. A fine place, one could tell even in the darkness: there were trees, a rarity in these parts, a river, thin and clear, for water, at their backs rose the steep slopes of the Gaeni hills. The baggage, inevitably, was still far behind them on the plain, 'We'll sleep better tomorrow,' Acol the squad commander told them, 'it'll all be here by first light.' The wind changed as they were getting themselves settled down to sleep, blew hard from the north bringing a faint smell of smoke. A hint of orange light, on the horizon to the north. 'And there'll be a good breakfast tomorrow morning,' Acol said. Up in the hills torchlights flickered, their soldiers up there looking down protecting them, looking out from the brow of the hill away to the south at lands still to be won. The King was up in the hills, Lidae felt that suddenly, looking down over them watching over them like mother watches a child, turning to look out into the dark to the lands yet unconquered with yearning in His heart. Every one of them camped down there on the plains knew it, even in their sleep men's faces turned towards Him.

So many of them. If they turned on him. Just a handful, no more, three, four of them, angry, mourning, if they rushed forward now, swords and spears, empty-handed, he thinks, even, he stands alone one frail slim figure, two or three of them in their heavy armour, strong with rage against him, if they knocked him down, punched him, kicked him. The crowd of them there in front of him, all they have to do is walk forward together, and they could trample him. All he has to do is draw his sword, run towards them. He catches his breath, clenches his hand on his sword hilt. You know what I've done to you, he wants to shout to them. He breathes out a long deep sigh and his hand is so tight on his sword hilt it hurts him. Far back in the ranks, a man holds a spear at a bad angle so that the point seems to drive straight at his throat. A hawk screams high in the sky overhead.

Waste of space, waste of bloody air, you are, gods, if you hadn't been born, how much better the world would be. But you can't bring yourself to do it, can you? So useless you can't even do that one fucking thing.

Kill yourself, Marith. Get it over with, do it, you useless worthless shit.

He turns his back on them, bends his head down like a man at the block. Their cheers fill his head so loud beyond thinking. He walks through them, like walking through the sea with the waves parting before him, back to his tent.

idae woke at dawn. Eager-hearted. Crows circled overhead, huge numbers of them, fighting over something in the air. A slave woman was kneeling making up a cookfire. Her face had a grey pallor to it: the baggage train must have marched all night to catch up with them. Two sutler women came walking through the camp carrying baskets. The dew gilded their bare feet, stained the hems of their long skirts; they left green footprints on the silver-wet grass. Thin hard faces weathered by years following the Army of Amrath. They could be twenty or fifty years old. Their dresses were silk brocade, one pink and green and yellow, one peacock blue and gold. Bracelets and necklaces jangled as they walked.

'Fresh meat!' the women in blue shouted. 'We sacked a village last night! Fresh meat!'

'Here's some coin.' Lidae handed three in iron to the slavewoman at the fire. 'Go and get enough for all of us.'

The slave looked back at her painfully.

'Get enough for yourself as well,' Lidae said. The slave blinked.

'They'll be bringing bread rations round soon,' said Emmas. He was sitting up, rubbing his eyes, yawning. 'Get the meat well cooking by then.' He took out a pan from his marching pack, and a pouch of salt.

The slave came back. Frightened. 'She says ... the woman says six in iron.' The slave's voice shook with fear.

'Six? She can fuck right off.' Emmas went over there; Lidae followed him. The slave bent by the fire, tending it. It burned very strong and bright, a good clear fire, catching well; she was clever at it. Tended it carefully, like it was barely burning and needed coaxing still. Lidae thought: she is afraid we will blame her for the price of the meat.

'Six in iron,' the sutler woman in blue said. She had silk flowers in her hair like the flower garlands the Queen sometimes wore, huge glass earrings one green one amber that shook as she shook her head. From her basket the strong metal smell of fresh meat. Flies buzzing at the white cloth covering it. The crows circled overhead, looking down, hoping.

'Six in iron?' said Emmas. 'Six?'

The sutler woman's hands were as crusted with blood as their own. Ground in deep beneath her nails, marking out the folds of her skin. The lines on her palms that some believed told secrets were written out in blood. There were maggots crawling in the blood and filth clotting her strong thin wrists.

'Six.' Her eyes were grey, outlined with black kohl. Owl eyes, animal eyes. Amongst the gold and jewels and gewgaws she wore a live beetle pierced and hung on a leather cord around her neck as a luck charm. The movement of the beetle's legs made the chains around it shift. 'It's good fresh meat,' she said. 'Worth the price. I cut it myself barely an hour ago. Give you strength for the coming battle.'

'There'll be dead in their thousands, after the coming battle,' said Emmas. 'Piles of them, your knives will be blunted before you can cut them all.'

The sutler woman gave him a smile. 'Who's going to portion it up for you, though? Are you going to do it, soldier man? You want to be what I am, do you?' Her earrings and her necklaces rattled at her laughing. 'Six in iron. Fresh, clean, well-cut meat.'

'Six in iron. The best cuts.'

Lidae dropped six coins into the outstretched hand. Clawed like crows' feet. Maggots crawling up the skin. The woman's eyes looked at her like the eyes painted on pictures of war ships. The sutler handed her the basket with a cold hard mother's grin. 'Keep you strong, girl.'

'Six! Six!' Emmas was spitting all the way back to the cookfire. 'Six! *You want to be what I am, do you?* Rich is what she bloody is! Gods, I should give this up and be a fucking sutler myself.'

They got the meat cooking, fine thick steaks of it with the fat bubbling in the skillet pan, char it black on the outside, red and bloody at the heart of it, sprinkled with salt grains and the last of the hot spices looted from Balkash. A rind of fat that Emmas chewed at length with a happy smile on his face. The slavewoman was good at cooking it. Looked sick and white at eating it. Afterwards a bowl each of thick barley porridge, the barley-meal starting to get stale. Sammik's man brought Sammik's boys to join them; the younger painted himself in porridge.

'Strong soldiers they'll be, soon enough,' said Sammik.

'They'll need new clothes in Gaeth,' said her man. 'Look at them, they're getting tall.'

'We should start them training properly,' said Emmas. The older boy was four, old enough to understand, he clapped his hands in delight.

'We'll get you a little sword made,' said Sammik.

'And a helmet! A helmet mummy, a helmet!'

'What about armour, little man?'

Lidae's corselet was lying waiting to be cleaned, the boy went over, tried to lift it: 'Heave. Heave.' He carried it a few steps, looked set to drop it, took it all the way over to Lidae and dropped it at her feet. 'Heave. See? I can lift it. I can wear it.'

'You want to?' She dressed him carefully. The corselet came down to his ankles. The shoulders covered his upper arms. He laughed and walked about like a tortoise until even the slavewoman laughed.

Someone did try to kill him, once. He remembers it dimly: a dark tent, a thing all of shadow, a twist of light, a hiss of breath. He remembers clearly the man dying later under a hail of stones, the men of his army, the camp followers, screaming and throwing stones, they kissed the stones before they threw them, prayed to him to guide their aim, shouted his name when they threw true. They would have torn the man apart with their bare hands, he remembers; they tore the body apart after the man was dead. A thousand spears, he remembers, they raised up each proudly bearing a scrap of dead flesh. They danced and sang all night, crowned with flowers, because they had killed the beast who had wanted their beloved king dead. For days afterwards they knelt at his feet if he passed them, kiss the earth he trod on with tears in their eyes and swear that they would have died a thousand times in his stead. They set up shrines outside their tents and made a prayer: take my first-born child, my mother, the sight from my eyes, oh you gods, but only spare the King. They took the tears that came into his eyes for gratitude, and loved him the more for it. They watched over him all night in a great crowd around his tent.

He thinks, sometimes: if I offered a thousand gold thalers … Hired someone to hire someone to put a price on my head …

He remembers the knife coming down, the man's face raw with hate. He remembers lying very still, waiting. He remembers the knife not touching him. He remembers the man dropping the knife, kneeling before him, begging him to forgive.

Gods, boy. What a joke you are, yeah? I mean, pathetic, or what?

Marith Altrersyr: such a fucking failure he fucking failed to fucking die when someone tried to fucking kill him.

The army reached Gaeth two days later. The camp buzzed with excitement. Tomorrow. Tomorrow. Tomorrow. Break the walls and shatter the gates and kill them all inside. A small city, barely worth noting, its walls are made of bricks and mortar, its houses are roofed in straw. A rich city, they say: it sits on the road from Calchas to Cen Elora, levies tolls on all who make the journey west in search of wonders. But the land here is barren and dry and very little grows. They dig gold in the dry hills, lapis stone as blue as a summer dusk. They eat dried fish carried ten days' on horseback from the Small Sea and think themselves blessed to have it.

The King drew them up in long rows, all of the soldiers in the Army of Amrath, column after column of them stretching from horizon to horizon, wheat ripening in the fields, waves on the bottomless pitiless dark sea. Bronze armour polished and gleaming. Red banners proud in the wind. They stood in silence, graven faces like the faces of statues, still and frozen, looking yearning longing towards Him. Men from all across the world now, from every corner of Irlast.

His people from the lands He ruled over before His wars began, from the White Isles, Ith, Illyr, haughty in their boasting: we were first above all men to know Him, we who were born in the very lands He was sprung from, we who crowned Him!

Soldiers from the lands He had conquered, who threw down their weapons at His coming, knelt at His feet to acknowledge Him. He forgave them, He told them kindly, 'Kill your brothers who do not surrender to me, your parents, your husbands and wives, your daughter and your sons. Your servants and your kings.' Their love for Him, their happiness at His receiving them, sparing them.

Soldiers from the lands He had yet to conquer, who left their families to serve Him, talked with eager hope of the day He might turn His eyes towards their home. He stood before them in his blood-covered cloak, crowned in silver, his sword Joy in His beautiful slender hand. His shining black-red hair, His skin like white moonlight, His grey eyes soft as moth's wings that no man dares look upon and live.

'My soldiers! My beloveds! My own! You who have butchered the world for me!'

Of all that is and was and will be, of all that lives and dies and dreams of life. Of all that weeps in sorrow, of all that is shame and ruin, of all that is dirt and filth. Of all that is wonder. Of all that is glory. Of all that is blank blind emptiness. Of all things on all the black earth of Irlast, He is the most beautiful, the most terrible, the most loved.

'We have marched from Illyr in the north where the sea freezes, we have burned all that our shadow has fallen upon, we stand now in the dry plains with the world open to us west and south. We will take Gaeth this evening with the sunset, we will feast there for three days, we will march again. Are you with me?'

Ten times a thousand swords beating on bronze armour. Ten times a thousand spears beating on the dry ground.

'The earth here is dust, good for nothing. Let us make it wet with blood.'

They screamed His name, they screamed the paean. They stamped their feet and the earth shook.

I *just want to die. Please. Kill me. Kill me!*

You must … someone must want to kill me.

There must be such hatred of him. He shattered endless countless lives, wiped whole cities from the face of the earth. There are soldiers in his own army who have lost everything they ever loved at his hands. A second army of slaves trails after his soldiers. A third army of beggars, destitute, starving, stumbles in his slaves' wake.

And yet—and yet—one man once tried to kill him, and now no one thinks to rise up against him.

There are cities and kingdoms he has not yet conquered, and they must know, surely, that he will come for them? This city, Gaeth: tomorrow it will be destroyed as if it had never been. It sits here waiting for him. Every man and woman within its wall, the youngest child there, they must have known, surely, that he would come for them? What he would do to them? They will have heard the stories, refugees will have clamoured at their walls talking of the atrocities he has inflicted. The wind blows from the east and it stinks of rot and burning, they must smell it. Flies and human ashes blow on the wind across the world. Yet no one dares try to stop him.

It is as though they see him as something unavoidable. A harsh winter and then a bad summer, and so the crops fail and famine comes. A disease that spreads unchecked through a city for which no one has a cure. One day we wake up, go quietly about our business, and then suddenly the earth shakes, brings the house down on our heads. There was nothing, the survivors say when it was over, against such a thing, there was nothing we could do. What could we do? The history books are filled with king killings. Great fat tomes filled with them. He used to sit once by the fire in his bedchamber dreaming over them. The king must fall!

The only way we can save our lives, our city, our freedom! A knife in the dark, an arrow from the alley, a traitor in the court, a full out assault on the throne room … they've all been done and done and done and done. But he, King Death, King Ruin, pestilence, filth, he who has killed babies in the cradle, who has destroyed whole cities, he who killed his father, his brother, his best and only friend—no one thinks now to do it to him. As no one thinks to kill an earthquake, a flood, a drought that will bring famine. They rush to fight his soldiers, line up against his soldiers to kill and die again and again and again. But they cannot conceive, now, of trying to kill him.

Small indeed, crouched on the dry plain behind high mud walls, searching out for any trace of wet green. There's a marsh, cool wetlands rich with fish and birds and flowers, five days walk from here on the shores of the Closed Sea. In the hills behind Gaeth there are green valleys, the hills run dun and green to the shores of the Small Sea where the earth is black and good. Stinks of life. Between the hills and the marsh the people of Gaeth live in dry dust on the dry plain hacking their crops out of stone-soil, because the road must come through here between the hills and the marshes and thus here the money comes. The houses are old crumbling mud brick, low and lumped, staring inwards; the richest men of Gaeth may have in their courtyards a rose bush or a peach tree or a fig tree. The skin of the people of Gaeth is dry and wrinkled, their hair is rubbed with oil, their lips are thin and white. They dress in satin, they adorn themselves with jewels, they account a man's wealth in water and milk. The wind blows cold through the streets of Gaeth, rubbing the skin of the people red. Two children in three die before they are six months old.

And here we are. We march. We take it. We shatter it, we kill it, we go on to lush rich soil beyond. A happenstance, a milestone on the journey. It happened to be here and we happened to come this way towards it. Nothing personal, the King and His generals say as they prepare the troops for battle. You are here and we are here and … well. That's how it has to happen. In war. Please understand that.

They worship a stone, they say, in Gaeth. It fell from the sky in a blaze of fire, and the people carried it into their city and built it a temple of mud bricks. Placing one's hands on it can cure leprosy. It glows in the night, they say, in the silent dark of its shrine. It is dark green in colour, almost the colour of the green jade marble they quarry in Maun and Medana: so perhaps it is simply a lump broken from an old building, carted a thousand miles and more across Irlast. If one squints at it, they say, it looks like a tree in spring leaf.

'Form up, Blades,' Acol ordered. 'Form up there.'

Lidae took her place in the second row behind Emmas, looking at her face reflected in his bronze helmet. Marcras beside her began to mutter his prayers.

'King Amrath. God Amrath. King Amrath. God Amrath—'

'Silence in the ranks,' Acol ordered, and Lidae could have blessed him, although Marcras's lips still moved and he'd soon start up again. Sammik on her other side shuffled her feet in her bronze leg-guards. Sammik looked very calm apart from that.

They pressed up closer. Going forwards. Close up to the front. The war machines loosed and the mud walls of Gaeth were coming open, cracking. 'Spray them with water, why don't we?' Emmas whispered.

The dragons rose in the evening sky. Acol choked and Lidae choked from seeing it. However many times one saw it. Forever and forever one could watch the dragons rising, throwing off all of themselves at the enemy, free of all things but death. Red and black, green and silver. 'Sorrow' and 'Joy', the Army had named them, after the King's swords. If they had names, no one could hold the sound of them in their minds. If the King knew their names, He said nothing.

'Oh fuck. Oh gods. Beautiful.'

The dragon that was called Sorrow clawed at the mud walls of Gaeth, tore them open. Arrows showered over it: Lidae, watching to go in, heard the rattle of them on its scales, useless. It twisted its head. A voice called from the wall, screaming to surrender to them. Green wings beat the air thick and dark. The crack in the wall widened, a great chunk of it came down in a cloud of dust. Blown into their faces making them spit. Eyes blinking. Lidae drank water to wash the taste from her mouth.

Going in through the breach.

The column marched forward. No rushing. Slow and steady, over the rubble. Already the corpses of the city's dying, stretched out broken over broken bricks, hands thrown out in supplication, mouths open with a prayer for surrender on their lips. Dragon fire; a war engine loosing. Ten of their own men before them fell dead in the mouth of the breach.

'Keep marching,' Acol called to them. Dragon fire licked around his helmet. He walked through a wall of fire. Arrows clattering on his helmet. Emmas followed him, and Lidae followed Emmas. The yawning gap in the shattered walls. Dry dust smell of baked mud.

Right up at the front of the lines. Fighting to hold it. The enemy was cowering behind the walls, pressed close, burning running liquid trying to hold them off. Press of spears facing them, wavering, shaking in the defenders hands but the spears are holding, we with our swords must go onto them. Lines behind pressing forward. On and in. On and in. Hacking, cutting, we choke from the mud dust, Lidae's face is stained grey. All the pain before us, the defenders weep as they fight, we cut them, press them, the world runs red with dragon fire the air is thick with dust. Someone falling there beside Lidae: Marcras, she thinks, not Sammik with her children, oh please no, but not Marcras either, poor sweet boy still a child himself. Her feet trample over him as she presses on. They are fighting hanging knotted in the shadow of the wall breach. The dragon screams overhead. The earth shakes the city is falling. The defenders the enemy push hard against us, bracing themselves, crying out knowing they have nothing left to live for but to die in our beautiful blood. When the poets tell of this victory, they will say that the men of Gaeth were strong, died meeting the enemy face to face.

Lidae drove her sword into a spear shaft. Into a weeping screaming body clawing blood. The red glass in the hilt winked at her. The blade bit home sweetly, warm slide into a man's fat flesh. The enemy line was crumbling, spears falling, men falling. Dead mouths gasping in the dust. Pressing forwards, churning through the breach. And a roar beyond swimming in her ears, men's voices and the dragon and the sound of the wall falling, as another breach was opened up. She pressed forward in pain with a spear point cutting her. Coughing in the mud dust. Her feet slipping in red liquid mud.

The enemy were falling back. The line of spears broke helplessly. Push and stab onwards with the enemy falling back falling back. Sliding on our dead, their dead. A voice shrieking, 'Hold! Hold! To me, men of Gaeth!' until it was drowned and gone. Lidae ran forward with her sword clutched tight bloody in bloody hands. See the smile on her face. The dragon Sorrow lashed the air, its flames running over the dark of the city. Tearing all the life away from within the city's walls. All of our army pushing up behind. Houses barred and shuttered begging to be broken open. Storerooms of household treasures, buried hoards of coin, the temple and the king's house all adorned with silver and gold. Soft-fingered soft-eyed children, narrow-hipped girls running on slender ankles, cowering away in hiding, dirt on their shining clothing, their lovely hair unbound. The city of Gaeth surrenders, holds itself out to us, kneels and begs for us, yearning. We are tearing through the narrow streets in the killing light in the killing fire, our swords bloody in our hands. The city bares itself for us. Begs for killing. Through the streets, through the houses, we run free and wild, we grant it what it seeks.

By dawn there was nothing left of Gaeth but muddy corpses. A few slaves being dragged away back to the camp. Lucky or unlucky, those that have survived it: toss a coin which is the better outcome, life or death.

'Went well,' said Emmas. They had found a place to stop and drink in a square where three streets met beneath an awning of green silk. There was a trough holding dirty stinking water, carved with a feast scene of veiled women dancing. They had taken a barrel of wine from a wine shop, sat around it. Fine and sweet and strong and red. The people of Gaeth were great drinkers, the water being scarce and stained with mud.

'You build a city where there's no water, because that puts you on a trade route for the merchants bringing wine that you need to buy to replace the water that you haven't got because you built the city where there's no water.' Emmas said slowly, 'Seems somewhat … circular.'

'It does, yeah,' said Acol. He raised his cup to them, smiled. 'Well done. A good night's work.'

'It was. Oh yes.' Emmas was wearing a necklace he had taken from a girl a few hours earlier. A complex, heavy thing, multiple strands of glass beads and gold. Two of the strands were broken, the beads smashed. 'I might get it fixed,' he said. 'Or might not bother. I didn't notice until afterwards that it was damaged. Stupid girl must have rolled on it. Either of your boys want it, Sammik?'

'Erist might like it. No … no, he's too old not to see it's broken. Mar would love it, but he's too young, I don't like him putting things around his neck.'

'Shame,' said Emmas. 'It can't be worth much. Probably not worth repairing.'

'Do we know that Marcras is dead?' Lidae asked Acol.

Acol shook his head. 'I don't know, no.'

You should know, Lidae thought. I'd know, if I were squad commander; I'd find out somehow before I sat and drank wine to celebrate. Marcras could be lying in the filth, in pain, wounded, the sutler women could be at him now with their knives, pleased at the strong freshness of his meat. You should be looking for him, getting him treated or putting him out of his pain or saying goodbye to him. May the King's peace rest on him.

'I saw him go down,' Lidae said, 'but I didn't see anything more than that.' All the offerings Marcras had made, his chants and prayers grating on their nerves, the panoply of arms and armour he set up after every battle, dragged in the baggage train all across Irlast: for nothing. 'Did he have any family, do you know?' Lidae asked Emmas.

Shrug. 'He must have had a mother once, I'd guess. Father too, for one night at least.'

'He talked about a sister, once,' said Sammik. 'Older than him, I think, from the way he spoke about her. I don't know, I can't remember her name.' Sammik frowned, a shadow came over her face.

'We'll divide his stuff up between us, then,' said Sammik. 'Apart from that stupid panoply. That gets dumped.'

'We could sell it,' said Emmas. 'It's beautiful work.' Enamel flowers on the breastplate, and the helmet crest had copper wire set amongst the horsehair.

'He took it from a dead man, he made offerings before it for his life to be preserved in battle and then he died in battle,' said Sammik. 'We dump it.'

'Pity.'

The armour was very fine. A pity, yes. Lidea said, 'Have it yourself, then, Emmas, if you want it.'

'I …' Emmas's eyes went to the body of a woman, sprawled on the street cut up. It had still been moving, a little, when they sat down there by the water trough, one hand had moved reaching towards them, a faint wordless sound had come whistling from its lips. 'No,' Emmas said.

Sammik raised her cup. 'To Marcras and his armour. I'm done here. I'll go back to camp now, I think.'

'I'll come with you.' Lidae got to her feet. 'Ransack some more houses for us, Emmas.' Two men were walking ahead of them dragging a cart loaded with looted rubbish. The carved legs of a table stuck up, jerking as the cart jerked. One of the cartwheels was smashed up. They never, Lidae thought, never had enough working baggage carts.

Back at the camp Mar and Erist came up dancing to greet them, Sammik's man laughing behind.

'Presents?' the boys shouted. Butting up around Sammik like little bull calves. 'Presents! Presents!'

'Well, now, let's see shall we …'

A messenger came later, from Acol: 'Marcras is alive. He is with the rest of our injured.'

'How bad is it?'

Acol said, 'Bad enough.'

The injured were housed was at the very furthest edge of the camp. Near the latrines, far away from the horse lines and the generals' tents. Two tents, small and rotting, a few men dumped down on a covered cart. We of the Army of Amrath, we do not take much account of the wounded. Fight for the King, win triumph and glory, die in the glory of dying for Him. Being weak and wounded … we can fight wounded, many have done it; well, then, if we cannot fight, we are not soldiers. The smell of death hangs over the tents of the wounded. The sound of them, that drifts out of the tents. Lidae had gone there once before to look for a comrade who was wounded, had put a knife in his throat to spare him.

'A sutler woman found him,' said Acol. 'He was lucky, she was reminded of her own son, she said, who died in battle. She brought him here.'

It was bright warm sunshine, hazy through the dust they had thrown up. Midday, noisy with song birds and crows. Around the tents of the wounded was only the whisper of dying men. They hung on the threshold together, taking a deep breath like diving beneath cold water, stepped as they had stepped into the city's breached walls. The wounded were huddled in clumps together, holding each other, limbs pressed against limbs. Where their bodies were torn in shreds they merged together, wrapped into each other, penetrated each other. Lovers' embraces and many-limbed many-headed beasts. Bones and entrails spilling tangled. The quiet soft drip of their blood.

'Marcras?'

He was in the furthest corner of the tent, propped upright. His face was gashed so that his eyes were hidden. He seemed otherwise unharmed.

A slow, slow death.

His lips moved. 'King Amrath. God Amrath. King Amrath. God Amrath.'

Kneeling before his panoply. The fear on his face. Eager, when he leapt into battle, a young lion, a wolf in the winter hungry for flesh. No man can say of him that he did not deserve his glory.

'Marcras,' Lidae said.

He did not reply, he was far beyond them now. The death sweat showed clammy on his face.

'We could take him outside, let him die in the sunlight,' said Lidae.

'He'd die,' said Acol. 'If we try to move him.'

Lidae thought: I know. But we have to say it. We shouldn't have come. I wish I hadn't known that he was here. Imagined him cleanly dead. A hero at the breach where another city fell.

'I'll do it,' said Acol. 'Unless you want to?'

There was a stirring behind them in the tent doorway. A hissing, a whispering, a murmur like the wind in green trees. A single bright clear shout: 'The King! Way for the King!'

The doorcurtain moved. White light flooded the tent.

He was there in the doorway, a shadow against the light on the threshold and then He came in amongst them, standing in the midst of His wounded men. His hair was red-black silk, shining, His skin was white as white blossoms, He was dressed in black and cloaked in stinking red blood. On His head was a crown of silver. The sword Joy hung at His hip. The God. The King.

Lidae knelt. Her heart beating and shivering. A thousand shadows followed Him, moved around Him, they curled about the tent caressed the faces of the dying, licked at wounds, drank the drops of Marcras's fever sweat. Acol knelt, his face lit and radiant. A praise song for Him:

Lidae joined him in whispering it. The old woman had fallen on her face, trembling.

The dying men turned, every one of them, their maimed eyes looking at Him.

'Carn.' He bent down beside a young man. Flesh mottled white and green, changing, sinking back down into the earth, mould grew on his face and his limbs. The man held out his broken hands, and the King held them. A crack as the skin of his wounds broke.

'My Lord King,' the man whispered. 'My Lord King. My Lord. I fought for you. I didn't give up, even wounded. I lay in the dirt and still I killed them.'

'Yes, you did, I am sure,' the King said. His voice was very gentle. His eyes were pale and soft. Lidae saw them without looking, felt His gaze searching over all the men there. 'A hero,' the King said. 'I am grateful for what you did.' The dying man smiled, his hand clutched at the King's white hand. There was great peace in him. A silent fragile whisper of music, the cool song of a summer dawn when the dew rises as white mist in the meadows and the air is fresh and clean and sweet. The tent was filled with that joyous melancholy of the morning, a breeze stirring the branches of the lilac, a blackbird singing to greet the dawn, the world is made of wonder and mystery. In the east the sky is rose petals; the stars are faded in the west to nothing, in the west the sky is blue water like a cool distant unknown sea. The dying man held the King's hand to him, clutched to his chest where his sickening heart beat. Lidae watched the man die looking up in rapture into the face of the King.

Those that could move themselves crowded around Him, kneeling, holding out their hands. He touched them, held them, rested His pale gaze on them. Some died. Some stirred themselves, sat up more strongly, colour and hope coming back into them. A glory, Lidae thought, a glory beyond all, gods, to lie here wounded, to know that He sees them wounded and suffering for Him. When He came to Marcras sitting still and rigid the

King bent, went down on one knee, Marcras's blood-face turned to the King, raw red holes where his boy's eyes had been, searching, searching. A sleeping face stirring in the sun.

'What is his name?' the King said to Acol.

'Marcras.'

'Marcras. Thank you for fighting for me, Marcras,' the King said. 'I hope that you are soon healed and well.'

He went out then, His shadows following at His heels.

A pause, a long strange sweet silence. A breath and a scent and a new warmth in the air.

Marcras let out a great laugh. Got to feet. His face was shining and well.

'Healed! Healed! I'm well! Praise the King!'

They camped in the ruins of Gaeth for three more days, they moved on west with the afternoon sun golden on their faces, the promise of richer lands before them in the sunsets, the smell of fruit trees and wheat fields and soft plump weak men. Marcras could run and fight as well as if he had never been wounded, by the time they left Gaeth.

Lidea's heart was bright with excitement. Every day, as they marched, new things unfolding before her, new landscapes, new peoples. Striding across the world tall and glorious. I have a sword in my hand and I am powerful. I am someone in the world. I kill.

A cheap form of power.

A cruel one.

Perhaps, yes.

But glorious.

Glorious beyond all things.

Thank you, she would pray each night. Thank you, My King.

Take your sword, Marith, hold it to your throat, push it in.

Pour yourself a cup of poison, sweeten it with honey, drink. You do so like to drink.

Take off your stupid over-elaborate armour, it makes you look a right cock anyway, Marith, a right bloody dickhead, take off your armour, your sword, wrap a cloth round your head to disguise yourself, go out into the camp one evening and start a fight.

Look at all this power you've got. So bloody special, so mighty, like you're a stupid bloody god. But will all that bloody power … I mean: everything in this fucking world dies, Marith. Apart from you.

He travels in a wagon for the new journey, shut away because he can't bear to see the eager faces look at him. Every night he thinks: if one of them tried … just one or two of them, angry, grieving, ambitious, and I lie here alone with my head spinning with drink. There must be someone, somewhere, who has the courage. The renown they'd claim, afterwards. Such a glorious vengeance they could shout. Or one of my lords, he thinks, they could take my place, have all this, have everything, be king. Hail me, behold me, king of light and hope and living, who has freed us all, risked my life to strike down the demon beast!

And he thinks: and that's why no one will do it. Because they all look at me, and they know what I am, and no one on all the black earth of Irlast wants to be as I am. They made me what I am, thus they are so afraid, all of them, of what will come to them in turn if they kill me. They cannot, they dare not, kill me. They want to, all of them, how can they not, but they dare not kill me because they know how it will be for them if they are become like me.

And he knows that's a lie also.

Without me, he thinks, they would have no one to blame for what they are doing. The king, the demon, the monster who oppresses us, he made us, he told us, he ordered it, blame him. If they kill me, think of killing me, they will admit they are guilty also. And my enemies, the armies that stand against me—while I live, there is nothing they can do that they cannot justify as good and righteous, because it was done in the name of defeating the demon beast.

The king must fall, yes.

But as long as the king lives, they can blame him.

THE BOOK BURNER'S FALL

Anthony Ryan

Chapter One

For the briefest moment she thought killing Baron Colbyn might not be possible after all. She had come to this drab, rain-drenched west-Renfaelin mill town expecting to commit an unhesitant murder. For weeks she had carried with her the faces of the two dozen Ascendants Colbyn and his retainers had left in the forest, hacked and empty eyed, naked flesh greyed by the absence of blood, several children lying amongst the slain. In their frenzy, the baron's party had even killed the dogs in that cluster of hidden hovels. So, his death should have been a simple matter requiring no more than an instant of effort, and yet …

It was his manner that gave her pause. As Baron Colbyn, followed by his sons and retainers, rode along the muddy thoroughfare that formed the town's only street, she saw more in his face than the mindless prejudice and brutality common to persecutors the world over. He met every dull, hungry, accusing gaze in this ragged town with unwavering fortitude and, more surprisingly, compassion. This was not a landholding noble intent only on extracting his due rents and subservience. This man felt a weight of responsibility for the plight of his people, even if the true author of their beggared state sat in a palace many miles to the south.

She tried to steel herself to the task, summoning the faces of the slain Ascendants, buttressing her conviction with the numerous previous horrors she had witnessed. So many crimes, so much slaughter, not all the work of the baron, of course, but certainly of his ilk. So what if he cared about his peasants? She had a massacre to avenge this day and would see it done.

Once again, Baron Colbyn contrived to frustrate her when he reined his fine steed to a halt beneath the stalled sails of the town's principal mill. People had already begun to form a line, clutching the purses and sacks containing what meagre produce they hoped to tender in lieu of rent. Some, inevitably, had nothing to offer but still shuffled forward to await their lord's judgment, heads bowed and shoulders slumped in anticipation of the shameful excuses they would stutter. However, their baron had no use for either rent, goods, or excuses this day.

Raising a hand, he called out a greeting, his voice strong and vibrant in the chilly, late autumn air. "Hear me, good people of, Hulesberth! I know that the Lord Collector has already visited this town and that the Crown Levy Agent came the month before that. Rest assured I have been visited by both myself and trying company they were."

It was a measure of the regard Colbyn enjoyed here that some of the townsfolk consented to laugh at this, although most simply stared in either trepidation or bafflement.

"Therefore," the baron went on, "today is not a rent day. Nor will there be another until the summer harvest. Instead, I invite you, good folk of Hulesberth, to join me in a feast!"

Colbyn raised his hand towards the far end of the town where a trio of ox-drawn carts was making its way along the rutted road. As they drew near, the assembled townsfolk let out a chorus of surprised grasps at the sight of the sacks of grain and barrels of ale. Some people even burst into grateful tears and bowed low to the baron. His unworthiness as a murder victim became yet more starkly apparent in the way he hastily dismounted to raise the commoners up from their grovelling before ordering his sons to marshal the tables and sundries for the feast.

Torn by indecision, she concealed herself within the throng of people crowding the carts. Short of stature and slight of build, she was distinguished by features many had told her were of remarkably feline prettiness. Consequently, in moments like these she concealed her face with a smearing of grime and an unruly cascade of chestnut coloured hair. Therefore, few paid heed to the stranger in their midst, most taking her for a wandering beggar girl. It also helped that she appeared far younger than her thirty-two years. Thankfully, none of the townspeople were so mean of disposition as to deny a youthful itinerant a share of the baron's largesse. So, it was a simple matter to move amongst them, slipping between the carts with carefully crafted blank-eyed wonder at such bounty. So intent was the crowd on the novel prospect of a full belly, she was able to approach to within a half-dozen yards of the baron himself without arousing any notice at all.

Her indecision still roiled like a restless beast at the sight of Colbyn exchanging a greeting with the town factor, all warm sympathy for the man's worries. The baron may have lived out the day, and many more besides, if her eye hadn't caught the pile of clothes being unloaded at his side. They were plain and homespun, but well made, nonetheless. Recently laundered and neatly folded too. She may have failed to discern their significance if she hadn't overheard the baron's offhand comment to the factor.

"These should help keep the chill off, eh?" he asked, clapping a hand to the gaunt fellow's shoulder. "Stripped them from that gaggle of Deniers we rooted out in the Green Woods a few weeks ago. Don't worry, had the blood scrubbed out." Then he laughed, a bluff, hearty laugh that damned him.

The beast within her coiled anew, but with predatory anticipation rather than confusion. It was a hungry thing and liked to be fed, often growing truculent at the extended periods in which she starved it. But now it sensed a meal at hand and hissed its gratitude much like these people had wept for their lord's beneficence.

She moved closer to Colbyn, allowing the beast to fully uncoil itself and fill her with its dark need. At times like this there was always a terrible delight in the moment, something she despised but could never suppress. It was part of her gift, and, therefore, part of her. It blossomed to a shuddering thrill as, for the briefest second, the baron's gaze slipped towards her. She parted the matted strands of hair veiling her face and captured his eyes, snaring him tighter than any trap. Within her, the beast's hiss became a full-throated snarl and she shuddered again, this time in pain rather than pleasure; this was an act that took a toll on the body.

Although Baron Colbyn's death appeared instantaneous to those who witnessed it, she knew it hurt a great deal, for she felt it too. The moment their eyes met created an unseen bridge between them, across which the beast could strike. So, when it lashed out and sank its ravening self deep into her victim, she felt the pain that wracked him as first his lungs collapsed and then his heart burst. Years of such shared horrors had left her with an intimate knowledge of the body's workings at the instant of death, so she knew that whilst blood no longer flowed through the baron's veins, it lingered in his brain. Consequently, he was fully aware of the inescapable reality of his end, the helpless terror and agony of feeling all vestige of life seep away in a few seconds. It was too short a payment for his crime, but it was something.

The beast withdrew the moment Colbyn's life flickered out, retreating to a tight, satiated coil at her core whilst she allowed her hair to conceal her face once more and mimicked the shocked, frozen state of those around her. Baron Colbyn stiffened and shuddered for his final few heartbeats, mouth gaping to release a brief, bloody surge before collapsing to the ground in a decidedly ignoble heap.

"Father?" the taller of his two sons said, voice curiously small and childlike for one so well built. He repeated the word several times as he knelt beside the baron's unmoving bulk, the words coloured by sobs. The crowd began to thicken around the scene, the clustering folk rendered silent by the sheer unexpectedness of the moment. The baron's retainers forced their way through, rushing to join the forlorn son's pointless attempts to revive a man so obviously dead.

As she had noticed many times, people were always drawn to, rather than repelled by scenes of sudden death, a useful if morbid human trait for it usually enabled her to slip away. But not today.

"She did it!"

The voice rang out just as she began to withdraw from the scene, enveloping herself in the growing crush of onlookers. Another, less useful attribute of crowds was their instinctive urge to move away from one marked as not of their kind, and so it proved now. She quickly found herself standing alone in a bare patch of mud, the townsfolk forming a circle around her whilst a woman with sparse, straggling hair sprouting from a near bald head dragged a small, emaciated child forward. The woman kept her finger pointed at the slight, now isolated stranger, her other hand tight around the child's wrist. It was a boy of no more than eight years, squirming in the woman's grip whilst shooting guarded, almost apologetic glances at the object of the crowd's interest.

"My nephew marked her as a witch!" Straggle Hair said, finger jabbing at the stranger with knife-like insistence. "He's never wrong. You all know that."

The word 'witch' spread through the throng in a murmur. The baron's sudden demise may well have denied them a feast, but a witch in need of killing promised at least some entertainment.

Had she been known here she might have talked herself clear. However, not a soul in this town had clapped eyes upon her before today. Furthermore, it was apparent that this boy, regret writ large in his tearful eyes, had a history of marking out those with gifted blood. The reason was clear to her, if not his aunt. His gift, whatever its nature might be, burned bright enough for her to sense it, as he could sense it in others.

"Witch!" the gifted boy's aunt cried out, finger jabbing with increased violence with each step as she drew near, voice hissing with more than a passing resemblance to that of the beast. "Killer!"

This, naturally, was swiftly taken up by the crowd. "Killer! Witch! Killer!" The discordant echo built into a chant as the space between stranger and townsfolk began to diminish. She considered running but there was no way through. She had knives hidden about her person in expert concealment, and was entirely capable of leaving more bodies on the ground before they closed in. But she hadn't come here for them; she came for the baron, and he was dead. So, she did nothing, simply stood at the eye of their burgeoning storm and felt oddly detached from the unfolding scene. When the first hand lashed out and struck a blow to the side of her head she wondered if they would hang her or burn her. As yet more blows rained down, bearing her to the mud where punches became kicks, she felt a growing certainty that it was far more likely they would beat her to death.

For a time, the world became a foggy chaos of pain and brief glimpses of descending kicks and leering, hate-filled faces. She had suffered beatings before, but none quite so overwhelming. She found it curious that the pain of individual blows merged into one great throbbing ache, filling her senses, flooding her vision with a dark red mist that soon shifted to grey. She knew it wouldn't be long before it turned black and then at least there would be no pain.

"Move back!" The shout was dim at first, a faraway echo barely penetrating her clouded awareness. More shouts followed, punctuated by the signature thud of hard things striking flesh. Then the scrape of a sword being drawn from a scabbard summoned her back from the grey fog. She was on her hands and knees, wrist deep in the mud. The patch directly beneath her face was red with her blood. She caught sight of her reflection in the red puddle, a more frightened face than she expected. Perhaps she wasn't as prepared for death as she thought. Then hands reached down to grasp her shoulders and haul her upright.

"Get away!" The voice was imbued with well-accustomed authority, the vowels smoothed by privilege. A noble's voice. Blinking the blood from her eyes she saw the baron's elder son standing between her and the crowd, longsword bared.

"She's a witch, Lord Edwird!" the straggle-haired aunt cried, finger still jabbing at the bloodied woman sagging in the grip of the baron's retainers. "It was her! We all know it! Justice for your father!"

Once again, the crowd proved a swift author of chants and the cry went up almost immediately. "Justice! Justice! Justice!"

"QUIET!" the baron's son roared, silencing the chant and causing the crowd to retreat a step.

"You want justice," the young noble said, glancing over his shoulder at his captive. "You'll have it, under the law. As my father would have decreed." He paused, lowering his face in momentary sorrow before turning back to the throng and speaking on. "As I also decree, for I am now baron of these holdings, and you are bound by my word as I am bound by the crown's laws. This woman." He pointed his sword at the stranger. "Will be held and the Crown Magistrate summoned to hear the accusations against her. This is the law. Those who would contest it will taste my steel, I swear by the Faith!"

His voice was hoarse, but the unwavering grip he maintained on his sword, and the line his retainers had formed to either side of him, convinced the townsfolk that their entertainment would be denied them this day.

"The goods in these carts are yours, by my father's order," Lord Edwird said as the crowd receded. Most wore faces that were dark with disapproval, but also lowered in contrite obedience. She wondered if they submitted because most were too starved to mount a serious riot. Edwird kept a steady glare upon them until they began to disperse, most returning to the half-unloaded carts. "Take it with his blessing," the new baron said in a strained mutter, sliding his sword back into its scabbard before turning to his captive.

She should have averted her gaze as he came closer, pretended dumb ignorance or played the simpleton. But she didn't. Her life had been rich in deceit and, whilst she hadn't yet exhausted her capacity for murder, she found to her surprise that she had no more stomach for lies.

"They're not wrong, are they?" Lord Edwird asked, leaning closer to meet her uncowed stare through the mud-caked mess of her hair. The noble's face was pale now, the raw pain of grief shining bright in his unblinking eyes as he spoke through clenched teeth. "I saw you. I saw you *look* at him."

She blinked against the spatter of spittle that accompanied his words, her voice flat as she replied, "Do you know why, my lord?"

The small twitch to his features told her the answer plainly, as did the absence of puzzlement in his eyes.

"Where you there?" she asked, feeling the beast stir. Summoning it again so soon would exact a high, perhaps even fatal price. Given her current circumstance, she didn't find the prospect fearful. "Did you strip any murdered children of those clothes? Or did you just content yourself with slaughtering the dogs?"

His features paled yet further and he retreated from her with a demeanour that mirrored the commoners he had just humbled. Coughing, he turned away, casting his parting words over his shoulder as he stomped towards his father's body. "You'll get your trial, witch. But don't expect it to be long."

Chapter Two

K estra Saero?"

The man standing in the open door of her cell phrased his question in a light, enquiring tone, only partially coloured by doubt. She deduced that, due to some innate sense of courtesy, he was trying to conceal his inability to connect her small, rag-clad and unwashed person with the name he had spoken. It was known to few, but the mere fact that he had spoken it told her a great deal. More significant still was the man's garb. For weeks her only companions besides the rats were the guards employed by the newly ascended Baron Edwird to keep watch in this grim, stunted tower. They all wore his household livery of black-and-grey tunics, somewhat besmirched, for these gaolers were not his best men. This newcomer proved a stark contrast with his dark blue cloak, hardy clothes, and the sword of the Asraelin pattern he wore on his back.

The light was dim despite it being nearly noon as her cell featured no windows and her captors were content to leave her in shadows. Therefore, she was unable to discern much of the man's face save that illuminated by the glow of the lantern held by the gaoler at his back. It outlined a head of close-cropped hair and dark skin which seemed at odds with an accent possessed of the broad vowels of southern Asrael. A curious figure, then, but not one with whom she was willing to converse, at least whilst the door remained open to inquisitive ears.

The blue-cloaked man let out a brief, amused huff at her silence then turned to the gaoler. "My thanks, good sergeant," he said, relieving the blunt-faced brute of his lantern. She caught the gaoler's resentful grimace before he stalked off down the passage, though he was wise enough to still his tongue. People with any sense did not argue with a brother of the Sixth Order.

"I am remiss," the brother said, stepping fully into her cell, lantern in hand. "In not offering my own name first. Please forgive me. Brother Lesander Doren, at your service." He paused to offer her a short bow before adding in a far quieter voice, "Sister."

Kestra shifted on the chill floor and rested her head against the wall, eyes closed. "I don't know what you're talking about," she told him in a tired, flat drawl. "Go away."

A brief interval of silence then the sound of her visitor softly closing the door, or as softly as one could close a ten-inch thick slab of oak and iron. She caught his scent as he returned to crouch at her side, the leathery, sweat tinged cloud that accompanied all warriors, but still preferable to the damp straw and rat shit with which she had become so familiar.

"You took quite some finding, I must say," the brother told her. "I've been on the road for two months now. I'd begun to suspect I might never pick up your trail, but your Aspect assured me that, eventually, you'd leave me a track to follow. 'Kestra just can't help herself,' he said. 'She's like an addict, only her drug is murder.'"

Her eyes flashed open, finding him regarding her with brows raised in placid curiosity. "And you do not kill the deserving, then, brother?" she asked him. "Or is that blade on your back just for show?"

His lips curved into a bland smile. "War is the province of my Order. But I've a preference for avoiding the killing stroke where possible."

"I marvel at your compassion." She angled her head, speaking with cold precision. "I've never heard the name you spoke and have no notion why you imagine I would answer to an Aspect, since I'll have no truck with your nonsensical Faith."

"I am sorry to hear it. I came a long way to return something to the woman who bears that name, something of great value." She heard a rustling of fabric then the faint metallic tick of a small chain. "Will you not, at least, look at what I brought?"

She knew what she would see before opening her eyes, yet the lure of it was treacherously irresistible. The medallion was a small thing crafted from base iron. It was formed of a circular band enclosing the overlapping motifs of a goblet and a snake. The trinket caught a dull gleam as it dangled from the chain. He held close enough for her to see the small nick in the band from when she had once dropped it. It was undoubtedly her own medallion, a once prized possession discarded in a fit of anger. She was both irked and surprised by the pang it provoked and she had to quell the urge to reach for it.

"A curious object," she said, swallowing to banish the catch in her throat. "But I know not why you came so far to show it to me."

"Because the Aspects of our Faith required it." He maintained the same affable half-smile, but his voice had acquired an edge of impatience. He shifted on his haunches and tilted his head towards the door in a manner that told her he was checking for eavesdroppers. Apparently satisfied, he turned back to her and murmured, "Conclave was held, in secret. It's been decided: the Book Burner has to fall."

Kestra contained a shudder provoked by the sudden lurch in her chest. Stirred by a reawakened, long-nurtured hunger, the beast began to coil and hiss. She closed her mouth to stem a plethora of questions, keeping her features bland and forcing calm into her voice. "It appears you are privy to some dangerous knowledge, brother."

His smile broadened. "I think we both are, sister."

"Why now?" she asked. "After all these years of tyranny, deprivation, and murder, why finally stir themselves to act?"

"I was not privy to the Aspects' discussions. All I know is that plans have been laid and you and I are required to ensure their success, unless," he reclined, gesturing to the damp, streaked walls of her prison, "you would rather skulk here in your self-inflicted misery. I passed a magistrate's party on the road, not two days away, by my reckoning, so you won't have long to wait, at least."

Kestra nodded to the medallion dangling from his hand. "Did they tell you my role when I wore that? Do you know what I am?"

His humour slipped away, gaze narrowing into the cool appraisal of a shrewd and dangerous man. "The deadliest living soul to walk this earth," he said. "According to your Aspect."

"He's not my Aspect, not any longer, and I've no intention of ever wearing that thing again. However," she grimaced, groaning as she put her hands beneath her in an attempt to rise, "I do have a yen to meet our beloved king."

She had difficulty standing thanks to weakened muscles. She had seen little point in exercise whilst languishing in her cell, finding some amusement in the prospect of her executioners carrying her to her doom. Lesander moved to offer a helping hand, but she waved him away in irritation.

"I'll need your word," she told him, propping herself against the wall. "Swear to me as Brother of the Sixth Order that you'll put me face-to-face with the Book Burner, and I'll go with you."

She knew she was asking something of signal importance, for a brother's word was not lightly given. Even though Lesander's confirmation came swiftly, he spoke it with grave, hard-eyed certainty. "You are not the only one with a keen desire to meet King Lakril," he said. "So yes, sister, you have my solemn promise that I will put you in front of him, or die in the attempt."

Kestra nodded, moving to the door on legs that contrived to feel both stiff and jelly-like. "I trust you brought me a horse. I'm not walking all the way to Varinshold."

Chapter Three

The gaolers insisted on being tied up before Lesander departed the tower with their prisoner.

"Looks bad for us otherwise, y'see, brother," the brutish sergeant explained in a chagrined mutter. "Lord Edwird's a decent sort, for the most part, but he can have a bit of temper when things go against him.'

The sergeant and his three comrades stood in the tower's guard room, faces downcast, sword belts removed, and weapons stacked in a corner. Although hardly the finest examples of soldierly conduct, they were all strong men of impressive stature. Yet none had dared speak a word of protest in response to Lesander's cheerful statement that he would be relieving them of the burden of caring for their Dark-afflicted charge.

"Few bruises wouldn't go amiss either," the sergeant added, darting a glance at Lesander. "If you're so minded."

"Of course," Lesander told him before slamming his hand, palm open, into the sergeant's nose. Having produced a suitably bloody result, the brother obliged the other gaolers with blows resulting in visible but not overly serious damage. When it came time to bind them, they shrank away from Kestra when she began to loop the rope about their chests and arms.

"I'll abide a brother's punch but not a witch's touch," said one, the largest but also the youngest, cowering from her, bloodied lips quivering.

"Too late," Kestra told him, reaching out to press a hand to his forehead. She held it in place whilst he shivered and squirmed. "Now," she said, withdrawing her hand, "I know all your secrets." She stood, shaking her head in disgust. "To do *that* to a goat. What manner of man are you?"

Before leaving the tower, they were obliged to gag the young gaoler else his loud protestations of innocence, evidently disbelieved by his comrades, might attract unwanted attention. The tower rose beside the bridge spanning a small river that ran through a nameless village in the southerly portion of the baron's holdings. The village wasn't important, but the bridge provided a crossing substantial enough to support the weight of an army marching either into the heart of Renfael or the north Asraelin borderland. Whilst Lesander untethered the horses, Kestra indulged in some idle speculation: should their mission succeed, this bridge might well see a great many soldiers tramping across it before long.

A king's fall is like a stone tumbling into a placid lake, yet instead of a ripple, it brings a storm. A line recalled from a translated Far Western text she read in her youth, one of the more highly prized tomes in her father's collection. As ever, memories of her father's books stirred images of flames rising high into the night sky, ashes swirling like a million fireflies. She remembered how the bonfire that birthed those embers, a veritable mountain of piled books, had roared when the soldiers' torches set light to it. But even that roar, monstrous as it had been, couldn't muffle her ears to the sound of her father weeping …

"She's called Forelock," Lesander said, cutting through her unsought reverie. "For obvious reasons." He handed her the reins to a young mare with a pale brown coat and a thick tendril of ivory-hued mane cascading over her forehead. The horse stepped closer to Kestra, head angled to regard her new rider with a bright, inquisitive eye.

"Friendly, isn't she?" Lesander commented, climbing into the saddle of his own, far larger mount, a black-coated stallion plainly bred for speed and aggression. The sheen of the animal's flanks was marred by several long, intersecting scars and Kestra saw only suspicion and dislike in the brief glance of his eye. "Unlike old Nolnen here." The brother laughed and smoothed a hand over the stallion's neck. "Fellow in the borderlands a few weeks back tried to steal him, crawled off with an arm and leg broken."

"Can we get on?" Kestra said, grunting with the effort of heaving herself onto Forelock's back. "We'd best be very far from here before the new baron comes to welcome the magistrate."

Lesander inclined his head and, without further pause, kicked his heels to Nolnen's flanks, spurring the beast to a full gallop. Sighing, Kestra urged Forelock to follow. The mare tossed her head and consented only to trot until they were a mile clear of the tower where the stone walls lining the road ended. Here the gravelled track snaked through the rolling, tree-spotted hills of south-Renfael.

Leaving the road, Forelock let out a joyous whinny and spurred to a full gallop across the fields. She kept roughly parallel to the road so Kestra was content to give her free rein, feeling a small blossoming of exhilaration at the almost forgotten sensation of riding a speeding horse. In her youth she had done so many times, her missions for the Aspect taking her to all corners of the Realm and occasionally beyond. It was strange, even perverse to think of those days as a time of happiness and freedom, yet even now the sense of nostalgia was strong. The regretful pang that rose in her breast was sharpened by the knowledge that there was no recovering those days, for they had been a lie, a dream she had awoken from and could never return to.

♛

I assume you had a reason," Lesander said. "The old baron, I mean."

He tended the stewpot whilst he spoke, sprinkling herbs into a bubbling concoction of rabbit and mushrooms. They had encamped after a long ride, the brother calling a halt when the sky had darkened so much that Kestra doubted they had light enough to find a suitable spot to rest. Lesander, however, led them to a thickly wooded hill a quarter mile from the road, lit a fire and had the meal underway in a remarkably short time. She was no stranger to the wilds but the unconscious alacrity with which this man conducted a brief scouting of their surroundings before going about his chores spoke of someone who lived the bulk of his life out of doors.

"I once heard tell," she said, evading his question, "of a young, dark-hued brother who journeyed through the Great Northern Forest alone and unmolested. I always found the tale hard to credit."

He smiled, not looking up from his cookery. "You wish to hear the story of my famous sojourn?"

She shrugged. "It would pass the time."

"One tale demands another in return." His eyes slipped to hers. "Your reasons for killing the baron, for instance."

Kestra hardened her face and she turned away from him, resuming the task of stuffing the fur of the skinned rabbit into her shoes. Having relieved the least bulky gaoler of his footwear, she found them a poor fit. "Suffice to say I had reasons," she replied, voice clipped to signify that no elaboration would be forthcoming. Brother Lesander, however, seemed blithely immune to such nuances.

"And the outlaw leader in Nilsael six months ago?" he enquired, raising a wooden spoon to his lips to taste the stew.

Kestra said nothing. She felt the weight of Lesander's gaze upon her but didn't find it cause to provide an answer.

"If we're to share the difficult task ahead," he said, "we should at least form some measure of understanding, don't you think?"

"I kill those deserving of death," she said, pulling on one of her newly stuffed shoes. "That is all the understanding you require."

"But who decides?"

She glanced up at him, finding his gaze steady through the steam rising from the pot. "What?" she asked.

"The people you kill. Who decides if they deserve it?"

"I do."

"And is your judgement always faultless?"

"So far." Kestra wiggled her toes, pursing her lips in satisfaction at the absence of chafing.

"Forgive me, sister, but you appear somewhat complacent regarding the power you've been given. The ability to kill with a mere look is ..." He grimaced and shook his head. "It strikes me as more burden than gift."

"All gifts are burdens. That's how it is with the Dark. And it's not just a matter of looking. If it were so easy, I assure you there would be a great many more corpses in my wake. That's how I know those I kill deserve it: my gift doesn't work if they don't."

"So, the gift decides?"

"In a way, I suppose."

"How?"

Kestra shifted under his unwavering stare, feeling she had said enough. "Is that ready yet?" she said, nodding to the stew pot. Lesander had enough sense to let the matter drop, although she could tell his curiosity continued to nag him. She supposed he found it novel to travel with someone who posed more of a threat than he did.

"I should take the first watch," she said when the meal was done. She had wolfed it down with unabashed relish, her denuded body finding it as fine a meal as she had ever eaten.

"No need," Lesander told her. Having removed the saddles and tack from both horses he groomed them then settled beside the dwindling fire, wrapping his cloak about him.

"You intend to sleep?" she asked.

"We are surrounded on all sides by dry bracken that will warn of any approach," he said, closing his eyes. "Besides, Nolnen is a light sleeper. Worry not, sister, and get some rest. I'm sure you need it."

The bonfire of books returned to torment her dreams, as it often did after unwanted memories rose to plague her waking hours. In this version of the nightmare the blaze stood as tall as a mountain, its roar louder than ever as the fire ate the countless pages and bindings. The surrounding streets of Varinshold were painted in garish hues, the houses seeming to sway and tilt in concert with the flames. As usual, the most disconcerting sight was not the altered reality of the scene, but the one aspect that remained true to her memory:

Her father knelt in the middle of the street of the artisan's quarter, shuddering as the sobs wracked him. He stared up at the flaming mountain of books just as he had all those years ago, his face bloodied by the beating the soldiers had given him when he tried to stop them emptying his library.

Your precious bloody library, Kestra's mother called it more than once during one of their frequent screaming matches. *You'd let your daughter starve just to buy another book!* Her mother had been a hard woman, made harder by privation and the trials of concealing a Dark-afflicted daughter, but Kestra never called her a liar. She wasn't there that night so didn't feature in this hideous pantomime; however, Kestra's sadistic mind conspired to summon forth another soul who hadn't been present either:

Your father's stupid, the little girl taunted, face set in a sneer that Kestra recalled as her only expression. Her name had been Lehla, a farrier's daughter from the poorer end of the street. Thanks to the vagaries of childhood, nature had seen fit to make her both taller and meaner than other children her age. She also had parents who beat her almost every day for the slightest misbehaviour, real or imagined. Kestra wouldn't discover this until years later when her mother, lying pale faced and near death, told her the tale.

No one makes themself a bully, Kessie, she said, smiling sadly as the tears fell from her daughter's eyes. *You weren't to know.*

But, self-made or not, Lehla had been one of the worst bullies Kestra encountered in a life rich in the experience of cruel souls. It wasn't just the unexpected punches or pisspot drenchings, it was her unending torrent of insults, and always Kestra's father was her principal target.

Stupid Kestra's stupid, scribbling da, she taunted now, the bonfire's glow adding a demented glow to the hateful rictus of her face. *Stupid Kestra's stupid da!*

Shut up, Kestra told her, the voice that emerged from her lips a small, tremulous thing, just as it had been that terrible morning when Lehla ambushed her in an alley near the docks. Kestra had felt the beast stir before, a strange roiling in her core that her mother told her was just trapped wind from stuffing her face so much. It would be years later that Kestra remembered the flicker of fear on her mother's face when she had dismissed her complaints. Gifts, she knew now, followed the female line. Sometimes they skipped a generation, but it was rare. Whatever the nature of her mother's Dark ability, however, Kestra never learned it. Even when she sat beside the woman's death bed, she allowed her to slip away with the secret unsaid.

Kestra's stupid da! Lehla screeched, face livid with enjoyment of her victim's destress, the face of a soul fully deserving of all the hate it provoked. *Kestra's stupid da!*

SHUT UP!

The beast had struck swift and sure that day in the alley, ravening its way through the small organs and bones of a ten-year-old girl then snapping back into Kestra with jolt that left her reeling. At the time she had spent several frozen seconds staring at Lehla's limp, unmoving form lying amidst the straw and detritus of the alley, eyes wide but unseeing, features slack and bloody. Then she fled, both hands clamped over her mouth, keeping her gaze averted from every face. She never told her parents what happened, but also never doubted that her mother knew. From that day on, Kestra was kept home, forbidden from playing with other children. She didn't feel the beast stir again until the soldiers came to break down their door and take her father's books for the fire.

She was sixteen years old by then, resentful and bitter at her mother for making her a prisoner in a house that seemed to shrink by the day. Her father's library had been her window on a far larger world, one he was happy to show her. Volumes of Alpiran legend, the histories of the Third Order, philosophy from the Far West, all stolen and burnt in a single night on a mad king's whim.

Her victim that night had been the captain of the palace guard who oversaw the crime. He was also the man who had struck her father down when his grief blossomed into rage. The captain was a tall veteran of dignified bearing and, Kestra would realise later, wore an expression that failed to conceal his dislike of the task he had been given. She couldn't see his reluctance that night, nor did she think it would have saved him if she had. All she saw was her kneeling, weeping father suddenly transform into something feral. The captain had made the mistake of standing at the fringe of the bonfire, snapping out curt orders to his men to hurry it up as they cast more armfuls of books into the flames. So, when Kestra's father charged at him, he came perilously close to finding himself propelled into the blaze.

A hard shove to the small, enraged man's chest, the flash of a hastily drawn sword, and her father lay on the cobbles, blood seeping thick and fast from the gash in his chest. It was Kestra's anguished howl that drew the captain's eye, and the beast that held it. Its ravenings caused him to spasm and collapse into the fire. His men dragged him clear in moments, but the beast had already done its work. Some instinct for danger drew their attention to the small girl with the strange, unwavering stare. She would surely have killed them all too if a heavy hand hadn't landed on her shoulder at that moment.

"Calm now, little sister," a deep, rumbling voice told her. Kestra looked up to see a very large man regarding her with brows creased in stern disapproval but also a keen interest lighting his eyes. "Ink and paper, though valuable, aren't worth a life."

"They killed my father," she sobbed. The large raised his brows as he surveyed the scene afresh. "No," he told her, striding forward with such assured authority that the soldiers raised no hand against him. "He's merely fallen."

That image of the Aspect pressing his hand to her father's sundered chest, the feel of his blossoming gift as he summoned it to stitch the wound closed, froze then fractured as the dream collapsed around her, banished by a sudden intrusion of sound from the waking world. Kestra jerked awake, instinctively reaching for her knives then swallowing a curse when she recalled they had been taken from her. Nor had Lesander seen fit to provide any replacements.

She shifted onto her front and gathered her legs beneath her, ears alive to the tumult that had roused her. It was a dolefully familiar collection of grunts and thwacks: the tune of combat. Raising herself up, she peered into the gloom, catching the flicker of moonlight through the trees as it played upon the fighters. Lesander's absence from his spot on the opposite side of their extinguished fire made it plain that he was one of the combatants. But was he winning?

Kestra's gaze snapped to the horses, fidgeting in agitation. With the combatants so close she wouldn't have time to saddle Forelock, but she had ridden bareback before. *Go,* she told herself, looking back to the flickering shapes in the woods. *Forget his plans … the Aspect's plans.* Plans, she remembered with a reluctant sigh, that would put her in front of the Book Burner.

Arming herself with one of the heftier stones Lesander had used to ring the fire, she started towards the struggle in a crouch. The nature of her work for the Seventh Order had imbued her with a facility for stealth and an eye for where to deliver an effective blow. As she drew nearer, however, it became clear that she would have need of neither.

A bulky shape loomed out of the shadows to her left, and she raised her stone in readiness as she made out the glint of moonlight on the buckles of a soldier's hauberk. Yet, instead of lunging for her, the soldier promptly collided with the trunk of an ash, his skull making a sickening, hollow thunk as it rebounded from the rough bark. He slumped unmoving to the bracken. Kestra sidestepped him and whirled about as she heard the hard thud of another body falling. The sound was accompanied by the muffled crack she recognised as breaking bone followed by a loud and profane outburst of cursing.

"You treasonous fuck!" a voice she knew snarled. She caught the flicker of a slashing longsword, the blade meeting only air. Soon she made out the form of its wielder, a tall man struggling on the ground whilst a cloaked figure of roughly equal stature stood beyond the reach of his weapon.

"Have a care, my lord," Lesander chided Baron Edwird. "I'm a tolerant man but I've scant patience for discourtesy."

Two more hauberk clad soldiers lay nearby, both groaning. Drawing closer to Lesander, she saw that he held his sheathed sword in two hands, one on the scabbard and the other the hilt. Apparently, he hadn't felt the need to draw it.

"That one's a tracker," the brother explained to Kestra, nodding to one of the groaners. "He's good. We didn't ride far and fast enough, it seems."

"Witch!" Edwird raged at her, attempting to swing his sword at her head then abruptly stiffening to let out a shout of pain, one hand clutching his broken leg. "This woman," he grated at Lesander, eyes blazing in the dark, "is a servant of the Dark and a murderer. By allying with her you disgrace yourself and your Order. I demand—"

Whatever his demand may have been would forever remain unknown, for Kestra leapt atop him, placed her left knee on the upper part of his sword arm and pinned his other with her foot before swiftly snatched the dagger from his belt. The young baron stopped struggling when she pricked the flesh beneath his chin with the point of the blade.

"Sister ..." Lesander cautioned.

"Don't call me that," she told him, fixing her eyes on Edwird's. They were wide with fear and hate, a hate she prepared to return in full. "Not long ago," she said, "I asked you a question, my lord. I should like the answer." She leaned closer, tightening her grip on the dagger. "Were you there?"

She watched his pride and detestation war with his terror, but also saw a tremble to his lips that told of shame, the same shame she had glimpsed in Hulesberth. "No," he croaked. The way he continued to return her stare told her this was no lie, but she wanted more.

"Why not?" she asked, voice mild as she pressed the dagger's tip a fraction deeper. "Hunting Deniers is such fine sport, is it not?"

"I ..." he faltered, and she felt him quell a shudder as his eyes finally gave up the contest between them, the shame blossoming in full now. "I had no stomach for it. My father and I quarrelled over it. He called me a coward, said a craven could never be his heir ..." Edwird closed his eyes, nostrils flaring and lips tightened. "A man cannot choose his father, nor his sons. But blood is blood and murder demands a reckoning. Strike home if you must, I'll not beg. Spare me and know I will spend all the days I have hunting you down."

Kestra was not unused to such promises. By her calculation there were at least a dozen people on this earth who had dedicated their lives towards her end. One more would make scant difference. Besides, the beast remained quiescent.

"As you wish, my lord," she said, removing the dagger. She leapt clear of him and stood. "However, I'd advise you look to your own holdings for the foreseeable future. This realm is about to become a good deal more troubled."

She stalked away, holding the dagger aloft. "I'll be keeping this. I trust you don't mind." Hearing Lesander fall in at her side, she spared him a short, sidelong glance. "Hate," she said. "That's how it works. I can't kill them if I don't hate them. Now, brother, you owe me a story."

Chapter Four

So, you never saw the Seordah for the duration of the journey?"

Lesander grinned in response to her dubious squint. "Not one. An entire month or more spent beneath the trees of the Great Northern Forest and they found no cause to trouble me. It must be said that they hadn't been so merciful to the band I was hunting, a truly vile bunch of Denier fanatics given to the worship of extinct Volarian gods, if you can credit such a thing. Every few miles I would come upon one taken by a single arrow, each aimed precisely at the same portion of the neck. Curiously, the Seordah left the leader alive for me to find. He was completely mad with fear by then, gibbering in old Volarian about his gods and so forth. I tied a rope around him and attempted to lead him out, but it became swiftly apparent that I was, by then, thoroughly lost."

Kestra's squinted at him. "You mean to tell me a Brother of the Sixth Order got lost in the woods?"

Lesander laughed. "Ah, but the Great Northern Forest is not just the woods, is it, sister? Have you never seen it?"

She shifted in her saddle, recalling her one visit to the northern hills of Nilsael where the vast green sea of the Great Northern Forest stretched away into the distance. The sight of it had been enough to dispel any notion of venturing inside; the darkness beneath the canopy seemed to shout its lack of welcome. Yet more disconcerting was the way it stirred her gift, not in the usual predatory animus, but a rare tightening of fearful agitation.

"No," she said. "Those with gifts tend to avoid it."

"As well they might." The humour in Lesander's voice faded as they turned the bend in the track and saw a small village. They were in the outer fringes of the Urlish Forest now, several miles north of Varinshold. In the early days of King Lakril's reign the region around his capital was spared the worst of his avarice. The Lord Collector's ever-growing army of Excise Men would range further afield and the even less popular agents of the Crown Levy inflicted their presence mainly on the lesser fiefs. In recent years, however, as Lakril's unquenchable thirst for gold increased, Asrael's protected status had dwindled then vanished. This village appeared to be a more recent victim, the roofs not yet fallen in and fencing still mostly intact. However, it was plain that the inhabitants were gone, most likely fled when the Levy Agents took their last sack of charcoal or dug out their last hidden purse. Kestra had seen a half-dozen such places over the last few days, causing her to wonder at the state of the capital. With no farmers to work the land, how did a city feed itself?

Her eyes caught the dim glimmer of a fire outlining the shutters of one cottage, a thin pall of grey smoke blossoming from its chimney. A careful inspection of their environs also revealed several blue-cloaked figures amongst the trees. She knew she wouldn't have seen them unless they allowed it. One, his face hidden in his hood, raised a hand to Lesander in a familiar wave; the brother returning the greeting with a grave nod. His affability had abruptly vanished, replaced by the stiffness of a brother performing a difficult duty with all required diligence and seriousness of bearing.

"Who's in there?" Kestra asked as they guided their mounts towards the cottage with the smoking chimney.

"You didn't imagine we were going to do this alone, did you?" Lesander said, bringing Nolnen to a halt.

Eyeing the dim glow behind the shutters, Kestra quelled the urge wheel Forelock about and gallop back along the track. It would have been pointless since the picket of brothers would surely bring her down before she covered a dozen yards, yet the urge to flee remained strong.

"The man you captured," she said, staying in the saddle whilst Lesander dismounted. "What became of him."

"We wandered for a time," the brother said. "Yet I could find no track that would take us clear of the forest. Landmarks I had noted were nowhere to be seen and what I could glimpse of the sun, moon and stars made little sense. It was strange …" He trailed off, gaze taking on a puzzled distance. "Even though I was utterly lost, I felt completely at home. I hadn't heard a word spoken since entering the forest save the ravings of a mad-man, and yet I have never experienced a stronger sense of welcome. It was as if the forest wanted me to stay." He blinked, shaking his head. "Of course, I couldn't. So, we spent several more days traipsing until one morning I woke to find my prisoner had hung himself from the branch of a very old oak. His bonds had been cut, by who I'll never know. I do know that suddenly the path out of the forest was abundantly clear to me."

He gestured to the door of the cottage. "Shall we, sister?"

She wanted to ask more, mainly as a means of delaying the confrontation that awaited her behind that door, but his story also intrigued her. "You've never been back?"

"No." His voice held a note of regret as well as finality. "I think I would find it too tempting." He smiled, the expression absent of his usual humour and gestured again at the door.

Sighing, Kestra loosed her foot from the stirrup and swung her leg over the saddle. *Please*, she implored the Departed souls of a Faith she no longer held to, *not Drisha. I can just about stomach the Aspect. But not Drisha.*

Drisha Al Veys had been a renowned beauty in her youth, her likeness being a popular and sought-after subject for the Realm's finest portraitists. Kestra knew this because Drisha had commissioned all their portraits and never tired of showing them to visitors. They adorned the walls of her mansion alongside tapestries that also depicted her in varied, often outlandish finery. In addition, there were a number of busts, both marble and bronze, and a large statue that formed the centrepiece of the fountain in her garden. Her parents, wealthy even by the standards of high Asraelin nobility, had died when Drisha was barely old enough to legally claim their fortune. She swiftly proved to be a terrible custodian of such riches, losing at least half her holdings due to poor management over the course of the next few years. However, as a patron of the arts, she excelled, even if the subject matter remained limited.

Upon seeing her for the first time in nigh a decade, Kestra was surprised to note how little her old mentor had changed. Never entirely sure of the woman's age, a subject Drisha avoided with stern and close-mouthed dedication, she was struck by how the woman retained the same austere high-cheek-boned beauty and poised elegance. Save for a few extra lines around her eyes and an additional leanness to her neck, age had appeared to pass her by.

Drisha wore a black velvet dress today, plain by her standards though the silver thread that embroidered the sleeves would have paid the rent of this entire village for a season. Offering no greeting as Lesander led Kestra into the cottage, she remained seated at a dust-covered table, back stiff and eyes narrowed in patent hostility. The large man warming himself by the fire was a marked contrast, turning to reveal blocky, strong-jawed features set in a smile of forced welcome. Kestra had reflected before on the paradox of a man who lived his life mostly in shadow yet possessed scant facility for artifice.

"Sister," the Aspect said, coming forward, hands extended to grasp hers. He wore a fur-trimmed cloak over jerkin and trews that were of good quality but not so much as to draw the eye. A man of his size would inevitably garner notice, but most would see only the avuncular, middlingly successful cloth merchant he pretended to be. His smile faltered when she moved her hands beyond his reach and stepped away. She ignored his frown and turned her attention to the other occupants of the cottage, a man and a woman seated at the table alongside Drisha, one she knew and one she didn't.

Blench, like Drisha, was much as she remembered him, a picture of slumped, unwashed sullenness as he worked a curve-bladed knife to into an apple, lifting the slices to his mouth and eating with a mechanical lack of relish. She fancied there was more grey in his shaggy mane these days. Also, the much-besmirched leather jerkin he wore was an even more ragged version of its younger self. Like Drisha, he offered no greeting, though she did detect a bunching of cheeks beneath his unkempt beard that might have signalled a grudging smile.

Seated to his left was an auburn-haired young woman in the well-tailored riding garb favoured by nobility. Kestra's eye picked out the tell-tale stitching and creases that marked it as the product of Drisha's favoured dressmaker. *Her latest student,* Kestra concluded, surprised by a sudden pang of envy. *A commoner, though,* she added to herself, noting how the girl's fidgeting betrayed a discomfort in her attire. *Just like me.*

"Sister Ulaine is a recent addition to our ranks," the Aspect explained as Kestra's gaze lingered, the younger woman squirming under the scrutiny.

"Another orphan or did you buy her?" Kestra saw the girl flinch at her words, guessing her distress arose more from the word 'orphan' than her harsh tone. There were only two avenues to joining the Seventh Order: you were either born into it or, like her, drawn in when, by chance or careful enquiry, they discovered your true nature. Consequently, those lacking the protection of family were most likely to be detected and their recruitment was not always a pleasant business. She was also grimly aware that the Aspect and his predecessors had not been averse to filling the purses of foreign slavers willing to hand over the gifted children found amongst their cargo.

The Aspect's blocky features took on a strained smile that more resembled the grimace of an important man forcing himself to patience. Drisha, as ever, was never prone to such restraint.

"Her origin is of no concern to you," she stated, fixing Kestra with a hard glower. Drisha raised her chin to a familiar imperious angle and added in her clipped, noble accent, "Renegade." A protective attitude towards her students had always been one of Drisha's more admirable traits, though Kestra suspected her intervention now stemmed more from basic antipathy.

Meeting her gaze, Kestra formed her lips into the sweet, demure smile Drisha had taught her during one of those endless, tedious lessons in comportment. "My lady," she said, curtseying, "please do me the kind favour of finding a cow's arse to lick."

Drisha jerked to her feet, hands forming into the talons that signified an impending use of her gift. Her anger was such that she had no reluctance in meeting Kestra's eye. Within her, the beast hissed but didn't stir, which surprised her. It was ever a better judge of her feelings than she was, knowing the truth of her hate when she did not. So, it appeared she didn't hate Drisha, which left her defenceless save for her dagger.

"Now, now!" the Aspect said, moving between the two of them, hands raised. "We haven't gathered here to indulge in old arguments." He focused a steady gaze upon Kestra that reminded her that he too was dangerous. "I'm sure good Brother Lesander has acquainted you with our shared purpose, sister. Else I doubt you would be here."

At the table, Blench let out a soft chuckle, scattering fragments of apple. "Keen to kill a king, are you, Kes?" he asked in his rough Nislaelin brogue. "Aren't we all?"

His words sufficed to leech the tension from the room, just enough for Drisha to relax her talons and resume her seat. Young Sister Ulaine's eyes moved between each of them, bright and fearful, but also inquisitive. *At least she's no fool*, Kestra surmised, hoping the girl had a gift that matched her wits.

"Perhaps I'm just curious," Kestra said, turning back to the Aspect. "So many years suffering under the yoke of a mad tyrant yet the Orders only trouble themselves to unseat him now. Did he learn of the Seventh's existence? Is that it? Is this all just a matter of self-preservation?"

"If the king knew of the Seventh's presence in this Realm," the Aspect said, "I suspect most of it would already be in flames. By all accounts he's as fearful of the Dark as he is cats."

Kestra frowned. "Cats?"

"Yes, he's terrified of them. Our sources in the palace tell us he believes they are all possessed by some malign entity that lurks in the Beyond. A year or so ago he ordered every cat in Varinshold slaughtered." The Aspect's face clouded as he shuddered. "They say the Bonfire of Books was his worst crime, but the Massacre of the Cats runs a close second."

If he fears cats, Kestra mused, playing a half-smile over her lips, *he's like to be terrified of me.* "You didn't answer my question," she reminded the Aspect. "Why now?"

The Aspect turned to Lesander who had positioned himself by the doorway, arms folded and viewing the fractious reunion with mild amusement. "Brother?" the Aspect prompted. "The intelligence was acquired by your Order. It seems fitting you should report it."

"In point of fact, Aspect," Lesander said, "the information originates with our brothers in the Fourth Order. You can always trust a bureaucrat to ferret out the most valued secrets."

"Such as?" Kestra said, impatience and anger piqued by his failure to relate said secret during their journey. The reason was clear if surprising in the resentment it provoked: *He wasn't sure he could trust me.*

"Eight weeks ago," Lesander began, "a senior chamberlain in King Lakril's court took ship from Warnsclave on a merchantman bound for Volarian ports. He travelled in disguise and without escort, but in his possession were sealed letters signed by Lakril himself, letters proposing a mercantile arrangement with the Volarian Ruling Council."

Kestra's mind raced ahead to the conclusion before he voiced it. "Slaves," she said. "He offers slaves in return for gold."

"Yes, sister." Lesander inclined his head in admiration. "Lakril proposes a gift of one thousand prisoners currently languishing in his over-stuffed gaols, to be followed by regular shipments in return for suitable recompense. He even professes himself open to the whole scheme being overseen by Volarian soldiery."

"It's no secret that the royal treasury sits empty," the Aspect added.

"Lakril's madness has always been entwined with boundless greed and a passion for indulging his nonsensical whims. The royal palace in Varinshold is now four times its original size, a sprawling maze of gardens, halls and follies, all garishly mismatched since our king has a fondness for executing his architects when their efforts fail to match his imagination. Fortunately, while one such victim awaited the noose, he saw fit to craft this."

The Aspect reached into his cloak, produced a small scroll of rough parchment, and unfurled it before Kestra's eyes. A career in murder had left her expert in recognising floorplans, though this one seemed to be of smaller than expected dimensions. "That can't be the entire palace," she said, squinting at the lines on the parchment which appeared to have been hastily inscribed with charcoal.

"It isn't," the Aspect said. "Merely the recently constructed western wing, currently lacking furnishings and occupants. Apparently, by the time it was complete Lakril couldn't remember why he ordered it built and grew enraged at his own forgetfulness. Hence the unlucky architect's appointment with the noose. Most importantly for our purposes," he traced a large finger from the lower end of the plan to the top, describing a wayward route, "it offers an almost uninterrupted and mostly unpatrolled pathway to the palace's central keep."

"It's still within the walls," Kestra pointed out. "High walls, as I recall, with very few gates."

At the table, Blench chuckled again before taking a final bite of his apple and tossing the core into the fireplace. "Why the fuck do you think I'm here, luv?" he asked, letting out a burp.

"And her?" she asked, nodding to the young woman at his side. The sister began to fidget again under the weight of her gaze, but soon stiffened her posture, forcing herself to return the stare. Kestra concealed a soft grunt of satisfaction; the task ahead was not one for spineless children.

"Sister Ulaine's gift will be vital in gaining access to the central keep," the Aspect explained. "Sister Drisha, as you know, is well practised in dealing with apparently impassable barriers and Brother Lesander's sword will, I'm sure, fend off any more mundane threats."

Kestra took the parchment from him and moved to the fireplace. The desire to unleash the beast upon the king was a long-nurtured ambition, but the level of protection he enjoyed had always made it impossible. Additionally, she had accrued a fair amount of knowledge regarding the much-augmented palace he never left, none of it encouraging.

"The palace is renowned as a place of horrors," she murmured, still studying the plan. "Lakril imprisoned his entire family there years ago, never to be seen again. It's said to be guarded by things both Dark and deadly. And I hear tell that Lakril has acquired the services of a Verehlan sorcerer, though I hoped it might be mere rumour."

The Aspect winced apologetically. "Sadly, it's no rumour. We have little information on the fellow in question, save that he sports the name Aertis Vezuri, which apparently translates as Flame Weaver. Perhaps a clue to the nature of his gift. We should assume his abilities to be considerable, but," he smiled, gesturing to the others, "in all the Seventh Order there are none more capable, and powerful, than those gathered here. Rest assured, you have my fullest confidence."

"Thank you, Aspect," Drisha said promptly, inclining her head in grave respect. Ulaine followed suit with a subdued mutter of appreciation whilst Blench merely ran his fingers through is beard.

"Assuming we succeed," Kestra said, "what then? The moment the king dies the Realm will slip into chaos."

"It's already in chaos," Drisha said, arching an eyebrow at her. "I would have thought one so well-travelled would have noticed."

"Conclave has long discussed the matter," the Aspect cut in, forestalling Kestra's venomous retort. "Three full companies of Brothers from the Sixth Order have been mustered in Varinshold, with great care and secrecy. When the mission is complete, they will storm the palace. As far as history will be concerned, King Lakril the Mad was deposed by the Servants of the Faith. Even now, some amongst the nobility may not react well to the violent usurpation of a lawful monarch. But, once his disgusting Volarian scheme is made known, I'm sure none of them will be willing to openly decry the Book Burner's fall. As for the wider Realm, although Lakril has been energetic in murdering his kin, several members of the royal family remain unaccounted for, including his sister, Princess Luvehla, one of the few souls he ever expressed any true affection for. With luck, we shall soon have a queen in place of a king."

"All very neat," Kestra observed. "And absurd. Have no doubt of it, when Lakril falls there will be blood, and the Realm will fracture."

"Then what would you have us do?" Drisha demanded. "Sit idle whilst an insane tyrant lays waste to the Realm and sells our children into Volarian servitude?"

"No, I'll kill him." Kestra angled her head at her former mentor, smiling the sweet demure smile once again. "I just wanted to make sure we were all aware of the consequences, my lady." She turned to the Aspect, handing him the parchment. "When do we leave?"

Chapter Five

It was inevitable that they would approach the smallest and least well-guarded of the five gates offering entry through the palace walls. It sat at the end of a narrow footbridge spanning the Brinewash River, an entrance reserved for servants and commoners. As they crossed the bridge, Kestra gained a true impression of the formidable scale of the walls. She hadn't visited the capital for several years and it appeared that, despite his many obvious faults, Lakril was not guilty of idleness. The walls ascended like an unnaturally smooth cliff-face from the riverbank to a height beyond one hundred feet from base to battlement. The gateway and its small, protruding guard house interrupted the otherwise featureless edifice, save for the streaks of moss and dark rivulets of effluent from the privy spigots dotting the brickwork. As they drew nearer, the stench made it plain why this portal was reserved for the lower orders, and few in this realm were regarded as lower than the guise they wore this evening.

"Trussed up like a fucking jackanapes," Blench muttered, heavy brows glowering beneath the flopping tassels of his cap. Kestra laughed, having always thought him indifferent to all matters sartorial.

"It suits you," she said. "I fancy you may have missed your true vocation. Prance about a bit, recite a limerick or two. They'll expect it."

"Piss off. Least I don't look like a strumpet."

For reasons she had never fathomed, the many insults cast her way by this man never succeeded in stirring her anger. She supposed it would have been akin to blaming the rain for being wet. "I, sir," she replied, spreading her arms beyond the confines of her cloak to reveal the beaded bodice and skirt she wore over tights of black cotton, "am a dancer. As you well know."

She twirled briefly, laughing again, for gaiety would add to their disguise, something her fellow dancer appeared not to realise. Ulaine walked with her head lowered save for the fearful glances she darted at the fast-approaching gate. With her violet eyeshadow and her auburn tresses arranged in a pleasing bun and decorated with pins of silver, she made quite an impression, but her patent fear did much to dissipate the distraction it provided.

"Too glum," Kestra said, catching hold of Ulaine's wrists and pulling her into a whirl. "Laugh," she instructed, maintaining her own facade of humour as they reeled along the bridge. "Be a dancer."

Ulaine consented to force out a somewhat shrill giggle and continued to whirl until they came within a dozen yards of the gate where a leathery-faced sergeant held up a hand to bring their party to a halt. "Wasn't told to expect any players tonight," he said. His voice held a note of routine tedium, but a suspicious frown began to crease his forehead as he surveyed the crew of motley performers. The guise had been chosen due to the king's famed fondness for performance. Troupes were regularly summoned to the palace to provide entertainment and paid handsomely for their efforts. Players were also one of the few elements of society usually spared Lakril's often fatal caprice and they tended to emerge unmolested the next day.

The sergeant's eye lingered on Kestra and Ulaine, interested, but not unduly so, by the sweet smile offered by the cat-faced one. He proved himself a dutiful and keen-eyed watchman by barely glancing at Drisha, her face painted alabaster and dressed in sombre black gown as was often the custom for singers. Instead, the sergeant focused most of his attention first on Blench's stocky, sour-faced jackanapes before shifting to Lesander.

The initial plan had been for the brother to adopt much the same garb as Blench, presenting them as twin fools come to caper for the king. However, Lesander displayed even less acting skill than Ulaine and the fool's garments did nothing to diminish his obvious martial bearing. So he had been cast in the role of porter, laden with a sturdy pole across the shoulders from which their various players' accoutrements dangled in two leather packs. Naturally, several weapons, including the brother's sword, were concealed inside. Kestra had hoped the burden would have borne Lesander down to the extent that he made a more convincing porter than he did a jackanapes. Sadly, his strength, posture and colouring attracted closer scrutiny.

"Where're you from, then?" the sergeant asked, moving to bar Lesander's path. As he did so, Kestra rolled her eyes in apparent boredom, taking measure of the other guards. To her annoyance, they were more numerous than expected, no less than six stationed where the bridge met the gate and another four silhouetted in the passage beyond. Turning to Blench, she raised a questioning eyebrow. She had witnessed the power of his gift before, but never had she seen him wield it on so many people at once.

His beard had been shorn down to a less rampant version of its former self, allowing her to see the rueful grimace that told of severe doubt. Kestra turned back to Ulaine, giggling and leaning close to whisper a girlish confidence in her ear. "This is likely to go bad. Be ready, and don't spare in killing. Falter even a little, and they'll kill us."

She had been afforded a brief demonstration of Ulaine's abilities at the cottage, gaining a healthy respect for the sister's power. However, seeing the way her throat constricted and the rapid blinking of her eyes, Kestra wasn't at all sure she had the resolve to use it to deadly effect.

"South Tower," Lesander told the sergeant, offering him the weary smile of one answering an oft-answered question. "Washed up on the shore as a babe. Luckily they didn't see fit to throw me back."

"You've a notable face, for sure," the sergeant observed, peering closer at Lesander. "One I fancy I've seen before, 'cept you were wearing blue as I recall …"

Kestra's hand slipped into her cloak, grasping the knife concealed beneath her bodice, then stopped as she felt the blossoming of Blench's gift.

"No," he said, turning to stare hard at the sergeant. His voice possessed a strange tone that resembled a whisper but, to the un-gifted, rose to an irresistible screaming command in the mind. "You don't recall him at all."

For a second the sergeant stiffened, standing rigid until the full force of Blench's will seeped into his being. The man's face became a blank mask, eyes empty and mouth slack, a puppet awaiting the master's pull on the strings.

"See us through the gate," Blench instructed in the same odd voice. Kestra could see how use of his gift took its toll on him. His temples hollowed and jawed clenched, a faint shudder in his form as he tracked the Sergeant's stiff-backed progress towards the portal.

"He'll manage those on the bridge," Kestra murmured to Ulaine, taking her hand and leading her along whilst Blench followed the sergeant. "We have to ensure the others don't seal this gate." She gave the sister's hand a hard squeeze. "Understand?'

"So close." The younger woman's voice was a thin whisper, her eyes shaded in fear. "It could kill them all."

"No one forced them to take the Book Burner's coin." Kestra used her free hand to draw her knife from her bodice, keeping it concealed beneath her cloak. "They know the manner of the man they serve. Save your mercy for the deserving."

The other guards stirred as they neared, then halted as Blench spoke his commanding whisper again: "Stand aside." His back was bowed with strain now, reddened features taking on an increasing quiver. When Kestra had seen him employ his ability before, it had always been a brief thing, a curt hiss to look the other way or, in one instance, a brief instruction for a smuggler to throw himself over the side of his own brig. Forcing passage through so well-guarded an entrance required all his strength and Kestra could tell it was fast giving out.

"Wait until I tell you," she murmured to Ulaine, releasing her hand as the torchlit gloom of the passage enveloped them. The surrounding guards had retreated several paces, each face the same blank gape. Those standing directly ahead, however, were taking on a far more alert stance, warned by the innate human instinct for sensing the strange or unfamiliar. The sturdiest of the silhouetted figures began a purposeful approach, shifting the grip on his poleaxe in preparation for a thrust. Just then, she felt Blench's gift dwindle and vanish like a snuffed candle. He staggered and she saw the gleam of torchlight on the blood seeping from his nose.

"What ...?" she heard the sergeant mutter in startled bafflement. She pivoted, preparing to silence him with her dagger but Lesander had already seen the danger. Dropping the pack-laden pole, he wrapped both arms around the sergeant's neck. A swift twist and jerk produced a familiar, muffled snap. Most of the other nearby guards, still blinking in the confusion created by the sudden removal of Blench's hold, failed to notice the sergeant's demise. One keen-eyed fellow, however, recovered his wits enough to witness the event in full.

"Ward the gate!" he called in an oddly unmanly screech. "Intruders—"

Kestra leapt on the guard, dagger spearing him through the eye. It was too late. His warning was immediately echoed by the other guards, their voices quickly swallowed by the loud rattle of chains scraping over gears releasing the portcullis.

Kestra turned and sprinted towards the opening, hoping to dive under the iron barrier before it descended, knowing it was hopeless notion but still determined to try. Drisha, however, moved into her path, causing her to veer away. Kestra rounded on the older woman, an obscene curse dying on her lips when she saw Drisha raise her taloned hands.

Drisha lashed the air above her head with an energy that belied her years. Although it appeared that she tore the iron lattice apart with her bare hands, Kestra knew that her gift in fact transformed the air surrounding them, making it harder than steel. No part of the plummeting iron grid came close to even touching her, Drisha's talons shredding rivet and bar like parchment. Knowing the consequences of being near Drisha's unleashed power, Kestra crouched and threw her arm over her face to shield against the hail of metal fragments that filled the passage. The nearby guards, of course, had no such experience and were left reeling in an iron blizzard. When it faded, most had fallen, screaming and clutching bloodied faces and lacerated limbs.

Looking up, Kestra saw Drisha collapse to her knees, spent by the effort of rending the portcullis into scrap. Beyond her, about half the remaining guards had been felled by the iron hail, but five remained on their feet. Although beset by fearful confusion, Kestra knew they would soon recover to cry out for reinforcements.

"Now, sister!" she shouted to Ulaine, pointing urgently at the hesitating guards. However, the novice appeared frozen by fear and shock. Slumped against the passage wall, she stared at the groaning, screaming men littering the ground around her. Kestra sensed no welling of her gift.

Cursing, Kestra surged to her feet, drawing her second dagger from its sheath at the small of her back and preparing to charge the remaining guards. With luck, she could cut down two or three before the rest recovered their wits. After that, things would get far more fraught, but she would at least have a chance to escape into the palace grounds in the chaos.

She had covered only a few steps when Lesander sprinted past her. Having already gained an impression of his abilities, she was surprised when, in the space of a few heartbeats, he clearly demonstrated that she had underestimated his skill. Two guards died almost instantly, each felled by a single stroke of the brother's sword. Another managed to half level his poleaxe before Lesander ducked under it and skewered him in the groin. Of the remaining two, one had the wit to drop his weapon whilst the other, more courageous than wise, attempted a slash at Lesander's head. Kestra had noted before how truly skilled fighters often appeared slower than their opponents, the precision of their movements and ability to anticipate action resembled a warrior at practice rather than engaged in a deadly duel. So it proved now as Lesander swayed gently backward, allowing the guard's poleaxe to pass within a quarter inch of his face. As he righted himself, Lesander flicked his sword and the guard staggered away, blood gushing from his throat.

"I …" the craven but sensible guard said, hands raised as he backed away from his abandoned poleaxe. "I'm a poor man, sir … Press-ganged, I was …"

"Go," Leander said, jerking his head at the bridge. The guard gabbled out his thanks and ran, hurdling his prone comrades then pelting across the bridge.

"What is wrong with you?" Kestra demanded, advancing towards Ulaine and shoving her against the wall.

"Can we get on?"

Turning, Kestra saw Drisha clambering to her feet, helped by a grey-faced Blench. "The guards on the battlements will have heard all this," the elder sister said. "Leave her be!" she snapped when Kestra rounded on Ulaine once more. "We've no time."

Kestra wanted to remind her, forcefully, that they were no longer novice and mistress, but knew the older woman was right. Soon the gate would be swarming with soldiers. "If you're not going to be of use, get out of here," she hissed at Ulaine before releasing her and following Lesander as he ran for the palace grounds.

Chapter Six

The gardens began only a short distance from the walls. Kestra quickly realised that this un-tended forest of interwoven trees and sprawling undergrowth could not truly be termed a garden. Lakril's passion for ornamental landscapes was legendary; much of the taxes he squeezed from his subjects were said to be spent on vast lawns, intricate flowerbeds and grandiose statuary. However, upon following Lesander into the welcome cover of the dense mass of vegetation, she saw only a jungle.

They were obliged to pause whilst the others caught up. Drisha came to a stumbling halt and slumped against the winding trunk of a puzzle tree, gasping for breath and dabbing the blood from her nose with a lace kerchief. Blench wasn't much better: hands on his thighs, bent double and staggering on weakened legs. The state of their exhaustion compelled Kestra to consider something that would once have been unthinkable: *Leave them. They'll slow us down.*

A rustle of disturbed foliage snapped her gaze to the sight of Ulaine coming to a halt nearby. The sister's face was downcast save for the glance she dared in Kestra's direction. *At least she didn't run,* she thought. She cast away her cape and the thin lace skirt before pulling the ties that would loosen her bodice, a cunning contrivance of armour plate beneath embroidered fabric which also concealed two more knives. It was heavier than she would have liked, but she fancied she would be grateful for it before long.

Seeing Lesander crouched in the lee of a juniper bush, she moved to his side. His eyes were closed but she could tell he was straining to catch any sign of a threat in the discordant maze of shadows ahead. From the sudden appearance of a crease in his brow, she divined he had found one.

"What is it?" she murmured.

"It's … unusual." He opened his eyes, turning to her with a grimace. "Which can't be good."

A tumult of shouting from the direction of the gate caused them to stiffen. Through the trees Kestra caught the gleam of torches flaring to life along the battlements, a great many torches.

"Unusual or not," she said, "we can't linger."

"The western wing is this way." Lesander rose and started on a leftward track. Kestra gestured for the others to follow. They did so with aggravating slowness, Drisha helped along by Ulaine whilst Blench followed behind. It was clear both needed a considerably longer rest, but that was impossible now.

"The brother tells me there's a threat in here with us," she told Ulaine, meeting the girl's eye. "Your mistress and brother are in no condition to fight, which means it falls to you." She held her gaze a moment longer. "Don't fail again."

"So harsh have you become," Drisha observed as they laboured on through the thick undergrowth. "What happened to that whimpering girl who sobbed her way through our first task together?"

"Task," Kestra repeated, scanning the surrounding jungle. "Such fondness for euphemism, my lady. As I recall our first *task* was in fact a squalid murder in the back room of a brothel, the first of many."

"Everything we did was done for the good of the Order," Drisha snapped. "And everything the Order does is in service of the Faith and thereby the world."

"Spare me your mantras, old woman. I had my fill of them years ago."

"You used to have Faith," Drisha persisted, undaunted by the acid colouring Kestra's tone. "What happened to you?"

"The Aspect lied to me." Kestra cast a glance over her shoulder, offering her former mentor one of the empty smiles she had taught her. "And so did you."

She heard Drisha draw breath for another retort but, mercifully, Lesander forestalled it with a raised hand, bringing them to an abrupt halt. Kestra took a firmer grip on her dagger, crouching in readiness, but neither saw nor heard a threat. However, she did see the focus of Lesander's interest, a tall, overgrown object rising from the mass of bushes a short distance off. They had found one of Lakril's statues.

The subject was hard to make out as they drew nearer. Although plainly intended as some form of human representation, the manner of it was obscured by vines covering it from base to head. Peering closer, Kestra saw that what she had initially taken as weathered granite was something else entirely.

"A skeleton," Ulaine whispered, squinting at the ribcage visible through the covering. "Why carve such a thing?"

"It's no carving, sister," Lesander told her.

The ribs and limbs were hard to make out beneath the shroud of vines, but the dark, cracked surface of old bones was something Kestra had seen before. These had been affixed to a rusted steel framework, itself arranged to convey a pose. The figure had been positioned with straight-backed elegance, one arm raised. Amidst the interwoven strands enveloping the wrist, Kestra glimpsed the sparkle of gems. They also gleamed dully within the cage of the skeleton's ribs, dangling from a silver chain that had once adorned the neck.

"Aihlsin Al Varnen," Drisha said. "The king's aunt. A woman of peerless vanity, so they say, who loved her jewels above all. They called her the Lady of Rubies. At least he let her keep them."

Looking around, Kestra saw other vine-covered figures through the trees, counting at least a dozen. "So here resides the royal family," she said. "It seems the prospect of putting his sister on the throne is somewhat remote."

"We won't know that until he's dead," Drisha pointed out. "Which won't happen if we continue to dawdle here—"

A lithe, long tailed silhouette separated from the matrix of branches above to descend upon Drisha. Although it appeared to have been crafted from the stuff of shadow, its teeth and claws shone bright as it fell, ready to deliver a killing bite to the neck of its prey.

A sound like the single beat of a vast drum filled Kestra's right ear, accompanied by a blast of air that sent her reeling. Spun by the force of the wind, she saw Ulaine raising her hand, face once again livid with panic but this time lacking the same frozen immobility. The gust of air she unleashed caught the beast just as its claws were about to latch onto Drisha's shoulders, sending it spinning away. The feline shadow collided with several trees before disappearing from view. Kestra knew it would resemble just a collection of bloody fur and broken bones when it eventually fell to earth.

"That's enough!" she called to Ulaine as the sister continue to send her spiralling gale through the trees. The jungle twisted and swayed in the storm, sending several more cats tumbling away before Ulaine dropped her arm and sagged in a way that made it plain she had expended far too much strength too quickly.

A short interval of creaking branches and falling leaves preceded a rising chorus of yowls and hissing. Clearly, Ulaine had not scoured the jungle clean of enemies.

"What are they?" Kestra wondered aloud, eyes flicking between a succession of lithe, black shapes loping through the trees.

"Tree panthers," Lesander replied, sword held low as he moved in a slow circle. "Common to the jungles of southern Volaria. Our king has a liking for exotic pets." Kestra saw him wince as the feline chorus increased in volume. "And he keeps them starved." He jerked his head at Kestra. "Best make for the western wing, I'll hold them off."

"No," Blench said, moving to stand in front of Lesander. "Your sword is still needed, brother."

Blench straightened and fixed his gaze on a patch of vegetation where the long tail of a panther coiled with snake-like anticipation. "No food here," Blench said. The tail's coiling halted at the sound of his whisper-shout. "There." Blench pointed towards the outer wall. They could hear the clipped, barking commands of captains and sergeants hectoring their subordinates into action. A great many soldiers would soon be sweeping these grounds.

"There is prey," Blench said. Kestra saw blood streaming thickly from his nose. With a hungry growl, the panther bounded in the opposite direction.

"Prey!" Blench raised his Gift-infused voice louder than Kestra had ever heard it, the surrounding foliage roiling as it spread from cat to cat. The jungle came alive with fleeting shadows, the air filled with the screams of unleashed blood lust, soon joined by the sound of human screams as they found their first victims.

"Brother," Kestra said, starting towards Blench's side then stopping when he turned to her with a raised hand. Red tears seeped from his eyes, a sign that any further use of his gift would be fatal.

"Best get on with it, Kes," he grunted, pointing a finger over his shoulder then turning away. He staggered off into the jungle, still casting out his whispered commands as the sounds of dying cats and guards rose to a crescendo.

"Come on." Lesander gave an urgent tug to Kestra's arm as she continued to stare in Blench's wake. All the dangers they had shared in years past and he had never suffered a single scratch. Of all of them, she had felt him the most likely to survive this mission.

"Move, girl!" Drisha instructed with a hard shove, dragging a sagging Ulaine along as she followed Lesander. Kestra spared a last glance at the trees, their swaying more gentle now, the sounds of death fading, then turned and ran.

Chapter Seven

Lesander gained entry to the western wing by the simple expedient of heaving an earthenware plant pot through one of the tall, stained glass windows. They had encountered only one guard upon leaving the jungle-like garden to traverse the flat expanse of lawn separating the palace proper from its overgrown grounds. He had been a sturdy fellow of keen eyes made yet more alert by the alarms from the walls. He wielded his poleaxe with considerable skill and speed, stalwart in his duty. Lesander killed him with two strokes of his sword and spared the corpse only the briefest glance before crouching to heft the plant pot.

As predicted, they found the interior of the western wing bare of furnishings, the floors unswept and the air musty with the deadened atmosphere unique to unused places. "Fifty yards on then left for twenty yards," Kestra said, reciting the dimensions of the plan as she started down the corridor. "Right for another twenty yards to the ballroom. We can access the roof there."

Drisha and Ulaine were incapable of more than a shuffling trot, forcing them to adopt what Kestra felt to be a perilously slow pace. Once again, the notion of abandoning her comrades rose to mind, although this time she quickly discounted it, her reluctance arising not from sentiment but pragmatism. Ulaine's gift was too powerful an asset to be discarded and Drisha probably retained enough strength to tear down another obstacle or two.

How harsh have you become. Kestra quelled the uncomfortable churn of emotions that rose in response to Drisha's words, and the pain of Blench's sacrifice. Perhaps the hardest lesson she had learned in over a decade of surreptitious murder was the need for unwavering focus. Grief, fear, and loss were distractions. All that mattered was the target's demise, and no one was more deserving of death than the monster lurking at the heart of this palace of horrors.

They found another guard stationed at the ornate doors to the ballroom. A far less assiduous fellow than the fearless poleaxe wielder, he barely had time to look up from the brandy flask he held to his lips before Lesander's throwing knife sank into his eye. He tottered about and gibbered for the few seconds it took for the brother to close the distance and finish him with a swift thrust of his sword. Kestra rushed past to heave open the doors.

The revealed ballroom was so vast its marble floor resembled a frozen lake. Kestra found herself halting in admiration. Her gaze swept the space from end to end, taking in the gold-inlaid filigree of the pillars and the silver veins that traced through the floor like a great spider's web. In its centre, a small figure crouched amidst a circle of torches on stanchions.

The air was still, save for a faint, repeating scratch, so the echo of their feet seemed an outrage as they entered the ballroom. Kestra scanned the pillars and distant windows for threats but kept returning to the small figure at the core of the silver web. Progressing deeper into the space she realised the scratching noise was coming from this huddled shape. As they neared, she saw how the tiles surrounding the figure were covered in a circular matrix of script, the letters rendered in some form brown ink that had faded to obscure much of the meaning. Kestra picked out the partly smeared words 'treachery' and 'deceit' amongst the confusion of text before her eyes came to rest upon the small woman in a thin muslin shift who had assuredly created it all.

She muttered as she worked, paying her visitors no heed. "Conspired we did ..." Kestra heard her say. Shifting to gain a better look at the scribe's face she saw a young woman with emaciated features that hadn't felt the sun for many years. Her expression was set in a childish mode of concentration, chewing her lip and frowning as she contemplated her next words. Her hair was an unkempt nest of black shot through with grey, so matted in places it was clear she hadn't washed for months, if not longer. Kestra's rising sense of dismay and disgust increased as she looked at the woman's hands, finding she held no quill or brush. The scratch arose from the bone of her index finger, which jutted from receding and corrupted flesh. Her other fingers were in a similarly ruined state, her hands blackened claws and tendrils of corruption veining the pale skin of her arms. A small bowl filled with blood sat at her side and she occasionally paused to dip her mutilated digit into the contents before continuing to write.

"Chamberlain Al Simlin too ..." she muttered. "He was part of it. A vile traitor who corrupted me ..."

"Princess Luvehla?"

The question came from Drisha as she moved to stand in front of the huddled, muttering scribe. Drisha's brows were raised in an uneven arc, lips drawn as if containing a sob. Kestra had never seen her exhibit compassion before, at least not to this degree, and found it jarring.

The scratch of the woman's finger stopped abruptly. "Princess," she repeated, her dry, cracked voice faltering over the word. "They called me that … Not anymore. He won't let them." Her head snapped up and she stared at Drisha with wide, terrorised eyes. "You shouldn't either!" she hissed. "He'll know. Traitors are not princesses. It cannot be …"

Her voice faded and she slowly dipped her bone quill into the bowl once again. "Princesses get no dresses," she said in a sing-song voice. "Princesses get no horses. Princesses get nothing. Not when they turn traitor. Then," more scratching as she inscribed the words *'lying whore'* on the marble tiles, "then they get to write down their sins so all can see them …"

Kestra was no stranger to maddened souls. A tendency to lose one's grasp on reality was a common ailment in the Seventh Order, thanks to the varied price exacted by the gifts they wielded. Consequently, she had gained an ability to judge those who could be brought back to a semblance of reason, and those who could not. Her brief acquaintance with Princess Luvehla left her in no doubt that this was a soul forever lost.

"Behold our future queen," Kestra muttered, drawing a fierce glare from Drisha.

"Do you have no heart at all?" she rasped.

The urge to snap back with another acid-laced insult rose then fell from Kestra's lips, smothered by a sudden and unexpected surge of shamed self-reproach. She coughed and moved away with a purposeful stride. "The skylight we need is this way …"

"We can't leave her like this."

The hard, commanding grate of Drisha's voice brought Kestra to a halt. The sister slipped a knife from her sleeve but hesitated, continuing to stare at the kneeling, tortured soul before her. Kestra raised a hand and shook her head when she saw Lesander draw breath to remind Drisha of the urgency.

"I remember your mother," Drisha said finally, dropping to her knees and shuffling to the princess's side. "We played together as girls, for our fathers were very good friends. She was so beautiful." Drisha played a hand through the mane of matted, prematurely greyed hair. "Just like you."

Moving closer, she drew the princess into a tight embrace. Luvehla's face took on a last spasm of comprehension then, a faint smile of what Kestra chose to take as gratitude curving her cracked lips. When Drisha brought the knife to the princess's neck, Kestra turned away and went looking for the skylight.

Chapter Eight

Climbing onto the roof was easy for Kestra and Lesander, less so for their companions. Thanks to her youth, Ulaine had recovered a good deal of strength but proved an inexpert climber.

"She's been neglecting your education," Kestra grunted, taking hold of Ulaine's upraised arm to haul her up to the skylight's frame.

"I've only been her student for few months," the young sister said, scrambling onto the tiled roof. Her voice held a note of pique as she added, "And I feel I have, in truth, learned a great deal from Mistress Drisha."

"Did she make you kill anyone yet?" Kestra asked. Although the question was directed at Ulaine, she looked down to meet Drisha's upraised gaze. "Perhaps someone she told you was a vile rapist and murderer of children but in fact turned out to be an overly inquisitive scholar with a few dangerous books in his hidden library?"

Drisha returned her stare with a glower, her forehead spotted by a princess's blood. "Is this really the right time?" she asked.

"Our sister makes a fair point," Lesander said, reaching down to offer Drisha his arm. As he hauled her up, Kestra heard the mingled discord of hunting dogs and shouted orders from all around. The rooftop offered a comprehensive view of the inner wards of the palace. The gardens here were also overgrown but lacked the jungle-like appearance of those fringing the walls. Dozens of torches blazed amongst the bushes and flowerbeds as soldiers ran to and fro. From the corridor below came the echo of further alarm signifying their pursuers had now reached the ballroom.

"That scholar was a thief," Drisha said, teeth clenched with the effort of dragging herself clear of the skylight. "A stealer of knowledge that was not his to share. If he had had his way the existence of the Seventh Order would have been exposed for all to see. I'll offer no apology for ensuring that never came to pass. Neither should you."

"You," Kestra leaned closer to Drisha, the beast hissing with predatory interest, "do not tell me what to do anymore."

"We've no time to chat, sisters," Lesander said. He began to move along the rooftop in a low, rapid crouch, keeping clear of the apex to conceal his silhouette. Kestra broke the glare of mutual antipathy with Drisha, placating the beast with thoughts of what lay ahead as she turned to follow Lesander. The prospect of ravaging the innards of the soul she hated most of all in this world caused it to partially uncoil in readiness, its hunger adding speed to her progress.

Their course had appeared far shorter on the unfortunate architect's scribbled plan, just a hundred yards or so with two sharp turns and a short leap from one tiled slope to another. However, as the din of those hunting them filled the air with a discordant chorus, it felt far longer. Kestra expected to hear the thrum of a bowstring or the shout of alarm with every step. By dint of luck and skill, however, they reached the terminus of the western wing without discovery. The high towers and halls of the palace's central keep loomed above.

"It's quite a distance, sister," Lesander observed, turning to Ulaine with a doubtful crease to his brow.

As she surveyed the broad gap separating them from the tower, Ulaine's face bunched in uncertainty. Kestra saw her throat constrict in a swallow before she exchanged a glance with Drisha. The older woman forced a tight smile and gripped her arm, displaying far more encouragement and regard in one gesture than Kestra had seen in all the years of their acquaintance.

"I have to," Ulaine said, drawing a deep breath. "Do I not?"

"Yes," Kestra told her simply. A clatter of displaced tiles from behind and a fresh upsurge of shouting from the gardens below prompted her to add, "And without delay."

Nodding, Ulaine rose to her full height, stepping back and extending her arms. "It's best if you hold yourselves limp," she said. "Don't fight the wind, it'll break you."

"Get yourself gone from this spot as soon as we're across," Drisha told her, voice stern but also possessed of a poorly suppressed quaver. "Hide and wait for the Sixth Order. With luck, they won't be long in coming."

Ulaine smiled, blinked tears and unleashed her gift. The very suddenness of the gale that struck Kestra helped her survived the initial blast, the force of it was so irresistible. In accordance with Ulaine's warning she stifled the instinct to struggle against the invisible hand that lifted and cast her high into the air, allowing herself to tumble and flail in its grip. The world became a swirl of sky and palace that set her guts roiling. Then the walls of the tower loomed closer, a cliff of broad granite and windows that seemed very small. The image of a fly swatted and smeared on a wall, sprang into Kestra's mind and she hated the realisation that her final seconds of life would be lost to panic.

It was then that Ulaine's skill and precision became apparent. Abruptly, the wind released its hold on Kestra, tossing her towards a narrow window. Just before she collided with the surely fatal combination of glass and lead, Ulaine's gale flared a final time, more powerfully than before. The window shattered and Kestra's landed hard, though uninjured on the marble floor beyond. Ulaine had judged the angle of her throw perfectly. Still, the impact was jarring; Kestra rolled and collided with the wall opposite the destroyed portal.

She expended precious seconds gasping air into her winded lungs before rising. Next to her, Lesander levered himself to a sitting position, palming blood from a cut to his forehead. Drisha was already on her feet, standing at the shattered window and staring at the rooftop far below.

"She's not there," she said.

Kestra moved to her side, glancing down to see a half-dozen torches clustered at the end of the western wing. The distance was too great to make out details, but Kestra felt sure the torches would be moving with more animation had the soldiers holding them found a captive.

"It seems she took your advice," she told Drisha. She moved away but the sister continued to linger at the window, face stricken with worry. "The task is all," Kestra reminded her.

Drisha's face bunched before she nodded and stepped back. "She's a good girl," she said, swallowing to banish the catch in her voice. "A good student."

"Better than me?" Kestra asked. Drisha followed as she started down the wide curve of the corridor towards the descending staircase she knew lay at its end, Lesander falling in behind.

Drisha let out a rare laugh. "Your status as my worst ever student," she assured Kestra, "could never be outdo—"

The clatter and snap of a crossbow warned them both to dive aside, but the range was too close to avoid the bolt that came streaking out of the shadows. Drisha gasped and collapsed, clutching at the fletching protruding from her side. Something flashed across her eyes an instant before Lesander charged past and plucked the throwing knife from the throat of the fallen crossbowman. He held his sword ready, but it appeared this guard had been alone.

"Don't pull it out!" Kestra said, rushing to Drisha's side. The sister hissed blood through gritted teeth and forced her hands away from the bolt. Crouching to inspect the wound, Kestra saw the projectile had chanced upon a gap in Drisha's armoured bodice, sinking deep into the flesh beneath. From the woman's increasingly pallid skin and shuddering breaths, Kestra divined the bolt head had found an important vein.

"Go!" Drisha grated. "Finish the task!"

"It requires all of us," Kestra said, looping Drisha's arm over her shoulder. "You know that."

The elder sister bit down on a scream as Kestra hauled her upright but voiced no further protests. They hobbled along in Lesander's wake as he led the way to the staircase. Descending the stairs brought a harsher pitch to Drisha's gasps. With every step Kestra felt blood wash over the hand she held to the bolt in the sister's side. The stairwell seemed unnaturally quiet save for Drisha's pain, an unnerving contrast to the confusion raging outside. Consequently, when Drisha spoke in a voice that was little more than a murmur, Kestra had no difficulty hearing it.

"It was fear …" Drisha said. They had paused on a landing only one storey up from the base of the tower where, Kestra knew, they would find a wide, pillar-lined hallway leading straight to the huge doors guarding Lakril's throne room. Turning to regard Drisha's face, Kestra found it bleached to a near alabaster shade, the sister's eyes hooded by pain and exhaustion.

"Fear?" Kestra asked.

"How I was … with you," Drisha groaned. "I feared what would happen … if we became too close. For love … can so easily become … hate." Her pallid brows bunched together in a frown that was sorrowful and reflective in equal measure. "It is not easy … to play the mother to a girl who can kill with a look."

"I didn't need a mother," Kestra muttered back, taking a firmer grip on Drisha's slender form and resuming the descent. "I needed a teacher who told me the truth."

"Concealment … is our protection." Drisha sucked in a sharp breath, shuddering in Kestra's grasp but her feet never faltering on the steps. "Once … when the Seventh Order worked in the open … its mere existence almost brought an end to … everything. We must stay hidden. Although …" she sagged, forcing Kestra to tighten her hold, "… I am sorry. For the scholar … and the lies."

"Hold," Lesander instructed softly as he paused at the base of the stairwell. Lowering himself to a crouch, he slowly inched his head forward to glance around the corner. Turning back to Kestra, he whispered, "Four guards."

"The doors?"

"Closed and barred, with chains."

"Just get me to the doors," Drisha grunted, spattering her lips red. She raised her hand and formed it into a familiar talon. "The task is all."

Chapter Nine

Lesander slid his sword into the sheath on his back then bade Kestra wait a moment. He then surprised her by straightening and walking around the corner. Kestra peeked from her cover to find the brother making for the throne room with a confident stride and the purposeful air of one who had every right to do so. His appearance and lack of regard for the guards stationed along the corridor enabled him to pass by the first two without a challenge. It wasn't until he drew level with the next pair that they stepped forward to bar his way.

"Stand aside," Lesander snapped, waving a hand. "Brother Lesander Doren bearing despatches from the Aspect of the Sixth Order. For the king's eyes only."

"We were given no notice of your coming," the guard replied, marked as a captain by the small plume of peacock feathers fixed to the side of his helm. Hearing the suspicion in his voice the other guards shifted from their stations to form a loose circle around the brother. Kestra crept from concealment, moving slowly and bearing most of Drisha's weight to prevent an audible footfall.

"Have you not heard what's happening outside, man?" Lesander demanded. "Rebellion has broken out in the city. Whilst you force me to dither here my brothers fight to keep the rioters from these walls."

Kestra used the pillars lining the hallway for cover, dragging Drisha from one to the other. She made it halfway along the passage whilst the argument rose in volume and neared its inevitable conclusion.

"No one sees the king unless he summons them," the guard captain stated. "And we've heard no news of riots."

"You have now," Lesander said. He made a show of calming himself, sighing and gesturing at the barred doors. "Very well. Tell him I'm here and crave leave for an audience."

The captain stiffened and coughed in discomfort. "I have orders to keep this door sealed," he stated. "And that is all."

"I have vital news for the king's ears," Lesander told him, leaning closer to the man. "What precisely do you find so difficult to understand, sir?"

"The last guard to open this door without leave was nailed to it." The captain let out another flustered cough. "Servants bring the king's supper in two hours." He extended a gauntleted hand. "Give me your missive and I'll put it in the hands of his chamberlain. I can do no more."

Kestra risked a glance beyond the pillar to see Lesander's face creasing in annoyance as he reached inside his jerkin for a message she knew he didn't have. "Be ready," she told Drisha. The sister groaned softly in response.

"It bears the Order's seal," Lesander warned the captain as his hand began to emerge. "I assume I can trust you not to break—" He jerked the dagger from his jerkin and stabbed it into the captain's eye. As the three guards began to level their poleaxes, Lesander plucked the dagger from the captain's eye and thrust it into the throat of the soldier to his left.

Lesander ducked and whirled, pulling his sword from its scabbard. The third guard's poleaxe sliced the air above his head. The brother parried a thrust from the fourth, stepped in close and punched him square in the face, sending him reeling and allowing enough space to fend off an overhead swing of his comrade's poleaxe. Lesander jerked his blade, forcing the guardsman's poleaxe up then delivering a blurring slash to the man's face. He screamed and staggered back, poleaxe falling as he clutched at ruined eyes. The surviving guardsman lunged at Lesander, succeeding in spearing his upper thigh with the spike of his axe blade.

Lesander backed away, pulling the steel from his flesh. He collided with a pillar and fell, trying vainly to raise his sword and parry the killing blow the guardsman aimed at his head. Kestra had been well tutored in seeking out vulnerabilities in soldiers' armour. Sprinting from cover, she slipped her blade into the gap between the guardsman's backplate and the lower rim of his helm. He stiffened as she drove it home, working the blade back and forth to sever the appropriate veins before drawing it clear. He fell face first onto the marble floor at Lesander's side, twitching as his blood spread out across the tiles.

"Can you walk?" Kestra asked, offering a hand to Lesander.

He gave no answer save for an aggrieved and agonised grunt as he clasped her forearm and heaved himself upright, blood leaking from his thigh. Kestra recognised his anger as that of an expert reproaching himself for a foolish mistake.

"We all have our bad days, brother," she said, unable to contain a grin before hurrying to raise Drisha from the spot where she had been forced to leave her. Moving with stiff determination, Lesander helped convey the sister to the doors.

"You …" Drisha gasped, sending a spatter of blood onto the gold-inlaid, white-painted timbers. "You had both best … stand back."

They did so, casting worried glances at the corpse-strewn hall as it echoed with the sound of the blinded guard's screams soon joined by the tumult of many running feet. The clatter of a falling chain drew Kestra's gaze back to the doors. Drisha had already used her talons to slice the iron links and heavy lock to pieces. The door itself remained locked and the sister paused, drawing in a breath before unleashing her gift in full. The doors disappeared in a blizzard of splinters and shredded gold leaf, the cloud of powdered timber dense enough to briefly obscure Drisha from view. When it cleared, the sister lay in the ragged portal she had created, utterly still and spent. Kestra found herself transfixed by Drisha's slack features; all vestige of life vanished from her eyes.

"Come, sister," Lesander said, taking her arm and dragging her forward. "We've a task to finish."

A fresh drumbeat of fast approaching boots provoked her into movement, ducking through the remnants of the doors and into the throne room at last. She had her dagger ready for more guards, Lesander crouching in a defensive stance at her side, but no enemies greeted them. Blazing torches flickered in the influx of air from the opened door, casting dancing light around the vast, bare, windowless chamber. In the centre of the room a small, thin man sat on a throne, a far more imposing man standing at his side.

Kestra was entertained by the amusing notion that whoever had constructed that throne had done so as a joke, so starkly did it emphasise the unimpressive dimensions of its occupant. The small man's crown wobbled on his head as he squirmed in his overlarge perch. He wore the finery of a king, but it too sat ill upon him. The ermine hemmed robe and heavy chain of office making him appear a child playing dress up. Then came his voice, a high-pitched, shrill piping that completed the impression of an infant confronted by adult anger.

"Intruders!" he shrieked, jerking in his throne, hands reaching out to clutch at the plain black robe of the tall man standing at his side. "Rebels! Assassins! Kill them, Aertis!"

"So," Kestra said, starting forward, her feet echoing long on the marble floor. "You'd be the sorcerer, I suppose?" She addressed the tall man but mostly kept her eyes on the squirming king.

Aertis Vezuri's glared at her with poised and arch disdain as she neared. She put his age at somewhere near fifty, but his grey beard, trimmed into a neat point to match his moustache, made her think he might be several years older. His robe was a floor-length, all black affair save for the symbol embroidered in white upon his chest. She recognised the intertwined snakes as a sigil relating one of the many Alpiran gods, but couldn't place the name, not that it mattered, for despite his apparent absence of fear, she felt no gift as she drew closer. Whatever abilities this man possessed, they didn't arise from the Dark, which made him just a man, one Lesander could deal with if need be.

"You can leave if you like," she told the Verehlan, keeping her principal focus on the king. "We're not here for you."

"Aertis!" The small man's crown slipped from his head as he clutched at the Verehlan's robe with desperate, twitching fingers. "She looks like a cat," he whimpered, eyes spilling terrorised tears as he stared at Kestra. "The thing in the Beyond has sent a cat to kill me!"

Aertis Vezuri frowned and Kestra couldn't decide if the man's disdain was directed at her or the king. "To betray one's employer," Aertis said in a smooth, cultured accent, raising his arm as he spoke, "is to be dishonoured. That, I will not abide."

"Brother," Kestra said but Lesander was already palming a throwing knife from his belt. Strangely, the Verehlan betrayed only faint concern when Lesander drew his arm back in readiness. Aertis formed his outstretched hand into a fist and Kestra heard the metallic snick of some hidden device. A torrent of thick grey smoke issued from the sleeve of his robe and Kestra and Lesander were instantly blinded.

Kestra found herself in an anonymous swirl of grey fog, Lesander lost to sight along with the sorcerer and the king. Cursing, she spurred to a run hoping she was heading toward the throne. Upon reaching it, however, she found it empty. Casting about for any glimpse of the little man, she heard the heavy thud of something impacting the marble tiles close by. She glanced down and saw an iron cylinder about six inches long, decorated with a swirling brass motif that resembled a flame. A sparkling wick protruded from one end. *Flame weaver*, she recalled, the literal meaning of the sorcerer's name. Despite never having seen the like of this thing before, she knew she had best not linger to see what would happen when the sparks met the decorated cylinder.

She caught hold of the throne's sturdy, oaken back, swung herself around it and sprinted away, covering barely three yards before a sudden roar filled her ears and an invisible fist swatted her to the floor. Her dagger spun free of her grasp as she collided with the tiles, feeling the sting of splinters on her lower legs. She glanced back and saw the blast had partially banished the fog and the throne lay in very small pieces, but it had served to shield her from grievous injury. King Lakril Al Vernon cowered on the floor in a pool of his own piss barely a dozen feet away.

He shrieked as she closed on him with a rapid crawl that surely made her resemble the cat he believed her to be. "Please," he begged as she clamped a hand to his chin, forcing his tear-filled eyes to meet hers. "Please …"

She waited for the invisible bridge to form so she could unleash the roused beast. But the beast wouldn't stir.

"I …" Lakril gibbered. "I'm sorry …"

"Shut your mouth!" Kestra tightened her grip. "Book burner! Murderer! I saw what you did to your family! Your own sister!"

"I couldn't help it!" he said in a cloud of spittle, the peevish, pathetic excuse of a soul that had been indulged for all its years. Detestable, certainly, but more deserving of pity than hate.

Wake up! she raged at the beast, willing it to stir, but all it consented to offer was a disgusted hiss. The king, apparently, wasn't worthy of its hunger. Yet, she had other means of killing. "If you would be so good, Highness," she said, placing a knee on Lakril's chest and reaching for the dagger at the small of her back, "as to hold still."

She had half raised the blade when another thud sounded close by, and another flame decorated iron cylinder rolled to a halt barely a yard away. This time the sparking wick was only an inch from reaching its end.

A hard shove sent Kestra rolling off the king. She glimpsed Lesander rushing to place himself between her and the sorcerer's infernal device. The blast pushed her across the marble floor, leaving her deafened and numb. The throne room disappeared for a time, Kestra struggling amidst a void of sound and sight. When her hearing returned, she heard what sounded like a swarm of angry hornets which then subsided into a voice.

"Are you another of its servants?" Lakril, uninjured apart from a scratch on his cheek, stood over Lesander's smoking, broken body. Incredibly, Kestra saw that the brother continued to cling to life. His hands moved in jerking spasms, as if trying to grasp something. "It sent you, didn't it?" Lakril persisted, crouching at Lesander's side. Kestra realised his voice was now far deeper than that of the whimpering child who had begged for his life only moments before. Also, his fear seemed to have vanished. Instead, as he peered closer at Lesander's burnt features, the king's face was that of a man fully confident in his cruelty.

"Highness," Aertis said, moving into view. "We had best retire to your private quarters. Your loyal guards come to escort you."

"Later." Lakril waved a dismissive hand, not looking up from Lesander. "First I must get the truth from this one, then the other." His eyes slid to Kestra as he prodded Lesander's burns. "You hear me, cat?" he asked, pressing his finger deep and drawing forth a moan from Lesander. "We shall have so many games together, you and I."

At last, the beast uncoiled, roused to a pitch of ferocity beyond any she could remember. Lakril's face became a frozen mask of shock as invisible bridge formed between him and Kestra. The beast issued from her with lightning speed, sinking itself into Lakril's core with such fury that blood instantly gushed from his mouth, nose and ears as his insides were shredded and spilled from his body. It was the most complete and satisfying feast the beast had ever enjoyed, one it savoured, ravening with far more thoroughness than usual before it finally withdrew.

At the moment of his death Lakril Al Vernon, King of the Realm, deflated rather than fell. The bloodied husk of his body subsided to the throne room floor amidst the mess of his innards with a sound like wet leather cast upon stone. Kestra spared the corpse a brief glance before turning to Aertis. Although plainly a man of dutiful instincts, he was also no fool, turning and fleeing before her eyes could meet his. He raised his arm as he ran, letting out another pall of thick grey smoke that obscured her gaze and that of the palace guards rushing into chamber.

Unable to stand, Kestra crawled towards Lesander. The exhaustion of the beast's exertions made it a difficult and prolonged journey. She heard combat through the smoke but ignored it, intent only on reaching Lesander's side. Shadowy, blue-cloaked figures swirled around them as she rested her head on the brother's chest, feeling the soft but diminishing thrum of his heart.

"Little sister." The Aspect's voice seemed very far away at first, a murmur from a dream that only became real when he crouched to gather her up. "Let us help you," he said, arms enfolding her.

"No." Her refusal was a tremulous thing, but she summoned all her will to turn it into a shout. "No!" She pushed back from the Aspect, looking down at Lesander's body. "Heal him," she instructed. "Bring him back."

The Aspect pressed a hand to the brother's chest, letting out a regretful sigh. "I can't. It's been too long …"

"Bring him back!" Kestra slapped her hands to the Aspect's face, staring deep into his eyes. "The hatred I had for the king is as nothing to what I feel for you. Now do what I say."

Chapter Ten

Does it still feel like home?"

Brother Lesander surveyed the dark mass of the Great Northern Forest with little change to the troubled frown that Kestra felt be his permanent expression now. Still, there was a small glimmer of something, a burgeoning light to the eyes that had been absent throughout their journey from Varinshold. Ever since he first woke hours after the Aspect had set his healing touch upon him, Kestra had known the kind, cheerful, if deadly soul she had met in Renfael was gone. In his place was a sombre man who rarely smiled and endured nightmare-filled slumber ever night. Also, although it pained her to admit, he scared her. He had exhibited no violence since waking, and yet the sense he exuded was that of a man striving to contain a restless, perhaps dangerous shift in character. Watching him look upon the forest Kestra wondered, not for the first time, if she had done right in forcing the Aspect to bring him back.

"It's different," Lesander said eventually. "But I still feel its welcome." Kestra was relieved to note his slight smile. Coming here had been her idea, one he had initially refused. However, the Aspect of the Sixth Order had persuaded him otherwise. She didn't know what had passed between Aspect and brother, but Lesander had left his blue cloak behind when they set off. He had kept his sword, but no longer wore it on his back, instead keeping it strapped to Nolnen's saddle.

The stallion nickered in impatience as Lesander continued to sit. "The Realm is troubled," he said, turning to Kestra. "As you said it would be. My Order may have need of me ..."

"Your Order will persist," she cut in. "With or without you. As will the Seventh. Should this Realm crumble they'll just make another, though I fancy it will require the labour of many years."

It was true that, with no rightful heir to sit the throne, rebellion and strife had arisen in all four Fiefs of the Realm. *Kill a king and you kill his kingdom,* Kestra had mused more than once as they passed many a burnt village and untended field. Yet, she felt no guilt, nor the slightest doubt. Those, apparently, were now Lesander's province along with the terrors that haunted his sleep. She hadn't asked him what set him screaming and thrashing every night, her only clue being a cryptic warning from the Aspect of her former Order whilst she sat at the brother's sick bed: *What lies in the Beyond is not meant for the living to see.*

"What will you do?" Lesander asked her. "Continue your self-appointed mission?"

"I don't know," she said, as honest an answer as she could manage. The beast remained within, as hungry as ever, and she wondered what might happen should she fail to feed it. Also, the face of Aertis Vezuri had fastened itself to her memory. After storming the palace, the Sixth Order had found no sign of the Verehlan and discreet enquiries at the harbour revealed no clue as to his avenue of escape. Kestra sought out his chamber in the palace, collecting several interesting maps and books: apparently Lakril's injunctions didn't extend to his most trusted servant. Her examination of the material so far bespoke a man of particular interests, especially in the field of alchemy, an art most famously practised in the sorcerer's home city. The journey to Verehl would be long and probably perilous, but not impossible. And his face did vex her so …

"Sister Ulaine would benefit from a mentor's guidance," Lesander suggested. "And I feel your Order would be improved by your presence."

Ulaine had been found unconscious but alive in a ruined corner of the gardens amidst the broken bodies of several guards. Fortunately, she hadn't required the Aspect's touch to restore her; Kestra doubted the young sister would enjoy the nightmares.

"Ulaine has her own path," she told Lesander. "And it hasn't been my Order for a long time."

"Still so bitter." He shook his head and took up Nolnen's reins. "There is another path you could follow," he said, nodding to the forest. "In there you will find nothing to hate."

Without hate, what am I? She left the words unsaid, pausing to quell the tremor in her voice and forcing a smile. "Its welcome is for you, brother. Not me."

Lesander nodded, eyes lingering on hers for a second longer, perhaps striving to commit her face to memory, then he turned, kicked his heels to Nolnen's flanks and galloped away. Beneath her, Forelock stirred, keen to follow.

"No," Kestra told her, scratching the tuft of hair between her ears, which usually served to calm her. "Not for us." She watched Lesander shrink to a small speck that merged with the dark wall of trees, then vanished. For reasons she couldn't fathom, Kestra doubted Brother Lesander Doren would ever range across the four fiefs of this land again.

"He's gone home," she told Forelock, tugging the mare's reins to turn her head south. "Perhaps we will too, one day. Until then, we have a sorcerer to find."

MOTHER DEATH

Michael R. Fletcher

I woke screaming, buried in the cold weight of dead flesh. Vacant faces and heavy limbs pressed against me. I hung, trapped like a fly in a web, suspended in a mountain of cooling meat. Blood trickled through my hair, pooled in my eyes, clogged my nose. Seeping down from the corpses higher in the pile, it was thick by the time it reached me.

Early spring, a northern wind leached the last of the heat from my dead companions. In time, I'd be encased in a hill of frozen corpses.

I blinked bloody tears.

Impossibly, I was alive. I'd survived the Wilzi stone sorcerer and having the back of my skull caved in. My thoughts were jumbled, soggy.

I wanted to touch my head, feel the shattered bone that it must surely be, but the dead held me trapped. I recalled the sharp edge of cold obsidian the sorcerer pressed the into my forehead like he meant to cleave clear through to my brain.

He took something, stole it. A piece of me.

Too old to be accepted by his tribe and too young to fight, my boys had been harvested and killed.

The stone sorcerer took everything.

Mother of nothing. A ghost of a woman.

Buried in corpses, I squirmed for a more comfortable position, creating a small opening. Dim sunlight, pale and cold, penetrated the gap, reached down to me.

With our own warriors dead, the Wilzi stripped the women, children, and elders of our furs, forced us to our knees in the mud, our weight cracking the thin crust of spring ice. A line of shivering women, children, and old men.

First, they harvested the elderly. A Wilzi warrior sporting dripping trophies of scalps and noses, stood behind the person they claimed. Holding them helpless, they pressed a small rock between their victim's eyes. The sorcerer chanted and danced. He wore a necklace of pebbles carrying the souls and memories of his tribe's ancient sorcerers. The stones clacked and clattered like the rattle of dry bones. He tore hard won skills and memories from our elderly, stored them in the warrior's stone. When the sorcerer proclaimed a man drained, the warrior caved in his victim's skull with a heavy cudgel. They had killed our warriors. Now they murdered our past.

The women were forced to watch as, one by one, our children were brought before the stone sorcerer. Bent and jagged like a long dead tree, he looked into their eyes, searching out their strengths. When he had their measure, he called forward a waiting warrior. The warriors held our children as they had our elders. Helpless, we bore witness to the harvesting of our young. The sorcerer stole their bravery, robbed them of intellect, loyalty, and confidence, and locked them in pebbles and rocks. Once they had what they wanted, they killed our children.

I watched as my sons were harvested.

When they lifted the cudgel over my child's skull, I screamed and begged, *Please, please, leave what little is left.*

I saw.

I saw and I can never unsee.

When I lay dead and buried, wriggling with maggots, I will still see that scene over and over.

Our children dead, they took the women last. Numb, I knelt in the frozen mud as a young warrior stood behind me. He didn't even bother restraining me. There was no need. I'd lost everything. I wanted the cudgel, the last bright splash before my soul made the journey to Vyraj. Arms bent like splintered branches, the stone sorcerer once again danced. Pieces of me slipped away, stolen. I couldn't know what was taken. What traits would a Wilzi warrior find valuable in a mother?

There was no bright splash, only black agony.

My boys were gone, hollowed ghosts in stone.

As I lay crushed in death, the blood of the men and women I'd lived my life with trickling through my hair, I thought perhaps they had left me something in return. In taking one trait they freed another to rise to the surface.

The Wilzi took everything and left me nothing.

I could be that nothing, lay here until the last of the heat leaked from this mountain of corpses.

Or I could fill that nothing.

I could fill it with vengeance and pain.

I could fill it with death unending.

I clawed free of my prison.

Lifting my hand to touch the back of my skull, I hesitated. I knew what I'd find and wasn't brave enough to face the confirmation.

My sister had been a warrior. She wore our father's soul stone, had his skill in battle. Fearless, she'd collected the trait stones of half a dozen fallen enemies over the years. When the invaders crossed into our lands and hunted the herds of colossal aurochs and steppe mammoths we relied upon, she took up her spear. That was never me. I'd never stabbed someone, never thrown a punch. We are who we are and each of us finds a place. I knew mine. I collected berries and skinned the aurochs the hunters brought back. I tanned hides and helped raise all the children of the tribe. This year, seven youngsters called me Mother. In the last two decades there had been scores of them. They were gone now, harvested and slaughtered. All of them.

The icy wind whipping across the steppes scoured me. Blood dried, tightening my flesh. Caked in tangled ropes of gore, the long braids of my hair hardened.

In taking one thing, the Wilzi stone sorcerer left me something else. Maybe he saw in me my capacity for love, the strength of my mothering nature, and took it to give to one of his own tribe. I didn't know. Something was gone and I had no words for it, only the hole left behind.

I studied the heaped corpses. Staring eyes. Pale skin. Blood darkening as it chilled. My boys were in there. All my children.

I had been mother to many.

Now, I would be mother to death.

No tears fell and I understood the strangeness. I should want to beat my chest and tear at my hair. I should want to scream and cry, rage at the stone gods who failed us. I should want to hunt through that mound and find my boys, cradle them one last time in my arms before death took me. Because it was going to take me.

One woman, alone. No tribe.

No future.

I scavenged what clothing hadn't been stolen by the Wilzi. Hide leggings from a fallen warrior. A heavy cotton shirt. A fur vest. All of it so caked in gore as to be not worth stealing. I found a broken spear in the long grass, the tip a wedge of knapped flint. It felt right in my fist. Simple. Brutal.

As the sun set, I followed the Wilzi north. Having slaughtered their enemy, they made no attempt at hiding their tracks.

I ate their leavings. I chewed denuded bones, sucking what marrow remained from their core. Finding several unripe dwarf cherries, probably tossed aside for being too sour and devoured them, tasting nothing.

Night fell and my breath misted before me. For a long time I stood, head tilted back. The Black River, a slashed wound of nothing dividing the night sky, drew my eye..

The peace and silence reminded me of everything lost.

Ruthbo Vell had worn the storytellers stone. One of our tribe's most valued rocks, it contained the memories of our chroniclers dating back scores of generations. Many nights my boys and I listened to Ruthbo tell the tale of the war of the gods that threatened to shatter the world. She spoke of their eventual truce, and how they decided to split the night sky. The fire breathing Azhdaya claimed half. Ravenous demons, they loathed all life, claimed the souls of those who died selfish deaths. Gromma and Volosa ruled the other half, collecting the souls of those who died serving their tribe's needs.

Ruthbo Vell was gone now, dead. The Wilzi, uninterested in our past, shattered her stone.

Spotting a sparse kolky of stunted trees, I entered the grove. I slept there, back against a rotted and hollowed aspen, dead to the world, dead to the horrors of life. I dreamt that Mother Mokoshaa stepped from her stone prison and pushed her hand through the softness of shattered bone in the back of my skull. She lifted me and I swung loose like a puppet.

I too was a mother, I told her. *And now I am nothing.*

From nothing comes something, she answered. *That is always the way.*

I am tired. Though I had clawed free of my grave and walked an entire day, my will and body failed. I was not my sister. I was no warrior.

I am the giver of life, said Mother Mokosha, *but that which is given can also be taken.*

Mokosha leaned close, whispered in my ear: *Fill the nothing.*

Broken spear still clutched in my fist, I woke to a morning sky of pale raspberries receiving the first blushing kiss of spring. The air tasted of clover honey and earthworms. Dew glistened on a flowering spiderweb, each drop a sparkling diamond. I imagined they were memory stones, the souls of my children given one last moment of light.

Again, I lifted a hand to touch the back of my head and hesitated. What was the point? At best, I'd learn my skull had been broken and I was slowly dying, alone, hunting an entire war party.

"I am nothing," I whispered. "Fill the nothing."

After a meal of leaves, slugs, and fat worms, I continued north, following the bent grass wake of the Wilzi. I watched flies flit through the air, not bothering to brush them away when they landed on me. Drawn by the caked gore, they crawled through my hair. I listened to the ancient sigh of long grass, enjoyed the cool wind of the steppes on my exposed arms. Herds of mighty auroch darkened the horizon. I felt the thunder of their hooves through my bones. Off to the west I saw one of the towering obsidian obelisks that littered our world.

Heading up another rolling hill I saw a man awaiting me at the top. Tall and broad shouldered, he wore a necklace of many stones. He leaned casually against his spear, unhurried and unworried. A quiver of arrows and a longbow of black locust wood tipped with bone hung across his back. A cudgel sat in a loop in his belt, its head black with dried blood, clumps of hair still clinging to the mess.

The mother I had been would have screamed and fled, floundered off into the grass only to be cut down. The mother I had become never broke step. I carved a path through the grass, straight toward the waiting man.

"I am Kai Serkai," he said when I reached him, "the greatest Wilzi warrior."

Running blunt fingers across the pebbles and stones, he displayed his collection. Scores of souls. The harvested traits of countless warriors. Were my boys in there somewhere?

"You're not afraid?" he asked, when I neither spoke nor fled.

I wasn't. The stone sorcerer had taken something he thought useful, and the void left me changed. Perhaps he took my fear, thought I couldn't imagine what use he'd have for it.

When I remained silent, Kai Serkai shrugged and said, "You have walked a long way to die."

Words would not fill the nothing in me.

I stabbed him through the throat with my broken spear.

He toppled backward, gagging and clutching at the ragged wound, I stood over him, driving my spear into the softness of his guts until he lay quiet and still. A pink bubbled formed in his parted lips, expanded, quivered, and popped.

I knelt at his side, reached tentative fingers to caress one of the stones hanging about his neck. Memories of war flooded me. I smashed my enemies, crushing their bones. A massive steppe mammoth trampled me, left me broken and dying in the grass. I recalled the tribe's stone sorcerer hurrying to my side to harvest what he could before I passed.

Touching another stone, I knew how to craft powerful bone-tipped longbows and which feathers made the best fletchings. My arms and eyes knew how to send a barbed arrow into the heart of a charging sabretooth.

Another stone and I understood how to blend herbs and grasses to make healing poultices. Another, and I was a hunter stalking the grasslands, quieter than a ratsnake. Stone after stone, I touched upon memories of the past, felt the skills and traits stored within. Brave. Adaptable. Calm and clear headed. Logical. Murderous and cold. Honest. Perceptive. Tolerant, and patient. Kai Serkai hadn't simply been a great warrior: he'd been a dozen great warriors, the best of each man and woman his stones had been harvested from.

I found nothing of my sons, nothing of anyone I recognized.

I took his necklace, hung it about my neck.

I was nothing. And now, so was the great warrior, Kai Serkai.

Frowning at my broken spear, I studied the lustrous gloss of blood slicking its stone tip. When I walked with it held in my hand it was nothing, a functionless stick. When I pushed it into a man's throat, it sang with purpose.

"I am a broken spear," I told the dead warrior, tossing the useless stick aside.

I took his dagger, a sabretooth fang hardened in fire, and tucked it in my belt. He had a pouch of tough dried meat wrapped in leaves. I sniffed it and tossed it away. I was nothing and nothing must be empty.

After collecting his bow and quiver of arrows and slinging them across my back, I took his spear and walked north.

Like a shaking bowl of pebbles and sand, the new memories and traits jostled within me, searching for their place. Some had been harvested by master stone sorceries and were pure knowledge, untainted by personality. Others had been taken more clumsily and came tied to emotions. Fragments of past selves demanded attention as they wrestled with the change. They'd been part of a great warrior in a long line of great warriors.

What are we now? they demanded of me, for they knew what I was not.

"Nothing," I told them.

And they were. But each nothing filled a little something in me.

When the Wilzi killed my boys, I never expected to be a mother again. But these souls were nothing without me. They needed me. I was mother to them.

Uncomfortable, I set aside that thought and continued north.

I had changed. No longer did I blunder blindly across the vastness of the steppe. Now, I crept low, parting the long grass no more than the skittering mound mice whose dirt homes tripped the unwary. I stopped often to test the air, breathing deep, following the sweat smell of men, the dusty char of burnt meat.

I stalked the Wilzi as I remembered hunting mammoth and auroch a thousand times before.

The relentless unchanging march of history nagged at me like a child demanding attention. Some of the stones I wore were truly ancient. They remembered a winter lasting many years, how almost all the animals died, and the tribes were reduced to a score of souls each. Even then, even with the world covered in snow and ice and the deadly white cave bears coming south, it was more of the same. We hunted, following once great herds of auroch reduced to a few scrawny beasts along migratory paths writ deep in their bones. When we crossed paths with our enemies, we went to war. It didn't matter that the tribes were dwindling, that each death was a loss that might doom us all.

As mindless as the mammoth we tracked, we were animals. We bickered like children too ignorant to know better.

Recalling the way my boys used to fight, scrabbling in the dirt screeching like savage cats, I stopped to cry. The first tears since I found myself in the mountain of cooling dead, they fell to dampen the earth. Seeing the relentless cycle of life, war, and death as I now did, I understood that my boys were always doomed to die. A spear in the back. Pulled down by a sabretooth. Trampled by a mammoth.

The backs of their skulls smashed in after they'd been harvested.

Unlike the men whose memories I now wore, my boys were gone. Forever gone. As children they had no skills or memories worth taking. They had nothing but their beautiful personalities to offer. My oldest, with his serious eyes and unwavering loyalty to tribe and family. My youngest with his ability to love and forgive and the way he saw beauty in even the simplest things. I could kill every Wilzi warrior and take their stones, and I would find no trace of my boys except ghosts of temperament.

The tears stopped, my face drying in the breeze. The steppes were alive. The grass inhaled and sighed around me, a beast with no end and no beginning.

Knowing I was close, I sat cross-legged, swaying with the breath of the world, waiting. When the sun fell and the fireflies grew in brilliance until they shone hard, I studied the Black River dividing the night sky. It was easy to think of one side as good and the other as evil. Azhdaya, Gromma, and Volosa. Mothers of all creation. Our most ancient and distant gods, these were not the hungers our ancestors long ago trapped in the obsidian monoliths dotting the landscape. The Black River cut the sky long before the decades of winter and would be there long after the last auroch died. There was, I decided, a comfort in such unknowable distance. As if knowing that, even though I and all my world would someday end, the Black River would remain.

I breathed in the night, listened to the chittering hiss of insects, the bloated warbling belch of frogs. A dire wolf howled, muted and distant. Another answered, even farther away. Wise to the dangers of man, they'd avoid the Wilzi.

I stood and unslung my bow. Though I'd never loosed an arrow I knew its deepest essence. My fingers knew the grain of black locust, the texture of gut-string. My arms knew the feel of the pull. My lungs knew when to still and my thoughts when to calm to a quiet nothing in preparation to loosing. My skin knew the wind, its effect on my aim. My eyes knew the path and arc of every arrow.

It was time to hunt.

As a mother my senses had been attuned to the sounds of my children. I knew which cry was real and which a call for attention. I knew squeals of delight from squeals of pain and could judge the seriousness of an injury by the timbre. Children have one silence for when they are focussed on a task and an entirely different silence when they are causing trouble.

With these stones I possessed the senses of a hunter. The steppes spoke to me. The birds told me where the Wilzi posted young warriors to watch the camp as the rest slept. The breeze brought me wisps of their conversation, wafts of the leaves they smoked to pass the time. Back in their own hunting grounds, they'd grown lax.

Circling the camp until the wind took my own scent and sounds away, I stalked through the long grass like a panther. Move with the wind, breathe with the world. Stop. Listen. Patience.

I found the young warrior sitting cross-legged, his spear across his knees. He held a wood bowl under his nose, inhaling smoke from the fragrant leaves smouldering within. Even from behind, I knew the shape of him, the set of his shoulders, the shape of his head. I'd watched him hold his sliver of obsidian between the eyes of one of my boys. Helpless, I watched him smash my child's skull with his cudgel.

There is no screaming rage in emptiness.

There is no anger in nothing.

Heart calm. Breath slow and measured. Patience.

Far above, the Black River drifted as Gromma and Volosa battled Azhdaya to once again lift the sun into the sky.

Move slow enough and it is easy to sneak up on a man. Our complexity is our downfall. Thoughts wander, and the world is a constant source of distractions. Young men, pulled as they are in so many directions, are particularly easy prey.

Behind.

Hand over mouth.

Stab him through the side of the throat with the sabretooth fang, severing the big vein, and closing his throat.

Tuck in and hold against the kicking.

Small, gagged noises. Wet coughs.

Feel him weakening.

The young warrior made a sob of understanding and surrender.

Kill enough things and you learn that life fights until the moment it gives up and accepts.

Silence and blood.

I took the youth's necklace, touching each stone until I found the one with my youngest son's love of flowers and mist in the valleys of the steppes. Clutching it tight, I knew I could never again let it go.

I cut a small gash in the flesh over my heart and pushed the stone in. Searching the corpse at my feet, I found the thin twine I knew he would carry and stitched the wound closed. Sewing my boys' shirts. Sewing flesh. The skill was the same. Never again would I be without this small part of my boy.

I prowled the camp perimeter, killing men and women, taking their stones. On my fourth victim I found a stone containing aspects I recognized from my eldest boy. Again I cut myself, pushed the stone in, and sewed it closed.

After the sixth I crossed paths with a seasoned warrior pissing against a stunted tree. I stabbed him through the back with my spear. Slipping it between ribs, skewering a lung, I angled it upward to impale his heart. He farted, collapsed forward, and hung in the crook of the tree. I stood in silence, listening and waiting, while his body coughed a few last breaths.

I took his stones. Hunters and warriors long dead. Fragments of people harvested over generations. He wore the soul of his father in a wedge of crystal and that too went into my emptiness. The memories of hundreds filled my head and the stolen personality traits of those they'd murdered. Each became a part of me, and I knew them all as I'd known my boys. Existing within, they saw the nothing, understood they too were now a part of it.

I'd been mother to my boys, mother to all the children of my tribe.

Now, I was mother to the dead.

I looked at Jedhe Arne hanging in the crotch of a tree. I knew his name from his father's memories. He'd been a precocious boy, always in trouble, always bleeding from scraps and scrapes. Not yet stored in stone, he wasn't part of me. He was gone forever, lost to the world. In a way, I had murdered him far more successfully than he'd killed any of my tribe.

Failure is the fear of all mothers.

I could be no mother to the dead if I lost them.

I pulled Jedhe from the tree and laid him in the grass. I stood for a long moment listening to the night. I knew so much now. A thousand stolen skills. Memories dating back to the decades of winter. I recalled animals the steppes hadn't seen in many lifetimes of man, strange loping bison with too long legs, and gaunt dogs shaped like starved rats. I remembered being Wilzi warriors, but I also remembered being a Wilzi mother. Some of them were centuries dead, their children also long fallen. Some died more recently, and I'd murdered their children this night.

The dead were lost to me as I lacked the skill of a stone sorcerer.

I closed my eyes, saw the spindly arms like broken branches flail in a disjointed dance. The man who harvested my boys wasn't far. Like the others, he wore necklaces of stones, traits, memories, and skills. Some would be those taken from his ancestors, rocks and crystals carrying the memories of the tribe's previous stone sorcerers passed from master to apprentice.

The camp's sentries dead, it was time to change tactics.

I stripped Jedhe. Donning his furs, I dressed myself as a blooded Wilzi warrior.

At first, I'd thought to fill my nothing with blood and vengeance. I'd tasted that, felt the souls of the mothers I wore twitch and cry at the deaths of their children. I understood their pain all too well. Vengeance, I now knew, could never fill the nothing.

"I was a broken spear," I told Jedhe's corpse. "Without purpose."

Setting my spear aside I took his and studied the crassus feathers decorating the flint head. Each tribe had their own customs. My own people used the feathers of the deadly brontornis. Too large and dangerous for a single warrior, the trophies were a sign of both skill and cooperation. When young hunters reached the age of blood, four would leave together to earn their feathers.

I headed toward the heart of the camp.

Though some slept under the stars—mostly those too young to have found mates and made tents together—many slept in shelters of tanned hide stretched across a light but strong wood frame. I knew how to build one, how to collapse and pack it away in moments if needed. More warlike than my people, the Wilzi were all about speed and mobility. Whereas my own tribe stayed in one place for an entire season, they roved with the herds, constantly moving. I knew now that they saw our ways as a weakness.

I wended between tents.

Life without purpose was death, could end no other way. But emptiness was all potential, room for infinite change. Since the moment I knew I was pregnant, I'd defined my purpose as *Mother*. I thought that had changed after their deaths. It hadn't. I was still their mother. I would always be a mother.

Now I would be *the* mother.

Dressed in the style of the Wilzi, most ignored me as I strolled toward the stone sorcerer's shelter. Some few noticed my many necklaces and ducked their heads in respect. Spear in hand, bone-tipped bow over my back, and sabretooth fang dagger at my belt, I was clearly a great warrior. It bothered no one that they didn't recognize me; the Wilzi were a great tribe, with many bands littered across the steppes.

Stooping low, I entered the stone sorcerer's tent.

The sorcerer sat at the centre, a wooden bowl nestled in the crook of his crossed legs. Thick smoke rose from the pungent blend of roots, mushrooms, and leaves burning within. Head lowered, flat nostrils flared, he inhaled the smoke deep into his lungs. Liquid eyes, wet shards of obsidian, rose to study me. His lips and lids were tattooed in swirling black lines, his teeth filed to vicious daggers. Hair tied in tangled ropes hung in a knotted mass about thin shoulders.

He coughed, sunken chest convulsing, and said, "Not Wilzi."

"Not Wilzi," I agreed, approaching to stand over him.

Looking up, he said, "I recognize you. Your concern for your children was impressive. More than anything, you were afraid of failing them. You used it for nothing."

"Raising children isn't nothing."

He ignored me. "Carved from your familial ties, directed toward something useful, the potential was incredible." Lifting his head, he sniffed at me as if he might catch the scent of my soul. "Ah, I understand. Your fear held you back."

He was right, but he was wrong too. Lying in that pile of corpses, I had been unafraid of death. It wasn't a simple lack of fear that pushed me into action. In truth, he had no understanding of what I had become.

The sorcerer gestured at the many necklaces I wore. "It's too many. So many souls, so many lives and memories, will break your mind."

I smiled at him, wan and patient. His warriors had already done that for me.

"The souls fight in me," he said, glancing at the bowl, as if drowning himself in narcotic bliss needed explanation. "Constant war. Wrestling for dominance." He grinned black teeth. "I win. I am the strongest. I dominate." He winced, bowing his head again for a moment to breathe in the fumes. "But they never stop."

I felt no such battle within myself. Of its own accord, my hand reached up toward the back of my skull and hesitated. "Sometimes we continue on because we don't know we're already dead."

"Sometimes knowing is death," he agreed. He focussed on my spear, eyes narrowing. "Jedhe?"

"He knows he's dead."

"You came for vengeance." Arms of bone and wrinkled flesh spread wide as if expecting a hug.

"Yes. No."

I examined this sunken old man. Like me, he wore more stones than any warrior I'd seen. Unlike me, they were a burden on his soul. Every tragedy we survive is a weight upon us, and here, in the steppes, there was no life without tragedy. This stone sorcerer carried lifetimes of calamity, decades of adversity and failure.

I knew his mother's reaction to what he had become. We all dream bright futures for our children. Long lives, rich with love and family. He had none of that. He was alone with his stones and souls.

"You carry stones," I said, "and yet you are alone."

"This is how—"

"It would be different, were you a mother."

He scowled. "Women can't be stone sorcerers. They're too—"

I stabbed the sitting man in the belly. "They're too what?"

Teeth bared in agony, he clutched the wound. Blood spilled over his fingers. "They're too—"

I stabbed him again. "They're too what, old man? Too slow to learn?"

Hand falling away from his gut, he sat back, blinking at me.

Was this vengeance? Was this what vengeance felt like. It was worse than nothing.

Standing over the sitting man, I pushed my spear through his chest until it stuck out his lower back. He remained sitting, propped upright by the spear. I took his stones, the souls, the personalities and memories, and made them a part of myself. His master was there, harvested on his deathbed by his apprentice. His master's master too. Dozens of men who'd done nothing with their lives but harvest others. I knew them and I knew all they knew.

I was a mother, and I was a stone sorcerer.

"You are children," I told the dead man.

I picked up a pebble from the dirt floor of his tent and harvested him of everything. I took his soul, all his memories, every last aspect of his personality and trapped it in dull stone. Diamond, I knew, would have been better. Crystalline structures better stored information, preserved against deterioration of that which was stored. Locked in this little stone, the man would last only a few generations before he began to fragment. Even rubbing it with my thumb scraped away memories and bits of personality.

"Sorry," I said. "We make do with what's available."

I turned to leave and stopped.

I knew why women couldn't be stone sorcerers: Unlike men, we embraced the souls, made them a part of ourselves. Carrying life was no burden.

Women couldn't be stone sorcerers because there was no limit to how much we could carry, to how much we could bear.

Azhdaya, Gromma, and Volosa. Mothers of all creation. Women couldn't be stone sorcerers, because we carried the seeds of divinity. All those gods littering the steppes, bound in their stone prisons, were women. The stone sorcerers trapped them out of fear.

I stepped from the tent, stood in the centre of the Wilzi camp. The eastern sky showed the first hints of dawn, the night's chill receding.

Band after band. Tribe after tribe. Soul after soul. I would take them all. I would watch over and protect them from an uncaring world. They would live on forever, never suffer the brutal fate of my boys.

I would be mother to all.

THE
BLACK HORSE

Jeremy Szal

They butchered the humans first. With the Kin, they could take their time, and they always like to take their time with us.

I watch the bodies swaying in the sour wind, hanging from trees by lengths of creaking rope. They're little more than skeletons now. A sign says they've been hanged as thieves, but more than likely there's no truth to that. The humans around here don't need much of a reason to see us dead.

I stand high above Kharkov on a mossy parapet, fists clenched by my sides. My ears are pricked sharp, my breath steaming in the frigid night, the city spreading out before me. The light comes and goes as thick clouds sail briskly past the full moon, revealing the maze of iron-coloured stone buildings and the gleaming wood of ragged rooftops and sweeping balconies. They merge with the green tops of leafy trees in parks, with spires and onion-domed churches and temples rising above them all, painted blue and red and gold. Smoke rises from industrial yards and alchemical factories. But it's the creaking old tavern at the heart of it that holds my interest. Two drunks blunder out, leaning against each other, braying with laughter and singing loud enough to wake the dead bodies swinging from the trees. It's the perfect safehouse for a king seamlessly blending into this city of humans. Unlike me.

The humans all insist we Bolokov resemble horses standing upright. Sure, I've got a dark brown coat with a black crest of hair riding up the back of my neck, the pointed ears and long snout, but last time I checked I'm missing the tail, hooves and stupid, dull-eyed look. Besides, I've got hands and feet just like the humans do. Though I'm tall compared to them, I'm small and slender for a Bolokov, with a thin waist to show for it. I've got to wear these suspenders, hooked into my pants, just to keep them up.

Gods above, am I really going do this? I feel like fear should have gripped me by now. But all I feel is a cold, iron resolve. And that worries me.

'We don't have much time, Yharv.' A small, hazy ache grows in my skull like a bad hangover as our mage transmits Guildmaster Vesemir's voice directly into my head. 'Bring the Heir of the Elderblood back to us, unharmed. Whatever the cost.'

'If I was going to desert you, betray you, I'd have done so already,' I say.

'I know you won't betray us,' Vesemir says, his firm but cautious voice distorted by the magic. 'You're a Bolokov, true enough. But you're also a sworn member of the Guild. That means your word is your bond. Doesn't it?'

I don't like being interrupted when I'm on a job. It's distracting, and getting distracted when you're wearing my skin can be a death sentence. But Vesemir is possibly the only person I don't dislike, and I give him the respect my Guildmaster deserves. 'I won't let the Horde take our city,' I promise him. 'I won't fail you.'

'We can't have another Molengaard, Yharv. For your species and mine and everyone else's. For the Guild.'

'For the Guild,' I echo.

The link snaps, hurting more than the connection. I turn into the howling wind, carrying the stink of distant fire from beyond Kharkov's sweeping, armoured walls. Tents and siege weapons and darkly gleaming ballista and all the rest are spread out along the rolling hills, with little guttering fires like twinkling orange points of light against the darkness. The Horde. I swallow, the fear threatening to grip me.

I can't be sure if the tavern's empty yet. But Vesemir's right—we don't have much time. Besides, once you've set yourself a task, you've got to throw yourself at it until it's done. Hesitating gets you a knife in the back. Hesitating lets someone else take your moment. I'm a hunter, and hesitating lets you become the hunted. Never again.

I tighten the X-shaped harness clamped over my back and shoulders, crisscrossing over my chest and winding around my waist and thighs, then park my hand on the pommel of the longsword sheathed at my waist, near the small daggers I keep strapped around me. When you look like me, steel is one of the only things you can trust to do its job reliably. I ease my nimble body down the ledge towards the greasy cobbled laneway hugging the tavern's edge. Posters half-peeling from the walls announce the death of King Alexander almost two months ago at the hands of a Horde assassin, leaving the city vulnerable for attack. I barge inside.

The bare-rafted tavern's old enough to have seen five Kings. Tongues of buttery light spread from alchemical lamps, and a roaring fire burns in a soot-stained hearth. Ale-stained floorboards creak under my leather-swaddled boots. It's sweltering inside and I'm sweating before I've taken five steps. Wheels of cheese and salted meat and coffee beans scent the air. It's cosy and surprisingly pleasant on a cold winter's night.

The company, less so.

The place is empty besides three men, all baring the Guild's tattoo across the back of their hands. They wear thick, furred greatcoats over their leather mail. They're armed, of course. They're staring at me, unblinking. 'You're a Bolokov,' sputters a chestnut-haired man with a scraggy wisp of beard.

'A Bolokov!' another lad echoes.

I grip the chest straps of my harness, keeping my hands close to the hilt of my longsword. 'Oh, really? Well, thank you so much for inform-ing me.'

'A Bolokov. In our Guild,' the same chestnut-haired man says.

'In our Guild!' the lad echoes again.

'Is this conversation going somewhere?' I ask.

Of course, their surprise is at how unrepentant I am about what I am. Those few of us Kin who aren't yet extinct will wear armour or helmets to disguise their leathery or furred skin, their pointed ears and hooves. I don't. I wear a leather brigandine beneath my suspenders and harness for protection, but my arms and shoulder blades are bare, exposing the clan tattoos scrawling up my arms and all the rest of my features.

I'm a Bolokov. One of the last of my Kin. And I don't care *who* knows it.

Although, I do understand that the Guild that manages the Royal Affairs and all city council bureaucracy employing one of my kind is a startling sight. It doesn't mean I won't get the pleasure of exploiting it.

I hook a chair out from the peeling table and plant myself down, before helping myself to their coffee, meat, cheese and dark ale without asking. 'If you Paleskins are done with the stimulating questions, I've got a long-lost King to deliver.' More stares. 'No hurry at all. It's not as if the Horde's at our gates or besieging this fine city or anything of the sort.'

'Paleskins?' the lad says indignantly.

'My kind look like horses to you, and yours look like pale-skinned worms to me. A fair exchange, don't you think?' I carve myself a good wedge of cheese, wash it down with a long swig of dark ale, and prop my boots up on an adjoining chair. 'Now that the pleasantries are over, could you bring the King in? If it's not too much trouble, that is.'

The least stupid of the three Guildsmen has had the sense to bolt the tavern door shut. He's a tall bastard with a mane of white hair, breath that stinks of ale, and hands that are gnarled and callused from long years of repairing machinery. He sits uncomfortably close to me, the armpits of his leather jerkin dark with sweat.

'I could smell that Beast stink of yours a mile off.' He sniffs me. 'Like burnt grass and leather. It's the smell that gets my blood up.'

Beast. I was wondering when that insult was going to present itself. 'You're hardly a meadow in springtime either, Paleskin,' I tell him as I eat another slice of cheese. Gods above, this cheese is good.

He turns to the others. 'You know what the Guild calls this bastard? The Black Horse. Their best hunter.'

He slings his arm around my neck and grips the back of my harness.

And then I see the tattoo emblazoned on his arm. A crude circle dissected with three diagonal slashes. My ears curl back and flatten against my skull; I can't help it.

'Ah. Yes,' he says. 'The Beastie finally noticed. Maybe you aren't as dumb as you look. See, I hunted your kind back in the Great Purge, when you were the enemy. Butchered 'em in the fields like pigs for slaughter. The grass was black with that devil's blood of yours.' His hot breath tickles my snout as he leans in. 'Your kind really do scream and kick like horses when you catch on fire. Especially your young. Pity we won't be hearing it anytime again, what with your kind getting wiped out and all.'

'You sound,' I say slowly, my knuckles white against the edge of the table, 'like a man sick of wearing his guts on the inside.'

'Hey, hey. I'm just making sure we know where we stand,' he says. 'After all, we wouldn't want you to be mistaken for traitor, like the rest of your kind, and take an arrow in the back. It's awfully hard to see in these dark alleyways.'

'Leave him be, Tark,' the young lad says. 'We're all Guild now, right?

That means he's our brother. All sins forgotten, past blood washed away when we took the oath, all that.'

'Aye, that's true,' Tark says. 'You killed countless of my kind, and I killed countless of yours. Now here we are, working together to stop this city all going to the hells. Life's full of little ironies, eh?'

In a moment of weakness, I almost tell him the truth. Tell him what I really did—what the tattoo across my back really means, just to see him squirm. But one moment of weakness can kill you just as easily as a knife.

So, instead, I rip out my blade and slam it down, impaling his hand to the table. Tark shrieks, lurches backwards, ale and mulled wine spilling and spattering, the pommel gently wobbling, blood welling around the blade. The other two gasp, but don't move.

Exactly as I said. Steel is reliable. Paleskins, even among my own Guild, aren't.

'The past is the past,' I say when Tark stops shrieking. 'But if you take pride in hurting a child, then the way I see it, that blood is still on your hands.'

I hear the scuffing of boots on the creaking floorboards behind me. A sharp pain explodes across my shoulder blades. I twist around and see my assailant coming at me, swinging a thick stick for my skull. I catch it in mid-air. If it hit me, he'd have smashed my skull in.

I'm about to rip the weapon out of the little bastard's hand and clobber him across the face with it when I freeze. My eyes go wide.

Oh, gods.

At a noise, I glance back and see the three Guildsmen, even Tark, all thumping their clenched fists on their chests and bowing their heads in reverence to the Heir of the Elderblood.

I don't.

Because the future King of Kharkov and all the Eastern Province is a Beast, like me. His skin glistens with dark green scales, his hands and feet hook into savage claws. Between his legs, a long, slender tail thrashes back and forth across the dusty floorboards. Even though he's terrified, his reptilian face is still twisted up in a snarl. He's hardly even a man. Barely past the age of a child.

He's a Korvian. Extinct.

And now he's under my care.

'Let go!' the Korvian snarls and tries to wrench the stick out of my hand, even though I'm a head taller than him. The lad's got a fighting spirit, no question.

I pull my blade from Tark's hand, earning a whimper from him, and wipe it on his fur coat to clean it before slamming it back into its sheath and facing the king. 'You want to keep hitting me? Or do you want to get out of here before the Horde burns this city to the ground?'

His name is Kievar and he's the opposite of what I expected from a king. He wears every emotion and opinion plain to see on his face, most of which includes glaring daggers at my back. I'm not sure who he was expecting to guide him across the city, but clearly that person is not me. But it's not my duty to make him happy. Gods know I struggle enough with that myself.

Kievar wears black suspenders over a stained white shirt with scraggy pants. I'm about to tell him to disguise his Beast features but I see him pulling on a thick, hooded jacket and a padded leather cap with some big leather boots, tucking his tail into his pants. Smart lad.

The cold wind nips at my ears as we bundle back out into the night. But the cold keeps me alert. Keeps me on edge. And I'm going to need that edge. There's nothing more dangerous than becoming comfortable on a night when there's a lot of sharpened steel about. Besides, my Kin are from the mountain ranges, in the howling tundras of the Northern Realms. The cold's second nature to us Bolokovs.

We pass the river that winds through central Kharkov. The moonlight glints off the broad white sails of the great creaking barges tied up at the docks and along the rooflines of the fisheries and cream-coloured warehouses. The warehouses are now all used as armouries and emergency stockpiles. Past them all, southward at the mouth of the river, is the Guildhall. A magnificent building the colour of iron, with broad archways and ranging watchtowers, supported by battlements and flying buttresses. Our destination.

There's a sludgy, thick taste in my mouth, like wood and ashes. It could have been from that cheap dark ale, but more than likely it's thanks to the ash and smoke, pluming into the sky. The Horde, burning and pillaging the villages and granaries along the city outskirts. Slaughtering and raping. A foreshadowing of the horrors to come. Just like they did at Molengaard. They left every tenth inhabitant alive, so they could report the horrors there. Their eyes glassy, their words hollow. More than half killed themselves rather than relive what was done to them.

And there it is at last. The fear. The dread. Gods above, it hits me like a mailed fist in the chest.

'You do everything I say, when I say it,' I tell Kievar. 'Keep your head low, stay away from lights, mind your own business, and we might make it there alive.'

'Aren't you supposed to have a vanguard? A troupe of armoured soldiers, at least?' Kievar asks. If our impending deaths unsettle him, he doesn't show it. He's used to being on the run with men of violence looking to cut his throat to the bone, then. He smells of forest wetlands and moss, at odds with the brine and grease dripping from the city.

'Sorry, I've misplaced the royal precession, flags and grand parade to announce your arrival,' I say, my harness creaking as I roll my burning shoulders. 'It seemed unwise, with the city seething with Horde spies, the Horde knocking at our gates desperate to torture you to death, and half the folk inside looking to hand you over to them if it'll spare the city.'

'So instead they've saddled me with a rusty, old codger,' Kievar hisses.

I feel my ears flattening. 'Saddled? Is that a horse insult? And gods above, who are you calling *old*?' My mane isn't even greying yet, I'll have you know.

'It's true, isn't it?' he snaps. His reptilian tongue slurs the edge of his words when he's angry.

'Listen here,' I poke him hard in the chest. 'I'm tasked with getting you to the Guildhall, and that means I'll tie you up and drag you along if I have to.'

'You wouldn't dare.'

No. I wouldn't. But he doesn't know that. 'If we're lucky enough to survive, you can complain to the Guild about my attitude when we arrive,' I say. 'But right now, we're safer in fewer numbers.'

'Can you give me a weapon at least?'

'Are you going to hurt me with it again?'

'Hey! I could have killed you, if I wanted,' Kievar says. He runs a very pink tongue across a bank of very white teeth. 'I've got acid glands, you know. I can melt flesh, steel, wood, anything. But before you ask, it takes time to gather it up, and it's not much use in a fight. So. Steel, please.'

Pity. Spitting acid could have come in real handy. 'If I do, are you going to attack me with it?' I repeat.

The lad folds his arms across his chest. 'I just might if you try to tie me up.'

There's that fighting spirit again. I smile. Despite the smarting bruises between my shoulders, I'm starting to like Kievar. Even if he reminds me far too much of myself when I was his age. I unsheathe a blade from my harness and hand it to him. Good and sharp, of course. There's nothing worse than a blunt one and nothing better than a sharp one. He admires the blade like he's never held one before. Maybe he hasn't. I ask him.

'I've used blunted steel with the Guild quartermaster,' he says.

I snort. 'That's not real steel. Tell me you know how to use it, at least.'

He scratches the back of his neck with a yellow nail. 'You stab them with the sharp end until they stop moving?'

'That's the essence of it,' I say. 'The Paleskins are a feeble sort, usually easy to take down. Aim for the meaty, soft bits if you can.'

'That seems a little gruesome,' he says with a grimace.

'All killing's gruesome. That's the point of it.'

'You've got a lot of experience with it, don't you?'

'I hunt people the Guild wants hunted. When you're crowned, I'll hunt the people *you* want hunted. That's what I do.'

Kievar's silent for a time as we scramble through the city. A thick fog swaddles the city, no doubt concealing us from view, which is exactly what we want. But it's also getting in my ears, making it damned hard to hear, even with ears like mine. We're stealthy and full of purpose, going along a carefully prepared route of back alleys and flaking courtyards, of unregarded shortcuts and neglected stairs, through dimly lit tenements and rusty gates, across canals and rickety wharfs. Everything's creaking around us: railings, bridges, carts, lamps on poles at corners.

'Just ask me,' Kievar says as we leap over a short fence. 'I know you want to. Everyone does.'

I do, too. I wanted to hide that fact, but now he's brought it up I can't keep it down. 'So,' I say, turning back to him, 'how does a Kin, an extinct Kin at that, become the only descendant of the Elderblood?'

Kievar shrugs. 'I know as much as you, I suspect. The mages' alchemy drew them to me years ago. It doesn't matter what emperor, sovereign or king my ancestors were or what they ruled over, as long as they're descendants of the Elderbloods. That same bone, blood and lifeforce that ran through them runs through me. You know how the Guild respects lineage.'

I snort. 'Seems awfully ironic, doesn't it?'

'What?'

'That ancient magic doesn't care what race or Kin you are, but our modern, advanced society will happily butcher us by the thousands for looking different.'

I glance at the ranging, curving walls that fortify our city and countless cities like it. Walls constructed with ancient magic, veined with powerful alchemy, impenetrable to any Horde siege weapon or destructive attack. But only as long as a descendant of the Elderblood sits on the throne. If the alchemical energy powering the walls dies, so does our city. A story we've all heard over and over, but no less true because of it. A very real, very dangerous story I'm now part of.

'The Great Purge was decades ago,' Kievar says.

Painful memories stab at me and loom large in the fog. Burning. Screaming. The wet crunch of Paleskin longswords and battle-axes chopping down. The screaming of Bolokovs, mine the loudest of all. 'It was,' I grind out. 'And yet, for piss-bucket maggots like Tark, it was only yesterday.'

We're approaching Kharkov's central market square. Alchemical lamps shower spears of glowing light across the brick walls of narrow alleyways, balconies with missing balustrades jutting like ribs above us. There's inns, coffeehouses, printing presses, taverns. In a red-bricked apartment above, a violinist violently butchers a symphony, setting my teeth on edge.

Kievar huddles close to me, his scales jabbing hard through his jacket and into my side. I press my back up against a stone pillar and steal a glance out. It's madness. Mountains of furniture have been piled high against the steel gates of each little precinct in a feeble attempt to blockade the incoming Horde. Armed guardsmen patrol watchtowers, holding longbows and rifles, long spreads of cannons at the ready, banners and flags snapping against the moonlit sky. Dray carts and wagons clatter across the cobblestones as families flee for their lives, although I'm sure they've got no idea where they're headed. Conversely, the common folk, fully expecting the Guild to come through, are going about their business, visiting market stalls to purchase cheese and wine and crowding inside ale halls for mead and ale. It's two worlds colliding.

I find a hooded leather cloak snagged on a splintered beam, abandoned by someone in a hurry, and pull it over my body as we plunge into the draughty town square. I keep my obviously-not human-shaped head low under my hood. Kievar stays close as we slice through the crowd. My hand's wrapped tight around the hilt of my blade. I hear a drunk woman laughing as she stumbles in her high shoes, knocking into a red-faced man with a beard like an overgrown shrub. A wealthy man of medicine haggles desperately with the local guard for safe passage out of the city for him and his family, making me feel personally responsible for their safety, for getting them and their loved ones out alive. Gods above, I wish we took the long way around. I huddle deeper into my coat. But Kievar sways, uncomfortable, each desperate individual's cry hitting him harder than the last. The lad's got a tender heart, no doubt. That'll serve him well when he's on the throne, but tonight it's a curse. I pull him away and into the darkness of a piss-smelling alleyway.

Darkness. It's a hunter's best friend, and it's not failed me yet. I shed my cloak, and pick up the pace.

'Hey, Yharv,' asks Kievar when we're a good distance away, 'why weren't you covered up before? Why show who you are when it's so dangerous?'

'Because the world's never going to let us forget it,' I say, my voice low and quiet, boots creaking against the cobblestones. 'They'll use what we are like a weapon. So we use it like armour. Only then can it never be used to hurt us.'

'Like in the Great Purge?' Kievar says.

Wind tousles my black hair into my face. 'Not exactly. I was kidnapped as a boy, long before that. Brought here and sold for the price of sick livestock, with all the other Beasts.' Sweat pools in my armpits and slithers down my ribs, my knuckles white where I'm clenching my harness. Remembering the stink of my cell. My chains and bonds. The muzzle fixed to my face. The way the Paleskins blindfolded me and kept my keys just out of reach and laughed as I struggled and struggled to reach them. How they poked and prodded and played with me, week after week, month after month.

'I'm sorry,' Kievar says. 'What happened to my people ... to your people will never happen again. There will never be another Great Purge. You have my word.'

'Don't make promises you can't keep.' I narrow my eyes at him. 'Especially *that* kind. You don't know what you're talking about.'

But then I see the anger on Kievar's face. That same righteous fire burning in him, utterly fearless. The kind of fire fit for a King. 'I know it was a clan of Bolokovs who turned on humans and broke their peace treaty,' he snarls, breath steaming between his hacksaw teeth. 'One little clan in one little town, and it gave the humans the excuse to butcher whole Beast populations. Not just yours. *All* of ours. Great cities desecrated. Temples and sacred places torn down, airships blasted from the skies, our people dragged out of their homes, set on fire and fed to wild dogs.' Tears fill Kievar's eyes as he grapples my shoulders. 'My family, our ancestral home, all of them ashes and blood. Now, I might be the last one remaining. And I won't let it go to waste.'

'Like I said.' My voice wobbles as I struggle to keep myself under control. 'Don't make promises like that.' I frown. 'What did you mean, you *might* be the last one remaining?'

'You thought Korvians were extinct, didn't you? Well, alchemists put a curse on us, killing every living male, making it impossible for us to have children. The curse only lasted twenty years, but the damage was done.' His slitted eyes—a brilliant topaz that gleams in the dark—blink slowly at me. 'Maybe my Elderblood protected me from the alchemy. I don't know. But I've heard … whispers. Of entire towns, of cities filled with Kin in the northwest reaches of the Realms. Who's to say there's not more of my kind there? More of yours?'

'That sort of hope,' I say slowly, 'can get you killed.'

'Then why are we here? What are you fighting for, if not to stop the Horde from destroying this city, from destroying all of our people again, this time for good?'

A familiar, hard lump surfaces in my throat. 'A debt.'

Kievar goes silent, likely sensing he's prodded at something terrible and raw. I could leave it there to fester, like I always have. Maybe it's because I like the lad, maybe because the dread and hopelessness of the city's rearing over us like the shadow of these great walls, but I find myself speaking.

'I've … I've never told anyone what happened to me before,' I say. That sludgy, splintered wood taste has returned to my mouth. It's absurd, standing here in a piss-smelling alleyway on the eve of a great and bloody siege, confessing my past to the future King of Kharkov. But I say it anyway. 'Thank you, Kievar. For listening.'

Kievar shuffles awkwardly. Have I ruined the moment? But then he smiles. 'Thank you for trusting me with this, Yharv. Truly. I … I want to be a King who can be approached. Be trusted with these things. I'm glad you told me.' He pats me awkwardly on the shoulder, and I can't help but smile in return. 'And I truly do mean to make good on that promise, Yharv. I won't let there be another genocide, to Beasts or humans. On my honour as an Elderblood, on my honour as a King, I won't.'

And I can't tell you why, but for the first time, I believe it.

My mood's starting to perk up when the gods correct my thinking by sending rain.

I *hate* rain.

The guttering rain soaks my coat, makes my grip slippery around my sword hilt. It makes it impossible to see, though I try to wipe the water from my eyes every second, turning the alleyways into a wet smear.

Kievar, of course, *loves* it. 'There's three weeks of dust coated in my scales,' he says, his arms spread wide with joy, his head tilted up to the downpour. 'Ahhhh. That's better. I feel as good as new!'

I miserably scrape another tuft of hair out of my eyes. Despite the weather, I can hear and smell the clatter of war on the other side of the walls. Folks in the surrounding villages and towns scattered along the valleys, caught outside before Kharkov's gates shut for good are likely being slaughtered. Brave warriors attempting one last final stand, cut down into twitches and flayed shreds of meat by the Horde.

It's not an hour later when they start catapulting severed heads over the walls. Splattering down in dark smears on the cobblestones and along the alleyways. We bypass a market square, where a man's skull, half-melted into his great-helm, leaves a streak of stinking smoke as it smashes down into a stall, throwing up a great crowd of splinters. Foreshadowing the fate of everyone in Kharkov.

There it is again. The dread. Hammering nails down into my skull.

We pick up the pace, down a series of stone steps slick with rain. At this rate, we'll be at the Guildhall in two hours. Perhaps less. I imagine limping through the great halls to shocked surprise and thunderous cheers. Sinking down into a chair by the roaring hearth, demanding the biggest and best jug of dark ale while the entire Guild prostrates themselves in front of a baffled Kievar, before the machines taste his Elderblood and crown him as King, hardening the ancient magic in the walls and repelling our savage invaders once again. We're almost—

My ears prick up. I grab Kievar and attempt to flee, but it's too late. Shadows step from dark alleyways towards us in a broad circle. Their flatbows and crossbows and rifles gleam in the moonlight, all pointed directly at us. There's ten of them. Maybe two more, concealed in my blindspots. Far too many to fight.

'Well, well, well. Look here, boys.' A gaunt, skeleton of a man wearing a broad-brimmed hat and a broad grin struts forward to stand in front of us. 'Our Beasts are exactly where Tark said they'd be. We got ourselves a special prize tonight!' His eyes gleam. 'The deal was that we'd only take the Bolokov and get the other one to the Guildhall … but I think it'd be a real waste to have a scaly Beastie as fine-looking as you walking around free.'

Tark. That gutter rat sold me, and now Kievar, out to the Snatchers. A Black Guild that profits in the capture, trade and slavery of Beasts.

Kievar huddles away from them, breathing hard. We were so godsdamned close. I'm going to rip Tark's heart out his throat for this.

'I don't suppose it'll make any difference if I say we've got crucial, urgent business with the Guildhall,' I say, biding my time, hand crawling to my weapon.

'None whatsoever,' their leader says cheerfully, as I expected.

If we're taken, we're as good as dead. Like I've said, hesitation is defeat.

I rip blade from my harness and slash at a man holding a crossbow close to me. I hack his hand off at the wrist, his crossbow clattering away across the slick cobbles, and he lets off a piercing scream. Kievar dives for the weapon, but a boot crunches into his face. I whip around to help him, when something hard and heavy *cracks* across the back of my skull.

My legs puddle beneath me. Blood trickles down my neck. I taste the muddy cobblestones, my lips numb. Kievar is pressed down next to me, his eyes wide with fear. I want to tell him it's going to be okay, that we'll make it.

But I don't.

I'm many, many things. But I'm not a liar.

We're tied up and caged in an alchemy-powered carriage and driven back through the damned city. Away from the Guildshall. Away from any hope of bringing an end to this nightmare.

Hours later, we arrive in a decrepit room inside a decrepit house. We're stripped of our gear, leaving us only in our trousers and suspenders. They fit me with a muzzle after I bite someone's finger off and spit the stump in his face, and then fit Kievar with one for good measure. We're strapped into mechanized iron chairs designed to restrain strong Kin like us. Thick restraints and manacles are snapped tight around my wrists, waist, chest, ankles, and then Kievar and I are bound back to back, leaning against each other for support. Our bonds are so tight the faintest movement could choke us.

Our prison chamber stinks of wood shavings and dust and blood. It's lit with a drowsy orange glow, the temperature hideously blood-warm. There are gouges and dents in the metal armrest of my seat, made by claws of Kin who sat here before me. The only lasting memories of so many Kin whose lives ended here.

Our captor is a Paleskin named Dmitri, with a tremble in his left hand. He enjoys watching as we're inspected, prodded, poked, and tested. A dozen men and women crowd around us, most of them armed, daring us to put up a struggle. Knowing I'm going to cause trouble, they coat my skin with powder that tickles and itches like wasps are about to burst through my flesh, and has me bucking in my straps. But it's the humiliation I hate more than the pain. They take samples of my blood, my hair, my nails, stare into my eyes, measure my heartbeat. We're both sweating hard, our muscles tight with tension. Kievar's shoulder blades dig into my back as he flinches from the experiments.

'The scaly one is in very good condition.' A Paleskin physician sniffs and adjusts his spectacles. His breath smells like rye bread. 'But the Bolokov has poor health. He'll fetch a poor price if we don't take care.'

'I'm healthy enough to rip your throat out,' I snarl, one eye pinned shut against the bright white glare of the alchemical lamps shining in our faces. The stained-glass windowpanes rattle, reflecting a distant tongue of fire as screams pierce the night. The onset of slaughter is ignored by all in the room.

'How *frustrating* for you,' smiles Dmitri at me, 'not being the strongest creature in the room for once. You look like a tough old Beast. But I pride myself on breaking Beasts just like you all the time.'

'You grew bored with hunting down animals, then?' I snarl.

'Animals are too easy. It's you Beasts who provide a challenge.' Mania dances inside Dmitri's eyes like wildfire. 'The thrill of a hunt, of an enemy conquered and broken, is the sweetest thing the gods have bestowed upon us. So why not take advantage of it?'

'Because we're all about to be the hunted, you fool.' I rattle my restraints and twist in my seat. 'What's the point of this? The Horde's about to burn this city down.'

'Oh, indeed,' says Dmitri, patting my heaving chest. 'But we'll have taken you away from the city long before that happens. You know, in the southern parts of Jalensvok, they still allow Beasts to be caged and sold as livestock? Well, that's where we'll take you. Not for your meat. Not for a long time, anyway. We'll sell your hair, scales, nails, coat, anything else we can cut from you. Some savages still think there's magic and omens to be had from Beast parts. Nonsense, of course, but still, who are we to deny a well-paying client?'

The horrors sound too awful to be true. But I've learned long ago that it's these kinds of horrors, the ones we never want to think about, that often are true. So I won't deny them.

I seethe in my straps, studying my captor. The evil in this world isn't some grand, tyrannical god. It's not even the Horde. It's these small men with their small ways and small schemes and small cruelties that cause suffering. And yet, these small men have us, have everything we struggled for, under in their power, because some small bastard like Tark wanted revenge.

A torrent of anger fills me, so savagely strong I feel dizzy. I hate these bastards even more than I hate myself.

'Your Paleskin ancestors must feel so proud of you,' I say, saliva dripping from my mouth. 'Torturing Kin for profit. Continuing your little genocide, right down to the present day.'

'Well, well, well. The irony!' Dmitri leans down, grips my jaw with frosty fingers and wrenches my head sideways to tap the Black Horse tattoo on my shoulder. 'Have you told your little scaly friend here what you did to earn this tattoo, hmm?'

I freeze. 'No,' I rasp. My bonds bite into my flesh as I struggle. '*No.*'

'When the Great Purge happened, you turned on your own kind,' Dmitri continues, undeterred, his lips parted at the pleasure of dominating and humiliating a Beast like me. 'You participated in the genocide.'

'I ... I hadn't seen my people for decades.' Bilgewater sloshes around in my guts as I fumble for words. 'I believed the propaganda. Believed they were slaughtering children, burning villages, like the mad warriors were.'

'Yharv?' Kievar asks in a small voice that cuts me deeply.

'Now, now, now. The story isn't done!' Dmitri cries. 'You tell him, Black Horse, or I hurt you.'

'In exchange for freedom, I helped the Paleskin armies. Pointed out areas where we lived. Strongholds. Armouries. I ... I led them to my people.' My thundering heart is wedged in my throat, as if it's trying to contain the words. 'They said they'd question them, come to an agreement through a new peace treaty. Instead, they tortured them and slaughtered them like animals. Burned everything they had.'

Dmitri pats me gently on the shoulder. 'Little wonder they call you The Black Horse. And they branded you with that tattoo to show for it. No good deed goes unpunished, eh?' He leans in close. 'Was it worth it, Yharv? Being a good little Beastie for the humans?'

My ragged breath saws in my throat, closing up around the words. Gods, I feel like I'm drowning.

Satisfied, Dmitri backs off and speaks to his comrades. 'Turn up the heating and let these two sweat it out in here for a bit before we set off. I'm sure The Black Horse has a lot of thinking he wants to do.'

The room is a sweatbox. The internal heaters radiate warmth that leaves us both sheened in sweat and panting for breath.

I killed them.

The Horde are still outside the walls, preparing their weapons. In less than a day, the gates will crumble and the full bloodthirsty might of the Horde will seethe into Kharkov.

I killed them.

Escape is impossible with skin-tight, mechanical bonds like these. Our captors know how to treat Bolokov. Just like my captors did when I was first kidnapped and strapped deep in that wet dungeon.

I killed them.

I betrayed them all.

'You've never forgiven yourself, have you?' Kievar's voice shoves me back from my own thoughts. 'And that debt you spoke of ... it's the debt to your people, isn't it?'

'It is,' I say softly. 'I've been trying for the past twenty years as a Guild member to pay off that debt. To find some sort of peace with myself. And

I haven't found it yet. I don't think I ever will.'

'I don't believe that.' Kievar's scales rub against my back, itching against my wounds, as he twists back around towards me. 'And I don't think you do, either.'

I almost bark with laughter. Gods above, I'm going mad. 'What difference does it make, now that we've got one foot in the grave?'

'Because,' Kievar says softly, and I can hear the nervous smile in his voice, 'I can get us out.'

'How? You planning to dazzle these brigands with your pretty scales or something?'

'Yharv, can you please shut up for once? Remember when I said that we Korvian have glands that excrete venom?'

'Yes?'

'Well, perhaps my acid can melt through iron. Melt through our restraints.'

It's a mad plan, if it constitutes a plan at all. But as I've said, once you've got yourself a task, you've got to throw yourself at it until it's done. Hesitating gets you killed. Hesitating now could get the whole of Kharkov killed.

My spine feels like a branch of a withered old tree and my limbs have gone to sleep, but I still twist around as far as my straps allow. Kievar draws his long head back, makes an obscene sucking sound with his cheeks. A thin stream of colourless acid trickles out between his sharp teeth. The metal of his muzzle melts inwards, leaving an opening, and the acid drips down towards me, splashes on the iron shackle that's clamped hard over my right wrist. Metal sizzles. Stinking black smoke wafts up as the lock melts inwards, frustratingly slow. Pain shoots up my arm as some poorly-aimed drops spatter against my flesh, but I've had worse, and I force myself to remain still.

The lock snaps. Almost choking on the pain, I rip my arm free, flinging away the last few drops of acid to sizzle harmlessly on the wall. More carefully, Kievar burns through each metal shackle. Sweat drools down my armpits, down my ribs. I know that poor aim is the only thing between us and an agonizingly slow death.

But the lad does it. He *does* it.

The shackles around my wrists broken, I pull my hands free, undo my muzzle and set about unlocking my legs. Kievar's freeing himself when the door unlocks and swings open, revealing someone standing in the doorway. Dmitri. His eyes fly wide, his mouth agape. 'Whaaa—'

But I'm already out of my straps and darting across the room. I claw for the dagger sheathed at his belt and thrust it up into his throat up to the crosspiece. His beard tickles my snout, our eyes inches apart, the blade piercing through his tongue to the roof of his mouth. He sputters, claws pointlessly at my arm, a curtain of black blood dripping down my fingers.

I kick him away, and he's dead before he hits the ground. Together, Kievar and I burst out of the sweatbox. I find the room where they've stashed my harness, brigandine and weapons, and promptly and strap them back on. I unsheathe my longsword from its scabbard. The blade gleams in the low light. It always feels good to have sharpened steel in your hand.

'You want to show them how primitive we Beasts really are?' I ask Kievar. I reach over to where finely-sharpened axes are propped up on the wall, take one down and hand it to him. He accepts it with a firm, grim nod. Elderblood or not, there's steel in him now.

Screams of alarm rise up as we burst out onto a long, lichen-spattered battlement over a small courtyard, dotted with small braziers. My ears prick up at the jingling of mail and steel. I shield Kievar with my body, my teeth clenched hard enough to crack. A big bastard with small eyes hacks his axe inches from my face, the sharpened edge squealing against the stone rampart, spraying sparks. I slash my sword around in a full-body swing, chopping down into his shoulder, the blade's edge jarring off bone, pain rattling all the way up to my arm socket. Enraged, Big Bastard grabs the front of my harness to send me off balance. My head whips forward, but I hack a long gash in his neck, bringing him spinning down with a high-pitched howl.

Ripping my blade free, I reel backwards as a vicious strike rips past my chest, smashing into an old beam and throwing up a cloud of wet splinters. Blinking grit from my eyes, I'm off balance as my attacker bowls into me, grappling me. His hairy face is inches from mine, our expressions twisted up in a grimace, our teeth clenched, our muscles straining as we claw at each other. My steel is too long, awkwardly wedged against my chest and I can't rip it free. So I smash the pommel once, twice, into his face, staving in his helmet with ear-splitting cracks. He flops down to the ground, his sword clattering away across the stone.

Kievar bellows a warning as I hear the creak of flatbows being pulled back. Dragging the lad with me, I swerve sideways as arrows come flitting down from the watchtower, narrowly missing us, instead thudding into the enemy's flesh. A big, black-haired man lunges towards us, his bastard sword gleaming in the fiery brazier light. He slashes it in a steel blur, my own longsword wobbling in front of my face as I parry, drawing sparks. He's stronger than me and he pushes down, hard. My back grinds against the lichen-streaked stone as he pins me there. I'm bent backwards, sweaty tufts of black hair blurring my vision. He smashes his forehead into mine, the metal of his helmet gouging into my flesh and dashing blood down into eyes. I'm only distracted for a second, but it's enough for him to break my defences, my sword twisting aside and clanging against the stone. He raises his longsword for the kill.

But Kievar pounces on him, fast, stabbing him hard in the gut, once, twice, three times. The bastard reels back, sword in mid-swing, twisting around madly in his final breaths, but we both grapple with him. Our boots scuffling hard against the slippery stone, we wrench the bastard sideways and spin him over the edge of the parapet, smashing down on a group of armed men below with a great clattering of metal.

'I see now,' Kievar grins from beside me, panting. 'Stick their soft bits with the sharp end until they stop moving. Simple.'

I grin at him. I pull him away from the ledge and we charge down the steps towards the carriage used to abduct us, a few stray arrows flying towards us and falling short. Kievar gets the alchemical engine fluids charging up with a sound like a fat man drowning in syrup. A crossbow bolt grazes the top of my head and crunches into the carriage's flank.

We bundle inside in a sweaty heap. The carriage *jerks* forward across the courtyard, wheels rattling against the greasy cobblestones, and then goes tearing through the gates, smashing them off their hinges. The carriage lurches and races down the winding cobbled street like a missile. Back into the city. Our captors fire off a few arrows and bolts in pursuit, all falling short.

My spine creaks like an ancient tree as I ease myself into a seat, breathing hard. My blood and sweat stain the upholstery. The engine's got enough power to take us all the way to the Guildhall. It's not stealthy, but that can't be helped now. We check each other for wounds but find nothing that can't be treated later. But I can't relax until we're safely behind those armoured walls.

'You should have taken transport, like I asked.' Kievar grins as he seats himself across from me. 'We'd be there much faster.'

It hurts my chest to laugh, but I laugh anyway. When was the last time I actually laughed? I thump my fist to my chest. 'As a sworn servant of the Elderblood, I'll obey whatever you command.'

Kievar rolls his eyes. 'And my first command as Elderblood is none of that tripe. I forbid it. Not from you, Yharv. Not from you.'

The carriage squeals on the great flagstones of the Guildhall's courtyard. A massive building of onion-domes and belvederes rising up above me, its grand sweeping arches strung with red silk drapery.

About damn time.

The armoured gates, flung open with barely enough time for our carriage to squeeze through, clang shut again. I squeeze my eyes open and shut, open and shut.

Guildmaster Vesemir stands waiting there. His dark, shoulder-length hair is flecked with iron. His leather mail creaks as he leans in. Behind him are dozens of Guildsmen, all open-mouthed and wide-eyed, unable to believe I made it. *I* can scarcely believe we made it.

At seeing Kievar, as one, they thump their fists against their chests, bowing their head in reverence to the Elderblood. To their new king.

I try to speak. But everything goes white.

♛

Freshly bathed and groomed, I'm sitting in a private chamber, warming myself by the roaring hearth fire. I'm dressed in a fresh white shirt and black trousers. My wounds have been dressed and I'm nursing a mug of creamy dark ale. Frothy and bitter, the way I like it. It feels strange to be this clean, this presentable. It's a feeling I could very well get used to.

I wonder if Kievar will still see me when he's King. I certainly hope so. I have no plans to leave the Guild anytime soon. I can't wait to see the faces of the common folk when their new King is revealed, with his scales and tail. There'll be outrage, certainly. Protests, perhaps. Too bad. The old magic protecting our city doesn't lie. They'll have to understand how things are going to be.

And if anyone tries to take him out, like they did with the last King, well, they'll have to get through me, first.

The heavy wooden door creaks open against the flagstones. Vesemir glides into the room with the slow grace of great, battle-hardened ship. His usual retinue of armoured Guild members march in alongside him. Vesemir grips my shoulders with both hands, his fingers like gnarled tree roots, and gives me a gentle shake. 'You've done it, Yharv.' His voice trembles with joy. 'You've saved Kharkov. I could kiss you, you big, hairy bastard.'

'I'll settle for more ale instead,' I grin, hands cupped behind my head.

Vesemir seats himself down and pours us both some dark ale. He's got purple bags under his eyes so big they could be used as holsters. 'The wait's been a nightmare, and no question. But once Kievar's Elderblood is inducted into the alchemist's machine, the walls will be restrengthened and will hold for generations. Generations! The Horde will have lost. They'll attempt to flee, and will be totally vulnerable. We'll surround them, and water the fields with their blood.

As if on cue, the ominous creaking of siege weapons and screams echo through the fort's thick stone walls. A little while longer and those dreadful sounds and the horrors they herald will disappear into the fog of memory. Perhaps I'll get some sleep at long last. Gods above, how I need *sleep*.

I hook my thumbs behind my suspenders. 'How soon can you start the process?'

'It's already happening,' Vesemir tells me. 'We can't delay any longer. The walls' magic is almost depleted, and every hour weakens it further. Which has made things ... complicated.'

I frown. 'Complicated?'

'Yes. The walls must recharged to full strength to function. We'll need to harvest Kievar completely.'

A long silence stretches out. My body goes very, very cold. That same icy dread returns in full force like a raging blizzard. 'No,' I hear myself say. I sit up. 'You can't. You can't mean it.'

'It's the only way,' Vesemir tells me in a firm but anxious voice. Set on his course, but desperately trying to convince himself of its righteousness. 'We've tried everything, Yharv. Everything.'

'Then find someone else,' I snarl. An armoured Guildman narrows his eyes at my outburst.

'Who?' Vesemir says. 'It's taken years of planning to find a true descendant of the Elderblood. And now we have until dawn before Kharkov's gates are breached, and we're lucky to have that.'

'He's one of the last of his Kin! Perhaps the only living male.' I scramble for an answer like a drowning man at a piece of driftwood. 'What if there are more of his Kin out there in the Realms? A mate? What if their race could be saved?'

'We can't gamble the lives of everyone in this city on that uncertainty.'

'Uncertainty? We'd be killing our King,' I roar. 'We'd be committing *regicide.* A *genocide.* Another Great Purge. *That's* not a gamble. Killing the last living male of an entire race will make that a cold, dead certainty.'

'You don't think I've wrestled with this over and over and over? You don't think we all have?' Vesemir grips my shoulder, but I shrug it off. His eyes shine with the onset of tears. 'You're fond of the lad, aren't you, Yharv?' I clench my teeth but hold my silence. 'It's understandable. Truly. I would kill anyone who hurt my children. But Kievar isn't your child, Yharv. He's our King.'

'You didn't even give Kievar the dignity of a choice, did you?' I ask bitterly. 'You're forcing this upon him.'

Vesemir wrings his hands, answering for me. The screech of siege weaponry and savagery plumes in the night. 'You hear all that scream-ing, Yharv? Those are the lives on the line. Countless men, women and children, balanced up against one.'

'Those with the least always lose the most in war. And in killing Kievar, you've doomed an entire race before it's even had a chance.' I jump to my feet, fists clenched by my sides. Half a dozen Guild members stiffen around me, their hands creeping towards blades and crossbows. 'All those dead Beasts, all that mass slaughter, burning, raping. Have we learned nothing from it?'

'Which is exactly why we can't let Kharkov fall to the same fate,' Vesemir says softly. 'What of our hopes for a brighter future? Of bring-ing sanctity and industry to our great city? A place where all our races, all Kin, could live in harmony.'

'I was promised a dream like that once, too,' I say bitterly. 'More empty promises. More shedding of innocent blood at the hands of hu-mans just like *you.*'

The room turns icy. I stiffen. Vesemir's face tightens.

In that moment I become the enemy.

'I'm sorry, Yharv,' Vesemir tells me, his eyes filled with regret, but his voice steely with resolve. He speaks to his vanguard of Guildsmen. 'Take Yharv to the dungeons and strap him down until the procedure is finished. If he resists, kill him if you must. The Elderblood can't be endangered, no matter what.'

Vesemir leaves. Four armed and armoured men sweep forward to surround me. Moments ago, they were my allies, and now there's a cold, callous hatred burning in their eyes. The sight ignites something primal inside me, kept buried deep inside my mind. Something that was first born when I was a young lad, when after days of starvation and torture, my drunken captor forgot to restrain my left wrist to the bloodstained table they'd strapped me to; when he leaned over me his blade was within easy reach at his belt. When it finally dawned upon me that I could never please my Paleskin kidnappers. That, in the end, I was just a Beast. Something savage and feral, to be tamed and broken.

So I became what I needed to be to survive.

The Black Horse.

The Betrayer. The turncoat. The killer of his own people, once again.

No. *Never* again.

That same fire blazes inside me as I rear back with all my Bolokov strength and smash my heavy boot between the legs of the nearest Guildsman. He shrieks and puddles to his knees, hands clutching his groin. Steel scrapes as I tear his longsword from his scabbard and cut him down in single swing.

The other three charge me as one, weapons whispering out of their sheaths, cold murder in their eyes. But I'm on a rampage, now. In a gnashing blur of bright steel, clenched teeth, smashed furniture, sweating faces, broken bones, I cut the three of them down. All the Guildsmen are dead, lying still, the room around us a whirlwind of destruction. I recognize the black-haired one. Eren, I think he was called. I used to drink small beer with him on the southern battlements before dawn, when the weather was good.

Now, his life's blood is pumping from a savage wound in his neck.

I tear my eyes way. It's too late for any regrets, even if I had them. I scrounge around for some mail and a weapons harness. I buckle it on, slotting a crossbow into the holster. I light a torch with the fire in the furnace and blunder outside. The alarm will have been raised. My window of opportunity shrinks by the second.

I run down a great hall towards the throne room, where Kievar's transformation is taking place. Halberds are stapled to the walls, their brilliant edges glinting in the glow of alchemical lamps. I tear down the banners strung up overhead and bundle them up in the middle of the hall, and then set fire to them with my torch. I conceal myself in the shadows of a great suit of battle-hardened armour as Guildsmen stream out of the room in a panic to put out the flames rapidly spreading along the carpet. By the time they notice me dashing into the room behind them, it's too late. I slam the heavy door shut and activate the mechanism. No one's breaking in from that side.

I turn into the throne room. A huge hearth burns to my right, a stovepot bubbling away there, and is surrounded by plush furniture. But the air's as thick and warm as a summer bog and heady with a sulphuric smell like volcanic soil. Magic. It plucks the strings of my stomach. I glance up towards the high vaulted ceiling. A great bronze machine looms overhead like a spider, intricate tangles of thick pipes carved with arcane runes that gleam in the darkness, spewing bursts of steam. Vats filled with murky fluid bubble away in the dark. And at the centre of it, gagged and strapped to a bloodstained operating table, is Kievar.

He's dazed, likely drugged, but he's fully conscious and aware. He's lying right below the machine, surrounded by Guildsmen clad in purple alchemists' robes. They're holding obscene, sharp instruments, preparing to carve him open and harvest the Elderblood from his veins, his marrow, his brain.

The Guildsmen standing guard notice me. Their boots squeal on the flagstones as they charge me, blocking my access to Kievar and the alchemists.

They all charge me as one. My boot scuffs on stone as I reel backwards, the silver blur of a short sword whipping past and chopping a chair to pieces, splinters jumping up into my face. I growl and lunge forward with an upward thrust, ram my sword through his gut, sliding it up to the hilt. He sputters, spittle flying, face ragged with rage. I kick his body off the sword, into the path of the charging Guildsmen. But they're too fast. I feint around the piercing edge of a sword to drop to my knees. A black-haired Guildsman with a missing eye steals forward, hacks at me like a madman. Teeth gritted, I parry the blow, metal shrieking against metal, and I haul myself up to my feet. The drifting tip of his sword slashes a stinging wound open across my forehead and sheaves a chunk of my left ear off. My vision a dark smear from the blood sheeting down into my eyes, I totter against the brick-lined side of the furnace. It's painfully hot and I jerk away. The Guildsmen are nearly on me. I fumble for the stovepot, grab the wooden handle and hurl it across the room, spraying scalding hot soup into the Guildsmens' faces. They scream in pain, including One Eye, who's almost on me.

With him distracted, I duck low, bowling hard into him and sending him tottering off balance. I reel up and smash my skull into his face, hearing the wet *pop* of his nose breaking. I twist sideways, his eyes bulging wide as he stumbles against the scalding furnace, his left arm dragging across the coals and catching fire. The smell of burnt flesh fills the air as he howls and feebly rolls across the stone floor.

I drag my tongue over my teeth, and hawk out a ball of saliva. Fools. All of us. The Horde are hours from breaching our gates and ravaging our city, and here we are, too busy butchering each other instead of saving the city together like we were meant to. My head swims. Sweat drips from my tangled hair.

Gods, what have we done?

Nothing that can be undone now.

A Guildsman wearing thick mailed gloves lunges forward, and I scoop up a light table, use it as a shield. His bastard sword cleaves through the flimsy wood, inches from my throat, throwing up a great cloud of splinters. I wrench the table sideways, sending him reeling off-balance and giving me the window to chop through his throat, sending him crashing down to the stone. I see a silver blur over my shoulder, and jerk forward as a sword slashes painfully across my side. It's like I've got a cold line of fire under my ribcage. My attacker grabs a fistful of my mane, wrenches my head back, and punches his mailed fist between my shoulder blades. I feel my hair ripping as I stagger sideways, boots skidding on the blood-slick flagstones, trip over pile of smashed furniture and almost cut myself open on my own sword. My fingers are numb around its blood-slick hilt. Can't get them to work.

I'm going to die. I'm going to die here.

No. I can't. I should have died decades ago, all the gods know that. But I can't let Kievar's blood, the blood of an entire Kin, go to waste with me.

Face down, blood and sweat growing cold on my skin, I draw on one last burst of strength and feint upwards. The Guildsman's short sword hacks past with a gust of wind, clangs into the mantelpiece and sends chips of stone spraying. I slash my sword around in a vicious two-handed swing, chopping hard into the Guildsman's ribs. He grunts, jerks sideways, reels back to stab me again. I hack at him again, again, again. In the sword's reflection, I see the bodies of my people scattered and broken across the grasslands I once called home. All dead. All dying. All because of me.

Never again.

There's a supercharged whine of energy, the air around me distorting with a colourless haze. My guts feel like they're tying themselves into knots. The alchemists are turning their magic on me. Their hands are down by their sides, but their eyes are gleaming, their muscles tense. It's like there's an invisible, gut-wrenching shockwave crashing down on me with every ragged breath, but infinitely worse. How could so much pain exist?

But I push through.

Through the hazy shockwaves heaving through the room, I see one of the alchemists raising a single, trembling finger, the veins swelling. A blue bolt crackles from the finger, scarring the air with spots of light, and I wrench my body sideways. The spell sears past my ribs and explodes into the furniture behind me with a great, ear-splitting crack, splinters raining down on my back.

One of the alchemists peels away, knowing I can't be stopped, and raises his blade to kill Kievar. But with one last shove, I lurch forward and get in range, cutting both alchemists down in a single swing.

The energy dissolves from the room. I can breathe again. I rear upwards, smearing blood out of my eyes with the back of my hand. I go to Kievar and rip the gag from his mouth. He moans my name, his mind hazy from the drugs. 'Are you hurt?' I say.

'No,' Kievar coughs. In the ghostly light, he looks so young. So feeble. 'Almost. They were … they were going to …'

'I know, I know.' I clutch the lad to my chest, feeling his heart pounding and his body shaking. Shaking like so many young Kin did when they witnessed the slaughter of the Great Purge. 'It's okay. I've got you. We're getting out of here.'

For a moment, I think Kievar will refuse. That he'll agree to be slaughtered to save his people. Maybe he still would, if I asked him. Maybe he *wants* me to ask him.

But I don't. I can't.

And he doesn't ask me, either.

I quickly free him. Secreted behind a doorway at the back of the throne room is a passage that leads to a mechanical elevator for the royal families to make an emergency escape. But as we push through into the corridor, Vesemir is standing there, a length of gleaming steel in his hand. I snatch up my crossbow and level it, staring at him down the sights.

'Get out of the way,' I say. I'm not commanding him. I'm begging him.

'You don't have to do this,' my friend says. His voice is hesitant and kind, with an undercurrent of hope. I hate hearing it. 'We can still save the city, Yharv. We can still save the Guild.' He takes a step forward. 'Just leave Kievar and walk away. All will be forgiven, I swear it. We can still do the right thing.'

'That's exactly what I'm doing.' A wave of exhaustion swamps me. My shirt's dark with sweat, and blood's snaking down my bruised ribs. I want this nightmare to all be over. 'I'm undoing the damage that I did, that *we* did, decades ago.'

'You're angry, Yharv. Frustrated. Torn. I understand. But think of the children in the city. The families. The innocent.' Vesemir's gimlet eyes are filled with tears. As are mine. 'Please.'

'Shut up,' I shout, my throat locking up around the words. I can't look at Kievar. 'Just shut up.'

'You swore an oath, didn't you? To stand by the King, by your brothers, by your Guild? The same oath we all swore, no matter how hard it is to uphold?'

'Not for this,' I rasp. 'Never for this.'

'You want to undo the horrors of the Great Purge? We start by saving *this* city. Ours. Not sacrificing it,' Vesemir pleads. 'Even if there are more of your Kin out there, you'll never find them. You know what people will do to you two. You'll be butchered, skinned, torn apart, raped and tortured.' He takes another step. And another. The crossbow trembles in my grip. 'What our people did to yours was wrong. But that doesn't mean you can sentence us, sentence this city filled with innocents, to the same fate. And you know it.' Another step. 'If you do, it'll haunt you until the end of your days.'

'I'm already haunted,' I say, refusing to let him sway me. 'Nothing will ever change that. But I can change this.'

'Then why haven't you shot me already?' Another step. He's almost close enough to reach me with his sword. 'Because you're no traitor, Yharv. Don't throw away your honour now. Don't become a traitor. Please.'

A traitor.

Maybe I am. Maybe I'm the most cowardly, callow, turncoat to ever stand in the grand throne room of the Guildhall. Maybe I am The Black Horse, like they say.

But I am not a tyrant. I won't have the blood of an entire race staining my hands. Not again.

Vesemir's forlorn eyes meet mine over the crossbow bolt. He's fighting for his own people's redemption, as I am for mine. He knows there's no stopping me, and knows he won't be able to let me go.

He stares at me, long and hard, as if asking forgiveness for what he's about to do. Willing himself to forgive me what for I'm doing to do.

He closes his eyes, straightens his spine, and raises his sword high.

I aim at my friend's head and I pull the trigger.

It's peaceful here outside the city walls. The brilliant blue sky is crowned with creamy clouds from horizon to horizon, painted a soft tangerine-pink by the dawn light. The ground is loamy and springy underfoot, the rolling grasslands sparkling with fat dewdrops. Birds sing in the sprawling boughs of a great weatherworn tree to our left. A gentle, sweet breeze tousles my mane.

I spread my arms and take in a wide, chest-heaving breath. It tastes like freedom. It's like I'm breathing for the first time since I was kidnapped and imprisoned.

We snuck out through the viaduct that led past the city walls, to a small muddy lake. My wet, blood-flecked shirt clings to my skin, starting to dry. My arms and sides are lacerated with a multitude of wounds. Some new and bleeding, some old and reopened, all hurting the same way.

I glance over my shoulder as Kievar picks his way down the rolling slopes. Behind us, the sweeping city walls loom tall like a wave of iron, shavings of light spilling over the mossy battlements. Whatever magic that once ran through the walls will wither and die.

The wind shifts and carries the sound of the Horde falling upon the great city of Kharkov. Screams of horror and terror. Fortifications crumbling. The clash of metal. The echoes of slaughter in the streets. The *thwack* of ballistae and trebuchets crushing the battlements and ramparts and laying siege to the city. Yellow clouds of alchemical weapons churn with oily plumes of stinking black smoke. The sounds and smells of a city being killed.

The wind changes and it disappears.

'How much further?' Kievar asks me.

I grip the chest straps of my braces. 'Viziden's a few days away. From there, we'll head north, look for your people.'

'You think we'll find them?'

'I think we've got a chance. A chance no one's had before. And maybe that's got to be enough.' I smile, shove my hands deep into my trouser pockets. 'I'll be with you all the way.'

'What'll you do then?' Kievar's voice is hesitant as he asks, like he's worried of the answer. But he needn't be. I made my choice the moment I left the Guild.

'You're still the Elderblood,' I say. 'You're still my King, and I swore an oath to protect you and get you to safety. The way I see things, that hasn't changed. And until you tell me otherwise, it won't change.'

'You swear it?' Kievar asks.

'I swear it,' I say, sealing our new, updated oath.

Kievar smiles broadly at me. Gods, he's so young. Then he stoops down and digs his leathery hands through the olive-green grass, inhaling the earthy scent. He's back with nature he was deprived of for so long. Will I feel the same way we reach the mountain ranges and snowy slopes of my home? The sounds of the wind whispering through the trees and the trickle of a nearby stream fills my ears. Gliding specks of birds wheel lazily overhead. In the distance is a hazy caravan of refugees that escaped Kharkov. With our hoods, we'll blend in easily enough.

'Yharv.'

I know what Kievar's going to say before he says it. His slender, reptilian body stands silhouetted against the city walls, his golden eyes bouncing back and forth as they search my face. 'Tell me we did the right thing,' he says. 'Tell me my life was worth more than all of theirs.'

'I'm not sure I've ever done the right thing. Not once. Sometimes, there's only the burden you're willing to carry.' I grip Kievar's shoulder and pull him close. 'But maybe I can help someone else live so they can do the right thing. And maybe, that's the start of something for me, too.'

Kievar smiles tightly, nods. Maybe he's expecting more. But I can't give him more. The decision is set in stone, the die is cast.

After all, once you've set yourself a task, you've got to throw yourself at it until it's done.

And my new task is helping Kievar find his people again.

We take once last look at the burning, smouldering, besieged city. Then we throw on our hoods, turn and break into a run, heading northwest towards the distant horizon. Towards home.

THRALL

Lee Murray

Solander Island, Southern Coast of New Zealand, 1805

Soaked to the thigh, Ethan Pollard shivered in the bitter southern wind. It was November, spring in the Antipodes, yet the cold bit him to the marrow, stiffening his fingers around the wooden sealing club. He lifted his torch and hastened forward, carefully picking his way over the glistening black rocks. He wouldn't be the first man to tumble into the brine. The lucky ones washed up bloated and blue on the island's sole stretch of beach days later.

"Bunch of 'em just up yonder," Simon Flett cried over squalls.

Ethan swore under his breath. *Bloody idiot.* At his rate, he'll have the entire rookery lumbering into the sea. If that happened, Captain Molloy and the *Endeavour* would surely abandon the lot of them to this blasted rock for eternity. As it was, they'd been freezing their fecking balls off in this hell hole since May. An entire winter living on ship's biscuits and salted pork. They'd worked their arses off during those months, slaughtering scores of seal pups, drying the skins, and boiling the blubber for oil. They were all set for Molloy's return, each man dreaming of the fortune in lay, when they'd been attacked by a gang of sea rats come ashore in a slew of whaleboats. Ethan had no idea which ship the bastards hailed from. Maybe they'd been stationed on a nearby island. Whatever their provenance, they'd stolen in at dawn and slit poor Mowat's throat afore the wretched beggar could shout the alarm. When Tulloch went to his aid, the bastards had blown his face off with a musket. Awakened by the noise, his own gang had scattered, Ethan included. Good thing too, or else they'd all be dead. They'd hidden in the island's caves, or among the tussock, while the sea rats, maybe forty men, took what plunder they could carry and burned the rest to keep the prices keen.

Ethan hadn't worried they would starve, not given Heddle's skill with a spear and Robertson's knack for foraging the eggs of seabirds. It was Molloy's ire at the loss of the valuable cargo that worried him.

Today, though, it seemed their luck had turned because the seals were back for mating. Ethan rounded the bluff to a wall of noise, the animals bellowing and crying like a crowd at a hanging. His heart leapt with hope, though his breath caught at the stench. He crept up to the other survivors and asked, "How many do you reckon?"

"Hard to tell," Budge said, his red beard flecked with foam.

"Hundreds," said Flett. "Maybe thousands."

Ethan nodded. Flett could barely count, but he likely wasn't far off, if the noise and the stink were anything to go by. With just five survivors, they had their work cut out for them. "We best get to it then," he said.

Flett spat and took off. Ethan lingered a moment to wedge his torch in a cleft in the cliff, then, gripping his club, he clambered over the rocks as the sun's first rays breached the horizon.

His muscles hot with effort, and sweat freezing on his face, Ethan smashed his club down, the splinter of bone giving way to mush as the weapon smashed into the seal's brain. The seal trembled and slumped, and once again Ethan felt a dull thrill. It was a young female of around a hundred pounds. Unblemished, the skin should fetch a good price.

Stepping over the dead animal, Ethan rolled his shoulders and arched his back. A carnage of carcasses lay on the slick red rocks around him, his own arm accounting for scores of them. Would it satisfy Molloy? Ethan didn't know. What he did know was that he was tired to the bone. He'd stopped only once all day, to take a drink and help Budge down to the shore. Caught unawares by a lusty wig, the man had taken a vicious bite to the thigh. Since they had no vitriol left, Ethan had packed the wound with moss. He hoped it wouldn't fester. Now, with Budge useless, that left just four of them to skin the beasts. Flett, Heddle, and Robertson had already made a start, their backs bowed, straddling the seals, knives flashing in the afternoon sun.

Ethan stashed his club near the burned-out torch and took out his skinning knife. He gave the blade a few swipes on a flattened stone to sharpen it, then heaved the dead female onto her back, and sliced off the flippers at the joints. That done, he slit the pelt vertically and, gagging at the stink, began separating the pelt from the fatty carcass. He was just about to douse the pelt in salt water when Flett bellowed across the rocks.

Ethan whipped up his head.

Flett was leaping over the rocks, his club in the air, pursuing a straggling seal and a late season pup who were making a run for the ocean. Dropping his blade, Heddle stepped into their path, waving his arms to chase the seals back towards Flett.

"Get 'em," Robertson yelled. His shout confused the pup, and it swerved away from its mother. The loyal cow lumbered after it, but Flett was faster. He lunged, grasping the pup by its flippers, and lifted it into the air.

The cow moaned.

Flett pivoted on his heel, swinging the animal sideways like a hammer thrower.

"No!" a woman screamed.

Ethan looked around. He blinked. Stopped in his tracks. All at once, the seal mother reared up on her back flippers, her skin splitting lengthwise. A woman stepped out of the silver pelt.

Flett spun mid-swing.

The woman screamed again. "No, please!" She ran at Flett, stumbling barefoot over the craggy rocks, hands outstretched …

Ethan was too startled to move.

Flett smashed the pup's skull against a rock. It connected with a sickening crack. Flett dropped the carcass on the rocks, then wiped a fleck of bone from his face with the back of his hand. On the ground, the pup's pulped head drooped and lay still.

"No!" The woman rushed over, gathering the baby to her breast and cradling it gently in her arms. She buried her face in the pup's silky grey fur and began to keen.

"What the hell?" Flett breathed.

Heddle, who'd seen what Ethan had, dropped to his knees, his hands clasped before him. Robertson opened his mouth like a gull, then closed it again.

"Where the feck did the woman spring from?" Flett said.

Ethan stepped over to the discarded skin and picked it up. The soft fur smelled of musk and brine. He turned the pelt in his hands, examining the cut that ran from snout to tail. It was clean. Like it'd been made with a blade. Maybe Ethan was mistaken? Maybe his mind, giddy with lack of water, was playing tricks on him. His wishful thoughts come to life? Heaven knows, it'd been an age since he'd laid eyes on a woman, and he'd only ever seen one as bonny as this one.

Except Heddle and Robertson had seen her step from the sealskin, too.

"Pollard?" Flett demanded.

The woman cradled the dead pup in her slender arms and lifted her chin, fixing Ethan with eyes the colour of kelp and deeper than the ocean.

Ethan shuddered. They were in even worse shit than he thought. "Not a woman," he whispered. "She's a selkie."

His back to the wind, Ethan stirred the fire, sending orange sparks whirling in the darkness above them.

"I say we give her skin back and let her go," Heddle said. Higher up the beach, the selkie woman probably couldn't hear him, not over the crash of the surf and the crack of the fire, still Heddle kept his voice low. "Selkies are an ill omen."

"No," Flett said, the creature's skin tucked under his arm. "We can't let her go. We kilt her pup. She'll fetch her Mer kin to avenge us."

"*You* killed the pup, Flett," Robertson reminded him.

Flett pointed a stick at him. "You think they'll care? The beach is spread with sealskins. They'll slaughter us all before Molloy returns with the *Endeavour*."

"Kill her then," Budge said.

"So that's your answer," Ethan said. "And will you be the one to do it?"

His face aglow, Budge raised his hand. "Not me. I wasn't even there."

Robertson rose to his feet. "I can't believe we're even talking about harming the woman. Look at her. What threat is she, over there singing to herself, clinging to her babe?"

Flett clucked his tongue. "It's a seal pup, man."

"You saw her turn," Heddle added.

"She's grieving," Robertson insisted.

Ethan shivered despite the blaze. Woman or selkie, this was a bad business. Already, Robertson fancied himself in love with the creature.

"Pollard, what say you?" Budge said. "What do we do with her?"

They all turned to him, their gang leader, although he'd done a sorry job of it with five of their number dead in as many months and only a handful of skins to show for it. They were bound for ill luck whatever they did. Ethan had no answer. He was just a sealer.

"Pollard," Budge said again.

"The fur belongs to the company. I say we let Captain Molloy decide."

♛

Captain Thomas Molloy stood on the beach watching the men load the long boats. "Pollard, a word."

The sealer jogged over. "Captain." The man's voice was coarse as salt and his weathered face looked to have aged a decade in the months since the *Endeavour* had last anchored in these straits.

"I count five men. Where's the rest of your gang?"

"Killed, sir. Raiders got them. Like bloody ghosts, they were. Got Mowat and Tulloch before they rose from their beds. Two others we lost to the sea."

Molloy suppressed a curse. He'd counted on Pollard's gang to replenish the crew after a dozen of the hands had succumbed to fever. "I left you with ten men. What of the other?"

Pollard shook his head and dug his toes into the sand. Suicide then. Molloy pursed his lips. He tilted his head at the red beard leaning on a stick. "And him?" The bandage around the man's leg was stained with pus. Molloy wagered he'd smell the putrefaction if the wind were blowing the right way.

"Budge? Seal bit him, sir."

"The *Endeavour* doesn't carry passengers, Ethan."

"Mr Budge is handy with a needle, Captain."

Molloy gazed off to the horizon. "As far as Tasmania. Either the leg's mended or he sets down there." It was as fair as he could do. He wasn't running a charity.

Pollard nodded grimly.

"Now tell me about the pelts."

"Four hundred and thirty-two, Captain. Mostly females. Skins have been drying a week. Free of marks and holes, so they should be worth good coin …"

Four hundred and thirty-two. Molloy's blood bulged in his veins. Three gross. It was pitiful. Not nearly enough to fill the hold, even accounting for the potatoes. Molloy could almost hear his brother's laughter from the other end of the map.

"What good is a merchant ship if her captain doesn't know the first thing about business?" James had chortled to their father. "Mark my words, he'll be sailing home with his tail between his legs inside two years."

Molloy had no idea where his brother was now. Shining his officer buttons and exchanging cannon with Napoleon somewhere while Thomas was expected to pay for it all.

"Sir, there's something …"

Molloy interrupted him. "Why has that man got a pelt?" he barked, pointing out the young sealer. "Is the blighter stealing it under my very nose? Tell him to load it in the boat with the rest, Pollard, or I'll cut off his hands and leave him to rot on this godforsaken rock."

"Captain," Pollard mumbled.

"What is it?"

"We … that seal …"

"Out with it, man."

"We had to keep that skin aside. It's not like the others, you see? Belongs to a selkie, sir."

Molloy shook his head in disbelief. God knows, sailors were a superstitious bunch, but a selkie? The man was surely touched in the head, plagued by events and too long with the wind and the gulls for company. It was a pity the *Endeavour* was in dire need of seamen. He snorted. "A selkie, you say?"

"Yessir."

"And how do you know that?"

The man's eyes flickered. "On account of we all seen the woman step out of her skin."

Preposterous. Although, what if the gang were suffering some strange malaise picked up on this damnable island? Wary, Molloy took a step back. He should keep his distance. It would not do to bring the plague aboard the *Endeavour,* or they might all perish. James would not be gentle with his eulogy. Molloy glanced across the beach to where the crew were loading the boats. Still, there was time yet before the tide turned, enough to assuage any fears of the peste. He would humour the man a moment. "Well," he said, brushing the salt spray off his jacket. "Where is she, then? This selkie-woman of yours."

The sealer grinned. "Flett! To me," he shouted, then he gestured towards the cliffs. "This way, Captain."

Molloy followed the two men off the beach and up a narrow track to a crack in the rocks, the opening barely wide enough for a man's shoulders to pass. Pollard nodded for him to enter. Molloy felt his suspicion grow. What treachery were they plotting? He could no longer see the boats. Out of instinct, he dropped his hand to his pistol.

But a woman's voice carried from the cave, her song pure as a bellbird's.

Pollard nodded again. "She's in there, Captain."

Molloy turned sideways and stepped inside, blinking in the dim torchlight.

Not a selkie, Pollard had been wrong about that: it was a woman—a native woman. Naked but for a man's ragged chemise, she was a beauty. Raven-haired, with dark skin, tracks of salt crusted on her hollowed cheeks. She was kneeling on the rocky ground, pitching back and forth, cradling a child wrapped in a sealskin.

At his approach, she hunched her shoulders and cringed away.

"Don't touch her," she hissed.

Molloy turned to Pollard. "How long has she been here?"

"Not more than a fortnight. Since the raiders came."

Molloy nodded. He'd wager she'd been kidnapped, used, then dumped to make room for the stolen pelts. How else would a native woman have learned to speak English? Perhaps she'd evaded her captors whilst they'd been ashore pillaging, hoping to travel inland and reunite with her kinsmen and incite them to vengeance. Molloy himself had only seen the natives from a distance, but by all accounts, the Māori were a fearful murderous people. She must have been sorely disappointed to discover herself still a captive on the island.

Molloy's vision adjusted to the gloom, and he saw she was thin, her skin chapped and cracked. "Looks like she's been treated poorly," he said.

Pollard straightened. "Not by us, sir. Flett killed the pup, for sure, but I swear we didn't lay a hand on her."

A pup? Molloy stepped closer to the woman, then quickly retreated, disgusted by the pungent waft of blood and rot. It was indeed a seal pup the woman was clutching. That explained the seaman's outlandish selkie story. Molloy chuckled. The first selkie in captivity. Wouldn't that be a *cause célèbre* in England's parlours? The notion was even shinier than the brass buttons on his brother's naval dress coat …

A thought struck him: being the first ship to bear a New Zealand native to Britain might also be lucrative, if only for the novelty. The country was gagging for news of the colonies. And if not, Molloy knew some slavers in Liverpool. "Bring her aboard," he said.

Hovering near the cave's entrance, Pollard hesitated. Scratched at his neck. "Sir, you know it's bad luck …"

Molloy snatched the pelt from Flett and bundled it under his arm. "Enough with your delusions. By whatever manner she came to be here, this woman is traumatised and in need of care. We will not abandon her on this island alone."

The *Endeavour* had been a day at sea. His face buffeted by the wind, Molloy stood on the quarterdeck, watching a pod of fur seals.

Pollard joined him. "It's Mr Budge, Captain."

"What of him?" Molloy said absently, his telescope still trained on the black patch in the distance. Every now and then a glossy back would break the surface then dive again, break and dive, break and dive. It was mesmerising …

"The surgeon says he's dying."

… so many pelts. If only those skins were safely in the *Endeavour's* cargo hold, bound for market; they'd fetch a pretty price in tea.

Molloy was reminded of Pollard's presence. "The leg? Oh yes. I recall it had festered. Can't Mr Matthews remove it?"

"Too late, he says. The mortification has set in. Would you come below decks, sir?" Pollard cast his gaze aft. "I wouldn't ask, only Budge is saying some things. He's got the men spooked."

Molloy sighed heavily. It would have been kinder to shoot the man on the beach. "Lead the way, Pollard."

Below decks, Molloy resisted the urge to hold his nose. It was ripe enough down here without the added stench of Budge's festering limb. A bunch of seamen crowded the hammock.

"Move aside, men," the surgeon said. "Captain's here."

Molloy took off his hat and leaned in. "Bad situation we've got here, Mr Budge."

"Yessir."

"Shall I have one of my officers dictate a letter to your family?"

The seaman grasped Molloy by the lapels, his grip surprisingly strong for a dying man. He dragged Molloy's face close, his breath as rank as his rotting leg. "The selkie-woman, sir," he rasped. "Either kill her or give her back her skin and set her free. She'll curse you. All of you. I beg you, throw it over the side."

"Mr Budge. I assure you, that woman is not a selkie—"

"I've seen it, Captain. The *Endeavour* on fire, men cloaked in flames, no way to escape."

Molloy smiled. He patted the man on the forearm. "Mr Budge, calm yourself. It is the fever talking."

Budge let go Molloy's lapels and fell back in his hammock. "I'm dying, sir. I tell you, the ship is cursed. Why would I lie?" He closed his eyes.

"Mr Budge?" Molloy coughed. He took a step back and smoothed his jacket. Budge gave no answer. The man's chest still rose and fell, but it was clear there would be no need for a letter. Molloy turned to go, then slowed, startled to see ten men staring at him from the gloom, their faces grim with doubt.

"What are you all looking at? It's the fever!" he hissed. "The man is quite clearly delirious."

"I saw her change from seal to maid," a man said.

Pollard batted him on the arm. "Quiet, Heddle."

"You saw it too, Ethan. Saw her change right there in front of us."

"Enough!" Molloy said through clenched teeth. "The woman is not a selkie."

"Captain," the surgeon began.

Molloy glowered. Even his officers were questioning him now? Let this insubordination continue and he'd have a full-blown mutiny on his hands. Molloy knew how to deal with this. "Well, since you all insist," he said, keeping his voice even. "I shall prove it to you." You will fetch the woman from the steward's cabin, Mr Matthews, and meet me above deck."

Molloy charged back to his captain's quarters. Selkies! He took a key from his pocket and opened the sturdy oak chest at the foot of his bed. For a moment, as he shook out the crumpled pelt and inhaled its fading musk, he wondered why, if he was certain the woman wasn't a selkie, he'd thought to store the pelt? He snorted. It was as well he did. Otherwise, how could he prove to the men that she was not? He snatched it up and stormed out of his cabin onto the quarterdeck. The crew had congregated around the woman, who was still clutching the dead seal pup.

"Here," he said, flapping the pelt in her direction. "You want this? Come and take it."

The woman looked up. Her eyes narrowed. "You're giving me this pelt?"

Molloy stepped aside, clearing a path to the rail. "My men seem to think you are a selkie, madam. If you are, I am offering you the opportunity to take your skin and return to the sea." He waved an arm to the horizon.

The woman shifted nervously.

Molloy grinned. "It's quite simple, really. All you have to do is transform into your true self. I shall let you go, and my crew will go back to their duties."

Cradling the pup to her chest, the woman shook off Pollard's grasp and sidled forward. "And you'll let me go?"

"Of course." Molloy held out the silky pelt.

She gazed about, looking from one man to the next, then she turned and tore the pelt from him. In one smooth movement, she slung it about her shoulders.

A cry went up. Molloy felt his mouth drop. No, no, no. It wasn't possible. It was pure superstition. Tales told by crofters' wives. Yet there was no denying it: the woman was gone, and a seal stood on the deck in its stead, one flipper curled about the dead pup. The creature was indeed a selkie. Molloy almost laughed. To think he'd imagined parading her about England as the country's first Māori voyager. Where was the *cause célèbre* in that? It was nothing compared to this marvel, this creature of myth. Why, she would outshine even an admiral's epaulettes. His mouth went dry. Molloy knew the shapeshifter would never see England. He had no choice but to let her go—he'd given his word before the crew.

The woman-turned-seal lumbered awkwardly for the portside, rolling the dead infant before her. The men drew back to let her pass, their eyes wide with terror. Flett moaned. Heddle kissed the cross he wore on a string about his neck. A few more clumsy paces and the beast would be gone, gliding through the waves to join her seal kin.

Yet, instead of slipping into the sea, the cow turned at the rail, bellowing softly. Molloy saw her dilemma: she was a *seal* and in her seal form, she was unable to lift the pup.

Molloy's mind raced; he would fill the hold yet.

By now, Pollard, the *Endeavour's* only crew member with any balls, was on the move, about to retrieve the pup. Molloy shoved the seaman out of the way, pulled the knife from its sheath, skewered the pup, and raised the macabre morsel above his head so its putrid juice rolled down his arm.

The seal screeched.

"We're going to die," Heddle cried out.

"Shut up!" Molloy yelled.

"Captain." Pollard grimaced. "Please. Let me help her. Remember Budge's vision."

Molloy shook his head. He fixed his eyes on the seal. "Change back," he told her.

The creature turned its gaze to the ocean and the black patch of seals in the distance, and for a moment, Molloy feared all was lost, that the cow would abandon the pup and slither into the sea. But it lowered its head, shucked off the pelt, and once again the native woman appeared on the deck. Molloy placed a boot on the sealskin.

"You lied," she hissed, rounding on him. "You said you would let me go." Her brown eyes, dark as obsidian, glittered with anger and, once again, Molloy was struck by the wild beauty of her.

"You're right, I did," Molloy replied. "But unfortunately, I did not specify when."

She lunged at him then, shrieking.

Molloy merely leaned to his left and dangled the grisly corpse over the rail.

The woman gasped and drew back.

"Calm yourself, madam," Molloy drawled, excitement thrumming beneath his ribs. "A small favour is all I ask. Then you can return to the sea."

"Give me my pup," the woman wailed.

Molloy flung the carcass over the rail. "I made no promises about the pup." He sheathed his knife and wiped his hand on his breast. "When you've done as I ask, you can recover your infant."

In the end, Molloy allowed her to resume her seal form after Pollard went on and on in his ear, insisting that if the selkie died they would surely be cursed to hell.

"The woman will drown, sir," he'd said. "The sea is too cruel. Too full of foul creatures. She can't call her kin to her if she's dead."

He had a point. Come to think on it, Molloy doubted her seal kin would recognise a human voice. His plan depended upon it, so he had conceded. Blocking off all avenues for escape, he'd handed over the pelt a second time. Still, the lure of the pelt was clearly too much for her because she slipped the skin around her shoulders, transforming once more. She should have been grateful, instead the woman was as bitter as a fish wife.

"I won't help you," she stormed before she was fully altered. "I won't call them. You'll never force me to sacrifice my kin. Never!"

Pollard and Heddle seized her, holding the writhing creature still while Flett tightened the rope around her waist.

Molloy grinned. He'd known she would resist. It was of no matter. All it required was a nick through the pelt …

She moaned softly when the blade bit her flesh. Molloy was careful not to push it too deep, just enough that her animal self would cry out in pain, and the wound would leave a bloody trail in their wake.

After that, they tied her to the gunwale and lowered her into the water, so she thrashed in the boarding nets hastily re-purposed to the task. By the time they'd delivered Budge's miserable corpse to the sea and pronounced a few words of respect, the waters around the *Endeavour* were churning with seals come to the sea-maiden's rescue. It was touching really. Almost too easy.

"Pull her up!" Molloy yelled when the nets were fit to bursting. "And keep the ropes tight until we've clubbed 'em all. We don't want wigs thundering all over the midship."

He appointed Flett and Heddle to haul the seal-woman from the seething mass. They delivered her skin to Molloy, wrapped her in a blanket, then fixed her to the mainmast. All the while, Heddle mumbled his prayers and the woman screamed. She was like any woman in that respect, her screeching penetrating Molloy's skull. When it got too much to bear, he stomped over and pressed a boarding axe to her breast. "You will cease your caterwauling, madam, or I will stuff your mouth with your own skin." That quieted her. Or perhaps it was the blood loss.

The sealers set to, and with the sailors' help, by mid-afternoon another two hundred skins were ready for salting, the seals' skinned bodies mouldering on the deck, their exposed fat glistening under a weak sun. An officer—Sinclair—ordered the seamen to throw the carcasses over the rail.

Molloy halted them. "Wait. Pollard, what of the oil?"

"Cold drawn oil takes time to press, sir."

"And if we trim and boil the fat? We have the jars."

"You're suggesting we build a fire on the ship, Captain?"

"Yes. We could burn one of the long boats."

Pollard winced.

Molloy felt his nostrils flare. "Something to add, Ethan?"

Then man took a step back. "I ... I ... It's just that wind and fire make a poor combination, sir."

Molloy paused. He ought to flog the ignorant sea rat. But of all of them, his officers included, at least the man was not afeared to speak his mind. Molloy respected him for that. He thumped the gunwale with the flat of his hand. "You're right, lad, the risk of fire is too great. Carry on, Sinclair. We'll press what fat we can and dump the rest overboard."

"And the selkie-woman, Captain?"

Molloy's skin prickled on the back of his neck. He turned to Pollard. "When the *Endeavour's* hold is full," he said, "we'll release her. Tomorrow perhaps."

Still, the gnarly sealer lingered. The man was fair begging for a flogging.

"What now, Pollard?" Molloy snapped.

"Robertson asked if we might give her a drink, Captain."

Molloy frowned. Were the men succumbing to her selkie thrall? There was no denying in her human form she was handsome to look at.

Still, where was the harm in giving her a little water if it would keep the crew happy? Besides, Molloy didn't want the woman dying on them. They would never fill the hold that way. "Of course, Ethan. Tell Robertson to go ahead. We're not barbarians, are we?"

Grinning, Molloy pushed away from the rail. All this talk of curses, yet nothing untoward had happened. If anything, their fortunes were looking up.

But when he passed by the mainmast on the way to his quarters, the blasted woman followed him with her eyes.

♛

Sinclair woke him in the night. "Storm, sir. Caught us unawares. Mr Arthur says we've lost two topsails. One of them torn clean in half."

Molloy swung his legs from the bed and pulled on his breeches. "Dammit. Have the men reef the sails, Sinclair. Leave the mizzen, nothing more."

"Yessir."

Molloy dragged on his coat. The ship rocked beneath him. Although she was old, he was confident that in a heavy gale no sea could hurt the *Endeavour*. After all, she'd survived the voyage to the Antipodes and back many a time. Nevertheless, his blood clotted when he emerged on the quarterdeck, and he was thankful for the obscurity of the night because the way the deck pitched and rolled, the waves must be mountainous.

His officers ran asunder. Molloy shouted orders until he was hoarse. His face and hands were numb, the wind stinging him from every direction. For hours, the sea and the sky assailed them, and the *Endeavour* groaned and shivered and strained with the effort. Molloy and his crew could do little but pray to the Virgin that they would prevail.

At some hour of the night, Molloy saw someone had cut the woman down from the mainmast and taken her below decks. In truth, he didn't see it—the night was so black that he could hardly see two yards before him—yet, somehow, he'd felt her presence beneath the boards—mocking him. Then, in a rare lull in the squalls, he heard her singing, the melody echoing upwards from the ship's bowels. Her voice so low and pitiful that it made his bones ache. Molloy would have preferred to hear her screaming. "Someone shut that woman up," he roared.

Sinclair's voice carried to him on a gust. "The men are saying she was whistling into the wind earlier."

"Shhh, man," said Matthews. "The captain'll hear you."

"In this gale?" Sinclair said. "I tell you, John, it's not the captain we have to fear."

"Back to your stations, or I'll throw you overboard myself," Molloy screamed. There was no need: the sea rose again, and the men scattered.

Molloy lost the course of time. Dawn came and he scarce noticed. The waves still crashing over the bowsprit with such force that Molloy wondered how the timbers did not splinter. Some time ago, they had lost a man to the surges, swallowed by a wall of white foam, his corpse likely in the Americas by now. Did Molloy fear death? He'd asked himself the question more than once this night. He did not, he decided. A merchant seaman must know that drowning is a probability. No, what galled him most was that his brother would claim the last word. It was that fear that drove him hardest.

When Molloy's throat was raw from screaming and his body cramped and wracked with fatigue, the storm began to wane. The rain persisted, everything beyond the rail as grey as a London street, but the waves were hills, not mountains, and the wind was no longer a gale. In his forty years, it was the bleakest morning Molloy had seen, yet he allowed himself a smile. They were not drowned. Whatever gods held their fate, the woman below decks held no sway.

"I believe I will have some coffee," he called to his steward.

Before the man could reply, timbers screeched and the ship foundered. The bark had struck something. Molloy shivered. It made no sense. The *Endeavour* was flat-bottomed, and they were in the middle of the Southern Ocean—at least, they had been the last time he had charted their position. Molloy held his breath. Perhaps the waves would lift them free.

The grinding continued.

♕

Molloy had no choice but to go below decks with his officers to inspect the damage. The situation was grim. The ship lay holed and fast upon a reef; although, for now, the hole was small and she was taking little water. A small mercy. Still, Molloy was sick to his gut. If she sank, the company, and the Molloy name, would be ruined and even James's reputation might not withstand the indignity, although it was scant consolation.

"We should hoist out the boats, sir," Sinclair gibbered.

"There's no saving her, then?" Molloy said.

"None, sir. We should leave while we yet can. By God's grace, Mr Arthur has spied some land, an isle to the south."

Abandoning the pumps, Pollard rushed over, gesturing at the gushing water. "We could try fothering her, sir. Haul a length of sailcloth over the hole. But we'll need to float her first."

Pollard was right. It had been done before, and on this very ship. "Yes, yes. Let's do as Pollard says. Have the men heave the ballast overboard, casks, anchors, anything of weight."

Sinclair dithered like a maid beside him. "Captain Molloy, please. At the very least, we should get the officers into the boats. This will not work, and even if it should, we cannot spare the sail."

Molloy swore. In his exhaustion, he'd forgotten the ruined topsails. They would need all the sail left to them to get home.

"Then we use the pelts," Pollard ventured.

Molloy whirled and almost collided with a blasted lantern. "No, not the pelts. I will not have it. Already the potatoes are spoiled. We cannot pay for this voyage without those damned pelts."

"Then I fear we will pay for it with our lives, sir," Matthews whispered.

Molloy clenched his fists, his blood thundering in his veins. It was as Colonel Monro described it: *they were betwixt the devill and deep sea.* Without sufficient sail, the *Endeavour* would become a ghost ship, doomed to drift at the mercy of the current.

"Goddamn it. All right, use the pelts."

When the men turned to go, Molloy grabbed Sinclair by the arm. "Sit in a boat if you must, but the woman stays aboard. If the *Endeavour* founders, I'll have her go down with it.

"Aye sir."

E than wiped the sweat from his eyes, then bent to shoulder another sack of potatoes.

"This is God's punishment for our sins," Heddle whined beside him. "We should never have brought that cursed witch aboard."

"The storm was not the woman's fault," Robertson said.

Flett heaved a barrel onto his shoulders. "Yeah? What about her whistling, aye? I reckon she called it down upon us. My ol' da said women are bad luck on a vessel," he wheedled.

"Our bad luck started when you butchered her pup," Heddle said.

Climbing to the upper deck, Heddle grunted. "We're all cursed now."

Ethan hefted the sack onto the deck, then clambered up himself. He carried the sack to the rail, dodging items left behind on the deck by the crew in their haste to lighten the ship. Casks, barrels, a sealing club. He rested the sack on the gunwale a moment and looked out. The sea was calm now. Fifty yards off the stern, a dozen men bobbed on the waves in the *Endeavour's* pinnace. Beyond them, dark patches scattered the sea's surface, signs of coral glass. Ethan let the sack go and watched it disappear under the surface. Heddle was mistaken. Raiders. Pestilence. Suicide. The way Pollard saw it, this voyage had been ill-fated before any of them had laid eyes on the sea-maid.

Matthews stopped them when the gang were returning below decks. He handed Ethan a ring of keys. "The hold is empty, the ballast too, and we've dumped the spare anchor. We're working on the cannon, and the powder lads are emptying the magazine. These are the steward's keys. You're to clear the captain's cabin of anything heavy. The desk, chests. Look smart now, the sailmakers are nearly finished readying the pelts."

"Right, sir."

"And, Pollard, take an axe. You won't be able to lift them." Matthews ran back below decks.

Ethan's heart thrummed. The sealers gathered around him as he turned the keys over in his hand. Robertson groaned softly. Heddle sucked air through his teeth.

"Damn," whispered Flett.

The selkie's pelt was stashed in the captain's quarters.

They were come full circle.

Ethan threw open the chest. The selkie's skin lay alongside a stack of books and the captain's dress coat. In the days since Ethan had last held it, the fur had lost its sheen. It was shabby and thin, and there was a rip where Molloy had pierced the selkie's side to make her bleed. Ethan lifted the pelt to his face and inhaled its scent of musk and brine. His heart jumped—he was reminded of someone. Someone from long ago, back when he was a younger softer man.

The selkie's voice carried up from the steward's quarters. The tune was sweet. Romantic. The kind to make you long for a woman's arms. Ethan shivered. Perhaps Heddle was wrong and there was time yet to make a better choice. Ethan tucked the pelt into his breeches. He tossed the steward's keys to Robertson. "Fetch the woman and bring her on deck. We're letting her go."

Robertson arched an eyebrow, but he turned and disappeared along the gangway. Flett cursed. Heddle said nothing, just brought the axe down on the chest, splitting the timber.

"If we live, I take responsibility for freeing her," Ethan said, even as the ship lurched.

They might still die, but at least he would sleep better.

Molloy leaned over the gunwale and grinned. The day was improving. Pushed inwards by the current, the bundle of tarred pelts had stuffed the hole like a stopper in a wine cask. It wasn't pretty, but it would hold until they reached the isle where they could beach the bark and make the necessary repairs to get them safely home. No need for a cargo now, not when his leadership would get him a commission and his own command. The captain who survived a storm, a reef, and a selkie's curse. He couldn't wait to see James's face.

Molloy took one last look at the hull, then turned away from the rail.

Robertson was escorting the selkie-woman to the rail. What the hell was he about? Hadn't Molloy said she was to remain on board? And dammit, if that wasn't Pollard stepping onto the quarterdeck carrying the creature's pelt.

"Stop!" Molloy yelled, but no one moved to do his bidding. He had no allies on deck. Sinclair was out in a long boat, and Matthews was below decks seeing to the patched-up hull.

Then Flett, the young one, charged from the great cabin, wielding a boarding axe. Screaming, he ran at Pollard, knocking over a powder boy in his haste, and snatched the precious pelt. They grappled like a pair of sea urchins. The seamen gathered to watch. Molloy would have liked to take a wager. Pollard was smarter, but Flett was a scrapper, and he had the axe …

Turning away, Molloy scooped a sealing club off the deck. He crept up behind Robertson and quietly brained the man.

That would teach the bastard to disobey orders.

Robertson crumpled, knocking over a cask of seal oil. Molloy grasped for the woman's arm, but she had edged closer to the pair battling over the pelt. Seemed she was hoping for her chance to grab it.

The pelt flew free. The woman seized it. Slipping the pelt over her shoulders, she ran for the rail.

"Stop her!"

Still, the mutinous bastards didn't obey. It was no matter; he would deal with them later.

Molloy drew his pistol. Not to kill her. To frighten her. Prevent her escape. What good were stories without proof? He raised his arm …

The ship bucked on a wave.

He fired.

The shot went wide, glanced off a lantern hanging from the yard. Time stood still as Molloy watched it fall. Powder and oil ignited in a whoosh of flame.

Dear God. A powder crate.

From the corner of his eye, he spied the selkie-woman slipping over the rail.

The *Endeavour* exploded, spewing men and timber. Flaming men panicked and ran. The topsail yard cracked and toppled. The timber clubbed Flett, caving in his skull as he rolled away from Pollard.

Molloy was thrown in the air, his flesh on fire.

Ethan fell through the water. He was drowning. He knew it. It was the strangest thing. Lit from above, the water was green and full of silhouettes. Sinking timbers. Bodies. Heddle, his chest impaled with a chair leg. And hundreds of seals, diving and soaring.

The selkie's seal kin.

The *Endeavour*, too, was taking her last breath, the sea eddying around her. The old girl tipped, and the stern plunged.

The selkie glided up beside him as graceful as a scarf in the wind; Ethan knew her from the wound in her side and the song in his ears. He had a flicker of hope that she might save him, but she sped away, chasing Molloy.

The selkie-woman slid her arm through the slit in her pelt and grasped a floating rope. She coiled it around the captain's neck and wrapped the loose end around a cleat on the sinking ship.

Ethan lost sight of her after that. But he saw the captain's eyes widen as the *Endeavour* plummeted to the seafloor.

Ethan's chest ached with the rightness of it.

KING FOR
A DAY

DANIEL POLANSKY

When the rain began to fall Cuauhtemotzín, Emperor of Civilization from the Swallowing Sea to the Peaks Beyond the Clouds, went to the window to let in the evening, a journey of twenty paces made in silent, graceless pain. Cuauhtemotzín did not mind the pain. When the pain was gone he knew he would be gone as well. The pain was almost gone.

From his window atop his Pyramid atop his Mountain Cuauhtemotzín gazed at his City; the Hundred Bridges like cataracts of colored stone, the perpetual shadows they cast on the squares and tenements below. With the moon hidden it was too dark to make out the Moat but he could hear its gurgling loop, the permanent backdrop to everything else that happened in the City.

Cuauhtemotzín tilted his head out the window and took a deep breath as the rain fell against dirt and dry stone. There should be a name for that, he thought. Perhaps there was. Cuauhtemotzín did not know everything. He followed the scent through the worn folds of memory: A spring afternoon when his uncle had taken him hunting jaguar in the forests north of the city; the morning he had led his armies against an incursion from the East, his rumbling war chariots, the packed mass of spears. The early winter's evening when Yaotl had fled the court, the shouts of the guards and the threats of his lords soon lost to the torrential downpour.

The King sneered and turned away from the past though not the vista. A man could live too long. Sixty-five years he had been above the ground, and for forty-three of those he had worn the Torc, since his mother had died one evening, face down in a bowl of marrow porridge. He had spent the night in the prescribed rituals of mourning and greeted the dawn from atop the Pyramid. With the first rays of the sun, the Torc had seared to his flesh and revealed its secrets: the words of power that discharged the city's defenses, the oaths and ceremonies that that sustained the outward boundaries of existence, the true name of the serpent that lay sleeping in the Moat.

There would be no such ceremony this time, the Emperor was sure. With his son in exile, the jackals gathered. They could slaughter themselves for it, so far as Cuauhtemotzín was concerned. What did it matter? What did any of it matter? At the end of the day came the night, and the night was forever, and what was anything when held against forever? Nothing.

Evening bled in through the window. The rain turned to a steady patter. The Emperor's blanket lay forgotten on the floor.

How fares our sovereign?" asked the Warden of the East. Against the walls, his shadow was a writhing mass of serpents.

"Sleeping peacefully," said Itotia, closing the door to the king's bed-room.

"Surely the Gods will bless us with his presence for a hundred years," said the Warden of the South. Like her counterparts the Warden of the South had not bothered to withdraw her mantle and passing beside her, the Emperor's attendant shivered at the sudden change of temperature, the frost piercing his voluminous robes.

"Surely," agreed Itotia.

In the sitting room outside of the Emperor's chambers waited the four great Lords of the Empire, withdrawn from their distant borders to comfort the Emperor in his time of trouble.

"A travesty that the Emperor should face his reward unsupported," said the Warden of the North. She was the size of the other three Wardens set together, and her skin was hard-flaked obsidian.

"Are we not all the Emperor's children?" asked the Warden of the West. His staff reached nearly to the vaulted ceiling and had already begun to sprout roots into the stone floor. "Faithful in his time of need?"

"Indisputably," agreed the Warden of the East. The snakes in his silhouette writhed atop one another, a shifting, sharp-fanged tumult.

Itotia had served the King since before he'd sprouted his first hairs, had lapped up the lies of the court as he had his mother's milk, and still, he struggled to keep a straight face. As if each Warden had not conspired to turn the Emperor's favor from his only son, as if they hadn't spent his dotage maneuvering against one another, as if they were not all, just then, waiting only for his death to tear the City apart over the Torc. In the end, not one of his servants had stayed true to the Emperor, Itotia thought with a frown—no, not one!

Itotia bowed once to each of the Wardens then left the room. Like all of the Emperor's personal servants he had been born within the walls of the Pyramid and had never left—though he considered this no kind of hardship, the Pyramid being itself a synecdoche for all of Civilization, albeit of finer make. He moved swiftly to the southeastern ascensor and rang the bell. Far below the slaves turned to their wheel and the glass cage rattled slowly down from its perch, rain beating against its frame. There would be chaos along the Moat tonight, as the poorest of the City's inhabitants, those who lived beside the waters and the yet more desperate boat dwellers, fled the rising tides. This did not cause Itotia any particular unhappiness—it was an indifferent observation, neutral in its objectivity. It was the way of the clouds to rain, the Moat to flood, and the poor to suffer.

The top rung of the Pyramid was reserved for the highest of the Lords and Ladies of Civilization and their servants, but the second was the province of every officeholder and administrator within the vast Empire. Even so late in the evening, its food halls and taverns and smokeries were busy with passing courtiers, with soldiers of indifferent ability, with the third cousins of cadet branches of minor houses of nobility. Itotia lost himself in the crowd as a toad to a stream, hurrying through the cavernous hallways and paying faint attention to the scrum of conversation.

"—won't last another week."

"—live for another five years just to spite them."

"—a thousand serpent drawn caleche just east of the City—"

"—all the forests of the West come marching—"

"War will come—"

"Slaughter and blood—"

"—enough bodies to build another Pyramid."

"—war—"

"—war—"

"—war—"

"Hail and well met," said Meztli, stopping Itotia as he reached the end of the pavilion. He was dressed in that summer's style: high-fastened sandals and a robe and rich headdress of peacock feathers—though with his keen eye Itotia could tell these last were false, plucked parrot or swan died vermilion and chartreuse. A ceremonial dagger hung in a sheathe on his chest, the jewel in the pommel too large to be anything but glass.

"May the Emperor recall you in his prayers." Itotia managed his part without slowing his pace, and the courtier fell along beside him.

"And what brings you to the basement, and so late in the evening? I hope this happy surprise signals no ill news of our Lord?"

It was, Itotia thought, the same conversation that was happening across the length of the Pyramid and the breadth of the city. When would the Emperor die? Who would take the Torc? "The Son of All Creation remains as hale and healthy as feather grass, praise be."

"A thousand praises."

"A thousand by a thousand," agreed Itotia, hurrying on through the great obsidian gates that led to the outer battlements.

Meztli proved as tenacious as a candiru, immune to the evening air and the rain which was no longer a drizzle. "And yet, the Gods call all of us to their feet, Emperors and paupers alike."

"What keen insight. Such poetry will earn you a high prize at the harvest festival."

"I hope only to last that long," Meztli said with a rueful and exaggerated sigh. "Alas, I've had a run of bad luck lately."

"Fortune is a fickle mistress," Itotia assured him, "you'll be back in her arms again soon."

They had walked far from the bustling center of the pyramid, alone along the walls.

"And you might offer that introduction."

"I?"

"The whole City waits to hear news of the Emperor—a word, a hint of his condition, could be parlayed into coin."

Itotia wondered absently what debt to which Underbridge gambling house could have made Meztli so desperate. "The Emperor is hale and healthy," Itotia assured the fop, pressing onwards, "thank the Seven Gods and Hundred Spirits."

But Meztli would not be put off so easily, pulling at Itotia robes to reveal a faint glimpse of gold, "If I don't come up with something by dawn, I'll—"

Itotia tore away and Meztli stumbled backward, his hand going to the ceremonial dagger at his side. "By the Things That Scuttle and the Things That Float," he gasped, "you took it!"

Storm is picking up," said Zuma.

"Going to be a bad one," agreed Patli.

Tecocoa poked at the fire and said nothing.

It was the sixth hour of the evening, and in the seventh gatehouse on the eastern wall, the three members of the watch struggled to stay awake. As dull a shift as any but the punishment for inattention remained in place—a finger for the first offense, an ear for the second, decortication with a barbed whip for the third. Zuma and Patli were best friends and twenty-year veterans of the Pyramid guard and could be trusted to cover the others' indiscretion. But Tecococa was newly transferred, a taciturn, unsmiling soldier, not the sort to inspire confidence.

The inner door opened to reveal an overdressed buffoon, one of Pyramid's innumerable courtiers, an army larger than the guard itself. "Good fortune to you this evening sirs," he began with a flourishing bow, "may the blessings of the Emperor descend upon you like the rain."

"Evening," said Zuma.

Patli grunted.

Tecococa said nothing.

The fop pulled his robes tight around his chest. The feathers in his headdress were badly dyed and had started to run.

"What business has you leaving the Pyramid so late in the evening?" asked Patli.

"For a cat a mouse, for a soldier a blade, for a poet a rhyme, for a man a woman," said the courtier.

Patli laughed and Zuma smirked.

Tecocoa remained by the fire. He had spent ten years on the Eastern March, along the far borders where the things that were bled into the things that were not. His service had gained him a serpent-tooth macuahuitl, a scar that split his nose in two, and no sense of humor that anyone could detect.

"She must be a fine one," said Zuma, "to bring you out in the rain."

"An Underbridge widow, with gray hair and a thick seat," the courtier explained, "but what she lacks in beauty she makes up for in wealth."

"Wiser than you look," said Zuma. "Beauty fades, but copper can always be buffed."

"Any news of our Emperor?" asked Patli. "They say he's not long for this world."

"Rumor runs faster than a chaparral cock," said the fop. "Our Lord will live for years."

"He could live another fifty. Without an heir to give the Torc to, he only delays the inevitable." Zuma shook his head sadly. "There will be blood in the streets before long."

The fop made a noise that could have meant anything; it was part of the genius of his genus. "In any event. If you would be so kind as to allow me passage—I'd best not keep my matron waiting long."

"Far be it for us to interrupt," laughed Patli, heading to release the latch on the outer gate. "Give her one for—"

But whatever Patli intended to offer this hypothetical widow remained unclear, silenced by a ringing that spread from the top of the Pyramid and reverberated throughout the City. Only once before in living memory had the tocsin been sounded—when Prince Yaotl had fled the court, all the might of the Empire in swift pursuit.

"Strange," said Zuma.

"If you wouldn't mind, masters," the fop continued, trying to brush past.

"You'll have to wait until we get the all-clear," said Patli.

"My mistress has many virtues, but alas, her sense of patience remains—"

"What did you say your name was?"

"Meztli of the House of the Seven Winds," said the fop, bowing once more, "now if you wouldn't mind—"

Zuma pulled down the fop's cheap robes. The golden blaze of the Torc shone beneath them.

"Let me out and I'll give you anything you want," the fop promised. "In three hours the sun will rise and I'll be Lord of All Creation."

"In three hours any man wearing the Torc will be the same," observed Patli, "and you can't split the throne, nor the Pyramid."

"No," agreed Zuma, turning slowly to face his oldest friend, "you can't."

A flash, a stroke, a scream. Patli lay in one corner and Zuma in another. Tecocoa had lost three fangs from his war club. Chunks of pink brain stained the fop's face. He was too frightened to scream.

When Tecocoa left the Pyramid, the rain had turned torrential and the tocsin drummed across the city. He wore the fop's robes over his uniform and his macuahuitl strapped to his back, and he walked swiftly, with no trace of regret. The thing to do now was to move downslope as quickly as possible, walk the streets or find a wine house to wile away the remainder of the evening. Beyond this, Tecocoa thought no further. Twenty years stationed at the edge of reality, where mistaking a shadow for a jaguar might bring the thing to life, had given him no gift for imagination. Tomorrow, when the first rays of the sun struck his Torc and he had become a living God, there would be time for plans—now there was only the task itself. Tecocoa hurried past the shuttered businesses that buttressed the Pyramid, the district abandoned except for a black bird perched atop a parapet. He crossed the Bridge of a Thousand Sighs and turned down the Descent of the Unforgotten, coming to stop in Seven Widows Plaza. It was busier here, with streetwalkers taking shelter beneath the awning of a wine shop and a mad beggar so far gone as to remain indifferent to the storm, talking nonsense to the black bird that nested on a pipe above him.

Tecocoa hurried on, his head a cautious swivel. He had only been in the City a few months, and in that short time had rarely left the Pyramid. After so many years in the wilderness, it was too crowded, too busy, too loud. He got lost in the maze of alleyways spreading out from Seven Widow's Plaza, found himself in the shade of one of the Hundred Bridges, the name of which he didn't know. It didn't matter—all that mattered was to keep moving. This late at night the City was composed of gamblers, whores, petty thieves, drunks, smoke addicts, and vagrants. A black bird hooted at him from the shadow of the unnamed bridge. Tecocoa was staring at it when he heard a voice call out from behind.

Oughtn't have done that," thought Worm, after it had finished with the brain and was creeping out through the ear canal, "not up so high."

But Zyanya didn't answer, attention focused on the glittering bit of metal she had taken off the corpse. Humans were like that, Worm had learned, easily distracted and with the most warped priorities. Worm stretched himself upright from atop the ravaged carrion and wiggled its antennae.

"Oughtn't have—"

"I heard you," Zyanya snapped in voiceless thought-speech. A black bird hooted at her from the underside of the Bridge of Loss and Longing, but she paid it no mind. "Suck up your marrow and keep still."

"Careless," thought Worm, stretching sulkily around Zyanya's wrist and wriggling into her voluminous black robes

Zyanya ran her fingers around the Torc a moment longer. Then she set it carefully around her neck, smiling despite the rain. She slipped backed into the alleyways, leaving the ravaged body behind. She knew the City as she did the whirls of Worm's skin, making a swift series of turns that left her standing atop the Broken Bridge, a jut of stone giving abrupt way to nothing. From the precipice, she watched the rain fall past the foundries and slaughterhouses of Underbridge, towards the shacks and tenements of Moatside. Then she stepped out into air.

An instant of free fall before Worm wrapped a mucosal tendril around a piece of masonry, stretching taught and depositing her a hundred feet below, on a darkened trellis beside the Bridge of Tortoiseshell.

"Metal is not meat," Worm thought.

This was far from the first time that Zyanya had tried to explain money to Worm. A composite of sin and darkness, man-eater, spreader of filth, her strength and her damnation, still Worm was no capitalist. "This is better than metal," Zyanya explained.

Worm hooked itself around a parapet and dropped them down another level. "Better?"

"Better."

"How?"

Five years they had been one, since Zyanya had summoned it from the ether with flattery and prayer, with rotting offal and the fresh flesh of an old man she had lured into a drainpipe. "Special metal. Metal to become Emperor."

"Emperor? Emperor means more meat?"

"All the meat," promised Zyanya.

Worm swelled ripe.

Soon they were deep into the forever shadow of Underbridge. Without a tyrannical sun to dictate schedule, its taverns and dice dens were busy at all hours and swallowed in silhouette, and few bothered to look too hard at what they saw. Amid its eternal gloom Zyanya passed unsmiling Anthracites, mixed-breeds from the borders with extra arms and useless gills, things yet stranger, things without names. The Hole in Keg was a cramped warren of side rooms and closets built into the side of an aqueduct, no different from a dozen others within a few minutes' walk. Zyanya nodded at the heavy who scowled at her from the door, then went to find a dice game. Apart from his brain meat and the golden Torc, she had taken the man's purse, a modest weight of copper with which she would fritter away the hours before sunrise.

The place was packed, the patrons loud, the drums manic. It took Zyanya some time to find an open seat, landing finally at a table where a priest of Jaguar was losing his tithings to a flint merchant and a hulking stevedore up from Moatside.

Zyanya put three stolen coins on the table. The stevedore set one between his teeth, gnawed at it a moment, then nodded. "Game is colors. New arrival picks her hue."

"Indigo," said Zyanya.

The stevedore rattled the dice cup, uncovered it, revealed two crimsons, then passed it on to the Priest.

"Is that ringing ever going to stop?" asked the flint merchant, an Anthracite, short and stubbed, face flat as a river rock.

"Not till they catch whoever stole the Emperor's Torc," said the stevedore.

"May his soul rise swiftly," said the priest, the blessing of less interest than his roll, which came up crimson and obsidian and earned a swift curse.

"Stole the Torc?" asked the Anthracite, his sediment shifting slightly in surprise. "Out of the Pyramid? Past the Four Wardens, past a thousand lords, past the battlements and the guards?"

"The storm is wet, the Tocsin is loud, the evening long," said Zyanya. "Are you going to roll, or are you going to pass?"

"Trouble," thought Worm.

The Anthracite rolled, scowled, then passed his play to Zyanya.

She held the cup for a moment, Worm tugging tightly at her wrist.

"Trouble," it thought again.

"What does it matter who wears the Torc?" Zyanya asked. "The Emperor doesn't care what happens outside of the Pyramid. This Emperor, the next—Underbridge might as well be the far borders."

"Trouble," insisted worm.

Zyanya realized the other three players were staring at her—then that they were, in fact, staring past her.

"It's been a long time."

The thing standing behind her was tall and smelled faintly of sugar. Beyond that there was nothing Zyanya could say about it, its figure lost completely in heavy, ratty robes.

"I don't know you," said Zyanya.

"I wasn't talking to you," said a voice from within the robes.

"Trouble trouble trouble trouble trouble—"

Zyanya launched herself from her chair, Worm turning to a lash, an asp, an arrow, a—.

The host died in an instant but the parasite was halfway across the room and stretching fast for freedom before Shuck struck, skewering the worm against the floor with its poisoned, pointed tail, then depositing the still wriggling body into a glass jar. With one hand Shuck capped the jar and with another hand, it cleaned the host's blood from its curved dagger, and with a third it adjusted its robes. It was as neat a catch as any Shuck had made, which was to say that it was perfect, the entire operation taking place in a few seconds.

In that time the rest of the table and much of the bar had already come to see what was clasped around the dead girl's neck. Shuck put the jar into one of the pockets of its robe and looked up to discover a sea of scowling faces, wide eyes and unsheathed weapons.

"Shit," Shuck said.

Shuck would have left it there on the ground—Shuck would as soon be a slave as Emperor, indeed saw little distinction between the two—but it never had the opportunity. The priest of Jaguar called to its god and launched himself forward, jaws howling, claws ripping out from his hands. Shuck turned aside only to be caught full force by the diving Anthracite, who saw no reason why a foreigner ought not become Lord of Civilization. With one hand Shuck pierced the eye of the howling Anthracite and with another, it held the stevedore at bay, and with another, it tore the Torc from the host's throat. Its tail lashed out at the resurgent priest, a small cut but its poison was swift-acting. In an instant, the devotee was on his way to meeting the deity he had long worshiped.

"She's got it!"

"He's got it!"

"It's got it!"

In an instant the Hole in Keg had turned to a packed scrum of flesh, every patron turned against every other. An off-duty soldier broke a jug over the head of the porter with whom he'd been flirting, a doxy pulled a knife from her stockings and threw herself into the fray, a wine sot looked up from his inebriated daze vomited on himself, then went back to sleep. With three hands holding curved blades and the last clasping the Torc, Shuck cut its way to an open window and dove through the glass, rolling as it struck the stone below, upright in an instant and sprinting onward.

Outside, the rain still fell and the Tocsin still rang and the evening inhabitants of Underbridge went about their shadowy business, as yet unaware of the prize in their midst. A black bird perched on a sign, indifferent to the wet. Shuck lost itself in the labyrinth of side streets, hood pulled tight over its body. Its first thought was to leave the Torc somewhere or toss it into the Moat and let fortune determine who would become Emperor, but conscience, as hard and implacable as Shuck itself, would not allow it. To leave the Torc to any passerby was to give the Torc to at best a fool and at worst a monster, and if Shuck had no desire to be Emperor, neither would it hold itself responsible for gifting the Throne to some random savage. But to hide it forever was to consign the City and all the Realm to war, to turn the Wardens and every minor potentate against each other, an anarchy worse than tyranny.

Shuck had not yet come to a solution—there was no solution at which to arrive—when a shift in the air alerted it to trouble. It whipped its tail out in an instant, and—

Yaotl, the true born son of Cuauhtemotzín, honest heir to the Empire, caught an air current and rose above Underbridge. The rain beat against his feathers, the Torc rested around his throat. He wanted to caw with joy, to perch atop the Pyramid and roar like a morning cock. Three years since he had been forced into exile by the connivings of the Wardens and the jealous paranoia of an old man. Deprived of his birthright, marked as a traitor, a bounty on his head, every hand set against him.

Best to forget all of that, even if he could not forgive. By morning he would be in his rightful place once more. The Wardens would need to be replaced, of course, stripped of their power and broken on the wheel, but beyond that Yaotl hoped the purge would be brief. There was so much to do! It was a hidden blessing that he had been cast out onto the roads, forced to wander the City and the Empire, to see with his own eyes the incompetence and corruption, the waste, the ruin. The state of the roads and the borders, the tax collectors grown fat off the sweat of the people, the nobles indifferent to their suffering and the good of the realm. But all that would change on the morrow, Yaotl thought, his wings grown strangely heavy. Once he was atop the Pyramid he would have the power to right the many wrongs he had seen, to ease the people's suffering. He stopped to rest on the ledge of a building, only then noticing the wound that he had taken, a bare scratch, not enough to cause his sudden weakness, nor the darkness that surrounded him.

You're late," said Tepin, when Ōlli finally came in from his shift.

Tepin was busy preparing a late supper—a maize and squash stew, with a few measly acocils waiting to be shucked, the same thing they had every night, or nearly. Ōlli took a long look at her, as he hadn't for years. A knobby nose below squinting eyes, the graying hair pulled atop her head, a fading bruise on her cheek he'd given her the week before.

She looked up from chopping the squash. "What's wrong with you? You're white as the full moon."

Ōlli didn't answer, taking a seat at the table and offering an appraising look at the apartment as he had his wife. Their marriage bed was dank and faded, their table and two chairs pocked and pitted, the tiny window leering out over a back alley. It was a wretched place to spend a life, he thought, smiling strangely.

"Don't tell me you're drunk again?" Tepin said. "If you're going to be sick, by the Gods you'll use the window or—"

Ōlli's smile turned to a broad laugh. "You should watch how you speak to the Emperor," he said.

Tepin finished dicing the squash and turned to a thick red pepper. "Have you been mixing wine with lamp oil again?"

Ōlli reached slowly into his grimy robes and put the Torc on the table beside Tepin's finely diced squash.

"What's that?" she asked, though the answer was as obvious as the nose on her fat face. "What's that?"

"What do you think it is?"

But he couldn't say it out loud, and neither could she, as if frightened to put the thing into words.

"How did you get it?" Tepin asked.

"I found it in an alley by the Moat."

"By the Moat?"

"Next to a dead bird."

"A dead bird?"

"Are you going to repeat everything I say all night, or are you going to finish dinner?"

"You think people just go around leaving things like that in the mud?"

"Why not? Why not a bit of luck?"

"When does luck come for people like us?"

"And what should I have done? Left it lying there for the next fool to find? You have to grab your chance when it comes," Ōlli snapped, "and I'm as good a man as any."

Tepin looked at her husband for a long moment without answering, then grunted and went back to the food. Ōlli turned his attention to the Torc, dreaming of the morning and the mornings to come. Atop the Pyramid, far from the stink and swell of the Moat, far from everything that he had ever known, everything and everyone. Woken by the touch of a concubine to a breakfast of cocoa and tapir meat, his days spent in revelry and pleasure, every want satisfied, every delight—

Leaving her house, Tepin found the neighborhood in chaos, rain streaming through the streets and puddling into houses, the dykes themselves near to overflowing. The desperate inhabitants of Moatside bailed water out of their barges, and carried possessions to higher floors and picked through their neighbors' flooded goods. From some impossibly distant perch, the Tocsin still blared its pointless alarm but no one paid it any attention, like worrying about a broken small toe while your leg was on fire.

She would make it better soon, Tepin promised herself. When she was Empress she would strengthen the levees and rebuild the aqueducts. There would be no more tax farmers breaking fingers for their tithe, no more copper-pinching money lenders. The merchants on the Bridges and the nobles in the Pyramid would learn what it was to be wet, to be cold, to wake every morning with an ache in their stomachs and go to sleep every evening with that ache unfilled.

But why stop there? If the nobles were brutes and the merchants parasites, were their victims any better? Tepin watched as Ahuic from next door rummaged through the floating stock of Ueman the tailor, who was at this very moment no doubt drunk in some back-alley wine house. Two street urchins squabbled over a cask that had come floating downstream, moving swiftly from fists to knives. Forty-five years Tepin had lived and labored in Moatside, and she had learned with cruel certainty that misfortune did not breed nobility, that suffering leads only to hardness and further suffering. Man was a tyrant to his wife, his wife a despot to her child, and their child cruel to the cat. There were none worthy of salvation, there was no salvation even to be offered. There was only the lash, and which end you found yourself holding.

Tepin hurried through the main square, forgetting the rain, forgetting the chaos the rain had caused, forgetting the rising Moat and the blaring Tocsin, forgetting everything, lost in dreams of a future both bloody and bright—a reverie broken only when she looked up to find herself at the foot of the Warden of the North.

"Give it to me," she said, "and I'll kill you quick." Her thighs were as thick as Tepin's chest, her arms were as long as Tepin's body, her eyes were little pricks of black lost in dense obsidian skin.

"As charming as ever," said the Warden of the South, arriving as if on the wind. The rain froze around her, shattering into pieces as it struck the earth.

"Why lie?" asked the Warden of the North.

"Why say anything?" asked the Warden of the East, slithering from the shadows, his silhouette rising to blot out the night.

The Warden of the East struck the killing blow but it would be the Warden of the North who took the Torc, knocking her serpentine counterpart against a wall and ripping the necklace from the poisoned corpse. The Warden of the South was a scant instant slower, the air cooling from verglas to thin rime to firm ice, locking around the Warden of the North who screamed and dropped the Torc.

The Wardens were the first to arrive but they were followed closely by their entourages, picked bands of soldiers taken from the distant borders, veteran warriors of indisputable courage and as yet unbroken loyalty. They surged against one another, obsidian cracking against obsidian, war clubs breaking, spears piercing flesh. The Moatsiders dispersed in all directions. In a moment, the square had become an abattoir, and the floodwaters ran red.

Amid the tumult a foot soldier from the Eastern March caught a flash of gold in the muck, grabbed it and sprinted for an alleyway—to keep it safe for his master, no doubt, though before he could find refuge, roots burst from the stone pavement, tangled themselves over his ankles and thighs and groin, the soldier screaming then not screaming then dropping the Torc. The roots became the Warden of the West and for an instant he held the Torc in his stoloniferous hands, even allowing himself a smile in the instant before the Warden of the East slammed against him, the two grappling, the Torc scattered once more.

A captain from the Northern Reaches snatched it, took three steps, dodged a spiraling javelin but not the sling stone behind it, the front of his forehead burst like a ripe melon—

—held the Torc but only for a moment, already dying from the wound in his neck though he did not yet realize it—

—her hand severed at the root—

—shattered throat, sinking to her knees, asphyxiating even before she reached the water—

—halfway to the Moat when the knife caught him.

—blood—

—death—

—blood—

꙳

The two struggling along the precipice, one hand holding the Torc, the other trying to hold off the blade which came closer, closer, screaming as it pierced his flesh, falling backward over the barriers and into the moat, the current carrying him away.

꙳

When Izel woke fitfully, just before dawn, the rain had stopped and Nahuatal was down by the river finishing up his morning piss. The drums from the City had finally gone silent, but the pounding in his head made up for it. Last night's wine was as close to poison as Izel had ever drank, and Izel was a man who would drink anything, indeed whose days consisted of little more than finding or stealing or scavenging enough coin to inebriate himself come evening.

He found the empty bottle beside him, cursed himself for his predictable lack of moderation. At least it wouldn't be hard to come by more. A hard rain was a blessing for those who lived along the river, carrying off the City's detritus, tools and pans and spoiled foodstuffs and occasionally other minor treasures.

Nahuatal came back to the campsite with one of these last, a bit of metal covered in swamp mud.

"What's that?" asked Izel.

"Dunno," said Nahutaal, "found it in the reeds."

The two had been kipping together for the better part of five years, brothers in squalor, unhoused scavengers nesting along the river.

"Looks like a necklace," said Izel.

Nahuatal slipped it over his head and smiled. "Suits me nice, don't you think?"

"It's beautiful," Izel said. His hand tightened around the neck of the bottle.

THE KING-KILLING QUEEN

Shawn Speakman

1

High King Alafair Goode lay dying, and Death advanced to finish the work.

It was not upon a battlefield, where a glorious end fighting enemies led to an afterlife of honey-soaked crème cakes, rivers of rubywine, and the warmth of a woman's flesh. It was not at the hands of jealous lovers, which always resulted in the king hale and women disappearing. And it wasn't the result of Serath the Shadow's many assassination attempts. Or the Fall Hunt when the great tusked boar Barak skewered the High King's chest. Or being exposed to the Feverpox that struck down the northern city of Herrick. No, Death did not have a hold on High King Alafair Goode as it did others. After all, a witch magicked the orphan boy during his quest to destroy Mordreadth the Great Darkness and that enchantment held true all his days as foretold. Until the death arrived that none may escape—that of singular old age.

Sylvie Raventress knew all the tales, having been apprenticed to Master Historian Kell for more than twenty winters. But when she entered the King's Tower master suite on the heels of her old mentor and saw the bedridden form of High King Alafair clinging to life upon the room's circular dais, it left Sylvie cold inside.

"Child, be mindful," Kell growled as they walked through the parting sea of onlookers who filled the bedroom, all there to witness the passing of their patriarch. "You stepped on my robe. I nearly tumbled."

"Apologies, Master Kell."

"Remember what I told you, Sylvianna. We are here to aid a man to the Beyond. It does not matter if it is the High King. Or my stepbrother."

It matters a great deal, she wanted to say.

She remained as silent as a mouse, though. She would not embarrass her master in front of the kingdom's royalty.

She was no child and would not be petty like one.

But she knew her history. It was a day for decorum—one that would see the passing of a High King whose exploits had long been legend. Sylvie would have questioned that legend were it not for Master Kell's account of their fight to destroy Mordreadth. Then there were the relics that authenticated the stories too. The sword Lumiere, forged from fallenlight. The ring Verite, a granite truth circle discovered in the crook of a willow tree near the Fae rivers of the Twilight Lands. And Pridwen, a shield hammered into being from a scale of the dragon Shurtuth. Sylvie had seen them all—even touched Verite—and they were as real as the restorative elixirs and terrible poisons she carried in her master's goldfiligreed steel box.

All of that mattered little. The man would die and one of the people in the room would be named heir to the kingdom the High King had carved out of blood and death.

When Master Kell ascended the steps to the bed, Sylvie steeled herself for what was to come. The future of the kingdom depended on this moment. Wielding his gold staff of office, Pontiff Scorus stood behind the High King's head, his crimson vestments failing to conceal his massive paunch. He was there to not only oversee the spiritual needs of High King Alafair's end but also to hear the king's choice of successor. Also standing about the bed were five men and a woman, royal scions like several others in the room but these were considered the High King's favorites. They were as invulnerable to death as Alafair, a strange aftereffect of the witch's curse. They awaited the choice their father would make.

Sylvie looked at High King Alafair Goode. There was no doubt he was dying. Pain lingered in every deep line of his face. Blue eyes that once sparkled with life seemed muted as if leached of color. Even his white beard, which had always appeared as alive as he was, lay limp like wilted moss. Time had caught up with the legend. Lumiere, the High King's fabled sword, lay alongside him.

"My king, my brother," Master Kell said, sitting down on the edge of the bed, his white robe a stark contrast to the High King's royal blue bedspread. He took the other's hand.

High King Alafair squeezed Kell's fingers in return, but Sylvie noted it lacked true strength. "Brother. The day has come, hasn't it?"

Master Kell nodded. "The Mother willing, it will not be today."

"You've never been good at lying."

"You've never been good at anything besides being who you were born to be."

High King Alafair croaked a laugh. "We did great things together."

"You stole the whole world from the Great Darkness and created one kingdom from many," Master Kell said, eyes welling with tears. "Peace. Prosperity. And a world in which your children have no want. You did this. You."

The High King closed his eyes and took a deep, shuddering breath. Sylvie heard the rattle in his throat. She had no siblings, but the love the two brothers shared almost brought tears to her eyes. The day would be difficult for most in attendance, but it would be hardest on her mentor.

"Do you think she will come? At this end of all things?" High King Alafair asked.

Master Kell smiled but it was tinged with sadness. "If she yet lives … perhaps."

Sylvie knew of whom they spoke. They all did. The witch. When young Alafair Goode went on his quest to find Lumiere, a dark agent of Mordreadth wounded him. The witch saved Alafair. Some called her Morgause or Gwyar or Anna, names often given to a powerful woman born centuries earlier. However, separating folklore from history had never been easy, and Master Kell's account of that day stunned Sylvie when she first heard it—a boy given life without injury the rest of his mortal days. No one could know then the magic would pass down to High King Alafair's children, grandchildren, and even those great-grandchildren who now stood waiting in the bedroom.

Sylvie wondered what life would be like if nothing could kill you.

High King Alafair took another deep breath. Pain made him twist to the side. Then he fixed his watery eyes on Sylvie's.

Blue eyes to blue eyes. She couldn't look away.

"Child, are you prepared for this day?"

The way he said it seemed to suggest something other than the obvious. Sylvie nodded. She didn't want to upset her liege. And she certainly didn't want the High King's family or her mentor to think she held any disrespect toward him.

"When you look at me, do you see a perfect High King?" High King Alafair asked. The sincerity of the question caught Sylvie off guard. "Or a flawed man?"

She didn't respond. Not immediately. Master Kell had taught her to treat every question as important, and every answer as a possible trap. "I see a man who is High King, and that man has done right by his kingdom," she said.

The High King snorted. "Are you sure about that?"

"No, High King Alafair," she answered. Sylvie felt all eyes upon her.

The High King chuckled until it became a cough that shook the bed. Once he had recovered, he stared at her. "Honesty. Such a rare trait here among my children and children's children." He paused, his gaze never deviating. "Your eyes, so blue. Like mine. That pleases me a great deal."

Sylvie had no idea why it would. Many people had blue eyes this far north. Rather than reply, she thought it best to simply nod. High King Alafair only had so long left to live, and it shouldn't be spent focused on her.

"My king," Lord Pike Goode said, stepping forward to place a caring hand upon his father's arm. An act of tenderness that would only upset the High King, Sylvie thought. Pike was Alafair's eldest son, a grandfather in his own right, but the two had always had a contentious relationship. "Are you well enough to fulfill your duty this day, Father?"

"No, I am not well enough, you dolt," High King Alafair growled. "I'm dying. Let me do this day my way before the vultures pick my bones."

Lord Pike darkened and stepped back. Lady Erlina looked away, the eldest daughter repressing her amusement at her half-brother's ineffectual attempt at drawing their father's attention. Lords Idlor, Collin, and Yankton remained quiet. Each man was born a different decade, and each hoped to be named High King. Only the youngish Lord Kent seemed to take no interest, intent upon studying his fingernails as if he had better things to do with his day.

Sylvie kept her satisfaction at Pike's discomfort hidden. She hoped to be Master Historian one day, shaping the kingdom's future as a High King's personal counselor, and that meant treading carefully amidst the family.

"Now, since Pike opened his yap, let him be the first," High King Alafair said.

"The first what, Father?" Pike asked.

"To receive the first question," the High King said. Sylvie saw a glimmer of impish life in his eyes. Alafair was enjoying this, she realized, and had a plan beyond just selecting his heir. "Of the Seven Virtues, which would best aid the High King of the kingdom to keep the peace between the Fae and the Winter Trolls?"

Lord Pike cleared his throat, stalling as he searched for an answer. "I believe Morality," he said tremulously. "Yes, Morality. Morality leads to the justice that is clearly needed to keep the two factions from killing one another. Fairness is needed. Balance. Morality gives that."

"And Erlina," High King Alafair continued as if he hadn't even heard his first son. No woman had ever been crowned before. It made her inclusion all the more interesting. "A High King—or in this case, a High Queen—is faced with an invasion from the Isles of Raston. They've been hit hard with winter, are starving, and are in search of the hunt. Which Virtue best serves?"

Having seen how her older brother was caught off guard, Lady Erlina answered with conviction. "Fortitude," she said. "Courage to do the right thing. Fortitude to confront the attack, courage to repel it."

High King Alafair nodded. "And what of you, Idlor. Heated fallen-light falls from the stars, and you as High King have the chance to forge a new weapon or shield from the metal. Which Virtue helps you make that decision?"

"Prudence, Father," Lord Idlor said, eyes hard set. He clearly did not like the questions. Sylvie knew him to be vain, and in his vanity owed the crown. "Prudence is the wisdom of our age. The needs of the kingdom would determine how best the fallen-light should be used and that requires wisdom."

The High King then turned his gaze upon Lords Collin, Yankton, and Kent. They were younger than the others and were rumored to hold great favor with their father. The only one who even spoke to Sylvie was Lord Kent, though she thought he only did so to retain Master Kell's high opinion. She doubted any of them were being truly considered for High King of the kingdom, but she couldn't discount it either.

"Collin. Yankton. Kent. Which of you would make the best High King?" Alafair asked, surprising everyone with the directness of the question.

Lord Collin, known for his quick wit, began, "Becoming High King would be an honor I'd take wi—"

"I would," Lord Yankton said, standing tall.

Lord Collin frowned. "No, it'd be *my* honor."

"It'd be an honor for you, all right," Lord Yankton laughed. "An honor for all of those concubines you keep locked in your bedroom."

Collin and Yankton erupted into a finger-pointing argument. Master Kell shook his head. Lord Kent hadn't answered.

"Father, I protest this," Lord Pike said over the commotion, drawing his father's glare. "If this was to be a test, we should have been made awar—"

"Life is a test. Ruling is a test every moment," High King Alafair said as everyone quieted. "And these are my choices?"

"Temperance," Lord Kent said out of nowhere. All eyes turned to him. No one dared cross the cogitative lord. Even his older siblings kept clear of his machinations. "Extremism is a path a ruler cannot afford to embrace," he said, looking back and forth between Sylvie and his father as if no one else in the room mattered. "Recklessness has destroyed kingdoms. The choice of your successor, Father, must be determined by moderation and tradition. Any choice outside those boundaries could be disastrous for the kingdom and your family."

Sylvie realized then that the king's questions were planned and directed specifically at each family member based on their weaknesses. Lord Pike was known for his unwillingness to compromise. Lady Erlina knew nothing of war. And no amount of wisdom could overcome Lord Idlor's selfish heart. The sons and daughter of High King Alafair had been given serious questions, but Sylvie now realized it had all been a ploy.

As if sensing her thoughts, High King Alafair looked at Sylvie again.

"Can you answer these questions, child?"

Sylvie had spent all her years with Master Kell in study. Whether it be history, philosophy, anatomy, or the chem of elixirs and poisons, her training had been rigorous, especially with word games. The High King had phrased this question with purpose too.

"Not answers, Your Highness. Answer," Sylvie said.

"Go on."

She stared at the royal blue bedding as she spoke. She didn't want the king's children to think she was rising above her station, or that she was making them look like fools. "A ruler requires all of the Virtues," Sylvie said. "To make a decision based on only one is folly. Therefore, each of your questions has the same answer. All the Virtues."

Sylvie thought High King Alafair would respond to her answer. Instead, he lifted a weak finger toward his stepbrother.

"Will you aid me in my final burden, Kell?"

"You know I will, my brother. Then I will give you the Last Shade."

Master Kell said, motioning toward the pontiff. He stood once more and raised his voice. "High King Alafair Goode shall plant the future in this present with the help of Pontiff Scorus, for all of us in this room and for everyone who lives in this mighty kingdom we have sworn to protect."

At that, Pontiff Scorus summoned his assistant from the crowd below.

A boy of no more than ten winters, flanked by two knights, hurried up the stairs holding a large black leather tome clasped and hinged with the same fallen-light metal that forged Lumiere. There, within the pages of the Covenant Codex of St. Emmer, High King Alafair Goode would write the name of his successor, renewing the peace between Fae and Man with a stroke of pen and ink, the Naming such potent magic that even the Fae would know the chosen successor.

The boy knelt before Pontiff Scorus, and the Leader of the Citadel took the tome in his plump-fingered hands. The boy returned to his place with the hundreds of observers below while the Knights remained. Pontiff Scorus turned toward the High King, and Alafair tried to push himself up into a sitting position. Sylvie was about to help him, but Kell shoved a pillow behind the High King's back. Alafair took a deep breath and placed his hand on Lumiere, the magnificent sword lying lengthwise along his right leg.

"High King Alafair Goode, He Who Wields The Light of Lumiere, the Final Bane of Mordreadth," Pontiff Scorus said, his voice echoing about the chamber. The man loved attention. "We are here to witness the Naming. By which Man once again renews his oath of peace with the Fae. And the Fae again consent to the terms of the original compact of so long ago." He gently put the book on the High King's lap, and then returned to stand just behind the king.

"My children," High King Alafair began, picking up the book of peace with hands that had killed thousands of his enemies. The irony was not lost on Sylvie. "Each of you represents a different aspect of me. My strengths. My weaknesses. The hopes and dreams of a dying father. Each of you has a role to play when I am gone, which I hope will preserve what we've worked so hard to build. The kingdom needs you. Remember this if you falter from the path I have decided." He drew in a steadying breath as if he were going to war one last time. "It is time for the Naming."

Pontiff Scorus stepped to the High King's side, offering a quill while holding an inkwell. Alafair opened the book and turned the pages to the one he wanted. Sylvie was curious who the High King would select, but not for the same reason as the others. One day, when Kell joined his brother in the Beyond, she hoped to become Master Historian to the new High King. This day would tell her who that man would be.

She and the others watched High King Alafair draw another deep breath, steady his hand, and press his quill to the paper.

And magic filled the room.

"By my own hand, with quill and ink to mark the Covenant Codex of St. Emmer, I Name my heir." High King Alafair scribbled into the book, his breath labored. A hush hung over the room. The king's children around the bed tried to see what he wrote but the High King clutched the book so close that Sylvie doubted anyone other than Pontiff Scorus could view it. When the High King lifted his quill free from the page, the Citadel leader gaped at Sylvie. Alafair sank back into his pillows, the book falling to his lap with the pen in its inner hinge. Magic lingered in the air about them, renewing the compact between Fae and Man, and raising the hair on Sylvie's arms.

"It is done," High King Alafair Goode whispered.

Then he closed his eyes, his breath shallow, his skin pasty white. Kell took the gold-filigreed box from Sylvie, opened it, and began mixing two vials, Pontiff Scorus withdrew the Covenant Codex of St. Emmer from the High King's lap. He stared at the open page. Then he closed the tome and clutched it to his chest.

"Read the name," Lord Pike snarled.

Pontiff Scorus took a steadying breath. "High King Alafair Goode, slayer of Mordreadth the Great Darkness, wielder of Lumiere and strength of the kingdom has chosen his successor," the robed man said. "The newest name inscribed in the Covenant Codex of St. Emmer is legible and clear. On this day and all of those henceforth, the Light from the Heavens Above illuminates those below in our blessed kingdom."

"Out with it, Scorus!" Lady Erlina hissed.

"High King Alafair Goode has selected Sylvianna Goode," Pontiff Scorus muttered. "The first of her name and the first High Queen of the kingdom. As ordained by the compact between St. Emmer and Wise Belloch, the heir has been Named before the careful regard of the Citadel, the Ecclesia, and the Masters."

Sylvie couldn't believe her ears. The hundreds of scions whispered among one another, their murmured voices growing to curses and shouting. All the while, Alafair breathed upon his bed, eyes closed, as if worries could no longer touch him.

Sylvie looked to Master Kell, but even he was not looking at her. He continued to mix the concoction that would aid his brother to the Beyond with neither pain nor awareness.

Like Kell had known all along.

"That cannot be!" Lord Pike shouted, bringing Sylvie back to the moment.

"This is outrageous, Father!" Lord Idlor roared and stepped down from the dais to storm from the room.

"She isn't of your blood!" Lady Erlina spat.

High King Alafair did not open his eyes. "Kell, the dagger," he said.

Master Kell drew his weapon from the folds of his white robe. "Come sit, Sylvianna," he said, patting the bed. "For all to see and witness."

Master Kell moved aside, and Sylvie sat. Dagger in hand, High King Alafair opened his eyes and looked at her. She regarded Kell behind her—and suddenly felt like she had been punched in the chest by a giant.

She looked down and saw the hilt of the dagger jutting from her chest.

"Pull it out, Sylvie," Kell said.

Sylvie gulped. With a shaking hand, she gripped the knife's handle and pulled the blood-slick blade from her body. As she withdrew it, power swept through her. It was magic, she realized. She couldn't pinpoint its source, but it was potent and ancient, a warmth she sensed connected to the world as it thrummed in the wound. Barely any blood stained her robe. She felt the magic mend bone, muscle, and skin back together until the wound closed. Then the unknown power left her like nothing had happened.

"Am I … your daughter?" Sylvie asked, still trying to grasp it all.

"Remember what Father did with Mikkel," Lord Pike growled to his siblings before the High King could answer, his face red with anger. "Father chose a boy to become his heir apparent with full command of the Ecclesia Knights. Mikkel had to be stripped of his titles and imprisoned when he rebelled against the kingdom. He wasn't ready. This girl isn't ready. It's the same thing!"

"None of you are as prepared as Sylvianna," High King Alafair rasped. "Either *you* aren't ready or *she* is."

Lord Pike snorted. "How do you know she is *ready*, Father?"

"She is my choice, and you will abide by it," the High King said.

"No. Many of your subjects will not simply abide by it."

"It will be up to Sylvianna to set them right, then." Kell placed a vial to the king's lips. The High King drank from it and grimaced. "Farewell, Sylvianna. I wish I knew you as my brother knows you. My dreams are with you. And farewell Kell, my first friend and brother. I will miss you."

"I will miss you too, my brother," Kell said, clutching the king's hand again. Even though a mortal potion like Last Shade could not kill the High King, it would free him of pain until his natural death arrived.

Long minutes passed. Sylvie reached out and placed her hand on Kell's, hoping to give her mentor some solace. Alafair's breathing was so light it was impossible to know if he yet lived. Then he gasped several breaths and finally lay completely still.

Master Kell checked his brother's pulse, and then announced, "The High King is dead." Tears streamed down his weathered cheeks. Sylvie removed her hand even as Kell placed his stepbrother's lifeless hand on Lumiere's hilt. Then the Master Historian knelt before Sylvie, head bowed out of respect she had not yet earned.

Dozens of the other Goode scions took a knee as well, save for a few who took their leave of the room instead.

Of those around the bed, only Lords Pike and Idlor did not kneel.

"The High King is dead. Long live the High Queen," Kell said, his voice ringing throughout the room, all eyes on her.

Sylvie stood, unsure what to do.

But with stunning clarity that frightened even her, she realized just how much danger she was in.

2

The witch was real then," Sylvie mused, falling into her plush chair in the quarters she shared with Master Kell. She still couldn't quite grasp what Alafair—her father—had done and what it all meant for her past, her present, and her future.

After Alafair passed into the Beyond, Pontiff Scorus led a prayer, and once concluded, the bedroom emptied of everyone except a few. Kell and Sylvie waited in silence as the pontiff led the two attending Ecclesia Knights in wrapping the body in a white, myrrh-scented shroud. Together, they left the bedroom and the King's Tower to walk Alafair's body to the Citadel, where his remains would be cleansed and prepared for his funeral at sea. Afterward, Sylvie and the Master Historian walked the High Gardens under the stars. He informed her a Knight of the Ecclesia secretly warded them from the shadows, a bodyguard for the new High Queen to be. She did not mind. Sylvie knew she needed protection. As the two strolled through the night, he answered as many questions as he could until they eventually arrived at the Masters Tower where routine and home helped calm her anxiety.

The memory of steel buried in her chest still lingered. Sylvie marveled she suffered no ill effects even as she considered the day's events.

"You doubted?" Kell said with a short laugh as he lit candles to chase back the room's gloom. "That's not like you. I witnessed it with my own eyes. Felt the magic, saw my brother's wound close. Alafair would have died an uncrowned orphan of a royal family, and the world would have followed in that death if not for the witch."

"Apologies, Master Kell. I did not doubt," Sylvie said. She needed to talk it out to make sense of it all. "I know the witch was real. I meant more about the magic that kept Alafair alive for so long. Does it mean I'm invulnerable too? And more importantly, did the witch know what she was doing? If so, why did she make the Goode bloodline long-lived? What purpose would that serve once Mordreadth was destroyed?"

"All questions that have plagued my life, Sylvianna," Kell said, also taking a seat. The hearth burned bright, warming the night's chill from them.

"And beyond that," Sylvie said, "I thought I was an orphan. How is this possible?"

"Well, you *were* an orphan," Kell said, shrugging. "Not unlike Alafair. When he discovered his parentage, he wanted nothing to do with any of it. Save the world? Why him? He rebelled as I think anyone would, given the circumstances. He eventually came to terms with it. You will too, my dear."

"Did you know? About me, I mean?"

"Did I know that your sire was my stepbrother?" Kell asked. "No, although I have always suspected. Alafair was a good man, but he did welcome a great many women to his bed after the queen died." He paused, considering her. "I believe your mother was a baker in the kitchens. Lovely jet-black hair, just like your own."

"I'm sad I didn't know her," Sylvie said. "What happened to her?"

"I was told she died in childbirth," Kell said, drawing his pipe from the pocket of his robe and scraping it free of ash. "You were brought to me as a newborn. I never married. Too busy keeping the kingdom together after the destruction of Mordreadth and the chaos that followed."

"I was lucky then."

Master Kell shrugged. "I like to think we were a good match."

"In a way, you are my uncle. Though not by blood."

"No, not by blood," Kell said. "But some bonds are stronger than blood."

Sylvie nodded. It was something he had said often, especially when she was a child. She had always looked up to Kell like a father. He was a man capable of great life lessons and stern but fair love. They had fought. They had laughed. She had received an education rivaling that of even the wealthiest merchant princes. Most children were not so lucky.

"What about this witch's magic. This curse … if that's what it should be called," Sylvie said, letting the fire and his voice relax her. "Am I unkillable like … like my father was?"

Kell tamped smoke-weed into his cleaned pipe. "We could test it if you wish it."

"But I might not like the consequences."

The old man grinned. "You might not. Magic is fickle that way. Few witches can be trusted. Worse, at this very hour, though it be late, some of your father's children are testing whether they are immune to death like he was. It is going to be a bloody few days."

Sylvie frowned. "What do you mean?"

"Well, how does one examine such a thing?" Kell asked.

"I suppose sticking a knife into someone's chest might do it," Sylvie said with a grin. When he didn't respond, she continued. "And since one cannot exactly do that to themselves …"

"Correct," he said. "I don't know this for sure, but I could easily see someone like Lord Idlor finding a lowborn son of Alafair's loins."

"And if magic no longer protects the family, that child will die," she said, horrified.

"Sad but true."

"I will do no such test," Sylvie said.

"Nor can we stop the others from trying. We cannot protect so many against the ill will of the few."

"Well, what happens next? I know I will be crowned by Pontiff Scorus the morning after my father's farewell. But when will the funeral pyre be lit? Tomorrow? The day after? There is little information about all of this."

"The Covenant Codex of St. Emmer is quite clear on the coronation and quite vague about the funeral," Kell said, placing a kettle over the fire to prepare his nighttime tea. "The coronation is to happen the day after the funeral, true. But grace has been given when it comes to the sea pyre. It merely needs to happen within a month." He paused, rubbing his beard as if expecting the answers to fall out. "I do not want my brother rotting that long, to be fair. He deserves better. I imagine preparations for the funeral will be two, maybe three days at most. The kingdom needs its High Queen. But it is largely out of my control. Pontiff Scorus will oversee the bulk of duties now. My brother has fulfilled all of his own."

"Did you know what Alafair had planned for me?" Sylvie asked.

"I wouldn't be much of a brother or counselor if he hadn't confided in me," Kell said. "Yet the final decision was his alone."

"There were other candidates?"

Kell nodded. "Though none as bright as you."

Before Sylvie could ask more, she heard a knock at the room's window.

"Ahh. I've been waiting for this," Kell said.

Curious, Sylvie watched her mentor open the window to the night. From the darkness, two tiny bodies flew into the room, circling it with dizzying speed. She sunk deeper into her chair. Finally, the two creatures settled delicately near a plate with a honey crumble cake upon it, gossamer wings flexing rainbow hues even in the candle and firelight.

Sprites. Fae from the Twilight Lands—one an old, white-bearded man with wispy hair on his head, the other much younger, beardless, and broad-shouldered. Both appeared to be made from bits and pieces of the forest, their skin like bark and their clothing woven from moss and leaves.

"Well met, Grumtil and friend, of course," Kell said, giving a short bow to their tiny visitors. "Pleased you could join us despite the sorrow of the day."

"Good evening, Master Kell the Historian," the older sprite said, tugging at a beard so long Sylvie wondered how it didn't hinder his flight. "It is indeed a sad day, but also one of hope."

Sylvie had never seen one of the Fae. Perhaps her mentor kept stranger secrets than she could have guessed. She remained quiet, observing, and listening.

"Yes, I have hope as well," Kell agreed, glancing at Sylvie before returning his attention to Grumtil. "And who accompanies you this evening? Your replacement?"

"I like to think no one can replace me," Grumtil sniffed.

"True, what was I thinking?" Kell said, grinning.

"You have always enjoyed antagonizing me. Like your brother. If you weren't so ugly, I would teach you manners." The old sprite crossed his arms over his beard. "I am sorry that the most important aspects of Alafair are no longer with us." He lowered his head, and a tear ran down his dark brown cheek. "He was my friend."

"You shared a bond. You were close. I think a refreshment is in order, if you are interested?"

"We are. The journey was long," Grumtil said. Master Kell went to the dresser and took a sewing kit from a drawer, withdrawing two wooden thimbles that he washed and then dipped into his tea. He added a sprinkle of sugar to each. The two sprites accepted them with nods and sipped the hot liquid. "Kell, the journey was made more exhausting by the Court. The Elders care more about the drama of the succession, not what it means for the compact. They are apparently not worried about these swamp vipers Alafair called children. I am not so sure." He paused, considering Sylvie for the first time. "The Fae's obligation to the Covenant Codex is realized, though. Sizmor here was chosen. And while young, he serves with wisdom."

"Ahh, the Court of Elders," Kell said, shaking his head. "They do not see how tenuous the compact is at all times. Nothing lasts forever and, if we let it, all that Alafair fought for could be undone. Even destroyed."

"So," Grumtil said, waving a tiny hand at Sylvie. "Your little apprentice has grown into a young woman. And she is the heir? Amazing."

"Please don't speak of me like I am not here, Master Kell," Sylvie said finally.

"Apologies, Sylvianna," her mentor said as he sat back down in his chair, teacup in hand. "May I introduce Grumtil Hodgemurkin. He is a Fae from the Twilight Lands and a member of the Shadow Court who ensures the compact by St. Emmer of Man and Wise Belloch of Fae is maintained. They guard it, even as we do our best to uphold it here." He sipped his tea. "Grumtil was Fae advisor to the crown. He knew my brother better than anyone. Except me, of course."

"Grumtil lived here?" Sylvie asked, surprised. "I never saw him. And no one has mentioned him."

"My Lady," the old sprite said, bowing.

And then he vanished.

Before Sylvie could say a word, the sprite returned. A wry grin twisted

Grumtil's face. "The Fae have many abilities Man cannot fathom. We are among you without your knowledge. Though the Covenant Codex of St. Emmer does not allow my brethren to interfere in your affairs."

Sylvie leaned forward in her chair. "But you helped the High King? Does that not constitute interference?"

"It is the only relationship between Fae and Man the Covenant Codex allows," Grumtil said. "I served faithfully all of the years of High King Alafair Goode's rule."

"I did not know him," she said, shrugging. "At least not that way."

"He was a good man. Prone to women and other vices. But good, nevertheless."

"Yes," Sylvie said.

"You have many brothers and sisters," Grumtil continued, stroking his beard. "Brothers and sisters who would see you removed from ruling before you even begin."

"And therein lies my worry," Kell said, eyeing her.

Sylvie remembered the dagger-like stares she received from those in the bedroom accompanied by their muttered curses. "Who are you most worried about? Pike? Idlor?"

"Pike is one, though he lacks the spine required to do much more than whine," Kell said, waving that idea aside. "Idlor could be dangerous. He is friends with Pontiff Scorus too, which creates an unequal power balance within the kingdom. Scorus controls the coronation. That worries me. But honestly, there are too many threats to count. And some are smart enough to keep their interest in the throne secret until they make their move."

"Like?" she asked.

Kell shrugged. "Lord Kent, for one. He has always been a man possessed of keen intellect and quiet ambition. That's why it is so important for you to have eyes and ears in places you otherwise would not have access to. Sizmor will aid you during your transition, even as I will help too."

"Sylvianna Goode," the younger sprite said, inclining his head slightly. "I am Sizmor Darkinmoor."

Sylvie looked at Sizmor. "You are to be my Grumtil," she said. "Once I'm High Queen of the kingdom. I have questions about that. But first, how did you know to come here? The High King only just passed into the Beyond. How did this Shadow Court convene and send you here so quickly?"

Kell stared into the fire, cup held before him but forgotten for the moment. "There are aspects to it that few know. As Master Historian, I am one of them. The Shadow Court is another. You will know these secrets now too, Sylvie. The moment my brother signed your name into the Covenant Codex of St. Emmer a matching signature appeared in the Covenant Codex of Wise Belloch."

"Wait, there are two books?" she asked.

"There are," Grumptil said. "Connected by a magic far older than most in the world. One book here with Man, one book in the Twilight Lands with the Fae. In this way, the compact is maintained. When a change occurs in one book, it affects the other. Equal knowledge between equal partners."

"I see," Sylvie said. She looked at the younger sprite. "How do you feel about all of this, Sizmor?"

The younger sprite puffed out his chest. "I was chosen to assist you on behalf of the Fae once you have been crowned High Queen of the kingdom. It will be an honor to do so."

Sylvie knew little about ruling, only what she had read in history and philosophy books. While they walked back to Kell's quarters, she wondered if she even wanted to be High Queen. Could she refuse the succession? How firm was the Covenant Codex of St. Emmer once her name was written there? The weight of responsibility would crush her if she were not prepared.

"Master Kell, this is all quite overwhelming," Sylvie admitted.

"I know it is, child," her mentor said, leaning forward and patting her knee. "I remember when Alafair discovered the truth of his parentage. It was daunting, to say the least. But I promise you this: I will prepare you for the coronation and be there while you rule. You also have Sizmor as a confidante, a spy, and wise counsel when you have need. The other Masters will aid you as they deem fit. Even Grumtil will be here, at least until my brother is put to rest."

"But I know nothing about how to rule, Master," Sylvie said. "Are you not worried that my father made this decision in error?"

Grumptil replied, "The questions you are asking yourself are natural."

"I agree with Grumtil," Kell said, looking deep into her eyes. "I will add this. High King Alafair Goode knew people. He could read them. I know you as I knew him. You have the same ability he had. You are learned. Strong. Capable. My brother's choice was wise."

Growing up, Kell's insights had always soothed her. They did so here, though she still worried.

"Relax tonight," Kell added. "Spend some time with that squire who is so fond of you. I will entertain Grumtil and Sizmor. Return here tomorrow morning and we will help you realize what the rest of us see."

Sylvie nodded. "Thank you, Master. You've always been there for me. I appreciate it more than you can know."

He nodded, smiled, and took another sip of his tea.

With Kell by her side in the days to come, Sylvie knew she could overcome the hardships that would challenge her in the days to come.

♔

Sylvie awoke to the touch of fingertips on her naked back.

"Good morn, Love," Darian whispered in her ear.

Languishing in the warmth of his body next to hers, she drew a deep breath, content, even as a kiss graced her shoulder with a feathery touch. She smiled, opening her eyes. Sunlight entered the squire's small room through a slit in the wall, motes of dust swirling in the air. Most of the blankets were piled on the floor next to the narrow bed. Only a sheet remained, twined about her legs, hiding little of her nakedness. She loved the feeling. They had slept little but regretted nothing. She kissed his lips. He returned it, firm but gentle. She liked his lips, his chin, his strength. But her love for him went beyond the physical even if that's how it started. With his quick smile and wicked humor, Darian offered a contrast to Kell's serious studies. It's why she continued to see the squire when she otherwise would have grown bored.

She hadn't told him about the High King. When she arrived at his door late in the night, she pushed her way into his room and delivered a passionate kiss on his lips. He had wrapped his arms about her and shut the door. Sylvie had wasted no time. She pressed him to the bed and then disrobed, removing all pretense about why she was there.

Their pleasure had been hot and furious to start, but the second and third rounds they had taken their time, enjoying one another's touch in more intimate ways.

She rolled onto her back, to view his handsome face above her. Sunlight played across his blonde-red stubble. He smiled, green eyes kind.

In his hand, a cup.

"You went out this morning and got my favorite drink?" she asked, surprised she hadn't heard him leave.

Darian smiled, giving her the cup. "You deserve it. What got into you last night?"

"You did," she said, sitting up and taking a sip, enjoying the sweet juice. "Several times, as I recall."

He laughed. She loved the sound.

"That's not exactly what I meant, Sylvie," he said. "You were like a crazed highland cat when you knocked on my door."

"This cat may need more attention," she said, reaching down between his legs. When his manhood didn't respond, she let him go. "I thought a knight favored as many jousts as possible when a tournament came around?"

"Who would have thought I'd rather talk than fuck." Darian disentangled from both her legs and the sheet, and sat on the edge of the bed, naked. Then he stood and relieved himself in the chamber pot in the corner of the room. Sylvie sat up, covering her breasts with the sheet and stared at his body.

"If you would rather talk," she said, "then you know what occurred yesterday."

"High King Alafair died," Darian said over his shoulder, his urine hitting the bottom of the pot with tinkling splashes.

"Never underestimate the power of news spreading," Sylvie said, shaking her head. "I should have known Sir Gwain would tell you.

"He didn't tell me," Darian said, pulling on breeches and shirt.

"Then who?"

Darian grabbed her white robe and handed it to her. "Lord Idlor."

Sylvie shrank inward. Her future came crashing down on her again. She swung her legs off the bed and dressed herself, feeling the comfortable white robe fall upon her shoulders and, with it, some semblance of her own authority returned.

"What did Lord Idlor want?" she asked. "Did he come here? Or find you in the training yard?"

Darian took a deep breath. "He came here."

"Why? It wasn't to share news of the High King's death, I bet."

"Sylvie, I didn't want to be put in this position. Know that, my love," Darian said. He went to her, his calloused hands gently taking her own. "He came to me with a proposition."

"And?" she asked, feeling her jaw tighten.

"Surely, you don't want to be High Queen of the kingdom, do you?" Darian asked, their previous playfulness gone. "I mean, yes, he mentioned you were named Alafair's heir. That it was proven you were his child. It has … upset a lot of people." He paused and squeezed her hands. "And if I am to be fully honest, I'm one of the upset."

"It sounds like Lord Idlor came here with one purpose," Sylvie said, removing her hands from Darian.

"You didn't answer my question," Darian said. "Do you want to be High Queen of the kingdom?"

"I'm not sure what I want."

Darian paced across the small room. He turned and glared at her. "You just came here for one last fuck, is that it?"

Darian's barb missed its mark. Sylvie just shrugged. "You think I should give up the throne, don't you?" she asked. "For a prize that Idlor dangled in front of you. One you would use against my heart to help Idlor play his little game."

"I think you need to at least entertain the idea," Darian said, hands on hips. "There are other ways to lead a comfortable life aside from ruling the kingdom. Plus, if you were queen, Pontiff Scorus would never let me be with you. You'd have to marry a prince or something."

"You mentioned other ways," Sylvie said. "What did you mean by that? What did Idlor promise?"

"Sylvie, I love you. I want to marry you and have children with you. Lord Idlor is prepared to offer a large swath of his personal estate to create a new lordship, one we could govern together and leave to our children one day, title and lands both."

She took a deep breath. "If I abdicate the throne."

Darian nodded.

"And you'd be knighted as well?"

"I would. Sir Gwain has said I am ready to take the trials. I think I am too. The knighthood is a formality, though I would welcome it. Most knights are not given lands like Lord Idlor is offering."

Sylvie thought on it. It was a princely offer. Not only would they receive lands and titles but servants and workers. But whether Darian realized it or not, Lord Idlor had struck against her. If she had been younger, she would have stormed from the room. Instead, she cooled as Kell had taught her.

"What do you think?" Darian asked.

"I think I should be the one deciding the direction of my life."

"Wait, Sylvie, I didn't mean—"

"No, you just decided to do Lord Idlor's bidding."

Darian frowned. "For us. For our future!"

"No. For you," she spat.

"I think you really shou—"

"No one tells me what I *should* do, Darian. I have enough to think about without adding you to the mix. I'm leaving."

As she stormed toward the door, Darian stepped in front of her and grabbed the handle before she reached it. "I was worried I wouldn't do this right," he said, opening the door.

Standing outside in the hallway, Lord Idlor, dressed in the finest clothing the kingdom offered, stood glaring at her. Sylvie saw the morning clearly. When Darian left to retrieve her favorite morning drink, he had found the time to bring Lord Idlor to his chamber to ambush her. It left her even more furious.

Before Sylvie could utter a word, Idlor Goode pushed past her into the room and Darian closed the door behind him.

Trapping her.

"Sylvianna Raventress," he said with a smile.

It took her a moment to realize that Idlor used her orphan surname as opposed to their shared one. That Idlor knew about Darian meant he either had spies in Mont Saint-Michel or her lover told him.

She remembered a quote from St. Emmer then, one he had made while trying to form the compact with the Fae: *The supreme art of war is to subdue the enemy without fighting.*

"Lord Idlor," Sylvie replied, trying to maintain the decorum that Master Kell had taught her. "This is an unexpected visit."

"But a necessary one," Idlor said. He found the room's one chair and took a seat, leaving Darian and Sylvie standing. Apparently, he did not intend to kill her. "Yesterday saw the passing of the greatest king the world has known. It also has demonstrated a need for family to come together. The kingdom needs us. We cannot be divided. We cannot show weakness now. Or ever. There are forces that would see the kingdom undone. Strong leadership is required." He paused. "And that is why I am here now."

"Darian has told me your offer," Sylvie began. She knew men like Idlor. The expensive clothing. The perfectly trimmed pepper beard. Even his teeth gleamed. "It is a generous proposition. It speaks to how powerful you are as a man and as a son of High King Alafair Goode."

"I welcome you to consider it," Idlor said, leaning forward. Being so close to him made her almost nauseous. "I do not want to see the kingdom that our father built ripped apart. I will do everything in my power to prevent that from happening."

"A noble conviction," Sylvie said. "I will say this, though. Master Kell taught me well. The first lesson he ever taught me was how an offer always hides what the offeror wants."

"I see where you lead," her half-brother said, his grin deepening the beginnings of crow's feet at his eyes. "You think I make my offer for personal gain."

"Becoming High King of the kingdom would be gain, yes."

"There is no guarantee that Pontiff Scorus would crown me," Idlor said, waving her accusation aside. "Our father had many children, evidently more than we knew of."

"Just so long as it isn't me, I take it." Sylvie bore her gaze into his. "I think you consider me weak because I am a woman. Or because you consider me low born. Or any number of other reasons." She paused. "Do not consider me weak. That would be a grave error."

His smile vanished. "Quite the contrary, I understand why Father chose you. I find you talented and capable. There is a reason you were permitted to stay with Kell when so many of us warned him and Father against creating another Mikkel." He stopped and glanced from Darian to her again. "Nevertheless, a woman lacks the fortitude of kingly leadership. There are times when a king's heart must be stone. And, as a woman, you lack that."

"Was Mikkel a woman?" Sylvie asked, moving the conversation where she wanted it to go. "The stories I've heard said he was quite the fearsome man. Like you."

Lord Idlor's gaze narrowed. "Mikkel was mad for power. When Father had him silenced—even though it hurt him to do it—it was in service to the kingdom and its future."

"Master Kell shared details about Mikkel during my history lessons," she said. "A boy of extraordinary intellect and strength of mind. He became his father's First Knight, commanding a position reserved for the most chivalrous. But Mikkel wanted to carve out a life of his own. The conflict resulted in the only rebellion attempted against High King Alafair Goode, one orchestrated by his own son." She paused. "How are you different from Mikkel? Father made me heir to the crown. It was his wish. It seems like you are doing the same as our half-brother, just quieter and with a bit more nuance."

"I only want to rule as father did," Idlor replied. He took a deep breath and shook his head. "I cannot simply take the crown from you. There were too many people in Father's bedroom when he announced you and they have already spread the news far and wide. A woman is too much of an unknown for the Knights of the Ecclesia and the Masters. For the Church with its male priests, male bishops, and male pontiff. Even for the common folk, who will see you as weak just because you bleed every four weeks. I will admit you have a tough mind, like Father. But it won't be enough. Let's stop being coy. Abdicate the throne. I do not care what you tell Pontiff Scorus and the family. Swear to me that you will do so."

She looked at Darian. "I must go. I've outstayed my welcome here."

"Let me make this more plain," Idlor said, also standing. "Abdicate the throne or I will discredit you. Time is of the essence. Tomorrow night, our father's funeral pyre will be lit. The new ruler will be crowned the following morning. Preparations must be made with Pontiff Scorus for you to relinquish the crown." He paused, steely eyes burrowing into her. "I suggest you consider the trajectory of your life."

"Threats are the actions of a desperate man," she said.

Lord Idlor stepped aside as she walked toward the door.

"Sylvie! Wait!" Darian yelled, reaching out for her. She ignored him.

In moments, she exited the building into brilliant sunshine.

"What you did to that boy, riding him like a horse, was … repulsive," a voice at her ear whispered.

She almost yelped. Sizmor hovered over her shoulder, invisible to anyone looking her way. Sylvie took a calming breath. "*That's* what you were worried about? The sex? Not the attempt to steal the crown?"

"Well, that too, of course," Sizmor said. "I still feel ill though."

"Oh yeah? Well, how do the Fae have sex?"

"I do not think a human can understand," the sprite said as they passed a group of children playing in Mont Saint-Michel's grassy inner courtyard. "Let's just say it involves more play—days of it, sometimes— and less grunting and panting and sweating."

Sylvie laughed. "Master Kell and Grumtil said you are to be my counselor when I need it," she said. "What am I going to do about Lord Idlor? He is a powerful man who knows other powerful men. In other words, he is dangerous."

"Grumtil shared a great deal about the kingdom and its politics. Idlor did command Grumtil's respect. Still, the lord endangers the compact. That cannot be allowed."

"Is there even a way for me to refuse the crown," Sylvie asked as she made her way into the High Garden. Privacy, shade, and blooming flowers in an array of colors always helped her find peace. She went to her favorite bench and sat. "Some way to erase my name in the codex?"

"That, I do not know. The magic of the compact between Fae and Man is complex. Perhaps the Elders of the Shadow Court would know. Or Master Historian Kell."

Sylvie sighed. "It feels wrong to betray my father's wishes."

"If that is your choice," Sizmor said, "then accept it. Life is short for humans and regrets are plentiful, from what Grumtil tells me."

"Speaking of Grumtil, where is he? Is he flying beside my other ear?"

"He is paying his final respects to High King Alafair Goode."

Sylvie wondered if her father had been close friends with the sprite. If so, the little Fae might have some insight. "I would like Grumtil's advice about this, yes," she said. "He saw much as an advisor to my father. He likely knows Idlor better than anyone."

"I think that would please High King Alafair," Sizmor said. "However, Grumtil flies back to the Twilight Lands upon the winds of the funeral pyre. He will never return here. There can never be more than two Fae present once a coronation is completed, so says the compact."

Sylvie nodded and closed her eyes, enjoying the sun on her face. Birds sang in the High Garden's willows, and children ran about laughing and screeching. They paid her no mind—they didn't even know who she was. She knew all of that would change soon.

"You have gone quiet," Sizmor said finally. "Is there anything more you require?"

"I think I am recovered from Lord Idlor," she said, shaking her head.

"What of your boy?"

Sylvie hadn't spent much time thinking about Darian since she'd run out of his bedroom. "I know what I must do. But I have larger worries right now," she said. "I need Master Kell's knowledge. He knows more about the Covenant Codex of St. Emmer than anyone else in the kingdom. He also knows Idlor and will know how to counter what he's trying to do."

"Does this mean you wish to be High Queen of the kingdom?"

"I do wish it," she said, not realizing the truth until the words had escaped her mouth. "Yes. I do. It is my duty. I will honor my father's wishes."

Sylvie got to her feet and began walking back toward the Masters Tower. She had chosen. Now she needed Kell's help in dealing with Idlor. She climbed the steps two at a time, feeling the thrill of hope. She reached her quarters and was about to unlock the door when movement at the end of the corridor caught her eye.

She froze, uncertain. Outside the window, a shadow blocked the sunlight and then vanished.

"Who was that?" Sizmor asked at her ear.

"I don't know," Sylvie said. "But it is quite normal here. When I was younger, I moved about the castle roof."

Finding the door already unlocked, she pushed it open.

The tea kettle was whistling and hissing. It continued to do so as she entered the living quarters she shared with Master Kell. She wondered why he was not attending it. Remembering the shadow outside the window, she crept in silently, the hair along the nape of her neck standing up.

In the main sitting room, between his plush chair and fireplace, lay Master Kell, the front of his white robe crimson, his throat slashed and a dagger buried in his chest.

She wanted to scream, but she remembered the Master's teachings. She moved across the room as cautiously and quietly as she could and knelt next to her mentor's side. His glazed eyes stared up at the ceiling.

Sizmor materialized on her shoulder. "Who would do such a thing?" the Fae whispered.

"I have a guess, but nothing matters without the facts," she said, tears stinging her eyes. She wouldn't cry. Resolve mattered more than sorrow. The tea over the fireplace made her believe his killer had been familiar. Kell always offered tea to his guests and since the kettle hadn't boiled out, the murder must have happened recently. Sylvie looked her mentor over and felt his flesh—still warm. She smelled the air above his open mouth—no poisons she could discern. Then she looked at the long dagger in his chest, a weapon he had gifted her long ago.

"My knife," Sylvie said, shaking her head. "A present, for passing my battle history trials. It was in my room."

"Someone wants this to look like you did it then," Sizmor said. The sprite pointed at the floor next to Kell. "What is written there, Sylvianna?"

She bent to examine the letters.

The blood there had been smeared into writing.

"Mikkel Dung," Sylvie read. "He must not have died immediately from his neck wound. There is blood on his fingers, his hands. He wrote this before the killing blow to his heart."

"What does it mean?"

"Mikkel is the name of a rebel who wanted to take the throne before I was born. A son of High King Alafair who rose in rebellion against his father's kingdom. Just like Alafair and the others, Mikkel could not be killed."

"Did this Mikkel kill your master, do you think?"

"Possibly. But if he did, why now? Why not before? No, it doesn't feel right. Master Kell had been making tea for someone he knew. He would not have done so for Mikkel. No, this means something else." She paused. "And why did Kell capitalize 'dung?' That's far more interesting."

"Maybe because Mikkel sounds like a proper shit?" Sizmor said with a straight face.

Sylvie ignored him. "What if Kell died before he could finish writing the word? And the smearing is someone trying to erase what was written?

"It makes sense."

Sylvie checked Kell's fingers. His hands and forearms were covered in blood, undoubtedly from attempting to stop the wound at his neck.

She remembered what Idlor had said then. That if she didn't choose what he wished, there would be repercussions.

"I did this," she whispered.

Just then, she heard a heavy door crash open.

Sizmor flew to the front entryway. "Knights of the Ecclesia," he yelled at her.

Sylvie ripped the dagger from Kell's chest. She had to escape. The Knights would be in the corridor and already flooding into her quarters. She went to the window, threw it wide, and pulled herself out. The sun was blazing and the roof sizzling hot; she looked down and felt dizzy. She would not fall. She moved across the roof and through a maze of chimneys and smaller turrets and towers.

She wanted to cry for Kell. Needed to. But tears would blur her vision. She kept moving, the Fae creature hovering beside her. They needed to hide, and she knew many secret passageways through Mont Saint-Michel.

"Where do we go?" Sizmor asked.

"Do you have a problem with stone and darkness?"

3

The lowest depths of Mont Saint-Michel were as formidable and dank as she remembered.

Sylvie and Sizmor ventured deep into the castle's bowels, her torch held high to light their way. The two moved through narrow corridors that seemingly had no end. This was the world Sylvie had grown up in. As a child, she and her friends explored the endless maze of the depths, looking for lost treasure or hunting deadly creatures from Fae stories. The corridors were chiseled from rock beneath the city. She knew these secret places as well as her own name. That's how she had discovered the dungeons—had even spoken to prisoners who regaled her with stories of their ludicrous deeds—but she had never met Mikkel. Now much older, she returned to discover the harsh reality of who had killed Kell. She knew her mentor had been trying to help her with his cryptic message in blood and she needed help more than anything right now.

"You think Mikkel's down here?" Sizmor asked.

"I do," she said. "Kell was trying to help me. I don't know how yet. How attuned are your Fae senses to the natural world? I've heard so many stories about sprites, but I do not know what is real and what is Fae story."

Sizmor snorted. "We Fae are quite different from humans. There is a world of magic that is largely invisible to your kind."

"Do you think you could find a hidden room down here?"

The sprite shrugged. "Possibly. If one exists."

Sylvie held her torch high as they ventured through the secret corridors. She remembered every corner, crook, and cranny like old friends. Eventually, the carved rock ended at a wall built from stone blocks. She touched two places. The hidden door swung outward; the dark tunnel to the dungeons lay beyond. Sylvie held a finger to her lips. Sizmor nodded.

They stepped quietly into the tunnel, past empty cell after empty cell.

"What is that smell?" Sizmor whispered.

"Humans living. Humans dying."

"I hate it here. Oppressive and evil. We Fae do not have such places," Sizmor said. "Rather than look for a door or hidden room, wouldn't it be easier to see signs where someone has entered an area that they shouldn't be able to?"

"You can do that?"

"Sometimes. Though the air leaves the least trace of passage. I might find nothing," the sprite said.

"I have a lot to learn about you," Sylvie admitted, suddenly sad her mentor would not be there to help. She had a lot of questions. Could one of High King Alafair's children starve, despite the witch's curse? Was that a natural death? She didn't know. But she doubted Kell would have sent her into the dungeons on a fool's errand. Mikkel had to be here. "See what you can find," she said.

Sizmor scouted ahead, sweeping the corridor from side to side. "There, Sylvianna." He pointed at a wall between empty cells.

It looked like just another wall of dark stone.

"How do we open it?"

Sizmor hovered next to the wall. "Here. There are many human hand-prints here. Use the palm of your hand, fingers out."

Sylvie pressed her hand on the cold stone, but nothing happened. She pushed harder and heard a series of clicks. The wall swung inward, creating a passage barely wide enough for her to use. On the other side, a narrow corridor vanished into darkness. She gave the sprite a look. He shrugged and flew ahead. The tunnel turned to the left, deep enough now to be behind the other cells. She saw flickering candlelight ahead, and then a door. It was made of thick bars, rusty and old, but it was the large room beyond it that left Sylvie stunned. It was at least five times the size of the other cells and looked almost like a merchant's sitting room.

Tapestries on the walls, tall shelves of books, a bed larger than any Sylvie had slept in, and a desk with quill, ink, and parchment. It was a room for a prince in a most unprincely place.

A man sat at the desk. Long salt-and-pepper hair hung lank over his shoulders and a thick beard hid most of his face. He wore a simple brown tunic that appeared quite warm over broad shoulders and a wide chest that was built for war.

It wasn't until they locked stares that Sylvie worried about Kell's message.

For those eyes burned with madness.

"Well," the man said. "It seems we have a visitor. And a beautiful one at that."

Sylvie let the flattery go. "We? Is there someone else in there with you?"

He shrugged. "I have so few visitors. I contrived someone to talk to. One cannot debate philosophy, power, or even love without a willing partner." He looked her over. "You are not here to feed me or remove my pot. You aren't supposed to be here at all."

"No, I am not," Sylvie said, taking a deep breath of cold air. "And I don't have long, either. Will you listen to me?"

"Do I have a choice?"

"You are Mikkel Goode," Sylvie said. "I am Sylvianna Goode, your half-sister. We share a father. In that way, we are bound. Master Kell also binds us. I was his student."

"Then Sylvianna Goode, you are educated. I like that," Mikkel said. "I do not like how you just used a past tense though. Did you learn all you could from Kell and left him?"

"He's dead."

Mikkel looked away for a moment. "That is unfortunate. He was a good man. Perhaps the best I've ever known. This must have happened in the last few days?"

Sylvie frowned. "Why do you think that?"

"He visited me three days ago."

Sylvie had not expected that, but it made sense that someone had brought this stuff here.

"What did you talk about?" she asked.

"A question first," Mikkel said, a scarred hand tugging at his beard. "You could be anyone. How do I know you are Alafair's issue?"

"You likely cannot," Sylvie admitted. "I know I am, though. Alafair stabbed me in the chest on his deathbed to prove to the pontiff and all in attendance that I could not be killed."

"And therefore, it made you one of his children. Ahh yes, that sounds like our father. Not a thing most people would lie about, that's for sure," he said. "I remember when I discovered I could not be killed. I was eight. Knife to the chest, same as you. I pulled the blade out and killed the boy who had done it." He grinned, staring off at a past only he could see. "My first kill. Not clean, either. Tomas was his name. He was fifteen."

Sylvie shivered. She knew little about Mikkel. Master Kell had told her a great deal on his military victories as First Knight but not much else. She wondered if Kell had done that purposefully, to shield her from some truth.

"Why was Master Kell here?" she asked.

"To tell me that our father lay dying. Then yesterday, I felt the change in my heart the moment Alafair died."

"You could feel it?"

Mikkel stood and walked to the cell door, folding his arms across his broad chest. "We are no longer unkillable. A man who spent a great deal of time surrounded by death can feel when it is coming for him. It is a natural thing for a knight to know." He paused, considering her. "I expected armed knights to come for me the moment he died. A final parting gift for the hatred Alafair had for me."

"I am not here to kill you. I am here for a different reason," Sylvie said. "Master Kell was murdered. He wrote your name in blood on the floor. It's what brought me here."

"That is sad news. Why would he write my name?"

"I do not know but I learned to not second guess him."

"I hope you learned that faster than I did," Mikkel said. "Who killed him? And why?"

"I don't know who did it. Though I have my suspicions."

Mikkel grabbed the bars with thick-fingered hands. "But you know the why."

Sylvie nodded. "On his deathbed, High King Alafair Goode made me his heir."

She expected him to laugh, but he just gathered his thick, greasy hair and twisted it into a bun upon his head. "Our siblings must be quite chagrined."

"Lord Idlor attempted to bribe me to give up the crown."

"Ahh. Idlor," Mikkel growled and pursed his lips. "Not the most cunning of the bunch, but he has power."

"He told me if I didn't refuse the crown, he would discredit me. And he did that by proclaiming me Kell's murderer. Sent the Ecclesia Knights after me."

"Yes, that sounds exactly like Idlor. When our father needed help to dishonor me, Idlor was right there with a handy lie about my allegedly conspiring to remove father from the throne, trying to gain favor," Mikkel said. He paused, shaking his head. "If you've been named heir, I expect you've met Grumtil."

Sizmor materialized then, flying out of the cell.

"Well, well, a thief in the shadows," Mikkel said, eyeing the little Fae creature. "Grumtil's replacement for the new queen, I would think. Spying on me, dear sprite?"

Sizmor landed on Sylvie's shoulder. "You can learn a great deal about a man by what he reads."

Mikkel nodded. "True enough. How is old Grumtil doing, by the way?"

"He's deeply saddened by the loss of his friend," Sizmor said.

"That makes one of us," Mikkel grunted.

Sylvie stepped closer to the door. "You hated him, didn't you? Alafair, I mean."

"I did not hate him. He was my father and my High King. I devoted myself to his bloody cause with fervor and honor. Do you have Lumiere? If you do, it will go a long way in securing the crown for that head of yours."

The thought hadn't even occurred to Sylvie. The famous blade had belonged to the kings of history as far back as Kell's books had recorded. Forged from fallen-light, it not only carried with it a proclamation of kingship but it was said to possess powerful magic on the battlefield.

"I know not where it is," Sylvie admitted. "I saw it when Pontiff Scorus moved father's body to the Citadel. The sword lay on the king's chest, in his hands. The pontiff and other bishops of the Citadel have it for the funeral."

"Then it is with your enemies," Mikkel said.

Sizmor moved to Sylvie's palm. "As far as we know, Pontiff Scorus is a good man."

Mikkel snorted. "Do not believe it. Scorus helped put me in here when he was bishop of Mont Saint-Michel. Do not think he's an ally simply because he's a holy man. He will use Lumiere as leverage, especially if he believes you should not be High Queen of the kingdom. Every man who gains power wields it for his benefit."

"Like you did?" Sylvie asked.

"You know not of what you speak, *girl*. I never abused my power."

"You merely tried to usurp the kingdom from Father."

Mikkel laughed then, an echoing guffaw. Sylvie cringed, hoping the stone around them muffled the sound.

When he finished, he had tears in his eyes. "Thank you, Sylvianna Goode, for the laugh," he said. "Though perhaps crying would be more appropriate."

"What do you mean?" she asked.

"You are as wrong about history as you could be. Is that the tale Kell told you? Perhaps his mind grew soft as he aged. Worse, he protected his brother's role in it." Mikkel shook his head. "I did not want the kingdom. I was the High King's First Knight, the only honor I ever strove for after I saw my first tourney when I was six. By the time I was fifteen, I was one of the best warriors in the city. By nineteen, Father dubbed me his First Knight. We finished quelling the outlying territories and unified the land under one banner for the first time. I was his man. In some ways, he was less a father and more a best friend."

"Then why did you turn on him? Master Kell told me your story but never explained the why of it all."

"The why is never what you expect. Especially after the victor has chiseled his story into history. The why, you ask? Love. Love put me here."

"You tried to overthrow the crown … for love?"

"I did nothing save protect the love of my life." He turned away from her for a moment and cleared his throat. "After the Battle of the Three Immortals by which the kingdom finally became one, I went home. Alafair said I had earned a rest. I took the offer. I went to take stock of my new landholdings. To set up the government of my lordship. If Kell taught you as he did me, you learned how best to lead. I went right to work." Mikkel sighed. "I should have listened more to bards. They sing of love happening when one least expects it. It was true for me."

"Who was she?" Sizmor asked before Sylvie had the chance. "She must have been quite the woman to capture a First Knight's heart."

"Chelle was unlike any woman I had met," Mikkel said. "A beauty, to be sure, but my feelings for her ran much deeper. She was smart. A wry humor that made me laugh more than I had right to, given the death I had doled out. And she cared for what I attempted to build. We were happy."

"What happened?" Sylvie asked.

"I brought her to court, and she dazzled. It pleased me to share our happiness with my Ecclesia friends. After so much bloodshed, believing a life after war was possible meant a great deal to me. Chelle charmed everyone, including the other women at court."

"Did one of the other Ecclesia Knights pursue her then?" Sylvie guessed.

"Not exactly. I could have dealt with that in a test of arms. No, the man you are asking about was our father."

Sylvie and Sizmor looked at one another. She most certainly had never heard this part of the tale, but the moment Mikkel shared it, she knew it to be true. She saw how the pieces of the puzzle fit perfectly. The High King who lost his queen and, to fill the void, bedded as many women as he could.

"I am so sorry," Sylvie said. "I had no idea. It must have been horrible."

"At first, I thought Alafair jested," he continued. "But then I saw how he changed toward me. And I saw how in err I was. Our father became infatuated with Chelle. First, he tried to woo her without my knowledge. He did not get far. She spurned him as nicely as she could. When she told me of it, I knew I had to act. I sent her home to Bavar. Then, I confronted him in private. He tried to tell me Chelle misunderstood his intentions and asked me to quell a small uprising in the north." He paused and rubbed his scarred hands. "It was a terrible time."

"Because the uprising was not real," Sizmor said. "A fool's errand to remove you so he could pursue your woman."

"Sprite, you cut to the bone. I was indeed a fool. There was no uprising. Alafair sent me north even as he traveled to Bavar to woo Chelle. Once I realized what he had done, I sent a raven with a note to my steward ordering him to bar the castle. Alafair had not been prepared for that. He hadn't brought an army. Unable to get what he wanted, he returned here to prepare the Ecclesia Knights and I prepared my army for what was to come."

"So .... you weren't after the kingdom."

"Hardly. I was merely protecting my life and my love. The rest you know from what Kell taught you, I'd wager." He paused, and Sylvie thought she saw tears welling in his dark eyes. "What would you have done in my stead, Sylvie?"

Sylvie thought about it a moment. "I … I don't know."

"What happened to the Lady Chelle?" Sizmor asked.

"After the armies of the kingdom destroyed Bavar, Alafair had his way with her," Mikkel turned his back to them again. "He discarded her after that. Kell told me she joined the St. Ives Monastery."

"And since you could not be killed, they put you here. In these dungeons," Sylvie said. "No wonder Kell continued to visit you. You were not in the wrong."

"It is the past," Mikkel said with a dismissive wave. He walked over to his desk and straightened some papers and books. "Nothing can undo it. I cannot regain the lost decades. I cannot unmake a nun once she has given her oath."

"You can help me, though," Sylvie said.

"How so?"

"Swear fealty to me as High Queen of the kingdom."

Mikkel snorted another laugh and turned to face her. "I will say you are tenacious. You will need that if you are to set right the wrong that has been done to you." He shook his head. "But I will not swear fealty again. Not until you make the hardest of decisions. Perhaps I will consider your offer then."

"Very well. Where do we begin?" she asked.

"Lord Idlor will not be working alone. He could be working with any of our siblings. Or those of the Citadel. Or even the Masters. He is the first enemy you must stop because he is known. The others can be dealt with later." Mikkel eyed her. "Before these dungeons became my home, I always found the best way to weed out the dishonest is to be direct. Being direct is unexpected. Sets people on edge. Gives insight into what they are thinking. We go to Idlor."

She nodded to the sprite, who flew to the door's locking mechanism and studied it. "And if he is wishing a crown upon his head, take the head. Leave the crown."

Mikkel grinned. "I like you, Sylvianna Goode."

Through some Fae means, Sizmor unlocked the cell door. Sylvie pulled it creaking open. Mikkel just stood there, eyes wide. Then he grabbed a dark sweater and pulled it over his head.

"I need a sword," Mikkel said.

A light at the end of the corridor outlined the hidden door to Idlor's quarters.

After she freed Mikkel, they had gone back and gathered supplies. She went to the kitchens first; they were empty due to the late hour. She took cheeses, breads, and salted meats—enough to last them several days. Even sugar cubes for Sizmor. After that, she gathered two heavy blankets for them from linen closets and a black robe which she changed into. She returned to Kell's quarters, which had been ransacked and the body removed, and took his elixir and poison box. Then, Mikkel led her to a small armory where he took a sword, daggers, and a thick leather vest. Confident they had what they needed, the three of them went back through the secret passages to the King's Tower. As far as Sylvie knew, they had avoided detection.

The King's Tower not only housed the High King's quarters on its uppermost floor, but also the royal suites of many of Alafair's children, including Idlor's rooms. If she could confront him without inference from the Knights of the Ecclesia, she was confident she could expose the traitor. The plan she had formed depended on her most.

Sylvie nodded to Mikkel and Sizmor before she pressed her ear up to Idlor's hidden door.

She could just make out voices.

"The Knights of the Ecclesia will be in place by then, yes?" Idlor said. She recognized his voice from her encounter with him the day before. "All safety measures must be in place to maintain a peaceful farewell to my father. And I want them there during coronation too. I do not want havoc when I'm supposed to reassure the kingdom."

"The Knights will guard both ceremonies, my King," another male assured. She had heard the voice before but didn't recognize it.

"Good," Idlor said. "Whatever she is planning with Mikkel cannot be allowed."

"I still cannot believe she found him. I thought he was buried down there."

"She is smart and determined, which I can't really say of you. How *did* you rise to Bishop of Mont Saint-Michel if you so underestimate your enemies?"

"My friends are well paid, and they outnumber my enemies, my King."

"Kell," Idlor cursed. "Even in death, he is a nuisance."

There seemed to be only the two men. It made sense. The fewer people who knew, the safer they were. Sylvie took a deep breath. She steadied herself and triggered the door's release. A bit more light entered the tunnel. Then she nodded to Mikkel and pushed on the panel.

The room Sylvie entered was ornate, filled with art, fine furniture, a fireplace of dying red embers, and the thick odor of perfumed candles. The voices had come from an adjoining room to her left. To her right was probably Idlor's bedchamber. She crept silently to the bedroom and peered there, to make sure there was no one else present. It was empty.

She then made her way to the open room with the two men. Idlor sat behind a large desk, sifting through paperwork, three tall stained-glass windows behind him, the other walls covered in bookshelves. The second man sat across from him, scribbling notes into a book. He wore a simple robe with a large hood lying flat on his back. Pudgy rolls bulged at his neck and his bald head glistened in the candlelight.

That wasn't all. She saw Lumiere laying across the desk between the two men, sheathed but unmistakable in its craftsmanship and beauty.

She steeled herself and stepped into the room. "Is that the High Queen's sword?"

Idlor glanced up. The fat man turned too, and Sylvie recognized Pontiff Scorus. He gaped at her, his jutting lower lip trembling. The latter gave her more pleasure than it should have. Idlor was not so surprised. He leaned back in his chair, hands steepled before him, watching her and the knife in her hand.

"Bold move, Sylvianna," Idlor said. "Most unexpected. As my door is guarded, it seems you've scurried in like a rat. Though I remember having that hidden passage sealed long ago, I believe."

"You thought wrong," she said.

Idlor nodded. "Pray tell, is that the knife you murdered Master Kell with?"

"*I* did not kill him."

"Oh, but you did," Idlor said, standing. She could tell he hadn't slept much by the dark circles under his eyes. "I told you. Choices have consequences. You chose and that decision ended Kell's life. His blood is on your hands, not mine." He grinned, took Lumiere from the desk, and held it up for her to see. "But that matters little. I have Lumiere. Pontiff Scorus already conducted the Rites of Kingship witnessed by the Knights of the Ecclesia and most of the Masters. What's done is done. There is no changing it. I am High King of the kingdom."

Sylvie should have known Idlor would twist precedent to his desires. It changed little for her plan though. It meant the days ahead would be more difficult than she had anticipated but she was ready for them. "Not when the truth is known," she said. "As I learned earlier today, the truth can never be buried because there is always someone with a shovel."

"But how will you dig that truth up, Sylvianna?" Idlor asked, stepping around his desk. "Word has spread through Mont Saint-Michel and is likely already in the other cities and villages. You killed Master Kell. Knights of the Ecclesia—the most noble men in all the kingdom—saw you flee your quarters with your bloody dagger in hand. You are a murderer."

"Guilt. Innocence. Rumor. They are only words," she said, watching Pontiff Scorus heave his round body out of his chair. She did not see the Covenant Codex of St. Emmer on the table though, which meant she'd have to find it.

"Ahh, yes, your vaunted studies," Idlor chuckled. He unsheathed Lumiere. "Philosophy will not save you."

"You are right about that, despite being wrong about so many things," Sylvie said. "You have Lumiere. Yet you need the Knights of the Ecclesia to keep you safe during the funeral and coronation."

"She's been listening to our plans," Scorus hissed.

"Listening is the first lesson a great ruler learns," Sylvie said, shaking her head. She pointed her dagger at Scorus. "You've forgotten that."

"And you've no one to keep you safe from me," Idlor said. "I have never liked killing but I think I will enjoy it tonight."

Idlor stepped toward her, but Sizmor materialized between them.

"Sylvianna Goode is not alone," the sprite said.

"That thing is unholy!" Scorus yelled, pointing at Sizmor. He turned to Sylvie with an accusing finger, eyes bulging. "You're in league with them. You are a witch! My King, we need to kill her and that *thing* now. Now. Guards! Knights!"

Then Mikkel stepped into the room from behind Sylvie. Idlor froze, his bravado snuffed like a candle. The pontiff paled.

"I will leave when my work here is done," Sylvie said, nodding to Mikkel.

The former First Knight of High King Alafair Goode moved into the room, a simple soldier's sword in his hand, eyes fixed on Idlor. Sylvie stepped back to give Mikkel more space to maneuver. Idlor moved away from his desk toward the windows. Mikkel said nothing. He crept steadily toward Idlor's desk and around its corner. Idlor raised Lumiere before him. Sylvie doubted the man had held a sword since the kingdom's formation. Mikkel hadn't wielded a sword either, in that time.

On the other side of the desk, Scorus pushed up against the wall. He squeezed his rotund shape by his chair and stumbled to the suite's main door. Sizmor looked to Sylvie; she grinned and nodded. The pontiff reached the key sticking out of the locked door. With shaking, fat fingers, he fumbled to get the door open. "Knights! Knights! To me!" he thundered and pushed on the heavy door. It swung wide and struck something on the floor outside.

"The Knights on watch will not be joining us," Sylvie said. "My little friend here put them to sleep. You might as well come back into the room. We have much to discuss."

Sizmor waved a tiny hand and a gust of wind drove Scorus back into the room and slammed the door.

"Mercy. Mercy," Scorus said, quivering in fear.

"I wonder if you stabbed Master Kell with my knife," Sylvie said.

"He did it!" Scorus yelled, pointing at Idlor. "He did it all!"

Sylvie glared at Idlor. Mikkel stepped toward him. Idlor had to know Mikkel was one of the best swordsmen to ever step on the battlefield, but the scion still had the fallen-light sword. It would balance the fight between the two men.

Mikkel feinted. Idlor didn't fall for it. Mikkel stepped to the side. The two men circled one another before the stained-glass windows, their breathing and Scorus's whimpering the only sounds in the room. The former First Knight grinned, his eyes bright. Sylvie realized Mikkel was enjoying this, a cat playing with a mouse.

Idlor must have sensed it as well. He roared and attacked, feinting left and thrusting right. Mikkel brought his sword up to parry—his first mistake, Sylvie thought.

Lumiere shattered Mikkel's sword, shards exploding into both men.

Idlor swung Lumiere back and forth, pushing his advantage. He brought Lumiere against his weaponless enemy, hitting Mikkel's shattered sword at its hilt again and again, driving the larger man back toward the wall of books. His back to shelves, Mikkel kept his broken blade in front of him, parrying each strike. Just as Sylvie was about to shout at Sizmor to help, Idlor drove Lumiere down at his foe—but this time Mikkel caught it with his sword's cross guard. The two men stood frozen, snarling hate.

Then Mikkel drove Lumiere upward with one hand, grasped Idlor's sword hand with the other, and dug his thumb into his foe's wrist.

Lumiere clattered to the floor.

"That was fun," Mikkel growled, discarding his broken sword. He grabbed the dazed Idlor and slammed his face into his desk. Blood welled up from a cut on the man's forehead. Then Mikkel turned him over and pinned him—knee on Idlor's chest and both of Idlor's wrists in his hands.

Mikkel nodded to Sylvie. She approached, dagger firmly in hand.

"I will not grovel like Scorus there," Idlor said, blood seeping into his blinking left eye.

Mikkel's grin widened. "She isn't asking you to."

"I was doing what is best for the kingdom!" Idlor screamed.

Sylvie shook her head. "Then Master Kell would still be alive," she said, hardening her heart for what would come next. "He will live on in me and I'll grant you one final lesson, to you from him. 'When a man lies, he murders a part of the world.' You lied. And there is only one way to deal with a murderer."

Bringing the dagger up so Idlor could see it clearly, Sylvie drove her dagger down into his mouth and pinned him to his desk. Blood sprayed in crimson spurts as Idlor gagged and coughed. Its hot touch felt like a baptism on Sylvie's arms and face. Idlor tried to grasp her dagger, but she pressed it harder into his mouth. Idlor would die slowly knowing that she had bested him. And whoever found his corpse would know not to cross her.

At last, the light in Idlor's gray eyes went out and his struggle ceased.

"For you, Father," Sylvie said, removing the dagger and wiping it clean on Idlor's finery.

"What would your father say?" Pontiff Scorus stammered, still cowering behind his chair.

"Master Kell was my father," Sylvie said. "He raised me. I think he'd be proud. But if you mean High King Alafair Goode, he chose me to be his heir. And his heir, I shall be."

Sylvie nodded to Mikkel, and he picked Lumiere off the bloody carpet. Then he walked over to Pontiff Scorus and slashed his flabby throat.

They will find the bodies," Mikkel said next to Sylvie, arms folded over his chest. "The Knights will wake and realize they failed. Or the Citadel bishops will come looking when Idlor and Scorus don't show up at the funeral."

Sylvie nodded, already thinking about it. They stood outside the walls of Mont Saint-Michel. From their cliff-side vantage, they looked down on the ocean waves beating at the white sandy beach, the water glimmering like a million fire diamonds. A large stone pier jutted into the sea, built for only one purpose—the funeral of royal family members. A large wooden boat with a single mast and unfurled sails stood at the ready, rocking gently, the day's final sunlight a swath of warm gold. On a tinderbox of dry wood and colorful flower wreaths lay High King Alafair Goode—He Who Once Wielded The Light of Lumiere, the Final Bane of Mordreadth. Even at a distance, Sylvie saw the Citadel had dressed him in regal finery, hands folded at peace upon his chest.

On the beach, the remaining members of the Goode family gathered alongside Masters, Bishops of the Citadel, and Knights of the Ecclesia with their squires. Behind Sylvie, on the city's outer walls, the castle's commoners paid their respects. The sun descended toward the horizon where it would vanish into a salty sea—and the High King's funeral pyre would chase it, lit by a flaming arrow to honor the dead's life.

"They are already looking for them," Sylvie said. "But we have the time we need to set right the wrongs done."

"The Knights of the Ecclesia will hunt you," Mikkel said.

"They will. But they will fail."

"I like hearing calm certainty from you," Mikkel said, looking at her. "It is a powerful strength to possess. I will likely always be angry at Father, but I think he made a wise choice in naming you heir. Holding onto that honor will be the difficult part."

"Without a pontiff, no one can be crowned." Sylvie thought about the days ahead. She looked down at Lumiere, sheathed and cradled in her arms like a baby. "The Bishops of the Citadel will clash to decide who the next pontiff will be before the smoke blows for the next leader of the Citadel. Perhaps even longer for him to disentangle the morass of rules and knowledge required to erase my name from the Covenant Codex of St. Emmer, if it can even be done. I will prove my innocence in that time and become High Queen of the kingdom."

"First, you must find the Covenant Codex of St. Emmer," Mikkel said. "It contains the proof you need. Scorus was a snake, but he was a smart one. It will be hidden. You may never find it."

"Or she could journey to the Twilight Lands and convince the Shadow Court to share the Covenant Codex of Wise Bulloch," Sizmor suggested from her shoulder. "Remember, there are two matching copies. Though convincing the Fae to become involved in the political intrigues of Man may be far more arduous."

Sylvie watched as the two most powerful Citadel bishops gave their final benedictions upon the stone pier below, their shared song upon the evening air as they unfurled the sails and the boat began to move away from land into the great sea beyond. She agreed with both Mikkel and Sizmor. The days ahead would be hard ones. But she had to begin somewhere. She would have to learn everything about the compact between Man and Fae, how the magic worked, and what problems could arise if no coronation took place in the expected time.

That meant a secret visit to the Bodleian Library.

A dark speck flew from below, growing larger as it approached.

"That was quite beautiful," Grumtil said when he arrived, hovering beside Sylvie and Sizmor. "I think High King Alafair Goode would be pleased. He is at peace."

"Did you do as I asked?" Sylvie questioned.

"I did as you commanded," Grumtil said, stroking his silvery beard, wings ablur. "The boy was shocked to see me hovering at his shoulder, but he left Sir Gwain's side when he heard you were here. He is headed here now."

"Did he alert Ser Gwain?" Mikkel asked. "Or any of the other knights?"

"No. He told Ser Gwain he had to piss in the dunes."

"Thank you, Grumtil," Sylvie said. "I owe you."

The old sprite bowed in mid-air. Together they continued to watch the funeral. Once the pyre was far enough out to sea, it would be set ablaze by Archery Master Kael. The ocean would consume what remained, spreading all that High King Alafair Goode had been to the far reaches of their world. It was a fitting tribute to a man who had saved it from Mordreadth.

Sylvie saw the fruits of Grumtil's efforts. Darian had left the gathering below and now approached them on the cliff. The two sprites disappeared. When he saw her, Darian smiled, shaking his head in disbelief. She knew what she had to do. Yet as much as it hurt, she would do what was right by the kingdom.

"Darian, my love," Sylvie said, turning to him with a smile.

Dressed in his squire's best, Darian came right to her and wrapped his arms about her. She kissed him hard. Sylvie held the kiss for as long as she could. Fate would take care of the rest.

"I've been so worried," Darian said, rubbing her arms. He gave Mikkel a curious look but returned his attention to her. "I know you didn't kill Kell. I've been telling Ser Gwain and even some of the others that. But they won't listen. They have made up their minds."

"They have. Idlor used his poison well." Sylvie lightly touched his face, memorizing his handsome features. "Now it has spread."

"Why didn't you accept Lord Idlor's offer?" Darian pressed.

"Duty is an individual choice," she said. "High King Alafair did his duty by naming his heir. I am doing my duty by accepting. Idlor thought he was doing his duty by protecting the kingdom from a woman. But as he said, choices have consequences."

"But we could have been together and still lived a fine life."

"It is not the life the High King wanted for me."

Darian frowned. "You aren't right in the head, Sylvie. I think we need to go find Lord Idlor right now and straighten this out. Though no one seems to know where he is. The pontiff, too. They are not at the funeral. It's like they just disappeared."

"Lord Idlor walked his own path, and that path has ended," Sylvie said.

Darian took a step back. He looked at Mikkel and then at Sylvie. He blinked several times, took a deep breath, and shook his head. His cheeks reddened despite the cooling wind.

"I am sorry, Darian," Sylvie said. "Know that I loved you. Sadly, sometimes love isn't enough."

Horror twisted those features she had so come to love. He stumbled backward, tripping, and falling hard on the dirt trail. She went to his side. She could have chosen to look away, to not view her handiwork. But Master Kell had taught her to take responsibility for all aspects of her life. She owed it to Darian to be there at his end, his death upon her lips when she kissed him. His breathing became shallow, and he seemed lost in a daze.

A few moments later, Darian died, staring up at the sky.

"I see you have learned a difficult lesson," Mikkel said, nodding. "To rule, one must be dispassionate. Ultimately, he would have joined your enemies. He would have been used against you."

"I loved him," Sylvie said, wiping a tear from her cheek. She closed Darian's eyes. "Love is a powerful thing. Poets know it. Bards know it. You know it. Now, I know it. It makes me vulnerable. I cannot become the queen the kingdom needs me to be if my enemies have such an easy pathway to my heart."

"The world is only as bright as its darkest hole," Mikkel grunted. He said nothing more. She wondered if he was thinking of his long-lost beloved.

"What will you do now?" Sylvie asked him, still kneeling at Darian's side.

"You have given me my freedom. I never dreamed this day would come," Mikkel said, looking out at the sea. "They will never stop trying to kill you. You represent the power they all crave. One will succeed. At some point. Unless you steel your resolve and surround yourself with those you fully trust."

"I know," Sylvie said, looking at him. "Will you consider becoming my First Knight?"

Mikkel studied her. "Why would you do such a thing?" he asked finally. "I've done terrible things. I'm hated."

"You are hated for all the wrong reasons. Just as I am." Sylvie rose from Darian and stood at Mikkel's side. She put her hand on his forearm. "You are a good man, Mikkel Goode. History may not understand that, but Master Kell did. He wanted you to keep me safe. I offer you the title of First Knight for that reason. But I realize now he had one last lesson to teach. He wanted me to listen to your tale. To prevent it from happening to me. Love is a beautiful thing, but it can also be a weapon." She paused, considering her words carefully as she gazed at Darian's body. "Without you, I may have fallen prey as you did. I thank you for sharing your story, despite the pain it causes you. I will never forget that."

Mikkel looked away, a light wind tousling his hair. Sylvie looked to the sprites who had materialized once more. Sizmor shrugged. Grumtil flew to Mikkel and whispered in the knight's ear. Sylvie could not hear what he said.

Finally, her half-brother squared his shoulders and knelt before her.

"I would be honored to be your champion," he said, dropping his head to respectfully avert his eyes in respect. "I will serve you and the kingdom faithfully as First Knight, to honor and protect the realm in life and by death, if need be."

Sylvie took Lumiere and, rather than unsheathe the blade and touch his shoulders as was customary, placed the round pommel to his forehead.

She needed his new start to be different than the last.

"Rise, Ser Mikkel Goode," she said.

Mikkel did so. Sylvie breathed in the air, heavy with cool salt and coming night. It was a start. They watched the funeral pyre drift into the distance. Just when she thought Archery Master Kael wouldn't be able to reach the boat, he lifted his bow, lit the end of a large ceremonial arrow, pulled it back, and loosed it at the purpling sky, its fire an arc of flame.

Soon the boat was ablaze. A sting came to Sylvie's eyes. Not out of sadness for the dead, but for what High King Alafair Goode had given her.

At last, Mikkel rose and asked, "What will you do when our brothers and sisters fight for the throne, High Queen Sylvianna Goode? Not all of them will be as bold and forthright as Idlor. When word spreads about him, they will conspire in the shadows. Even now, some plan a return to their lands, to raise armies and announce they are the true High King of the kingdom. What will you do when one challenges you? Or two. Or five. All blood-related with true claims to the throne."

"I will kill them," Sylvie said. "I will kill them all."

THE FACE
OF THE KING

ADRIAN TCHAIKOVSKY

As King of Narad-Var, you go before your people masked, so the unworthy may not look upon your divine features. So your royal pronouncements are lent a stern gravitas, any flecks of individual temperament smoothed from them. Proper regal dignity imparted by the implacable gold face that all know as their king.

Which tradition also means that, when your vizier Enephet decides to murder his young master and take your place, the job is pathetically easy. A paralytic poison in your cup, excuses for the royal personage retiring early. Your memory of him staring down at your locked body, the divine ribs showing the faintest rise and fall, at his mercy. No longer the animate personage of rulership but something to be disposed of.

Trying to foresee how Enephet will go about it; imagination the only part of you that can move. Cut your throat, shed the blood divine? Who can say what curse might alight on the hand that does such a thing? The final wrath of the last scion of the royal line. No mere superstition. Such curses have killed before. History is replete with them.

Dump your dying body in some alley of the lower city for the scavengers, perhaps? After all, who would recognise your face? Drawing off that mask he stares down at the divine features. No god strikes him down for heresy. Perhaps the conservative pantheon of the city have already accepted this change to the status quo. He tries the mask on. It seems to fit him better than ever it did you.

Enephet draws off his gloves. Some master tattooist has already gifted him the elaborate, geometrical designs that decorate your own fingers. Those same patterns, a birthmark, and a scar mean he can't just dump your corpse on a trash pile. *Someone* might still ask questions about a distinctive cadaver. Worse, if you somehow recovered from the poison's slow death and started talking. A madman, people would think, yet Narad-Var's lower city holds an inconvenient number of enquiring minds within its cults and scholars' rings and acquirers' guilds.

Perhaps he is thinking of acid or the hungry mouths of beasts, to rid him of the last vestiges of your inconvenience. But you see the fear of your dying curse in his eyes—stare helplessly at that fear because your own eyelids are frozen.

And so he begins dragging away your still living remains. Enephet will lose you somewhere nobody will find you. Time and the poison eke out your death, so that he can stand before the gods and say his hands are clean.

Narad-Var is built on the ruins of older places, and those in turn paved over elder still. There are cellars within cellars, pits and shafts, dungeons and oubliettes. Those who venture unwisely into the dark do not return. So it is Enephet makes a midnight visit to a certain buried well that descends beyond knowledge, the waters of which bring terrible nightmares.

With none to see, he casts you down the shaft, doubtless listening for the faint splash. *It is not I who slew the king. It was the waters. Let any curse disperse amongst the ripples.* So ends, as far as Enephet is concerned, your whole dynasty. Though none will ever know. How many times has such a substitution happened, while the faintly smiling mask rules on?

Pel-Adarm, third of your name. You awake on the shore of a sunless sea and know only that you have been betrayed.

Weak as a fever victim. Vomiting foul water, wracked by shudders. Alive, wishing you were dead. Every limb of you tortured, your skin on fire. You return to consciousness trying to scream; the sound is just a rattle and a cough.

You lie on your back. Above are strange stars: carnivorous constellations of luminous insects clinging to an unseen ceiling. They twitch and shudder into new patterns as their trailing threads catch bats and moths. The only fortunes foretold by such lights are bad ones.

At first you cannot remember your own name. Only that you had trusted, and that trust had been broken. Your existence is a knot of pain. It hurts to breathe. Your guts cramp. Your very eyes and teeth feel bruised, your tongue a strip of sand-crusted leather. You lie at the borderlands of sea and shore, life and death, and wait to see which will claim you. Darkness rises within you and you slip into it gratefully, feeling you will not wake again. And yet you do.

No stronger, surely, but some of the leaching poison has withdrawn from you. Hunger jostles with death and sickness. Blind fish butt against your bare feet. You grope, just as blind, trying to seize them. Imagine yourself tearing into their watery flesh with your teeth. You are too weak, they too fleet. Enephet chose wisely. The dark and the cold, the hunger, or else some subterranean predator, these things will kill the king. The hidden usurper need fear no retribution, mortal or divine.

You recall draining the cup, fitting its spout to the slot of your mask with the ease of long practice. Enephet sitting across from you, watching you slyly. But then slyness was what one expects from one's vizier, is it not? Enephet the all-capable, who had insinuated himself between you and the world until he oversaw every aspect of the royal life. Including its end.

Betrayed! The thought brings a surge of improbable strength to your limbs and you stand. *Revenge!* The passion filling you, but only as water fills a sieve. Already leaking from all the places where the poison broke you, even as you lurch away from the water. Reaching for the cavern walls. Gashing your hands on the rock. Knowing that, the moment you stop moving, you'll collapse again, measure your length on the lightless stone and that will be the end of you.

It will be a mercy, when it happens. Everything hurts, and you are no warrior-king used to privation. A privileged child who inherited the world, and everyone in it placed there to serve and adore you, or at least the mask you wore. Now your face is naked to the cave's dank air. As though you've been flayed, only raw twitching muscle left, flinching from every breath.

Your feet strike something and you fall forwards, battering your body against a rank of hard edges. Weeping with the pain, the indignity, how *hard* it is. Only that fading echo of *Revenge!* has you on your feet again. You try to cry, "I shall return! I shall reclaim my throne!" and hear only a deathly croak from your throat. It lends you strength, though, and in the echo you realise you've fallen against the worn edges of stone steps. Above, a greyish radiance that is not just the hungry stars above the lost sea, but something new. A weak pre-dawn forever on the point of breaking. A buried day that will never escape its own tomb.

Your city is built on ruins, and those ruins were ill-omened long before the first stones of Narad-Var were laid. The work of sinister peoples whom your bold ancestors put to the sword and, before them, the crumbled edifices raised by hands not human at all. Venture deep enough and the very air is made of ghosts and history.

But light. Even that unhealthy grey pallor is better than utter darkness. You stride up the steps. You stagger. You crawl up them, bloodying your knees, feeling the last of your strength slicking their chipped edges. Until you come in sight of the altar, and you fall. The last of the poison, the exertion, cold, hunger, they haul you down like a gang of lower-city bravos.

A temple, lost to time, illuminated by a sourceless, leaden light. A deity, nameless now but honoured once. Heaps of finery are mounded behind the altar. Jewelled icons of jade, knives of chalcedony. And here you lie, a final offering to a dead deity.

Save that something moves in your failing sight. For the altar is alive and so is the god.

What you see at first: a great stone block carved with a writhing mass of worms and centipedes, lizards, serpents, formless tentacled things. Rats and ravening wolves and shapes like men yet not human. The carvings seem to pour from the altar's face, down its sides and out across the intricately worked basalt floor towards you. Yet they are not carvings and the altar is not stone. Motion ripples there, the intricate figures welling up from the depths of the gelid mass, crawling over its surface, fighting their way clear of it only to deliquesce into the rotting substance of the floor. A sluggish life pervades the altar, a mindless drive towards fecund creation that lies shackled here beneath the Earth. You have the sense of *something* crouching invisibly over the altar. A great, mute giant filling all the space within the shrine. The god, locked away beneath such a burden of stone, patron of a vanished people, frustrated and maddened at centuries of disuse.

You are fading, by then. Dying. Already half lost in your own mind, the messengers of your senses bringing only unreliable and cryptic news.

What will you give me?

Anything, you cry in your head. *I shall raise temples in your name! I shall shed blood on your altars, if only …*

What is it you wish?

What are the last desires of Pel-Adarm III, dethroned king of Narad-Var?

Revenge! you cry into the void. *Revenge and the strength to achieve it! Make me whole and let me return to the sun to have my revenge!*

Later. Days later, whole moons, who could say, a man crawls out of a lightless crack in the wall of a tomb and stumbles into the streets of Narad-Var's lower city. He wears ancient robes, papery with time and fortified with gold thread. He carries a knife of obsidian and a sack of treasure. He has a face nobody knows. And though the man is you, at the same time he seems a stranger.

You look up at the moon. You feel the night on your skin, a world away from the chill exhalation of the underworld. You cannot know what days you have lost, but you have returned. And in the high city, in your palace, Enephet sits upon your throne, enjoys your pleasures, wears your mask. But not for long.

A second chance. The blessing of some pre-human thing of crawling growth and life that has given you this new vitality because, in all the world, you were its one votary. And then, renewed and strong again, you filled a sack with its offerings and treasure, swearing *I will raise a temple* and knowing you never will. Not when you are king again and have other diversions.

But you cannot simply walk into the palace and demand all bow before you. Who would know you? They kneel to the mask, not the man. You will have to be an intruder in your own halls until you can serve Enephet the way he tried to serve you. And to invade the palace of the king, against all those vigilant guards and wards, demands skills that your life of indolence never prepared you for.

But if Narad-Var is blessed with one thing in excess, it is villains. The lower city seethes with resourceful malcontents. A thousand guilds and sects and secret societies fester there. And though they mostly prey upon each other, neither the houses of the rich nor the palace itself are proof against their attentions. And you have treasure to whet their appetites, and the promise of more to come. And so it is that you set out to make the worst of your subjects serve their rightful king.

👑

Ollec the Borquan is a heavy woman, so massive that the world seems to bend inwards towards her as though whispering secrets in her ears. And secrets are her business, that a man with a sack of treasure can pry from her one by one by feeding her gold like grapes. A jowly, ill-tempered face. Absurdly luxurious dark hair piled elegantly atop her head and, you suspect, stored elegantly on a stand when she sleeps. Yet you've won her over, with the fire of your purpose and riches you stole from a god.

"Into the palace? She pours you both some wine and scratches at her chins. "It's been done. Not often but in living memory. You remember when they turned the whole city over, looking for the Arch-Steward's sword?"

You do indeed. Your father was incandescent with fury. They hung a hundred thieves and vagabonds and never found the true culprit. Now, looking at Ollec the Borquan's coarse features, you know you could hear the whole story if only you asked carefully enough.

You don't even know what a Borquan is.

"What do you bring besides seed money?" she asks.

"I know the palace inside out," you tell her. You were, you say, a servant there. And the servants have many secret ways so they may be where needed without offending the eye in crossing from place to place. And, of all things, you were never a servant in the palace, but you were a child there once. Children get everywhere they're not supposed to.

She pays for a meal with your money, in a nearly windowless taverna stinking of stale beer; of the sweat, vomit and blood of its patrons. She picks over what you can tell her of how the riches of the king are defended. Because of course you've told her it's all about the riches, not the king. And though certain choice trinkets have been abstracted from the palace, no-one has ever reached the treasury itself. The challenge speaks to Ollec.

"Too many guards patrol the lowest floors," she decides. "Each with a whistle and a loud voice, and a bronze gorget to stop a garotte from conveniently silencing either. But the roof gardens give more cover. A good climber, a soft-shoe cove, someone to get up, get in, get you all in." And so she introduces you to Elemi the Ape.

There's precious little of the ape in Elemi. She's small, precise, elegant, restrained. She doesn't brag. She doesn't smile. Mention of the palace neither makes her blanch nor ruddies her cheeks with greed. It's a job. The down payment is good, the promise of plunging her hands into the royal treasury is satisfactory. Her approach to parting the wealthy from their valuables is so clinical you can't tell why she's even in the trade.

"Of course," Elemi says, in her sparse little back room above a cooper's shop, "the palace wardens know full well the weaknesses of their charge. There's a reason the roof garden has no human guards. The grounds likewise. They are not safe from dusk to dawn." And so Ollec introduces you to Yance the Silent.

He's anything but silent when you meet. A broad, squat man, gnarled by outdoor life, from some nomad tribe you never heard of. Exiled to Narad-Var for crimes you don't even have words for in your language. Drinking fermented milk and roaring greetings to this regular or that, in the filthy gambling den you find him in. "I'm your man!" he confirms happily, and it's not for the riches or the daring. He has some grudge against the crown, or the king, or the city, or perhaps the whole concept of civilization. He will guide you through the savage wilderness of the palace grounds, through the shadows of the garden.

"But the palace itself!" Yance shakes his beard at you. "A thousand clever locks and magical wards. Curses and fire and poisonous needles."

Elemi's contemptuous look says she can deal with locks, but magic is another matter. The lower city has a thousand quacksalvers and failed apprentices and hedge witches, but a little knowledge is often worse than none at all, and nobody wants to rely on a magician who's *almost* good enough. So it is that Ollec brings you to Tenebric, the spider cultist.

There are far too many spider cults in Narad-Var for you to know this one. They're all forbidden, all secretive, and their arachnid iconographies are very similar. Tenebric shuffles up in a grey robe, face and voice sexless. You sit on stone benches in the shadow of a hideous icon whose eight barbed limbs arc down towards the grooved and red-marked sacrificial stone. Tenebric lights up a pipe with a spark from their finger and listens to Ollec's pitch. You expect the cultist to be on fire with arachnid heresies, striking a blow against the orthodox pantheon. Except Tenebric is all about the money, because being a devotee of the spider god pays very poorly. The gifts of the spider will undo the magics of the palace, so long as Tenebric gets first pick of the treasure.

So Ollec the Borquan furnishes you with your team, and one night soon after, you gather within sight of the palace. The thief, the wild man, the cultist, slinking through the shadows of rich houses, dodging the patrols of the king's own guard. Here to rob the king. Here to thumb their noses at the king. Here, though they don't know it, to restore the king to his throne.

The walls of the palace grounds are tall, capped with broken shards of sword blades—every weapon used by the Uthrani war host when they came and battered themselves to death against the city. Their edges are too sharp for a rope to find purchase amongst them and the walls are too smooth for even a lizard to climb. Elemi the Ape is up and over them in three breaths and has a side gate open in another half-dozen. As swiftly as that you become an intruder in your own home.

The grounds themselves are a patchwork of pleasure gardens, fountain-decked groves and broad open parades. You have often spent afternoons with your favourites here, reaping the pleasures of power while men like Enephet gave the orders that ran your city. Only while the sun shone, however. After dark, not even the king could safely walk these shadowed haunts. Your servants saw to that, letting slip the great barred gates to the pens, giving the beasts free roam. More than one opportunistic rogue has left only a few scraps of bloodied clothing as testament to the palace's defences.

They come slavering out of the night. They do not bark: why warn those doomed to die? Not dogs, not cats, not crocodiles. Something of the bear, of the hyena, in the front-heavy way they stand. Great spines crest their backs. Their tusks are murder. Your royal blood is no more to them than that of the least beggar.

Yance steps forwards and becomes true to his name. A quiet gathers about the hirsute, barbaric little man, as though the whole ground and air, the trees, the night itself bends low to listen. He locks eyes with the lead beast and approaches it, one hand extended. The silence of Yance the Silent slowly clenches into a fist so tight you cannot breathe. Elemi's eyes are wide. Tenebric thoughtfully rubs fingertip against chin.

Yance lays a hand upon the beast's muzzle. His lips move, but his words are only for the monster, not for you. A moment later the creature licks his hand, nuzzles at him with its appalling tusked head, and then the pack lopes off as though none of you are there. Even though it's what you counted on, the dereliction of their duty hurts you. When you are restored, you will have better beasts, more savage, less amenable to these primitive wiles.

Soon, you are at the argent walls of the palace itself. You crouch low as guards move past, peering out of each narrow window as though they, too, fear the beasts. You know an army of servants will be abroad in the hundred rooms within, cleaning and mending and making everything perfect so that the king—the false king—might see no fleck of dust, no stain, no mark. Any thieves entering the palace's lower floors would be detected at once. Even disguising yourselves would not serve: the age-old dance of the palace staff has been honed to meticulous perfection over generations. Every one of them precisely placed so that an errant thief tripping through the halls would stand out as monstrously as one of the beasts from outside drinking tea in the aviary.

So: the roof garden.

Elemi scales the impossibly smooth wall without hesitating, more nimbly than any true ape, letting down a rope for those less talented, such as yourself. And in the end they must haul you up because a life as king has not prepared you for such exertions. You sense their contempt. Even the studious cultist Tenebric can climb a rope. You bear both the indignity and the scorn. Betrayal has taught you patience.

The roof garden of the palace of Narad-Var is no safer than the grounds. There are night-blooming plants here that can and have devoured intruders. These Yance identifies and guides you around. There are traps and deadfalls set by the palace gardeners, and these Elemi spots with her dark-adapted eyes.

When the spider descends on Yance and sinks its fangs into him, it is a surprise to all. He has time for one shocked exhalation and then the venom has him and the monster is threatening you all with its hooked legs, its sickle mandibles. You have no idea if this is some guardian you never heard tell of, or whether the roof garden was already harbouring an intruder. Perhaps there have been absences amongst the staff nobody has been able to account for.

Too late for Yance, but Tenebric raises the symbol of their cult and speaks certain words that twist and sear in the ear, and the monstrous arachnid calms and stares at you with its many eyes. Tenebric speaks with it, or at least makes sounds, and seems to listen to replies. The spider tells Tenebric where its brood is, and what parts of the roof garden to steer clear of. You do not recover Yance's body. What would you do with it? It has become the spider god's due, consecrated by the cultist post facto.

The gates that lead into the upper floors of the palace are warded with magic and barred with iron locks. The ease with which Tenebric and Elemi together can dismantle these protections is demoralising. In your head you are building quite the list of changes to the palace's defences.

There are certain lax functionaries who will be hauled before the king—the newly reinstated king—who will hold them to a stern accounting of their failures.

Once inside, it is time for your own contribution to this venture. You lead them from chamber to chamber, through the servants' doors you used as a child to hide from your tutor's rod or your father's hand. Into dusty, unused little rooms when you hear the scuff of sandals ahead. Out through paintings and false panels and sliding stone blocks, all the strange workings decreed by generations of seneschals and viziers and bored royalty.

The upper stories of the palace at night are a maze of locks and wards. Only a handful of servants are permitted here, and each knows only one path. You were an industrious child, though. You found many of them, and you can circumvent much of your own defences. When you come across a lock you cannot find a way round, Elemi attacks it with picks and springs it too swiftly. When you find a ward or a watchful ghost or a protective sigil, the subtle machinations of the spider cult suffice to circumvent it. Even though this is all slaved to your purpose, you are slick with cold sweat at how close an assassin might have come, had not your own vizier got to you first.

And then the door to the royal chambers. Eight feet tall, faced with bronze panels showing the great victories of your forefathers, who were so mighty that their descendant never needed to be strong or determined or even particularly clever. Until now. How odd that only betrayal served to wake the king within you!

And even you, untrained, can see the shimmer of the magics defending the portal. *A thousand royal curses on the unworthy hand that defiles these doors!* But Tenebric is undaunted, kneeling and drawing runes in blood and soot around the frame, building a stealthy web that catches all the power of your ancestors and holds it, helpless and raging. A hundred years of forbiddance and royal privilege, undone as simply as that. And Tenebric executes a magicianly flourish at their own cleverness and lays a hand upon the ring of the door. And hisses in pain as the simple needle set there breaks skin and discharges its load of venom.

The cultist collapses, twitching, fitting, foaming. Dead in seconds before your eyes. And that makes two, half your number. Elemi looks grim. You do not care. The door is open despite Tenebric's death. You step into your own chambers, knowing that here there are no more traps, no wards, no beasts. Only you and the usurper.

Elemi pads across the antechamber. You have explained that the king's own treasure is held within a secret room accessed by a panel on a certain wall. She sets about searching for the catch with professional care.

You creep to the next door, inch it open. See the mounded form lying in the bed beyond, hear its steady breath. Beside the bed, the golden mask of the king rests crooked on its stand. The air tastes of imminent revenge, but you have one last piece of business to deal with.

Elemi is still searching, glancing at you with a frown. "Where's the catch?" she murmurs, so consumed with the rigors of her profession she doesn't even note the obsidian knife in your fist.

You drive it into her side, under her ribs, then again, and then into her neck. Her scream, after so much silent work, is shocking. You stab her again to make sure and then drive the knife into her corpse. There is no catch. There is no secret panel. You will have no thieves sullying your treasure.

And the usurper needed a wake-up call, because you will not simply slit his throat in his sleep. He must *know* before he dies.

He has a lamp lit. He has the mask on when you enter. The golden visage stares serenely at you, sheets pulled up to that metal chin. You look for panic in the eyes behind it, but instead find something else. A raw emotion you have no words for.

"So," says the muffled, metal tone the mask lends to the king. Hard to understand, really. Small wonder the voice of the vizier was always louder.

"That's right, Enephet," you say, showing him the knife, letting the lamplight glisten on Elemi's blood. "I'm back. You cannot keep the true royal line in darkness. And when I've finished with you, I shall have every member of your family excruciated, yes, even those who have the least drop of your blood. I shall have magicians locate your least acknowledged bastards and flay each last one, even be they babes in arms."

And he laughs.

Not a happy laugh. Not the sound of vizierly cunning about to turn the tables on the intruder. A terrible bleak sound of a man who's lost far more than life or kin.

"You're too late." That empty, hollow voice. "It's been done. Exactly as you describe, to the last one of them."

You blink, taken aback, but perhaps all of Enephet's family were as treacherous as he, and even the man himself could not trust them.

"Then I shall finish the task here and now," you tell him, and close with him.

He slips from the sheets, naked; a younger, leaner body than you'd expect from the vizier. That laugh again.

"You don't know," he tells you. "You never know." Arms spread, inviting the knife. "O gods! Do it, then. Just get it over with. I'm tired."

You'd wanted pleading. You'd wanted misery. Enephet's last moments should have been drowned in agony and fear, not this weird relief. With a snarl you reach forwards and do what no man might do save the rightful king himself—you tear the royal mask from his face.

It is not his face.

You know whose face it is. The weak chin, the long nose, the watery, flinching eyes. A face inferior to the calm majesty of the mask in every way. A face the bronze of your mirror showed you each morning. Your face.

You recoil. The mask—the king's sacred mask—falls from your fingers and clangs to the floor. You stand before yourself and you—that other you—trembles and laughs and sobs, all at once.

"Enephet is dead, with all his line," that other you tells you. "I saw to it myself. I had the torturers teach me, so I could tear his skin off a strip at a time. I had my revenge. I retook my throne and the mask. That should have been the end of it."

It is a trick. Some magic, some sleight of hand. You menace yourself with the knife, forcing that other you back against the wall. There's no fear of the blade in him, but there is fear. A terrible fear that goes far beyond that of pain or even death. Fear of a universe grown vast and cancerous behind the walls you thought were unscalable, the doors that should have remained locked.

"You keep coming," he says with your lips. "I can't stop it." That terrible broken laugh again. "I have seen *eighteen* of you, of me, dead. Some in the lower city. Some come straight to the palace gates, ranting about being the true king. Some torn apart in the grounds, killed by the guards, poisoned by the traps, blasted by the wards. Eighteen. And now this. One of us more patient and cunning than the others, and here you are, breaching the royal bedchamber. Just as I did months before when I came for Enephet."

"Lies," you spit, but he's not even listening.

"I don't know how many others of us died, that I didn't even see," he tells you earnestly. "I just know … we don't stop coming. We keep crawling out of the dark down there. Knowing only one thing. That we want revenge."

"Lies," you repeat desperately.

"Eighteen corpses with our face," he whispers. "People are starting to notice that, when they find intruders in the grounds, they all look the same. And nobody knows the face, of course. Except me. Except us. And down there in the dark, they're still coming, one after another. An eternal act of creation. Because we demanded it. Because we asked for it, and it was a god of life, generous beyond our wildest dreams."

He has your wrist. You try to draw back but he won't let you. Inexorably he guides the knife until the blade is at his throat, which is your throat, perfect in every detail.

"I can't live like this," he tells you, wild-eyed. "Take the knowledge from me. Take it all. You'll never be safe. Because you'll always be coming for you. Untold legions of you. You'll never sleep soundly. And the last thing you'll ever see will be your own face."

"No," you croak and then he forces your hand, literally. Opens his own throat with your blade. Royal blood flooding out down your arm, slicking the floor. Except perhaps the blood royal isn't so precious anymore. What gives a thing value, after all, save scarcity?

The body, your body, collapses down the wall and sprawls on the royal floor. You've had your revenge. You've reclaimed your throne. Again. You're king once more. Until the next time. Until the temple deep below vomits out the next *you* resourceful enough to evade your traps and guardians and find you here. Until the lower city fills with displaced kings all conspiring to retake a throne that's been taken and retaken until it holds no meaning any more. Until the whole city groans and cracks with the burden of so many true heirs, drowns in an ocean of royal blood.

You sit on the bed; the knife tumbles from numb hands. Outside, beyond the antechamber, there is a soft footstep, the stealthy tread of a new intruder. You close your eyes. You don't want to see their face.

HAND OF
THE ARTIST

TRUDI CANAVAN

So, young man, this is all your fault. If I'd known you were going to write down everything I said last time you interviewed me, word for word, I would not have mentioned anything about a scandal. But I did, and you did, and here we are now, under orders by our fresh young king to record that particular episode of my life.

Well, I'm not sure if I mind. I've longed to tell this story, even if doing so will mean admitting to great foolishness. Only time will tell if I regret it, and at my age, that is not much time at all. So we best get on with it.

Hmm.

No, I do not hesitate because I am reluctant. These events happened so long ago that all for whom it was most painful are dead, save myself.

It is only living so long with a magical restriction preventing me from speaking that makes me pause. Though Master Towan assured me that I won't lose the ability to breathe now, the memory of suffocating is strong and I fear it will manifest merely from habit. I have only ever deliberately attempted to speak of it once, to my father, so that he might guess from the consequences of me trying that shame was not the sole reason I'd stayed away. My mother was dying, you see, and if they thought I might not have been to blame for the scandal, perhaps it would have eased her passing and his own heart.

Though it would not have if they'd know the full truth: that my actions led to the murder of a king.

There. I have said it and not choked to death.

You look a little pale. You've stopped writing. Are you well?

Good. Let us begin properly.

My childhood home was a country estate a week's carriage ride from the Mountain. All my young life I'd prepared for the day my family would visit the palace and I would meet the king, queen and prince and the rest of the court. There we would stay until I found a husband—perhaps even the prince, my mother said—and begin my life wherever and however he chose.

I had the good looks of youth, though not those of a great beauty, but I had been well groomed in all the expected ways, from memorizing lineages to courtly manners to how to fake losing a game or a bet convincingly. Court sounded like a great deal of fun, and I was looking forward to joining it, but as I neared the age when such a journey ought to have occurred, events prevented me. The queen was ill. The queen had died and the court was in mourning. All the available young men were undesirable and my prospects would be better next year. A disfiguring sickness was going around court … I suspect my parents invented that last one.

My parents hired all manner of tutors to add more skills to my repertoire, but I began to suspect their true purpose was to keep me distracted. That is how I became so skilled a painter, you see. I spent many, *many* hours learning and honing my craft.

Then one day my parents told me that some important people were coming from the palace to check my father's books and ensure we were paying our taxes. She said I was not to join them at dinner, or be seen by any of them, and arranged activities that would keep me away from the house all day. I was furious. Even a tax collector sounded fascinating and glamorous to a young woman raised on stories of the court.

My annoyance kept me awake at night, so I would slip down to the kitchens to make myself a warm drink. One night I found a man I did not know helping himself to the contents of the larder.

He exclaimed in surprise as he noticed me; then, as he took in my overrobe, which was too fine for a servant, he bowed. "I apologise, lady. I should have called for a servant but I did not wish to wake anyone."

"It is I who should apologise for startling you, lord," I said, as I had noted that his clothing was also too fine for a servant. "Are you with the tax collectors?" I asked. "From the Mountain."

"I am," he replied. "A mere assistant. Please, forgive me for my intrusion."

In the dim light of the lamp I carried, I could see he was a slight but leanly muscled man, pleasingly symmetrical. The artist in me wanted to see him in better light, while the curious young woman in me did not want to let the opportunity pass to meet someone from the Mountain, so I turned up the light and sat at the kitchen table.

"I will," I told him boldly, "if you tell me about the Mountain."

He smiled at that. "It would be my pleasure," he said, then he expressed astonishment that I had not yet visited the city, as most young women my age had. I explained, not quite managing to hide the bitterness from my voice, that my parents had found reasons each year to delay taking me there.

We talked late into the night. He was amiable and funny, a good listener but not reticent about his own life, which had taken him from a lesser son of a noble to one of the palace's senior talliers. After that encounter we met every night. When he learned that I liked to paint, he asked to see my work and professed to be amazed at my talent. He told me it was a shame that I had not had the opportunities and admiration of the court and that any man who won my hand would be the envy of the Mountain. I drank down all his praise and anger on my behalf and wondered aloud if we might, between us, manipulate my parents into returning to the Mountain with him. Perhaps he might invite my family to court in a way that would be rude to refuse. He said he would raise it with his master.

The next night he told me that my parents had turned down the tax collector's invitation on the basis of my poor health. I was shocked by their outright lie and my anger deepened. He saw this and took my hand.

"I will take you to the Mountain myself!" he declared.

My heart filled with hope and joy, but both quickly subsided. If I did so, there would be such a scandal I would never be welcome in good company again, let alone find a husband worthy of my family name. Though I found I cared less about that than I expected, I did not want to hurt my parents.

Seeing my hesitation, he got down on his knees. "I must beg your forgiveness again," he told me. "All this time I have lied to you. I am not an assistant to the tax collector. I *am* the head tallier. I am the King's Pen."

"What are you saying?" I demanded, though I already knew since he had told me about the hierarchy of the court and the titles of the most important men and women.

"I am also the king's closest and most loyal friend," he told me, meeting my gaze. "When I arrived here, I sensed that something was being hidden from me. I disguised myself in order to secretly check that the house's stores were as your father recorded. I had not reckoned on finding you. Nor of … of falling instantly in love with you. Every night my appreciation of you has deepened." He took my hand. "Marry me."

If I recall correctly, I gaped at him in a most undignified way.

"Come back with me to the Mountain," he urged. "We will be wed there. Your parents will be angry, yes, but they will forgive us once they know you are happy and well positioned at court."

My surprise gave way to excitement, yet I could not make an affirmation pass my lips. My thoughts were spinning, doubts rising. He responded to my hesitation with a kind nod.

"You are right to be wary. Tomorrow, let me prove my identity. Come to your father's office at midday."

The next day at the appointed hour, I reached the door of my father's office and stopped as I overheard a loud argument. The content of it convinced me of my suitor's identity, but also that my father disliked him intensely. As if sensing me listening, my ally asked if I would ever be well enough to visit the court, and my father rudely snapped his reply that I would never go there even if I were hale and healthy.

Filled with dismay and bitterness, I returned to my room to consider my options. If my parents did not intend to take me to the Mountain, what were their plans? To marry me off to one of the few local nobles' sons, none of whom I liked? For me to be unwed and childless for the rest of my days? My suitor and ally was the best chance I had of the future I wanted. To throw my lot in with the King's Pen would be no hardship. He was rich, powerful, handsome and charming. Under his influence, the scandal would be seen as a romantic elopement. My parents would have to see it as a suitable match eventually.

I laugh now to think I was once desired such mundane things so badly and that I thought myself better able to judge people than my parents, but I would not go back and advise myself differently. My mistakes have made me and this land what they are now. It is up to others to decide if the result is better or worse.

On the evening of the following day, I slipped out of the house with a small bag of my most precious belongings and met his carriage beside the road. To my dismay, the presence of his assistants prevented private conversation. Each night of our journey we stayed at an estate house, where he insisted I eat and sleep in my own room, saying we must behave correctly until the king had approved our betrothal. He could have found moments in which to express reassurance and affection, but he was strangely aloof. As days passed with little sign of the affection he'd shown before, my doubts began to grow. He had lied to me about his identity. Had he concealed anything else? Was he really the king's closest friend? Did he have a purpose other than love for marrying me? Did he have debts and thought to ransom me back to my parents? Was there another benefit to an alliance with my family that I could not discern?

The first sight of the Mountain amazed me so much it silenced those thoughts for a while, and I was reassured when we finally entered the palace precinct and his identity was confirmed. He left me in the care of a friend to preserve my reputation until our wedding, then left to seek an audience with the king.

The unease I'd felt on the journey faded, so I did not sense the wrongness about the palace when we arrived. I had no real concept of how it should be, so no comparison to make. His friend, a widow, treated me well but with no true warmth or desire to know me. She told me the king was ill. My suitor visited each morning, assuring me he would raise the issue of our betrothal when the monarch recovered. I noted that, whenever he said this, the widow looked at me with a strange expression—a mix of pity and contempt. Though she advised me to not leave her rooms without an escort, she declined my request for a tour of the Mountain and mostly ignored me. As days passed, I grew bored and unable to sleep from lack of activity, so one night I slipped out of her rooms to explore the palace alone.

It was not difficult to remain unnoticed. Most of the lights were broken, so I could retreat into one of the shadows whenever I heard someone approaching. Signs of neglect and decay were everywhere. Paintings had darkened, some to full black. Strange smells wafted from rooms or lingered in odd corners of the corridors. Servants hurried about and when addressed were either fearful or disdainful. The few courtiers I saw walked quickly and intently or else gathered in whispering groups. All spoke softly and wore soft shoes that muffled footsteps, so it seemed as if something was thickening the air and dampening all sound. The palace itself seemed as ill as the king.

Then, on the third night, I heard a sound of such contrasting brightness I could not resist its lure: many voices, some of them laughing, some singing. Memories rose of the yearly festivals held for the commoners that worked and lived around my home. The sound drew me to the entrance of a large room, but I could not see inside without stepping out of the shadows, and as I dared to, a group of men and women came up behind me. Seeing my hesitation, they invited me to join them. Their warmth seemed genuine, so I accepted.

That room, you may have guessed, was the Chalice. I'd never been to a tavern before, so I did not know how special this one was, being inside the palace. It was for the servants, artisans, and performers, but it was so popular, some members of court occasionally gathered there to eat and drink.

The men and women who invited me in would eventually become my friends, some of them lifelong ones. Each night I slipped away to meet them. Afraid that they would reject me should they learn I was of the nobility, I told them I was an artist's assistant. They challenged me to show them my work, so the next night I brought my drawing materials and sketched their portraits, and after that they accepted my story.

Several nights later, the subject of the king came up. Someone had heard the monarch had mostly recovered from his latest bout of illness and would soon call for entertainment. They looked surprisingly grim at the news, so I asked why this was not good.

"You don't know?" someone asked—it is so long ago I do not recall who said what—and as I nodded another leaned close and spoke in a low voice. "The king is quite mad," he explained. "Mad and cruel."

"Best hope he never even lay eyes on you," one of the women warned. "Especially when he's in one of his moods."

I pretended fear. As a noble woman, I would be immune to such abuse, but they didn't know that. "And if I can't avoid it?"

I do recall it was one of the acrobats, his tongue loosened by spirits, who sagged toward me then. "Let's just say, the claims about the king's prowess are true," he told me. "The man has bedded every woman he has laid his eyes on, no matter their status. Servant or noble. Married or unwed. Enemy or friend."

"Only below a certain age," a female acrobat said, winking at me. "Which is I why I dress and paint myself to look older."

Now I was caught between disbelief and worry. "But surely not everyone," I said. "Powerful families would not want their daughters ..."

"The Mountain is full of his bastards, from the Lower Slopes to the High Peaks," the drunk acrobat added. "Though I've heard he's too old and sick to sire bastards now."

They all nodded in agreement. "Which is why he plays nasty games with people instead, I reckon," someone pointed out. "Not being able to ... you know ... makes him angry." The acrobat then turned to me and sighed. "The queen was able to keep him in check, but after she died nobody's been brave enough to stand up to him."

"Because nobody refuses the king and lives," someone pointed out, to which they all nodded in agreement.

"Not even the prince dares refuse him," the drunk said, but the others warned him not to speak of the prince and turned the conversation to the cruelties the king had inflicted on performers and artisans, to the traders ruined when the king had seized their stock or neglected to pay for orders, and decent nobles exiled. As they began to speak over one another, the stories grew worse and I turned to the man next to me.

"What of the King's Pen?" I asked. "Surely he ..."

The man screwed up his nose in distaste. "He's the one who ensures the king's desires are met. Whatever the king wants, the Pen delivers."

Needless to say, I was truly frightened. Was this the real reason my supposed suitor had brought me here? My parents' reasons for keeping me at home finally made sense. Years later my father explained that they hadn't told me because they did not want me to be afraid of something that might never happen

But I had run straight into danger. What could I do now? Could I escape the palace as easily as I did the widow's rooms each night? Where would I go then? I couldn't return to my parents. Even if they forgave my disobedience, it was the first place the King's Pen would look for me. The only alternative was to disappear among the common people, with no money and no skills to earn any. The poor do not commission portraits.

I asked the female acrobat if she would teach me how to change my appearance to look older, and we agreed on a time. I also decided to ask her, when we met, if she or the others could help me escape the Mountain and find work as a painter elsewhere.

I did not get the chance, however.

The next morning, when the King's Pen came to join me for the morning meal, he told me the king was feeling much better and wanted to meet me and have his portrait painted. My stomach turned to stone, and he interpreted my fear as intimidation.

"Don't be nervous," he told me, placing a hand on my shoulder. "The king may be better but he is still very tired. He will not expect you to follow formalities. Just be a pleasant distraction to him—a balm for the pain." He sighed. "It saddens me to see him so diminished. We are old friends, you know. I may be the last person he trusts, and he fears that if I take a wife he will lose me. Show him that instead he will gain another friend."

I was too appalled by his lies to speak. He took me to through the palace to a circular hall where we joined a handful of courtiers relaxing on divans. My betrayer introduced me and I was welcomed, but I was too frightened to give more than the simplest answers to their questions and their interest waned quickly. He told them I was nervous about meeting the king and would be my usual bold and interesting self afterwards, then he left to check on the king. All too soon he returned, took my hand and led me up a curved staircase to the balcony that overlooked the hall. After leading me to a grand pair of doors, he pushed one open and ushered me through.

The smell assailed me first. The air was thick with perfume that clashed with something medicinal, under which lay the taint of sickness. The sight of an enormous bed seemed to confirm my tavern friends' warnings. A bedroom was not an appropriate place for a young woman of noble birth to meet with any man, be he king or commoner. Heavy wooden furniture stood against the walls like menacing guards. An easel had been set up at the corner of the bed, with paints laid out on a table beside it.

Then I saw him, sitting in a chair beside the bed.

"You took it off," the King's Pen said, leaving me standing behind the easel.

Though my heart was racing, a part of my mind began making notes. The king looked older than I had been told, but illness might have aged him prematurely. Painting him younger would be prudent. He was both fat and thin, flesh hanging where it had once been plumper, like a water float that had been partially deflated. Should I paint him rounder or thinner? I decided rounder, as it was probably how he had most recently been known. Dark shadows ringed his eyes, making his brows jut out, but that could be compensated for with a more flattering depiction of lighting. Hair in all shades of grey had been smoothed into the current slick style except at his brow where he had rubbed it into chaos again, as he was doing then.

His clothes were fine and flowing, conveying regality, but no ornament proclaimed his importance and power. The King's Pen walked over to the bed, where a heavy gold bib lay, huge gemstones glinting in the soft lamplight.

"It gives me a headache. She can paint it in later," the king growled.

His voice sent a jolt through me. The king might look diminished, but his voice held all the arrogance and authority I had expected.

"Of course," the King's Pen replied. He turned and introduced me.

"It is an honour to meet you, your majesty," I managed to say, my voice tight with nerves.

The king merely squinted at me. "Is the lighting suitable?" he asked.

I glanced around slowly as if considering. "May the lamps be brought closer?"

He jerked his chin at his friend. "Do it."

I asked for the easel to be moved, then moved again, and for the king to shift his position in the chair. A part of me enjoyed this small moment of control—this delay—until the king abruptly dismissed my betrayer, who bowed and left the room.

It took all my courage to not flee after him.

I began painting.

Usually, a calm comes over me as I work. This time my heart continued to race. I sketched out rough details to get the proportions right, deciding to paint only his face. To distract him, I should have started a conversation, but I did not know how and then it occurred to me that protocol required that I wait for him to begin, then follow his lead.

But he didn't speak. As the silence lengthened, he began to twitch and shift. One leg began jumping up and down, then his attention moved to something beyond my shoulder, turning his head into a different pose than I was painting. I nearly asked him to turn back, but when my mouth opened he gave me such a forbidding expression I said nothing.

Then his hand moved and he began scratching.

He didn't stop, and after one glance at the source of his itch I fixed my attention on mixing paint, hoping he would stop soon. My embarrassment must have shown, because he looked amused. Then a gleam of meanness crept into his eyes, and his lips curled into a sneer. Sensing the start of a cruel game, I fixed my eyes on his forehead and concentrated all my attention upon it.

My awareness flew forth and fixed on that patch of skin. I could sense the texture of it. The heat. The salty sweat of lingering fever. Looking deeper, I was drawn to a stronger, sharper impression. Pain. A throbbing, hovering, merciless pressure. It was something neither alien, nor belonging, but it was slowly winning the battle for space within the hard confines of his skull.

I thought, "No wonder he is mad." Despite all I knew about him, I felt pity. I wished to paint away that pain, along with the sagging flesh and shadows. I imagined my brush moving deeper, easing the pressure, blotting out the wrongness and smoothing the tortured substance within.

A grunt from the king distracted me. My awareness came back to the room to find him staring at me in shock. His hands rose and rubbed at his brow again, further messing up his hair, then he looked up and his eyes widened.

"What did you do?" he asked, his voice no longer forceful, but husky and weak.

I could not answer him, but I could see by the shift of his gaze that his mind had already moved elsewhere. Somewhere that horrified him, by the way he winced. He groaned, then jumped to his feet.

"I've done such terrible things," he said. His eyes filled with tears and he looked down at himself. "I am a monster."

He suddenly rushed toward me, a strange fire in his gaze. Alarmed, I backed away but his attention was fixed beyond me. He strode past me then pushed through the door. I hesitated, unsure what I should do, then put my brush down and approached the doorway, hoping to slip away.

The king had crossed to the balcony overlooking the circular hall where I'd waited for the King's Pen to fetch me and he was looking down at the people.

"I'm sorry," he told them. "I have wronged so many of you. I'm so sorry."

I do not know how the audience responded, except that they remained silent. The king began speaking to individuals, admitting what he had done to them or their kin and begging their forgiveness. I approached the balcony and looked down at the disbelieving and surprised faces, and then at the King's Pen. He was staring at the king in astonishment, but as he saw me he frowned and rose to his feet with the air of someone used to taking charge.

"Father."

The voice came from behind me. I turned to see two young men approaching from another door to the balcony. Both were finely dressed and I realized who the foremost was as he spoke.

"Father," the prince repeated. "I cannot let you—"

"Son." The king turned to face him, then he reached out to embrace the prince. "I am sorry. I am so sorry."

The prince's first reaction was to recoil, but as his father's arms touched his shoulders he pushed the king away. The monarch stumbled back onto the balcony railing. I heard a creak, looked down, and saw that several of the supports were cracked, one broken right through.

Time seemed to pause, and the king caught his balance. I looked up at the prince. He glanced at me briefly, then back at his father. Then he reached out as if to return the king's embrace …

… and pushed.

I heard a crack. As the king's arms flew wide my first thought was to grab one, but then a thought made me freeze. *Whatever I had healed, if that is what I did, was not there all his life. No one had said he was a decent man who inexplicably changed to a monster.* So I did not move.

Even so, one of the king's hands caught my arm and I realized, as he pulled me over the edge, I could not have supported his weight anyway.

All I remember after that were flashes of consciousness that came with pain so terrible, I welcomed oblivion. In one moment of awareness, I heard voices chanting the prince's name, but they called him 'king'. In another I saw the prince's young companion hovering above me and, in the background, someone begging and their words ending suddenly.

When I woke properly, I found myself on a bed with my legs wrapped in bandages and still hurting badly. I called out and a healer came. He told me I was in the infirmary and explained that I had broken both of my legs. The prince had ordered me to be cared for in a private room. I spent a few hours alone, thinking over everything that had happened: what I had sensed and intended as I painted the king, his sudden change in behaviour, and his murder by the prince. I decided I'd imagined the association between painting and the king's sudden apologies. The idea was ridiculous. I wasn't sure what to think about the prince's actions and decided to pretend I hadn't noticed.

Of course, my first two visitors were the prince and his companion, who I learned was the palace sorcerer, Master Towan. I did not have a chance to speak. The prince—now king—ordered me to be silent. He told me I must never speak of the events of that day to anyone, ever. To ensure that, Master Towan placed a charm on my mind that would stop my breathing if I ever made such an attempt.

Years later, a Sorcerers' School teacher claimed that a sorcerer with healing powers was born just once in a lifetime, but none had manifested in more than a hundred years. I pointed out that those powers would be wasted, since the School did not admit women. In truth, I don't know if healers are more likely to be women or men, but I did enjoy his confusion and then skepticism.

Oh, I am not angry that the king ordered me silenced. I would have done it were I in his place. He was a better king than his father. Who knows what this new one will be like? Kings come, kings go. I'm too old to take it personally.

Now? My powers have waned with age. I doubt I could do much even if I had been trained. It would be dangerous to try. I could as easily harm someone as heal them. Which is what I will tell our fresh new king if he asks, which I'm sure he will.

I wasn't *displeased* to learn that the King's Pen was beheaded that night. I did wonder, for a long time afterwards, what his true motivation was. The widow came to visit me in the infirmary, you see. She gave me a document she said she had found in his rooms when clearing them out. It was a formal announcement of his intention to marry me, which only required the king's sign of approval.

Yes, perhaps he did. Perhaps it was only to keep me believing the lie, should I start to suspect. I will never know.

What did I do then? My new friends visited me in the infirmary. They'd heard that I'd been present at the accident that had killed the king. I couldn't tell them much, of course. The widow had brought me my painting materials and, as I'd been moved to the general ward, I kept myself entertained making portraits of other patients, and a few were purchased by relatives of those who died. By the time I was well enough to leave I had a few commissions lined up, and eventually I was able to support myself as a painter of miniatures. Which I did until I discovered another magical property of painting which was to change the world.

But that is a whole other story, and I am too tired to speak of it today.

THE CONSPIRACY AGAINST THE TWENTY-THIRD CANTON

Alex Marshall

The history of the Star is written in the blood of queens and kings. From the greatest empire to the humblest fiefdom, the fortunes of every realm are inseparable from the fate of its rulers. This is the way of all worlds. Even the devils had their king, before he abdicated his throne, plunging the First Dark into a deeper shade of chaos … or so the old song goes. To know the story of a people, whether one's own or another, is to know who led them, by right of birth or strength of arm or wits; for as long as there are mortals there will be those who command, those who heed, and those who rebel. Learn their names, trace their struggles, memorize their deeds, and you will know the song of all days.

The only thing Vhumi Bensi found more tedious than ancient history was her future as Tapai of the Twenty-third Canton of Ugrakar. Ever since her sixth birthday—when her father had spoiled a perfectly frivolous tea party with a lecture on how she should treat her dolls as peons instead of peers—the shadow of responsibility had loomed on the horizon, darkening what should have been the bright days of her youth. Trying to enjoy one's life knowing it will inexorably lead to a somber throne room is like attempting to savor a homecoming feast knowing your dessert will be fishhook soufflé.

According to Vhumi's father, her antipathy toward her role was definitive proof of her worthiness for it. When the Living Saint had decreed his thirty-six disciples should divide their country equally and then adhere to dynastic succession at all costs, he had intended to foster this very sentiment. To be born to the burden was the only way of ensuring that tapais ruled from a place of duty, not ambition.

Not that any system is foolproof. Vhumi's father felt the same reluctance, at first, only to fall deeper in love with his liabilities with each passing year. Now as he lay on his deathbed, stricken with a wasting disease that would render the ritual consumption of his flesh by his family a sparse repast, Vhumi tried one last time to pawn her title off on her Aunt Agaja.

"She knows our land and people better than anyone, maybe even better than you," said Vhumi, spooning buttered chai into her father's trembling mouth.

The dying tapai slurped the thick tea. "True, true. And if some tragedy were to befall both you and Krish, I have no doubt my sister would make as worthy a tapai as I—but she is not next in line. You were born to be Twenty-third Tapai, Vhumi."

"You thought I was born a boy, too," said Vhumi. "You believed me when I told you I was a girl, so believe me now when I tell you I am not a tapai."

His wizened face creased into one of those infuriatingly condescending parental smiles. "Sweet Vhumi, to rule well you must learn that some things are fixed at birth. Just as you were given a body that you alone may govern, so too were you given a canton that you alone must rule. You can decide what shape your governance will take, but you cannot say, 'this is not mine.'"

"I thought the tapai could say anything she wants," said Vhumi, regretting the petulance as soon as it left her lips. This wasn't how she'd wanted what might be their last conversation to go.

"If you decide to be the first tapai in Ugrakar to abdicate her birthright, I will be in no position to stop you." He shook his head when she tried to spoon him more chai. "But if you choose to ride such a shameful yak, it won't be my sister who takes your place—it will be Krish. Is that what you want for the Twenty-third Canton?"

This was as close as he'd ever come to acknowledging the unsuitability of her little brother to rule. Krish Bensi coveted their father's throne as openly as Vhumi wished to avoid it, a sure sign he would make a terrible tapai. Patting her quaking hand with his, he said, "I know it wasn't always easy, but in time you found peace with your flesh—now you must do the same with your title. Our people shall soon look to you whether you want them to or not. What will you show them?"

The old tapai didn't have much time left, and Vhumi knew she should spend her every waking hour at his bedside, soaking up all she could of statecraft. Yet the dawn bell found her not joining him to review the dueling petitions of bickering millet farmers but saddling her dire yak in the royal stables. From the moment she assumed rule of the canton she would never be free to ride without a retinue of guards and courtiers; this was her last chance to find salvation beyond the city's walls since it would not be found within them. Technically she wasn't supposed to leave without her father's permission and a pair of bodyguards, but here, on the eve of her absolute capitulation to tradition, she finally mustered the courage to buck it, small and fruitless a rebellion though it should surely prove.

The stable door creaked behind her. A figure stood silhouetted in the misty morning gloom. Her adventure already undone by a royal guard?

"Awfully early to be setting out," said her brother, the golden beads on his embroidered robe clicking as he crossed his arms. "Almost as if you were trying to sneak away."

"An early return demands an early start," said she, leading her yak out the stable door. As always, her brother moved out of her way at the last moment.

"That it does," said Krish. "But it would also allow you to put that many mountains between you and the yoke of service that seems too heavy for such a skinny neck as yours."

She forced a smile. "You think me capable of such a betrayal to Ugrakar?"

Would that she were, would that she were.

"Dearest sister, I am not so blinded by sentiment as Father." He always puffed out his chest when he launched one of his carefully prepared little speeches. "If you were to ride far away and leave the throne to a more deserving bottom, I should not consider it a betrayal at all—nay, such a sacrifice would be the ultimate proof of your devotion to the realm. I would see to it that all offerings were made to clear your name with the Living Saint, and you should always be welcomed back as a dutiful servant of the new regent. Not that I *wish* to rule, of course, simply that I would be willing to accept the burden if you could not."

"As always, your thoughtfulness warms my heart," said Vhumi, for truly, the only thing in all the Star that made her think she should accept her fate was the thought of Krish becoming tapai in her stead. "But rest easy, dear brother. However far I ride and late I may return, so long as there is life in my lungs I shall never shoulder you with such dread responsibility—it is my destiny, not yours."

"Of course it is," said Krish as she climbed onto her saddle in the dim courtyard. "But while the Living Saint tells us destiny is what we make of it, I still urge you caution riding alone on such a dark morning. The summer storms have made the roads treacherous, and I hear bandits lurk in the woods and passes."

"I appreciate your concern for my safety."

"I am concerned for the safety of the canton."

Vhumi left him without another word, and only after she'd passed under the ever-chiding glare of the carven yeti that squatted atop the western gate and found herself alone on the open road did it occur to her that her little brother might mean genuine menace. Did he want the throne badly enough to orchestrate an assassination and tell their father she'd fallen prey to cutthroats?

Vhumi should be so lucky to have her burdens lifted by such a plot! She spent the next few miles imagining how she would dispatch the hired killers, bringing one back to testify to her brother's involvement—Krish would be banished from the canton, and Vhumi could risk the wrath of fate by passing the crown to Aunt Agaja.

Alas, fine a daydream though it was, no true Ugrakari would ever stoop to such treachery. Whatever else Krish might be, they came from the same noble blood. If Vhumi were to dodge the arrow of destiny, she must do so on her own.

That left one path open to her, a road she had oft considered on sleepless nights only to shy away from in the light of morning—the faint yak trail that forked off from the base of Devil's Breath Bridge. The only road up Ghosthead Mountain.

Vhumi rode down from the high country, where their capital nested amongst the crags overlooking the terraced fields and misty pinewoods of the Twenty-third Canton; though waking villages, where peasants knelt at the passing of her black steed, the tinkling bells set in his horns announcing the arrival of royalty; out across naked ridges, where only the pica and the marmot plied the fields of lichen; and down, down, down into the steep valleys stitched with rushing streams and precarious crossings.

The sun must have been high when she reached the groaning cables of Devil's Breath Bridge, but the fog exhaled by the cataract upstream cloaked the deep forest in eternal twilight. After thrice circling the shale stupa in the road, her yak carried her on clattering hooves across the swaying bridge and out of the Twenty-third Canton. Were she to follow the track through the twisted juniper that girded the steep banks, she would enter the Twenty-fourth Canton, and from there it was simply a matter of minding the signposts to reach any Arm of the Star.

Ugrakari are not known for their wanderlust. Indeed, the Second Chamber of Ugrakar warns that to leave home you must first open your door, and, in doing so, invite in trouble. Yet for a girl with unfettered access to her mother's library and a court echoing with the songs of visiting griots, the lands beyond their borders teemed with possibilities far more appealing than a lifetime of civil servitude at the top of the world. Vhumi longed to sail through the Immaculate Isles and brave the burgeoning settlements of Jex Toth, to explore the prehistoric ruins of Flintland freshly exposed by receding glaciers, to watch glass storms rage over the canyons of Usba and ride a racing catfish through the sunken labyrinth at the heart of the Raniputri Dominions. She even dared to daydream of an expedition into lost Emeritus and a pilgrimage to dread Diadem, capital of Samoth and all the Crimson Empire, where an itinerant throat singer had told her the people ruled themselves with neither tapai nor queen ever since the Final Truce.

Gazing down the well-worn path into the Twenty-fourth Canton, all Vhumi had to decide was where to sojourn first. If she but goaded her yak forward, both her wish and her brother's would be granted, neat as deviltry.

Instead, she steered her yak off the road, into the hazy trees.

Vhumi never would have been able to find her way on foot, so faint was the trail, but her sure-footed steed picked his way nimbly between mossy branch and mossy boulder, up, up, up the wall of the valley. Only when she emerged from the gloomy wood into the sun-kissed field of wild saam that marked the treeline did she see he'd led her true, for a clear track meandered through the skunk-scented weeds.

She had no head for the stuff herself, but she broke off a cola as long as her forearm as they rode through the field, thinking to add it to her other offerings. The purple hairs curling from the green flower shone silver in the sun. Unlike the saam they grew in the Twenty-third Canton, the enormous bud cradled nary a single seed.

Not a wildflower, after all. It was a tapai's obligation to know the business of every crop in their realm as intimately as a farmer; if but a single male plant was allowed to bloom within leagues of these girls they'd be riddled with seeds. She plucked another. Again, no seeds.

A breeze as refreshing as snow mead rustled through the field. She gazed over the tidal wave of saam breaking over the mountainside. Witchcraft seemed the only way such a vast tract could be kept free of male influence. Perhaps the legends were true, then, and her quest more than a fool's errand. Vhumi shivered in the sunlight.

Up they climbed, leaving the susurrating sisterhood of saam to whisper in the wind below. Now only grass and lichen cloaked the flinty shoulder of Ghosthead Mountain, its face slipping behind a veil of hanging cloud. After countless switchbacks, the trail terminated in a sheer slab of rock that vanished into the clouds above and dropped hundreds of feet to the scree below. Metal posts were hammered into the granite, ancient boards balanced atop them to make a narrow walkway across the cliff face. The crude bridge looked far too precarious to lead her yak over. Vhumi dismounted, fed herself and her steed, and, after filling a bole in a rock from her waterskin, continued alone. Her old friend would be waiting when she returned … assuming the boards held.

Vhumi didn't look down. Her pack scraped against the cliff with each step. It couldn't be more than a hundred feet across, but her legs shook and her heart hiccupped with every puff of wind. Ugrakari are not scared of heights, as a rule, but neither are they fools. When she finally stepped off the last board onto the steep trail that continued up the mountain, she thanked the mercurial gusts of Ugrakar for seeing her safely across, even if an ignoble plunge to certain death would have neatly spared her the fate of tapai. She dared hope her courage would be repaid with a less terminal solution.

The trail zigzagged upward once more, scarcely less steep than the cliff, and when she breathlessly crested the rise, she saw she'd only reached a false summit. Here a glassy lake filled the clavicle of Ghosthead Mountain. Beyond, the trail continued up to where the witches must dwell—a plateau that that jutted out like the chin of the cloud-crowned peak.

A twisted ankle and a pint of sweat later, Vhumi gained the plateau. The sun drooped low over the countless peaks at her back. This must be the witching place. Against all laws of altitude and season, wild orange roses bloomed across the deep hollow in the mountainside, climbing through the trellis of rotting cartwheels and up the side of the little house-shaped wagon that had once rolled over every Arm of the Star, if the songs told true.

Behind the now-grounded vardo, a complex of typical Ugrakari huts nestled against the cheek of Ghosthead Mountain, but what took Vhumi's breath away was the sun-bleached skeleton of an enormous horned wolf sprawled between the fallen posts of the wagon's yoke, as if it had just lied down for a rest. No flowers entwined themselves around the remains as they did the cairn erected beside its regal skull, but when Vhumi approached to read the inscription on the limestone monument a low growl froze her in place.

A horned wolf emerged from the far side of the vardo. Though smaller than the fallen titan, it stood as tall as Vhumi, its ivory pelt shimmering in the setting sun. It stalked toward her, unhurried enough for Vhumi to reach for her bow—only to remember she had left it on her yak. Her hand went to her kukri instead, drawing the curved blade as two more of the hulking, shaggy beasts emerged from the shadowy huts.

Vhumi had come here to find a way to avoid the responsibility of becoming tapai, and now she'd found it. As far as epic ways to die went, being torn apart by a pack of horned wolves beat falling off a bridge. If only her brother were here to see their hopes realized!

The lead monster snarled through jagged yellow teeth, lowering its head to charge. Its twisted horns were longer than her kukri and looked every bit as sharp. Vhumi's nerve failed her and she nearly swooned. She leaned against the cairn to stay upright.

A door in the back of the vardo banged open. A little old woman with a face full of gleaming hoop, studs, and chains stepped out and jabbed a finger at the beasts. "Bvām'sō! Rücker! Oisín! What have I told you?!"

With a low whine and a flick of its tail, the pack leader turned away and slunk back to the shadows of the huts, the others following as if their horns suddenly carried the weight of the Kutumbans. The bespectacled crone blinked at Vhumi like an owlbat caught by dawn. "What do you expect, barging in here without ringing the bell? Count yourself lucky they didn't eat you alive."

"What bell?" asked Vhumi.

"The bell by the lake," said the witch. "The one that says *Ring this bell or face death.*"

"Forgive me," said Vhumi, wondering how she could have missed such a thing on the barren trail below. "I saw no sign nor bell."

"No?" The tempest of the old woman's features darkened, and for a moment she seemed so wroth Vhumi feared she might call her pet monsters back, but then all the bad weather blew out with a sigh. "Well, they didn't eat you, so no harm done. My apologies for the uncivil welcome—I am Nemi of the Honeyed Laughter, whom do I have the honor of receiving?"

"I am Vhumi Bensi," said she with a deep bow, "heir to the Twenty-third Canton."

"Hmm," said the crone. "In all my years and grimoires, I've encountered few portents more ominous than neighbors arriving uninvited at sundown. I suppose you had better come inside and tell me your business."

Vhumi followed the frail woman into the vardo and found herself in that holiest of sanctums—a library. Shelves bowed under the weight of tomes and scrolls. The back wall was given over to a less welcoming collection of jars, boxes, and curios ranging from skulls, feathers, and fossils to less mortal remains. A window looked out onto the brambly yard, a closed door presumably led deeper into the complex, and between them squatted an iron woodstove, two comfortable chairs of Imperial design, and a low driftwood table set with an Immaculate tea service.

The strangest bird Vhumi had ever seen hopped out of a hutch built into the rear wall, its head covered by a black leather hood, its snowy feathers puffed up and its long grey lizard tail lashing the floor as it bawked.

"Yes, yes, I know, such a travesty," the witch said, shooing it back into its coop and latching the wire door. "What will it be, neighbor mine, chai or chaang or something stronger?"

"Tea would be most welcome," said Vhumi, swiftly removing her offerings from her satchel and laying them on the edge of the table. She'd been raised better than to lose the age-old Ugrakari race between guest and host to bestow gifts on one another. "I hope you will accept these modest offerings of my regard. Three pounds of golden grain from our lowest fields, two wheels of the richest cheese from our deepest caves, a pouch of tubāq blended for the tapai himself, and these saam buds, which I thought most fine."

"Queenly gifts." The witch hobbled back to the table, one gnarled hand white-knuckled on her feather-topped walking stick, the other clutching a glittering egg. "Be a dear and pack my pipe with this royal tubāq, my mouth is watering already."

Vhumi took the knobby templewarden from a simple wooden stand beside a gilded Raniputri ashtray with a cork knocker rising from its center like a toadstool. As Vhumi loaded the bowl, the woman cracked her egg into one of the teacups, dropping the iridescent eggshell into a wicker wastebasket beside the woodstove. Seeing what had laid the egg, Vhumi really, really hoped the witch wouldn't ask her to eat it … and had her prayers answered in record time. The old woman knocked back the egg with obvious relish. Closing her eyes and reclining deeper in her chair, she said, "Pardon my rudeness, I need but a moment. If you would be so kind as to pour the tea …"

Vhumi returned the packed pipe to its stand and took the teapot from atop the stove. She paused over the witch's slimy cup, and though the old woman's eyes were still locked tight, she said, "Go on, I never waste the dregs."

When both cups were brimming with oily brown chai, Vhumi returned the pot to the stove … and despite her commitment not to act the superstitious rube, she gasped. In the time it had taken her to pour the tea, a transformation had overtaken the crone. Her thin grey hair had turned tawny and thick, the lines of her cheeks melted away to reveal a fit woman of middle age. As Vhumi gawped, the witch opened her eyes and let out a satisfied sigh as she cracked her knuckles, the silver and gemstones in her lips, eyebrows, nose, and ears sparkling as she turned her head this way and that.

"That's better." The woman picked up the pipe and gave the tubāq a sniff. "Oh, this smells lovely. Thank you for your grace as well as your patience. I know the approach to my house is a difficult one. Now that we are free of distractions I am dying to learn what brings a tapai-in-waiting to Ghosthead Mountain."

Before Vhumi could reply, a tumult erupted deeper in the complex, a flapping commotion like the flock of harpy eagles descending on her father as he opened his bag of sacrificial bones on the uppermost balcony. The door in the back wall burst open and half a dozen little girls swarmed the room, waving their arms and crying, "Mama! Mama! Mama!"

All the vigor of the egg seemed to drain from the witch. Closing her eyes again, she said, "I have company, children."

"Mama!"

"Mama!"

"Look!"

"Look!"

"Mama!"

"Look!"

"Well, what have we here?" The witch opened her eyes and surveyed the mob crowding her chair. All of the girls were about the same age, eight or ten, but there the similarities ended. Each wore her hair in a different fashion, this one with braids and that one with a bun, this one shorn and stubbly and that one with a sparrow's nest of wild locks, this one with skin as light as Vhumi's own and the next one with the rich walnut complexion of the witch herself. They all wore different styles of clothing, the pigtailed child in a Rajput coat big enough to be a dress, the braided girl draped under an Immaculate jacket and hat that slipped so far down her sharp face she peered through the mesh crown like the witch's bird through its cage.

"My, my, my," said the witch. "Not only do I host a tapai-in-waiting, but also an Usban pilgrim, a Serpentine fop, a Flintland chieftain, a Rajput sellsword, an Immaculate dignitary, and, um, what are you supposed to be, Hassandra?"

"I'm Cold Cobalt, the Banshee with a Blade!" crowed the girl with a blue bedsheet tied around her neck.

"Of course you are," said the witch. "Be careful with that hat, Sully, you'll bend the brim."

"I'm Din!" The girl in Immaculate garb laughed, and all the other children shrieked with such shrill delight Vhumi's eyes watered.

"What have I told you about that game?" the witch used her long-stemmed pipe to hammer the hat lower on the girl's head.

"*You'll get stuck that way!*" They cried in unison. To Vhumi's alarm, several of the brood finally took notice of her and began to advance. She wasn't good with kids. She took a sip of the sweet chai to stall, then said, "Good evening."

They stared at her, then whispered to each other, and laughed louder than ever.

"Fabulous a delegation as you may be," said the witch, "I can't help but notice Ugrakar is absent from your coalition." Raising her voice, she called out, "Vere!"

An older girl appeared in the doorway, so swiftly she must have been waiting just out of sight. She looked much older than the others, perhaps Vhumi's age, as short and sturdy as any daughter of Ugrakar yet as dark of complexion as the witch. Dour as the young ones were merry, the first words out of what Vhumi couldn't help but notice was a rather lovely mouth were, "It's not my fault. Mom let them play dress up and—"

"Nemi! Nemi!" A stocky woman pushed past the teenager. "Look! Look!"

This last arrival was a middle-aged Ugrakari draped in a white pelt, jagged horns curling down from the hood. "Still fits!" she cried triumphantly, giving a twirl. "Can you believe it?"

"We have company, my love," said the witch.

"We do?" The Ugrakari stopped spinning and blinked at Vhumi. "We do! Why didn't you ring the bell?"

"An excellent question," said Nemi. "Apparently one of your daughters hid it again."

"So now they're mine, huh?" The Ugrakari said, hands on her hips. "Girls, what have I told you? You think it'd be funny if the pups gobbled up this poor yak herder?"

From the peals of laughter, the children thought it would be.

"Our guest is no yak herder," said Nemi. "She's a tapai-in-in-waiting who's waited quite long enough, if you catch my drift."

"Right!" The Ugrakari snapped into a semblance of military discipline and bawled. "Line up, Mini-Moochers."

To Vhumi's surprise and relief, the unruly mob stood at attention. "If the bell isn't back up by moonrise, no pudding rations for a week. Rolllll out!"

The girls blasted out of the vardo, raising a flurry of barks from the deepening night.

"You, too, Private Vere," the Ugrakari said, flipping back her hood and revealing a smiling, pleasant face.

"But moms—" the girl began but the witch cut her off with that most powerful of parental invocations: a full name.

"Vere Thomassina Antigram."

"*Fine.*" The girl rolled her eyes at Vhumi, the first sign she'd given that she'd even noticed her. Then she stalked off after her sisters, slamming the door behind her.

"Are these for us?" The Ugrakari picked up the saam buds and gave them an appreciative huff. "So sweet! It's been ages since anyone brought me flowers—hint hint."

"Plucked from our own garden, you'll notice," the witch said in the Crimson tongue, and Vhumi hoped her blush didn't betray her fluency in the language.

"So grouchy!" the Ugrakari responded in kind. "Have you had your egg yet?"

"Have I—" The witch's eyes flashed behind her spectacles and then her haughty frown twisted into a wolfish grin. "Just you wait until I have her out of here, Tapai Purna. They get it from you, you know."

"So do you, and I don't hear any complaints," said the Ugrakari, sticking out a monstrous black tongue as she poured herself some tea.

"Excuse us," the witch said to Vhumi in Ugrakari. "You must think our hospitality quite barbaric compared to what the Twenty-third Canton offers its guests."

"I came unannounced and uninvited at a late hour," said Vhumi, not volunteering that as grim and spooky a reception as she'd expected from the mysterious witches of Ghosthead Mountain, this scene of domestic anarchy came as something of a relief. "It is my place to apologize for the intrusion."

"No intrusion," said the Ugrakari, taking the unlit pipe from the witch's lap and lighting it on a candle. Between puffs, she said, "Guests. Are always. Welcome."

"But you may wish to bring your own bell next time," said Nemi, commandeering the pipe from her partner and taking a long draw for herself. "My, but that's nice."

"So you're a tapai-in-waiting," Purna said, waving Vhumi back down when she rose and offered her chair. The Ugrakari sat on the floor next to Nemi so they could pass the pipe back and forth. "Reckon you want us to take care of the whole in-waiting part, go straight to tapai?"

"Quite the opposite," said Vhumi, relieved and anxious all at once to finally be at the heart of it. "I'll be tapai in a matter of days, maybe hours, unless you can help me get out of it."

"That's a bit backward, isn't it?" said Purna. "Usually folk seek witches to help catch the crown, not dodge it."

"The peculiarity of my circumstance is not lost on me," said Vhumi. "But I find myself ensnared by fate. My father, the tapai, is dying and expects me to take his place. But I can't imagine anything worse—I've seen the drudgery of rule firsthand and long to experience all that this world has to offer, not be trapped in our castle until the end of my days. I do appreciate the obligation of my birth, of course, and if I had any hope, I might do some good in the position I would accept my unhappy lot. But I can imagine few people less suited for the responsibility. For the good of the Twenty-third Canton, I must not become tapai."

"Easy fix!" said Purna. "Just fake your own death and start over somewhere new. It's a classic move, never goes out of fashion."

"Oft have I daydreamed just such a ruse," said Vhumi. "Sadly, when I said I could imagine few less suited to rule in my stead, I had someone particular in mind. My younger brother, Krish. He will ascend to tapai if I do not, and he is a selfish, scheming twit. I cannot doom my people to his rule. If it were anyone else, anyone else at all …"

"Still an easy fix," said Purna. "Kill your brother, *then* fake your death. Hopefully whoever's in line after him will—"

"I will not assassinate my brother." Vhumi set down her teacup harder than she intended, ashamed of how many times that evil notion had flirted with her imagination. "We are not savage Imperials, we are Ugrakari. We do not turn against our own."

"Purna," the witch said, the first word she'd uttered after listening with snakebit lips pursed around her pipe.

"Well, what about your pops?" Purna continued. "You say he's dying, but maybe my old lady can fix him, buy you a few more years."

"Alas, my father now refuses all treatment," said Vhumi. "He says his sun is setting, and he longs to join my mother in the First Dark."

"Well, what he doesn't know *really* won't hurt him in this case," said Purna. "We slip him a special omelet and—"

"Purna, *enough*," Nemi snapped in Crimson. "It wasn't my idea to retire to your homeland. When we made peace with your aunt and uncle and brokered the terms of our emigration with the tapais, what was the one condition we agreed to?"

"This doesn't count!"

"Purna."

"This poor kid's just like I was, Nemi. She's got bedbugs in her britches and needs to'em shake them out with a turn around the Star. We wouldn't be—"

"Purna. The one condition you swore on the memory of your parents."

"My parents were cool, they'd dig it!"

"Purna."

"But—"

"*Purna.*"

The woman hung her head and said something so low Vhumi couldn't hear it. Apparently, the witch couldn't, either. "What was that?"

"No meddling in Ugrakari politics," grumbled Purna.

"And what do you call helping a tapai-in-waiting subvert the lawful succession of her canton?"

Purna sighed and offered Vhumi a sad, forced smile. "Sorry, kid, mom says we can't help."

Well, it had been worth a shot.

"We can offer you hospitality," said Nemi. "Please join us for dinner and stay the night in our humble home. You have journeyed far and—"

"Thank you, but no." Vhumi forgot her manners in her hurry to be away from these witches, lest the tremor in her chest begin to rattle out tears. She hadn't been able to imagine how exactly they could possibly help her, but she'd hoped nonetheless, and the death of hope is the cruelest loss. "My father doesn't have much time, and I do not trust my brother to delay his homecoming until my return."

"You sure?" asked Purna. "It's getting dark and they say bandits grow bolder along the roads. And it's been *ages* since we had company."

"I have my bow and my yak waiting on the far side of your bridge, and the moon is full," said Vhumi.

Despite their warm offer, the witches didn't seem terribly sorry to see her go. Vhumi couldn't blame them. After a few more pleasantries—and a plate of salty cheese biscuits Purna insisted she try—they saw her to the door, the pack of children and horned wolves coming up the trail from the lake to frolic in the moonlit yard. Any one of the beasts could have eaten the whole family and still had room for dessert, but these monsters of legend behaved not unlike overgrown puppies with their diminutive charges.

Picking her way down the slope, Vhumi indulged in a few bitter tears. She would never experience what these women enjoyed, a life unburdened by the urgent needs of an entire queendom. At least they seemed to appreciate what they had.

The lake shimmered in the moonlight. Watching her reflection stride along the rocky shore, she tripped several times but couldn't look away. Childish a fancy though it surely was, she imagined this second self had received what she'd come for, and in the mirror realm of the lake, she'd start a new life free from the responsibility of fate or its dire double, the worry of her brother ascending to tapai in her place.

"Nice night, isn't it?"

Vhumi almost tumbled into the drink. The eldest sister, Vere, stood in the moonglow beside a freshly erected plaque with a dangling brass bell. Vhumi had been so preoccupied with her reflection she'd walked right up on the waiting girl without noticing.

"It is," Vhumi said sharply, offering Vere a nod as she walked around her.

"They all are, when you're free to spend them as you wish." Vhumi didn't appreciate the observation one bit and quickened her pace, but what the girl said next brought her up short: "My mothers can't help, but I swore no oath to any tapai. I pity your predicament and offer salvation."

"You heard?" Vhumi willed her heart too slow, not turning to look at the girl lest her face betray the pathetic resurrection of hope.

"Sat under the window right up until they gave you the brush-off." A yellow flash muddled the moonlight as the girl lit a coalstick and applied it to a stubby clay pipe. The sour scent of saam filled the air. Holding in her smoke, she offered the pipe to Vhumi, who shook her head—her thoughts were clouded enough.

"And what is your solution?" Vhumi knew she should be more polite but was too tired and heartsick to play the usual games. "What sorcery or stratagem have you concocted in half an hour that that will free me of my lifelong trap, and without putting my brother on the throne or harming either of us in the bargain?"

"A skeptic." Vere exhaled another dark cloud. "I like that. Good quality in a tapai."

"A pragmatist," said Vhumi.

"A woman free to live any life she's bold enough to choose, if she heeds my counsel."

"Counsel I'm still waiting to receive."

"It's simple," said the witchling. "I take your place."

"You *what*?"

"It's an easy trick, me and my sisters used to do it all the time. I use my cunning to take on your appearance, and you take on mine."

"So I stay here and become babysitter to a troupe of bloodthirsty brats while you ride home and become tapai?"

"I become tapai and you do whatever you like. After I heard your tale, I left my mothers a note informing them of my departure. They've been expecting it—you won't be followed."

"A fine deal for a tapai wishing to walk away from her crown and finer one for a witch looking to escape her family," said Vhumi, going along with the girl's mad proposal for the sake of argument. "But not such a fine deal for the Twenty-third Canton. My brother is unfit to rule, but why should I think you'd be any better? You might be far worse, and I'd condemn my people to an unproven devil instead of one familiar."

"You said anyone would be better than your brother. I'm anyone."

"Fair enough. Yet my father cautioned me that any who actively seek the crown do not deserve it."

"Further proof I'm just the woman for the job," said Vere. "I don't give a moldy peach about being tapai, I just don't want to spend all my days on Ghosthead Mountain. You've offered me an out—I've thought it over and believe I'm up for the job of tapai."

"Thought it over for half an hour," said Vhumi. "You'd take on the highest honor and gravest responsibility of any mortal, simple as that?"

"See, now it doesn't sound like you actually want your wish granted."

"I want what's best for my people, which I know isn't me or my brother. But while I intend no offense, I'm not sure a random witch is much of an improvement."

"It's true I don't know the first thing about the position, but you could teach me. You'll have my appearance, remember. Stay on as a new friend that Tapai Vhumi met in the mountains until you're satisfied the Twenty-third Canton is in firm hands."

"You make it sound simple."

"It is simple. We swap bodies, you coach me on everything I need to know to play the part, and then you set off on your adventures and leave me to rule in your stead."

"Simple as that?"

"Simple as that."

Vhumi turned it this way and that. "Even if you really could exchange our bodies—"

"I can. As I said, my sisters and I used to do it all the time. Even the little ones have figured it out."

Tempting, actually tempting … and yet. "Thank you, Vere, for your generous offer, but I cannot take it on faith that you would be a good steward of the Twenty-third Canton."

"I suppose not." She relit her pipe, but Vhumi couldn't bring herself to walk away, not yet, a part of her hoping this witch would say the magic words to convince her. "But then you don't know why I stayed long after all my sisters flew away."

"Didn't I meet your sisters?"

"Bah, that's the new clutch," said Vere, waving away the specter of her younger siblings along with another smoky exhalation. "I mean my real sisters who came of age with me. One by one they all went off on their own—well, except Diggilise and Marota, they left together.

"But I chose to stay because I'm the most Ugrakari of the lot. I love this land the way this lake loves the moon, so why should I go journeying when wherever I should go I'd pine for these mountains and valleys? Even when my mothers were less than subtle in suggesting I quit the nest, I declined, for I know Ugrakar is my destiny. All I've ever wanted is to spend my life in the high country, nurturing my homeland as it's nurtured me. So while I admit I don't know anything about running a canton, I swear on the bones of my old nursemaid that I desire only what's best for Ugrakar. Should fate burden me with the responsibilities of tapai, I shall devote myself to doing right by this place and its people."

That shouldn't have been enough for Vhumi, not nearly. But seeing how earnestly the young witch spoke, her pretty face turned not to Vhumi but the star-crowned brow of Ghosthead Mountain, she found herself saying, "Alright."

"Alright?"

"Alright."

"Alright!" The witch pocketed her pipe in her voluminous skirt and slapped her hands together. "Now, it'll hurt a little, but only for a minute. The quicker you follow my instructions, the quicker it'll pass."

"I'm not afraid of pain." Vhumi tried to convince herself as much as Vere. "What do I need to do?"

"Eat this." Vere pulled a jet-black egg from her belt pouch. When

Vhumi reached for it, though, the witch held up her other hand and knelt, setting the egg on the path by her feet. "First, close your eyes."

Vhumi did.

"Now stick out your hand."

Vhumi did.

"Now stick out a finger."

Vhumi opened her eyes and saw she'd led with her fist.

"No peeking, it'll spoil the spell," said Vere. "Eyes closed, finger pointing toward your future."

Vhumi couldn't help but return the girl's impish smile and she did as she was told; Vere really was a comely lass. Vhumi felt the witch wiggle her extended fingertip, making her smile all the wider, then Vere gave it a little tug. A tingling energy seemed to flow between them, raising the hairs on Vhumi's neck. This must be the spell, it must already be—

Pain.

Pain the likes of which Vhumi had never experienced. The witch broke her finger, she thought, reeling away, but when she forced her streaming eyes open she saw it was so much worse. Her finger was *gone*, the knuckle-stump jetting black blood. She reflexively clamped her other hand over the wound, which brought more pain and nausea on a wave of cold sweat.

"Sorry," the witch said, wiping the blood from her own small kukri and sheathing the curved blade. In her other hand, she held Vhumi's index finger. The sight of moonlight reflecting on her own fingernail made Vhumi faint, and as she returned to consciousness, the horrible witchling cracked the black egg into her moaning mouth.

"Almost over," cooed Vere, clapping her palm over Vhumi's gagging mouth so she couldn't spit it out. "Swallow it, swallow it."

Vhumi choked it down, if only to appease her tormentor long enough to draw her own weapon. But as soon as the slimy mouthful cleared her gullet, a fresh agony spread through every bone in Vhumi's body, eclipsing the throb in her hand. The last thing she saw before the rising anguish blinded her was her severed finger disappearing into the witch's grinning mouth.

Pain.

Every bone in her body splintered, every muscle tore, and her skin melted. Chai and clods of biscuit painted the rocks as she voided herself. Convulsions rolled her over the sharp rocks as she died the worst death imaginable—and then it was over.

Vhumi lay trembling, basted in sweat, the fire that gripped her banking to coals, then blowing away like ash on the balmy breeze of late summer. She stayed where she lay for a time, heart thundering, then crawled to the lake to soothe her raw throat and scalded skin. The cold, sweet water tasted good and felt better on her raw face.

Her face.

Vhumi blinked, water leaking through her fingers. Bright as the moon reflected on the water, she saw Vhumi was gone. In her place crouched Vere, a fair if rather frazzled witch. She gulped and the mirror image gulped; she sat back on her haunches and so did the double. Raising her hands to tentatively touch the unfamiliar cheekbones, the nub of a nose, her reflection did the same. She was Vere, exactly … save for her left hand, a knot of scar tissue at the knuckle where her pointer finger should be.

"Oh sugar," said an unfamiliar voice. A shadow appeared in the reflection and gently took Vhumi's left hand. "I was sure it would grow back when you changed. Whoops."

"Whoops? Whoops!" Vhumi turned on Vere—and turned on herself, confronting the face that had frowned back at her from the looking glass every morning. The strangeness of the sight almost sent her back into the First Dark for another spell, but she clung tight to consciousness, swaying as she stared at the witch who'd first taken her finger and now her whole body.

"A pretty big whoops, I'll grant, but a whoops all the same." Vhumi saw herself purse her lips. "If I'd known it wouldn't come back I would've told you to stick out your pinkie."

"It … it worked." Vhumi looked back at the reflection, two flustered girls on the edge of a lonely lake.

"Of course it worked," said Vere. "With my sisters, we'd just swap eggs, no harm no fowl, as mother says, but with you, I had to try something new. And now I know for next time—the offering doesn't grow back."

"Next time?" Vhumi turned her head this way and that, never vain before but unable to stop smiling at how fine her new face looked.

"Assuming you get tired of roaming someday and want to switch back," said Vere, and Vhumi felt a flash of pride in catching the witch likewise apprising herself favorably in the reflection, stroking her new chin. "You might get homesick you know. That's how it went with Mom—she couldn't wait to get out of here, but after a few years adventuring she felt the call of Ugrakar and came home tail between her legs. Whenever your sense catches up to you, return to the canton and we'll reverse the spell, easy as breakfast."

"Easy." Vhumi shuddered. Comforting though it was to think all this witchery could be undone if she changed her mind, she didn't relish the prospect of undergoing the ordeal a second time.

"Let's finish up and bounce out of here," Vere said. "You made a real racket and if either of my moms come down to investigate we're both in for it."

"Finish up?" Vhumi braced herself. "You mean there's more?"

"Can't have the tapai-in-waiting roll back home wearing her new best friend's kit, can we?" Vere winked as she unbuckled her belt. "The good news is I guarantee they'll fit like—oh!"

Vere froze with her skirt around her ankles, mid-shimmy out of her pantaloons. One hand slid over to cup her groin. Vhumi didn't understand—and then she did, an unconsidered consequence of their physical exchange dawning on her. Looking down over the swell of her breasts—her breasts!—she tentatively snaked a hand under her riding skirt, feeling through her leggings … and wake the Living Saint, it was gone! All of it!

Vhumi was so caught up in exploring her exciting new topography it took her a moment to remember she wasn't alone. Yanking her curious fingers out from her between her legs, she looked back at Vere, who stood on the bank, hand still warily moving around the front of her underwear like a marmot exploring a new rock pile.

"Sorry, I should have said." Vhumi had struggled with her body but had never been ashamed of who she was, but now she blushed and stammered. "I knew I was a girl from … from when I was a girl, and … and I didn't think we'd swap *that*."

"This …" Vere looked up at her, squeezing her new tackle. "This is going to be so much fun."

"Really? You're not …"

"I always wondered what it would be like." Vere's hand shifted things around and she giggled. "Oh wow, this is so weird. How do you not just sit on them all the time?"

"I'm sure you'll get the hang of it," Vhumi said primly, defensive of her old flesh.

"Hang is right," said Vere with another giggle, and then Vhumi got it and laughed, too. "So, wanna try them out?"

Vhumi was sure she'd misinterpreted, but the girl's leer confirmed she hadn't.

"I'm flattered, but no," said Vhumi. It was one thing to hit on yourself, but something else entirely to make a proposition with no semblance of romance.

"Your loss." Vere resumed stripping. "I'm quite the catch if I may say so myself."

Vhumi didn't know if she referred to her old body or her new one, but either way, she took it as a compliment.

They rode through the night and arrived home with the sun. Her yak had banished any doubts Vhumi may have harbored about the success of their deception. The faithful steed greeted Vere with his customary slobbery kisses and snuffled skeptically at his former mistress hidden in the guise of a witch. Squeezing onto his broad back behind Vere, Vhumi began to think their plan might actually work—if they could fool the wise old yak they could fool anyone.

Exhausted though she was, Vere kept Vhumi awake on the long ride by plying her with endless questions on the Twenty-third Canton, her family, and her daily life. No detail was too minor or personal for Vere to mine for richer material, and with each clever question, Vhumi's confidence grew.

Their next trial came in the royal stables, when Krish descended on them with the news that Father had become catatonic and not even the most optimistic barbers of the court expected him to wake again. Vere handled it well, brushing off Krish's needling better than Vhumi ever had.

"And who's your new friend?" Vhumi's stomach turned at the hungry way her brother sized her up.

"Vere Antigram," said Vere. "My new advisor and a witch of no small potency."

"So I see." Krish bowed so low his feeble mustache nearly swept the stable floor. "M'lady has already cast her spell upon me."

Vhumi had planned on staying at least a month or two to make sure Vere was fully prepared and to reassure herself the canton would be in capable hands, but now she felt a few days ought to suffice. She would stay until Father went and then Vere could handle Krish on her own.

A frantic week galloped by far too quickly. Everyone from her aunts and uncles to her handmaids questioned if it was really necessary for the tapai-in-waiting's new advisor to join her everywhere, even the baths, but none had the power to forbid her. Other than these grumblings, the plan went off without a hitch. Vhumi's chief concern was no longer being found out but the heroic quantities of saam Vere smoked, worried it would muddle her judgment and was out of character besides. The witch countered that such a new habit would perfectly explain any perceived changes in personality or lapses in memory. Besides, she added with a wink, the inferior flower they grew this far from

Ghosthead Mountain barely got her high.

Vhumi continued Vere's education late into each night, but eager a pupil though she proved, the more Vhumi explained the more she realized just how impossible a task it truly was. Reluctant as she'd always been to assume the throne, Vhumi had dutifully learned every lesson, closely minded her father's every move, and a lifetime of learning cannot be distilled into a handful of lectures. Vere's heart might be true and her mind eager, but there was too much she didn't know, too much Vhumi couldn't teach her. Old fears blossomed in her new breast—this Vhumi would not make a worthy tapai, either. Could she really trust the fate of the canton to a girl who'd only been here a matter of days?

Her doubts reached the tipping point when her father died and the homecoming festivities commenced. Vere played her part clever as ever, reveling as merrily as Krish and the rest of the family celebrating a loved one's return to the First Dark, but watching the witch with her face dancing and singing and throwing handfuls of bright-dyed powder with her young cousins, Vhumi became melancholy despite the joyfulness of the occasion. Much as she'd longed to escape her birthright, fit a replacement as she'd found, painful though she knew the sundering of the spell must be, they had to switch back.

"I completely understand," said Vere when Vhumi informed her of the difficult decision as they dressed in party silks for the feast.

"You do?" Relief made Vhumi weak in the knees. "Good. Let's hurry, then. I realized I wouldn't even be able to help my father home—only relations sit at the tapai's table, of course."

"Of course," said Vere, but she looked pained as she put a hand on Vhumi's shoulder. "But I'm afraid there's no time—it will take me at least a day to prepare another egg for a second spell."

It took a moment for the enormity of this to sink in, but when it did Vhumi committed the gravest trespass on the day of a loved one's homecoming—she wept in sorrow.

"There, there." Vere hugged her. "I'll hide a few bites for you in a napkin, and later tonight you can be the one who takes him the rest of the way home."

The thoughtfulness of the gesture almost made Vhumi second-guess her second-guessing—surely a woman as considerate as Vere should make at least as competent a ruler as Vhumi herself. But as she sat exiled at a table of drunken courtiers, dipping cabbage momos into tomato achaar while the Gatechef rolled out her roast father for Vere, Krish, Aunt Agaja, and their other relatives, Vhumi knew she had already failed the canton enough for one lifetime. Even if no one ever found out her father was consumed by someone other than a blood relation, a crime needs no witness to be criminal.

Watching Vere take the first bite of her father was more than Vhumi could bear. Her eyes filling with more wicked tears, she tried to rise from the bench to stop the travesty, even if it must cost both her and Vere the crown and hand it to her brother—but she had no strength to rise, nor even speak, her tongue fat and sluggish as a freshly fed rock python. The last words she heard were those of her neighbor at the table asking if the chaang was perhaps too strong for her, and then Vhumi blacked out.

Anguished dreams yielded to a yet more distressing reality, one cheek slapped, then the other. The crashing of a nearby cataract echoed painfully through her aching forehead. Hazily familiar faces of guards loomed over her in the mist.

"Up, witch." Esterval, a thick-bearded woman who had only ever shown Vhumi the utmost deference now snarled at her like a poorly trained mastiff.

"Esterval, what is the meaning of—" she began, too disoriented to even remember that the guards couldn't possibly know her for who she was. Esterval reminded Vhumi of this with another rude slap to her stinging cheek.

"Not a word, witch! The tapai warned us of your sorcery. Take your bag and our liege's mercy and be on your way—and if ever the nine-fingered witch returns to the Twenty-third, you shall be fed to the harpies. Your exile is absolute and immediate. Go."

Unaccustomed though Vhumi was to obeying orders instead of giving them, her father had always observed she was a quick study. Clambering to her feet with the worst hangover of her life—one brought on by something Vere had slipped into her millet beer, she suspected—she hoisted the satchel one of the po-faced guards offered. Blinking into the fog, she realized they had delivered her to the edge of the canton, and without another word she took the first tottering steps onto Devil's Breath Bridge. The guards mounted their yaks but did not ride homeward. They stayed and watched her shuffle miserably into exile.

On the far side, she looked up the faint track to Ghosthead Mountain. Nemi and Purna would surely be horrified to learn of their daughter's betrayal, and they could return to the capital together and unmask Vere … who would implicate Vhumi, guaranteeing she would be run out of the canton a second time and giving Krish control of the realm. Would that be any better than leaving it to Vere?

Vhumi considered the muddy trail through the pines, not relishing the climb to come with the heavy sack the guards had given her. She opened the drawstring to inspect its contents, and her jaw gaped wide as the mouth of the bag. Pouch after pouch of coins, crammed together with bricks of the blackest hashish from the royal coffers. Between the gold and the hash, she had enough to buy her own estate anywhere in the Star. And tucked into an interior pocket, the dearest treasure of all—one of her father's roast fingers wrapped in a monogrammed napkin.

A note written in sour hog plum sauce upon the yellow silk: *Sorry! It's for the good of the realm xoxo Tapai Vhumi*

"The good of the realm," Vhumi murmured, holding up her father's finger. She gave it a nibble. Salt and spice and the memory of his smiling face permeated the greasy morsel, and happy tears ran down Vhumi's cheeks as she delivered the last true Tapai of the Twenty-third Canton home. Only when she'd cracked the bones and scraped every fleck of marrow did she rise from her seat on a mossy rock and continue her journey—away from the Twenty-third Canton, and away from Ghost-head Mountain

Bandits ambushed her that night, leaving her with nothing but her sandals and her life. The next day an early snow nearly deprived her of the latter, but she persevered.

Grim a start as she suffered, in time Vhumi found her fortune. She fulfilled her childhood wish to see every Arm of the Star, and if she made foes on each as well as friends, it was simply proof that she learned to live up to her principles and never again let malice or folly go unanswered.

In her wanderings, she sailed beyond the borders of the old maps and was there in the risen kingdom of Jex Toth when the Final Truce proved not so final after all. No one was more surprised than Vhumi herself at the role she played in helping avert a crisis as catastrophic as that which had threatened the Star a generation past. She even met the last two living Villains of Cold Cobalt herself, saving the life of one and earning the eternal enmity of the other.

But these are songs for another night, and as the fire burns low you deserve the only proper ending of this one—which is how after many years abroad, Vhumi returned to the Twenty-third Canton.

'Twas her father's ghost that summoned her that chill autumn eve. After nary a parental nightmare for a solid decade, he had begun haunting her nightly, silently pointing the finger she'd eaten into the mist of Devil's Breath Bridge, up the trail to Ghosthead Mountain. Vhumi needed no oracle to unpack the meaning, simply grateful he'd given her so long a reprieve to adventure before he called her home.

When she at last arrived at the looking glass lake beneath the plateau, no sign nor bell awaited her. She'd brought her own; she spun the prayer wheel and clanged its bell until echoes rolled like thunder from the mouth of Ghosthead Mountain. Yet when she reached the darkening plateau, she found no horned wolves, living or dead—the great skeleton that had stolen her breath on the first visit was gone, as was the vardo where she had taken tea and biscuits with the witch and her wife. Only the cairn, the roses, and the small complex of huts remained, bramble-choked with neglect.

And there, in a clearing surrounded by wild orange roses, stoking a yellow fire in the purple twilight, sat the witch with Vhumi's face.

"What are you doing here?" Vhumi asked.

"Waiting for you." Vere grinned. "You got my summons, then."

"*Your* summons?"

"I knew you wouldn't come if I called, so I made the sending look like your old man. Apologies for the pretext, but it couldn't be helped. The Twenty-third Canton is in danger and needs its tapai."

Vhumi was too tired from the trek and the evening too cool for her to resist a seat by the fire. Much as she resented the witch's deception, it was a relief to know her father had not actually rematerialized out of the First Dark out of shame at his daughter. Ugrakari knew better than to believe in ghosts, and it served her right for being superstitious.

"Could there be a greater threat to the realm than a treacherous witch?" asked Vhumi as she plopped down in the dirt.

"Much greater," said Vere. "Your brother. He's exiled me and seized the crown for himself."

"Found out who you were, did he?" Krish must have grown smarter in her absence.

"No, damn it, the honorless cur never suspected a thing. He simply deposed his sister, beloved ruler these many years, as if Ugrakar were some barbaric Crimson backwater."

Not smarter, then, but even more devious. Vhumi's guts churned. She'd always known Krish was craven, but such a shame as this could not be borne.

"So I came to seek the witches of Ghosthead Mountain to get rid of the Twenty-third Tapai, and you did the same." Vhumi smiled at the quirk of fate.

"No," said Vere. "I knew my mothers moved on after my last little sister flew the nest—your typical morbid old timers' wish to see the Star one last time and all that. As I said, I came here to wait for you."

"Really?" Vhumi took the pipe her former five-fingered hand offered her, admiring how the rest of her had filled out over the years. All her young life she'd been so uncomfortable in her skin she never stopped long enough to appreciate its manifest charms.

"Really," said Vere, who seemed to be sizing her old self up in a similar fashion. "I like what you've done with my hair. The side-shave is sexy as the First Dark."

"Is that why you called me back, to flirt with yourself?"

"An added bonus," said Vere. "I called you back because I've got the perfect plan to overthrow your brother and restore the true tapai to her rightful place."

"And who might that be, me or you?" asked Vhumi.

"We can figure that out along the way. The most important thing, though, is that we get rid of your brother. I know you balked at striking against him before, but he's disgraced all true Ugrakaris and must be stopped."

"As always, I make a lot of sense," said Vhumi, lighting the pipe and shivering at the taste of the witch's saliva on the stem. "What's your plan?"

As the last light of late summer failed, the plot thickened along with the smoke drifting out from Ghosthead Mountain to mingle with the clouds gathering over the Twenty-third Canton.

THE BLADE-QUEEN AND THE STONEHEART

ANNA STEPHENS

Queen Alaya sat on her throne and placed the tip of one satin slipper beneath her husband's chin and lifted it until he was forced to look up and meet her eyes. He was sweaty, bloodstained and bruised, kneeling with his hands bound behind him at the feet of the woman, the wife, the queen, he'd betrayed. Alaya, in contrast, had changed into a white silk gown and rose-coloured slippers once Dorian was captured, abandoning her bloody armour for something softer and more vulnerable.

'Tut, tut, husband,' she said, shaking her head in theatrical dismay. 'You really are the worst traitor to ever disgrace my rule. How many is this?' she added to her chamberlain.

'Rebellions or husbands, Your Majesty?' he asked.

Alaya snorted. 'Aren't they one and the same? Both, then.'

'Seven uprisings against your gracious and bountiful rule, Your Majesty. Five husbands.'

'Five husbands,' she mused as she removed her toe from under Dorian's chin. 'Is that excessive? That seems a little excessive.' She leant forwards, braced her elbows on her knees and stared down at him. 'Why do you all play the same tired game?' she asked with genuine curiosity. 'Each of you pledges me loyalty and, within months, have convinced yourselves that you can do a better job of it than me and you've been somehow … belittled because I'm more powerful and wiser and a better killer than you. You go from adoring me to resenting me and it's so predictable. Why is it you think I still don't have an heir, Dorian? You think I'd let a weak, vacillating, greedy fool like you or the others father the next queen? And yet still I hope and scour the battlefields for someone my equal.'

'It isn't greed, you arrogant, cold-hearted bitch,' Dorian yelled.

Alaya sighed from the belly and leant back in her throne. She crossed her legs and waved one hand. 'Go on then,' she said. 'Astonish me.'

'You're a Blade-Sister,' Dorian began with a complete lack of originality. Alaya held up one finger. 'A Blade-Queen,' he corrected himself reluctantly. She was rare and powerful and destined by heredity and might to rule all lesser mortals, beginning with this land of Sistral and its capital, Sisterne. She was also, for now, the last of the Blade-Queens. Hence the husbands.

Hence the disappointment.

'Death is your nature, and conquest and conflict and—' Dorian continued, warming to his topic and apparently oblivious to his fate.

'You fought in my armies, Dorian. You distinguished yourself in two of those conquests you now pretend to abhor. It's why I chose you for my husband. Because you said you saw the world in the same colours as me and wanted what we could build together.'

'The same colours?' Dorian spat. 'You see only in red.'

'A common misconception,' Alaya said. 'I see mostly in black and white, but yes, there are shades that I believe you call red. Also blue. No one talks about how I see in blue, do they? I wonder why. Do they think I never look up from the bodies long enough to view the vastness of the sky?'

'Your poetry is fucking awful,' the prince spat.

Alaya narrowed her eyes. 'Easy, my sweet,' she murmured. 'There are limits to even my patience.'

'As if I care,' Dorian shouted, trying to lunge to his feet, though with his hands bound he just flailed comically upon the floor. 'You're not even human,' he added and the queen laughed and clapped her hands, settling herself back more comfortably in her throne. It was what all her husbands—and her other enemies—had thrown at her. Her lack of humanity. As if Alaya could change her own nature. As if she'd want to be like … everyone else. So much *lesser*.

'That's not what you said yesterday morning,' she purred and he blushed. 'Ah, husband of mine, but I thought you'd last longer. I thought I might have finally found someone worthy of me, worthy of creating a child in me. It seems not.' She stood and walked in a slow circle around him. 'What is it about me, about this,' she said and ran her hands down her flanks, 'that you find inhuman?' Alaya leant in to lick the blood from his mouth. Dorian shivered.

'How am I not the pinnacle and culmination of your every desire?' she breathed against his lips. 'This isn't about my being a Blade-Queen, or about Sistral's conquest. This is about my having more power than you. More influence and wealth and adoration. You want what I have, and you thought you could fuck your way to it. When that failed, you tried to take it by force and failed again. You are a failure, Dorian. A laughable, pathetic failure of a man.'

She returned to her throne and sprawled against the cushions in a swirl of white silk. 'What happened to your predecessors?' she asked abruptly.

Dorian swallowed, paling beneath the bruises and the blood. 'You ate them.'

Alaya laughed again. 'Ah, yes, that is a persistent rumour, isn't it? Did you know that despite being the last Blade-Queen until I birth an heir, there are other ways for me to increase the number of my sisters?' She glanced coyly at her chamberlain, who was flapping his hands uselessly.

'What?' Dorian croaked. 'What are you jabbering about? You ask why you haven't given me a child? Better to wonder why I didn't give you one!' Alaya supposed she had to admire his bluster, even bound and beaten on his knees before her. He really made a very pretty picture and she allowed herself to relish it for a long, unspeaking moment.

'Oh, my love,' she mocked. Then, when he was squirming with defiance and embarrassment both, 'As if I wouldn't smell any magic you might use to render yourself sterile.' She gestured to her chamberlain. 'Fetch them in.'

'Your Majesty,' he stuttered. 'The others are much further along than I. They'll suit your needs better, Your Majesty. P-please—'

'Fetch them,' she said again, still studying Dorian. He could have no idea what was going on, and suspicion sat uneasily with confusion amid the bruises on his face. The chamberlain had no choice but to carry out her order and it didn't take long for three more men to shuffle in and gather before her throne.

'Chamberlain Endine,' the queen said and then glanced at Dorian. 'Your most recent predecessor. And Alik, Deros and, ah'—she snapped her fingers—'someone, I don't remember now. The former princes of Sistral. All like you, dear husband. Each professing his undying love and devotion. Each of them betraying me. Trying to seize my throne and my power for themselves.'

Dorian gaped at the four men, three of whom were already blubbering and pleading. Only the nameless one stood straight and unmoved. His face was drawn with exhaustion and something suspiciously like relief. He even dared a tiny smile.

'What?' he said, voice at least an octave higher than before. 'But you … but they said … everyone said you *ate them!*'

Alaya tutted. 'Your stupidity is remarkable, Dorian, even for you. Why waste such potential when I have an entire species to rebuild?'

'Your Majesty,' Endine begged, throwing himself at Alaya's feet and pressing kisses to her slippers. 'Please. No. Please don't, *please!* Haven't I served you well, been faithful and steadfast and true? You don't need mine yet. Take them, take theirs.' He gestured wildly at the other three, two of whom renewed their wailing. 'I'm loyal, I've always been loyal.'

Alaya raised both eyebrows and jerked her foot from his clammy grip and too-wet mouth. 'You tried to kill me,' she reminded him primly and returned her attention to her current husband, leaving Endine blubbering. 'You wanted to know where the men who occupied your position before you went? Nowhere. The most recent serves as chamberlain until he has a replacement. Our marriage bought Endine three more years of life. Three years in which to fulfil a very special purpose, like the others. I have been the last Blade-Sister for too long, but no longer.'

'What are you—' Dorian began, this time successfully reaching his feet. He loomed over her on her throne, and Alaya cocked her head to look up at him. He really was too pretty to be this stupid. What a waste.

'I'd say not to worry,' she said sweetly as she stood to match him, and things began to shift inside her. 'I'd say it doesn't hurt, but you've lied enough for the both of us, haven't you?' There was the sound of shredding silk as Alaya's wings slid out of her back and destroyed her gown. Dorian had seen them before—anyone who'd faced her or stood with her on the battlefield had seen them—but he was only the fifth person in all Sistral to see the ovipositor that slid from the base of her spine.

Alaya leapt onto her throne, the remnants of her robe falling from her, and then jumped, her wings clattering as they caught at the air and slowed her descent. She drifted down onto Dorian like a feather, curling her blade-wings around him and caging him in. He froze, his gaze darting between her sharpest edges to all the places where she was soft and curved, places he had loved so much.

It was in that moment of stillness that her ovipositor pressed against his belly and then into it. He let out a high-pitched scream and threw himself backwards; her blades turned their flats to him and held him secure and Alaya groaned and unburdened herself of her eggs. Eleven this time. The largest clutch so far: her strength was growing.

The soporific effect of the liquid the eggs floated in slackened Dorian's features as it entered his system. His screams faded into silence within seconds and, by the time she was done, he was grinning mindlessly. The drug would last long enough for the eggs to settle and adhere to his organs; by the time he regained his senses, there'd be no digging them out.

The Blade-Queen opened her wings and let her now-ex-husband stumble free, retracting her ovipositor as she did. The pheromones from the laying wafted across the room and reached the others, triggering the hatching of the eggs each of them carried.

She could stop it in Endine if she wished—the simple application of a different pheromone from a saliva gland—but she was eager to finally begin her hive. Alaya settled her wings and sprawled naked in her throne, watching four of her five former husbands begin to twitch and then scream as the eighteen little Blade-Sisters ate their way free. They'd grow quickly with so much fresh meat to consume; by the time the four ex-princes of Sistral were piles of picked-clean bones, they'd already be learning to fly. The failed rebel leaders, held captive for years for just this purpose, would supply them with the remainder of the flesh they needed to grow swiftly, and then Alaya, with her sisters' aid, would close her hand around this land and secure it for herself and the Blade-Queen she'd finally breed.

The queen cooed as the first Blade-Sister emerged from Alik's ravaged gut. The little one shook herself, blood spraying from her skin and her tiny, almost translucent wings clattering like silver wind chimes. The first of her hive. Slightly larger than the rest and blinking sleepily, she climbed up into Alaya's lap and together they watched the rest of their sisters emerge.

'Rest, little one,' the queen crooned. 'Rest and grow swiftly. If this rebellion continues, I will give you such a spectacle to learn from. And if you're very good, I'll leave some of the traitors alive long enough for you to play with.'

👑

'Well, that was a shitshow and no mistake. Better luck next time, Holliday. I'll be taking my money and leaving now.'

Syl Stoneheart, famed warrior and captain—*former captain*—of the Iron Blades free mercenary company, held out a rather grubby palm. Since her second, Renn, had turned out to be a slimy, treacherous, betraying arsehole who'd left her bleeding to death in the dust two long years before, Syl had taken one bad contract after another in an increasingly desperate attempt to earn enough coin to set up a new company, arm it, train it, and then take it to find the Iron Blades and murder every last motherfucker of them. So far, she had a notched sword, two broken bowstrings, and a knee that ached in wet weather.

Holliday stared at her in dumb surprise. 'What? What about Alaya? She is a parasite, a mass murderer. She *eats people!* She cannot be allowed to continue her reign of terror.'

Syl thought back to the city streets she'd walked over the last month, how clean and prosperous the people of Sisterne were as they went about their business. She recalled the border guards who'd vetted her and let her pass into Sistral itself and the wide, tilled fields she'd ridden past. Reign of terror? Her own home city could do with such if this is what it got you. Still, she'd been paid to lead a rebellion and she'd done so. Or, and rather more pertinent, so far she *hadn't* been paid to lead a rebellion.

'Dorian was the head of this uprising, so if Alaya did eat him, then there is no more uprising, is there?' she pointed out with more patience than any of her former company would have believed she possessed.

'Dorian was a prince,' Holliday insisted. 'As his brother, that makes me a prince, too. And that means—'

'Is that how it works? That psychotic bitch with knives hidden in her back tell you that, did she? You planning on replacing the dear, departed

Dorian as the husband of Queen Alaya? Woman who can stab you in the back with her back?'

Holliday straightened, looking offended and, somewhere underneath, a little sheepish. Ah, so he had considered it. Why wasn't she surprised? Oh, right, he was a fool, much like his dead brother. Syl wasn't a fool. Syl had been hired by Prince Dorian, whose rebellion had fallen apart as soon as his erstwhile allies learnt he'd been the main attraction at brunch. She'd done all she could to fulfil her side of the contract up to and including exhorting fleeing soldiers to stand firm. Only a little, mind you, just enough for the look of the thing.

No need to get carried away and actually inspire them into a second attempt. Someone could get hurt doing that. Me. I could get hurt.

Still, it wasn't just Dorian's death that had taken the spines from his raggedy army. If the mewling, self-righteous little piss-stain had listened to Syl in the first place, they'd have taken the castle and then cut Alaya's wings from her back or whatever unpleasant end the prince had had in mind. Only Dorian hadn't listened to her. His honour as a soldier had bent far enough to recruit a mercenary to lead his troops, but not far enough to listen to said mercenary's wise and practical advice on how to storm a castle ruled by a terrifying creature that appeared human right up until she flew out of the sky *on wings made of steel* and slaughtered her way to her husband's side, swept him up and carried him off to her lair to eat at her leisure.

Syl could've prevented that. Well, maybe not that last part, but if she'd had her way, they'd have been into the castle and Dorian would have been out of Alaya's sight before she could so much as work up an appetite.

The mercenary wiggled her fingers. 'My coin,' she said. She didn't lace her tone with a threat; she didn't tickle her sword hilt with her free hand. She hated people who acted big when there was no need. No, Holliday would bluster and then he'd try and convince her to change her mind and then he'd pay her, and she could leave this monster-ruled country with the silver she needed to finally begin her new company. One step closer to vengeance.

'She's the last of her kind. If we kill her, we end the scourge. Free Sistral from her tyranny! Free the whole world!' Holliday's eyes were alight with passion and red-rimmed with exhaustion. Syl was very familiar with the recklessness that went with fatigue. Lines blurred and bad ideas could seem good when you hadn't slept in a couple of days. She had practice at reining in those wilder impulses. Holliday, drunk on exhaustion and the sound of his own voice, clearly didn't.

'Sounds like a blast. Good luck. Pay me before you canter out to die, there's a good nearly-prince.'

Holliday grimaced. 'Lady Stoneheart,' he began.

Syl recoiled. 'The fuck? *Captain* or *Stoneheart, Captain Stoneheart* if we're being particularly fancy. Just give me my coin, man. Rebellion's dead in the water, and I'm speaking as someone who's very nearly been dead in water on more than one occasion.'

'Double,' he said, too loud and too fast. 'Double your fee to bring an end to the Blade-Queen. I am not my brother, Lady. I am not emasculated by the fact that the officer in charge of this army is a woman.'

'Call me "lady" again and you will be,' Syl muttered automatically, but hesitated, nonetheless. That was a fuckload of coin and she needed all of it. Still …

'Dorian didn't tell me what Alaya actually is,' she said, playing for time and calculating how much of the rebellion remained intact and righteous enough to have another push at the castle.

Holliday's brow wrinkled. 'What she is? She's a Blade-Queen, the only one of her kind who can birth one like her and so somehow restore her people and grind the rest of us into slurry.'

'"Somehow?" You don't know how these monsters swork?'

'They are not native to Sistral and we know little of them,' Holliday said, as if this important fucking fact was of no importance at all. 'They've been little more than legends for several generations.'

Syl stared. 'Dead fucking gods. You sent me in there blind? You've not one of you a clue as to how to kill her, have you?'

'I would expect most of us thought they'd died out long ago—or perhaps never even existed at all—before Queen Alaya's arrival.' There was a touch of defensiveness to his tone now and Syl had to clench the hand she'd still been holding out for her coin and lower it so she didn't do something stupid with it, like punch him in the face until his nose was on the other side of his head.

'The arrival during which she slaughtered every member of your ruling family bar the king, who she promptly married to try and breed this next generation of flying fucking horror, you mean? That arrival?'

Holliday blushed. 'That's the one. You must understand, it happened very quickly.'

'Must I?' Syl demanded sourly. 'None of this explains why I was presumed to have known what a Blade-Queen is when, by your own admission, most of you think her a monster from an old tale. Where I come from, Blade-Queen sounds like a Name. I'm Named,' she added, pointing at her chest. 'A Name is a … characteristic, if you will. I knew a Lady Dagger back home, for instance, so when I heard Blade-Queen Alaya, I expected a normal fucking person with an affinity for weapons, not a monster. I was brought here under false pretences.'

'So Stoneheart?' Holliday tried.

'Means I want my coin and I'll walk out of here without giving a single fuck about the carnage I'm leaving you all to face. I'm not from Sistral, Sort-of-prince Holliday. I'm not even from this side of the Patient Sea, which is why I didn't know what I was facing, and now that I do, I'd be wise to walk away.' She hesitated again, willing her heart to the hardness her enemies—and few friends—believed it to have. *Fuck, he looks like someone just stole his puppy. He looks like a* puppy *whose puppy got stolen.*

Syl hesitated again, biting the inside of her lip and then pushing her filthy, sweat-lank hair back behind her shoulder. This was a stupid idea. 'Triple. Triple the coin and you've got a deal. I'll kill this Alaya myself.'

'Two and a half,' Holliday said immediately, confirming that he was, after all, the cleverer of the two brothers and possibly had a facility for acting that had gone hitherto unmentioned. It seemed Dorian had got the honourable outlook and martial instincts and Holliday the ability to haggle like a dockside whore.

'Done,' Syl said. Holliday grinned as if he'd got the better end of the bargain, and she had a vivid memory of Alaya gliding down into the narrow street where the rebellion was bottle-necked by the castle defenders and flicking out those dragonfly wings in a complex pattern that left seven rebels in at least fourteen pieces. The Stoneheart wondered if, perhaps, Holliday was cleverer than she was, too.

'Well, Captain Stoneheart,' the prince-once-removed said in brisk tones. 'What's the plan?'

Syl did tap her sword hilt this time, but not to unnerve him. She paced back and forth in the private room of the inn where Holliday had been hiding for the last two days and nights as the rebellion rose, splashed against the castle, and then drained away. The room was low-ceilinged and smoky, and Holliday's fine jacket, trousers, and haircut made him stick out like an erection at a funeral.

'You have access to the castle, right?' she asked as she prowled back towards him.

Holliday turned an interesting shade of oh, fuck. 'I do,' he squeaked.

Syl grinned and leant one hip against the table, looking down at where he sat wilting with dread. 'You're going to surrender to Alaya and beg her forgiveness,' she said. 'The rest of your army will be throwing themselves at the gates and walls again, and you'll be simpering on your knees in front of her. And that's all the distraction I'll need to kill her.'

Holliday's palm rasped over his stubble as he rubbed his jaw and mouth. 'That sounds … loose, for a plan.'

'Like a runny shit, Part-time-prince,' Syl said with more cheery confidence than she felt. 'Unexpected and impossible to get a grip on.' Holliday's lip curled. 'Two and a half times the coin, remember. I want to see you count it out now and I want to know where it's stashed for when this is over. I'll be coming with you to the castle, so you can be sure I won't steal it and run the second you walk through the gate.'

She waved her fingers again when he didn't move. 'Sooner you do it, the sooner we can get in there and get this over with. You'll be the hero, Holliday. They might even make you a prince for real once this Alaya thing's dead. You wouldn't begrudge an honest, hard-working mercenary a little silver in return for the crown of Sistral, would you?'

Holliday licked his lips and eased onto his feet. Syl's eyes flickered down as he put his hand on her vambrace and squeezed the metal as if it were her wrist. 'If I was so fortunate as to become prince, or even king, of Sistral, I'd need—'

'Don't do honour guarding.'

'A queen,' Holliday finished.

Her eyes bulged and then she bent over and put her hands on her knees and laughed herself silly. By the time she'd mastered her mirth, the prince-in-not-even-name was on the other side of the room projecting waves of icy fury that couldn't quite cool the furious blush staining his cheeks.

'I meant,' he tried, 'if you know any noblewomen of Talannest—that is where you're from, isn't it?'

Syl wiped the tears from her eyes. 'Course that's what you meant,' she said and had to pause to swallow a fresh giggle. 'And if you'd ever been to Talannest, you'd know the chances of meeting a decent, well-connected, wealthy noblewoman there are as likely as finding a virgin lad on a long-haul merchant ship.'

'How colourful,' Holliday said and sniffed. Syl rolled her eyes. 'Allow me to fetch your payment,' he added and stalked out of the room.

'Feisty for a little fucker,' Syl muttered and then put him from her mind. Despite her confidence, what came next was going to be far more complicated than simply knocking on the castle gate and asking for an audience with Blade-Queen Alaya. Although, as plans of last resort went, it could be worse. Syl had done worse. Question now was whether she could do better.

♛

Alaya stood on the roof of the tallest tower and squinted down into the morning. 'Really? They're actually trying again?' She had to admit to some surprise; had Dorian truly been the ringleader if these peasants would fight on without him? 'Fine, fine. Send someone out there to deal with them, will you?'

'At once, Your Majesty,' Chamberlain Dorian said. Either he'd settled into his new role without fuss, or he was still riding high on the lingering effects of his impregnation. He spun on his heel, a little wobbly, and tottered away, already calling for the castle's defenders.

Alaya threw herself from the roof, her wings punching out of her back after she'd dropped several body lengths and catching the air with a grating squeal. Her fall arrested, she began a smooth gliding circuit of the castle perimeter, where she discovered that all four entrances were under heavy attack. If anything, this push was even bigger than the one that had seen her capture Dorian.

'Perhaps it's a rescue mission,' she murmured to herself, the words vanishing behind her as she banked sharply to get a closer look at the small, private western gate. Despite the vicious fighting taking place in its vicinity, the gate itself was curiously unguarded. Even as she watched, two figures slipped over the wall beside it. Alaya grinned. *Assassins.*

Stretching her wings to their limit, the Blade-Queen glided down to the courtyard between the killers and her private quarters. The pair skulked near the wall, one shaking with nerves, the other still and watchful, their helmet ever-moving as they scanned the area. Alaya back-winged to cut her momentum and then landed lightly on the stone.

She prowled the last few steps towards them, her wings *snick-snicking* against each other. 'Tell me why I shouldn't kill you here and now.'

The man who wasn't wearing a helmet hurried to kneel before her.

'My name is Prince Holliday,' he began. 'Prince Dorian was my brother, though I had no part in his rebellion and I deplore that he would treat Your Majesty in such a way. I am here to pledge you my allegiance, My Queen. To offer you everything, anything, you desire.'

He wore barely any armour, Alaya noted, in sharp contrast to the figure next to him, who was shrouded in chainmail, plate, and leather and bristling with weapons. 'You come here to surrender and yet you bring an armed guard?'

Holliday was already frantically patting at the air. 'Captain Stoneheart, please lay down your weapons. There is no need for concern.'

The good captain stared at Holliday, and although the Blade-Queen couldn't see his face within the shadowed depths of the helmet, his frozen outrage was perfectly clear. 'I'd prefer not to, if it's all same to you.' His voice echoed strangely within the confines of the helmet. A pause, and then he added, 'You are my liege and your safety is my concern.'

Holliday grimaced and, at his Queen's nod, he rose to his feet. 'Perhaps then, Your Majesty, we might be permitted to speak at a distance from the captain here? There are things I would discuss with you in private.'

Alaya lifted one eyebrow and crossed her arms over her chest. 'You don't trust your man to hear what you have to say?'

Holliday licked his lips and glanced anxiously at Stoneheart, who'd twitched at her question. 'There are things, ah, things he does not need to know but which are of the utmost importance, Your Majesty.'

'Prince Holliday,' the captain began before Alaya could respond, 'you'd better not be doing what I think you're doing. Wherever your personal loyalties lie, your brother's rebels do not deserve your betrayal. If they want to protest the Queen's reign, they are within their rights to do so.'

Alaya peered intently into the shadows beneath the helmet but was unable to make out Stoneheart's features. She tapped her forefinger against her lower lip thoughtfully. 'You are a bold one, considering your master is surrendering himself into my control, Captain,' she said with a friendly edge to her voice that made it clear they were not friends at all. 'Perhaps you should let your … Prince do the talking. He has a wiser head on his shoulders than you.'

Captain Stoneheart muttered something she didn't quite make out but then nodded. There was a pause and then he leant his spear against the wall behind him and placed his sword beside it. He held his hands out from his sides, took three paces sideways, and halted again. 'I will be right here, Your Grace. And I will be watching, Your Majesty,' he added.

Alaya threw back her head and laughed, pleased by his lack of deference and his spite both. 'Oh, I like this one. I hope you can bring him to our side, Prince Holliday. It would be such a pity to have to eat him.' She laughed at Holliday's full-body flinch but didn't recant her words. Better to let people believe the rumour which would, after all, be fuelled soon enough by the piles of bones dumped outside the main castle entrance. The Blade-Queen preferred to keep the existence of her sisters a secret for as long as possible. Besides, she'd been newborn herself once, and while she had been born in fact, not hatched, her diet had been … varied.

Holliday was either constipated or attempting to smile as he politely gestured her away from the wall and his guard so they might speak in private. She already knew he must have taken over the rebellion when Dorian vanished—neither he nor his captain could act well enough to convince her otherwise—but she was willing to play the game if he would betray his associates to save his own skin.

'This has all been a terrible mistake, Your Majesty,' he began, clasping his hands in front of his chest. 'What my brother did was reprehensible. I can assure you that my loyalty is to you and you alone, My Queen.'

Alaya let her wings shift against each other, flashes of light reflecting from them and bouncing off the wall behind Holiday's head and across Captain Stoneheart's armour. 'If you want to prove your loyalty to me, Prince Holiday, you better give me something other than empty words. The longer you keep me out here babbling, the more inclined I am to think you are attempting to distract me from the battle outside my walls. Is that what you are doing?' she added, letting her face and eyes go cold and lethal.

Holliday blanched. 'Not at all, Your Majesty,' he squeaked, bringing up his clasped hands in supplication. 'I was hoping you would authorise me to negotiate the rebels' surrender. I'm sure I can do it, My Queen, and it will allow me to prove my loyalty to you.'

The Blade-Queen cocked her head and examined him. The proposal was interesting and she was, after all, in need of a new husband. Lucky number six. She let the corner of her mouth tilt upwards. 'And what is it you expect in return, little prince?'

Holliday stammered denials of wanting anything but peace within the realm, which was as transparent a lie as any she had ever heard. Then again, if he could indeed talk the rebels into surrendering, perhaps she would grant him a few weeks of life to see whether he could be trusted. Or at least trusted long enough.

'Very well. I accept. How do you plan to work this miracle exactly?' she asked.

Holliday gaped as if he hadn't expected her to agree. 'Would you allow me to ascend to the battlements above the gate, Your Majesty?' he asked. 'I have no armour, but your favour is protection enough,' he added so piously that the Blade-Queen was tempted to spit him on her wings out of pique.

'And I suspect you wish me to go up there with you, do you, and outline myself against the sky for rebel archers to shoot at?'

This time, he had the audacity to look affronted. He threw himself onto his knees and clutched at the fine material of her trousers. 'I would ask no such thing, My Queen,' he said fervently. 'Your health and survival are essential; it is you who has brought stability and prosperity to our ever-increasing kingdom—I mean queendom. Forgive me, queendom of course.'

Alaya watched a bead of sweat dribble down Holliday's temple and onto the curve of his cheekbone before she reached down and hauled him up by one arm. She leapt and unfurled her wings and then they were flying, a little laboured—the prince was not a light man—until they reached the battlements above the western gate. Alaya dropped him from a few strides above the walkway and enjoyed his screech as he landed and either twisted or broke his ankle.

Even paler than before, from shock or pain or the first-hand knowledge of his queen's strength, Prince Holliday leant on the battlements and stared down at the melee beyond the gate. He cupped trembling hands around his mouth.

'Citizens of Sisterne, it is time to lay down your weapons. Queen Alaya does not deserve your violence or your insurrection. All she has done since coming to power has been for the peace and stability of our'—he flicked her a glance—'great queendom. We are happier, healthier, and richer than we were under her predecessors. And so I ask you: why do you fight?'

As oratory went, it was fucking awful, but it served the purpose of pausing the fighting below and allowing hesitation and possibly doubt to creep into the first ranks of rebels crowding the narrow road.

Perhaps the fumbling idiot could convince them, she thought, whereupon said fumbling idiot threw himself at her chest, wrapped his arms and legs around her, and toppled them both off the wall.

Ah. Of course.

Alaya's wings opened on instinct and she twisted catlike in mid-air, but even so they landed heavily in the courtyard below, the queen's knees thudding hard onto the flagstones as Holliday hit the ground back-first, still clinging like a baby monkey. She heard his grunt as the air was forced out of his lungs and before she could rear back and curve a wing to take off his head, something slammed into her from behind.

Ah. Of course.

'Clever,' she murmured into Holliday's pained face, 'but not clever enough.'

'Really?' Stoneheart asked from somewhere behind her wings. 'You'd be surprised how clever I can be.' Alaya reared backwards but he was already looping a chain around her wings and cinching it tight. The Blade-Queen laughed and flexed, and the metal links gave a tortured scream:

they wouldn't last long. A knife jabbed at her side and screeched off her armour, almost clipping Holliday on its way.

'This is possibly the worst assassination attempt I have had the indignity to suffer,' she snarled and, despite the gibbering Holliday *still* gripping onto her, she fought her way to her feet and turned in time to catch Stoneheart's knife hand as the blade came in again. 'You're just embarrassing yourselves now.'

Alaya tore Holliday off her and flung him across the stone. She was unsurprised that Stoneheart didn't even blink; the prince was simply his way into the castle. Who cared whether he lived or died? Without his weight hampering her, the queen threw her arms wide and flexed her wings again. Metal screeched and part of the chain broke, freeing one of her four wings. She drove it directly for her assailant's face.

Stoneheart jerked up his arm. There was a clang when it met his vambrace and then both metal and man screamed as it cleaved through. Alaya heard the greenstick crack of bone and grinned as the captain fell to his knees, his wounded arm clutched to his chest and his silly little knife flailing in his other hand.

The Blade-Queen took two paces forwards and stood over him, flexing her wings until the chain fell in sundered links around her feet. She hissed in triumph. 'Little fool. No man can kill me.'

He got one foot under him and halfway to standing, an ugly laugh wheezing from his throat. He used his knife hand to pull off his helmet and Alaya's eyes widened as the face that was revealed was decidedly feminine.

'Bitch, please,' Stoneheart said and lunged upwards.

The point of her knife took the Blade-Queen under the chin, piercing her mouth, tongue, and soft palate and driving upwards into her brain. Alaya twitched once, in shock and bitter amusement, and died.

Syl Stoneheart, famed mercenary and former captain of the Iron Blades, sat on top of a mounting block and drank rum. The surgeon had said that, unless infection set in, her arm would heal and she'd live.

'"No man can kill me",' she muttered and snorted a laugh. 'What a fucking joke.' Holliday approached and she waved the bottle at him in acknowledgement. He was limping on a pair of crutches but there was a grim twist to his mouth that she didn't like. She forestalled whatever calamity he was about to drop on her. 'My coin. Triple, wasn't it?'

'Two and a half,' he said absently. 'Come with me, Captain, and bring your sword,' he added, voice strangely hollow. He didn't wait for her, just limped in a circle and headed back indoors. Syl eyed her bottle of rum and sighed with regret, then stashed it in the shadows and picked up her blade. She caught up with the prince-of-nothing as he was labouring up a twisting flight of stairs. He refused to answer any of her questions and when they finally reached the top and passed between half a dozen guards and into the room, she understood why. What could explain this, after all?

Nestled amid piles of bones and gobbets of flesh were dozens—a score? more?—of naked little girls, each with four translucent wings protruding from their backs. In the centre of the room, in the centre of the carnage, stood Prince Dorian.

'What the fuck.' Syl was impressed her voice came out with barely a tremble.

'You have to kill them,' Holliday said as Dorian put one hand over his belly.

Syl didn't blame him; she felt a mite nauseous herself. She looked from the brothers to the children in their beds of meat and back. 'No.'

'Triple,' Holliday tried. 'Captain, please—'

'Not a fucking chance. I don't do kids.'

'These aren't—'

'No,' Syl said. 'Give me my damn coin and do your own dirty work.'

Holliday tried one last time while Dorian stood silent and still, his arms wrapped around his midriff. In the end, Syl Stoneheart pressed the blade of her sword against Holliday's throat until he passed her the coin purse. She took one last look at the room and the people in it and stalked to the door. Holliday's hand was shaking as he pulled a knife, but it wasn't aimed at her. He was staring at the children; he was crying.

Syl closed the door and ran back down the stairs to the courtyard, weighing the purse in her hand and trying not to listen for when the screaming started.

Odds were even the brothers would die.

Odds were even better that Syl Stoneheart, famed mercenary who never knowingly ran into a fight she could run away from, was never coming back to this fucking country and the monsters—human or otherwise—who ruled it.

THE DAY THE GODS WENT SILENT

JUSTIN T. CALL

THE DIRGE OF LUMEA

Weep now, my daughters, for I sing to you the Dirge of Lumea. Listen well that you may sing it, too, and forget not that we were once loved by the Goddess of Light and Fire. Whither she has gone, we know not, but so long as her fiery star rises in the sky, there is hope. Lumea watches over us in silent vigil, and while her song remains unsung, we must sing for her.

Sing then and remember that terrible day—the day the Gods went silent.

Oh, the days are short, and the nights are long, but they were not always so.
In a time of peace, we once danced and sang and fed on Lumea's glow.
The land was large, and people were strong. The earth was lush and green.
And while of cities, we had none, the fruit was choice and sweet.
Dionach Lasair. Dionach Tobar. We all were friends of old.
They shared their cups, and we stoked their fires, and never a hearth was cold.

We lacked for nothing in those days we supped with Odar's sons.
And for Regaleus we often travelled south to old Speur Dún.
To celebrate that holyday, we swapped gifts beside the Well.
The lamps burned bright as we sang all night and the kinship 'tween us swelled.
For Odar's mind was keenest then, and Lumea's voice was strong,
And Keos was dead—or so t'was thought, though 'haps we all were wrong.

It was on that day the Diamagi were displayed for all to see:
Lumea's flute and Odar's staff—gifts to man from deity.
The Hammer of Keos lay there, too, though few were shown its face:
A wicked tool of war and blood that forged the vampyr race.
But on that day an Age did end; Speur Dún fell into shade,
For Keos sent his sons to steal the gifts his hands had made.

SHIT SQUAD

You have got to be rotting kidding me.'

The priest, the soldier, and the Artificer stood in the shadows of the Black Wall, the Kuar River at their backs. In front of them, looking out of place and more than a bit uncomfortable, were their conscripts: a half-naked man in shackles, a prim lady in a petticoat and black dress, and a lean nobleman with a bald head and a sharp smile.

'I'm afraid there is no kidding to be had,' Zedir said, his hands alternately fidgeting with his crimson clerical robes and spiked leather bracelets. 'The God-King was very explicit in his commands.'

'Believe me,' Urran said, frowning, 'I'm not pleased about the arrangement either.'

Captain Lucius Scalva shook his head, his gauntlet waving the writ in front of Urran's nose. 'Don't give me that bullshit, you derelict has-been. This is all because of you. You arranged this. You asked for it.'

Zedir raised a finger. 'Well, technically, it was—'

'Derelict?' Urran interrupted. 'You surprise me, Scalva. I would never have guessed that a cur like you possessed such a turgid vocabulary. How positively grandiloquent of you.'

'Turdy ... now listen here you little sh—'

'My lords!' Inquisitor Zemir shouted. 'Please ... consider our guests?' He nodded toward the three disparate Terrans standing before them. 'It does not help our case to have them see you argue like this.'

'Yeah? And what do I care for this lot, eh?' Scalva growled, unrolling the parchment once more. 'According to this, we've got ... what? A farmer, a mass murderer and ... oh, now I know this is a joke. A bleeding schoolmistress?' He spat on the parchment, crumpled it, and hurled it at Zedir's feet. 'I wouldn't lead these three to fetch a flaming pail of water, much less across a continent to break into the rotting Halcyon Knights' castle and steal their most guarded treasures. Oh—and lest we forget—you want to do it while they are crowning their rotting king, too. Fantastic. Bunch of bloody pricks.' He spat again, narrowly missing the Inquisitor's boots.

'Well,' Zedir said, scooping up the parchment and attempting to smooth the paper, 'it is not a joke—I can promise you that—but if it is leadership you are concerned about, you need not trouble yourself. Perhaps you missed it, but the directive explains that Master Urran will lead our endeavour. Your presence is merely for, ah, insurance, shall we say?'

'You mean when it all goes to shit,' Scalva said, sneering as he scratched the black veins just visible beneath his copper-toned skin. 'And you? Who the hell are you supposed to be?'

The priest laid a hand on his paunch. 'Me? I am Inquisitor Zedir Zemir. I work for—'

'The rotting Census Bureau. Yeah, I know you now. You're the one who keeps pestering us to clean up the quarantine in Casaria, yeah?'

'Well, yes ... or rather, that was true before this week. Now his Hematic Holiness has assigned me a critical supervisory role for your mission.'

'Eh? And what the hell does that mean?'

'Well,' Inquisitor Zemir stammered, 'it, uh ... means ...'

Urran chuckled. 'He's our babysitter, Lucius. He's here to make sure you and I don't kill each other.'

'Well, yes,' Zedir said, nodding sheepishly. 'Not just you two, though. There is also the issue of the mass murderer ... the one from Casaria?' He slowly inclined his head toward their three spectators who had finally warmed up enough to begin speaking with one another. The lanky fellow with the tailored suit, the shorn head, and the razor smile seemed to be sizing up his companions. After a cursory glance at the grubby man in shackles, he turned his attention to the redhead with chalk stains on her black blouse. He stuck out his hand, offering it to the petite woman.

'Pleasure to meet you. Name's Phwillym Ordshaw. Most folks call me Phwyll.' He smiled congenially. 'Did I hear that you're a teacher? May I ask what subjects?'

The woman hesitated then extended her hand and a timid smile. 'Mistress Sloen ... but I suppose you can just call me Piritta—or Riita.' They shook hands. 'I'm the headmistress of a small school near the Southern Plains. I teach all the subjects, actually, but I'm most fond of history.' She smiled demurely. 'Did I hear that you're a farmer, Phwyll?'

'Ach, no! That'd be me, I think.' The grubby lake-man waved his shackled hands, nearly dropping his torn kilt in the process. 'Gah! Sorry 'bout that. Had a bit of a tumble with Zedir over there. Just a misunderstandin', though, yeah?' He nodded at his manacles and raised his voice. 'Figure you can take these off now that we're all acquainted, yeah?'

The schoolmistress turned, her eyes a bit wild. 'I'm sorry ... you are the farmer?

'Aye, that's right. Mahuu Cropley, though my friends call me Maw on account I can't stop jawing.' He smiled, revealing a mouthful of ivory yellow teeth. 'Got meself a nice patch o' land between Lake Jeevir and the sulphur pits. Hard to grow most crops out that way, but my tatties do just fine. Well, they do when my bloody fields aren't flooded.' He swore again. 'Mud up to my arse right now! It's devastatin'. That's how I lost my boots, actually.' He lifted a knee, waggling his bare feet and a fair bit of what lay beneath the torn kilt. 'Did I hear your name was Riita? Capital! I had a marm named Riita, too. Foxy as hell—course I was only twelve at the time, so I s'pose anything with breasts was titillating.'

The mistress retreated another step then stopped, not knowing where to run. She shifted her gaze from Maw to Phwyll, then tried to attract the attention of Inquisitor Zedir, Artificer Urran, and Captain Scalva. 'Excuse me, milords. Does that mean ...?' She nodded at Phwyll. 'Is he ...?'

'A mass murderer?' Phwyll answered, his rakish grin still firmly in place. 'Yes, I'm afraid that's what they call you when you murder whole townships just to satisfy your ego.'

'I'd wager that's not the only thing they call him,' Urran whispered to Zedir. 'He seems a bit ... unbalanced. Will he be dangerous during our mission?'

'Most likely, yes.' Zedir shrugged. 'Sorry, Master Urran, but as they say, beggars cannot choose their meals, and if Master Ordshaw seems a bit wild, it's likely because he's spent the last two months conversing with no one but walking corpses.'

'Two months?'

Zedir smiled, his expression a bit sickly, his voice lowering to a conspiratorial whisper. 'I kept petitioning Captain Scalva to come and execute him, but as long as the quarantine in Casaria held, he wasn't in any hurry to answer my requests. One of the hazards of being part of the Inquisitorial Census Bureau, I'm afraid.'

'I ... see. Phwyll does have the requisite magic, though, yes?'

'Necromancy? Oh, yes, beyond a doubt. Master Ordshaw set himself up as mayor of his little hamlet and all its citizens were his undead puppets. As far as necromancy goes, you won't find such a strong talent in all of Eastern or Western Daroea.'

'Excellent. That resolves at least one part of my plan. Tell me, though, is he likely to try and murder us at some point?'

Zedir shrugged. 'I'd say the odds are about fifty-fifty.'

'That good, eh? And that doesn't fluster you?'

The Inquisitor gave a lopsided grin. 'Master Ordshaw is not a sadistic killer. When he chooses to kill, he does so quickly, out of pragmatism. Given my rapid healing abilities, I believe he poses no threat to me personally.'

'Just to the rest of us.'

'Yes.' Zedir paused. 'Yes, that about sums it up.'

'What about the other two?' Urran pressed.

'Ah, you mean the Sower and Skinchanger?' Zedir nodded at Maw and Riita then hesitated. 'But no, those titles are imprecise. I should say rather that these are their equivalents. Come to think of it, all three conscripts come from a line of Earthshapers, but Master Cropley's strain seems to have spontaneously mutated, whereas Mistress Sloen and Master Ordshaw have a bit of Bloodlord magic mixed with their heritage.'

'That interests you, does it?'

'Oh, yes. Very much so—or rather, it did. I suppose finding those with corrupted magic is no longer my job, but old habits are slow to erase.'

Urran chewed his lip, attempting—and failing—to ignore the withering gaze of Captain Scalva, who had been eavesdropping on their entire conversation. The captain laid a hand on Zedir's shoulder, causing the Inquisitor to jump.

'Just so I'm clear on all this, the God-King put Urran the Great in charge of this little operation, and his brilliant plan is to use these three citizens to break into Speur Dún. Not only that, but we're also supposed to steal the Staff of Odar, the Flute of Lumea, and the Hammer of Keos, and it needs to be done before the week's end?'

'Yes,' Urran said, answering on behalf of Zedir. 'I think that about covers it.'

Scalva scoffed, his scorn practically dripping from him. 'Did I hit my head? Am I missing something?'

'Well,' Zedir added, his eyes twinkling, 'if you're counting us three, it brings our total party up to six.' He smiled beatifically. 'All full-blooded Terrans, too! Just as the God-King requested.'

'Well, then,' the Bloodlord captain said, 'I'll take back what I said earlier. This mission literally can't go to shit because it's starting at the bottom of the bloody garderobe.' Scalva spat again and this time it hit the Inquisitor right in the eye.

Zedir carefully wiped his face, his smile still bolted in place. Scalva huffed, half-sneering half-smiling, then he stormed off to address their conscripts.

'Is he always like this?' Urran asked, beginning to wonder if perhaps the captain's colorful assessment was right.

'Lucius?' Zedir chuckled, though there was no mirth in it. 'No, no. Usually, he's much worse.'

THE TRIDENT KING

ir Lucas Valkar stared at the royal diadem cradled in his hands, his fingers alternately tracing the arching silver loops and angular golden lines that formed the arcane symbol of the Halcyonic Order of the Riddari Tavtyv.

'What do you think they'll call it?' he wondered.

'Beg your pardon, Sir Luc?' The answer came from the councillor standing behind him.

'This.' Lucas raised the two-toned band of metal, still amazed by its deceptive weight. 'The other royals have impressive names for their crowns—the Great Helm of Borderlund, the Halo of Odar, the Fisherman's Anadem.' He paused. 'Does Tir Reota have a crown? I didn't see one on either King Danjord or Queen Jana, just those jewels in his beard and her braids.'

The councillor nodded, his narrow figure wandering into view. 'That's typical for the Reotans, but if you ever set sail on their Whalebone Throne, you'll see the tiara from their first pirate queen fixed to the warship's mast.'

Lucas nodded, his thoughts still lingering on the braided circle of palladium in his hands. The artisan who had forged the treasure had hammered a slash of bright yellow gold into the shape of a horizontal lightning bolt, its zagging lines forming the head of an abstract trident. Jewels of sapphire and chrysoberyl ornamented the trident's first and third golden tines, the former cobalt blue, the latter a bright lemon yellow. A sparkling green emerald filled the triangular void beneath the arch of the middle prong, and a final curl of white platinum had been fixed to the top of that same central tine, its shape evoking the imagery of either a breaking wave or a stylized gust of wind.

'Lumea's light,' Lucas said, tracing the lightning bolt, 'and Odar's breath.' He tapped the platinum spiral with his thumb. 'The symbol of the Riddari Tavtyv immortalized in the emblem of a newborn kingdom.'

'Just so,' the councillor said, peering at the crown. He nodded at the three gemstones. 'I suppose those represent the three territories you'll be governing? Yellow cat's eye for the sands of Innistiul. Green for the wild jungles of Cunnart. That means the sapphire is for ... the Oracle of Speur Dún?'

Lucas inclined his head a second time, now smiling. 'Perceptive as always, Arch-Dionach Reeve. The gemstones also represent the Halcyon Knights' connection to the Gods: blue for Odar and the Darites, yellow for Lumea and the Ilumites, and green for the union of their children in the Halcyonic Order of the Riddari Tavtyv and the Siúl Riddari.'

At the first mention of the Riddari, Reeve's amusement seemed to wither; his jaw clenched and his lips pressed into a thin line. 'Sir Lucas, I realize you are still a knight, and the Riddari Tavtyv are extant, but in a few short hours neither will be so. No more Riddari. No Shildari. After your coronation, you will be King Lucas Valkar, first of his name, the wise Trident King of the North, first ruler of Ildarna and the Savage Lands—and the Halcyon Knights will be nothing but a memory.'

Lucas nodded, though he did so reluctantly. 'Trident King. That name seems to be sticking ... but perhaps it is as you say.'

The councillor nodded with satisfaction then turned his attention toward the window and the Regaleus celebration transpiring in the courtyard.

'Even so,' Lucas continued, his attention returning to the diadem, 'I prophesy that after the Halcyon Knights are gone, a piece of us will live on.'

Reeve seemed to stiffen at this, his head slowly turning to peer over his shoulder. 'And may I ask what has inspired this ... prophecy?'

Lucas waved the two-toned crown at the councillor and gave him a sardonic smile. 'If a pirate queen can be immortalized by nailing her tiara to a mast, then certainly the Halcyon Knights can be memorialized by the Trident Crown of Ildarna.'

Reeve's expression softened as he turned away from the window. 'Of course,' he said, bowing to expose his baldpate. 'Such a legacy will not be so easily forgotten, and I believe you've now answered your previous question.' Lucas tilted his head in confusion and the high priest nodded meaningfully at the jeweled coronet. 'Your words will indeed be prophetic. "The Trident Crown of Ildarna." You wondered what the history books would call it, yet you have named it yourself.'

Lucas chuckled, his expression wry. 'I suppose I have, but only because you named me first.'

'Mm,' Reeve said, head bobbing in agreement. 'There is much power in a name. It is the foundation of all Darite magic: what is said, what is intended, and what is written. Words have the ability to shape the past, present, and future. Indeed, that is why I must counsel you to refer to the Halcyon Knights in the past tense. Or better still, don't refer to them at all. Let your crown remember them. Let the symbols speak for them.'

'But—'

'You need to start thinking of them as your people, Lucas. Not as your brothers in arms, but your subjects—as the Ildari—because, after today's coronation, the Halcyon Knights and vagrant knights will be no more. You'll be king and you'll have your vassals and commoners, the same as every kingdom in the Empire. A debt repaid and balance restored, both long overdue.'

Lucas felt the smile slip from his face. 'You know I didn't want this, Reeve.' Lucas lifted the crown again, as though offering it to his councillor. 'I didn't seek this honor. Odar help me, but I voted against the Northern Accords.'

'And that is precisely why the High Council chose you to replace them.' Reeve ignored the palladium treasure and slipped his arm over the future king's shoulders, guiding him towards the window. 'You're a familiar face, Lucas. People like you. They trust you. You take counsel from all corners and all sides, yet you have your own voice and you're not afraid to speak.'

'That's true enough,' Lucas said, his attention turning to the celebrants outside his high window. 'I've never been concerned with popularity—more the opposite, I think—yet it seems my unpopular actions have endeared me all the more to my people.'

Reeve smiled. 'They called you a fool when you trusted your birthright to your cousins and traveled abroad with the Shildari.'

Lucas smiled, remembering. 'My father was furious, and the High Council even more so.'

'But it served you,' the councillor said. 'You and your people. You learned the customs of the Shildari. You travelled the length and breadth of the Empire, befriending kings and queens along the way.'

'That's not why—'

'Of course not,' Reeve interrupted. 'You never gave a thought to yourself nor the politics of your actions. You only sought "to educate and adjudicate" just as the Law of the Siúl Riddari demanded. You led by example, never claiming authority because of your station, yet receiving it because of your virtue. You listened to the vagrant knights and brought their concerns back to Speur Dún. What's more, you made certain their interests were protected, even when their desires and opinions conflicted with your own. You served the eternal servants. You listened to your people, Lucas. That's what a king does. That's why they chose you.'

Lucas heard the high priest's words, though his gaze lingered on the various peoples gathered in the courtyard below: kings and queens from all parts of the Darite Empire milled about with their royal retinues. Interspersed among them were the consecrated priests and priestesses of Odar and Lumea: the sober Dionachs Tobar and the joyful Dionachs Lasair. The Halcyon Knights and Shildari were in attendance, too— some in their ceremonial armour, others vying for a balance of formality and comfort by wearing either the Halcyonic robes of investiture or the Shildari's more rugged coats of vagrancy. A pang of regret stabbed Lucas when he saw the latter, wishing, not for the first time, that he had stayed among the vagrant knights and never returned to court.

Except Reeve was right. Lucas had seen firsthand how the council brushed aside the Shildari's interests, even though the vagrant knights were far more numerous. He'd also been unable to remain idle when Sir Lambert had abdicated his commission as the Shildari's vested emissary.

When the other Riddari Tavtyv then competed for the vacancy—not because they cared for the landless knights, but because they craved the political clout it would grant them—Lucas had been compelled to return to Speur Dún to challenge the others for the right to represent the vagrants.

And he'd done such an excellent job representing their interests that Sir Lucas, against his better judgment, had been the instrument of the Halcyon Knights' downfall.

'I never wanted this,' Lucas repeated, his eyes still fixed on the congregants' singing and dancing. 'I only fought for it because that's what so many of the Shildari had been requesting for the past two centuries, and not even the majority of them.'

'But the rest came around,' Reeve said, squeezing the knight's shoulder. 'Once they saw you had the High Council's ear, they changed their tune.'

'Most ... but not all, not me, anyway.'

'Again, that is precisely why they chose you. Who else could they trust to balance the wants of the many against the needs of the few? Only you, Lucas. That is why they chose you and why they deserve you.'

'Perhaps,' Lucas murmured, his voice little more than a whisper, 'but if I am doing what is right—if this is truly what is best for my people—why does my conscience prick me so? Why do I tremble beneath this horrible feeling of foreboding?'

Reeve's hand slipped to his side. 'I know your oaths don't permit you to use magic to manipulate other people's thoughts or emotions, but do they prevent you from sensing?'

Lucas hesitated, slowly shaking his head. 'I'm not sure I follow, councillor. What are you suggesting? Are you worried that I'm eavesdropping on something ... on someone?'

'Not intentionally, but yes. I thought you might be sensing a strong disturbance of emotion from something close by.'

Again, Lucas shook his head. 'You are speaking of the gift of Soulriding. I do possess that skill, but its strain is faint. I do not think ...'

He weighed his words against his few memories of accidentally sensing someone's emotions. 'It would have to be a very strong disturbance. Someone who is conflicted about what they are about to do—what they don't want to do.'

Reeve hesitated then nodded. 'As you said, that strain of magic is not strong in your bloodline. I think it is more likely that you're feeling jitters on the day of your coronation. Today marks the last day of the Age of Peace, and we stand at the dawn of a new millennium. The Halcyon Knights will soon be dissolved, and with that dissolution, we will witness the birth of a new kingdom. With such momentous events ahead of us, a sense of foreboding seems only natural.'

Lucas grunted in concession, yet he could not shake the sense that something very ominous was about to transpire.

THE DIAMAGI

It was two hours before the Trident King's coronation when the iridescent gates of Speur Dún were finally opened to the common Darite citizenry and the many Ilumite performers, all of whom had gathered to celebrate the crowning of the Empire's newest king and the creation of its newest nation, the northern kingdom of Ildarna. The towering doors of the Sky Citadel swung inward, admitting a wave of people from the vast reaches of the Darite Empire and beyond, mixing with the Halycon Knights, the vagrant Shildari knights, and the many guests who had already entered the castle. Chief among these were the Empire's four arch-monarchs and their retinues, the lesser monarch-chieftains from Southmarch and Tir Reota, and the heads of the orthodox clergy for both the Dionachs Tobar and Dionachs Lasair.

Amidst this maelstrom of activity, a small troupe of entertainers dressed in Ilumite merrymaker clothes strolled into Speur Dún's central courtyard. Each of their faces was painted a bright colour to match their clothes, the only exception being the black-and-white harlequin who wore an ornate mask.

'Well,' Maw whispered, readjusting his green silken langot, 'that part was easy enough. They didn't even check us for weapons.'

'Indeed,' Urran said, his voice low as he scanned for the easiest entry into the castle proper. 'But the gambit was never about getting into the keep. It was about finding the diamagi and successfully escaping with them.'

'And it seems finding them won't be difficult either,' Phwyll said, plucking a stray thread from his white-and-gold epaulettes. He nodded towards the three enormous display cases in the center of the courtyard. 'The Staff, the Flute, and the Hammer ... sitting right out in the open.'

'Blight me,' Scalva swore, then paused when he caught Riita glowering at him. 'Sorry, I mean ... well, look! They're sitting in plain sight.' He lowered his voice, though his bulging eyes belied the emotion he fought to conceal beneath his purple face paint. 'How in Keos's name are we supposed to steal the artifacts with a few thousand people watching us?'

'I don't believe they are in plain sight,' Urran said, edging the group closer to the three pedestals. 'The diamagi are the three most powerful tools ever forged by Keos. Despite what the stories say, I find it extremely unlikely the Halcyon Knights would put the genuine artifacts on display— not even for Regaleus. Not even for the coronation of their first king.'

'So,' Maw said, 'you're saying these are all fakes?' He side-eyed the shimmering silver staff in the nearest display case.

Urran nodded. 'The true treasures have always been locked in three of Speur Dún's tallest towers. I'd wager that's where the diamagi still reside, though I admit these replicas are quite convincing.' He beckoned the group to follow him and began pushing through the crowd, his voice raised just loud enough to be heard over the surrounding din but not beyond the circle of his immediate companions. 'I know you're all anxious about the parts you'll be playing in today's events, but you needn't be. I've created hundreds of artifacts to aid us if need requires and developed several dozen contingency plans for virtually any scenario we might encounter.'

'That's interesting,' Scalva breathed, 'because you've told us rot all about your plans up to this point—excepting some crazy shit about splitting up and storming the treasure towers. Rotting suicide missions, every one of them.'

'No, that's fair. I've been a bit scant on the details, but that has been intentional.' Urran tapped his temple. 'The Halcyon Knights have the ability to read people's thoughts and sense their feelings. If I had shared too much, it's possible you five might have given away something crucial. That is why I've devised so many contingencies.' He patted his bag. 'It's also why I've mostly kept you in the dark.'

'Hold up,' Scalva said, raising a hand. 'Did you just say the Halcyon Knights can read my mind?' He looked around, muscles tense as though preparing for combat.

'Ordinarily, yes, but you needn't worry.' He tapped the two halves of the pendant hanging around his neck. 'This artifact allows me to shield our thoughts and emotions from any mental or luminal scrying, but it will be difficult to maintain once we are separated.'

'How long have you been shielding us?'

'Since before we got to Speur Dún.'

Urran paused, having come to a halt in front of the pedestal that displayed the gold flute: an aura of white light seemed to hover about the artifact, and Urran stared at it in fascination. Then, very slowly, the blood began to drain from his face. 'Damn me,' he breathed, suddenly dancing back to the pedestal displaying the silvery staff. 'Shit,' he swore again, now dashing over to the farthest pedestal.

'Something wrong?' Riita asked, her fingers knotting the neck of her yellow drawstring blouse.

Instead of answering, Urran continued to work his way to the front of the small crowd lingering near the replica of the Hammer of Keos. Fewer celebrants had chosen to gather in that section of the courtyard, with the largest attention being focused on the flute and staff. Those that remained quickly left Urran alone once it became clear he intended to scrutinize the relic on the other side of the transparent barrier.

Though it appeared to be entirely metal, the material composing the hammer was white in colour, its surface entirely covered with an impressive, blood-red filigree. As the group of Terrans formed around Urran, he could also see the artifact possessed a scintillating, prismatic sheen. For a moment, no one spoke. Urran stared, his mouth hanging open, unable to find his words. After almost a minute, he stepped back from the pedestal and beckoned his five companions to do the same.

'They aren't replicas,' Urran said, his eyes unfocused. 'Why in the names of all the Elder Gods would the Halcon Knights display the actual treasures? It's ludicrous. Irresponsible.' He shook his head, one hand pressed to his apricot-coloured lips, then falling to rub the orange peel painted stubble growing around his mouth and chin. 'Godsdammit. Of all the eventualities, this was my least favorite.'

'So, they aren't replicas.' Maw smirked. 'You know, I usually like being right about things, but I can't say I'm feeling all that pleased about this one.'

'At least we don't have to split up now,' Riita offered, though her eyes looked wild. 'You can keep guarding our thoughts, yes?'

'Of course, yes, but ...' Urran groaned. 'Dammit. My least favorite plan.' He took a deep breath then shook his head. 'No matter. I've come prepared, so we'll make do.' He looked over at Zedir and Scalva. 'You aren't going to like what comes next.'

'Why not?' Scalva said, eyes narrowing. 'We gonna smash the glass, grab the artifacts, and run?'

'Gods, no!' Urran breathed. 'Don't you remember anything about the diamagi? They destroy anyone who touches them.' He paused. 'Actually, that's not completely true. The scriptures never specify whether the hammer has the same curse placed on it, but it's not something I want to test, either.' He sighed heavily. 'No, this has to do with the God-King. You may recall his instructions precluded us from using any outside help?'

Inquisitor Zemir nodded, his eyes shifting beneath his checkered harlequin mask as though to confirm Neruacanta himself weren't listening in on their conversation. When the priest spoke, his tone remained apologetic yet insistent. 'The God-King was quite explicit on that point.'

'Indeed,' Urran said, his fingers tapping the front of his chest. 'Well, the thing is ... that's not going to happen.'

'What's this now?' Scalva stepped closer, his eyes taking on a dangerous glint.

'Acquiring some outside help,' Urran repeated. 'I have several artifacts that will allow us to remove the diamagi from their glass cases, but that's as far as we'll get without help from our seventh party member.'

Scalva frowned, his head rotating to take in the full courtyard and all the people in it. 'I'm sorry. Did I miss the part where we had a seventh party member?'

Urran took another deep breath then slowly exhaled. 'I had hoped not to use her at all, or as a last resort—one of those contingency plans I mentioned earlier—but I fear we'll need her assistance in the more immediate future.'

'Her?' Riita said, raising an eyebrow. 'Does that mean there are two women in our party now?'

Urran wobbled his head, his eyes roaming the courtyard, searching for something, or someone. 'In a manner of speaking ... er ... she's a Lady, actually—not that you aren't a lady, my dear.' He inclined his head toward the schoolmistress. 'What I mean to say is she's a former member of the Halcyonic Order.'

'Hold up,' Phwyll said, piecing it together quicker than the others. 'You mean the seventh member of our party is a traitor Halcyon Knight?'

Urran nodded. 'Lady Sariah Inkpen. She possesses a skill with sound and illusions that will be the key to escaping with these artifacts.'

'How did you find her?' Riita asked, stepping closer. 'And what makes you think she's trustworthy?'

Urran hesitated, his attention shifting once more between Zedir and Scalva, both of whom were holding their tongues. 'Truthfully, Mistress

Sloen, I didn't know a thing about Lady Inkpen until very recently—but she was scouted out a few years ago by the First Vampyr.'

'Dortafola? You're getting your intel from him?' Scalva bit off a curse. 'Let me guess, he was asking her to become one of his Sïanar mercenaries, yeah?' He sniffed. 'I'm telling you, Urran, you can't trust those kraiks—or Dortafola, for that matter. He doesn't play by the same rules as the rest of us.'

Zedir murmured his agreement, his dour tone offset by the grinning harlequin mask. 'The God-King was very explicit about this, Master Urran. No help from the Younger Gods or their heretic worshippers. No interference from Dortafola or his Sïanar.'

'That's the thing,' Urran said, raising a finger. 'Lady Inkpen rejected Dortafola's offer. She isn't a member of the Six. She's not New Terran either, nor does she worship the Younger Gods. Technically, she falls outside all the God-King's restrictions.'

'A dubious distinction,' Zedir said. 'And I doubt the God-King would see things that way.'

'And let's not forget that she's a bloody Halcyon Knight,' Scalva hissed. Violet veins of his Bloodlord magic pulsed beneath Scalva's heliotrope-hued skin. 'What makes you think she would help us steal from her own flaming family?'

'They aren't my family anymore,' said a bodiless voice, its tone unmistakably feminine. The tight circle of disguised Terrans parted, each person searching for the speaker—all except for Urran, who was smiling. 'Besides,' the voice continued, 'once Lucas Valkar is crowned King of Ildarna, the Halcyon Knights will officially cease to exist. The moment that happens, the knights will forfeit all their claims to these artifacts.'

'But why help us?' Riita persisted, still searching for the invisible woman, though she did so more discreetly than the others.

'I want to see them fall just as much as you do,' Lady Inkpen said, her voice full of scorn. 'More than you, I'd wager—but I won't indenture myself to a vampyr just to see it happen.'

'Neither would I,' Riita admitted, her eyes crinkling with amusement, 'though I can't say I was given much choice in the matter.'

Urran cleared his throat, regathering everyone's attention. 'I asked the lady knight to shadow us in case we required her assistance. I just didn't expect I'd need to reveal her this early.' He looked around. 'Sariah, dear? If it's not too much trouble, could you show yourself to us?'

'Look at your reflections in the glass case.'

As one, the Terrans turned toward the pedestal displaying the Hammer of Keos. The glass enshrining the relic seemed almost perfectly transparent save for the rainbow-hued aura emanating from the sacred hammer. The glass case then reflected a portion of that divine light, serving as a faint mirror for the courtyard's nearest celebrants. Urran and the others spotted the seventh figure then standing amid their little cabal: a lean young woman with a fair complexion, dark brown hair, and the signature padded leather and silver-blue half plate armour worn by the vagrant knights known as the Shildari. As soon as Maw spotted her, he began waving his hand in the air, trying to grope the spectre.

'Stop it,' Urran shushed. 'You're drawing attention.'

'Sorry,' the lake-man said, grinning, his hand quickly dropping back to his side.

'It's just an illusion anyway,' Urran continued, turning his attention away from the enshrined relic and back towards the assembly of priests, performers, and royal attendants. 'Are you close, Sariah?'

'I am, though "just an illusion" is an insulting oversimplification.'

'I'm sure it is,' Urran said, his eyes still roving over the faces in the crowd. That was when he spotted Sariah: a fair knight in formal Shildari full plate leaning against the far western wall. She studied Urran from behind the bars of her open face great helm, and he gave a small nod of acknowledgment.

'Now you're the one drawing attention,' Sariah whispered, though she nodded before directing her gaze elsewhere. 'By the way, Urran, I'm only projecting my voice to you now.'

'Fair enough,' Urran said, stepping away from his companions. 'Now that introductions are over, I'm assuming you'd like to know your part in the plan?'

'Not really—I pieced all that together after eavesdropping on you and your companions. I just wanted to make sure Dortafola explained my conditions for helping you.'

'Something about needing to wait until after Valkar is crowned, yes?'

'That's right.'

'Yes,' Urran said, his disappointment evident. 'Given the unusual circumstances, I had hoped for an exception.'

'The circumstances are the exception.'

'Of course,' Urran said, 'but they'll be closing the gates in an hour, and I was sort of hoping we could be on the other side before that happened.'

'You've already dug your tunnel, so there's no need to concern yourself with something as simple as a gate.'

'True.' Urran narrowed his eyes. 'All the same, it'd be much easier if we could leave the same way we entered—before they close the gates.'

'Well, that won't be happening. So stop asking.'

'Not even if I say please?'

From across the courtyard, the lady knight shook her head. 'You'll get my help after Valkar is crowned king and not a moment before.'

'Right,' Urran said, shoulders slumping. 'Let's start from there. Once the crown touches his head, my companions and I will grab the artifacts.' He paused. 'Dortafola said you can maintain your projections even when the diamagi aren't nearby—even when they're moving. Is that true?'

'If it weren't, you'd be in a heap of trouble, yeah?'

'More like mountains of it. How does that work, exactly? I don't know any Ilumites with that ability.'

'Nor would you. Lightslingers can project and manipulate the light, but they are limited to only projecting images of something nearby. My illusions have a different source.'

'One conjured from your memories, no doubt. That's why it's a trick that only a Halcyon Knight can perform.'

For a long moment, Sariah said nothing, then she chuckled. 'I see now that your reputation as a problem solver is well earned.'

'It comes from practice. Lots and lots of practice.'

'Well, you won't be teasing out more secrets from me. Have your companions ready when the coronation ceremony starts. Projecting three pairs of illusions will be challenging. It will be easiest if everyone does their job and is ready to move at the same time. If you need an illusion covering your escape I could—'

'Don't stretch yourself,' Urran interrupted. 'We'll manage the details of the escape. Just do your part.'

'You can count on it.'

'Good.' Urran rejoined his companions who had retreated to another empty space in the courtyard. 'We'll keep the same pairings I mentioned before,' he told them, 'but we'll each take up positions near the relics we'll be stealing.' Urran stuck his hand into a mantis-green sack, which appeared to be empty, then withdrew three pairs of elbow-length riding gloves. He handed the first pair to Phwyll. 'Put these on, all of you.' He passed the other pairs to Riita and Maw. 'You recall my previous warning about not touching the diamagi with your bare hands?'

Phwyll nodded, flexing his gloved fingers. 'Something about being obliterated by the curse of Keos ... or the combined power of Odar and Lumea?'

'Correct,' Urran affirmed, extracting three more sets of gloves, two of which he passed to Scalva and Zemir, then he returned the hiding-sack to his breast pocket and donned the last pair. 'These garments were designed to generate thin shields of pliable air—like a second glove protecting the first—which will allow us to move and manipulate the diamagi without permitting the relics to touch either our skin or our clothing.'

'I can't touch my fingers,' Maw said, attempting to pinch his right thumb and forefinger together. He tried making a gloved fist but was similarly rebuffed.

'That's the enchantment,' Urran explained. 'It should also allow us to penetrate the shields protecting the diamagi.'

'You mean the glass cases?' Maw asked, still playing with his garments.

'Not glass—skywater. Observe.' Matching actions to words, Urran strolled over to the pedestal displaying the glowing hammer and swiped his glove through the transparent barrier. For an instant, the surface of the rectangular prism shuddered, then the case's enchantment reasserted itself, shimmering as it once again reflected the hammer's colourful aura.

'Enchanted glass is a Terran invention,' Urran said, returning to the group, 'but these knights don't use Terran magic.' He smirked, obviously pleased with himself.

'Hold on,' Scalva said, frowning. 'Did you know that would happen or were you gambling?'

Urran's smile broadened. He bit his lip. 'Best not to answer, I think.'

THE DALTA

Sir Lucas Valkar fixed his gaze on the diadem as its bearer wended her way through the crowd and towards the dais. As it drew closer, he fought the imagery of a ring-snake slithering towards him, climbing his body, and coiling around his neck.

'Steady,' the councillor said, his hand lightly resting on Valkar's shoulder plate. 'It'll all be over in a few minutes.'

'Reeve,' Lucas whispered, his hand obscuring his speech from the closest monarchs, 'how do we know this is Odar's will?'

The councillor chuckled. 'Lucas,' he chided, 'it's a little late for cold feet.'

'How do we know, Reeve?'

'It's the will of the people,' the Arch-Dionach blustered. 'The knights voted. The high council voted. It's done, lad. It's out of your hands. You've accepted their will, and now it falls to you to do your duty.' He nodded at the Trident Crown nestled on its velvet pillow, its bearer sashaying her way across the open-air gallery as she displayed the Ildari diadem. 'You remember the oaths, yes?'

Lucas nodded, though his fingers still itched to unlatch the heavy royal robe that had so recently been pinned to his shoulders. 'You and Arch-Dionach Helwig present the crown. I recite the oaths of monarchy and imperial fealty, then you and Tiersa put the crown on my head ... and I become the first king of Ildarna.'

'Excellent,' Reeve said, his attention returning to the bearer of the crown, who was now weaving between the display cases for the diamagi.

'And,' Lucas added, his voice lowering, 'I become known as the man who destroyed the Halcyonic Order of the Riddari Tavtyv—the man who brought an end to the Age of Peace.'

'Lucas,' Reeve said, now scolding. 'It is done. Stop acting childish. Accept the will of your people and behave like the king everyone expects you to be.'

Lucas frowned, wondering if he was indeed acting the petulant child. Even if he were, petulance by itself did not sufficiently explain his feelings of foreboding. 'I just ... I wish I knew for certain this is what Odar and Lumea wanted—not the people, but the Gods themselves.'

Once again, Lucas found his attention drawn to the approaching Trident Crown, whose bearer was nearly upon him. As she approached the foot of the dais, Lucas forced himself to look away, allowing his gaze to rest instead on the distant Flute of Lumea. A second hand fell on the knight's free shoulder just then, and Lucas turned to see Tiersa Helwig, the Matriarch of the Ilumites and High Priestess of the Dionachs Lasair. She nodded warmly to him, her presence both regal and reassuring.

Lucas blinked, his attention turning briefly from Dionach Helwig toward the diamagi—and then he smiled.

Madness, he thought. Sheer and utter madness.

But he was already lifting his hand to call a halt to the coronation. His heart hammered in his chest as Tiersa and Reeve's hands each fell from his shoulders. The high priestess looked at him with curiosity while Reeve seemed to glower in reproach—but it was too late. He had made his decision, and the Gods alone would tell him whether it was the right one.

'Bring out the diamagi!' Lucas said, raising his voice so it might be heard above the din. 'Bring me the Staff of Odar and the Flute of Lumea.'

Oh, hells.

'What's going on?' Maw said, his eyes wide as he fondled the small sack of seed potatoes hidden beneath his langot. 'Are we in trouble? Do we need to run?'

Urran slowly shook his head, his mind racing to form a response to current events even as he struggled to process what was happening.

'What is it?' Riita asked, abandoning her post with Inquisitor Zemir beside the case containing the Staff of Odar. 'Are we tattered?'

Again, Urran shook his head, relieved to see Lucius and Phwyll holding their positions next to the Hammer. He took a deep breath, trying not to hyperventilate, trying not to panic.

Calm yourself, he thought. Process the facts, identify the problem, and formulate the solution. A moment later, he exhaled and turned to face the schoolmarm. 'I could be wrong, but I believe the Trident King means to ascend.'

'Ascend?' Maw said, peering at the dais. 'Ain't he about as high as he can go?'

'The diamagi,' Urran said, stepping back with the other guests as the Halcyon Knights removed the Flute and Staff from their enchanted cases. 'He means to take them up ... to ascend and become a dalta—a child-god.'

'You mean ... he wants to hold the bloody things? Why? He's got a death wish?'

'Perhaps he does' Urran said, frozen as the knights carried the two artifacts toward their would-be king, '... but I don't think so.'

W hat are you doing?' Reeve growled, his eyes bulging as he gripped Lucas's arm.

'I don't want to be the first king of Ildarna unless it is the will of Odar and Lumea,' the knight said, his mind made up. 'I don't want to end the Halcyon Knights' legacy without being certain it is what our Gods desire.'

'This is ludicrous! You will die, Lucas. You'll be committing suicide right in front of all these people. This is the worst—'

'He's following his heart, Reeve.' Tiersa laid her own hand over the councillor's and pulled him away. 'Lucas knows what he's doing.'

'Does he though?'

Lucas nodded, his breath quickening as the guardians of the diamagi brought the staff and flute before him. 'Only those with Odar and Lumea's favor may wield the relics,' he breathed, his mind made up though his spirit quavered. 'I don't want to be king unless I have the God's favor—so, yes. I do know what I am doing.'

The high priest of the Darites rubbed his face, his hands trembling. 'This is the worst idea you've ever had.'

'No,' Lucas said, his mind and emotions finally calming. 'The worst idea I ever had was placing the esteem of men above the will of the Gods.' He stepped forward his hands outstretched to take both artifacts from their bearers.

Reeve inhaled, bracing himself as he stepped away from the would-be king. Tiersa smiled, tensed as if to move farther away, then held her place. Everyone else—monarchs and merrymakers both—held their collective breaths.

Lucas Valkar seized the Flute of Lumea and the Staff of Odar. In the space of a heartbeat, a pillar of fire roared down from the heavens, blasting the patch of stone on which he stood. At the same instant, a column of ice rose from the knight's feet, encasing him in wind and water as arcing tongues of electricity shot from his body and flew over the heads of the gathered assembly. At the sides of the dais, the monarchs and monarch-chieftains all leapt from the seats of their improvised thrones, while the venerable King of Odarnea literally threw himself to the ground.

Then suddenly, it was over. The smoke and vapor cleared, and when the sun shone on the spot where the knight Lucas Valkar had once stood … the man himself had been erased.

In his stead, still smoking from his ascendancy, was the first dalta of the new age: Valkar the Child-God, Trident King of Ildarna. And he was a king in truth, for as the assembly watched, a halo of blue and yellow light hovered in the air above his head and settled on his brow, not crowned by monarchs, men or priests … but by the Gods themselves.

'As Odar and Lumea command,' the Trident King boomed, his powerful voice carrying above the hushed crowd, 'so it shall be done. Let the will of the Gods determine our course … and may the Fifth Age commence on this sacred anniversary of the first Regaleus.'

King Valkar lowered his hands, barely registering that he had been holding the Staff and Flute aloft. As he passed the two artifacts back to his knightly retainers, the halo of light slowly faded from above his head. Then, Lucas felt the heavy gold-and-palladium crown of Ildarna float down to replace it, moved as if by the Gods themselves. The Ildari King glanced momentarily at Tiersa, silently inquiring if this was her doing, but the high priestess shook her head, her eyes full of both wonder and mischief. When she then nodded to Reeve, Lucas saw the lean councillor's look of concentration and instinctively knew the floating crown had been his doing. As Lucas met the high priest's gaze, the latter inclined his head in what might have been an apology.

'I still think that was unwise,' Reeve whispered telepathically to his mind, 'but seeing as the Gods didn't strike you down, I suppose there's no harm in adding my blessing to theirs.'

Lacking the ability to magically reply, Lucas touched the triangular emerald at the centre of his brow, inclining his head as he did so. 'Thank you, councillor. I was certain you'd understand—once I survived, I mean.'

Reeve huffed and snorted, suppressinghis characteristic dry laugh, then he discarded his stormcalling in favor of speaking aloud. 'Of course, your Majesty. Now, if you'll excuse me, I'm suddenly feeling a bit woozy.'

Lucas nodded, dismissing his old friend with a gesture and an empathetic smile. 'Nothing serious?'

'No,' Reeve said, his hands trembling. 'Just my nerves.' He flashed his teeth, an expression that seemed caught between a smile and a grimace. 'I'm afraid your little gamble with the artifacts may have given me some indigestion, but it will pass.' Another pained flash of teeth. 'Excuse me,' he said again, then he left the dais.

Rot and ashes!'

'Steady,' Urran said, redirecting the farmer's attention away from the Trident King and towards the Flute of Lumea. 'This changes nothing. As soon as the knights have the diamagi in their cases, we'll snatch them.'

'But he just—'

'Focus, Cropley.'

'Right,' Maw breathed, finally tearing his eyes away from the spectacle on the dais. 'Right, right, right. Stay focused. Stay focused.'

The two artifacts had been brought back to their pedestals, and the Halcyon Knights were in the process of reinstalling them in their protective cases. At the other end of the courtyard, Urran could see Captain Scalva and Phwyll waiting beside the pedestal displaying the Hammer of Keos. While keeping eye contact with Scalva, Urran whispered, 'Lady Inkpen? Are you still ready to proceed?'

A moment's hesitation and then, 'I am.'

Urran checked to make sure no one nearby was watching then touched the black-and-white pendant hanging around his neck. Using his Artificer abilities, he then amplified the pendant's magic and focused it on the Bloodlord captain, discouraging others from acknowledging what they might inadvertently witness in the next few seconds.

Urran nodded to Scalva. The Bloodlord immediately stepped forward and, using the gloves previously given to him, he reached through the barrier of skywater and grasped the Hammer of Keos. The artifact's prismatic aura flickered for just an instant, then Scalva's hand emerged from the case ... holding nothing. Yet even as Urran started to doubt the efficacy of his plan, his heart leapt as he saw Scalva's eyes suddenly widen, his trembling hand extended as though he held something quite heavy away from his chest. Blood drained from the irascible captain's face, and across the distance of the courtyard, Urran could see the Bloodlord mouth an inaudible oath.

Despite all evidence to the contrary—despite the fact that he could see the relic sitting on the pedestal inside its protective case—Urran the Great knew, beyond a doubt, that Captain Lucius Scalva was holding the diamagus.

They had stolen the Hammer of Keos.

One down, the Master Artificer thought, two to go.

The guardians had already moved away from the pedestals displaying the flute and staff, their attention shifting to the ascended king who had just held the Artifacts of the Gods and not been consumed by their magic. In centre of the courtyard, Zedir and Riita flanked the largest pedestal displaying silvery staff that once belonged to the God of Skywater. Zedir raised his harlequin mask and licked his lips, intent for Urran's signal.

'Lady Inkpen,' Urran whispered. 'I trust you are ready to fabricate two more illusions for us?'

'Four illusions,' came the whispered reply. 'I can't very well make copies of the artifacts only to have folks seeing you walking around with the genuine articles ... but yes, I'm ready.'

Urran smiled, touched his thumb to the pendant, and shifted its foci to the pedestals displaying the Flute of Lumea and Staff of Odar.. Then he glanced back at Zedir, who was still waiting for the Master Artificer's signal.

Urran gave the nod then immediately plunged his arm into the flute's display case. Just like the first time, the glove slipped past the skywater barrier with barely an effort, and an instant later his fingers were wrapped around the legendary artifact. Urran gasped, barely believing it could be so easy. For an instant, he saw the superimposed image of Lady Inkpen's illusory flute as it overlapped the genuine article. Urran jerked the diamagus free of its case then, withdrawing Lumea's golden flute even as the artifact itself turned invisible to the naked eye.

Urran didn't have to imagine what he looked like just then for he saw Inquisitor Zemir's face and knew it mirrored his own shocked expression—a potent mix of disbelief, elation, and even a touch of dread.

They had done it. His little group of Terran outcasts had achieved the impossible.

Well, half the impossible. They still needed to escape from Speur Dún with the stolen treasures. A quick glance down the gallery showed that Captain Scalva had the same notion, for he and Phwillym Ordshaw were already making their way to the part of the courtyard where Riita had excavated their escape tunnel. Urran moved to follow but was stopped short when he noticed Zedir wasn't following—In fact, he had completely disappeared.

'Damnation,' Urran swore, his eyes alighting on Riita, who, based on how awkwardly she held her hands before her, seemed to be holding the invisible Staff of Odar. The schoolmistress glanced back at Urran, eyes wide with terror, seeking help.

'Where ... is ... Zedir?' Urran mouthed, not even attempting to shout above the cheering crowd. From across the gallery, the schoolmistress gave an exaggerated shrug then quickly waved one hand towards the dais where the monarchs sat. Urran's gaze followed—and then he spotted him: the trembling Inquisitor had his mask in place once again and was mere steps from King Valkar, his hands and arms raised high above his head.

'What the hell is he doing?' Urran swore.

'What?' Maw pressed, and Urran realized it wasn't the first time the farmer had asked him the question. The Artificer pointed at the dais. 'Zedir is ... bowing to the Trident King?'

'Oh, come on! Be serious, mate.'

Only Urran was serious: Zedir Zemir, former minister of the Inquisitorial Census Bureau of New Terra, had prostrated himself at the feet of the new King of Ildarna. Urran shook his head, not quite believing it.

'Master Cropley.'

'Yes?'

'Could you please grab the empty sack hanging at my left hip?' Maw did so, careful to avoid the invisible relic in Urran's hands. Urran nodded. 'Now open it, please.'

Maw struggled to untie the knot and loose the drawstring, his hands moving clumsily as he tried to manipulate the bag using the magic shield that surrounded his gloves. 'I can't quite ... Ah, got it!' He opened the sack and Urran surreptitiously dropped the magic flute inside. The relic disappeared into its bottomless depths. Maw continued to wait, uncertain what had just happened. 'Did you, uh ... put something in there?'

'The Flute of Lumea,' Urran said, then reclaimed the green sack from his companion.

'Kraik and Keos!' Maw jerked his hand back from the green velvet bag. 'You could have warned me first.'

Urran ignored the farmer, first securing the hiding-sack and then checking on the safety of his other companions. He nodded to the location where Scalva, Phwyll, and Riita had congregated. 'Go join the others at the escape tunnel,' he said, waving Maw onward. 'I've got to check on Zedir. Keep your magic handy.'

The farmer nodded, quickly grasping the bulge at the front of his langot. 'None to worry! I have my tatties close, should it come to that.'

Back on the dais, the harlequin-dressed Inquisitor had thrown himself at King Valkar's feet, eliciting a shriek from the other gathered monarchs—save Valkar himself, who studied Zedir with bemused fascination.

'Who's this?' he said, stepping closer to the masked Terran. 'I've only been king a few minutes, but already I'm receiving auditions for a jester?' He laughed, and that single reaction seemed to melt the other monarchs' apprehension. The royals eased back onto their thrones and Valkar gestured for Zedir to rise.

Urran slowed, watching as Zedir climbed to his knees. Just as he got his feet under him, Zedir lunged a second time, his arms hugging the Trident King's calf.

'Ouch!' The King of Ildarna shook Zedir from his leg, delivering a kick to the supplicant's face before dashing back to the safety of his guards and his throne. 'Knights of … soldiers of Ildarna! Get this beggar away from me!'

But Urran was already there, and before any of the guards or former knights could grab Zedir, he stepped forward and swept the Inquisitor back onto his feet. 'So sorry, Your Majesty!' he said, bowing as he pulled his companion along after him. 'He's light-touched—I'm sure you sensed it—and the spectacle of your coronation disturbed him more than I realized. If it pleases you, I'll take him outside right now. Soothe him a bit?'

The Trident King fixed Urran with a hard glare. 'See that you do, Master Merrymaker.'

Urran dragged Zedir behind him, his quick steps taking him like an arrowshot towards the nearest set of doors. He passed the others as he did so, discreetly waving for them to join him. The group hesitated at first, though as soon as Riita followed, Maw and Phwyll came too, forcing Scalva to bring up the rear.

'What the hell are you two doing?' the captain growled, his voice still low.

'Improvising. Also, I'm fairly certain our underground escape route is compromised.' He gestured at the barred gates. 'You coming?'

As the troupe reached the exit, Urran waved to the first pair of guards then smiled apologetically, gesturing first at Zedir—who had wordlessly reclaimed the flute from Riita—and then back at King Valkar. 'I'm afraid we've been asked to leave.'

The guards studied Urran with uncertain looks, their brows furrowed. Finally, the captain shook her head. 'No one leaves. Not till morning.'

'Yes, but King Valkar asked us to leave.' Urran waved toward the dais, this time drawing the Trident King's attention. When Valkar caught his gaze, the king muttered something under his breath then waved them onward. The captain watched the exchange then clucked her tongue and issued the command to let the group pass.

And so it was that, despite all of Urran's preparations, the theft of the diamagi was accomplished by simply walking into Speur Dún ... and walking out again.

LOSS

Your Majesty ... they're gone.'

The news came less than an hour after the coronation, though it had taken almost twice that long for word to reach the Trident King. When Lucas was finally notified, it was his former councillor, Arch-Dionach Reeve, who brought him the news.

'Gone?' Lucas repeated, still not understanding. 'How could—'

'Stolen, your Majesty. A group of Terran thieves stole the Artifacts of the Gods. The Order of the Dionachs Tobar has already begun searching for the criminals. We will have them in custody shortly. In fact, we have already caught their accomplice. An outcast vagrant knight named Sariah Inkpen.'

'One of our Shildari?' Lucas thumped down into his chair, wincing as he did so. He touched the back of his calf. Blood and ashes ... was he bleeding again? Damn that jester and his clumsy embraces—and spiked bracelets! He'd outlaw those for all his future public audiences. He took a deep breath and slowly let it out. 'Where is she being held?'

'She ... isn't. I'm sorry to say the disgraced knight committed suicide just moments after being brought into custody. We didn't have time to question her.'

'Lady Inkpen killed herself?' Reeve nodded his affirmation and Lucas felt a renewed wave of foreboding crash into him. The artifacts have been stolen ... and one of the thieves has committed suicide? What did it all mean? That strange feeling of dread, almost forgotten during his coronation, now beat like a drum beneath Lucas's ribs. If anything, the premonition felt stronger, but how could that be so with all the criminals either dead or fled?

'Your Majesty?' Reeve pressed. 'Are you all right?'

'I don't know,' Lucas said. 'When did this happen? I swear I saw the artifacts just minutes ago. By the Gods, I held them just two hours past. How could they have been stolen during that time?'

'As best we can tell, the other thieves gained admittance to your coronation by masquerading as a troupe of performers. It seems they stole the artifacts immediately after your ... ascendancy.'

'Please don't call it that.'

Reeve frowned. 'But that is—'

'No, I know that's technically what happened, but I'd prefer to simply call it my coronation. Please.'

The councillor studied him then nodded. 'Of course, Your Majesty. As I was saying, the thieves waited until your ... coronation. Then they stole the artifacts in the resulting chaos. Lady Inkpen created an illusion to hide the theft. The infiltrators used a tunnel to escape. As soon as it was discovered, I authorized my people to flood the whole of it and then freeze the water inside. A tidy trap, but one I fear the thieves may still have escaped.'

Lucas sat stiffly on his throne, his back straightening. 'Reeve, why are you the one telling me this?'

'Beg pardon?'

'This whole issue with the diamagi. Why are you informing me? And why are the Dionachs Tobar conducting the search instead of my knights?'

'Your knights?' Reeve's brow furrowed and then his frown slipped into a condescending smile. 'Forgive me, Your Majesty, but ... the Halcyon Knights have been dissolved. The council has also abdicated its authority, so until you've been installed at the new palace in Cunnart, there is no clear line of command. Given all that has transpired, it seemed best to take matters into my own hands—for efficiency and to maintain decorum. Do you disagree?'

'No,' Lucas said, drawing out the word, 'but the artifacts—'

'—are no longer under your jurisdiction,' the high priest finished, his eyes flashing.

Lucas frowned, liking neither his councillor's tone nor his suddenly icy demeanour. 'But the diamagi are still under my stewardship,' he persisted. 'Even with the Halcyonic Order disbanded, so long as the artifacts remain at Speur Dún, they are mine to steward. That was also in the accords.'

'Beg pardon, Your Majesty, but the artifacts are no longer in Speur Dún. They also aren't in your custody, nor are they being transported to Innistiul or the Cunnart Isle.'

Lucas felt his self-assurance begin to waver. He glanced at each pair of guards standing vigil in the four corners of the former Council Hall, a room that had become both his formal audience chamber and throne room. Lucas knew at least two of the knights, but the rest were unfamiliar to him.

Something is wrong here, he thought. Something has felt wrong all day ... but I refused to see it ... my attention too focused on my own insecurities. He stood. 'Would you walk me to my chambers, councillor? I've more questions for you, but I would prefer a bit of privacy first.' He gestured to the door then began walking. 'How exactly did Lady Inkpen kill herself?'

The Arch-Dionach followed Lucas out of the hall, hastening to catch up. 'It seems she had a glyph prepared in case she got caught.'

'Seems?'

Reeve nodded. 'I believe the glyph was consumed by its own magic when she activated the spell.'

'You mean there is no evidence left from it?'

'Just Lady Inkpen's corpse dried out like a husk.' The councillor shook his head, sighing. 'It's not a pretty way to die, but it is effective. Very quick, too.' He hesitated. 'Did you want to see the body? I had it frozen in case you—'

'No, thank you,' the Trident King said, raising his hand. 'I've seen enough horrors. I am content simply imagining that one.' He turned to follow the intersecting corridor then felt Reeve's hand on his shoulder.

'Sorry, Your Majesty, but the royal chambers are ... unstable. It seems the thieves dug their tunnel right beneath it. I advise against sleeping there, at least until we've repaired the foundation.'

Lucas huffed. 'Shall I sleep on my feet then?'

Reeve chuckled. 'I expect there will be plenty of that once you've been king for a while—but no, I had thought to spare you that on your first night. Since the treasure towers are empty, I took the liberty of having one prepared for you.'

'Oh. That was ... very thoughtful. Thank you, Reeve.'

'Of course.' He gestured, redirecting Lucas toward the tower that typically held the Staff of Odar.

'Tell me, councillor,' Lucas said, walking beside his old friend. 'What are we currently doing to find the lost artifacts?'

'We are thawing the escape tunnel in sections, but it's over two miles long and will take time to properly investigate. I also suspect the thieves may have escaped that trap, so I've posted spies along every road leading to Daogort. I even have eyes watching the ocean and river passages.' Reeve continued his debriefing as they climbed the long flight of stairs leading to the top of the tower.

'These reports,' Lucas said, interrupting only after Reeve began repeating himself. 'I assume you are communicating telepathically with those outside Speur Dún?'

'Of course—well, for those in range anyway. For those at a distance, I've established a relay system.'

'And are the Halcyon Knights included in this system?'

The steps of the high priest faltered. 'I hadn't thought to do so. I wanted to talk to you first, but I welcome any assistance the Ildari might provide.'

'And the Dionachs Lasair? Are they helping with the recovery?'

'Arch-Dionach Helwig is currently investigating the enchantments that were left behind to conceal the nature and timing of the theft. I believe she has a few priests and priestesses assisting her.'

Lucas slowed his climb, finally pausing at the penultimate landing. They were five floors above ground level now, and a single glass-paned window peered out over the courtyard. Lucas gravitated towards it with Reeve following close behind him.

'So, you both knew before I did.' It wasn't quite an accusation, but it was close.

'Well … yes,' Reeve admitted, 'but Tiersa was only recently informed, and only with my magic. In Your Majesty's case, I felt it necessary to deliver the news in person.'

Lucas nodded, wanting to forgive the insult … yet he found he could not.

He wants to claim the artifacts for himself, Lucas decided. If he can reclaim the diamagi, he will use their theft as an excuse to return their stewardship to the Dionachs Tobar. Yes, that resonated with the dread Lucas had been feeling … yet something more ominous seemed to lurk beneath that realization. Lucas stared out the window of the spiraling tower and used his magic to scan the auras of the crowd below. 'Have you kept my guests in the courtyard?'

'Of course. That is your tradition, yes? All celebrants remain here until sunrise.'

'Yes, but why have you prevented them from entering the keep? The whole point of the tradition is to welcome our guests into Speur Dún, so they feel as though this is their home.'

'Yes,' Reeve said, drawing out the word, 'but given the recent theft, I thought it wise to limit people's movements inside the castle.' When Lucas did not respond, Reeve stepped closer. 'Do you disagree, Your Majesty?'

'Would it matter if I did?' Lucas whispered, his sense of foreboding having reached its pitch.

'Lucas,' Reeve purred, 'you know it would. Your people respect you. They—'

'Arch-Dionach Helwig isn't in the courtyard, Reeve. None of the Ilumites are there—none of my Ildari are there. Just your priests.'

Silence. A long and terrible silence.

'What did I do?' Lucas continued, no longer guarding his thoughts and feelings from his former councillor. 'What offense did I ever give you?'

'None.'

Lucas shook his head. 'Come now, old friend. Let's put the lies behind us. You stole the diamagi. That, or you permitted someone else to take them. Then you left me out of the loop so the Dionachs Tobar could reclaim them ... only they haven't. Something has gone wrong.'

Another long silence followed and was only broken when Reeve once again placed his hand on Lucas's shoulder—except this time it was different. This time, instead of reassuring warmth, Lucas felt the seeping chill of magic.

'It was your hubris, Lucas,' the high priest said, his fingers tightly gripping the king's shoulder. 'Not just yours, but all of the Halcyon Knights. So self-assured. So self-righteous. It was the only offense you ever gave me ... and it was the most damning.'

Lucas tried to turn—to scream or curse or otherwise fight back—but the bindings of skywater had already seized his limbs and a sound bubble had silenced his voice.

Reeve leaned closer, his eyes glittering with an intensity Lucas had rarely witnessed. It was as if the scales had finally fallen from the man's eyes, and now Lucas could peer into the heart of the person glaring back at him. The high priest clenched his fist, and a sneer curled his lip.

'That's what the history books will say about you, Lucas—not the name of your crown or any other inanity. They'll remember your hubris. That you were willing to risk the stability of a nation just to prove you had the Gods' favor. Then people will shake their heads as they talk about how the diamagi were stolen on the day of your coronation. Stolen right out from under your nose. But you're right: the Dionachs Tobar will reclaim diamagi. When we do, the artifacts will return with us to the Enclave, where they always should have been. You and the Halcyon Knights will become a footnote. Scholars will question your mental instability and wonder why anyone ever thought you fit to become Ildarna's first king—Its first and its last. When they talk about the fall of the Halcyon Knights—when they debate why you killed yourself—It will always come back to your hubris.'

Reeve shoved Lucas then, propelling the Trident King through the glass window and out into the open air. Lucas tumbled through the void, his voice still magically silenced, and then the world seemed to slow as he felt another wave of Reeve's magic gathering around him—not to aid him, he knew, but to accelerate his fall.

At the last instant, Lucas found himself spinning headfirst to meet the cobblestone courtyard just as it rushed up to greet him in a final crunch of betrayal.

THE DAY THE GODS WENT SILENT

Traitor!' Scalva howled. He raised the Hammer of Keos and rushed Urran.

'It's not betrayal if it's true!' Urran shouted back, raising the Flute of Lumea. Before the two weapons could connect, a crackle of yellow sparks encircled Urran, and an invisible shield seemed to repel both him and Scalva away from one another. The force of it drove Urran to his knees even as it propelled Scalva backward, sliding the captain's boots through the muck.

Urran leapt back to his feet and spun the flute in his gloved hands, its mouthpiece whistling as the air around him began to crackle once more.

His arms began to tingle and a faint halo of light blossomed around him just as Scalva rushed in a second time. Urran stopped his spinning and an arc of lightning suddenly shot from the flute, zapping the Bloodlord full in the chest. Scalva flew backwards, this time tumbling head-over-heels across the sodden field.

'Neruacanta is not a God!' Urran puffed, no longer advancing, merely holding the golden flute defensively in front of him. 'He is not Keos reincarnated, and we don't owe him our allegiance, much less our worship.'

'Blasphemy,' Zedir whispered.

Urran glanced back at the mausoleum where the others stood. None of his companions moved, though Zedir held the Staff of Odar in one hand and clutched his other fist in front of his mouth, his harlequin mask having been discarded. Urran waited to see if the Inquisitor would take up the fight for the Bloodlord.

But Zedir did not move, nor did any of the others. No one made a sound. Anticipation and dread hung heavy in the air along with the metallic tang of charged ions.

Beside the Inquisitor, Riita stood still as a statue in her bright yellow merrymaker dress. Yet as Urran watched, the woman's bright red hair shifted into coarse black bristles that spread across her scalp, face, and neck. Long claws began to grow from the schoolmistress's fingertips, and pointed teeth protruded from behind her lips, the perfume of violence coaxing the schoolmarm's body to respond even as she chose not to embrace it.

Maw stood just behind Riita and Zedir clutching a handful of seed potatoes, their roots creeping between his fingers, stretching from his fist toward the ground. Like the schoolmistress, his magic had responded instinctively to his need, and he was prepared to fight if his life was in danger.

Phwyll stood slightly apart from the group, his face impassive while his clever eyes weighed every detail of Urran and Scalva's altercation. The man seemed relaxed, but the bony fingers churning the cemetery's damp burial plots told an altogether different story.

'Blasphemer,' Scalva whispered, echoing Zedir's curse. The captain fumbled for the long knife hanging at his belt but was encumbered by the magic gloves and the Hammer of Keos in his other hand. Still, he did not remove the protective garments, nor did he set down the diamagus. 'Heretic,' he barked, finally drawing the blade and slicing his forearm. 'Infidel!' Ribbons of blood quickly rose from the captain's wound, compressed and innervated by Scalva's magic. 'You have lost your faith. The God-King is—'

'He is a man, Lucius!' Urran shouted back, his eyes following the twisting red tendrils, weary of their deadly grasp. 'Neruacanta is a Bloodlord just like you. He's just … like … you.'

'You lie. You have seen his divinity. You know he is Keos Reborn. We all do.' He waved distractedly at Zedir and the other Terrans with his knife, his cords of compressed blood unconsciously bobbing in response to his movements. 'But you are weak. You have always been so. Always tempted by the promise of another's blood magic. Easily lured away by the false promises of the demi-gods and the jealous siblings of Keos.' He stepped forward, his blood-whips writhing in the air like angry serpents, ready to strike.

'Lucius …' Urran pleaded. 'Please don't.'

'Or maybe,' Scalva continued, his eyes still wild, 'you just want the artifacts for yourself!' The crimson cords shot towards Urran then, a squad of razor-sharp tentacles spiraling outward, striking for the Artificer's hands and throat.

But Urran was ready. He spun the Flute of Lumea in his hands and a wave of fire crashed into the blood-whips, evaporating the nearest hemomantic tentacles into wine-red ash. Scalva howled his fury as the flailing stumps retreated, their crimson tendrils slithering back to the safety of his still-pulsing wound.

Cursing, the captain sheathed his plastun knife and once more took up the Hammer of Keos in both hands. He advanced again, slower than the first two times, though his intentions were much the same. 'I'm going to kill you now—going to execute you for crimes against our God—and if you raise that damn flute to defend yourself, I swear on all that is carnal, I will call upon the power of Keos himself and use the magic of his hammer to smite you where you stand.'

'You will do no such thing.'

Scalva blinked, his attention shifting to the unassuming Inquisitor, who had finally separated himself from his three conscripts.

Zedir waved his finger reproachfully at Scalva. 'Urran is an Artificer who knows the limits of his magic and the inherent dangers of the diamagi,' he said, his voice calm, almost detached. 'You, however, are a Bloodlord who knows nothing but violence. If you raise that hammer and attempt to call upon its magic, that is precisely what you'll get: more violence, but on an unimaginable scale.'

Scalva swallowed, his eyes drifting to the glowing hammer in his hands before finally lowering the weapon. 'That heretic wants to escape with all three of the diamagi,' the captain explained, almost petulant. 'If you think I'm dangerous with this hammer, how much more dangerous will this traitorous Master Artificer be once he decides to use the full power of Lumea's Flute?'

'But that can never be, Lucius,' Urran said, lowering his own instrument. 'I am not a dalta. I'm not even an Ilumite. The Flute of Lumea will never share its secrets with me. What little magic you saw me do tonight is rather a testament to the flute's sense of self-preservation. It has nothing to do with my skills as an Artificer. Mortals cannot use the full power of the diamagi, much less one who does not carry the blood and blessing of the Gods.'

'But you would solve that problem, too, given time,' Scalva insisted, accusing. 'That's the way your mind works! It's just a game to you. Another puzzle to solve with no consequences for your actions, like inventing a way to carry the diamagi without getting blasted.' He held the hammer aloft. 'For us believers, though, this is something sacred.'

'You think it's not sacred to me?' Urran spat at the earth between them, his temper flaring. 'Gods be good! Lucius, during the Second Age I walked with Keos! He used that same hammer to teach me how to artifice—how to be a Master Artificer. It's why I've never been able to abide that pretender sitting on his throne in Keokumot.'

'Watch your tongue, cur.'

Urran shook his head. 'I've stayed silent long enough. For centuries, I've watched that madman ruin our nation. I know exactly what devastation Neruacanta will cause if he gets his hands on these artifacts.' He pointed at Zedir. 'He knows it, too. The Inquisitor knows—hells, probably the whole bloody Inquisition knows—but no one has tried to stop him. If anything, the Inquisition is helping Neruacanta hide the truth. I'd wager that's why Zedir pounced on the Trident King.' Urran turned his eyes on the Inquisitor, whose lips were pursed. 'That's it, isn't it, Zedir? Neruacanta knows he can't use the full power of the diamagi—not unless he has the blood of a dalta—so he sent you to get it. You were probably hoping to find the blood of Breathanas on the diamagi themselves or on some other Halcyon Knight relic, but there was no need for that once you saw Lukas Valkar ascend and become a dalta. That's why you threw yourself at his feet. That's why he jerked back from you ... because you'd bled him with your wrist bracelet.'

As Urran spoke, the Inquisitor's eyes had grown wide. Now they narrowed, his gaze penetrating and full of spite. 'You know nothing.'

Urran shook his head, his glare matching Zedir's for intensity. 'I know Neruacanta's blood can't reproduce artifacts forged with the blood of Keos. And I know Neruacanta covets the diamagi because they allow him to seem more divine than he truly is. Wielding them is the only way mortals like him can feign parity with the Gods.'

'Wait,' Scalva stalled, uncertain. 'You said earlier that mortals can't use the diamagi.'

'I said they couldn't use their full power ... but a dalta could. Someone like Breathanas.' Urran turned his gaze on Zedir. 'Or someone like Lukas

Valkar—which is why Zedir wanted a sample of his blood. The priest has always known about Neruacanta's great deception. He knows and he's trying to help him conceal it.'

Scalva's fist began to tremble, his attention dancing between Zedir and Urran, no longer certain of anything. Again, the blood-whips crawled from his wound and skittered across his forearm, every edge sprouting a barb or a razor. A single deadly ribbon rose from his arm, its head bobbing like a viper as it leaned towards Urran. A second cord split off from the first, its path weaving towards the Inquisitor.

'Captain Scalva!' Zedir barked. 'Are you so easily deceived by the lies of a self-admitted traitor?'

Scalva's twin blood-whips wavered, their sharp crimson heads wilting and then crashing to the earth in a tangle of spongy gore.

'Thank you.' Zedir turned towards Maw, Riita, and Phwyll. 'You three remember why you're here, don't you? If all of these artifacts don't make it back to Daogort, you can forget about the God-King forgiving your blood heresies.'

'Say what now?' Maw said, stepping forward.

'Convince Urran to give us the flute,' Zedir continued, 'then we can be on our way. You don't even need to attack him, much less kill him.'

'Not that,' Maw said. 'I meant that bit about heresies. What's all that about?'

'Just what I said,' Zedir coaxed. 'If you help me bring the diamagi back to the God-King, he will absolve you of the sin of possessing corrupted magic.'

'Absolve us?' Riita said, forcing herself to enunciate around the fangs of her bear-badger muzzle. 'We have committed no crimes! We came willingly.'

'Did you? When I first tried to invite Master Cropley to join us, he attacked me with those tubers he's clutching in his fist—damn near smothered me, too. Master Ordshaw didn't attack me, but that's only because he's tried—and failed—to do so before. You yourself refused to come until we compelled you, but the issue is irrelevant. Your bloodlines have been corrupted and that requires purging. Bringing the diamagi back to Daogort is the only way you can absolve yourselves of those crimes.'

Riita looked to Maw who quietly shook his head. She then turned to Phwyll, her eyes silently pleading for answers, but he only gave her a huff of amusement.

'Come on, Piritta. Can you honestly say you didn't know about the purges? That's why Maw attacked Zedir when he spotted an Inquisitor at his door.' Phwyll flashed a smile that didn't extend to his hard, sharp eyes. 'It's also why they had me quarantined in Casaria,' he continued, his fingers twitching. 'They tried to purge me months ago, but they only sent Inquisitors who could sniff me out or detect my hemomancy. None of them could heal, like Zedir over there.'

Phwyll turned his queer grin on the Terran priest who stood scowling at him. 'Forgive me, Inquisitor Zemir, but I have a hard time believing the Inquisition will ignore my crimes in Casaria, much less pardon me for the perversion of necromancy.'

'They will,' Zedir insisted, 'but only if you help me deliver the diamagi to the God-King. Do that and you will get more than absolution: Keos will reward you. Anything you might hope or ask for can be yours.'

Phwyll's eyes narrowed. 'My lands and titles? My ancestral home?'

'All of it restored. All of it magnified. You can have it back, even better than before. Lord Phwillym of House Ordshaw.'

The Necromancer lifted an eyebrow, intrigued. He glanced at Urran, who tightened his grip on the Flute of Lumea. Phwyll huffed in amusement then shrugged. 'It doesn't matter what you promise me, Zedir. I'm no Inquisitor. I have no way to prove you're telling the truth.'

'No,' Zedir said, drawing his belt knife, 'but Captain Scalva can!' The Inquisitor slashed his forearm and whirled, extending his bleeding limb in the Bloodlord's direction. 'Quickly, Captain! Before my magic heals the wound.'

Scalva squinted at Zedir as though he were glimpsing him through a fog. Then the man's eyes widened. He nodded, and the languishing blood-whips suddenly flared to life, their sticky tendrils slithering and sliding across the cemetery's soil. When they reached Zedir's feet, the crimson cords began crawling up the Inquisitor's legs, stretching and then snaking their way toward the exposed blood. Even as they moved, Zedir's injury was beginning to heal, his bloody flesh knitting itself back together. Just before it could seal itself entirely, though, the blood-whips found Zedir's injury and sunk their gruesome claws into his open flesh. The Inquisitor winced, bracing himself as the hemomatic manifestation of Scalva's magic began to force itself beneath the skin's surface.

'That's enough!' Zedir said, gritting his teeth. 'You feel my pulse, yes?' Scalva nodded.

'Good. Now tell Master Ordshaw if I am lying.' He turned back to the Necromancer. 'I swear on my life, if you help me deliver the diamagi to the God-King in Keokumot, you will be rewarded with lands and titles that far outmatch those once held by your family. Your past crimes will be forgiven, and your necromancy will no longer be counted as a sin in the eyes of God or the Holy Terran Church. I offer similar terms to Master Cropley and Mistress Sloen.' He nodded in turn at Phwyll and the other two conscripts. Then they all turned to Captain Scalva to hear his verdict.

The Bloodlord licked his lips. 'He ... that is, Inquisitor Zemir ... speaks the truth.'

'And what of the God-King?' Urran shouted, recapturing their attention. 'Is he telling the truth about the God-King's divinity, Lucius?' Urran pointed the flute at Zedir. 'Tell him, Inquisitor. Tell all of us. Do you truly believe Neruacanta is Keos incarnate, or do you know, as I do, that he is a pretender and a usurper to the throne of Keos?'

Scalva and the conscripts swiveled their attention back to Zedir who had frozen, seeming to realize his mistake. He scoffed, fumbling for words. 'Heretics need not—'

'Answer him!' Scalva's voice rang out, its edge hard as stone, as certain as death. 'Is Urran telling the truth? Is Neruacanta a false god?'

Before answering, Zedir glanced at Phwyll. The Necromancer met Zedir's gaze and his enigmatic smile quickly disappeared, replaced by a mask of dark contemplation. He gave an almost imperceptible nod then slowly retreated to the shadows of the mausoleum.

The Inquisitor looked back at his captain. 'Lucius,' Zedir said. 'Do not be deceived by—'

'Answer the rotting question!' Scalva roared, his blood-whips undulating in response to his anger.

Zedir glanced down at the veins of hemomancy worming beneath his skin, at the black and purple fingers of invigorated blood swelling and spiderwebbing across his arm, shoulder, and chest. He winced as the blood-whips stretched and then further distorted his skin. 'Don't do this,' he hissed through gritted teeth. 'Don't ask this.'

'Why?' Scalva growled. 'Because it's true? Because our God is dead?'

'Not dead, Lucius.' The answer came from Urran, his soft voice carrying across the moonlit cemetery of Gods' Field. 'He's only separated from us—silent and asleep—but Keos will return. The true God of Earthblood will rise again.' He pointed at Zedir. 'Neruacanta and his Inquisitors have lied to us, Lucius, but we needn't lose hope. I still have faith in our silent God, and I won't let false priests destroy his church or his people. Will you?'

'Never!'

'Then help me. We'll take the diamagi and hide them from Neruacanta and his Inquisition. We'll hide them ... and wait for the real God of Earthblood to come and claim them.'

Zedir scoffed. 'Heresy! Lies and lunacy.'

The captain shook his head. 'Urran might be a lunatic'—Scalva flexed his arm and the black veins beneath Zedir's flesh spread further, to his neck, face, and other limbs—'but you are the one who's been lying.'

'No!' Zedir raised the Staff of Odar just as Scalva's tentacles burst from his chest in a mass of crimson claws and tangled intestines. The priest tried to scream, and a fountain of gore erupted from his mouth and eyes, his face disappearing behind a spray of scarlet serpents.

'Keos preserve us!' Maw swore, even as the blood-whips looped back to strike Zedir's body a second and third time.

'Grab the staff!' Urran shouted, taking a step forward. 'But be cautious, Captain! Don't let it touch you—not even your blood-whips.' Yet even as he spoke, the flayed creature that had once been Zedir swayed on his feet and swung the diamagus, smashing the silver stave into Scalva's invigorated blood before collapsing to the ground.

The effect was instantaneous. Blue lightning arced down the length of the magic tendrils, traveling to Scalva's bleeding arm before spreading outward to his other blood-whips. Those impacted by the Staff of Odar immediately shattered, scattering pink shards of frozen blood across the graveyard.

Captain Scalva fell to his knees, his body coated with a rime of ice and convulsing with electricity. He toppled onto his face. The Hammer of Keos slipped from his grasp.

Urran dashed toward Zedir, his gloved hand fumbling to open his bottomless sack. 'Grab that staff, Maw! Quickly! Before Zedir heals himself.'

'What! And end up like him?' Maw pointed at Scalva's frozen figure, his skin still steaming, his limbs twitching. 'I already returned my gloves!'

'Bah! Use your plant magic to keep you safe—or take Scalva's gloves! He won't be needing them.'

Maw looked dubious, but Urran didn't waste more time trying to convince him. Instead, he raced toward Zedir, whose bowels were already spooling back into his belly. As he ran, the Inquisitor's head turned toward Urran, exposing the optic nerves wriggling inside his empty sockets. Yet even as Urran stared, those nerves inflated into orbs, restoring the two baleful eyes that now glared back at him.

Urran muttered a curse and finally plunged his hand into the drawstring sack. When he was barely a dozen paces away, he flung a fistful of copper clips into the priest's face. Zedir raised the staff in defense and a few of the coins shot into the night, deflected by a burst of wind and a shower of sparks—yet a few still made it through, colliding into the

Inquisitor's chest and face before detonating in a flash of fire and fury. Zedir flipped through the air and the staff went spinning from his grasp, landing behind the fallen Inquisitor and barely a dozen feet from Maw.

'I can grab it!' the farmer declared, suddenly finding his nerve. He extended a fist filled with sprouting potatoes. His forearm twitched and the roots of the tubers swelled, growing long and thick, intertwining and then crawling towards the fallen artifact. Just before they could retrieve the staff, though, skeletal hands burst from the sodden soil, claiming the diamagus.

'No!' Urran sprinted and then launched himself at the staff. As he crashed to the ground, he scrambled to snatch the silver artifact, but the bony fingers had already pulled it into the mud-churned earth. Urran swore, his anger flaring as he turned to look for the cunning Necromancer.

'What now?' Maw said, appearing at Urran's side.

'You keep an eye on Zedir. Maybe tie him up before he heals again. I'll handle Phwyll.' He paused. 'Where's Riita?'

Maw gestured at the surrounding forest. 'I think the fighting triggered her. She went full bear-badger and raced off into the woods.'

Urran grunted, sad to hear of the schoolmarm's departure, yet also glad she'd not chosen to support Zedir or Phwyll.

'Keep an eye on the Inquisitor,' Urran repeated, his attention returning to the shadows.

'Ordshaw!' he shouted. 'Please ... you don't have to do this.' Urran carefully squatted in the muck, his fingers searching for any sign of the staff while his eyes searched the shadows of the moonlit graveyard. 'The Inquisition won't keep their promises, Phwillym. Their only goal is to keep Neruacanta on the throne and themselves in power. Your magic threatens that—and trust me, when either Neruacanta or the Inquisition feels threatened, they will come for you.'

'You think I don't already know that?' Phwyll's laughter echoed throughout the Halcyon Knights' cemetery, his wiry figure concealed amidst the shadows of its ancient trees and even more ancient mausoleums. 'That's precisely why I'm going to take Zedir's offer. Only a fool thinks he can win against the God-King.'

A chorus of bony hands suddenly shot from the soil, their fingers grasping for Urran's golden flute. One latched onto the artifact. More scrambled to follow. Urran stumbled, his enchanted gloves unable to keep a firm grip on the relic. He clambered to his feet and hoisted upwards, barely managing to prise the diamagus from the reanimated corpses. More skeletal hands clawed at his feet and ankles, tangling and entrapping him. Urran tried to escape but instead, he tripped over a solid mass slowly rising from the muck. He pitched forward, rolling onto his hands and knees, and found himself staring at the grinning skull of an undead Halcyon Knight. All around him, nechraict were struggling to climb from their graves.

Rot and hell.

The corpse-knight seized Urran, rolling him over and pressing his face into the mud. The Artificer spluttered, first struggling to escape, then fighting to breathe. More hands found him, their sharp fingers and bony talons tearing into Urran's clothes and flesh before trying to drag him down into the earth. He felt the Flute of Lumea being pulled from his fingers ...

Something large crashed into the Halcyon Knight sitting atop Urran's back. The force of it blasted the skeleton to pieces, disentangling it from whatever magic Phwyll had used to animate the long-dead corpse.

No longer pinned, Urran lifted his head from the soil and gasped deep lungfuls of air. A few breaths quickly restored both his strength and his grip on the Flute of Lumea. He fought to rise while his undead captors resisted him, still clinging to the Artificer's limbs, clothes, and torso.

A feral roar split the night air.

Urran peered over his shoulder at the enormous bear-badger approaching from behind. Through the dripping haze of mud and blood, he watched the beast rise onto her muscular hindlegs, stretching to nearly ten feet in height. The monster-that-was-Piritta raised her long forepaws, each one tipped with a quintet of curving seven-inch claws. One paw smashed into the half-exhumed skeletons, sending splinters of broken bone across the graveyard. Two more swipes freed Urran from his snare. Riita then scooped the Artificer out of the muddy pauper's grave before dumping him on the sodden topsoil.

'Nice of you to join me, Miss Sloen,' Urran said, painfully rising to his feet.

The bear-badger dropped to her feet and lowered her head until it was level with Urran. Then she bellowed such a roar of defiance that it shook Urran's jowls and nearly drove the Artificer back to his knees.

'Quite right,' he said, wiping mud and saliva from his face. 'We can exchange pleasantries later. Right now, I need you to clear this pit of nechraict so we can recover The Staff of Odar.' He pointed back at the grave where a half-dozen of Phwyll's corpses still crept and clambered. 'If you find it, be careful not to touch it. I'll use my gloves for that. Got it?'

Riita threw back her shaggy head and thundered her assent before immediately diving into the tangled mass of undead. Frenzied, the skeletons quickly latched onto the Skinchanger's legs and back, seizing hold of her thick, bristly fur. They couldn't pierce Riita's thick, rubbery hide, though, and the bear-badger's uncommonly loose skin made it easy for the schoolmistress to freely twist and turn within the confines of the grave. Ignoring her undead assailants, Riita set her powerful claws to work and started to excavate the place where the Staff of Odar had fallen.

Ominous clouds drifted over the face of the moon as Urran limped toward the spot he'd left Maw and Zedir.

'Master Cropley?' Urran slowed his pace, now squinting into the deeper darkness. 'Maw? Is all well?'

Twisted fingers brushed against Urran's leg. He jerked back, expecting another assault from Phwyll's undead minions, but as the clouds retreated and the moonlight shone once more on Gods' Field, the wan light revealed the twisting tubers and curling potato roots that had once secured Inquisitor Zemir's injured body.

Urran swore, discerning that something had breached the vegetable cocoon, allowing the resilient priest to escape. Worse still was the sight of Mahuu Cropley's eviscerated corpse, his looping entrails torn from his belly and tossed to the earth, left to mingle with the sprouts of his beloved tatties.

'If it's any consolation,' Phwyll said, emerging from the shadows of a toppled crypt, 'I rather liked him—always quick with a joke, always so self-effacing.' He shrugged. 'But he should have known better. In the end, the Inquisition always gets what it wants. He was a fool to oppose them.'

Urran shook his head, his anger quietly brewing. 'You think this was inevitable? You did this, Phwillym. If you'd just sided with me instead of helping Zedir, none of this would have happened.'

'Ah, but that's where you're wrong, Master Artificer.' Phwyll pointed east toward the cemetery's tallest hill, its silhouette limned with a flickering red light. 'Do you understand now, Urran? The Inquisition is already here. The God-King sent them a few days after we left Daogort. Them, and a full battalion of Bloodlords. They were insurance, both to make sure we didn't betray the God-King and to finish our jobs for us if we failed to escape with the diamagi.'

Urran blinked, trying to adapt his plans to this new bit of information. 'Is that why you sided with Zedir? Because you knew about the encampment?'

'I'd say that was a determining factor, yes.'

Urran shook his head, unable to make the pieces fit. 'How is it you calculated they'd be here ... yet I did not?'

Phwyll grinned, his hard, sharp eyes now tinged with madness. 'The same way I knew when it was time to pull up stakes and hide out in Casaria: the bones talk to me.' He reached beneath his shirt and withdrew a white necklace made entirely of clattering phalanges. 'A few years ago, I noticed that when I was performing my necromancy, I'd sometimes get ... premonitions. Glimpses of the future. Visions.' He laughed, replacing the necklace beneath his shirt. 'It sounds crazy, I know, but it's true.

Something about practicing necromancy gave me supernatural insight. I've come to rely on it, and it's why I ultimately sided with Zedir.'

Urran shook his head. 'Well, that makes perfect sense then.'

Phwyll frowned, suddenly uncertain. 'You're being sarcastic. You don't truly believe me.'

'On the contrary,' Urran said, surprised by the sorrow he suddenly felt for the man. 'I know you're telling the truth, Phwyll, because you just described the same magical mutation that's evolved among the New Terrans that worship the God of Death: their mages have all become Necromancers and Seers. The ones with both powers are called Marrow-Liches.' He sighed. 'All this time ... all those people you killed in Casaria? You were doing it to glimpse the future—but if someone had just taught you how to properly use your magic, you might not have become such a pariah.'

Phwyll smiled. Shrugged. 'What's done is done. I've chosen my path. I killed Maw and I freed Zedir—he's with that encampment, by the way. He must have smelled them coming, too, because he didn't seem at all surprised when I mentioned it to him.'

Urran frowned, sensing he had missed some vital detail. Then, just as had happened with every artificing schema he'd designed, the pieces suddenly fit and the answer revealed itself.

'That bastard,' Urran said, head shaking. 'Zedir doesn't work for the census—or if he does, it's a very deep cover.'

'Eh?'

'Inquisitor Zemir,' Urran said, forcing his brain to find a speed that didn't outpace his tongue. 'I thought he was being punished for something—that the God-King had sent him on a suicide mission along with the kingdom's other embarrassments—but that's not true. Neruacanta needs these artifacts. He's coveted them ever since he read my paper on theorycrafting, which speculates how artificing might allow a Terran mage to make use of the diamagi. He wants us to succeed. What I didn't guess, though, was the role Inquisitor Zemir had to play.' Urran shook his head in consternation, wondering why he hadn't seen it before.

'I'd thought Zedir was just a third-tier government official,' he continued. 'Just a glorified babysitter for Scalva and I, but Neruacanta didn't want a babysitter: he wanted an infiltrator. Someone who'd blend in with the rest of us outcasts while making sure our heist didn't go off the rails. More importantly, he needed someone who could travel to Speur Dún and return with the blood of a dalta—either living or dead—and he couldn't ask me to do it because that sort of task requires a subtle kind of Inquisitor. A Master Inquisitor.'

Phwyll frowned. 'Zedir is Grandmaster of the Imperial Inquisition?'

'Honestly, I don't know, but I'll tell you what I do know.' He tittered at the certainty of his revelation. 'Zedir is the God-King's spymaster.'

Phwyll sniffed. 'Well, if that's true, it also means Zedir is damn good at his job, which proves I made the right choice by siding with him.' Phwyll sniffed, his smile turning cold. 'Now if you'll excuse me, I told our little spymaster I'd take care of loose ends while he reconnoitered with the legions. That means you're going to hand over the Flute of Lumea and then do me the courtesy of dying quickly.' The Necromancer raised his hands and began plucking the air, his fingers manipulating the invisible threads tying physical bodies to their spirits.

Between them, Maw's corpse twitched. Then the dead farmer pushed himself to his feet and stalked towards Urran.

'You're forgetting something,' Urran said, his attention divided between Phwyll and the undead farmer. 'You don't have the other two artifacts.'

Phwyll laughed. 'You mean the one Mistress Sloen is trying to unearth? Keep up, Urran. The nechraict snuck it past you while your face was buried in the mud. Zedir has it with him right now, and he's with the legions.'

Urran's shoulders slumped. 'That is terribly unfortunate ... but no, that's not the artifact I'd had in mind.' Urran gave a queer smile then retreated one step from Maw's advancing form. 'You should have stolen the hammer as soon as Scalva fell.'

The nobleman frowned. 'You don't have the hammer. It's still with Scalva.'

'Precisely,' Urran said, his hard eyes now locked with Phwyll's.

The Necromancer's eyes narrowed, then widened, his realization dawning just as Scalva appeared at his flank with the Hammer of Keos. Phwyll spun toward the Bloodlord captain, attempting to dodge the attack, but instead he caught the warhammer full in the face. The force of the blow exploded into Phwyll's nose, caving in the Necromancer's skull, and scattering bone and brain matter across the disturbed graves at Gods' Field. In that same instant, Maw's corpse fell to the earth, dropping like a puppet with its strings cut. The same was true in other parts of the cemetery, with the undead Halcyon Knights suddenly collapsing to the ground, no longer bound by Phwyll's commands.

Urran looked at the Bloodlord, shaking his head. 'I can't believe you survived that. You should be dead.'

'I feel dead,' Scalva admitted, wincing at the pain of his frost-burned flesh. 'I guess the Gods' curses aren't holding up the way they used to.' He smiled—then he spied Maw's body and his tone grew solemn. 'We should probably go before Zedir returns with those legions.'

'And before the Halcyon Knights track us to this cemetery,' Urran said, nodding. He started to move then stopped, his attention transfixed by the sight of Riita's willowy figure stumbling towards them in the darkness. The schoolmarm's Skinchanger magic had fully worn off now. She'd somehow found a wool blanket to wrap herself in, though she clutched the tattered remains of her yellow merrymaker dress under one arm. 'We've got company,' Urran said, nodding at the schoolmistress.

'Great. She can come with us.' Scalva paused. 'Where exactly are we going?'

'Someplace far away from Daogort and Neruacanta.'

Scalva nodded, obviously still at a loss for words. 'Zedir's got the Staff of Odar,' he said at last. 'He's also got the blood from that Trident King, Lucas Valkar. Is that going to cause any problems?'

'More than likely,' Urran admitted, 'but what's done is done. We can only pray that my artificing schema proves faulty, or that Neruacanta mishandles the staff and blows himself up.'

'I'm still getting used to the notion that he's not divine,' Scalva admitted, his eyes distant. He shook himself then extended the hammer to Urran. 'I reckon you should take this.'

Urran reached out to take the artifact then stopped, his hand slowly falling to his side. 'Actually, I'm thinking you should hang onto it. The warhammer won't fit inside my bottomless sack, and the weapon suits you.'

'But,' Scalva protested, his body trembling, 'it's the bleeding Hammer of Keos!'

'That it is,' Urran agreed, gently patting Scalva's shoulder. "And speaking as someone who actually saw Keos wield that hammer, I think he'd be happy to have you as its guardian.'

They walked towards Riita as Scalva mulled that thought over, and when they shared news of Maw Cropley's death, she shed a silent tear in his memory.

The trio walked in silence then, travelling steadily south and leaving Gods' Field, the Terran legions, and the Halcyon Knights far behind them. Several days later, the group was passing east through the Vosgar when a merchant caravan shared the news they had all been dreading: colossal waves had just sunk half the continent of Ilumea, drowning most of the Ilumite people.

'Do you think that was Neruacanta?' Riita whispered. 'Could he do something like that with the Staff of Odar and the Trident King's blood?'

Urran nodded, his face ashen. 'That and worse—but there is one consolation. Neruacanta has only a limited supply of Valkar's blood. Once it is gone, the staff will cease responding to him.'

Over the next week, they searched for a suitable place to hide the Flute of Lumea and Hammer of Keos. When they reached the base of the Kalej Mountains, Urran spoke with the chaplain of a remote military outpost and learned the Dionachs Tobar had lost contact with Odar, the

Elder God of Skywater. Two days later, a pair of Ilumite dragonriders confessed that they could no longer hear Lumea's song. No matter where they went or who they spoke to, the news was the same: the Elder Gods were missing.

The Silence of the Gods had come upon them.

A PIECE OF MOVABLE TYPE

PETER ORULLIAN

By the light of a single candle, I sat at my smith's table, staring at hundreds of polished metal hand-mirrors. Useless things. King Frederick had delayed the exhibit of Charlemagne's relics for almost a year now. He claimed it was the floods. Whatever the reason, there'd come no pilgrims through Strasbourg in need of mirrors to capture holy light from the artifacts, which may not now be displayed for another seven years. My creditors couldn't wait so long, any more than could my soul. The king had put me in arrears to both.

In the quiet, my door pushed open. A gentleman with long brown hair entered, wearing a clean russet coat. He removed his hat and smiled. "Good evening, sir. My name is Konrad Witz, known with mixed affection as the Master of Playing Cards."

"You may call me Johannes," I replied. "But in truth, my evening hasn't been a good one."

Witz nodded. "I might have guessed as much, since like you—if the rumors may be trusted—I am an apostate."

I sat back. "Appealing to my spiritual malaise may prove a fruitless endeavor." I waved at the many unsold mirrors. "I've little more than reflections to sell you."

Witz crossed to my table and picked up a mirror. "For the delayed pilgrimage?"

"All my reserves and a lender's advance besides to fashion them." I summoned a weak laugh. "Frederick took me for a usurper—enabling laymen to gather Heaven's blessings without relying on his own beneficent hand. He issued my excommunication order."

Witz looked up from the mirror. "And this grieves you?"

I didn't hate God, and I had little use for a king whose order would separate me from the body of Christ. "Perhaps I grieve the society of believers."

"Those for whom you crafted your heretical mirrors," said Witz. "I can see how your apostasy might harm your profits"

"The mirrors are sold practically at cost," I argued, "and they're derived from the old Corinth stories of looking-glass used to receive glory."

Witz dropped the mirror, which clanged to rest. "Bible stories?"

"Apostates may pay no tax—which comes a blessing just now," I said, "but neither are we readily admitted to the gentler discussions that temper such long days as this one."

"You mean discussions of Our Lady's mourning cloak, the doomed Infant's swaddling, the loin clothes of the Crucified, John the Baptist's head gunny?" Witz huffed. "Are these the gentler discussions for which you pine? These relics whose light you'd empower each serf to gather for himself?"

I stood from my chair. "The very same. And your rough use of them tells me more than I care to know about you."

"Oh, my blasphemy runs far more scarlet than that," said Witz.

He produced a handful of playing cards from an inner vest pocket and handed them to me. Vibrantly colored in red ocher, azurite blue, and lead-tin yellow, the cards showed master craftsmanship in the plates used to press them. The Pope card—the Karnöffel—had been rendered with an open robe, putting on display the figure's testicles; the Kaiser was entirely nude—save his crown—seated on a pile of gold and jewels; and the Devil posed with a resplendent mane of flowing fire. Other suits—Unter, Ober, Sixes—were there too, and each depicting not just a societal class turned upside down, but its prominent figures engaged in the seven sins.

"To hear them tell it," explained Witz, "I am a purveyor of low amusement, encourager of carnal debasement, and abuser of moderation. Frederick's moral edicts have frightened those persons who enjoy a round of cards. I'm hard-pressed to scare up a hand of Karnöffel, myself."

"From my own experience," I said, fingering a mirror, "it would seem your illuminations might do better without such clear challenge to the clergy and proscriptions from civil authorities."

He laughed. "You and I are, then, well suited, are we not? A fine pair."

I'd made no secret of my feelings toward the king, but I couldn't see the value in further exciting his disfavor. "Your engraver doesn't need my help, if that's why you've come."

"I am a painter by training," continued Witz, "and carve, myself, the wood presses for my cards. Well enough, it would seem, to earn the dubious distinction I mentioned of being named Master of Playing Cards."

"As I said—"

"It is, however, an entirely different enterprise for which I require a goldsmith's expert burin." Witz smiled. "And more than a few artisans hereabouts have commended me to you."

I returned the cards. "I could certainly use a commission."

"You and the rest of Strasbourg's apostates." Witz laughed. "All of whom King Frederick will crusade against as readily as he does the caliphates, if the Habsburgs secure his ordination as Holy Roman Emperor."

A rush of panic stole down my legs. "The king's an autocrat, but he's peaceful."

Witz's jaw clenched. "As are most men until the Holy See invests them with the perception that they rule by divine right. Or do you need me to cite historical precedent for the same?"

I stared back at Witz. I'd read the histories of Charles V, Caligula, and others. The precedents churned in my head. "I've not heard that the Pope plans any such investiture for Frederick."

Witz placed a card face-up on the table. It showed the Kaiser, our king, only this time holding a bloody sword in one hand and a half-dozen severed heads in the other, dangling from hair queues. Wrath. "Our *peaceful* king Frederick made his pilgrimage to the Holy Land some eight years, accompanied by a legion from the Order of the Holy Sepulchre. Earned him a marked increase in reputation, and that came not purely for walking the shores of Galilee."

The problem of it came clear to me. "The Pope will end the interregnum, and Frederick will cease to tolerate the apostate for both his spiritual sloth and his many back tax payments."

Witz nodded. "Generations will suffer beneath the collector's boot and the pulpit's vain repetitions. The king may actually rationalize the consolidation of power as the only way to *keep* the peace. His court will nurture these lies. Trust me, lying is a freight I know in every measure."

"But what has any of this to do with a goldsmith's burin?" I asked.

Witz's eyes lit with excitement, and he pulled his wood plates from a pouch at his belt. "To create the many colors for my playing cards, I carve multiple pips and frame them together in a catch-press. I apply the die discreetly, then assemble the pips and print them all at once."

I nodded. "Yes, something similar is done with copper plates for intaglio printing."

"Precisely," said Witz. "But suppose an intaglio mount system could be devised to hold not only illuminations like mine ... but letters, words, punctuation, all meticulously carved in durable metal … by a goldsmith."

"It's feasible," I agreed, "but to what end? How would such a press prevent the coronation of a Holy Emperor."

Witz leaned out over my candle, his hair dangling close to the flame. "Quite simply, Johannes … we tell the people a story."

"A story," I said.

Witz clapped his hands with glee, nearly extinguishing my candle. "People are never so influenced as they are by a story."

I saw the cleverness immediately. It could be argued that scripture itself was little more than a collection of tales, and a press would allow us to produce one en masse.

"Not just any story," I said, half-smiling. "A prophecy."

"Of course, of course," said Witz. "Go on."

"I would need a thousand marks to purchase materials, build the press, craft each letter—"

"Anything," said Witz, producing a bag of coins and dropping it beside my candle.

He waited, eyes intent, as I picked up the money. His lips mirrored my smile, and a strange warmth rushed through my body, like the thrill of jumping from a precipice toward dark cold waters far below.

"Have you a prophecy in mind?" Wits finally asked.

Tucking the money away, my mind fixed on one of the old stories, in particular. "I do."

Huddled over my worktable, my barley stew cold and forgotten, I finished the final piece of movable type: the period. I'd saved it for last. A virtually anonymous part of stories that lent them all such cadence, architecture, comprehension, and everyday poetry. When I set it aside, my mechanical preparations were largely complete.

The press stood stoically in my back room. Its oak frame still smelled of its milling, the ink carried an acrid odor, and the paper's scent was clean in a way that calmed me. To the side, racks of type molds stood ready. This was the genius of the approach, separating the typesetting from the printing. I'd imagined there might be future texts.

I took a long, satisfied breath over my improvements to screw presses and other plate systems I'd seen, before reaching toward the bookshelves opposite my new machine. From the highest shelf, I drew down a brittle volume hand-lettered in Greek. Turning back the unmarked cover, I read the story's title: *The Tiburtine Sibyl.*

Finally picking up my cold stew, I slowly ate as I read, refamiliarizing myself with the centuries-old prophecy: from Adam and Eve on through nine generations of mankind, depicted by nine suns, each more bloodstained than the last; war with Gog and Magog brought to fruition as the End of Days hastened close; the fall of Man; the rise of a Final Emperor—a Holy Roman Emperor—who would vanquish all foes, all pagans, and convert all peoples to his holy dominion. It was an old prophecy, grounded in an even older warning: *The Apocalypse.*

The *Sibyl's* tenth tale would have frightened readers all on its own, this much of it anyway. But the end parts weren't conducive to our needs. It still needed something more to quash Frederick's ascendency to Holy Emperor, and stave off the blood and misery that would flow from his coronation.

I whispered my own question: "What would harm the King's reputation in the hearts of his people and the estimation of the Holy See …"

It came.

Such a simple idea.

I pushed my stew aside and gathered up a tray of type letters. In the stillness of my little back room, I began to set them into place. As I did, something in the slow revelation of the tale reminded me of my own apostasy, and my heart ached for it not to be so. *Could I yet be redeemed?* It seemed an unlikely proposition. So, letter by letter, I retold the apocalyptic prophecy, carefully modifying the ancient warning:

… not just any Roman Emperor, but Frederick, who would make war on the world to issue in the great hegemony …

… and as he assumed control, he would compel all who bent their knee to him in the name of the Empire to worship him … as God …

The Totenglock had just ceased to chime as I stepped into the cool still interior of the Cathedral of Our Lady. The resonant echoes of the death bell sounded out to silence in the empty nave. Not a soul. Though it had been a long while since I was welcome here, the vacancy disappointed and unsettled me. Moments later, our visiting French minister came fast-stepping up the right aisle.

"Johannes, thank you for coming," he said, extending his hand.

We shook. "I was surprised to receive your invitation, Father—"

"John will suffice." He smiled warmly.

Just then, the door opened, and in came the Master of Playing Cards. Witz caught sight of us and came directly over. "I'm behind my time, my apologies."

"Not at all," said John. "Thank you for agreeing to come."

I gestured toward the empty pews. "Either illness has swept the congregation, or apostasy is catching."

John laughed softly enough to be acceptable in God's house. "I'm sympathetic," he began, nodding to both Witz and me. "I'm a refugee here myself. The Geneva Council expelled me for reformative ideas it found … unpalatable. Not, I think, unlike your mirrors. But while Bishop Rupert is intractably unwilling to plead your position with King Frederick, his absence has created the vacancy I'm happy now to occupy."

"May we ask," said Witz, "why you've summoned us here?"

In response, John motioned us to follow. He led us beneath the great astronomical clock, which, as legend would have it, wound down toward Judgement, reminding me of my little publication. Just past the clock, John opened a door and ushered us through. Closing the door behind us, he turned us toward an equally barren room.

Shelves and coffers and cabinets all stood empty. It was the tithing closet, where monies and goods were stored for charitable distribution.

Without a word, John pulled a copy of *The Tiburtine Sibyl* from the folds of his robe.

It had worked. But in re-directing the prophecy at Frederick, I hadn't calculated that those adherents driven from the pew would cease to make offerings. *Apostates pay no tax.* My haste to harm the king had done damage to far more than him alone.

"John—"

The minister held up his hand and offered his same warm smile. "Your retelling of the *Sibyl's Tenth* is clever, and had, I would imagine, the intended effect. Parishioners have all read or heard its warning of Frederick's overreach, and have ceased to worship, either in protest or fear."

"Leaving them more time to do as they will," said Witz. "Isn't that the very promise of the agency we're taught to cherish? Be it at a pew or a table of cards?"

"I've been known to enjoy a brisk round of Karnöffel myself." John scanned the barren shelves and coffers. "But it never staid my hand to tithing, any more than it did the patricians, who now, as a result of your book, have ceased to make offerings."

Witz ran a finger over an empty coffer top. "What a shame."

John turned to me. "Clever thing to include a chronology of kings, tracing authority to Frederick, however honest the genealogy may or may not be."

I was, in fact, inauspiciously proud of that touch.

"These last months, we've spent all our reserves, distributed any food or clothing we had to share." John raised the copy of *The Tiburtine Sibyl*. "So, while I'll admit of your concern regarding Frederick's unification of faith and politics, in all practical terms, whatever impedance your little story will prove to Frederick, it is starving the poor and other refugees like me who rely on Our Lady for bread and clothes."

"It doesn't speak well of your congregation," said Witz, "that they cease to help when they fear the king's change of station may require more godly taxes, does it?"

I stared back at John. "We printed thousands. If doing so has prevented or even forestalled Frederick's consolidation of powers, I'm glad we did so." I sighed. "But on my family's name, I would not have wished to harm the proletariat."

John handed me the chapbook. "Quite an admission for a man whose patrician family was driven from Mainz during the uprising."

I took the prophecy gently back, nodded. "Like your tithe-payers, my agency is my own."

"Indeed," said John. He strode past us to a far door beyond the shelves and pushed out into the dreary midday light.

Witz and I followed, stepping onto a broad plaza, at the far side of which stood a lycee. All across the cobbled court, people were huddled around small fires or lying close together for warmth. Among them, I saw Kyle Anderson, a miller who'd actually bought one of my hand-mirrors. He sat staring at his own muted reflection, gaunt and listless.

"Most of those gathered here," John explained softly, "aren't like you and our Master of Playing Cards here. These people are afraid, hungry."

"And weary, it would seem," I added softly.

"My point," said John, "is that people with means won't come to receive absolution, such that they may make offerings as penance."

Witz leaned close. "If only there was a way to offer absolution in the sinner's home and thereby take receipt of donations without your patricians having to show themselves or rely upon Frederick's grace."

The feel of paper and ink on my fingers raised a thought. "We could print indulgences."

John's brow creased. "On your press, you mean? By the bushel?"

"If you'd like," I said. "You author the text, an enumeration of transgressions and their commensurate offering, with, perhaps, some mention of the Lord's grace. These can be purchased by anyone willing and able to pay, without their ever having to make an admission or ask forgiveness. It anonymizes the offender and puts coin back in your coffers."

John wrestled with the idea. While he did so, my chest loosened as if I'd been under a press from which a stone had just been removed.

"Help those in need without cowing to the threat," John muttered. He grew quiet, staring at me. "How quickly could you print a thousand?"

"Both a refugee *and* a rebel," said Witz, producing a set of cards tied with a scarlet ribbon and presenting them to John, "you and I are of a pair."

John graciously took the gift and shook my hand a second time. "Thank you. You are a blessing."

The words warmed me in a way I think only an apostate might ever know.

♛

In my back room, I hunched over my press, carefully laying out the indulgence text. It was beautiful. John had taken a good three days to compose it, and to my mind, it bore the hallmark of scripture. The words made no condemnation, but instead carried an invitation premised on responsibility. What a joy to place them on my rack.

Witz had also delivered an illumination, which required some modification to the press. But it seemed the Master of Playing Cards was as adept at depicting a benefactor stooping to offer alms as he was the testicles of an ecclesiastic. To his credit, he seemed to delight in our indulgence enterprise, where I'd expected complaints that it might be at odds with sewing discontent for Frederick.

When all was laid out proper, I stood, rubbing my back but feeling nevertheless content. It felt good to put my machine to use helping people, even if that help came by way of relieving them of the consequences of excessive vice. With one possible exception. Our city watchman, Erlich Schulz, was made aware of our indulgence plan. We'd commissioned him to deliver the indulgences and collect the contributions. He wandered in late one evening whilst I was printing the documents.

"Could you spare one for me?" he asked.

"You're no malefactor, Erlich," I answered. "These are for squanderers of virtue. Yours is a noble position in Strasbourg."

He nodded humbly. "I'd lay it up against a moment when my position may require something I'd want reassurance about. Men who enforce the law come upon such a need sooner or later."

I pulled the topmost Indulgence and handed it to him. "Should you ever need it."

He shared a wan smile and retreated out into the city darkness. I went back to my work.

As the days passed and with each Indulgence I pressed, it seemed more as though I'd embarked upon a new path. One less rooted in dissent and more enamored of peace.

Witz and I stood outside an immense set of arched doors in the vestibule of the King's Palace in Frankfurt. The stone carried a dry scent; the door guards' mail and weapons were freshly oiled. The election *beyond* the doors had been in session only an hour when an interior knock signaled that the doors be pulled back.

King's Hall. The very place the Golden Bull had declared a century earlier that all kings of the Holy Roman Empire would be named. The walls towered around us, swooping up to vaulted heights lost in a haze of smoky light produced by countless torches. A guard goaded us, and we hesitantly entered.

The great table lay at the center of the room. Frederick sat at its head and motioned us forward.

We approached, stopping a few paces from the king. The eyes of every man at the table fixed upon us with an unsettling lack of emotion. Beside the king's plate were copies of *The Tiburtine Sibyl* and John's indulgence letter.

"My little printers," said Frederick. "I will tell you first that I am most impressed by your ingenuity."

"Would that be mechanical or philosophical?" asked Witz.

"And sharp-tongued," added the king. "You'll want to go sparingly with that. Given the liberality of tonight's wine, I'm not possessed of my usual restraint."

I stepped forward. "They were *my* pressings. My editorial of the *Sibyl*. My idea to issue indulgences."

Frederick put down his wine glass. "You'd assume the responsibility, even though a card maker and French priest conspired with you?"

"It's not so simple as conspiracy," I said.

"Ah, another story, I'm sensing," said Frederick. He shifted in his seat. "Let us have it then."

"Mine is a brief, uninspiring tale," I began. "I'd thought to encourage common men with the enlightenment of a hand-mirror when Charlemagne's relics were to be shown. But Your Grace was apparently not prepared for common men to know such light. My efforts earned me the rank of apostate, communicated through Bishop Rupert."

The king rolled his hand. "This I know."

"There is little more to say, my lord." I concentrated to avoid shuffling my feet. "Except that apostates are, by and large, vindictive, in my experience."

That brought Frederick to laughter, the table of men joining the king. "Well, Johannes, just this last hour, the prince-electors," he nodded down the table, "have unanimously voted me Holy Roman Emperor. So, if undermining my influence was your aim, it would seem your vindictiveness has brought you no satisfaction."

I kept my tongue, awaiting my punishment.

Witz hadn't my patience. "It is all very intimidating to be summoned here and shown our failure. But brave of us, though, wouldn't you say, to play the hand we're dealt and come pliantly to the slaughter."

"This you call *pliant*," said Frederick, and laughed again.

Looking down the rows of men given responsibility for electing the Emperor, I noted some whom my family had trusted before we fled Mainz—Louis of Cologne, Sierk of Trier, von Erbach of Mainz itself. Had I been wrong? Should I have trusted Frederick more than my belief that people should have the tools to seek their own light and forgiveness? What had it earned me but a vengeful heart?

I stepped closer. A handful of guards closed in around me. Frederick waved them back.

"My Emperor," I said, my voice trembling, "while not an excuse, I never wanted to fight against you, or against God. On my name, I never even truly felt the apostate. But once upon a divergent path, I embraced it, if only to defy the one who placed me there."

Silence stretched throughout King's Hall. Even Witz found no smart remark.

"If I didn't know better, Johannes," said Frederick, "I'd say that sounds quite a lot like penance."

Witz sighed and rolled his eyes.

Frederick motioned for me to kneel, and I did so. He rested his hand on my shoulder. In its weight, I felt the authority of his office, and maybe … the capacity to forgive. Perhaps the ordination *had* invested him with something of the divine. My breathing slowed, relaxed.

"I forgive you," said the king. "But you do understand I can't have the people or our clergy looking elsewhere for direction or absolution."

"I do, Your Grace."

"Then," said Frederick, "you also understand why both you and Master Witz must be hanged for treason."

A chill shivered through me. I looked up at the king, silently pleading. I wasn't a bad man. I wasn't even, in my heart, an apostate. I'd mostly tried to do good.

"It gives me no pleasure," said the king. And I believed him. Despite the death sentence, I knew now that Frederick wasn't the enemy I'd made of him. My condemnation was a consequence of my own pride.

"How very unsurprising," said Witz. "But I'll wager, dear king, that we've more utility to you alive than dead. Wouldn't you say, Johannes? Perhaps you and I could help spread the gospel of Frederick?"

The king ignored Witz and motioned for the guards to take us. He then picked up his copies of the Sibyl's prophecy and the indulgence letter, preparing to tear them. My mind spun on Witz's words—*spread the gospel* …

"Wait," I barked. "Wait. My lord, what if we print another story. Something remarkable. Something that speaks to your beneficence and authority?"

Again, Frederick waved his guards back. "I should expect a deceit."

"No, lord," I said. "A book. *The* book. By your authority, the Holy Word may be copied. Give us leave to produce the most beautiful Bible the world has ever known."

Witz smiled. "With illuminations that give sight to the glories of God's Kingdom, rendered in vibrant multivariate colors unlike anything ever witnessed by man."

The Holy Roman Emperor's eyes danced at the idea. "To commute your sentence."

"If Your Grace would have it," I said. "But regardless, let this be my recompense. Commission us to create an artifact so sublime that its benefactor can only have been a true disciple of God. You, my lord."

Witz stepped up beside me. "What's more, Your Grace, I will underwrite the whole affair and count it a blessing to undertake the debt."

"For the Papacy and each Arch Diocese," said Frederick. "Two hundred volumes to mark my election. How long would this take?"

"Assign us your best copy of the Book," I said, "and we will commence the moment we arrive back in Strasbourg. A few years, perhaps, to achieve that number, I would think."

Softly, Frederick added, "A copy as a gift to the Holy See on the occasion of my formal ordination in Rome."

The electors fell silent as the king considered. My heart beat hard, less for a commutation, and more at the opportunity to print the oldest, most important stories, and in so doing finally let go my own rancor. Find release from my apostasy.

Frederick stood and raised a glass. "To your new enterprise, gentlemen." The elector-princes all raised their wine glasses. "And to maintain the surprise of it, make of this not a formal matter," said the king. "We will watch closely, and may your efforts be blessed."

I finally stole a breath, as Witz raised an empty hand, toasting with the rest whilst holding nothing.

I was never so happy as I was in those few years, letter by letter, setting out the Word of God. Though my back throbbed constantly with pain, and my eyes never ceased to sting from such close work, my heart knew healing.

I grew to love the parable of the Pharisee and the Publican, taking ever more care in the placement of its type. I was doing my part in humility for the people's tax collector—it's Publican—while forsaking the pharisaical pride that had left me feeling justified in my prior rebellion.

I wasn't so foolish as to believe our new Holy Roman Emperor was altogether pure. No man is. And my shop full of hand-mirrors were a constant reminder that I needn't look beyond my own reflection to find fault. But somewhere in those hours, I ceased to feel like an apostate.

Witz came by most evenings and brought me food—usually high cuts of pork, ripe plums, and fresh bread—as well as elderberry wine. We'd chat as I ate and he took my place at the press, placing his beautiful illuminations within the text. Somehow, the work seemed so very small, yet so very important.

On the night I completed the binding of the last volume, I placed it with the rest against the rear wall of my back room, unable to stop smiling at the culmination of so many countless hours. I only felt gratitude. And I was smart enough to savor that feeling.

As usual, Witz arrived. We'd both known today would see it finished.

He stepped into the back room with his usual flare and removed his hat. "Such a glorious sight, Johannes."

"At the risk of some conceit, my friend, I would agree." I sidled up next to him, and we stood staring.

"Could you have imagined where this all would lead," he said. "But a few years ago, I came through your shop door, looking to incite revolt against one man."

"A king," I reminded.

"Just so," said Witz. He gathered tonight's wine bottle and a pair of glasses. "A toast of our own?"

I laughed. "A perfect complement to the occasion."

Witz poured us full measures and stood poised, seeming to carefully choose his words. "To the silent workings of pride."

Odd phrasing, but I drank believing he'd meant to capture my parable in a paraphrase—we'd spoken on it more than once. He then drew from his inner vest several official-looking documents and handed them to me.

"What's this?" I asked.

He tapped them gently. "These are the ownership papers for the press and any materials related to the various printing it has produced, most especially our lovely Bible."

I scanned the notarized document. "What have these to do with anything?"

"They represent my legal claim to your machine and every book it has manufactured," he said.

"There's no need for that," I replied, my throat tightening. "We are under commission from the king—"

"A secret commission," Witz cut in, "and one I have funded from its inception."

I glanced worriedly at my two hundred Bibles, my beloved press. "I won't allow—"

The outer shop door opened again, and a dozen men flooded into my back room. Most wore rough wool coats, faces leathered by the sun, and carried hand weapons at their belts. Bandits, then. With them came our local watchman, Ehrlich, who looked to Witz, as though seeking cues.

"Ehrlich," I said, "don't do this. You know it is wrong. Appeal to the king for relief from whatever leverage Witz holds over you."

Ehrlich lowered his head and gently drew out a document of his own—the Indulgence I'd given him. He placed it on my worktable.

"You knew even then," I said. "You knew the scheme to seize my work."

"You've no legal recourse," said Witz, nodding to Ehrlich. "And in anticipation of your recalcitrance, I've hired these thick fellows to ensure an orderly conveyance of my property."

The men started toward my press.

"No!" I launched myself at the first, beating down his hands.

Witz laughed as another man wrapped me in an iron-like embrace. I kicked out wildly, writhing in his grip. "Even if you make away with it tonight," I hissed, "the king will set all his armies against you. He will see you utterly destroyed for this."

As his hired men began to dismantle my press, Witz sauntered towards me. "I very much doubt his success."

I stopped struggling. "Why would you do this? We've bought our freedom with this endeavor. And we've only just begun to print meaningful books."

Witz shook his head. "Oh, Johannes, do you truly believe that bowing to Frederick is freedom? Besides which, from our start, this hadn't a thing to do with the Tiburtine chapbook, or indulgences, or even our brotherhood as apostates. No, my friend, this was about your little press."

Piece by piece his men began carrying it from my shop.

"All for my printing press?" The familiar feeling of vengeance began to spread in my chest.

"Don't you see," said Witz, "there is now an efficient, replicable process for producing copies of the most authoritative book in all the world. We've created a template and machine."

I tried to push at him, but my binder held me fast. "To what end?"

Witz stepped close, grinning like a madman. "I will flood the Earth with this book. No longer will it be a tool for the patricians and diocese puppets. Every man and woman will have a copy. Isn't that essentially what you were trying to do with your mirrors? This is our true work, Johannes. We're giving the oldest stories directly to the people, to everyone. They will learn they can appeal to Heaven for forgiveness without having to first petition the likes of John or Frederick."

"You bastard." I spat at him. "Have you any idea the chaos and confusion this will wreak?"

Witz slowly wiped my sputum from his cheek, his smile never faltering. "That is precisely the point, Johannes. Schisms will form. Varying interpretations. Reformers. New Churches will rise by the thousands, all with their own virtuous ideology. They will compete for tithes, tearing one another down, as each declares a supreme understanding of God."

I looked over to the beautiful volumes we had published. "The Church will be decimated. Frederick will lose his authority to command the empire."

Witz patted my shoulder. "Seeing your newfound fondness for the king, let me assure you that this sort of change takes time. The Habsburgs will enjoy a long imperial reign."

I dropped to my knees. "Please Witz, don't do this. It's the Bible, for God's sake."

Witz gently placed his hand aside my head. "No, Johannes, not entirely. You see, your press and a thousand like it will be used to publish books of *all* kinds. Information will find durable and sharable form. The larger part of it, my friend … is that this information will *displace* belief."

My chest ached to hear it. I shook my head.

"More books than we can count," continued Witz, "appealing to man's greatest source of pride, his sanctimonious sense of reason. High-minded ideals that repudiate belief itself, as a matter of fact. The rational mind, they'll say. It will be a glorious clarion call to man's pride, drowning out the still small voice that has comforted him and his progenitors through grief and despair for generations."

I stared away. "They won't even recognize what is lost."

Witz laughed, though it struck me not as mean-spirited. "Now you see," he said. "New modes of thought will attempt to replace belief, and fail wonderfully, fracturing their minds, leading to dissent and war and hatred on a scale neither you nor I can imagine."

I slumped. "And shaming those who hold to whatever vestige of truth remains."

Witz slowly shook his head. "Maybe you *don't* yet see." He hunkered down to look me in the eyes. "The broad sharing of the old stories and of new books piquing every reader's prideful conceit will lead mankind to the conceit that the only truth to be found is each man's *own* story. Utter narcissism. Nothing like your publican."

I glared back at him, defiant at the invocation of my parable. "Some will survive it. You know they will."

"Well, of course, they will," he said, "but by then they'll be as a voice in the wilderness, if they've the fortitude, that is, to risk speaking at all. And everything owing to your little machine. Thank you," he said, then grinned and added, "God bless."

"So, it was a ruse from the beginning," I said. "You never meant to depose the king."

"Oh, Johannes, indeed I did," said Witz. "Just not, I'm sure, the king to which you refer."

The men finished removing my press and all the type and molds. My binder released me and took just one copy of the finished Bible on his way out. Witz had left me the ability to deliver my commission to Frederick and save myself. But that proved little comfort to me in the wake of these revelations.

Witz then stood, doffed his hat, and crossed the outer shop, where he stopped beneath the lintel of my door. "I'm curious," he said, looking back. "When you delivered *The Tiburtine Sibyl*, to my recollection, you refashioned its traditional conclusion."

I nodded. "Ours was meant to inspire suspicion of *Frederick*. If we'd had the emperor present the diadem to Christ, as he does in the original, it would have suggested we needn't fear the emperor's rule."

Witz shook his head. "No, Johannes, I'm referring to the concomitant event of the diadem's transfer."

My body began to tremble as I looked back at the Master of Playing Cards. "Dear God, the rise of the Prince of Errors, the very Son of Perdition."

"Indeed," said Witz, placing a set of his magnificent cards on the table near my door. "Good luck to you, Johannes. I still fancy that the pair of us are well suited."

The Master of Playing Cards pulled the door shut, leaving me to the silence of my workshop. What had I done? How masterfully had I been played, how carefully led, like a trump card in Witz's Karnöffel? The implications tumbled down upon me. Discord and nihilism and arrogance and selfishness … ramifications stretching for untold generations.

I couldn't fathom it.

Nor could I bear it.

I could do little more than stare into the vacant space where my press had stood.

Then, remembering a token I'd held back, I reached into my pocket and gently pulled forth a single piece of moveable type. The period. I uttered a mirthless laugh. I'd thought it might hold some kind of significance. A type of myself. Small. Inconspicuous. Both of us with the opportunity to leave behind something serviceable and poetic, and for all that, something profound.

But sitting on the rough floor of my workshop, staring at this small piece of tin, I simply could find no such meaning.

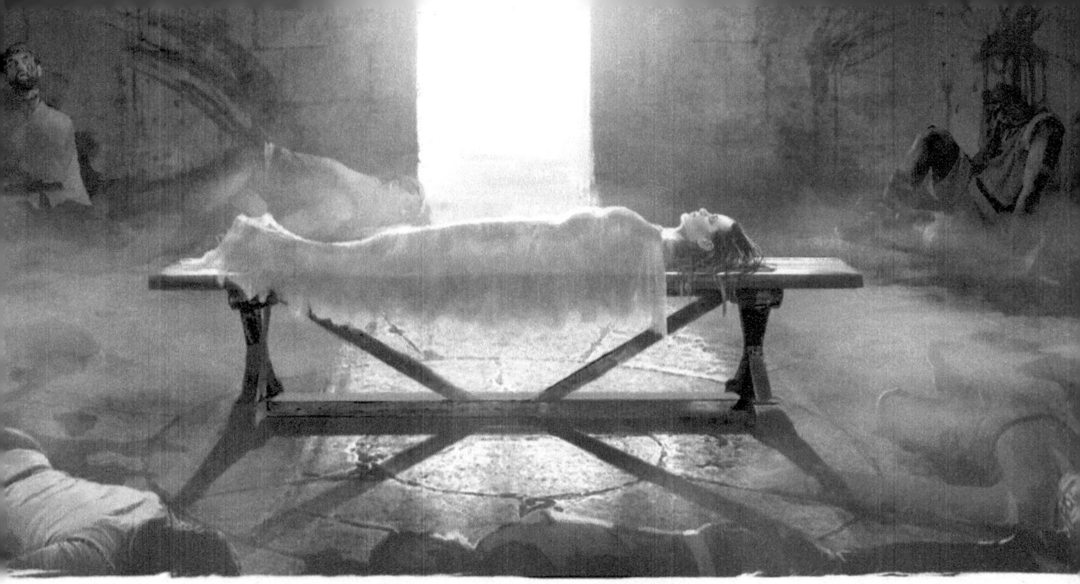

THE WIZARD
IN THE TOWER

KAMERON HURLEY

The surest way to tell if a body was too putrid for Nev's purposes was by touch: a useful corpse felt like a slumbering vessel; a useless one felt like a hunk of dead meat. But gloves were all the rage that autumn because the scarlet plague still haunted the steamy wharf and public houses of Balosovia. The style made it more difficult for him to connect with random passersby, as no one living would get within three paces of him, and all the dead were burned quickly and completely—far too quickly for him to remove his own gloves and lay hands on them.

The arrival of a caravan of cultists did not improve his situation. The hooded figures carried weapons openly as they churned through the leaves rotting in the streets. They posted crudely printed flyers in the public squares that warned of "corpse stealers" and "body doubles" in blocky red script:

BEWARE THE BODY-STEALER,
THE CORPSE-EATER, THE RISEN DEAD!
» Has your grandmother been miraculously healed,
but come back ... CHANGED?
» Has your child recovered from grave illness ...
only to speak in strange tongues?
BEWARE THE CORPSE WALKERS!
BEWARE THE PEACE-STEALERS

Fear during times of change brought out the worst in people. Nev had seen cults like this during other times of upheaval. The presence of the cultists chilled him and made him extra cautious in how he cared for his own, still living body. But he was out of coin, and with winter settling in, he would be stuck in this little town, with its gloves and cultists, until spring thawed the mountain passes.

And so it was that Nev sought out the nearest body dealer.

Over the time Nev had wandered the shifted patchwork of countries between the gaping teeth of the obsidian mountains to the north and the churning, violet sea in the south, he had encountered many types of body dealers. In his youth, the body dealers worked directly with the Corpse Mercenary Guild, securing useful bodies for fallen Corpse Soldiers to leap into upon expiration on the battlefield. Those times were only a dim memory for him now and dimmer still to those around him, whose fashions and names and government configurations he had long since ceased to follow. Over the years the types of people requiring bodies ebbed and flowed, but aside from those in his own profession, there was one type that always required a constant supply of human remains ...

The wizards.

Balosovia's most notorious body dealer was its local tyrant, a wizard called Kvesnia, who lived in a spiraling tower made of once liquified stone, long tempered, embedded with crystalline shards that peppered its face like studs. She had once been a close advisor to the queen, some said, and for her years of service, she was given run of Balosovia and the surrounding countryside to shape as she wished. She was a reclusive despot, locked away in her tower, but being under her protection provided Nev with the opportunity to gather as many bodies as he wished, without question.

She insisted he call her Master, and he felt that a slim price to pay for getting his hands on freshly dead meat.

Nev spent those early weeks of autumn tugging his forelock at her, driving her cart and its great squawking cassowary up the perilously steep circular path that wound around the outside of the tower. The city had its patchwork network of criminal gangs and petty neighborhood upstarts, but it soon became known he was Kvesnia's creature, and they let him be. Even so, some days were better than others. Most bodies were too far gone for his purposes, which made him anxious and jittery, like an addict deprived of a sniff.

And so it was that when he woke one chilly, rain-choked morning and checked the last secreted body in his dirt cellar, he found it too putrid to be of use any longer.

Dread soured his stomach. Today, if the cultists—wearing their fine gloves and long robes—murdered him, he would die as quickly and easily as anyone else. A fate he had avoided for quite some time and wished to avoid for some time more.

Nev wrapped the body and dumped it into the cart hitched outside his little workshop at the edge of the city. The cassowary wandered over and stamped its great taloned foot at him. Nev fished a slice of apple from his tunic and tossed it to the fat bird, which greedily swallowed the apple slice whole, shaking its double-wattle as it did. Cassowaries had the alien intensity of reptiles about them; he often suspected this one was part dragon. "We are on borrowed time, Bohdan," he said. "Let's hope your Master has more work for us, yes?"

Bohdan grumbled at him, more roar than squawk.

Nev took the bird by the lead and wound through the city's lesser streets, bumping along the cobbles. Though the streets were relatively quiet, the stink of the body announced what he carried, and the few people about made way for him. The scarlet plague still haunted the city, and it would only become more widespread as the weather worsened, driving people to gather inside. The streets were relatively quiet.

The wizard's tower bore only the most marginal of magical defenses. Most people in the city left Kvesnia to herself, putting up with her gory experiments on their kin because of both her abilities and her relationship to the Queen and her armies. Nev heard a whispered story at an inn one night about how a mob had once attacked the tower and Kvesnia had simply made a sign in the air and turned them all to stone. There had always been a wizard in the tower, the locals said, but this one, especially, needed to be left to go about her business—bodies and all.

Nev passed through the great iron arch above the main door and transferred the body to a hand cart. Down and down he went with his curious luggage. Water sweated from the walls.

He knocked twice at the wizard's workshop door. A strange humming came from within.

The humming ceased. Then, "Enter."

Nev cracked the door and said, "I have a delivery for you."

"Come inside," Kvesnia said.

He left the cart and stepped just over the threshold, careful not to touch anything. The room smelled faintly of sage and sulfur. A partially articulated skeleton lay on a table behind her, one hand waving at her as if still alive, but likely just animated by a spell or concoction. Kvesnia once told him she had a particular interest in what life remained in the body after death. Nev could have told her there was none.

"I need you to do a retrieval," Kvesnia said without turning, the red brocade of her robe dancing with shadows cast by the bright orange light of the spirit lamps. "A little cottage off Fen's Way, near the old Cykovoskova Temple. You know the area?"

"Yes," Nev said and added, "Master."

"There will be many bodies there, but I only want one of them. The others are of no interest to me."

He considered asking her who she had paid to murder all those bodies but swallowed it. Kvesnia's schemes and machinations were tolerated; she tended to murder the town's upstart citizens and petty criminals first. He suspected one day she would overstep and have to turn half the town into stone again. But today was not that day. He hoped he would be well away from here by then.

"Should I take away this one I've brought?"

"No, no, that's fine." Kvesnia half turned; most of her narrow face was consumed by shadow, and her body was made larger by her thick robes. She bore a single sliver of white hair above her left ear. The rest of her was dark, dour, as was fitting, considering her occupation. A twisted scar on the left side of her mouth made it look like she was always sneering. She seemed distracted by something in a crystal mirror to her left, so Nev waited for her, letting the silence hang between them.

Kvesnia drew a long tail of fire from a glass vial next to the mirror. Wrote a symbol in the air with it. Clapped her hands. The room chilled. "There will be a woman's body there," Kvesnia said. "Laid out on a table, wrapped in white muslin. Hers is the only body I want. And you must be discreet. You understand? She will not be a plague victim. It will be messier than that."

Nev bowed his head.

"You are to arrive precisely at thirteen in the morning." The bell in the town square tolled the hour. Kvesnia paused, let it finish, continued, "Not a moment earlier. Nor later. Precisely. I value your precision, you understand?"

Obeisance was an easy cowl to wear. "Yes, master."

"Good. Dump that one in the potting room."

Nev pressed a knuckle to his forehead. He rolled the body along, taking the winding ramp down a second level to what he had deemed the Body Library. Each door in the long, circular hall was marked with a cryptic symbol. He had only been permitted through three of them. The stench emanating from each differed, as did the sounds. A green light continually flickered from beneath one. Another occasionally released breathy puffs of blue fog. He once thought he heard moaning coming from one of them, but it did not last long. That had unnerved him: he did not care what Kvesnia did with the dead, but the living? The idea that she could have living subjects here chilled him.

The chamber Kvesnia called the potting room was less remarkable. Simply a room for rendering flesh from bone. He passed several large stone tubs filled with bodies in the process of having their bloody bits devoured by flesh beetles. Nev found a tub of beetles with room in it and deposited the new body there. The mix of beetles ate everything but bone; much more useful for the magician's purposes than feeding bodies to pigs, which often ate the corpses, bones and all. What she did with the bones, he did not ask, but he could guess. He had spent a long time in service to wizards.

Body deposited, he went back out to the courtyard where he'd left Bohdan and the cart. Bohdan insisted on more fruit, which he communicated by nipping at Nev's sleeve with his thick beak. Nev obliged him, fishing a bit more apple from his pocket and leading Bohdan and the cart into one of the city's lesser markets for fresh produce. The body had not leaked much, so he loaded the cart with various tough-skinned fruits and a bag of hardy tubers.

Nev did not spend much time on housekeeping. His home was a simple one-room box, strewn with sweet-smelling rushes. The loft was for storage, mostly food, and of course, there was the cellar, which was mostly for bodies. He whiled away his afternoon and early evening in pursuit of one of his many hobbies, making a few extra coins by crafting small animal figurines and repairing tools and furniture for those neighbors not repulsed by his primary source of income. As the plague progressed, though, those clients had become fewer and fewer. Now his figurines took up three long shelves above his sleeping platform.

Nev slept only a few hours that night. He found he needed only four or five hours of sleep in most bodies, and that left him great gulfs of time for busywork because if he did not stay busy, he spent too long thinking. There was a time when he had soaked his body in alcohol and opium to prevent all that thinking; he had lost decades to that, much of it simply extinguished. Blackness.

When the bell tolled the twelfth hour, he woke Bohdan, who thundered at him, and hitched the bird to the cart for the walk to Fen's Way. Nev enjoyed the city most at night. Many residents kept long hours, and their spirit lamps cast warm orange light across the cobbled streets. He liked to imagine the lives of the families, most of whom lived above street level in wattle-and-daub apartments lining Fen's Way. If he saw figures at all, they were mere shadows. Most would have retreated to interior courtyards. Others sat up darning clothes or entertaining. A few certainly were making preparations for the upcoming fertility festival, baking penis-shaped cakes and vulva-like pastries ahead of the week's celebration. What was it like, inside those warm walls, so full of life and vigor? He knew it was not all laughter and genital-shaped cakes. He had been a part of too many households to think that. But certainly, there would be joy. Secrets. Bitter rivalries. Warmth. Companionship.

Fen's Way was a dirty, cramped side street that veered behind the Cykovoskova Temple, wending past the pyre platforms and family tombs commemorating the dead. Ashes were usually buried under the dirt floors of homes, but memorials to the dead all ended up here, in the shadow of the temple. He knew the little cottage Kvesnia meant because he had been this way many times before. Families mainly used the cottage to stage wakes for the dead; no one ever came there at night.

As he approached, the cottage appeared cold and empty. No flickering lamps. No smoke in the chimney. A shiver crawled down his spine. Bodies were one thing, but he did not like sorcery, ironic perhaps, considering whom he worked for. Nev hitched Bohdan to the pillar of a tomb just outside the cottage. The bird pecked at his pocket, hard enough to bruise, but Nev batted his head away. The door lay open, just a crack. Dark fingerprints smeared the frame. A thick liquid puddled on the stoop. The smell of blood and voided bowels wafted out from the interior.

Death, he did not mind so much. Death, he understood. No sorcery, then? Perhaps this would be as simple as Kvesnia indicated. Kvesnia was nothing if not precise.

Nev pushed the door open, using just two fingers and turning his body so he presented less of a target to anyone inside who was still living. The scene before him made his heart leap.

Bodies lay against the walls, slumped in chairs, crumpled before the fireplace; heads bashed in, guts drooling from smiling torsos. Nev followed the bloody prints and smears, trying to recreate the slaughter in his mind, but his attention kept being drawn to the figure on the table, all tucked up into a great white shroud. No stains on that shroud. No prints. The creeping feeling came over him again. There was sorcery involved here; he could almost smell it.

Nev hesitated in the doorway. He had not lived this long by simply walking into messes like this. But his hands itched to take hold of a body—any of them, all of them!—to ensure he had a corpse to jump into should his current vessel fail him. Desperation often trumped good judgment. He knew that. He did it anyway.

He pulled off his gloves and gripped the forearm of a corpse next to the table, skin-to-skin. The body was already cool to the touch and had the delicious feel of the empty vessel about it. He breathed a sigh of relief and moved farther into the room.

Kvesnia only wanted one body, the shrouded one on the table, but Nev needed at least two of the others for his cellar. He worked quickly, choosing slender men with head injuries that were less likely to spill viscera.

After depositing the bodies in his cart, he came back for the shrouded figure. The shroud had not been completely stitched closed; the head and torso were still visible. A thick needle still dangled from a thread. Had all of these people been here for a wake? They did not strike him as family-types—more like young mercenaries, based on their dress and age. Three had tattoos on their faces marking them as belonging to a local street gang, one he certainly didn't want to get on the wrong side of.

He took up the needle and began to complete the sewing. The body inside appeared unmarred: a moon-faced young woman with a spill of dark curls, a twist to one lip that may have been from a cleft lip or injury in childhood. It reminded him vaguely of Kvesnia's scar.

The body's eyes opened.

Nev froze, needle raised.

Her arm snapped out of the shroud and she yanked his wrist, us-ing his body as leverage to leap off the table. She knocked him to the ground, turned his arm behind his back, and knelt on it, pinning him to the bloody floor.

"Where is she?" the woman hissed, spitting blood on the back of his neck.

"Where is who?"

"Kvesnia!"

"She's in her tower. Where she always is."

"No, she's here. She *must* be here. She would come for me *personally*."

"She sent me. It's just me, and Bohdan."

"Bohdan?" Her grip tightened.

"Sorry, the bird. Just … for the cart. We are no threat to you."

"I'll be the judge of that."

She went quiet, and he worried. Quiet meant she was thinking of what to do with him. "What happened here?" he said, interrupting her.

"Are you armed?"

"No."

A hiss, from behind her. A wet thunk.

"Fuck." She fell back against the table, and he twisted away.

Nev scrambled for the door. Glancing back, he saw one of the bodies was up, holding an ax in one hand and his own guts in the other. He regarded the woman the way Nev gazed at the bodies he needed to inhabit.

The woman yanked the knife he'd thrown out of her own shoulder and threw it back at the shambling man. The knife slid into the man's eye cleanly. He sagged to his knees, knocking over a chair. She tripped on the table behind her, stumbled. The man yanked one leg out from under her as she fell; she went down hard on her other leg, twisting it beneath her.

Nev heard the bone snap. She flopped onto the floor with a small cry. She struck the hilt of the dagger protruding from the man's eye once, twice, and he shuddered. Went limp. Fell back.

Nev made it to the doorway, heart surging.

The woman clutched at her leg. A shard of cracked bone peeked through the flesh just above the ankle.

Experience told Nev to take the two bodies already in his cart and run.

The woman stared at him with her big, dark eyes. Her rage and pain were palpable. "Well, you shit," she said, "will you take me back to her like this? Try and come for me! I'll slit your throat."

The words were out before he could stop himself. "Let me bind the break. You cannot get far on that."

"It not broken."

"I assure you it is."

"I'm fine."

Nev put his back to her and made it two steps out the door. He tried, but could not get himself to let go of the door handle. She did not cry out or hiss. She did not make a sound. She certainly did not beg. But the longer he kept his back to her, the more pain he felt.

He gritted his teeth and stepped back into the room.

She said, "I told you to leave me alone."

"And I respect that. I also feel a moral imperative to not leave you here to die. I can call a doctor … a mother, a relative? Someone you trust?"

"No doctors. No law."

"I realize you feel vulnerable." He knew what that was like. "What if you ride in the back of the cart, just until town? Let me get you nearer someone who can help. Out here"—he gestured to the wreck of bodies around them—"this is no place for the living."

"Why would you help me?"

"Because it pains me not to."

She gripped the edge of the table, tried to stand on her good leg. The broken foot hung sideways. She would not look at it.

"I could take you to Kvesnia now," Nev said, "as you are, but I suspect that will not go as you hoped, in your present state."

"What do you know about Kvesnia?"

"Only that you went to a great deal of trouble to lure her here or some purpose."

"She should have come for me."

"I can take you to town. On the back of the cart. I'll keep the cart between us."

She clenched her teeth. "To town, then."

"To town." He approached her carefully. "I should mend the break, first. All right?"

She nodded and fell into a chair, leg outstretched.

Nev pulled the bones together. She bit her own wrist to keep from crying out. He broke the spine of a chair and a length of cord from the belt of the dead man and fashioned a makeshift splint. She hissed and muttered, but did not protest.

He helped her up. She leaned into him, warm and soft. It was the first time in more than a year that he'd been this close to another living human being.

"What are you doing with these bodies?" she asked as they approached the cart.

"They are for Kvesnia."

"You said she sent you for me."

"She did. But she always requires fresh bodies. I'm not going to waste these."

"So this is what you do for her? You're her little henchman, her body dealer?"

Bhodan squalled at her and stomped his foot.

"It's an honest profession," Nev said. He helped her into the back of the cart, moving the legs of the corpses out of the way.

She grimaced. Gripped the edge of the cart tightly. "Where do you live?"

"On the other side of the village. I'll take a route straight through the central square."

"There will be no one awake but the law."

"Perhaps."

She eyed Bhodan, who ducked his head at her and squalled again. "What kind of bird is that?"

"A cassowary." He didn't mention that Bohdan and the cart belong to Kvesnia. "His name is Bohdan. I'm Nev."

"Well, Nev … Let's leave this place."

Nev unwrapped Bohdan's lead. He clicked at the bird to urge him forward, and the cart began to trundle along again.

"She's evil, you know," the woman said over her shoulder.

"Kvesnia? Undoubtedly. She's committed any number of atrocities in this city."

"Then why do you work for her?"

"I need to eat. Why do you hate her so much?" She did not respond, so he asked, "What does she want with you?"

"It's not what she wants with me. It's what I want with *her*, now."

"And that's …?"

She made a face, half snarl, half grimace. "She locked me in that tower cellar for six years. Six years of my life. A prisoner."

Nev shivered. "Why would she do that?"

"You don't believe me?"

"That was not my question."

She stared into her blood-crusted palms. "She believed I was a monster. Or that I would become one. She said she read it in my mother's entrails."

"How exactly—"

"How do you think?" she said bitterly. "Twenty years ago she wasn't as she is now. She stood at the side of Queen Rostovya, her personal sorcerer. Oh, she loved that power. Loved wielding it. Twisting people with it. This was before Rostovya brought the South under her shroud. To us, the new queen was a minor figure from a minor country, but with Kvesnia at her side, and with the pacts she made with the rulers in the east, she gained in power. Her people swept through my village, slaughtered everyone. My sisters, brothers, fathers … cousins, friends, old lovers. You don't know what it is to lose everything in one breath, a moment in an ordinary day. That place, those people were my world. They were everything. She took it away."

"And Kvesnia took you."

"Yes."

Nev suspected the answer, but asked anyway, "For what purpose?"

"For her depraved experiments and manipulations, to indulge in her monstrous theories on the nature of magic and its ability to render and unmake flesh. There was no one to look for me. I was a perfect subject. Just some body, like these, to her."

"She is obsessed with bodies," Nev muttered.

"And you retrieve them for her. Why not deliver me to her like this, as well?"

"I was tasked with retrieving a corpse. You are not a corpse."

"You could make me one."

Nev shook his head. "No."

"No? Is the body stealer a pacifist?"

"I choose to avoid conflict unless it's absolutely necessary."

"You could choose other employment. There is always a choice. You could go somewhere else. Work for someone else."

"I would be risking a great deal. Now is not the time."

They arrived at the edge of the village proper and began winding through the tanning district, whose stink permeated the air. Neither spoke; Nev to reduce the amount of air he needed to inhale, and the woman, well—when he looked back at her, she appeared deep in contemplation, brow furrowed. He did not envy her choices, or her rage. He knew what it was to be that angry, seething with the need for revenge, and he had never liked feeling it.

When they came out of the tanning district and headed up toward the open main square, she said, "Stop the cart, please."

Nev pulled on Bohdan's lead.

She put her elbow up on the side of the cart. Fixed him with an intense gaze. "My name is Renniv."

"Hello, Renniv."

"Look," she said, "if I stay with you, it will only be until I am mended by a chirgheon. I can afford one, you know. They can fix this in two weeks at most. And then I'm going to kill Kvesnia."

"All right."

"All … right? You aren't upset that I'm going to kill your employer, the tyrant who rules this town?"

"Not at all. Though succeeding at that will be easier said than done."

"You don't know me."

"I don't," he said, "but I'd like to." The last part slipped out, surprising even him.

"I'm going to *kill* her."

"All right."

They waited in silence for a long breath, gazes locked.

Bohdan hissed at them.

Nev said, "The square's just up here, or we can go on."

"Go on," she said.

Nev had never had anyone else in his hovel, not anyone living, anyway. As they approached, the sky was growing gray with the promise of dawn to come, and in the runny light, all the defects of his house were thrown into sharp relief. He had always lived humbly, as it drew less attention.

He tied Bohdan's lead and helped Renniv out of the cart and into the dim house. There was no lock on the door. He had nothing of worth. The room smelled of smoke and the sweet rushes lining the floor.

"Will you take those bodies back to her tonight?" Renniv asked.

"No, I'll store them in the cellar out back."

Nev pulled back the coverlet on his narrow bed and settled her into it. "You stay here. There's a pot to piss in, there." He was relieved that he had remembered to empty it before he left that night. "I'm going to stoke a fire and get us some light. I need to ensure you won't get an infection between now and the chirgheon's arrival."

He put his back to her and stirred up the fire, nurturing a little coal until it became a flame, then began to feed it.

"Did you make all of these?" Renniv asked. She was staring at the wooden figures.

"Yes, for a bit of side money."

"That wizard-tyrant is stingy? I'm not surprised."

"Are you hungry? I have some hard cheese and bread."

"No. I hurt, though."

"I'll brew something up for the pain." He swung up into the loft and sifted through the herb trays, retrieving a mixture of willow bark, turmeric, and his last bottle of eucalyptus oil.

"You have a regular pharmacy," Renniv said.

"My mother was healer," he said. The truth tripped easily off his tongue, though he had not spoken of his real mother for longer than he could remember. "I've learned much since then, of course."

"Oh, have you? You're barely twenty, if a day!"

"Older than I look," Nev said. Also not a lie. He had always found the truth easier than lying, as it didn't require remembering anything.

He made her tea and sat at the little table across from the bed to drink his own watered-down version as he prepared a salve for her wound.

"How long have you worked for her?" Renniv asked.

"Not long."

"How long have you lived here?"

"About the same amount of time."

"Where did you come from?"

Nev sipped his tea. Focused on mixing the salve. "Here and there. But how did you escape the wizard?"

"I was clever," Renniv said. "I faked my death."

"As you did tonight."

"Yes."

"Odd, a wizard falling for the same trick twice."

"I'm very convincing."

He brought over the salve and clean linen strips and knelt beside the bed. "Hold out your leg, please, if that's all right."

She gently extended it, wincing.

Nev removed his crude splint. Blood had thickened and formed crusted ridges around the area where the bone had burst through the skin. Her skin was deeply bruised around the fracture. In the light of the fire, he saw other scars here, though, and as she pulled her skirt up to her knees to give him more light, he noted the crisscross patterns of flesh worm damage. There was a thick hunk missing from the back of her thigh, just above her knee, as if something had taken a bite from it. He was aware of her hot gaze as he did his work. She did not let her eyes off him.

"What do you see?" she asked.

"A clean break. One that hopefully will not fester ahead of the chirgheon." He washed the wound and slathered it over with salve.

"You have very gentle hands," she said. "Is that from handling bodies? Are they very brittle?"

Nev chewed that over a moment. He knew he was very tired. "No," he said, "that is from dealing with animals. Animals spook easily, as they should. Not all humans are kind. They are right to be spooked. So one must earn their trust."

"I see."

He stood, quickly. "I'll fashion some better wood for the splint."

Nev rushed out of the warm cottage and into the cooler night. His cheeks felt hot, and his heart was hammering.

Bohdan raised his head and stared at Nev accusingly.

"What am I doing with this woman in my house?" Nev whispered.

Bohdan began pecking at his trouser pockets in search of an apple. Nev batted him away.

He unloaded the bodies from the back of the cart and hauled them to the cellar, then went out to the woodpile and burned off some energy splitting firewood into splints. After he had two suitable ones, he continued for a few minutes more. If she reported him to the cultists they would cut him up and burn him in the square and burn his house and these bodies as well. They would know how to deal with what he was.

He took up the two splints and went back into the cottage.

Renniv lay back on the bed now, injured leg sticking out, one arm draped over her eyes. The tea, the injury, and the evening were likely catching up to her.

He tied the splint, which roused her. She pulled her arm lazily from over her face. "That was good tea," she said. "Your mother was a good healer."

"She was." He knotted the splint, lifted her leg up, and settled her in the bed. Pulled the coverlet over her.

"I'll be in the cellar," he said.

"The cellar? For what?"

"To sleep."

"With the bodies?" she said, grimacing. "No, Nev. You're alive and you should sleep with the living."

He stood over her, watching the flickering firelight cast shadows across her skin. Her thick, curly hair fairly shone. He thought of the scars on her legs, the bite, and wondered what other horrors the wizard had written on her skin.

"I'm sorry for—" he began and realized his error. How trite would it sound for some stranger to apologize to him for all the harm someone else had caused him? All those decades of torture and experimentation at the hands of various organizations, and curious government agencies, and wild-eyed cultists. "I'm sorry the accommodations are modest," he finished.

She snorted. Pulled off her coverlet and handed it to him. "I've slept on rushes plenty of nights. Just sleep here, by the fire. We are adults."

Nev held the coverlet a long moment and then settled onto the rush floor. He watched her, and when she lifted her head to look at him, he turned over and put his back to her.

What was he doing with this woman in his house?

♛

Nev woke a few hours later, while Renniv still slept, and took Bohdan to fetch a chirgheon. The chirgheon was more hedge witch than specialist, a tall, stooped woman with a beak of a nose over which she peered at him skeptically. She reminded him of a heron.

When he arrived back at the hovel with the chirgheon, Renniv was awake and had hobbled outside to the rain barrel to wash her face and hands. The old woman clucked over her, and Nev left them to it.

He took Bohdan and the empty cart, more for security than practicality, and made his way back across town and up into the winding tower. He knocked three times, and the doors opened. Nev left Bohdan outside and went in search of the wizard. He found her in the potting room, cooing over the flesh beetles as they did their work on the corpse he had brought in the day before. She did not look up when he entered.

"Where is the body I charged you with retrieving?" she asked. "You did not return to me last night."

"There were many bodies," Nev said, "but no dead body on the table.

Your instructions were specific. I did not want to bring you a body you had not asked for."

Kvesnia raised her head slowly, and with a little flourish of her fingers, wrote a blazing symbol in the air. The flesh beetles hissed. "She was not there?"

Nev shrugged.

"Curious." Kvesnia straightened and rested one long, thin arm on the edge of the tub. "I will have to check my sources of information."

"Was there any reason you wanted that body in particular? Perhaps I could look for another with similar attributes."

"Her name is Rennivsaya Goborya," Kvesnia said, "and she's a very dangerous body. She burned her whole village, murdered every last one of her kin and neighbors. I attempted to rehabilitate her, but she was violent, crude, and ungrateful. She stabbed out the eye of her caretaker here and escaped. She has been trying to kill me ever since."

"I see."

"Do you? I wonder."

"Do you have another task for me?"

"Not today, no. But I would be wary of Rennivsaya. If she was nearby and saw you, your life may well be forfeit. She is a slender woman, dark curly hair, your height, and has a scar on her lip. You will know her at once if you see her. Come to me immediately if you do recognize her. I can protect you, of course."

"I understand," Nev said and tugged his forelock.

As he turned he felt a prickling thread of dread squirming in his stomach. He still knew very little about this wizard and her grip on the town, and even less still about Renniv. He knew the danger he was in by putting himself between them. He thought, again, of the villagers who had been turned to stone. If he was going to survive until spring, he needed to get Renniv out of his house or he needed to leave the wizard's employ and flee to a place well beyond her grasp, or both.

By the time Nev returned to his hovel, it was late afternoon, and he realized he hadn't eaten. He tied up Bohdan, stripped off his tunic, and washed up at the rain barrel, splashing water over his face and neck, still considering his options. He was a fool to bring Renniv here. When things went wrong at the cottage, he should have taken Bohdan and left town, maybe gone south to some smaller village like Doroteya or Inyessa.

He raised his head from the barrel and found Renniv staring at him from the doorway, leaning into it to favor her injured leg. She gazed at him as if she wanted to devour him, eyes wide, lips slightly parted. He was embarrassed at the intensity of that look. He reached for his tunic.

"Did it go well with the chirgheon?" he asked, face growing hot.

"She said I'll be good to stand on it in two weeks if I follow her prescriptions. She also says I should eat more citrus. Where would one find a lemon this time of year?"

He smiled. "I'm sure I have dried orange peels somewhere."

"You're full of surprises."

"I assure you, I'm a man of simple pleasures."

She tutted. "I don't believe you're as simple as you pretend."

"Are you hungry? I'm starving. I'll make us something."

He made a thick soup, which they ate sometime later in the firelight, dipping the stale bread in the stew to make it palatable. "I'll go out for more bread tomorrow," he said. "I have a little plot in the back. Some onions, parsley, kale. Not much this time of year, but we can supplement it. I can get a rasher of bacon."

"I can pay," she said. "I do have coin."

He shook his head. "It's not much. And I eat better when others are around."

"How long has it been," she asked, "since others were around?"

"A very long time." He met her black gaze, and could not help but note the curve of her cheek, her slender fingers, the way the firelight seemed to make her dark hair gleam.

"You like the solitude?"

"Yes. I find that people often bring … complications."

"Is that so? What did Kvesnia say about me, then?"

He sopped up more stew. It was mostly kale and parsley, butter and beans. He had learned to do much with little, over time. "She said you murdered your whole village."

Renniv snorted. "She would say that. Have you spent time locked up? Your freedom taken away from you?"

"Many times."

"How did you stand it?"

"I remembered every other time my freedom was taken away. I understood it was impermanent, that life went on afterward. For instance, in the spring the mountain passes will clear, and I will move on from Kvesnia to some new situation."

"You wouldn't have known you'd ever be free, the first time."

"You cannot take up the mantle of fate that others give you. You must bring it into being for yourself."

She seemed to consider that. "What happened to you?"

"May as well ask what didn't," he said. Memories flickered of the years after the dissolution of the Corpse Mercenary Guild, and what people did to body mercenaries when they found them. He pushed them away. "It was all a long time ago."

"And it's why you keep to yourself?"

"Yes. You seem to know something of that. How did you come to be in that cottage?"

"I was meeting someone who was supposed to help me. She didn't. Those men came instead."

He raised his brows. "*You* killed all those men?"

"Who did you think killed them, some murder troll?" she laughed. "You know the first thing I did when I got away from that … woman? I learned how to fight. How to kill. She made me do that. Made me into … whatever I am."

"We are not the sum of what is done to us," Nev said. "What makes us who we are is how we react to it."

She frowned. Stabbed at her stew. "Don't judge me."

"I'm not. Simply offering an alternative point of view. I understand that we know very little about one another. I am the last person to judge another. I carry around corpses for a living."

"You said it before I could."

"I do try to get ahead of that."

"Do you really know no one else here? No friends? No family? No … lovers?"

"I prefer no entanglements. No … engagements."

She laughed again; he liked the sound of her laugh. "Engagements?" she said. "You don't *fuck* much, do you?"

"I avoid people as much and as often as possible."

"Well," she said, still laughing, "I'm sorry to have messed up your life for a few weeks."

"I'm not," he said and got up before he could say more and make a fool of himself. "I'm going out to chop some firewood. Please get some rest."

That made her laugh again for some reason. He turned before she could see the flush in his face.

In the morning, someone knocked at the door.

Nev woke with a start. Renniv was already awake, spooning porridge into a bowl. She limped to the door.

"Don't," Nev said. "It's probably a beggar."

"This far from the city center?" Renniv said. "Hardly."

He heard the door squeak open, and then, "Hello, friend. Have you heard the righteous news?"

Nev sat bolt upright.

Two cultists stood on the other side of the door.

"I am Rippa," said the taller woman, her face all teeth, mouth spread wide in a grin that seemed to turn her eyes into two tiny beads of darkness. "And this is my associate, Calder." The little woman next to her curtsied.

"We have heard reports that a body dealer lives here."

Nev went to the door, moving just slightly in front of Renniv, who moved back into the house, brow furrowed.

"I work for the wizard, Kvesnia," Nev said.

Neither woman blinked at the name.

"Is that so?" said Rippa. "That means you deliver bodies to her, then?"

"Yes. It's all approved and legal here. Kvesnia is the ward of this town as well as the surrounding farmland."

Calder smiled. Nev didn't like that smile.

Rippa said, "I find that quite curious. You see, we received a report from a chirgheon that you were a bit unusual. She says you keep bodies *here*."

Nev winced. Had the chirgheon gone into the cellar? Had Renniv, and told her? "That's a curious accusation," he said.

He stepped out onto the stoop, and the women moved back. He glanced over their heads at the cellar door.

It was open. Wide open.

He cast a look at Bohdan. The bird pecked away at the grass, oblivious. Then he asked, "Have you illegally ransacked my property?"

"Are you illegally storing bodies here?" Rippa replied.

"What exactly is the issue?" Renniv said. "He says he works for the wizard, he works for the wizard. Maybe he doesn't always bring her bodies right away."

Nev smelled it then. The smoke. Burning.

No.

He pushed past the women and ran to the cellar doors. Below, flames fueled by large canisters of oil licked the beams of the cellar's roof. He tried to push the doors closed, but the heat was intense. Farther down the lane, a cart was hitched, and two more cultists waited there, both grinning the same mad grins as Rippa.

"What have you done?" Nev cried, rounding on Rippa and Calder.

"We would just like to do a few ... tests," Rippa said. "We have leave from the council."

Nev recoiled. "You will not touch me."

They raised their gloved hands. "Oh," said Rippa, "most assuredly not. We know what you are. We will not touch an abomination such as you with bare skin. We know that is how you steal our souls."

"You're mad," Nev said.

"You need to leave," Renniv said, limping out of the house. She had something in her hand that gleamed.

The two women reached for him. Nev ducked away and tried to take Renniv by the shoulder and get her back into the house, but she shrugged him away.

"Hey, fuck faces!" Renniv said. "You need to leave."

"This is nothing to do with you," Rippa said. "I suggest—"

Renniv stabbed her in the eye with the bread knife.

Rippa screamed. Calder squawked like a cassowary and rushed back toward the cart.

Blood and ocular fluid leaked from Rippa's eye.

"Go!" Renniv said, "or I'll stab the other one. And if you come back here … I'll stab the other one. And your friends' too."

"Miscreant!" Rippa shouted. "You have been deceived! This creature is a mimic, a soul-stealer."

"I'd worry more about your eye right now," Renniv said.

Rippa trotted back to the cart with the others. They turned the cart around and whistled at the four cassowaries that pulled it. The birds hissed and screeched, or perhaps that was the cultists. Nev could not be sure.

Nev went back to the cellar, but it was burning so hot he couldn't get within three paces of the doorway The bodies were destroyed, as were his other stores: potatoes, onions, garlic, apples. All gone.

Renniv limped up beside him, holding the bloody knife in her hand.

"Is that a signature of yours?" Nev said lightly. "You just … stab people in their eyes?"

"It's very effective."

They stood in silence for a long moment, watching the cellar burn.

"Why did you really keep bodies down there?" she asked.

He mulled over his answers. He had kept what he was from people before, and it never turned out well. He had also told a few what he was, and that hadn't turned out well either. But the cultists forced his hand. They already knew what he was, and they would be back.

"It was necessary," he said. "Because … I am much older than I look."

She turned her face to him. He could not meet her eyes. Her laugh was a little forced. "Surely, all that nuttery—"

He shook his head. "The stories exist for a reason."

"Corpse-jumpers are a myth."

"You understand now why I have to work for Kvesnia." He stuffed his hands in his pockets.

"Gods above," she muttered. "You're *serious.*"

She took his hand. He started, it was so unexpected.

"This isn't your body?" she said.

"It is now, but only for a few years."

"Where did you get it?"

"He died in an orchard. Fell out of a tree. Knocked his head. Dead."

"You can only take a dead body, right? Not a living one."

"It has to be dead, yes."

"So that part's true."

He sighed. "I don't want to—"

"Have you ever inhabited a woman's body?"

"I have inhabited many bodies."

He glanced at her. He had seen many reactions to his admission over his many seasons, but the way she looked at him, as if he were a fascinating curiosity, was not the most common.

"You were a soldier, then," she said. "That's what Corpse Mercenaries did in the stories."

"Yes."

"But now you just … gather bodies for wizards, and make stew, and whittle those figures?"

"Yes."

"You could be out there having adventures! Hunting monsters!"

"I've done all that," Nev said. "I don't hunt monsters anymore because far too often I've found myself the monster being hunted. You may have some insight into that."

"You are no monster," she said. "Nor am I. You just want to live the life of an honest coward?"

"Yes. Cowards live longer."

"What's being alive if you aren't really living at all?"

He pulled his hand from hers.

Nev worried about the bodies. He tossed and turned on the rushes that night and spent the next two days furiously weeding the garden and chopping more wood than necessary. He took Bohdan out for a few hours, but there were no bodies about—fresh or otherwise. He found himself hoping the plague would hurry up and get worse. It was a terrible feeling, and he hated himself for it. He even considered asking Kvesnia to protect him from the cultists, but to ask that would require him to admit to what he was, and he was no fool. If she knew what he was, he would be the next body she locked away in her tower.

Renniv came out to see him as he sweated over the cabbages that afternoon. She used a stout stick as a makeshift cane and stood over him, one hand on her hip.

"You know what my mother loved most?" Renniv said. "Cabbages. Plain, unassuming cabbages. She said you could live on cabbage and onions, and we did for a long time."

He sat back on his heels. Wiped his hands on his trousers.

She sat on a nearby stump. "I lived that way after Kvesnia, too. Bare, scrambled kind of living. Quiet. For years. I didn't know what to do with myself until I realized I wanted revenge."

"And what will you do when you have it?"

She laughed, but there was a bitterness in it. "I have no idea."

"Would it be so terrible to just … plant cabbages?"

"It would. I don't want my mother's life. She died with some seer picking through her guts."

"I'm sorry."

"It's what it is," she said, rising. "I just see you here, and I think of her and that other life and how my life would have been very different without Kvesnia. I suspect the life of this town would be different without her, too."

They ate early. Renniv insisted on going for a walk, after, to work on her strength. Nev spent the better part of the walk thinking about the cultists and when they would come back. He considered leaving the house, calling on Kvesnia for protection, and discarded each idea in turn. He had taken Renniv into his house, and it had complicated everything.

Renniv said suddenly, "Who has the best sexual apex?"

"What?"

"You appear deep in thought," she said. "You looked like you needed a distraction. So, the best sexual apex? Men or women?"

He shrugged. "They vary by body, not genitals. Each is different, just as—here." He saw a rogue, faded rambling rose still in flower on the side of the road and plucked it. "What color is this rose?"

"White."

"It's yellow to me. Pale yellow, certainly, but not white."

She lifted the rose from his fingers and caressed her face with it. "What are you getting at?"

"Bodies differ in many things. How we hear, the colors we see, the feeling of rose petals against our skin—"

"Or lips?" She brushed hers against his cheek.

He started. Desire overwhelmed him, so unexpected it took his breath.

She grinned. "You are skittish."

He kissed her. He had been wanting to kiss her from the moment he saw her. He'd wanted to kiss her by the firelight, at breakfast, in bed, here on this path. He wanted to kiss her and keep on kissing her until the breath left his body.

Renniv wrapped her arms around him.

He lost himself for one tremulous moment, then pulled away. "I'm … Should we? I don't want to give you a child, so we should—"

"Oh Nev," she said and she kissed him again, softly this time. "Kvesnia took that all away from me, along with the rest. We can do whatever we like."

"I'm sorry," he said.

"It is what it is." She kissed him again.

He carried her into the house.

Renniv lay back on the tangled bedding, panting. They were both covered in sweat, spent. Nev felt like he was floating on a warm cloud.

She said, "I thought … you didn't *fuck*."

"I did not say that. You assumed." Nev took a bit of her hair in his fingers.

"That's the last time I put words into your mouth."

"I do hope you'll put other things there."

They spent the better part of a week in various states of undress. They could not get enough of one another. Renniv was like a deep, sweet drink that slaked his thirst for an hour before rousing it again, and again. He found reasons not to go to the tower, reasons to stay home, to go on long walks with Renniv as she regained her strength, to teach her to cook a palatable stew—she was a terrible cook—and show her how to feed Bohdan without getting pecked. He was drunk on her, and being drunk on Renniv meant that, for the first time in a very long time, he did not think about the lack of bodies in his cellar. He did not think of the dead at all.

"What's this tattoo?" he asked one morning, tracing the intricate geometric pattern on her belly with his finger.

"A ward," she said. "I got it from another wizard, up in Kostoya a few years ago. It's supposed to protect me from magical *malfeasance.*"

"Does it?"

"I suppose I'll find out when I confront Kvesnia," she said, rolling onto her hip. "What were you like as a child?"

"A child? That was a long time ago." He closed his eyes, saw his own small feet running through a field of golden grass. He tried to recall his mother's face, but could only conjure up her smell, crushed sage and whey from the cheese room.

"I imagine you were a quiet, studious little boy," she said.

"I was a girl," he said, "in the beginning. Already wearing long trousers, though, trying to be like my brothers."

She raised her head. "A girl? Why haven't you stayed in girls' bodies, then? Surely it would be easier to get along in the world as a woman. You could certainly find better employment than ..." She gestured to the hovel.

"As I said, some bodies are more comfortable than others. I prefer male bodies."

"As do I," she said, kissing his throat. "In a much different way, of course."

Nev stared into the rafters, thinking of other conversations he'd had, just like this, with dozens of other lovers. In the end, it turned out the same way, again and again. They loved his bodies. They did not love the corpse-jumper who inhabited them. How could you know a man whose face changed so often?

"We should run away," Renniv said.

"What?"

"Far away from here."

He stroked her hair. "We can't do that."

"Why?"

"You'll tire of me."

"I won't!"

"You will. And you'll tire of the corpses. You'll get old and die and I won't."

"You could very well get old in this body."

"Old enough to outlast you? I don't know. And if I don't? If my faces changes? Think it through, Renniv. I've been here before."

She moved away from him and started dressing. "Of course you have. You've probably had thousands of lovers. I'm just a sideshow, then, in your epic immortal life."

"It's hardly an epic life. It's boring and gross most of the time."

"You could live so much better," she said, stomping into her boots. He noticed that the pressure she put into her injured leg was now almost equal to that she gave her good one. She had nearly healed. It was nearly over.

"I don't want to live better," he said. "I want to live quietly."

"You keep saying that!"

"It's true."

She went to the door. "I'm going to take a walk. Let me be for a bit."

When she came back that night, something had shifted in her. He felt it the moment she walked into the house. She was pulling away from him.

It was then he realized that morning was the first time in over a week she'd said Kvesnia's name out loud.

Nev woke alone.

The house was still.

He went outside to find Renniv and discovered Bohdan and the cart were gone. He swore, a long litany of grotesque epithets in a language he thought he had forgotten. He gazed toward the tower, and suddenly he wanted to take back everything back that he'd said to her the night before. What did he think she would do after he told her they had no future? What would *he* have done?

"Fuck!" he said and began to run.

Nev arrived at the tower out of breath, covered in sweat. He pounded on the door three times, and it opened for him. Bohdan squalled at him from the courtyard. The cart was draped in burlap. He took the cover off and found the cart empty save for his usual tools. He rummaged through the toolbox and found a long utility knife, which he looped onto his belt, and a crowbar he sometimes used to move rubble away from bodies at worksites.

He pounded up the stairs towards Kvesnia's workshop. Heard loud voices. The hiss and pop of some spell.

Renniv yelled, "You think I wouldn't come for you, eventually? You have strangled this town the way you strangled me. How many more people have you tortured here? How many more will you make dance for you?"

"You fool," Kvesnia said, laughing, "you are nothing to me, a bit of detritus, an insect—"

Nev pushed open the workshop door and found tables knocked over and braziers tumbled. Small, slimy creatures were wriggling from broken jars. The room smelled of sulfur and copper and lavender, making his eyes water.

Renniv wielded a knife in one hand and a rope with a small metal ball at the end in the other. A new bruise splashed across Kvesnia's temple. Kvesnia held one hand against her chest. It was her hands that danced to make the spells.

Renniv turned to look at him. "Nev, what?"

"You little shit," Kvesnia said. "She got to you, didn't she? She is a dangerous monster—"

"This isn't for—" Renniv shouted at Nev, and Kvesnia used the distraction to bring up her hand and begin to draw a spell.

Nev jumped over the broken table. He grabbed her bare wrist and stabbed her hand with his knife. She roared and pushed him away. He swung the crowbar, smashing it into her head. She crumpled like a doll, knocking over a weapons display. Two scimitars and half a dozen foreign implements clattered across the floor.

"What are you doing here?" Renniv said, running toward him.

"You left," he said. He bent over, exhausted, and dropped the crowbar. "You left. I was … fucking terrified, Renniv. Please don't leave me."

"You said—"

"I didn't say half the things you think I said. I love you, Renniv."

She raised an eyebrow. "I thought you didn't fight?"

"Why? Because I didn't fight you? Or the cultists? You make many assumptions."

She grinned. "Like the fucking."

He laughed, wincing at the pain in his chest. He was going to be sore tomorrow.

Renniv screamed.

Pain erupted from his left kidney. He looked down and saw the bloodied blade of a massive scimitar jutting from his belly.

Nev pushed Renniv away and staggered, turning just as Kvesnia yanked the blade from his body. Blood gushed across the stones.

Renniv swung the rope above her head and smacked Kvesnia in the face with the little metal ball once, twice, again, crushing the edge of her eye socket.

Nev clutched his gut. Kvesnia went down, head snapping back. Renniv stood over her and smashed in her head again and again, crumpling the wizard's face until it was a mess of blood, brain matter, and bone.

Nev lost his balance. "Ren—"

She turned, face splattered in blood. She panted heavily and at the sight of him, ran forward. Caught him just as he fell.

Renniv pulled him away. But his legs wouldn't hold him more than two steps. She dragged him with her, taking shelter behind the overturned worktable. Bits of broken glass bottles, feathers, and bone littered the floor beneath him, but he hardly noticed. Renniv had her hand over the wound in his belly, but he could feel the wet of the blood all around him, seeping from his back.

"Please," Renniv said, cradling his head in her arms. "Please don't die, Nev. I'm sorry. I love you. I shouldn't have come here. Please—"

"I'm sorry, I—" He could feel the darkness coming, and it terrified him.

He needed to *jump*, desperately. He coughed and hacked and smeared blood from his face. Blood bubbled up through Renniv's fingers. Of course the wound was mortal. He knew it the moment it happened. He'd been stabbed enough times. But Renniv was safe. Renniv would live.

He dug his fingers into her wrist. "I'm—" he swallowed the words. His brain was having trouble making connections now, starved of blood. He had been here many times before.

He needed to jump—

—but the bodies in the basement were gone, burned, and he hadn't touched …

He coughed more blood and gazed past Renniv to the crumpled body of the dead, gloveless wizard. The gloveless wizard whose bare wrist he had grabbed when he stabbed her hand.

"Ren—" He wanted to explain, to prepare her, but his body was going dark, his organs shutting down one by one.

He had to *jump*—

JUMP.

… and there was only one body.

He gurgled.

The world went soft.

Then dark.

A burst of awareness, shocking, like coming up out of a tub of ice.

Nev opened his eyes and gazed at the gnarled, bloodied hand of Kvesnia lying on the gritty floor. He couldn't breathe. A high, keening cry filled the air. A dozen paces away, Renniv held his old body in her arms. Renniv held his old body, an empty vessel. She clutched it to her as if he still inhabited it, sobbing.

Nev felt a surging heat flow through him. He got up on his hands and knees just in time to vomit a clotted mess of blood and bile onto the stone floor. His bowels voided, covering his robe in urine and bloody shit, and the body emitted a rank, violent odor: death. He stayed there on his hands and knees, waiting for his second wind. He was new enough to the body that it felt like he was operating a marionette.

"No!" Renniv yelled.

He jerked his head up. Fell back into his own shit.

Renniv scrambled for the scimitar, teeth bared.

"Renniv, it's me!" he croaked. "It's Nev, Renniv, I'm sorry!" He scrambled back.

She raised the scimitar high, pointing it at him. "Don't even say that!" she screamed. "Don't you dare try that foul trick, you fucking bitch!"

"It's not a trick. Renniv, you know—"

Her lower lip trembled. "You wouldn't. You … wouldn't."

"There was nowhere else to go."

"You fucking monster," she whispered. The scimitar fell from her hand and clattered to the floor. "You bloody fucking monster. You're everything they say you are."

"Please … Renniv."

"Don't say my name. Never say my name." Tears poured down her blood-spattered cheeks. She backed up to the door, took one last look at his former body. "How could you?"

"Please," he said. "Please."

"Monster," she hissed, and ran out the door.

Nev tried to get up and go after her, but he did not yet have his second wind. Adrenaline coursed through his body, a surge of energy repairing the body's wounds and damage, however slight. He vomited again. Stared at Kvesnia's hands as the wound he'd made in her palm closed.

A burst of alertness flowed through him, finally. He stood and tried to run down the stairs, but operating the new body was still awkward. He tripped twice on the long robe and tumbled down the last of the stairs.

When he arrived in the courtyard, she was nowhere to be seen. Bohdan cocked his head and squalled.

Nev limped to the open door of the tower courtyard and gazed out into the street. A little girl was walking alongside her mother, driving geese to the market.

"Look," the girl said, pointing at Nev. "It's the wizard in the tower."

Nev did not live in the tower long in Kvesnia's skin. Inhabiting her body made him sweat and itch, as if he wore an ill-fitting suit. Knowing what this body had done to Renniv made living in it doubly unbearable. He went through Kvesnia's cellars, opening doors belching green mist, cleaning out the stinking cauldrons. He found no living captives in the rooms, only the gory remains of various experiments. As he cleared each room, he could not help but wonder which one had once held Renniv. Which one might have held him, too, in time?

There were many bodies in the tower to choose from, and though he knew it was foolish, he found himself looking for one Renniv might like, one similar to his last, though he knew he had lost her, lost her terribly. Yet he kept looking into the bodies' faces, trying to find something of the face she had loved in them.

None of the faces felt right. But he found one body stacked in the potting room that would have to do. The body was that of a day laborer. Nev remembered bringing him to Kvesnia from an accident at a job site. The body was not handsome, but it was sturdy and broad-shouldered. Most importantly, it was of an age with the body that Renniv had loved.

Nev went up to the crystal mirror in the foyer and stared into his own face as he slit Kvesnia's throat. As he bled out, he jumped—

—into the body of the man in the potting room. Nev slipped into this new skin and made it his own. When he was done below, he went through Kvesnia's rooms in the upper tower, picking his way around magical traps, and found a chest full of coins, enough to last him six lifetimes. He thought of how stingily Kvesnia had paid him, and here she was, sitting on a hoard fit for a dragon.

He faced a decision. Leave the tower and strike off again, his pockets stuffed with what he could carry. Or take up the mantle of the wizard and stay.

It was a risky proposition. He did not like to inhabit bodies that drew attention. But how often did a wizard leave a tower? And in his heart, he knew that if he stuffed his pockets and ran, he would never find Renniv again. She would despise him for what he had done, for what he was, unless something changed.

He closed the trunk and stood.

His only hope of seeing Renniv again was if she came back to him.

Nev walked up the tower steps each morning at sunrise and again at sunset, bringing his tea with him. Whenever anyone came looking for a wizard, he told them she was indisposed, buried in her work. The town soon began to forget what it was to be under her sway; fewer and fewer scurried past the tower with heads bowed

Bohdan had the run of the courtyard and lived there happily until he began to slow and his squall became a true squawk, and then one morning when Nev went to rouse him, he did not move at all. Nev burned him and buried his ashes in the courtyard.

Nev paid a girl from the village to bring him bodies, and because they all assumed he spoke for the wizard now, they did not question him. He specified each body must be dead of natural causes. No more killing. That was what the wizard demanded, he said. When the girl grew older and went off to join the army, he employed her little nephew. And when the cultists came to town again, Nev watched them from the top of the tower. They put up their flyers and chanted their doom and gloom long into the night.

"I will outlast you," he whispered, and he did: for the next autumn, the cult was disbanded by the local magistrate for failure to pay its taxes.

The inquiry revealed the leader for a charlatan who had been siphoning the cult's funds for her own private depravities.

Typical.

How long he passed in that tower, Nev was uncertain. The town grew and shifted around him, the queen was deposed and the whole region shifted into the purview of some other empire, which left them well enough alone as long as the fields flourished. The body he inhabited began to slow and wither. In the crystal mirror in the foyer, Nev saw a face deeply lined, with a scraggly beard and bushy brows. His hair was thinning on top and stuck up in places where he had failed to clip it back evenly. When he woke he marveled at his veiny, wrinkled hands, the skin growing spotty and slightly translucent. Getting up the tower steps became more difficult, but he pushed on. He found himself examining his cellar of bodies more often, touching each of them as if for luck, asking for a few more days, a few more moments.

Waiting.

And so it was one cool autumn day when the leaves were rotting in the newly paved streets, he heard a gentle tap-tapping at the great tower door, so gentle he would have missed it if he had not waited for it for so long.

Nev unlatched the door and peered outside.

An old woman stood in the muddy road, a smudge of soot across one cheek, a new tattoo of a coiled serpent peeking out from under the collar of her loose shirt. An old woman, yes, with a thick mound of white hair twirled around her head, sagging jowls, and deep grooves at the sides of her mouth gave her a dour expression. But her eyes were the same—sharp and dark. When her gaze met his, his heart fluttered the same way it had when she first opened them on the table so many, many years ago.

He still loved her. It was a firm, aching longing that he had carried with him from body to body.

"I've been waiting for you," Nev said.

"All this time?"

"It's hardly been any time at all," he said and opened the door wide.

THE VÂRCOLAC

MATTHEW WARD

One moment the Immortal was an armoured, angular silhouette amid the bare Wintertide trees, given shape by waxing moon and midnight stars. The next, he was a lifeless shadow tumbling down the gorge-side's muddy scree.

"Shields! Shields!" Govadra Tiranas bellowed to be heard over urgent cries and the clatter of crossbows. "They're to the south!"

He shrugged his shield from its leather slings as his Immortals hurried to obey, the dark cloth that concealed its bright colours snagging on the brambles.

The shield shivered beneath a quarrel's impact. Ahead, where the forested crest met the night sky, ragged figures grounded their crossbows and wrestled with reloading cranks. The pale wolf-mask blazons on their tabards shone silver in the moonlight.

To Govadra's left and right, a gappy shield wall snaked beneath the skeletal trees. Cries of alarm yielded to the low, rising growl of men who were ashamed of their brief panic and determined to repay indignity with blood.

Quarrels rained down from the crest and thudded into branches and shields. One plucked at the red-lined cloak of the lone archer standing tall among the cloth-draped shields. Her hood was back, revealing tawny, braided hair and a calculating expression on a pale, youthful face. Another red-fletched quarrel set her cloak twitching, another rent to be repaired in a garment far older than she. She held her pose. Fearless. Unflinching. Her bowstring sang. A scream sounded among the trees.

Govadra grinned, pulling taut the twin scars on his left cheek. Now, as ever, he was proud to call Jennica his daughter, for all that they shared no blood.

As Jennica reached for another arrow, a nearby warrior cast down his shield. Govadra knew his face almost as well as his own. Indeed, it so very nearly *was* his own, the son the mirror of the father, his long, unbound hair and neat beard still dark with the vigour of youth where Govadra's steel grey was fading to white. Moving with a swiftness that belied the weight of golden-scaled armour, Ristane tackled Jennica to the ground.

Quarrels whipped above their heads, cheated by the moment's self-lessness.

Govadra grinned at the flash of Jennica's bared teeth. With a thrust of her elbow, she shoved her rescuer away. He couldn't hear her snarled complaint over the din of gathering battle, but he knew it existed all the same. Even when she'd nothing to prove, a woman still had *everything* to prove, but a brother's love paid such concerns little heed.

Another volley rippled from the crest. Fresh screams joined the moans of the dying. The Tressians on the summit would be weighing the balance as Govadra himself had so many times above a blazing farmstead or a corpse-choked roadway. Was there glory to be had in pressing the attack or wisdom in the retreat? Could the enemy be broken, or would they find their courage? The bleak arithmetic of the contested kingdom of Lasmanora for generations uncounted. It filled graves and fed funeral pyres like nothing else.

Govadra ripped his sword from its sheath. Held it high so the hawk of its crossguard gleamed in the moonlight. His Immortals needed their chieftain's voice. To hear it raised in challenge to the enemy skulking among the trees. "Tiranas Brigantim!"

"*Tiranas Brigantim!*"

The battle cry rippled to a throaty howl, chased on by the clamour of sword hilts striking shield rims. The hawks of Kentae were never prey for long. No matter that the plan was coming apart. No matter that Pieter Villem—the so-called King of Mountains, the self-styled Vârcolac of bloody myth—had likely already fled. There was only the enemy, and the call of steel.

The howl became a roar. Black shields went forward into the storm of quarrels. Cold, crisp air staled with sweat and bitter copper. A Tressian screamed beneath an Immortal's axe. The quarrels grew fitful. Orders rang out, the melodic language of a dying Republic rendered terse by urgency.

Govadra lumbered on, outpaced by younger warriors. An Immortal slumped against a tree, a quarrel protruding from his helm's eye-slit. Another hurled himself against the line of King's Blue shields on the summit. The thin wall buckled beneath his fury, then broke apart. Govadra thrust past a Tressian's belated parry and opened her throat. The woman's twitching body slumped against his shield. He heaved it aside and bellowed his victory skyward.

A tidemark of bodies lined the crest, Immortals' golden armour glinting beneath drab cloaks and patchwork Tressian plate half-hidden beneath blue tabards. More lay on the gentle downward slope beyond, eyes open to the night sky, some mewling with death's approach, others with the silent stillness of those already borne into Otherworld on the Raven's wings.

Fifty paces distant, beneath the trees, its shields locked and steady, a second Tressian line awaited. One thicker and longer than that which had launched the attack.

So this was how the night was to end? Not in vengeance overdue. Not with a monster brought to account. Just one more squalid skirmish against fools who fought and died for Villem's pride.

Govadra gazed down at the young woman he'd slain. Scarcely a few winters older than Jennica. She didn't look like a reiver, a slayer of the defenceless. Perhaps she'd thought herself a patriot, carrying the never-ending war between Republic and Empire into Lasmanora's troubled forests. It hardly mattered. She'd taken up the Vârcolac's wolf's-head blazon. Bound herself to a man who claimed kinship to blood-hungry monsters of legend.

"Form up!" he bellowed. "Make the line!"

Govadra thrust his sword into the rain sodden soil and tore the cloth covering from his shield, setting free the spread-winged hawk of his family emblem. The heraldry of Lasmanora, ever since Emperor Ceredic had named Govadra its regent, decades past. Along the crest, others followed his example. Immortals pressed close, shoulder to shoulder. Stifling. Reassuring. Brothers of the sword with whom Govadra had bloodied a thousand hillsides.

Kellerish, who'd broken the gate at Salleria. Brackon, who fought better drunk than most did sober. Tallavan who'd twice retired from war and had twice been lured back by the boredom of watching grandchildren grow.

On and on. A score of warriors in all. The finest Kentae had to offer. Most were veterans of Lasmanora's conquest. All had spilled blood in the endless battle against the Vârcolac. Duty drove them. Honour guided them. Villem's brigands would never understand, for they were no more soldiers than their master was truly royal.

"Saranal Amyradris!" Eyes on the Tressian line, Govadra offered the salute to an Empress too distant to hear his words. "For the Goddess and the Silver Kingdom! Let the sealanders feel our bite!"

"Father, you cannot," said Ristane.

Govadra stifled a scowl as he turned. Ristane had always been over-cautious, as like to his mother in character as he was his father in aspect, ever apt with a word to soothe or enflame as the course commanded. Not that he was a coward. No child of the Tiranas line could ever be that. But in his honest moments, Govadra recognised that his youngest son—his *only* son, ever since the Vârcolac had slaughtered Ralland and Haldra at Gairna Bridge—was but a shadow of his elders in so many ways.

"Choose your next words with care, boy."

Ristane cast down the splintered ruin of his shield, his left eyelid twitching but brought swiftly under control. "They are too many."

"Too many?" Govadra swept a hand at the Tressian line. "We match them blade for blade, and no Republic cur is equal to a son of Kentae!"

"They're *waiting*." Ristane frowned into his beard, a quirk borrowed from his father. "As many again approach from the east. They'll be here in minutes."

Govadra scowled. "You know this for certain? You've seen them?"

"Jennica has." He pointed to his sister, who stood leaning on her longbow behind the gathering shield wall, her quiver empty and her red-lined cloak open to reveal leather armour and a sword buckled at her waist.

So close, there was no disguising the bloodstains on her armour. Not all her work that night had been done with arrows. The patrol on the riverbank hadn't even seen her coming. Despite the chill, she'd waded into the river to wash the worst of it away while Govadra's men had slipped across the ford unseen and unremarked—slit throats were no friends to respectable attire, no matter how cleanly the work was done. The threadbare, red-lined cloak concealed the rest.

Grey eyes solemn, she offered a sharp nod of confirmation.

Govadra might doubt Ristane, but not Jennica. Never Jennica. She'd sharper eyes than any man Govadra had ever met and could read a trail of bruised leaves and churned mud with a deftness bordering on sorcery. She didn't make mistakes about such things. Had all Lasmanorans possessed her fire, they'd still rule their own land. Had her blood father shared her steel, he'd have claimed the throne after assassins had slain its queen.

Govadra turned back to Ristane. "What would you have me do?"

"We came here for a purpose. Would you lose sight of that?"

"We don't even know that the Vârcolac is still in his lair."

"He is." Jennica's assertion arrived level with Govadra's ear. Through iron self-control, he managed not to jump in surprise, even though he'd last seen her standing several paces distant. "The King of the Mountains cowers in the darkness, trusting to his soldiers to drive us off."

"You can't know that." Childhood petulance that manhood had done little to erase crept into Ristane's tone.

"I can. I do." Jennica folded her arms. "Before I killed the patrol, and I attended to his sentries. He'll have only a handful of guards with him. These others will have to march through us to reach him."

That much was true. Preferring comfort, the bulk of Villem's army had quartered itself in the nearby village. Only their captain and his personal guard squatted in the Marizan Caves like the beasts they claimed to be. Jennica had reported as much after one of her many forays behind the shifting territorial lines, and woodsmen had thereafter confirmed it as truth, those who would take Govadra's coin, at least. So close to the mountains, loyalty was a muddy concept.

They'd waited years for this opportunity. Villem never stayed long so deep in enemy territory. He'd slip away into the mountains as he had so many times before, returning only to drench some undefended village in misery—the bitter, spiteful deeds of a man who yearned to rule Lasmanora, but lacked the strength to hold it, and revelled in the fact that peasants thought him a blood-hungry beast. And it was always *Hadari* blood, for those native sons and daughters who could fight had fled their homeland long ago—a diaspora spread across the continent, begging and sell-swording to survive, dreaming of a homeland restored.

But what good had dreams ever done anyone? Only the sword mattered.

Jennica understood that—it was why she thrived. Her mother never had. For all that Halnica had come to accept Govadra's protection—had even come to return his love, in time—she'd never really grasped what it was to walk the warrior's path. The sacrifice it demanded. The regrettable but necessary cruelties. Understandable enough. War had killed Halnica's first husband and razed her home. It had seen the land of her fathers swallowed up first by the Republic and again by the Empire. It had almost cost her a daughter.

Jennica had fled the pyre of her family home the night the Vârcolac killed her father. A year she'd survived, a child of seven scant winters, before Govadra had found her alone in the deepwoods of the foothills. A muddy, wild-eyed sprite, bundled in the same red-lined cloak she wore tonight—her father's cloak. Govadra still bore scars from her thin, jagged knife. It had been worth the blood to see the gratitude in Halnica's eyes—for the first stirring of regard since he'd pulled her, lost and weeping, from the ashes of her manor house. For those harms alone, the Vârcolac deserved to die. A shame Halnica had not lived to see the promise fulfilled.

For all that his Immortals' eyes were on the sullen Tressian line, Govadra felt their thoughts upon him. Waiting for him to decide whether the night belonged to justice, or to retreat.

"Give me your counsel," he murmured.

Ristane opened his mouth. Jennica cut him off. "The man who killed my father dies tonight." She spoke flatly, her emotion in her welling grey eyes, not her voice. "The man who destroyed my family dies tonight."

Ristane shot her a weary, sidelong glance. Resentful for how, against all tradition, his father tolerated a woman's word in matters of war. Respectful because he understood why. She'd been Govadra's eyes in the Lasmanoran woodlands for half her young life. Never once had she steered her regent—her father—wrong. "The road back will be bloody regardless of our choice. I say we follow through."

Govadra nodded and raised his voice. "Then the Vârcolac dies tonight." His Immortals stood taller and straighter than before. All had lost comrades to Villem's predations. Most had lost kin. The price of a war that had never truly ended. "Tallavan. Can you buy us time?"

The grizzled Immortal flinched, a shadowed scowl visible beneath the close-set helm. "On my life, *savir*. We always knew some of us wouldn't make it back. Find the Vârcolac. Kill him. For my daughters."

A rumble of accord rippled along the shield wall. Brackon nodded. Kellerish offered a stony stare, offended that such a question need be asked. It took more than a sword to make a warrior, no matter what the Tressians believed.

One eye on the line of wolf's-head tabards below, Govadra clasped Tallavan's hand. "Then we finish this as family, for the family we have lost. Kithaga Narai."

"Kithaga Narai, my regent." Tallavan's scowl bled into a solemn smile as he echoed the words that promised a reunion in this world or the next. "Go."

Beckoning to the son of his blood and the daughter of his heart, Govadra plucked his sword from the soil, turned his back on the Tressian line, and descended into the gorge.

Jennica took the lead. Longbow and empty quiver abandoned, she passed like a ghost through the barren trees, retracing a path scouted hours before. She left barely a whisper to mark her passage—stark contrast to Govadra's own descent, betrayed at every step with the crackle of twigs and the heavy, labouring breath of a man with one foot in his prime and another in dotage. Ristâne hung close to his father, eyes as often on the path behind as ahead.

The first sounds of renewed battle rang out as they reached the gorge-bed and its swift-flowing stream. The wordless roar of men rushing head-long into death or glory echoed across the water. The ground shook with the thunder of feet.

"Blessed Ashana, witness your warriors' deeds," murmured Govadra.

Ristâne glanced back uphill. "Tallavan?"

"He's charged them," Jennica replied, her eyes shining with delight.

"Better to grind one enemy to powder than wound two."

"He does his part," said Govadra. "Now we do ours."

Before regret could overtake him, he plunged into the stream. Icy water rushed over the top of his boots and drenched his feet. Downhill over broken and jagged rocks, the stream veered south beneath a bower of black branches. Moonlight revealed a cave's ragged, pitted arch. Inky darkness pooled deeper in.

Govadra crouched. "Where are the sentries?" He spoke softly, though there was little need with battle yet raging to the north.

Jennica crept to his side. "Dead. I told you."

For the first time that night—for the first time in long memory—she sounded unsettled. Govadra's own disquiet rose to meet it. "Where are the bodies?"

There was no unease to be found in Jennica's soft, private smile. A more familiar sight, inherited from the girl she'd once been. It spoke of secrets and mischief, never to be shared. "Hidden."

Ristane grunted. "You *have* been busy."

"Absent sentries rouse less alarm than dead ones." She jerked her head northward. "Not that it matters with that racket, so watch your backs. Danger may be closer than you think."

"Suddenly you're a stranger." He flashed a smile tinged with mockery. "Jennica doesn't know the meaning of consequence. Who are you, and why are you wearing her skin?"

Jennica sniffed. "Perhaps you don't know me so well as you think."

Little chance of that. For ten years, the two had been constant companions. It might even have been their destiny to marry had more fondness—and less rivalry—lain between them.

Govadra waved for silence. "Hush. Anyone left inside will be expecting trouble."

He struck out for the cave. Some ancient hand had scored weathered runes deep into the granite of the lopsided arch. A thin trickle of mist danced above the water. The night air thickened with the stale scent of treasured memory and old friends long gone—of wives and sons dragged into Otherworld's pallid afterlife by the Raven's talons. Govadra shook his head. A Forbidden Place, it would be called in Tressia, what the Rhalesh priests called *cargastira*—thresholds where the ephemeral world bled into the divine. Only the arrogant or the desperate took refuge in such places. The Vârcolac was certainly both. Or perhaps he sought to harness its magic to his own wicked ends? Little would have surprised Govadra any longer.

Govadra's soul shivered as he passed into the cave. Eyes well-used to fighting after sundown took what shape they could from the dull orange light flickering somewhere beyond timeworn stalagmites.

He inched forward, placing each foot with exquisite care. Imagination conjured movement in every dance of shadow and eyes holding vigil in the dark.

The sounds of the gorge now belonged to another world, one not steeped in gentle mist, undimmed by the scent of yesterdays. The battle could have been raging still, or ended a minute, an hour, a month ago. Time's flow meandered through forbidden places, or else a man's perception of it did. With every step, the burden of Govadra's years grew. He gripped his sword tighter, seeking the younger man who'd once borne it to humble Lasmanora's pride—or even the man of middle years who'd spent decades locked in battle with the quarry he hoped to find within the cave.

He found neither, but inched on all the same until he rounded the corner into the wan flicker of torchlight.

The smell struck first, the cloying mist stifled beneath blood's rich, cloying copper. Then, the source. A wide-eyed Tressian corpse lay spreadeagled at the cramped cavern's heart, flesh and clothes gaping with ragged wounds inflicted not by steel, but fang and claw. A sword rested half-submerged in pooling gore that seemed almost alive through interplay of fleeting mist and flickering torchlight.

"Blessed Ashana," muttered Govadra, the simple prayer sour on his tongue.

The body lay with legs together and arms above its head, feet towards the tunnel by which Govadra had entered, and hands aligned with passageways leading deeper into the hillside. Too neatly arranged to have fallen thus. Smeared, swirling lines of bloody, eye-watering runes ran at head-height across bare stone. No language Govadra recognised, though in form they were kin to those graven at the cave's entrance. A back-broken table and two ruined chairs sat against the far wall. That made the victim a watchman, his vigil failed in spectacular fashion.

A sharp intake of breath and the wet swallow of a man fighting rebellious gorge marked Ristane's arrival. No shame in either. The brutality of the battlefield was one thing, this carnage quite another. One had to be steeped in it to hold one's nerve. Jennica ghosted into the chamber a moment after, her eyes more on the daubed, bloody runes than the man who'd served as their inkwell.

"What is this?" Ristane held his voice level, but his eyes darted about the chamber, from runes, to corpse, to the onwards passageways.

"The Vârcolac's work," Govadra replied, careful that his own voice didn't carry. Echoes were treacherous heralds.

"Why would he do this to his own man?"

Jennica sniffed. "Who knows why the Vârcolac does anything?"

Govadra nodded. Villem was no stranger to bloody deeds. That, at least, they shared. Though Govadra prided himself on ruling Lasmanora with justice and wisdom, there were always times when the populace refused to recognise that. Dissenters had to be dealt with firmly—in blood, if no other lesson would take.

But torture? Bloodletting of the kind now on display? That was something he'd reserved only for those who'd spat insults at Halnica. Dear, generous Halnica, who'd never wanted more than to live in peace with the man who'd rescued her from ruin and was as undeserving of a traitor's mantle as any soul Govadra had ever known. It had been mercy that they'd died so swiftly.

Careful of her trailing cloak, Jennica knelt beside the corpse. She dipped her fingers to the livid wound in its chest and raised them to her lips, almost touching, but not quite. Her brow tightening with revulsion, she wiped them clean on a rare patch of unsullied sleeve and glanced away. "No man did this."

"Villem is a man," said Ristane, his eyes fixed on the nearer of the onward tunnels and his voice trembling.

Jennica's eyes flashed. "Is he?"

Old memories gathered in the torchlight. Govadra closed his eyes and begged them to return to the past.

"You shouldn't believe tales spun by Lasmanoran peasants," said Ristane.

Jennica's voice hardened, the insult keener for her bloodline. "And you shouldn't—"

"This is what he wants! Don't you see? It's a warning to keep the superstitious away."

"The Vârcolac killed one of his own men just for that?"

"Don't call him that!" Ristane snapped softly. "He's a man. Flesh and blood. Vârcolacs are nothing but myth."

Govadra opened his eyes. "Enough." The two fell silent, though he'd barely breathed the word. "Even myth contains truth."

Ristane stared at him, eyes wide. "Father—"

Govadra gazed at the corpse. "I wasn't hunting the creature. I didn't believe they existed. No, I sought merely a wayward girl, lost and unloved." He offered Jennica a thin smile. "The miller of Gantrum claimed to have seen her in Brackwood, so I tested the truth of his words, an equerry as my only companion. As we set camp that night … something attacked us. I caught only a glimpse before it tore the lad apart. A wolf walking like a man, or a man wearing wolf's aspect, with a silver pelt and a snarling maw. Shaking with terror, I drove it off with my sword and a brand from the fire. The steel troubled it little, but the flame hurt it. That was the night I earned these." He tapped the twin scars on his cheek.

"You cannot be serious," breathed Ristane.

Jennica said nothing, her eyes pinched tight.

"When dawn came, I tracked the beast to a shallow cave, veiled in mist. Like this one. It was already dying. My efforts in the night had been greater than I'd known. When I took its heart, flesh flowed like water. The fire-blackened pelt melted away. What had lived a beast died a woman. You could have passed her in the street and never known. Perhaps I had."

Ristane grimaced, his face pale in the torchlight.

Jennica stared dully across the cave. "What did you do?"

Govadra shrugged. But even in the recounting, his pulse hammered with old fear. "What could I do? I cut off her head, scattered fleenroot across the body to ward off evil, and buried her. But I was not done with Brackwood. Three expeditions it took, but I finally found you, Jennica. As to the creature? I have never seen another in all my days since, but have no doubt, vârcolacs do not belong to legend alone. It may be that Villem's chosen name carries more meaning than we knew. All these years we named him a monster … The gods love irony."

Jennica stood, her eyes and thoughts still far afield, more ill at ease than Govadra had seen her in many a year. "How long have you known?"

He spat on the corpse to ward off its evil. The old fear receded, if only a little. "I still don't *know*. I have only suspicions and a tally of Villem's monstrous deeds. Your father. My sons. Tallavan's wife and daughters. A dozen villages in as many seasons. This is the first time … The first proof …" He shook his head. No weakness. Not now. He'd killed one such beast. He could kill another. "Man or monster, we kill him."

"If he's here," said Ristane.

"He's here," said Jennica, her voice steady as stone. "The man who killed my father dies tonight. The man who destroyed my family dies tonight."

"Even if he's no man at all?"

"Even then."

Ristane took a deep breath and unhooked a torch from its stanchion. "Two ways forward, and the Vârcolac could be waiting in the shadows of either. Father?"

Govadra nodded. "Go with him, Jennica. If you see Villem, you come back for me. If he attacks, you call for me. Do not face him alone. Keep one another safe."

They departed down the left-and passage, brows furrowed and eyes furtive. Govadra waited for shadow to claim them. Then, he sheathed his sword, tightened the straps of his shield, took the second torch from its stanchion, and set out down the right-hand passage.

Even with the torchlight to banish the shadows, Govadra's mind readily conjured snarling wolf-faces in the dark, and wet, throaty snarls on the edge of hearing. Soon, the passageway narrowed so much that the heavy shield became more encumbrance than protection, so he set it aside and took the torch to his left hand so his right could bear a naked sword. Still, he saw nothing—heard nothing save his own scuffed footsteps and shallow breaths that frosted the air.

Had Jennica been wrong? Had the Vârcolac already fled? Perhaps that would be better.

No. This ended tonight. He owed Jennica that much. More, he owed it to himself.

A choked, gurgling breath whispered down the stony passageway. Govadra froze … but heard no other. Was it his imagination at work? When at last a second ragged breath dispelled all doubt, he crept forward, torch raised and sword ready.

He found the Tressian where the tunnel wended hard to the right. She lay on her side among the stalagmites, hair bloody and matted to her scalp. A dark, smeared trail led deeper into the caves. Eyes wide in the torchlight, she reached out a trembling, filthy hand.

"Help me …" she gasped in Tressian low-tongue. "Blessed Lumestra, help me …"

Govadra spat at the evil of the sun goddess' name. "So he turned on you?" He glanced at the wide, livid gash at the woman's waist. There was no help for her in the ephemeral world, even had he been inclined to grant it. "You knew what manner of man he was."

"When night fell … Hunted us one by one."

Govadra crouched beside her. "Where is he? I can't save you, but I can avenge you."

But the woman was already gone.

"Useless sow. Rot in Otherworld." Rising, Govadra peered along the blood trail. That, at least, he could follow.

A bestial howl echoed out of the darkness.

Govadra froze mid-step. He'd known since the watchman's body. Perhaps a piece of him had known even before that. Villem had always favoured Forbidden Places as lairs, just as the creature of Brackwood had done. Maybe they called to such beasts. Maybe they made them what they were.

A second howl. A man's scream.

An icy fist closed about Govadra's heart and squeezed tight. "Ristane!"

He ran on through the echoes. He no longer feared what might be waiting in the dark, not for himself. But terror for his son—his only surviving son? It smothered his thoughts, stifled every breath. Numbed the pain of shin and knee striking stone. It blinded him to all save the need to keep moving, to close the distance.

"Ristane!"

The darkness offered no reply.

"Ristane!"

At last something moved on the edge of the torchlight. One staggering figure supporting another, her arm about his waist and his across her shoulder. A tattered, red-lined cloak snagged against stalagmites. Booted feet scuffed against loose stone. Even as Govadra closed the last of the distance, the crackling flame gave shape to Ristane and Jennica. The latter stumbled, pitching both to the ground.

"Jennica!"

She propped herself up on an elbow. The other arm, sheeted and sticky with blood, she tucked close to her chest. Her scabbard was empty. "Father?" she gasped. "He saved me. He saved me …"

The fist about Govadra's heart squeezed tighter still. Numbness crept across his chest as he fell to his knees beside Ristane. His sword slipped from slack fingers and clanged against the stone floor. His head hung to his chest for want of strength to keep it level.

"My son, my son … I told you to call for me. Why didn't you listen?" The words stuttered to silence as Govadra took in the ravaged throat and livid claw-marks to cheek and brow—the bloody, torn scales above Ristane's belly. "Why didn't you listen?"

The final words came more as howl than speech, thickened by sorrow and choked off by a sobbing fit beyond control. Time crawled, stretching heartbeats to agony. In that eternity, sorrow faded. Wrath burned away the numbness and the tears, for what use were tears to the dead? What worth was sorrow? Only blood reshaped the world. Only steel slew monsters.

"I was too slow," gasped Jennica. "I couldn't … I'm sorry …"

Head held high once more, Govadra turned from Ristane and gripped Jennica's chin in his hand, forcing her to meet his gaze. "You are not responsible. You'd have saved him if you could."

Jennica swallowed, eyes downcast.

Laughter echoed along the cavern. Even muffled by distance, Govadra marked the raw, broken notes of madness. Whatever sanity Villem had once known was long spent.

Govadra rose. Determination hardened sorrow to steel. "Did you see where he went?"

"There's a chamber. With a door." Bracing her back against a stalagmite, Jennica inched upright. She kept her arm tucked close, her hand pressed against the torn leathers above her ribs. She stifled a gasp as blood oozed between her fingers and grimaced a scowl away. "I'll show you."

Govadra set his hand against her shoulder, careful not to disturb her wounds. "No."

"I must …"

"Trust me. Honour me." He glanced towards Ristane's body, but his heart failed him and he looked hurriedly away. "You're all I have left. Stay with your brother. I'll return."

Reclaiming his sword, Govadra set off into the dark, beyond the side passage that had led Ristane to his doom. Past the mutilated bodies of those who'd stayed true to Villem through his madness and paid for their misplaced loyalty. Through it all, the laughter danced upon the mist. Govadra scarcely heard it. The hand about his heart was but a memory. No fear. No sorrow. Only need remained. Need, and the anger that gave it licence.

He gave no thought to the door that barred his way. Nor to the heavy, oiled bolt he slammed back with a jerk of his hand. The strike of his boot crashed the door back on its hinges. Sword in one hand, torch blazing in the other, he hurled himself into the space beyond.

"Villem!"

The chamber was not of the bare rock of the outer passages but dressed stone—a meeting place or feast hall for perhaps a dozen folk, lit by torches. A timber floor stretched between the walls, crowded with barrels and crates. At the room's heart, low benches sat before a broad table. And slumped on the nearest, head bowed so that his lank, white hair touched his knees, sat Pieter Villem, the King of the Mountains. The Vârcolac.

Whatever monster Villem had been minutes before, he now wore the form of a man. A tattered, unkempt wretch with a filthy, matted beard and unwashed face. Blood stained his pallid hair pink. His torn tabard was dark as wine. He'd always been wiry—the gift of a life lived hard, he'd boast to his victims—but gaunt, sunken features spoke to a man worn thin by disappointment. Pitiable, perhaps, had he been deserving of such largesse.

A pair of corpses lay at his feet, their wolf's-blazon tabards bloodied and ravaged in the manner long since familiar. A naked sword lay on the table. A length of rope, its strands split, lay strewn across the dead.

Villem raised his bloodshot eyes to Govadra's. "So you're here? Of course you are. You deserve everything that comes to pass this night. There's no running from it. Not for either of us."

"I deserve this?" Govadra roared. "You killed my sons!"

"And you hanged my wife for no other crime than that I loved her!" Villem shouted. "At Tannervale you slit my brother's throat and cast his body into the valley. When I wanted peace, you gave me nothing but slaughter and tears! We are both bloody to the neck."

"You're a monster!"

"We are both dead men and have earned it a hundred times over for making Lasmanora our battleground. So come, finish it if you can!" A dry, rotten chuckle crackled forth. "I'm tired of running, and it's the only satisfaction you'll have from me."

Villem snatched up his sword and flung himself across the room. Govadra swept his sword to the parry. Steel chimed as he struck aside the Tressian's blade. Flames roared as he swung the torch at Villem's face. The Vârcolac ducked the flames and lunged. Govadra twisted aside. The sword-point meant for his belly instead scraped harmlessly across golden scales.

Villem pressed his attack, howling, cursing and spitting as he struck at shoulder, hip and thigh. Govadra retreated, meeting each flash of steel with his own, alert for the inevitable moment when Villem tired of this game of swords, sloughed off the form of man, and let the beast run free.

"Where's your fire?" Villem crowed. "No wonder your whelps died so easily. They had a spineless cur for their father!"

"You'll not speak of my sons!"

Letting the torch fall, Govadra sidestepped Villem's lunge and sprang. He closed his fingers around a handful of grimy hair and yanked hard. The Vârcolac howled and stumbled. He howled all the louder when Govadra hacked down, the steel slicing through the cloth and flesh of Villem's shoulder and jarring on bone.

Villem's sword clattered from his hand. Growling his triumph, Govadra punched him in the face with his sword-hand. Revelling in the brief resistance of cartilage and bone, he yanked again on Villem's hair, reeling him in for another blow. Villem's teeth broke in a wet grisly crunch. Blood gushed from his ruined mouth.

"Show me the monster!" screamed Govadra. "Show me the monster who killed my son!"

Slick with blood and spittle, Villem's broken face contorted into a broken smile. "You'll … see it … soon enough." He spat away a tooth. "Always cruel … seldom clever …"

Govadra roared as red-hot pain lanced into his left thigh, the dagger's upward thrust cheating golden scales to find flesh. Blood slicked his leg and pooled in his boot.

His last shred of self-control turned to fire.

Letting his sword fall, Govadra took Villem's head in both hands and slammed it down onto the table's heavy timbers.

"For Ralland!"

Again.

"For Haldra!"

Again.

"For Ristane!"

His world wreathed in red, Govadra lost track of how many times he rammed Villem's head against the table. He'd only the memory of a dull crack and the distant awareness that at some point the Vârcolac's body had gone limp.

Only when the wet, pulpy mass beneath his hands was no longer recognisable as a man and his arms shook with exertion, did Govadra let the body fall. With trembling hand, he wrenched the dagger from his thigh and collapsed on a bench.

"Over …" Govadra murmured, somehow disappointed. Where was the swell of triumph? All these years at Villem's throat. *Something* should have stirred. Had the dagger done more damage than he'd thought? If Villem had pierced the artery, he was already dead. No. Not after everything the night had cost. "It's over."

"Not yet," said Jennica. "For you, there is a little more to come. But only a little."

She stood in the doorway, hunched to favour her wounded side, her eyes on the ruin that had once been the self-styled King of the Mountains.

"Jennica? It's done." One arm against the tabletop, Govadra made to stand. He sank to the bench as his wounded leg folded beneath him. "Help me."

Her gaze didn't flicker from the corpse. "The man who killed my father is dead."

"Jennica, if Villem's men corner us here—"

"By now, they're dead too."

Govadra shook his head, piecing together words through his weariness. "Tallavan might have destroyed the shield wall, but he hadn't the numbers to fight the others. At best, he has retreated. At worst …?"

At last, Jennica looked at him. *Through* him. "I lied. The second force wasn't Tressian. They're Borderers. Sons and daughters of Lasmanora who remember my family … and what was done to them. They'll settle whatever your Immortals and Villem's soldiers left of one another. I'll join them when I'm done here."

Govadra gazed at her, a chill creeping into his bones. The door had been bolted from the *outside*. He'd been too lost in rage to consider that before now. Villem hadn't been waiting. He'd been a prisoner … and Jennica had begun the night filthy with blood. "What is all this?"

She stepped into the chamber, a face that had seldom beheld him with aught save regard now contorted and bitter. "My mother was a proud woman, and she loved my father. I can only imagine how you twisted her to make her come willingly to your bed."

"Twisted her? I adored her!"

"You cared only that she legitimised your rule. And if she felt anything at all, she was afraid of you! You kept her walled up behind guards, controlled who she saw… even what she said!"

"That isn't so." Govadra sought words that would convince, but his thoughts were full of mist. "I'd have done anything to keep her from the Raven."

She drew closer, teeth gritted. "You drove her into his arms."

"I made her family. I made *you* family."

"I'd found one long before you shackled me to your keeping. There is kindness beneath the boughs of Brackwood that a man like you would never understand." Jennica gestured at Villem's corpse. "How else could I have survived when that butcher burned my home? I was seven years old, half-mad with terror and lost in a forest full of teeth! Amalie took me in. She'd no use for civilisation, nor it for her, but she cared for me for almost a year. Until you slaughtered her. Two families. You stripped both away."

Amalie. The vârcolac of Brackwood? "I didn't know, I swear. I couldn't have known."

"You wouldn't have cared if you had. Ten years I've waited. Ten long years, watching as the men who destroyed my life ravaged my homeland. You were both always so careful, never alone, even among family, but once I tracked the 'Vârcolac' to his lair I knew I could finally make an end of you both. To think, if you'd hated each other less, this would never have been possible. Two pretenders, fighting over a land not theirs. I enjoyed tonight more than I should, but it is such a small sin. I shall bear it."

"Why the deception with Ristane?" The words rasped at his throat. "Why save Villem for me? Why bring me here at all?"

"Because otherwise you might have died hoping that Ristane had survived. I wanted you to *know* your son was dead, and with him the last of your family. I wanted to see the hope slip from your eyes. As for the rest? In your way, you cared for me. Villem's death was my gift to you, to settle that debt. Yours is my gift to the mothers you destroyed. Before you killed her, Amalie gave me a piece of her to keep me safe. I've carried it with me all these years, coiled around my soul." Jennica looked sharply up. Grey eyes shone amber with something other than reflected torchlight. A sly, hungry smile touched her lips. "Would you like to see it?"

"Jennica, I beg you—"

She threw back her head and cried out. Blissful laughter became a throaty, rippling howl. Flesh flowed like water, drowned by a pelt's silvery sheen as young woman's features bled away into a lupine muzzle. Joints snapped and reshaped into a form not quite human nor wholly wolf, hunched and rippling with power. Too late, Govadra understood why she'd refused a coat of rigid golden scales in favour of looser-fitting leathers that night.

With a silent prayer that his wounded leg would hold, Govadra stumbled for the door. Jennica—what had *been* Jennica—lashed out. Black claws scattered golden scales from his armour and ripped deep into flesh. A second swipe struck him to the ground. Then she was atop him, fangs bared inches from his face.

"Ristane fought me. Be proud of that." The voice was still Jennica's, and yet someone else's also. Something old. "And he didn't beg, even when he knew he couldn't win. His spirit weeps that his father tried to run."

Govadra's right hand jerked, grasping blindly for something—anything—that might serve as a weapon. His fingers brushed the sculpted hawk-hilt of his sword. His heart leapt. "I gave you everything!"

"Not yet," Jennica growled. "But you will. The man who killed my father is dead. The man who destroyed my family dies now."

Govadra's straining fingers closed around the sword's hilt in the same moment Jennica's fangs tore out his throat.

ON WINGS
OF SONG

DEBORAH A. WOLF

The ship which would bear Lille away from all she had ever known bucked and strained against the mooring ropes, as eager to be away as she was. The sailors needed nothing less than one more girl to trip over, so Lille sat cross-legged atop a crate of figs and played her kithara. The cool salt air, the sweat-slicked men, the smell of ripe fruit rising from the crate spoke to her and, through her, to the music. Even through the anticipation of her first sea voyage and the confusion of sailors and travelers she could hear a new song calling to her, begging to be born. Lille bent her neck and let her fingers play across the strings of her instrument, straining to hear what it had to say.

And there it was, light as a gull's feather blown in on the wind, delicate as the pale foam that was all that remained of the sea king's court. A song dancing before her on newborn legs, tentative and lovely, a chorus like thunder, and the aria rising above—

"A perfect day for sailing, wouldn't you agree?"

And the song darted away like a little fish, back to the depths whence it had come. Lille looked up from her kithara, scowling. The young man who stood before her might have been half a god, he was that beautiful. His smile faltered as he looked at Lille, and his smooth cheeks reddened.

"I am, I ... forgive me, Blessed Lady. I did not mean to intrude."

"Then why did you?" Lille asked. The handsome stranger was staring at her face, at the smattering of wine-red scales and silvery eyes that marked her as having been touched by Allyr.

Blessed, indeed. She might have told him that such a blessing was as good as a curse, but she owed the man nothing. She bent back over her kithara, wishing he would leave.

"Your music," he answered at last and smiled. "You are quite good. Is that a new song by Arion? I have not heard it before."

"No," she answered without looking up.

He chose not to take the hint. "You wrote that, didn't you? I knew it! You must be headed to Taresia. It seems I will have competition after all."

She did look up, at that. "You are a bard."

He bowed again. "Even as you yourself, beautiful lady, and on my way to Taresia to compete for gold and glory. Though *I* have not had the great good fortune to have been touched by a god ... yet. All men know that the gods are drawn to beauty. I may get my chance." He winked at her.

She could not help but laugh. And after all, the day was glorious, the stranger was handsome, and she was setting off on her very first adventure.

"I am Lille," she said.

"Zymander," he answered.

Lille eyed him sidelong, mouth twitching in amusement. "Your mother named you after the King of Kings?"

Zymander spread his hands wide and shrugged. "What can I say?

My parents had high hopes for me. Alas, I became an artist."

Their laughter rang out across the amaranthine sea as the ship set sail.

Zymander entertained them one starlit night, when the sea was smooth as glass and the wind had died down to whispers. His kithara was fine—just not as fine as Lille's. And his voice was sweet—just not as sweet as Lille's. He should have studied the craft another year or two, she thought, listening to him sing about kings and gods, about battles and heartbreak. He should have gone out into the world and lived a little more, so that the words he sang would ring true.

He should have chosen any other year in which to compete because this year was hers.

"What about the Blessed One?" shouted one of the sailors, when Zymander stopped to sip some wine and smile at the men's praise. "Yes!" shouted another. "Let the girl sing too!"

Lille did not wish to outshine Zymander and cause bad blood between them. Neither did she wish to give him a closer look at what she could do before they were called to sing in Taresia. She tried to demur, pleading the late hour and the wine gone to her head.

Then Zymander turned such a smug look toward her that Lille climbed up on a wine barrel and struck a minstrel's pose.

"My kithara, if you please," she asked the first mate. A handsome enough man with the tongue-twisting name Berkhof, he had been captured and made a slave in some faraway war and had only recently purchased his soul back from the slave mages.

"Thank you," she said when he handed her kithara up to her and took a moment to tune it.

"Sing Arion's hymn to Hektos!" cried one sailor, whose skin was a prayer rug of tattoos.

"Sing Tathere's hymn to The Lovers," said Berkhof, ever hopeful.

"No," Lille said, and they quieted. "No. We have been blessed." she struck a note on her kithara, beautiful and true, and let it ripple across the waves like a call to prayer. "Blessed, I say, with a safe voyage, and true winds ... until tonight." There was some laughter at that among the sailors, and she smiled down at them from her wine-barrel stage. "Tonight, I will sing of the sea god and his twelve lovely daughters.

"I will sing of Allyr Golden-Tongue, king of the nine seas." Here she struck a strong chord that crashed and thundered like waves in a storm.

"I will sing of Khrissis, who loved him to her doom." She strummed a chord delicate and sad.

"And I will sing of the sirens, their daughters, each of them lovelier and more perilous than the last."

Then she raised her voice and played her kithara, knowing that for these poor souls it would be the most beautiful thing they would ever hear, though they spend their lives listening. She let the words and the music carry them far away to places and wonders they would never find, though they spend their lives seeking.

She sang of a sea captain and the ship who loved him. It was an old song, and tragic. It suited her mood.

Dolphins come to swim beside the boat. Perhaps they were drawn by her music—certainly, they were drawn by her music. The sight of them caused the ship's crew and her passengers to exclaim aloud. Beloved of Allyr, believed to possess the reincarnated souls of heroes lost at sea, dolphins were always a good omen.

As she gazed into the water, Lille saw what the others could not. There were siren faces among the dolphins, strange-eyed, sharp-toothed and smiling. One of them beckoned to her and they laughed like gulls. Lille's heart pounded wildly in her chest, glad despite the terrible danger. Sirens. Daughters of Allyr. Her sisters.

Just then the wind rose to fill their sails and the ship lurched forward. A cry rose among the sailors that the Blessed One's song had pleased the sea god, and her presence among them would bring them luck.

They were called back to their work by a stern-faced officer, thankfully before the smitten Berkhof could work up the courage to beg for her hand in marriage. The men and women who had heard Lille play moved about as if dazed. Some of them were trying to hum snatches of Lille's song. Some of them were crying. She smiled.

"That was cruel," Zymander said. He said the words lightly, as if in jest, but his eyes were dark and unhappy. "To show them a glimpse of a dream and snatch it away again."

Lille lifted her chin high. "We are bards," she reminded him. "It's what we do."

Where did you learn to play like that?" He asked later, after the rest of the passengers had retired and the moon-kissed the sea.

Lille shrugged. "I practice a lot." She might as well have said *the sea is wet* or *the stars are many*.

"Practice, huh." His mouth drew into a sharp frown. "I practice. A lot. Where did you *learn* to play?"

Lille drew her kithara close to her chest. "Tutors."

"Private tutors, I might have guessed from your golden rings and fancy manners," he said. "In your father's palace?"

She drew herself up to her full height, though she wasn't very tall, and spoke in a cool voice.

"In a palace, yes. The palace of my queen mother's husband. As they kept me locked away in a far tower, I had little else to do."

She could see him working it out, and his lush mouth softened into a little 'o' of dismay. "Because you are ..."

"A god's bastard. Too dangerous to kill, lest my death displease Al-lyr." She struck a dissonant chord. "Too dangerous to live among people who might use me for their own ends. I was kept in a marble cage day and night, weeping for the injustice of the world, until a kind servant brought me a kithara and taught me how to play."

"How did you escape?"

"The gods cursed me with a bastard's life, but they gave me three weapons." Lille held up three fingers one by one. "They gave me my wits, they gave me my voice, and they gave me music."

"You flew away on wings of song?" His tone was wry.

"Not at all. That just makes a better story." She smiled. "The truth is that the old king died, my mother married her captain of the guard and made him her consort, and they let me go free on the condition that I never return. My mother said I look too much like my father, and that it was dangerous to keep me around."

"Your father??"

Lille shrugged.

"I am a bastard, too," Zymander said. "Left on the temple steps with a milk goat, ten gold coins, and a Taresian short sword. My mother could not have children of her own, so she bought me for a good price—I was a handsome little thing, and the priests liked to whisper that I must have been fathered by a god—and here I am, dashing my parents' hopes of glory by entering a competition we both know you are going to win."

Lille inclined her head. It was true.

"Perhaps you are the son of a god," she said, half in jest. "Or at least a demigod. You are certainly pretty enough."

Zymander snorted. "More likely I am the son of a Taresian soldier who sweet-talked his way into some farm girl's bed and left when her belly grew big. But, Lille," he reached out and brushed a finger over her scaled cheek, "you are truly Blessed. I have never heard anyone play half as well as you do."

"Oh, that." Lille shrugged away from his touch and struck a chord that sounded like laughter. "I told you—I practice a lot."

"Well then, I'll just have to practice day and night, and in a hundred years I'll be as good as you." He laughed, but Lille could hear the anger lingering in his voice, like the feeling in the air after a storm.

"Maybe," Lille said.

Zymander did try. He sat at the ship's pointed bow, in a little space where he might keep out of the sailors' way, and played till his fingers bled and his voice broke. Then he bound his fingers with rags torn from his fine shirt and played some more. He was good—quite good, Lille admitted—and had the looks and style to earn any number of patrons and a seat at some king's table.

But Zymander's charm and skills would not be enough to let him win this year's competition, nor any other when Lille might play. Zymander was good, but she was brilliant.

From the moment Old Wylla had placed a kithara in her hands Lille had known that music was her path, her calling. Though walls might be built around her and a key turned in the lock, when Lille sang, when she played, she was free. She breathed song as others might breathe air, drank music like others might drink wine; these things, more than the scales on her face or her sea-silver eyes, marked her out as a Blessed favorite of the gods.

And she could see that Zymander knew it. Sweat dripped from his brow onto his instrument, but it would not be enough.

Thwarted by a complex transition that limped where it should leap and fell where it should fly, he lifted his kithara above his head as if he might smash it to the deck, his face twisted in anger.

"Don't!" Lille cried out. It was a lovely instrument, and she could not bear to see it hurt.

Zymander lowered the kithara and his guard, and for a moment Lille saw the raw anguish of his need. It was a hunger beyond feeding, she knew, a thirst beyond water and wine. It was the same mad passion that made men fashion wings of feathers and wax and fly too close to the sun. To tear one's soul free of mortal flesh and fly on wings of music. To soar.

"Let me show you. Here, your wrist is too stiff, you are holding your kithara too close. You can't clutch at the music. You have to hold it loosely. Gently. Like a bird cupped in your hands. Like a lover."

"If I had a kithara as fine as yours—"

She plucked Zymander's kithara from his hands, held it loosely. Gently. Stung by his petulance and excuses, she struck the first chord of a hymn that she had written in anger, with magic. A dangerous thing in these times, among these men. A challenge to king and god. Reckless.

Lille did not care. She sang:

Lo! is this the king whose glances
Weighed like golden manacles about my wrists?
These the wild, bewildering rages,
That with words of wrath and withering
As with walls of marble bound me ...

Four movements she played of her hymn, the likes of which had never been heard in the living world. Lille had invented the style just that spring and had named it *Tyrambus* after the bardic god of music and wine. It was a wildly enthusiastic form of long poetry meant to be improvised upon with each playing. Sung by a master bard, a *Tyrambus* had the power to excite an audience to dangerous passions.

Even though she did not play the fifth verse and complete the song's spell, Lille's voice rippled across a sea gone smooth as glass. She let the words, the music, and the magic fade away. It was as still and quiet as if the ship had borne them over the end of the world and into the Dead Sea.

A muffled sob broke the silence. Lille looked up and found every face turned toward her, wide-eyed and mute. Zymander was staring at her, and his cheeks were wet with tears.

She smiled.

"Who are you?" Zymander whispered. "Who *are* you?"

Lille shrugged. "I am just a girl," she said. "A girl who likes to sing." Her voice banished the last of the spell she'd woven over them, as a strong wind dispels the fog, and people began to stir. There was applause. There were tears. The audience was hers.

Zymander stepped closer. "I don't believe you. When you play ... when you play, you are as beautiful as Avanye. You are as dangerous as the sirens."

"Shush," she told him, handing his kithara back as if it were nothing. "They will hear you."

👑

That night Lille woke from a dream of drowning. She had to touch her unhurt skin many times before she was quite sure that the sea-thing she'd dreamt of had not wrapped its tentacles about her throat and dragged her down to a silent death. Her heart beat painfully hard, sending blood to pound in her ears like the angry sea.

When at last she had calmed herself a new sound caught Lille's attention, and she bolted upright in her hanging cot so that she cracked her head on the ship's wooden beam. Someone was playing *her song*.

The music faltered as its player struck a wrong chord, a man's voice whispered a curse, and the singer began anew.

Zymander, she thought, shocked and furious. He was trying to steal her song and likely meant to play it at the competition. Her song, over which she had wept and bled. That useless boy would play it before the court and then he would smile, basking in the praise that should be hers. Would be hers. Lille had one thing in this life, just this one thing, and she would die before she let him steal it.

"He will *not*," she spat, swinging her legs over the edge of the cot and dropping to the splintery wooden planks.

Lille scrambled up the ladder to the ship's deck wearing nothing but a short shift and her fury. Five angry strides carried her past a pair of sailors sleeping against the ship's mast. Zymander looked up from his kithara, eyes widening at the sight of her. Even as he opened his mouth to speak, she slapped him hard enough to snap his head back.

"*Mmmg!*" he grunted, pressing the fingers of one hand over his mouth, where she had split his lip open.

"You son of an ass, how dare you try to steal my song?" she shouted.

"*Ssssst,*" he hissed around his bloody fingers, eyes darting from side to side to see if anyone had heard.

Let them hear, Lille thought, let them wake! She would let the whole world know what Zymander had tried to do, that he was nothing but a thief. She drew back her arm and hit him again.

Zymander lunged at Lille, and she opened her mouth to yell. But he was faster than she had expected and surprisingly strong. He grabbed her about the waist and clapped one hand over her mouth.

"You had to spoil everything, didn't you, princess?" He whispered into her ear. You with your high airs and tutored voice and your fine instrument. It probably cost more than my whole village is worth, and you think you're so special. You think you're so good."

He was hurting her. His arm about her waist wrapped tight, squeezing like the sea-thing in her dreams, and his hand on her mouth pushed her head back. Lille rolled her eyes at him, angry and afraid.

Zymander smiled. He bent her neck so far back she was sure it was going to snap.

"Blessed one," he said in a mocking tone, "you were born with far too many gifts and I was given nothing. *Nothing.*" His breath stank. "So, I am going to take your music and your life and make them mine. I am going to play this song before the king. I am going to win the fortune and glory that might have been yours. And when they ask me how I did it, I will tell them—"

—he pressed his lips against her temple—

"—that I practiced a lot."

The sky grew dark, the stars dim and far away. There was a sharp crack and suddenly Lille was flying, tumbling through the air like a broken thing.

The warm water received her with hardly a splash, and Lille sank down, down, down, where the music could not find her.

Oh Sister, Sweet Sister, tell us where are you going?
The seagulls are crying,

The currents are flowing!
Your teeth are white as seed-pearls,
Your flesh soft and glowing,
But you should not be here,
Oh, sweet silly little land-sister,
Down here with the shipwrecks
And bones of drowned sailors,
Oh! Oh! La!

Lille was dragged to wakefulness as a fish caught in a net is dragged from dark waters, and when she woke, it was to such pain that she only wished to sink back down into the murk. To sleep, to forget, to cease.

But something sharp poked her cheek, and a sibilant *hsssssst* conjured an image of snakes and dragons. She was not alone.

Lille held her breath, waiting for terror to come—surely, she should be afraid—but nothing happened. She felt scooped out, hollow; the worst had already happened to her, many times over, and she had nothing left to fear. Still, she did not want to be eaten by snakes or dragons.

Lille opened her eyes the tiniest bit and found herself lying on a white sand beach, very near the water. Her mouth and eyes were caked with salt, and every breath crackled painfully in her lungs. She moaned, rolled over onto her side, and vomited. She squeezed her eyes shut again, feeling miserable and weak.

Well, she thought, shakes and dragons might not wish to eat such a wretched little piece of meat. And perhaps she did not very much wish to die.

She vomited again and rolled away from the stink of it, pressing her face into the soft hot sand. The snakes and dragons, whichever she had heard, would either kill her or let her be. There was nothing she could do about it.

The thing hissed again, an almost musical sound which rose and fell. It was not an animal noise at all, she realized, but a voice.

"*Sii nasss asssteh?*"

"*Asssteh esdodimoss?*" answered another sibilant voice. "*Assteh nossstimo?*"

Lille groaned again and struggled to her knees. If they were going to consider whether or not to eat her, she thought she should add something to the debate. Then she realized that she had understood them.

Lille's eyes flew open and she found herself staring at a girl perhaps a few years younger than herself. She was plump and dark, with very round eyes the same color as Lille's, that rare sea-washed silver which had marked her out as a god's bastard. Her face was scaled, as well. But where Lille had a spattering of crimson upon her face, this girl was masked all about the eyes with brightly colored scales. Her face glittered like a queen's jewels, red and blue and gold, and a thin line of black flowed upward from the corner of each eye like the stroke of a poet's brush.

She was beautiful. She was not remotely human.

The siren blinked back at Lille, as startled as she was, and then drew back with a hiss.

"*Mestissos!*"

"Well," Lille replied, "there is no need to be *rude.*" She drew herself into a seated position, legs crossed, and tried not to look half dead.

The girl stared. Lille stared back. Those *eyes.*

Another voice spoke in low and resonant tones, and Lille's heart lurched again. She turned her head and saw an older woman with those same silver eyes staring from a mask of yellow and blue scales. She stepped forward and bent at the waist, peering into Lille's face. Lille tried not to flinch at the woman's cold, fishy breath. The siren raised a slender, webbed hand, and ran short claws gently over the scales on Lille's cheek.

"*Asti issta,*" she said. Her voice was low, rough, strange but not unpleasant. "Little sister. We have saved your life. You owe us your mortal soul." And she smiled. Her teeth were very sharp.

"Well, now." Lille swallowed and tried to smile. "Of course, I am grateful—if indeed you have saved my life, and I did not simply wash up on this shore—but my soul is too steep a price to pay. Perhaps I can interest you in—in a golden ring, or perhaps a song—" Her voice faltered as the woman's grin widened.

"Ah," rasped the siren, "it is always a pleasure to barter with a mortal." She seated herself cross-legged before Lille and stretched her hand out in an imperious gesture, palm up. "Let us see this golden ring. Let us hear this song. And perhaps we will not eat you, after all."

The sirens laughed, and the bargaining began.

The older siren's name was Iloneth, her younger companion Sasra. Others emerged from the waves to join them, later: Essath and Pollonia, Carara and Nyssa. They were sisters, and they called Lille 'sister' as well. She wasn't sure how she felt about this, but certainly, it was better than being eaten.

They brought her to a little south-facing cave which was high enough on the cliff wall that an incoming tide would not drown her and deep enough to keep her dry in the worst of weather. She wove a mat for herself out of seagrasses and built a little fire in the back of her cave, though this frightened the sirens, and they would not come anywhere near it, nor eat the fish they'd brought her once she had cooked it. A day's exploration had discovered a small freshwater spring, a handful of olive trees perhaps planted by sailors and forgotten, and dozens of friendly, tailless little rodents which were good company and excellent eating.

When the sirens came to visit they would often bring small treasures to Lille: fish, bits of wood or torn sail, a broken harpoon. Sweet Nyssa, littlest sister, brought pretty shells and handfuls of sea-flowers that wilted as soon as they were out of the sea. One morning she shyly presented Lille with a splendid pearl almost as big as her fist, and Lille, in turn, gave her a golden ring like the one she'd given Iloneth. They had many beautiful things in their city below the waves, the sirens had explained, but no silver or gold of their own, and these were greatly coveted.

Lille wove necklets and wristlets out of palm fronds, which her sea-sisters decorated with shells and bits of coral. She drew pictures in the sand of cities and land beasts and told them stories, of which they never seemed to tire. It amused her that they dismissed dragons as uninteresting, having many such great serpents beneath the sea, but begged for tales of horses and birds, of cats and dogs. Lille promised that if ever she escaped to the mainland she would return and bring a dog with her and they might pet it. When the older sirens explained to Nyssa that she could not keep a dog in their home under the sea, and what would happen if she tried, she wept as if her little heart had broken.

They danced one time for Lille, though it pained them to do so, their finned and silver-scaled limbs being made for darting about the ocean and not treading upon the hard ground. When they moved it was with such grace that Lille felt ensorcelled. It was her turn to weep when the dance had ended, knowing that she might never see such beauty again once she had left her little island. And she would be allowed to leave, they had promised her, just as soon as she had fulfilled taught them how to sing.

They had finally agreed to this price: in return for saving her life, Lille would give them the gift of song. It had seemed a small price to pay, at first. She worried that their voices, low and harsh and unlovely, would not take well to song. She did not want them to think they had gotten a bad trade.

Had Lille understood the nature of sirens, she might have worried less and feared more. The first time the sisters raised their voices together in a hymn, magic washed over her like a cold wave. She could feel their voices pulling at her, commanding, cajoling, and she was filled at once with wild exultation and profound sorrow.

With a very great effort, Lille wrenched herself from the sirens' spell. All the hairs on her arms and the back of her neck were standing stiff, and the breath caught in her throat like fish bones. Iloneth smiled at Lille's reaction, sharp and satisfied.

But the bargain had been made, and Lille was true to her word. She continued to teach the sirens to sing even though she understood that in doing so she was giving them a terrible weapon.

And why not, after all? The god hunters might not dare to challenge mighty Allyr, but his daughters had long been considered easy prey. Many a sea-sister had met death at the end of a harpoon, bright scales and silver eyes gone dull in the dry sunlight, her corpse displayed before the gaping masses. Later her flesh would be hacked into bits and sold on the black market, a delicacy to those who hungered for power.

Lille thought of little Nyssa gutted and spitted for the greed of some high lord or king, and her heart grew cold and dark. Let the sirens sing, she thought. Let them fight back against those who would destroy them.

And what loyalty did Lille owe the mortal world? Humans had imprisoned her until she was of no use to them. A man had stolen her song and had tried to steal her life. This time the music, and the magic, were freely given. Let the sirens do with it as they would.

Time passed, and Lille supposed she was content. Though she did grow weary of raw fish, and the amiable little rodents had grown shy of her as their numbers dwindled.

She was standing that morning on her little beach, playing with a necklace of shells and bone she was making for Nyssa, and Iloneth was cooling her finned feet in the water. The sirens' song drifted back to them over the waves, tugging at Lille's heart. The sea-sisters were teaching this new magic to their friends, and those friends would teach it to others. In time, every maiden in the sea would have a weapon with which to protect herself against the depredations of men.

"You are helping to save all our lives," Iloneth said, "yet we gave you one life only. I feel ... strange."

Lille felt her mouth twitch with amusement. "You feel guilty."

The siren frowned. "I do not like it. I wish to do more for you." She balanced her hands like a set of merchant's scales until they drew even. "What would you have of me? Do not ask for your freedom," she added quickly. "That, I will not grant you until we have learned to sing the fifth verse of the … *shttthrambuss*." The word was clumsy in her mouth. "As we agreed."

"Tyrambus," Lille corrected absently, "and I would not ask for such a thing. It would be dishonorable."

"You humans and your honor." Sunlight sparkled on Iloneth's scales as she laughed. So pretty. "But surely you might seek another boon from me. I give this to you freely. What would you have of me? Pearls? Fish? A handsome sailor?"

"Ew, no," Lille said, making a face as she remembered the man Nyssa had brought for her.

"I could try not to drown this one," Iloneth said doubtfully, "though what one might want with a live man …" She shrugged.

"Still no," Lille said, laughing at the siren's grimace. "I suppose if you could manage it—"

"Yes?"

"Would you bring me word of the human kingdom Taresia? It is on the coast and should not be difficult for you to find. I would like to hear news of the great bards' competition that would have been held, oh, some months ago now. I would especially like to know if the bard Zymander sang—" her voice cracked with anger. "If he sang my song."

Iloneth tilted her head in a questioning manner. Without meaning to, Lille found herself spilling the ugly story of her life upon the sand before the siren. How she had been locked in a tower for being a bastard daughter of Allyr, allowed neither to live nor to die. How music and the king's death had set her free, and how that freedom had been snatched away from her by Zymander just as she was on her way to win fame and glory in a distant land. The sun had barely risen when she began her tale, and it sank towards the waves as she finished.

"That is *awful*," Nyssa cried, slapping her hands against the wet sand in righteous indignation. "What foul beasts men are!"

A murmur of agreement rose from the waves, and Lille glanced up, surprised to find many dark heads bobbing in the shallow waters of her cove. Iloneth stood then, straight and stern-faced, and her eyes were terrible. Lille stood as well, less gracefully, and reached out to clasp the siren's cold hands. It felt right.

"Sisters," Iloneth said. The sky grew dark. Thunder echoed across the sea. "Our darling Lille has been offered insult, and this we cannot allow. An insult to our sister is an insult to us all. We will search out this land—Taresia—and the bard Zymander. And when we find him—" She hissed. Her teeth were *very* sharp.

The sirens raised their voices in a wild hymn. In it, Lille could hear echoes of her own song, the roar of waves, the crying of sea-birds, and their own deep magic. It was ancient and ever new as the sea itself. A strange, beautiful new thing blossomed deep within her heart, and Lille added her voice, her magic, to theirs.

Home, she thought. I am home.

It was Nyssa who found her way to Taresia and back again. She brought the news Lille had asked for—and dreaded—and as Lille heard the tale, she trembled.

The great bards' competition had been a momentous event. Indeed, the telling of it was on every human's tongue as the ships sailed from Taresia to the six corners of the world. The sailors told any who would listen of the bard Zymander, Blessed and cursed bastard son of a queen and a god. Locked away from the world at birth, Zymander had freed himself at last with the magic of song. He had come to the competition and had presented an entirely new form, a hymn he called a Tyrambus. The sailors whispered that this new hymn was so beautiful, so powerful, that the statue of Allyr wept tears of joy as the bard sang.

So taken was the little princess of Taresia with the beautiful Zymander that she had been stricken dumb with love. The king, having no son, had declared himself willing to wed his daughter off to the golden-voiced youth and had made this Zymander his heir.

There was to be a grand celebration at the next full moon, and every bard who had come to compete for the king's gold had been invited to stay and play for the new king's wedding.

Lille listened to the littlest siren's words with a calm face, though her eyes and throat ached with angry tears. When Nyssa had finished, and as the other sirens looked on, Lille picked up a sharpened bit of conch shell, seized her braid in the other hand, and hacked her beautiful hair off close to the scalp.

Flushed with rage she turned back towards her cave, meaning to burn her hair, her clothes, perhaps to fling herself upon the fire and sear away the whole of her miserable existence.

But Iloneth's hand on her shoulder stopped her. "Wait," she said, "sister, wait."

Lille stopped. The tears came at last. She wailed buried her face in her hands and wept.

Then Iloneth's arms were around her, and Nyssa's, and Pollonia's—all the sirens, even those whose names she had not yet learned, were rising from the sea to embrace her. The sea-grey bodies were cold and strange, but their love warmed her more thoroughly than any fire might.

The storm of Lille's grief was over as quickly as it had begun. The sirens melted away and back into the waves. Being of the sea they were quick to anger; lacking a mortal soul, they were just as quick to forget. She was alone with Iloneth and Nyssa. The littlest sea-maid was sitting on the beach and chewing the edges of her fin in distress.

Iloneth took the severed braid from Lille and laid one clawed hand gently against her cheek, then pressed a thin-lipped kiss upon the scales at Lille's temple.

"You will stay?" she asked. "You will not ..." she waved a hand toward Lille's cave and the fire within.

"I will stay," Lille agreed, with a bone-weary sigh. "There isn't enough wood on this island for a proper funeral pyre, in any case."

Iloneth stared at her for a long moment, until Lille sighed again.

"I will stay. I promise."

"We will return," Iloneth answered, which was as close to 'goodbye' as Lille had ever heard from a siren. Still holding Lille's severed braid she took Nysse by the hand and then they, too, were gone.

When the sirens returned, Lille thought, she would beg them to carry her to Taresia. Though how a ragged girl without a coin to her name might hope to wreak her vengeance upon a king's heir—who would no doubt dispose of her more successfully a second time—was a riddle she had not yet solved. She paced the lonely sands, knowing that the price of the sirens' assistance would be high, knowing too that she had only one thing to offer, which might make the effort of bearing her across the sea to Taresia worth their while: her mortal soul.

What was a soul, after all? She asked herself. Iloneth and the other sirens seemed to do well enough without souls, though they did seem to lack ... something. A soul was passion, she decided at last. Love. Pain. The too-bright spark of a fleeting life. Infinitely small, infinitely precious. Such a price to pay, for the theft of a song.

And yet, for Lille, there was no real choice. She would not allow that thief to sit upon a golden throne and live the life he had stolen from her. If Zymander was to be a king, then the king must die.

Lille had been staring across the waves for hours, looking for the flash of sunlight on scales. Listening for their voices. So fixed was she on these things that she did not take notice of the tiny patch of cloud that wisped across the water until it had entered her little cove and taken shape. Sails. A hull. Oars.

It was a warship, swift and sleek, pale as a pearl, with baleful red eyes painted close to the waterline. Lille leaped to her feet, ready to flee to her cave until she saw that the sailors who stood upon her deck were not human at all but her sirens. Her sisters. Iloneth waved to her from the trierarch's chair. Lille waved back, dancing upon the sand. She waded out to meet them. When the water grew too deep, she swam.

When she reached the ship a ladder of pale rope was thrown down from its deck. Lille flinched back when she saw that the ladder's rungs were made of long bones, but then she took a deep breath and reached for the lowest rung. She pulled herself out of the water and climbed up the ladder of bones. The bones of men. She made herself think of that. Made her heart hard and cold, like a stone made smooth by the sea. They were taking her to kill a king. She must be like this, she thought, cold and brave.

As she climbed past the banks of oars, she saw that they were pulled by men. Dead men. A small crab crawled sideways out of the hole where one man's ear should have been, across his bloated grey cheek, and made itself comfortable in an empty eye socket. She kept climbing.

When she reached the top of the ladder many hands reached down and helped her onto the deck. Iloneth was there, smiling at her. The scales on her face blazed like jewels in the sunlight, as did her mother-of-pearl armor and the sword at her hip. Her hair—her beautiful hair—had been chopped as short as Lille's own.

"Are you ready, Sister?" she asked.

"How did you—" Lille choked. "How did—" She stopped. Words failed her. Tears shamed her.

Iloneth reached out and touched Lille's cheek. She said again, "An insult to our sister is an insult to us all."

Lille stared. She was a bard, but she didn't know what to say. There were no words big enough to express what she was thinking. What she was feeling.

Iloneth's smile was as wide as the sea. Her teeth were very sharp.

"Lille! Lille!" Nyssa cried as she scrambled up onto the deck. Her hair had been cut short as well. "Look! Look what I have for you!" She was staggering under the weight of a large bundle. It was not, Lille noted, large enough to be another drowned sailor.

Lille glanced at Iloneth. A question.

"Our father sends his regards," said the older siren.

"Our ... father?" Lille whispered. "Allyr?"

"He also sends you these gifts as a token of his affection," said Iloneth. An answer.

The package was laid before her and unwrapped to reveal a set of armor like the one Iloneth wore, complete with a red-plumed helm and a cape of sea-foam white. But the thing that caught Lille's attention, the gift that caused her throat to ache and her hands to tremble, was a kithara.

It was fashioned from the ebon-black horns of some great beast, inlaid with pearl and coral, mother-of-pearl and one great gold coin, and strung with what could only have been sirens' hair. An instrument fit for the daughter of a god.

An acknowledged daughter of a god, no longer a bastard at all.

Lille had been prepared to surrender her soul in exchange for passage to Taresia. But they were carrying her across the sea of their own free will. They gave her gifts from the sea god. A place among them. They would risk their lives to help her seek vengeance—because they loved her. They loved her.

Lille did not know what to say. She had been cared for, yes, by her mother's maids, and especially old Willa who had taught her to sing. She had been allowed to live when killing her would have been more convenient. She had even been sought as a bride by men who wanted a princess, even a bastard princess. But she had never been loved.

As she sailed with her sisters to Taresia, Lille taught them how to sing the fifth verse.

The first four verses of the Tyrambus were powerful, yes. They lured the singer's audience like fish to bait, drawing them into the song, setting its hook. But the fifth—

The fifth verse caught the listeners' souls.

"Oh," Iloneth breathed after Lille had played the entire hymn to them for the first time. Even the sirens, soulless though they were, had felt the song's pull. "Oh, sister, such a gift you give to us." And they embraced.

In that moment, between the sun and roiling sea, Lille came to understand that one human emotion which had always escaped her and, in doing so, attained the full power of her bardic gift.

An ethereal white ship sailed into the Taresian harbor on the morning of King Zymander's coronation. Splendid and sleek, and sailed by a crew of lissome young women whose beauty could only be guessed at behind their bejeweled sea-foam veils, it could have been sent by none other than Allyr himself.

The glittering troupe descended from the ship and glided through the streets of the city with an eerie grace. The red-plumed figure at their head played upon a splendid kithara. Such was the spectacle provided by these visitors, so exotic was their mien and enchanting their music, that every soul who saw, or heard, was drawn along in their wake.

Thus they made their slow way through the city and up the road to the mighty palace of Taresia, whose walls had never been breached, and the whole city followed behind.

Zymander sat upon his throne on the high dais on a golden throne at the king's right hand, a lovely princess beside him. He was stern-faced and proud. He looked, Lille thought, exactly as the son of a queen and a sea good should look.

Lille imagined herself leaping upon the dais, seizing Zymander by his ears, and beating his head against the floor. But she kept her hands light on the kithara and smiled behind her veil as she played. She stopped at the foot of the dais, let the music drift away into silence, and bowed low to the king.

The old king clapped, a delighted smile creasing his wrinkled face. "Bright strangers," he called to them, "who have come today to honor us, be welcome! I am sure your music will be a wonder and a delight! But will you not show us your face, great lady?"

Lille straightened, striking a bard's pose, and let her voice carry across the king's great hall.

"O king of men," she replied, "it is not I who honor you, but mighty Allyr, who has blessed me with a bard's gifts even as he blesses our ships with swift wind and friendly seas. Lo! We are veiled because our faces are not important. Our names are not important. Such things will be forgotten with the wind and tides. But men will speak of the gift we bring you today long after we have gone to sea-foam and stories."

Zymander froze at the sound of Lille's voice, wineglass halfway to his mouth. He looked very pale.

"A gift from Allyr!" cried the princess, clapping her little hands together in delight.

"Yes, Princess." Lille let a smile warm her voice. We bring you—" She brought her kithara up and struck a chord that resonated throughout the golden room, "—the song of sirens."

Lille bent her head over her kithara and brought the Tyrambus to life. The first notes flowed across the golden thrones, over the marble floors, out the door, and into the surrounding city like a mist rolled in from the sea. The sirens began to sway, to dance, to chant in chorus. Lille drew a deep breath, held it for a moment, and began to sing:

Away, away
Accursed thing
We shall lock you in ivory, marble, and bone
A prison of flesh, even as the soul of a king

Is held fast to this earth
You shall know no word but mine
No touch but mine
No love but mine
And I shall love you not …
The sirens answered,
Fly to the sea
Away to the sea
On wings of music
Send the sweet scent of burnt offerings up to Allyr
On the winds of destruction
Sing His praises …

Lille's voice drew the crowd in and made them hers, made them weep. The song built a storm of emotions in the heart of every listener. First came the grief of being unloved, unwanted, alone. Then hope as the listener was shown a path out of torment:

On wings of feather, wax, and song, I throw myself into the sky …

Betrayal as that hope was snatched away by one who wore the face of a friend:

Rise, he told me smiling, let the golden warmth of the sun kiss your face, your lips so sweet, come now, rise. But I did not see the feathers falling …

Grief renewed, as the song brought its audience back to a state of wretchedness and despair:

Down I plunged, towards the sea, down and down where the sea-things live, hungering for human flesh, and the words of the oracle rang in my ears: Alone. Alone. Alone. Alone.

And the sirens' chorus:
On the winds of destruction
Sing praise to Allyr ...
On the winds of destruction
Sing praise to his daughters ...

A storm built in the minds and hearts of the assembled kingdom until every upturned face was distorted, maddened. Even Zymander, who had begun to lean forward as at last he recognized the song and his own peril, was caught and held like a fish in the net.

The fourth verse thundered overhead and began to disperse. The little princess seated at Zymander's side gasped and began to weep.

Zymander leaned back into his throne, a look of relief growing on his face as the song's power began to fade. He gripped the golden armrests and opened his mouth to speak, but nothing came out. His eyes widened and he clutched at his throat.

The old king glanced at his new heir in growing alarm. "What—" he began.

Lille stepped forward, eliciting a gasp from one of the courtiers. She held up her hand for silence, paused for dramatic effect, and then brought it to her face, pulled her veil away, and let it fall.

Zymander, still clutching his throat, recoiled. The crowd drew back from the king's dais as the sirens dropped their veils as well. Little Nyssa revealed her face last and gave the audience a wide, hungry smile.

The princess fainted.

"This man who sits at your side," Lille told the king, "this false man, this false bard, this false prince, stole something from me."

She struck a chord on her kithara.

"I am taking it back."

Lille called to the music once more and it answered her gladly. She gathered the song to her breast, binding it to the anger in her soul, and unleashed her magic.

O why do you sit, king of kings
Upon your throne above our heads?
Do you not know that water is stronger
And more patient?
Do you not know we will bring you down
Down down
Do you not know that we will bring you down, and lay your palaces to waste?
Oh, false king, your golden palaces built upon the souls of your people
So long have you beaten our souls into sword and brick and bauble
To wear about your neck.
Let them strangle you now
Let the cities you have built with the bodies of our ancestors crumble.
And now may you fall
Down.
Now may you fall
Down.

The king's subjects, bound to her music, began to chant along with the sirens' chorus:

On the wings of song
Sing praise to Allyr ...
On the wings of song
Sing praise to his daughters ...
On the winds of destruction
There is no king but Allyr, sing praises to the sea!
On the winds of destruction
There is no king ...
There is no king ...
The king must die!
There is no king!

The people, wild-eyed and grotesque, turned upon the two kings. Drunk on wine and revelry, maddened by the song of the sirens, they began to move. They came as a trickle, and then a flood, flowing around the chanting sirens and the singing bard.

The old king turned to flee, and the new king as well. But as any sailor could have told them, there is no escaping the wrath of the sea—or the vengeance of the sea god's daughter.

The crowd crashed down upon the high dais like a storm-driven wave. They seized the old king, the new king, and the pretty little princess, and they tore them to pieces as the bard sang on.

THE LAST DAYS OF OLD SHARAKHAI

BRADLEY P. BEAULIEU

Chapter One

As the sun lowered in the west, an araba drawn by a pair of tall akhala horses bore Ihsan, the last of the Sharakhani Kings, toward his ancestral home along the slopes of Mount Tauriyat. The day was hot, the wind blustering. From Ihsan's high vantage, Sharakhai was laid bare, a sprawl of mudbrick hovels, stone manors, and crisscrossing streets. Beyond the city lay the rolling dunes of the Great Shangazi.

A relative calm had come over Sharakhai. The war with Mirea and Malasan had finally ended, but the peace was tentative. There was the all-too-real possibility that hostilities would resume, which was precisely why Ihsan was headed to his palace to meet with two of his grandsons, Mehmed and Zevi, who held much sway with the city's old guard.

A particularly strong gust of wind sent sand and dust billowing through the araba's cabin. Ihsan turned away from it and drew the linen blanket over the face of his daughter Ransaneh, who lay swaddled in his lap. Ransaneh stirred, but the rumble of the wheels on the rutted road soon sent her back to the land of slumber.

A moment later, the araba dipped violently. "My sincerest apologies, my Lord King." The driver, a middle-aged woman with a hunched back and an ever-present sneer, navigated the wagon over a series of deeper potholes. "Those bloody northern jackals left everything in a shambles."

She was referring to Queen Alansal and her host of Mirean invaders, who'd occupied Sharakhai and the House of Kings for months. But the Mireans were hardly the only ones to blame for the years of neglect. With the build-up to the war, the battles in the heart of Sharakhai, and the conflict with the gods, the roads had been the last thing on everyone's mind.

The driver glanced over her shoulder at Ransaneh. "She's precious, that daughter of yours."

"You have my thanks."

"Bet she's proud," she said, steering them around a switchback, "dealing with that foreign queen the way you did. Probably happy you're going home, too."

"I rather doubt she's aware of any of that."

"Oh, I don't know." The driver snapped the reins, and the akhalas redoubled their efforts. "I don't think we give 'em enough credit. Like my memma always said, the whelps know a lot more'n we think they do."

Annoyed by the woman's chatter, Ihsan let the conversation drop. Soon, a curtain wall with a series of watch towers came into view. The imposing palace beyond had been Ihsan's home for the past four centuries. He knew every room and every corner in the tall edifice intimately, yet it felt strange and foreign to him now. Long had he dreamed of becoming

Sharakhai's lone, remaining King, of ruling the city and the desert alone. He'd spent generations playing things just so to achieve it. And indeed, that dream was finally within his grasp. Other than Ihsan himself, the Sharakhani Kings were all dead, fallen to the blades of assassins, war, or, in the case of Husamettín, a duel to the death.

With little effort, he could consolidate his power, but he was faced with a simple yet very harsh truth: his rule wouldn't last. It couldn't. He'd been infected with the black mould, the very same disease that had struck Ransaneh's mother, Queen Nayyan. Sitting in the araba's cabin, he could feel the hard nodules inside his mouth, growing, multiplying. He didn't know how much time he had left, but he was certain it would be less than he wanted. As was true of any man whose days were numbered, he'd adjusted his priorities accordingly. He needed to see the city safe, thereby securing Ransaneh's future before he died, and the conversation he was about to have with his grandsons was the first step.

As the ground leveled, Ihsan glanced down and saw Ransaneh staring up at him. "Well, look who's awake!" he said with a smile.

Ransaneh smiled back, but it was a fleeting thing. She blinked her mismatched eyes—one hazel, one brown—and yawned.

As the araba's wheels thudded rhythmically against the planks of the drawbridge, Ihsan kissed her forehead and hugged her against his chest so she could see the curtain wall, its watchtowers, and the blue sky above. After passing through the barbican, the driver guided the araba along a gravel circle set before the palace proper. On the far side of the circle, standing at the base of a broad set of stairs, was Tolovan, Ihsan's long-trusted vizir. Beside him were Ransaneh's wet nurse, the palace steward, and a handful of other servants.

The araba came to a jingling stop. The servants bowed as the footman opened the door. Holding Ransaneh tight, Ihsan navigated the steps down, then handed his daughter to her stout wet nurse. She cradled Ransaneh lovingly, bowed, and took three steps back.

Beside her stood Tolovan, a long man with a long face. Wearing a dark khalat over a black thawb, he looked more hangman than counselor. "My Lord King"—Tolovan's voice was deep as a gorge, rough as a landslide—"your return is most welcome." He bowed again, offering the sort of smile he was famous for, which was to say he looked as if he were being forced, the edge of a knife to his throat.

Ihsan nodded, and the two fell into step as they made their way toward the top of the stairs.

"Has all been arranged?" Ihsan asked.

Tolovan bowed his head. "It has, Your Excellence. Your grandsons arrived a short while ago. They're waiting for you on the veranda."

"Their moods?"

"Tense, my Lord King."

"Given the circumstances, tension is understandable. Did they seem angry? Defensive?"

Tolovan shrugged. "Not that I could detect, but they *are* your progeny, sire. They're gifted at hiding their emotions, Mehmed especially."

Ihsan wasn't terribly surprised that his grandsons had risen to the fore of the opposition to Davud's plans for the city. Not only did Mehmed and Zevi stand to lose much in the new world order, Zevi was next in line for Ihsan's throne and Mehmed stood just behind him. It only made sense that the sons and daughters of the other, dead Kings would bid the two of them speak with Ihsan, to convince him to keep things as they were.

At the palace's entrance, a pair of Silver Spears in white uniforms snapped their heels, bowed, and swung the doors open. A putrid smell greeted Ihsan as he and Tolovan passed into the high entrance hall. The hall, once rich with artwork, was now bare as the day it was built. Halfway along its length, a fluted column was horribly chipped—from what, Ihsan wasn't certain. Near it, a wide swath of the marble floor was stained red. All were signs of the Mirean occupation of the city and the months of conflict that preceded it.

"Before you speak to your grandsons, Your Excellence, there's the matter of our new Crone …"

He gestured to the far end of the hall where a woman in a blood-red battle dress and turban leaned against a pillar. It took Ihsan a moment to recognize her, but once he had, a host of memories came rushing back. The woman, Shohreh, had once been an elite swordswoman known as a Kestrel, but circumstances had changed in recent months. Her former commander, the Crone, had died under mysterious circumstances in the Shallows, and Shohreh had risen to take her place.

Ihsan stopped and pulled Tolovan in front of him so that Shohreh was unable to see him—the woman was deaf but quite gifted at reading lips.

"Why is she here, Tolovan?"

"All she would say was that"—Tolovan's gaze drifted toward King's Harbor, where the Mireans were still camped—"given all that's happened, a courtesy visit with the last of the Sharakhani Kings seemed prudent."

Ihsan chuckled, a simple act that increasingly brought on a dull ache inside his mouth. "We both know it's more than a courtesy visit."

"That may be," replied Tolovan, "but she's an important ally. And she came without being asked. It's a good sign, the fates granting you favor after all you've been through."

"A blessing …" Ihsan snorted as he broke from Tolovan and headed toward the ornate door on his left. "I'll speak with her in here."

Soon, Ihsan was seated on his old throne in the audience chamber and Shohreh was pacing toward him down the aisle between the benches. As Tolovan closed the doors with a boom, she reached the foot of the dais and gave him a perfunctory bow. "My Lord King."

She stood at parade rest, her left hand on the pommel of her shamshir. The veil of her turban hung over her chest. Her expression was composed, emotionless, which made it seem as though it was all she could do to mask her bile. This close, he could see the scars along her cheeks and chin, the ragged gash along her neck that disappeared beneath her battle dress. There was also a bright, angry bruise over one cheek, a still-healing cut near her right eye, and abrasions over the backs of her knuckles.

Theirs had always been an icy relationship, and for good reason. Years ago, on the order of her then-commander, King Zeheb, she'd put out her own ears, deafening herself to resist the power of Ihsan's voice. Now she found herself beholden to the very man who'd driven her to such desperate straits.

"Why are you here?" Ihsan asked.

"You're about to take a meeting with your grandsons. I'd like to attend."

"Blunt," Ihsan said.

"You're a busy man, and I'm a busy woman."

"I can appreciate that, so let me return the favor. At this point, I have little reason to trust you, and I know you don't trust *me*, so why in the great wide desert should I agree to your request?"

"Because despite what you may think, I take my role as a protector of this city seriously, and I know the next few days will dictate much of what happens to Sharakhai in the months and years ahead."

The defiance in her eyes, as if she were daring him to say a word against her, convinced him of her sincerity. "Go on."

"News of Davud's document, the covenant he's written to secure peace with the Four Kingdoms, has spread like a fresh blaze in the slums. The highborn in Goldenhill and Hanging Gardens are now well aware he's making plans to form a representative government in Sharakhai."

Though Davud Mahzun'ava was a powerful blood mage, he was also a collegia scholar and one of the brightest minds the institution had ever seen. He'd developed a proposal, a covenant that would shake the foundations of Sharakhai's government. The most significant aspect of the covenant was to do away with the House of Kings and replace it with rule via a pair of co-equal houses, dubbed the House of Sand and the House of Stone. If put in place, those two houses would elect a new ruler, a Sultan who would reign for a six-year term.

"Davud has called for a council to be held in one week to decide the covenant's fate," Shohreh continued. "He's lured many high-ranking lords and ladies to his side, among them are several children of the former

Kings, the heirs to their fathers' thrones."

"Davud has proven to be quite persuasive," Ihsan said, "more than I ever gave him credit for."

Shohreh nodded. "It's an impressive bit of horse-trading, no doubt, but the outcome is still far from certain. An opposing camp has formed, comprised largely of Sharakhai's old guard. They're concerned about their prospects, but more than this, they feel disrespected. They're angry over what they see as a loss of status, a loss of power. They fear retribution from the populace as well—rightfully so, should the terms set out in the covenant be enacted."

"And in which of these two camps do *you* stand, Shohreh?"

She stared at him, nostrils flaring. "I should think that was obvious by now."

"I want to hear it in your own words."

Seconds passed in silence, Ihsan feeling the weight of her gaze, before she replied, "The city has seen enough war. It's time we heal. I've read the covenant—several times, in fact—and I think it provides a way, likely the *best* way, to do just that." She paused. "As *you* do, I presume?"

Ihsan narrowed his eyes. "You're well aware I'm in favor of the covenant."

"Yes, but while it seems to deal well with the *outside* threats to our city, there's the not-so-unlikely possibility it will plunge *us* into civil war."

"Should the covenant's terms come to pass, I have no doubt there will be resistance, even bloodshed, but I think we can chart a course that avoids the worst of the shoals."

"*Chart a course* is an apt way of putting it. You know as well as I that proper navigation takes time and skill. It takes precision. Your grandsons appear ready to oppose the covenant's passage. I'm requesting a presence in your meeting so I can weigh their words, their sincerity, which will aid me in guiding you in the days ahead."

It wasn't an unreasonable request—Ihsan's next meeting would no doubt have bearing on the coming council—but the truth was Shohreh was an unknown quantity. As such, she had to be kept at arm's length, at least until he had time to investigate and weigh her properly.

Perhaps sensing he was about to dismiss her, Shohreh pressed on, "You should know, there have been rumblings of discontent."

"Discontent …?"

"Rumors have begun to spread about your involvement with King Husamettín's death. Some say the reason *you* survived while the King of Swords was slain in his duel with Çedamihn Ahyanesh'ala was because the two of you were in league with one another from the beginning. Others disagree but wonder if you used your power on her and *forced* her to kill Husamettín."

Ihsan *hadn't* heard that last rumor, but he was hardly surprised. "And you? Do *you* think I forced Çeda's hand?"

"I wasn't there."

"That wasn't what I asked."

"My opinion hardly matters, my Lord King."

"Ah, but it very much *does* matter. What the Crone thinks shows where her loyalties lie, and the Crone's loyalties are important, now more than ever."

The muscles along Shohreh's jaw clenched. "I have no reason to think Husamettín's death was anything more than it seemed."

Ihsan tongued a painful bump along the side of his mouth while judging her words. Talking was painful these days, but it had been such a constant in his life he'd mostly learned to ignore it. Setting the pain aside, he found he believed Shohreh. He'd have to take care with her—she was clearly uncomfortable with *him*—but she was, by all accounts, *fiercely* loyal to Sharakhai and the House of Kings.

"The short of it," Shohreh went on, "is that, whether anyone likes it or not, you have become a powerful symbol. Throwing your lot in with Davud will sway some of the lords to his cause, which is precisely why others may want to prevent it from happening, by any means necessary. If the covenant is to succeed, your safety must be assured, and what is the Crone's primary responsibility if not that?"

The question was never whether Ihsan's life would be threatened by the steps he was about to take. He'd known it from the start and was willing to take that risk—he *had* to, for Ransaneh's sake. No, the real question was whether he could trust Shohreh. Would she protect him as she'd vowed, or had she already pledged her heart and soul to the old guard?

Part of Ihsan felt he hardly had a choice in the matter—he was woefully short on allies. Were the title of Crone held by anyone else, he probably *would* have accepted her offer. But Shohreh might have come to the palace for the sole purpose of ingratiating herself to him. She might have faked her wounds to garner sympathy.

"I have no need for the Crone's services at present," he said after a moment's reflection. "Perhaps you and I can speak in a few days, after I've had a chance to see how the sands have shifted—"

"There's one last matter Your Excellence should be made aware of. One of my Kestrels, Nazanin, returned not long ago from her mission in the desert. On learning about Davud's plan, she came to me and demanded we align ourselves with your grandsons."

"And your answer?"

"I serve at the pleasure of the Sharakhani Kings, and no other."

Ihsan gestured to the abrasions along her knuckles, the bruise on her cheek. "The result of your disagreement with Nazanin?"

Shohreh merely stared.

"I'll take the meeting alone, Shohreh."

"My King—"

"That will be all, my good Crone."

Shohreh looked as if she were ready to challenge him. Finally, she bowed, pulled her red veil across her face, and left without another word.

Chapter Two

When Ihsan reached the palace veranda, Mehmed and Zevi were seated at a table beneath a pergola positively choking with long wisteria vines. Both men wore high turbans and rich silk khalats over simpler thawbs.

Seeing Ihsan approach, they stood and bowed. "My Lord King," they intoned in unison.

Zevi, the taller of the two, had arresting blue eyes and a trim black beard. He was a mercurial racketeer, a simpler man than Mehmed, and so, easier to read. He was also the more violent of the two. On the surface, he ran a private security business that purported to offer protection against the city's thieves guilds. In reality, the business owners were often coerced, the threat being if they *didn't* pay, they'd find their places gutted or burned by Zevi's men.

Mehmed was closer to Ihsan's height. His beard was longer and kinkier than Zevi's and cut in a square style reminiscent of Sharakhai's elder days when Ihsan first came into power. Though Mehmed was generally soft-spoken, Ihsan knew him to be a conniving, vengeful man. To cross Mehmed, as some had learned to their deep regret, was to take one's life into one's own hands.

For many years, Mehmed had controlled the granting of a good number of the city's business licenses, along the Trough especially. Not content to simply *administer* such licenses, he'd been on the take for years, accepting bribes for prime locations along the city's busiest thoroughfare.

Both men appeared similar in age to Ihsan—roughly forty-five summers—but Ihsan had witnessed more than four centuries pass in the Great Shangazi. In years past, he would have thought little of the stark contrast in their ages, but things had changed. In every way that mattered, Mehmed and Zevi represented Sharakhai's future, while Ihsan was a fading symbol of its past. They recognized it, too, no doubt, which meant Ihsan would need to take care to steer them toward the future *he* wanted.

"Please," Ihsan said, while motioning to the chairs, "sit."

The scent of the hanging purple flowers filled the air as the three of them settled into the veranda's thick-cushioned chairs around a circular table. The air was hot but tolerable in the shade of the pergola. Bells sounded in the distance—the Mirean dunebreakers preparing to depart King's Harbor and journey north.

Zevi glanced toward the sound, then snatched up a bottle of araq from a tray at the center of the table. He poured three generous portions into the waiting glasses, distributed two of them, and took up the third. "To the Amber Jewel"—he lifted his glass high—"long may she shine."

Ihsan and Zevi raised their glasses. "Long may she shine."

All three men threw back their drinks. Ihsan used to adore araq, but the liquor felt dead on his tongue—another particularly tragic symptom of the black mould. *I suppose it's far from the cruelest thing the fates have done,* he mused while staring into his empty glass, *but how it burns to have lost my favorite pastime.*

Zevi shared an overly affectionate smile with Ihsan as he poured another round. "I'd like you to settle a bet for us, grandfather."

Ihsan took a deep breath, doing his best to hide his annoyance at Zevi's histrionics.

"When word reached us of the blood mage's plans for our city"—Zevi finished pouring and set the bottle down—"*I* said you were playing along, biding your time until you could organize the rest of us. Mehmed, meanwhile, spoke to several lords who witnessed your attempts to convince King Husamettín that the covenant was the proper way forward, the *only* way forward. He now has the fool notion that, for some unfathomable reason, you actually *want* the blood mage's covenant to pass." Glass in hand, Zevi leaned into his chair with an expression of mild curiosity, as if the conversation meant little to him. "So, which is it, Grandfather? Are you a traitor to your city or not?"

There was an ill-concealed rage behind Zevi's smile. Mehmed, meanwhile, waited calmly, betraying nothing.

Ihsan was about to give them the answer he'd prepared on his ride to the palace when something gave him pause. In his four centuries as a King, he'd developed a sense for when dark powers were being used. It manifested as a vague discomfort in the pit of his stomach, a slow wrenching that made his gut feel heavy. That was precisely what he felt as he sat with his two grandsons on the veranda.

He scanned the potted palms beyond Zevi and Mehmed, searching for the source of his unease. Near the veranda's travertine railing was a mottled patch of shadow moving in a way that seemed more complex than the palm's swaying fronds could account for. It reminded him of mud swirling, a frightened mudskipper wriggling deeper into the banks of the Haddah in spring.

"Are you feeling well, my Lord King?" Zevi asked.

Ihsan pulled his attention back to the table. "I'm fine."

"Then please, answer the question."

"Your question presents a false dichotomy, Zevi. It supposes that if one is in favor of anything beyond the continued rule of our twelve royal houses, one is a traitor. I hope to convince you of the many great opportunities presented by the covenant."

Zevi's eyebrows shot up. He laughed. "*Opportunities!*"

"Just so."

Zevi narrowed his eyes, then leaned back and laughed so hard his belly shook. "Surely you jest, Grandfather. What you're talking about is nothing less than ceding control of Sharakhai. Ceding control over the *desert*."

"Not entirely, no. You've no doubt heard details of the proposed House of Stone. The seats in that house are granted in perpetuity and passed down by blood. I've ensured you'll each be offered one."

Zevi put on an affected smile and spread his arms wide. "Two seats! How very *generous!*"

"Additionally, I'm well aware you both had thriving businesses once, and that the war affected them greatly." The gut-churning feeling was so strong Ihsan nearly peered into the shadows again, but he stifled the urge, keeping his focus squarely on Mehmed and Zevi. "The war is now over. We stand on the brink of a monumental recovery. I'm confident both of you will be able to expand on your old territories and gain even *more* influence than you once enjoyed."

All humor fled from Zevi's face. "Anything else?"

"Yes. I won trade rights from the largest winery in Qaimir and two of the largest distilleries. They're yours if you want them."

"What you're offering pales in comparison to ruling over Sharakhai," Zevi said.

"What I've presented is but the initial offer in an ongoing negotiation." Ihsan shrugged. "If you want more, tell me what it is."

Zevi's face turned blotchy, always a sign he was close to losing his temper. He clenched his jaw before responding in a tight voice, "What I want is my *birthright*."

Mehmed touched Zevi's arm, waited for him to compose himself. "What my cousin is trying to say," Mehmed said calmly, "is that a pair of seats in some fabricated house is cold comfort when we could help *you*, the last remaining King, rule city and desert both."

"That would cause years, perhaps decades, of further strife and bloodshed. I beg you to look toward peace and prosperity instead. Neither of you will suffer under this new arrangement, nor will anyone in our family. In a few short years, you'll be earning more than you ever did when the Kings ruled Sharakhai."

"But it's a future that could be changed with the swipe of a pen, could it not?"

"It could, but with your seats in the new government, you'll have a say in it."

Mehmed opened his mouth to speak, then seemed to think better of it. "Might I be frank, my Lord King?"

"Please."

"I know what you've long coveted, what you worked toward for generations. I know your queen, may she find peace in the land beyond, was helping you gain it." Mehmed pointed along the slopes above them, where several other palaces could be seen. "What you wanted was Eventide and, with it, sole rule over Sharakhai. So, I have to wonder, now that it's all within your grasp, what would possess you to give it up?"

I'm dying, you bloody fool.

Ihsan could hardly tell him that, though. To do so would be to show weakness, which would give them an opening, a reason to cast him aside and fight the coming wave of change.

"I know you weren't there," Ihsan began, "but coming face to face with the elder gods changes a man. Believe me when I tell you that you would feel small before them, inconsequential. That experience made me realize that the thing I'd been working so hard to take was built on naught but slipsand. Sooner or later, it would crumble and fall. What I truly want for Sharakhai is something solid, something made of the desert and its people. A thing that will stand for another age. *That's* what Davud's plan offers."

Mehmed, always so politic, gave a gentle wag of his head. "Davud has offered up *a* plan to achieve a lasting future for our city, but it's hardly the *only* plan that could work. You say you want something that lasts? Take Sharakhai's crown for your own. Rule the city. Find the stability you say you're searching for. Then pass it on. You wouldn't even have to do it as King. Appease Queen Alansal. Become the Sultan described in the covenant. We'll even form the Houses of Sand and Stone, if that's what it takes, but we'll ensure they're filled with representatives *we* want. Then, when you've ruled for as long as you wish, you can pass the mantle to Zevi."

Mehmed's words were like honey—Ihsan found himself wondering if he *could* rule the city for a time—but the taste soon turned bitter, and the realities of the situation returned to him.

"The desert tribes wouldn't stand for it," he finally said, "nor would Mirea or Malasan. If I made myself Sultan, we'd be back at the bargaining table, swords close at hand, in months, maybe weeks. Things could slip back into chaos with one wrong word, one small misjudgment. We can't risk it."

"*Now*, yes," Mehmed said, throwing one hand in the air, "but the new government will take time to arrange. By then the tribes will be gone. So will Mirea and Malasan." The bells rang again, and he leaned forward, stabbing his finger toward King's Harbor. "Then *we'll* be holding the trump cards, not them."

"What you're saying *sounds* reasonable, Mehmed, but I assure you, it won't work. Not in the long run. We have a chance to remake Sharakhai for the better. I say we take it."

The redness in Zevi's face had only deepened as the conversation wore on. He leaned forward and practically shouted, "I *beg* you to reconsider, Your Excellence."

Ihsan shook his head. "I've given this much thought," he replied. "The alternatives lead to continued occupation, war, or strife with the desert tribes for generations more. So while I'll think on it, dear Zevi, I beg *you* to do the same."

Zevi stabbed a finger at Ihsan. "You're making a mistake."

Ihsan paused. "If I didn't know you so well, Zevi, I'd think that a threat."

Zevi's jaw worked. Over several long seconds, his face paled. His expression became one of disappointment, except, in a manner that was strangely uncharacteristic of Zevi, Ihsan had the impression it was disappointment in *himself*, not Ihsan. "I admit, I was overjoyed when I heard Husamettín had died. I burned incense to honor Bakhi. My wife and I *danced* with our children. I thought our path to Eventide was assured. Now ..." He shook his head, then stood in a rush. "I'm embarrassed to share blood with you. Would that Bakhi had taken *you*, not the King of Swords." He stormed away, shouting over his shoulder, "At least *he* would have fought for our city."

With his cousin gone, Mehmed remained outwardly calm. He

smoothed down the rich silk of his khalat and said, "I hope you don't think too badly of him, my Lord King. Zevi has ever been guided by his heart first, his meditations later."

Ihsan waved dismissively. "Things were bound to grow heated sooner or later." Even so, Ihsan was worried over how much time would pass before Zevi felt it necessary to take matters into his own hands. Ihsan would need to stay ahead of him, lest things slip out of control.

Mehmed nodded. "Perhaps I haven't given Davud's plan enough credit. Give me some time to look over it again?"

"Of course," Ihsan said.

"I'll speak to Zevi as well, see if I can't calm him down." Mehmed stood and bowed. "May the sun shine on our next meeting, my Lord King."

Mehmed's tranquil departure left Ihsan feeling colder than Zevi's petulant exit. Mehmed was clearly lying—the *last* thing he would do was read Davud's proposal again. He was only biding his time until he could decide what to do with Ihsan, which made the situation doubly dangerous.

When Ihsan stood, he realized his earlier uneasiness was gone. He'd been so intent on his discussion with Mehmed that he wasn't precisely sure when the feeling had disappeared.

The wind shifted. The palm he'd been staring at earlier swayed. Ihsan approached it and stared into the shadows, but found nothing.

Just your imagination, he thought, and headed toward the palace.

Chapter Three

Ihsan found sleep difficult that night. Long after the sun had set, he gave up on it entirely. By then, the moons had risen, the palace had gone still, and Ransaneh was sleeping with her wet nurse in the adjoining room of his apartments. He struck a bulls-eye lantern and wandered the palace halls until he came to a long room with high ceilings, an alchemycal laboratory where he and Nayyan had spent many long days and nights.

The far wall was composed of stained glass windows through which the moonlight shone, ruby, emerald, and sapphire. Ihsan's lantern cast wild shadows as he strode toward the worktables. On his left were high bookshelves. For the most part, the abundance of books within them were stacked in an orderly manner, but here and there, a spill of them lay upon the shelves or across the floor, as if someone had conducted a frantic, haphazard search. Sourced from all five kingdoms and beyond, the books were largely dedicated to alchemy, herbology, medicines, even poisons.

Complementing the tomes, and telling more of the room's far-reaching tale, was a vast set of alchemycal equipment on the room's opposite side. Glass burners, beakers, vials, and jars were spread across wooden tables. Some were broken, dark stains beneath their shattered remnants. Others lay on their sides, mistreated and forgotten. Vials contained a kaleidoscope of diluted blood, venom, unguents, and more. Jars held exotic powders. Tall apothecary cabinets with hundreds of tiny drawers were filled with beetle casings, roots, petals, even the occasional bone of a rare animal.

All of it was covered in cobwebs and a fine layer of dust.

Nayyan had developed into quite the alchemyst. At Ihsan's direction, she'd experimented for years to produce the life-giving draughts meant to replace the fabled potions from the adichara trees. Though he now knew the laboratory was where everything had started to go wrong, back then he and Nayyan had been filled with so much hope. After long years of planning, they'd begun making moves that would see them become the sole rulers of Sharakhai. They'd been convinced they could outwit and outlast the other Kings, that they could reign over the Great Shangazi forever as immortals, gods themselves.

"We thought we'd come so close," Ihsan said into the murky shadows, "but it was a mirage all along."

The other Kings were indeed all gone, but so was Nayyan. And Ihsan himself had been cursed, struck by the black mould, an unforeseen side effect of the draught Nayyan had perfected in this very room.

Ihsan picked up an hourglass tipped on its side. He set it upright so that the uppermost portion was the one with nearly all its sand gone. Ihsan chuckled as he stared at it, feeling very much the same. It felt as if events were moving faster than ever, spinning out of control. He had only so much time to follow through on his promise to Nayyan: to chart a safe path forward for Sharakhai and, in doing so, ensure Ransaneh's safety.

At the sound of approaching footsteps, he turned to see a lantern approaching the room's entrance. Tolovan's gaunt form soon complicated the doorway. With the light from his lantern sending wild shadows across his craggy face, he looked like a ghul freshly risen from the grave. "Trouble sleeping, my King?"

"As ever."

Tolovan strode into the room. "The talk with your grandsons?"

"Among other things." Ihsan smiled. "Why they can't simply lie down and show me their bellies is beyond me."

The thickets that were Tolovan's eyebrows slowly rose. "You *could* always force them, you know."

"I *do* know. The trouble is it wouldn't last. They need to be convinced."

Tolovan opened his mouth to speak, closed it, then tried again. "I don't mean to press, my Lord King, but have you considered that their plan might be the better one?"

The question was hardly surprising. Tolovan, a man fully steeped in the traditions of Sharakhai and its House of Kings, would of course be predisposed to Zevi and Mehmed's way of thinking. It was only natural that he'd be confused by Ihsan's apparent about-face. Plus, he'd been Ihsan's vizir for decades. He'd gathered information, shared shrewd insights, worked tirelessly toward Ihsan's primacy. Ihsan owed him much, so much that he nearly told him the truth. The words were right there on his lips: *I'm dying, Tolovan. I only have so much time to set things right.*

In the end, however, he held his tongue. Sharing that secret, even with Tolovan, would put himself, and therefore Ransaneh, at risk. "I *have* considered it," he finally said, "at great length, in fact. As difficult as it may be to swallow, I'm convinced the covenant is the right way forward."

Tolovan nodded, slow as a desert titan. "Then suppose all goes as planned. Where will *you* go? Where will I and the others go?"

"Fear not, old friend. I've enough set aside to ensure your future and those of my other servants."

Tolovan winced and shook his head. "I'm afraid it's gone, my Lord King. All of it. The vaults were raided by the Kundhuni tribesmen. Anything of real value in the palace was stripped."

"I'm aware. Queen Alansal has agreed to speak to them, to return what she can, but even if she returns nothing, I have several small fortunes set aside."

"But you've only just returned to the city, my Lord King. You don't know what it's been like. Things may have changed, those small fortunes lost." Tolovan peered about, as if he'd just woken to find himself in a new, strange place. "The palace will be taken. *Everything* will be taken."

"I assure you, so long as we manage the threats from the old order, everything will be fine. The city will adjust. And you will not only survive, but live a life of dignity and leisure."

The apple in Tolovan's throat bobbed once, twice, then he nodded. "Of course, my Lord King."

"Good," replied Ihsan. "Now, there's something I need of you."

"Anything, Your Excellence."

"Are you aware of the Qaimiran drug lord they call the Widow?"

Tolovan shrugged. "I've heard the name."

"Apparently her husband died of the black mould. Before he succumbed to it, she moved heaven and earth to find a cure. Or so the story goes. She has a manor along the banks of the Haddah. Find her. Ask her about her efforts."

"Very well. Might I ask why?"

"As a precaution. The chance is small, but Nayyan may have passed the black mould to Ransaneh through her milk. If so, I want to be ready."

"Consider it done."

Ihsan patted his arm. "Find some rest, old friend. We have much to do tomorrow."

Tolovan nodded, then left, a swaying black pillar in the golden circle cast by his lantern. The vision shrank, dimmed, then faded altogether.

Retrieving his lamp, Ihsan returned to his apartments. The antechamber contained a pair of scalloped archways: one to the right, which led to Ransaneh's bedroom; another on the left, which led to Ihsan's.

He debated visiting Ransaneh to give her a quick peck on the cheek but didn't want to wake her, so went to his own room instead. His bed along the left wall had high wooden posts and veils to ward off night flies. With sleep still far off, he headed toward another high archway that led to a balcony. The drapes over it billowed in the cool night breeze. The city lay twinkling beyond them, a sea of calm after the harrowing events of recent days.

He blew out the lamp and set it on a small table, then parted the drapes and stepped onto the balcony. He was headed toward a hanging chair, the one he used to love sitting in while he watched the city lights, when his gut began to twist. Though not as strong, it was markedly similar to the feeling he'd had while speaking with Mehmed and Zevi on the veranda. He drew his knife and headed toward three massive pots containing ornamental lemon trees.

He peered into the darkness, finding naught save stone and shadow, but he was certain *something* was there, waiting for him, watching. He'd just taken a step toward the first of the lemon trees when he heard a soft mewling sound. A moment later, it came again, louder and more urgently. It was Ransaneh—he would know her cry anywhere. She sounded close. Only, she should be sleeping with her wet nurse.

He returned to his room via the archway and peered into the inky darkness. "Yelida?"

A heartbeat later, the hood of a small, brass lantern was lifted, casting the far end of the room in a crimson glow. Ihsan's mouth went dry.

The lantern was set on a low table meant for sharing araq, or smoking tabbaq from the tubes of a shisha. Beside the lantern was Ransaneh, wrapped tight in her linen swaddling. She was writhing, crying. Suspended by a thin rope from the chandelier above her was a greatspear, its point facing downward. The spear was a weighty thing, the sort King Onur, the Feasting King, might once have used in battle, and its edges were keen, the ruddy light from the lantern reflecting wickedly off the gleaming lines of its leaf-shaped head.

The rush of blood grew loud in Ihsan's ears as his gaze followed the rope from the chandelier to the room's far corner, where a shadowed woman wearing a red battle dress and turban sat in a low-backed chair. Leaning into the chair with her legs kicked out, she looked both calm and dangerous. It was that, more than the shamshir at her side, that marked her as a Kestrel. Ihsan had no doubts she was Nazanin, the very Kestrel whose argument with Shohreh had apparently come to blows.

"Before you think to take another step toward your daughter," she said, "or use your power on me, know that you and I are here to talk, nothing more. Furthermore"—she gave the rope a tug, which made the spear rise and lower slightly, made it sway—"the moment you decide to step closer, I will release this rope. Are we understood?"

Ihsan realized he recognized her voice. She was the woman from the araba, the driver who'd brought him and Ransaneh up from his sandship beyond King's Harbor. How she'd managed to insinuate herself into his life—and, more importantly, *why*—was beyond his reckoning.

Nazanin gave the rope another sharp tug. "My Good King," she boomed, "do we have an *understanding*?"

"Your position is clear," Ihsan said calmly. Thankfully by then, perhaps due to the sound of their voices, Ransaneh had stopped crying. "Now, where's Yelida?"

Nazanin leaned forward and twisted the lantern so it illuminated an unmoving body: Yelida's corpse, laying by the table, her throat slit. Blood glistened on the carpet beneath her, so dark in places it looked like a black mirror.

It took no small amount of effort, but Ihsan finally returned his attention to Nazanin. "Who sent you?"

Nazanin's laugh was a low rumble. "Sharakhai *itself* sent me, the city you vowed to protect."

"I *am* protecting it," Ihsan said.

"It may surprise you to learn this, but there are people who see it differently."

"And who are they, these people?"

Nazanin sneered as if disappointed by the question. "Know this, *O King*. You've made some rather poor decisions of late, and it's *those decisions* that have put you in the unfortunate position you and your daughter find yourselves in. Even so, this is no death sentence, but a warning. You could still live a prosperous life, so long as you follow orders."

Ihsan stepped to his left and sat on the bed, if only to give the sense he'd chosen the way of the dove instead of the hawk. "And what orders would those be?"

"Abandon the city. Leave in disgrace. Allow *us*, the *true* children of Sharakhai, those willing to sacrifice anything to safeguard her future, to lead the way."

"As I told Zevi—" Ihsan paused. "How is he, by the way?"

Nazanin only stared.

"Well, as I told him, there's no need to take a hard line. Amendments can still be made to the covenant. He can find more favorable terms, if he'll only tell me what they are. We might even add a clause to supply you with kittens to crush under your boot heel, or whatever it is you like to do in your spare time."

She tugged on the rope, causing the spear to lift. "You would jest, even at a time like this?"

"I was merely trying to illuminate the reality we find ourselves in. Your nameless benefactor doesn't like the proposal? Provide a counteroffer. I'll bring it to Davud personally."

Nazanin tilted her head. "Well, if you're going to bring it to the bread baker's son *personally* ..."

"Ah, see? That wasn't so hard, was it?"

She stood, holding the rope taut. "Davud's proposal is unacceptable." The spear above Ransaneh swayed gently with the Kestrel's movement. "Leave this city peacefully, for your daughter's sake if no one else's." With that, she tugged hard on the rope and released it.

"Halt!" Ihsan cried.

He put power into that simple command. It felt as if the flesh and bone inside his mouth were burning. It made his tongue ache. Yet Nazanin defied the order. As the spear plummeted, she flew toward the archway leading to the balcony. As Ihsan dove toward Ransaneh, the tip of the spear stabbed into the table with a resounding thud. Ransaneh shivered violently. A dark line appeared along her cheek. And she began to shriek.

Ihsan picked her up and held her close. Nazanin lingered in the archway. "I'll admit, I heard rumors your power was waning, but I didn't believe them until now." She was all but lost to the gently flowing drapes as she moved beyond the archway. "Think carefully on all I've said, O Honey-tongued King. My aim might not be so poor the next time around."

She leapt onto the baluster, as though she were preparing to jump. She paused, however, her gaze drawn toward the lemon tree on her right. Then she was gone.

Chapter Four

Ihsan pressed a corner of Ransaneh's swaddling against her cut to stem the bleeding. Her cries grew louder as he rushed toward the balcony. He arrived at the railing in time to see Nazanin far below, slipping along a rope. Moments later, she gained the mountain's rocky slopes and disappeared behind a cluster of boulders.

Ihsan was worried and angry, but just then all he could think about was the strange, gut-twisting sensation. It had shifted, moved farther away. Hoping to locate its source, he paced beyond the ornamental trees, feeling, searching. The sensation ebbed more with each step, then vanished altogether. Behind him, Ihsan heard servants approaching.

When he returned to his bedroom, the anteroom was bright with lantern light. Tolovan passed through the archway first. Behind him were the palace steward, his wife, and a cluster of five worried-looking Silver Spears brandishing shamshirs. Their arrival should have brought relief—in years past it would have—but Ihsan had been away from the palace for many long months. Several of his old servants were dead or gone, which was partly why it had been so easy for Nazanin to disguise herself as one of his drivers. Who else might Nazanin have turned in that time, either through bribery, coercion, or alignment with Zevi's cause?

It hurt to talk so soon after using his power, but just then he didn't care. "Out!" he shouted to the servants and guards behind Tolovan. "All of you, out!"

Tolovan, bless him, took charge and ushered servants and soldiers alike out of the anteroom and into the hall. "My Lord King, what happened?" Tolovan asked on his return.

Thankfully, Ransaneh's crying had subsided. "The Kestrel, Nazanin, was waiting for me in my apartments."

"Gods," Tolovan said when Ihsan had finished the tale, "to use your daughter as bait?"

"There's more. There was someone or some*thing* on the balcony." He went on to describe it in more detail. "I felt the same sort of thing while I was talking with Zevi and Mehmed."

"You've no idea what it was? *Who* it was?"

Ihsan shrugged. "None."

The steward, his wife, and the Silver Spears were still in the hall outside the antechamber. More servants had joined them. Some were glancing his way. Most of them were still faithful to him, surely, but how could he be certain there wasn't a traitor or two among them? He was tempted to interview them, to command them to tell the truth, but even assuming his power worked, he couldn't use it on so many of them at once. And some might resist, as Nazanin had. Worse, when his power waned, he couldn't tell if someone was speaking truths or lies.

I have to leave, he realized, staring down at Ransaneh. He needed a safe haven, a place to regroup. "Have everyone return to their rooms," he said to Tolovan. "No one is to leave until commanded otherwise, understand? You'll see to it yourself."

Tolovan paused a moment, rubbed his beard, then nodded dutifully. "Of course, Your Excellence."

"Bring an araba to the front of the palace when it's done."

Tolovan bowed and set off immediately.

Ihsan heard hushed murmuring in the hallway. Then it faded as Tolovan and the others shuffled away from his apartments. Ihsan lay Ransaneh on his bed and began stuffing his and Ransaneh's clothes into the same canvas bag he'd brought to the palace that morning. Often, he found himself peering at Yelida's gashed corpse, the black pool of blood beneath her, or into the dark corners of the room or other places the light of his lantern didn't reach. He felt like Nazanin would reappear any moment, wielding her wicked, curving shamshir.

Soon the bag was slung over his shoulder, Ransaneh was in his arms, and he was rushing down the palace's curving stairs toward the entrance. He saw no one, *heard* no one as he paced down the long hall. The entrance door clanked loudly as he opened it, boomed as he shut it. He felt even more exposed outside. He imagined a dozen assassins crouched on the palace walls, sighting him along the shafts of arrows, ready to release.

Yet the night remained blessedly silent, and no arrows flew. Soon enough the clatter of wagon wheels and the rattle of horses' tack rose from the stables around the corner. Tolovan, sitting in the driver's seat of the same araba that had delivered him to the palace, guided a two-horse team around the gravel circle and pulled to a stop at the foot of the stairs.

"Where shall I take you, my Lord King?"

Ihsan shook his head. "This is where we part, Tolovan. Ransaneh and I go alone."

"Your Excellence?"

"I need someone I trust inside Tauriyat."

Tolovan shifted in his seat and lowered the reins but stopped short of wrapping them around their iron hook. "What you need, My King, is someone to help protect the two of you."

"No, Tolovan. You're all I have left. I don't trust anyone else to help me. You need to remain here."

Tolovan, his jaw set grimly, shook his head as if he were fixing for an argument. Then he took a deep breath, nodded, and wrapped the reins around their hook. He stepped down, the gravel crunching beneath his boots. "How will I contact you?"

Holding Ransaneh tight, Ihsan climbed into the driver's bench. She hardly made a burble as he placed her swaddled form gently on the footboard between his feet and took up the reins. "I'll send word as soon as I can. Keep your eyes open, your ears sharp."

"Of course, my Lord King."

Ihsan snapped the reins, guided the araba through the barbican, and drove down along King's Road. To his right, Sharakhai sprawled, a field of fallen stars in the darkness of the night. As the wagon shook and the tack jingled, Ihsan looked down at Ransaneh.

"The city," he told her. "The city will see us safe."

Chapter Five

On a bright morning, five days after fleeing his palace, Ihsan left Ransaneh in the care of a gardener who worked at the small Kundhuni temple he'd chosen as their hiding place.

Ihsan would be lying if he said he hadn't thought about following Nazanin's orders. He could still leave the city, never to be seen again.

He could travel to Qaimir or Malasan and let the city's problems sort themselves out. But to do so would invite the very real possibility that Sharakhai would be dragged back into war. He owed it to Ransaneh, he owed it to the *city*, to prevent that.

From the temple, he trekked east through the poor western neighborhood known as the Red Crescent and headed along the Spear, one of Sharakhai's busiest thoroughfares. The day was scorchingly hot, with no breeze to speak of. The road, though wide, was packed cheek to jowl, especially when a wagon or two needed to pass. Normally a cause for irritation, the traffic was a blessing in disguise. It allowed Ihsan to blend in, which helped calm his fraying nerves. He'd been terrified Nazanin would find him in the temple, that she'd slay him and Ransaneh both for not having fled Sharakhai.

It had taken several days to establish a safe channel of communications with Tolovan, then a few more for Tolovan to arrange Ihsan's pending meeting with Davud, the covenant's chief architect. Now that the time had come, Ihsan wondered whether he was making a mistake, not because he didn't trust Davud—Davud was one of the few people he *did* trust—but because *any* meeting necessarily put him and Ransaneh at risk. The risk was necessary, though. Ihsan needed advice, he needed *help*. Just as important, he and Davud needed to decide what to do next.

Ahead, Ihsan heard a man roar, "Make way! Make way!"

He peered over the crowd. On spotting a mounted patrol of five Silver Spears headed his way, he pulled the hood of his thawb low and ducked into an alley. An old man pissing behind a stack of crates stared, but Ihsan paid him no mind and waited for the Spears to pass, then resumed his trek toward the center of the city.

He passed beneath the old walls of the city, broke from the Spear onto a much narrower street, and soon reached the spice market, a cavernous stone building with high archways along its length. Heading inside, the market was as loud and raucous as he remembered. The scents of anise, pepper, and garlic filled the air. His mouth watered at the aromas of thousand-layer sweets, roasted chicken, lamb on a spit, and savory potato pies.

He paused near a table laden with dozens of bags of spices and more beneath it. The spice monger, Seyhan, was haggling with a heavyset woman.

"Hoping to buy a bit of saffron?" came a melodic voice.

Ihsan turned to find a man standing beside him, a burly fellow with heavy jowls and deep bags under his eyes. He had a greasy pate. His black hair was curly and lank. He looked nothing like Davud, yet his voice was a perfect match. *And his eyes,* Ihsan mused. The expressive kindness in them mirrored Ihsan's memories of the young collegia scholar.

"You don't look so good," Ihsan said as the two of them headed deeper into the spice market. "Are you sure you're getting enough sleep?"

"I'm sleeping fine." Davud walked with a bit of a shuffle, as if one knee were bothering him. "You, however, look like you haven't slept in days."

"And can you blame me?"

"No," Davud said, "I suppose I can't."

Soon they arrived at a small tea shop near the center of the market, where they sat at a laughably small table and Davud ordered a pot of barley tea. A short while later, they were sipping from tiny cups, anonymous to the press of traffic flowing past the shop.

"Per your request," Davud began, "I did some digging into Nazanin. She returned to Sharakhai recently from a mission given to her by Husamettín himself. She was rather displeased to find the King of Swords dead."

"Do you know who she's working for now?"

"I'm still working on that bit."

"There are only two possibilities …" Ihsan prompted.

"I understand, but my time is quite limited."

"What news of Shohreh, then?"

"The Crone has gone missing. No one's seen her since the day of your meeting with Mehmed and Zevi. Her Kestrels-in-training have gone missing as well."

"All of them?"

"All of them."

The last Ihsan heard, more than a dozen young women were training to become Kestrels. "And what do you glean from this?"

Davud shrugged, leaned back in his chair. "Given the confrontation you reported between Nazanin and Shohreh, it could be that an internal war has begun within the ranks of the Kestrels."

"Or?"

"They've made amends and are plotting with one another, likely something big if they've both gone underground."

Ihsan thought back to how he'd dismissed Shohreh, how he'd stated, in no uncertain terms, that he didn't trust her. She'd hated him even *before* then. Might it have pushed her to align herself with Nazanin instead of him? Suddenly, it felt as though the throng outside the tea shop was pressing in on him, and that Nazanin and Shohreh were stealing through the crowd, ready to slit his and Davud's throats.

Davud glanced at the crowd, then returned his attention to his tea. "We're safe. I've ensured it."

"Couldn't you spend a bit of effort to find them? Or to find the truth about Mehmed and Zevi?" Ihsan bared his wrist. "Take a measure of my blood if it helps."

Davud's wry smile was the sort Ihsan might once have flashed. "As I said, I have quite a lot to do already. And there's a larger issue at hand. Zevi, along with Mehmed's younger brother, Yavin, have been pressing those who've been on the fence, plus those who were only *leaning* toward accepting the terms of the covenant. And it's working. Before Nazanin visited your palace, we had enough votes to ratify the covenant. Now it's very much in doubt, and there are still two days left."

"Do my ears deceive me, or are you're asking for my help?"

Davud gave an embarrassed grimace. "I know it's asking a lot—it puts you and your daughter at risk—but it can't be helped. We need this. *Sharakhai* needs it. So yes, I want your help with Zevi. He's the lynchpin to the coming vote. But let me be clear. Under no circumstances should you use your power to convince him."

"Then I suppose arranging it so that someone turns up missing is *also* out of the question?"

Davud leaned in and spoke in a low voice. "You're bloody well right, Ihsan. It would only turn more lords against us. If we're to succeed, Zevi must be convinced that the covenant is in his best interests."

"What about Mehmed?"

"He's been conspicuously absent the past several days. For now, we need to concentrate on Zevi."

Ihsan had to work to keep himself from laughing. *How perfectly the tables have turned.* Davud, once a minor figure in the great game, had risen to become a primary player, while Ihsan had been reduced to a pawn. "If you're asking me to coax the mule without a stick, then I need more carrots."

"Of course. Tell me what you want."

"What else? Land, business, money …"

"Done," Davud said. "Anything within my power."

"Very well"—Ihsan stood and held out his hand—"I'll speak to him."

Davud stood and clasped Ihsan's forearm. As the two of them shook, the proprietor rushed in and cleared their cups, saucers, and the pot of tea.

"Take care," Davud said.

"You as well. I'll be in contact soon."

Ihsan left the spice market and made for the Red Crescent. The news about Shohreh and Nazanin was disquieting. He'd have to take great care lest they catch him unawares. Knowing there was little to do about it just then, he concentrated his thoughts on Zevi. He was a venal, materialistic man. He'd earn more under the terms of the covenant—Ihsan just had to prove it to him.

He was working out how he might do so, and how much of his own fortune he'd be forced to use to sweeten the deal, when he reached the entrance to the temple, a narrow alley that led to an old stone arch. The briar rose carved into the arch's keystone was the sign of Naamdah, the Kundhuni goddess of good fortune. It was the very same temple he'd stayed in with Husamettín, Cahil, and Cahil's daughter Yndris during their search for King Zeheb. As then, the knowledge that Naamdah was secretly the patron goddess of thieves felt apropos.

Dark business for dark days, Ihsan mused.

The alley opened onto the temple's central courtyard, which was little more than a rock garden with four crabapple trees and a roughly hewn statue of Naamdah—one hand behind her back, the opposite arm held outward, palm up—standing tall at its center. Most who visited the temple took her posture to mean she was offering a boon to her devotees. Ihsan, knowing the truth about the goddess's nature, had always thought Naamdah looked as if she were demanding money from those who stood before her while holding a knife behind her back.

Against a stone wall to Ihsan's right was the nave, its tall, wooden doors open, the pews visible beyond. To the left of the nave, directly ahead of Ihsan, was a portico that shaded the paved flagstone walkway in front of the rooms set aside for the clergy. Ihsan had been given one. It was a place to sleep, a place to stay safe, hidden away from prying eyes. The room was where Ihsan had left Ransaneh with the temple's gardener.

Ihsan was headed toward it when he felt the now-familiar twisting in his gut. He stopped so quickly the soles of his boots skidded against the gravel.

Something or some*one* was hiding ahead of him, cloaked by magic. He peered into the shadows below the portico. Finding nothing, he studied the space behind the open doors of the temple, then below the crabapples trees. He'd just shifted his attention to the base of Naamdah's statue when the feeling intensified.

There, visible in the shadows below Naamdah's outstretched arm, was a girl of thirteen or fourteen summers. She wore a black dress and had curly, dark brown hair. She pushed off the statue and ran toward him. "Get down, my King!"

Ihsan tried to draw the kenshar at his belt, but the girl barreled into him before he could. They both fell hard onto the gravel.

Something blurred to Ihsan's left. He heard a sharp crunch, blinked, and saw a black arrow sticking out of the ground next to him.

The girl jumped up and tugged him toward Naamdah's statue. "Take cover!"

As Ihsan scrabbled toward it, he caught sight of someone crouched on the dormitory roof—a woman, he realized. She was barely visible above the roofline, but Ihsan saw her deep crimson turban and dress. Whether his would-be assassin was Nazanin or Shohreh, he couldn't say, but it hardly mattered just then. He had to get Ransaneh. He had to find another place for them to hide.

The girl grabbed a fistful of Ihsan's thawb and yanked him behind the statue as a second arrow came streaking in. He heard the rattlewing buzz of the fletching go past, felt its wind along his neck; it clacked against the stone statue a finger's breadth from his ear.

"You were told to leave the city, O King of Lies," called the woman on the roof.

Nazanin's voice. A moment later, he heard the rattle of clay tiles shifting, saw her creeping over the roof. A short bow at the ready, another black arrow laid across its string, she dropped to the courtyard ten paces away, then sidestepped, trying to get a better bead on Ihsan.

Ihsan kept the statue between them. The girl drew two short fighting swords from sheaths on her back. What she thought she could do against an elite swordswoman like Nazanin, Ihsan had no idea.

"Why don't you set the bow aside?" he called around the statue. "I'll send for some water and wine. Or araq, if you prefer. We can speak inside the temple, a place of peace and contemplation." When she lifted her bow and drew the string, Ihsan called upon the power of his voice. He felt it burn along his lower jaw, then his tongue, as he spoke slowly, "Set the bow *down*."

It worked much better than it had the other night in his palace.

Nazanin went stock still. Her body shook. Her breath became markedly more rapid. She'd even released the tension on the bowstring, but then she took another deep breath, groaned through gritted teeth, raised the bow again, and sent an arrow streaking toward him.

Perhaps it was because she was still in the throes of fighting his command, or perhaps it was merely a warning shot, but the arrow hit the rough stone of the wall behind him with a sharp crack.

Nazanin looked exhausted but defiant as well. "Why everyone fears you so is beyond me."

Ihsan paused, doing his best to hide his disappointment. "Are you saying you *wouldn't* like a bit of water and wine?"

The effects of Ihsan's voice wore off, and Nazanin stood tall and craned her neck. "You know, it's unfortunate you and your daughter have to die." She backed toward the room that held Ransaneh. "I think I might actually have enjoyed working for you."

Ihsan couldn't allow Nazanin to reach Ransaneh, but if he stepped out from behind the statue, she would pierce his heart with an arrow. He was about to try his voice again when the door to his room opened and Shohreh, wearing a red battle dress of her own, flew out holding a black shamshir.

Nazanin spun just in time to block Shohreh's swing with her bow. When Nazanin turned her head, the girl in black ran at her, brandishing her smaller blades.

"Wait!" Ihsan rasped at her. "You're going to get yourself killed!"

Nazanin retreated and drew her shamshir. She danced around a stone pillar, parried a blow from Shoreh, ran to the garden, and placed a bench between herself and the girl.

The girl leapt over the bench, and Nazanin sent her reeling with a blindingly quick slash at the girl's unprotected neck. Ihsan thought surely he was witnessing the girl's death, but she disappeared like so much smoke. The shadows shifted, and the girl reappeared, swinging for Nazanin's exposed midsection.

Nazanin, her eyes wide with shock, blocked the girl's swing with a sharp cry.

As the fight came nearer to Ihsan, he didn't bother using the kenshar at his belt. He wouldn't come anywhere close to Nazanin before she slit his throat, and he wouldn't have shadows to save him. He picked up a sizable rock instead. He was planning to throw it, to create a distraction, but no sooner had he lifted it than Nazanin sent a powerful blow against the girl, a thing the girl barely managed to block using both blades.

Nazanin ducked beneath a swing from Shohreh, and dove away across the gravel. She rolled over one shoulder and was back on her feet and sprinting for the courtyard wall. Ihsan, feeling perfectly useless, threw the rock anyway, but misjudged Nazanin's speed. She vaulted against the wall, leapt up to the lip, and Ihsan's rock clunked harmlessly against the mismatched stones and landed with a pathetic thud.

Nazanin was over the wall and gone.

Chapter Six

Two hours after Nazanin's attack in Naamdah's temple, Ihsan rode a particularly cantankerous mule over the dusty streets of Sharakhai. They were headed north along the Corona, toward temporary shelter and blessedly *away from* the Red Crescent. He'd given up his thawb for a homespun shirt, sirwal trousers tied at the knee, and sandals. And though he'd never enjoyed wearing hats or turbans, he'd wrapped a patterned blue shemagh around his head and neck. Even so, he was deathly afraid someone would recognize him, or that Nazanin herself would spy him from the rooftops. Despite his fear and the tenseness of the situation, he nearly laughed.

I was a King once. Now I'm a fugitive in my own city.

Shohreh had offered to hide them in a small room in a west-end tenement, but Ihsan declined. There were too many eyes that might see them. Too many potential informers. Instead, he'd reached out to Tolovan to arrange a much quieter hiding place that, if all went well, would give them a few days' reprieve. It should be long enough to figure out what to do about Zevi and the vote on the covenant.

As the mule plodded past a portly sweets vendor and his cart, Ihsan heard Ransaneh stir. She was in a lidded basket, one of two hanging over the mule's shoulders. She was the one most likely to give them away—Nazanin and her agents would surely be on the lookout for a middle-aged man with a babe—which was why he'd swaddled her and hidden her inside the onion basket.

Ahead of Ihsan, Shohreh rode on the back of a severely malnourished akhala. In the saddle behind her was Mala, the girl who'd helped save him from Nazanin. Behind Mala, slouched over the akhala's rump, was a large leather satchel that contained their effects. Both Shohreh and Mala wore simple dresses with homespun vests and white veils. The horse, mule, and change of clothes had all been provided by Shohreh—the woman was not only shrewd and resourceful, she was also well prepared. At Ransaneh's cry, Mala glanced over her shoulder, then fixed her gaze back on the dusty road ahead, perhaps not wanting to draw attention to it.

Ihsan lifted the lid of the basket, which spurred his mule to stop and attempt to bite him. Ihsan snapped the reins, then kicked the mule's sides. "Just follow the akhala, you miserable beast."

As the mule lumbered into motion, Ihsan stared down at Ransaneh. Wrapped in a nest of blankets, she stared up at him, red in the face. She was hungry and would become progressively more cranky about it. Indeed, as they passed by the northern harbor and its wide, sandy bay, she began to cry in earnest. Ihsan shushed her, rocked the basket with more gusto. He tried to ignore the passersby, a crew of sandsmen headed for the quays, but it was impossible.

Thankfully, the ship's crew made no fuss about it, and the traffic grew sparse beyond the harbor. Soon they arrived at an estate with a manor house, stables, and several servants' quarters. By the time they met Tolovan in the stables, Ransaneh was crying loud enough to awaken the dead.

Ihsan dropped to the ground and lifted her from the basket. Behind him, a man's voice called out. "A daughter …"

Ihsan turned to find a young man standing in the stable doorway, silhouetted by the trees and sunlight. He stepped further into the stables, and Ihsan got a better look at him. He had the sort of roguish good looks that women, not to mention a good number of men, melted over. His dusty blond hair was lighter on top, as if he'd been spending time in the sun, and his eyes were discerning, piercing, not so different from the man he'd inherited his fortune from.

Tolovan, who'd arranged the meeting at Ihsan's request, bowed, waved to the newcomer, and intoned in his deep voice, "My Lord King, please meet Tariq of the Shallows."

Tariq sauntered closer. He was taller than Ihsan, roughly the same height as Shohreh. He seemed to size Ihsan up, as he might any newcomer to the troubled streets of the city's west end where he'd grown up. "I understand you were in these stables before." He motioned to the straw-covered ground. "The story goes you were standing on this very spot when the Confessor King killed Osman."

Osman was the erstwhile owner of Sharakhai's fighting pits and a man who'd run no small number of rackets. Tariq had come up under his tutelage. When Osman had been imprisoned by the Kings, Tariq had taken the reins of his small empire. By all accounts, he'd done so deftly and had continued in that capacity when Osman returned frail in mind and spirit from his imprisonment. Osman had been a gladiator in the pits once, but his experiences in the House of Kings—with Cahil the Confessor King, in particular—had broken him. Later, when Cahil had taken his war hammer to Osman's head and killed him in a petty act of retribution, Tariq became the sole inheritor of his holdings.

Ihsan handed Ransaneh to Mala and gave Tariq a respectful nod. "What Cahil did was rash and cruel. May your former master find peace in the farther fields."

"The gods willing." Tariq crossed his arms over his chest. "Here's the important part. I'm told you tried to stop him?"

Ihsan nodded again, deeper this time. "I did."

"Well, know this, O Honey-tongued King. That is the only reason I agreed to grant you shelter. I consider myself in your debt. Stay a few days. Stay a week. When it's done, my debt to you will be paid."

Ihsan doubted that was the only reason he'd agreed to help him. Tariq's business had been all but crushed when the Mireans invaded Sharakhai. He wanted life to return to normal, too. He wanted *profits* to return to normal, which meant supporting Davud's efforts where he could.

"Whatever the reason," Ihsan said, "you have my thanks."

Tariq nodded and left. Shohreh retrieved the leather satchel from the akhala's rump and slung it over her shoulder, then Tolovan led them to the rooms they'd been given on the manor's upper floors. As Shohreh dropped her satchel off in a modestly appointed bedroom, Tariq's cook, a heavyset woman with arms like cordwood, brought a platter filled with bread, cheese, and red wine, plus some mashed peas with mint for Ransaneh, and placed it on the tall, rectangular table to one side of the much larger, high-ceilinged room across the hall.

Mala picked up the bowl of mashed peas and jutted her chin toward Ransaneh. "I can feed her if you like."

"You're certain?" Ihsan asked.

Mala smiled with teeth and dimples. She had striking brown eyes and curly black hair. "My mother used to force me to feed my little sister, Jein. I hated it then, but she's grown now. I miss it."

When Ihsan nodded, Mala carried Ransaneh over to the massive, four-poster bed, where she sat, cradled Ransaneh in the crook of her arm, and began feeding her with familiar ease. Ihsan opened the doors to the balcony, and the three adults brought the food and wine out to a small table. As Shohreh cut the bread and put slices of butter and cheese on them, Ihsan poured the wine, stopping short of Tolovan's glass when he raised a hand.

"Thank you, my Lord King, but I ate before you arrived, and wine upsets my stomach of late."

Ihsan shrugged, set the bottle down, and took a healthy swallow from his glass. He'd expected rotgut, but the wine was a more-than-drinkable red with notes of cherry, plum, and a hint of tomato leaf. Tolovan brooded in silence while Ihsan and Shohreh ate and downed half the wine. As the meal was winding down, Ihsan caught Shohreh's eye and said, "I suppose proper thanks are in order."

"There's no need to thank me," she replied. "I was only doing my duty."

"And yet I *do* thank you, O Crone, for having saved not only my life but that of my child."

Shohreh narrowed her eyes at him as she tore off a hunk of bread. "What I did, I did for Sharakhai."

Ihsan gave her a polite bow of his head. "As you say." He glanced toward the balcony doors. "The girl, she's a blood mage?"

Shohreh shook her head and popped the hunk of bread into her mouth. "She's a child of shadow," she said around her chewing, "a gift from the gods, apparently. Mala doesn't know where it came from."

"Is that why you chose the girl to become a Kestrel?"

Shohreh slowed her chewing then swallowed with a shrug. "Among other reasons."

"It was you who sent her, then, to spy on me at the palace?"

Tolovan shifted in his seat and pursed his lips. He would have been particularly aggrieved that Ihsan's palace—*his* palace—had been intruded upon not once, but twice, in a span of hours.

"I did," Shohreh said, "but I told no lie in your throne room. I was more interested in Mehmed and Zevi's plans than I was yours."

Ihsan considered this while he watched the wind play through the trees. "I'm still not certain if Nazanin is working for Mehmed, Zevi, or both. Do you know?"

Shohreh shrugged. "Not sure. I've been focused on finding a safe place for my girls, then on finding *you*."

Tolovan raised a finger. "As you asked, my Lord King, I've kept my ear to the ground. In the days since your departure from the House of Kings, Zevi has rallied many sons and daughters of the former Kings to his 'righteous crusade,' as he calls it. Given how closely his and Nazanin's interests align, I suspect it's he who's giving orders."

"And Mehmed? Davud told me he's remained far from the fray, conspicuously so."

Tolovan nodded. "That's true. I've heard little news of him these past several days."

Ihsan had suspected it was Zevi. "Likely Mehmed is allowing Zevi's anger dictate the course of events while he himself avoids perceptions of wrongdoing."

"I tend to agree," Tolovan said. "You aren't without power and influence, after all. Mehmed likely considers it too dangerous to make a move against you now." Tolovan turned to Shohreh. "What of our Crone? What resources does she have at her disposal?"

Shohreh glanced at the balcony doors. "I have Mala."

Tolovan's perpetual frown deepened. "Are there no other Kestrels you can call upon?"

Shohreh had another hunk of bread in her hands, but she dropped it onto the plate and dusted her hands of crumbs. "The war has decimated our ranks. Two Kestrels are confirmed dead. Two more were sent to gather information from Tsitsian and haven't returned. Another is in Malasan doing the same. Three more are unaccounted for and most likely dead. That leaves only Nazanin."

"And your apprentices?" Ihsan asked. "Are there no more like Mala?"

"None that I trust."

Ihsan tossed back the last of his wine to hide his disappointment. "Don't think me ungrateful, Shohreh, but it's impossible to note that it might have been easier for you to work with Zevi and Nazanin. Why align yourself with Davud? Why align yourself with *me*?"

"I told you—"

"I want more than a vague statement of concern over the city's welfare. There's more to the story, and I need to know it, for my own sake"—he waved toward the doors, toward Ransaneh—"and for hers."

Shohreh seemed to consider this for a time before speaking. "Our former Crone, Ulaan, was a cruel mistress. She'd marked Mala for death. She wanted Mala's family slaughtered as well, for the crime of being related to her." Her gaze shifted to Tauriyat, the top of which was visible over the acacias. "I know better than most the rot that has formed in Sharakhai."

When Shohreh drew her attention back to him, he said, "You told me Ulaan died of a random stabbing in the Shallows."

Shohreh shrugged. "Random, not random … The point is this. If there's a chance for us to retain our identity while we forge a better future for Sharakhai and the desert, then I think we should take it." She paused. "Since we're talking about resources, should we discuss the effectiveness of your power? It's waning, isn't it?"

Ihsan smiled. "What the gods giveth, they also taketh away."

Shohreh's nostrils flared. "It's gone entirely, then?"

"Not entirely, no. It's become … unpredictable."

Ihsan didn't know Shohreh well, but it hardly took a collegia scholar to figure out why she would be concerned, even angry, over the state of his god-given power. She'd taken her own hearing for the express purpose of protecting her master from Ihsan's power. Now Ihsan's power was waning. It would be a particularly galling turn of events, even for a dedicated woman like her.

"The important thing," Ihsan added quickly, "is that the vote on the covenant is happening the day after tomorrow. Zevi seems to be leading the effort, so we should focus on him. We need to convince him that it's in his best interests to call off Nazanin."

"My King," Tolovan broke in, "I feel it my duty to offer another path."

"Which is?"

"We have arrived at a day that you and Queen Nayyan long fought for. Is it so inconceivable that you would shift your not inconsiderable influence to the side of your grandsons? That you would lead them and the others? Could you not avoid repercussions from Queen Alansal by *pretending* to agree to the demands laid out in the covenant, then rebuilding the city as *you* see fit?"

Tolovan often hid behind a mask of stoicism, but Ihsan could see the pinched lips, the deepening of the already deep creases along his cheeks and the corners of his eyes, the way his left leg would bob, still, then bob again. Part of Ihsan wanted to confess everything—Tolovan, of all people, deserved to know the truth about his disease—but when Ransaneh burbled from the other room, he knew he couldn't. Not until he knew precisely what he would do with Ransaneh.

"I appreciate your thoughts on the matter," Ihsan said to Tolovan, "but I've made my decision."

Tolovan blinked once, twice, then nodded. "Of course, my Lord King." He stood in a rush. "Then by your leave, I will go. I have an appointment with the Widow."

Ihsan had all but forgotten his request that Tolovan contact her. "You've spoken with her?"

"Not as such. It took some days for her to reply to my initial request for an audience. That audience now awaits. The fates willing, she'll have good news."

If Shohreh was curious about the purpose behind the audience, she didn't say so. After Tolovan left, Ihsan returned his attention to her. "I need a way to reach Zevi."

"He spends much of his days at the silk market. But what's our plan? I assume you want something more permanent than the holding of a blade to his throat."

Ihsan did, indeed, which was why he'd ruled out using the power of his voice. Even assuming it worked, the chances of a command lasting more than a few hours were slim. He needed something else, something that could be counted on.

"How many men does Zevi have?"

"Roughly two dozen. Why?"

Ihsan stood. "Because I need to know how much this is going to cost me."

"How much *what* is going to cost you?"

"Why, paying people to hold a blade to Zevi's throat, dear Shohreh."

Chapter Seven

On the west side of the Trough was a small but rather famous building that for the past two hundred years had been home to Sharakhai's largest silk market. Ihsan himself had gifted the business to Zevi's father, Ihsan's son, decades ago. Zevi had inherited it on his father's death but hadn't had the foresight to do much with it since.

He might have expanded the business but had instead let it drift along with the prevailing winds of fate and commerce, using it as the primary base of operations for his 'security venture,' as he called it. The proposition to the other businesses along the Trough was simple: pay Zevi and his enforcers will ensure nothing untoward happened in or around their premises, be it thievery, roughhousing, or the presence of unsavory characters. Zevi had seen to it that his enforcers' wives, mothers, and sisters found jobs in the silk market, transforming the market into a cozy, familial affair that deepened their loyalty. But if Ihsan had learned anything over his centuries in Sharakhai, it was that even familial ties could be severed by greed.

The day following Ihsan's retreat to Tariq's manor, Zevi arrived at the market near noon, flanked by two rangy men in flowing white thawbs and blue skullcaps. All three men stopped just inside the threshold and stared about in wonder. Though the room was large enough to accommodate thirty seamstresses, not a single seat was filled. Ihsan sat in a chair before the rows of empty sewing tables, and Shohreh stood in one corner, beyond several low tables with pillows and shishas.

Zevi snapped his fingers and pointed at Ihsan. His enforcers unhooked studded clubs from their belts and brandished them.

"I wouldn't do that if I were you." Ihsan pointed at Shohreh.

Their eyes shifted toward her. All three men seemed startled to find Shohreh standing there. She wore her battle dress, her red veil drawn across her face. The arrow strung across her bow was aimed at the floor.

When one of the enforcers took a step toward her, she lifted the bow and drew the string, aiming for the man's chest. He stopped. A pregnant silence followed.

"I only wish to talk, Zevi," Ihsan said finally.

"So talk," Zevi replied.

"Alone."

A tense moment followed, but for all his bluster, Zevi had never been one to overplay his hand. He tilted his head toward the door, and his men marched from the room and closed the door behind them.

Shohreh eased the tension on the bowstring and lowered the bow.

Zevi seemed transfixed by Shohreh, seemingly afraid she'd shoot him the moment he looked away, but then he fixed his bulldog glare on Ihsan. "Where are my people?"

"I'll tell you soon enough. In the meantime, indulge me while I share with you a story."

Zevi crossed his arms over his ample chest. "A story ..."

"About a dancing spider and a singing frog."

Zevi frowned. "I'm too old for children's tales, Grandfather."

Anyone born and raised in Sharakhai knew the tale of the dancing spider and singing frog, unlikely allies who join forces to save Kundhun from a horde of voracious beetles. The tale had spread from Kundhun to the desert centuries ago and grown more fanciful—as all stories do—as time and distance bore it ever farther from its birthplace.

"What I'm about to share," Ihsan replied, "is no children's tale, but the truth behind the fable. Amidst the rolling hills of Kundhun can be found a particularly large spider known as the dancing butcher. The butcher burrows in the hills to lay its eggs and raise its young. It has a problem, however. Trapjaw ants plague those same hills. The trapjaws are predators themselves. They occasionally challenge the weak or unwary butcher, but that's far from the greatest threat they pose. The trapjaws, you see, have developed a taste for the dancing butcher's eggs. Should they manage to find an unguarded burrow, the trapjaws steal the butchers' eggs—their treasure, in essence—and take them to their *own* nest, where they're eaten or fed to their young. In response, the butcher has developed a unique defense mechanism. It invites another animal into its home."

"Let me guess," Zevi said with a flat stare, "a singing frog?"

"You always were the sharp one, Zevi. The black humming frog of Kundhun is a voracious little beast. It's perfectly happy to fill that appetite by devouring any and all ants, trapjaws or otherwise, that come across its path. The butcher finds this quite useful and so allows the frog to remain in its home. And for the frog's part, not only is it fed a steady diet, the butcher protects it from creatures that might find *it* tasty by the butcher's very presence. Thus, the dancing butcher's lair is safe, and the frog feasts happily."

Zevi's frown deepened. "Are you trying to tell me that, in this rather tortuous scenario, *you're* the dancing spider?"

"Tsk, tsk, Zevi. I thought it would be obvious by now that *you're* the spider."

"I don't see that."

"No?" Ihsan spread his arms. "Here is your lair, Grandson. The small empire you've built is your treasure, your clutch of eggs."

Zevi rolled his eyes. "And somehow you think *you're* the frog?"

Ihsan leaned forward in his chair. "I am very much that humming black frog. Earlier, you asked why this room isn't filled with happy seamstresses. It's because I paid them one day's labor to let us talk in peace. I paid them for tomorrow's work as well. In fact, I agreed to pay them for the entire week, and the week after that. I agreed to pay them for the next three years."

"You're going to *pay* them …?"

"I am, so long as I'm alive. Payments have been arranged through the moneylender Harivam."

Everyone in Sharakhai knew Harivam to be a fair lender, but a particularly ruthless enemy if crossed. He had the muscle and the reputation Ihsan required to ensure Zevi wouldn't try to influence him unduly before Ihsan was able to put Sharakhai on safe footing.

"Let's get to the details, shall we?" Ihsan stood and moved a chair so that it was across from his. "Time for the frog to sing."

Zevi glowered at the chair, then lumbered forward and sat in it.

"First," Ihsan continued, "the offer I made to you in my palace still stands: a permanent seat in the House of Stone, trade rights with some of the finest producers of wine and brandy in all of Qaimir. Second, as I've just mentioned, every week over the next three years, Harivam will make payments to your people to cover their wages, including a rather sizable bonus at the end—that is, so long as he gets a message from me indicating I'm still alive."

Zevi swallowed, tried to cover it up by working his jaw back and forth. "And if Harivam doesn't receive such a message?"

"I'm glad you asked. In that case, the entire three years' worth of wages and bonuses will be converted to a bounty on your head, which will be offered not only to your employees, but to the worst scoundrels, miscreants, and curs the west end has to offer. You won't be safe stepping foot outside the House of Kings, and I dare say you'd want to tread lightly *within* those walls as well. As we're both aware, the palaces of Tauriyat suffer not from a lack of opportunists."

Zevi's nostrils flared as he glanced at Shohreh. "And what, pray tell, does the humming frog require for such services?"

"No difficult thing for a wily predator such as yourself. First, you will speak to as many lords as you can, today, and convince them that the covenant's passage is in their best interests. You can start with Mehmed's excitable younger brother, Yavin."

"Yavin?"

"Come, Zevi. You know as well as I that he's been running around the city at your behest, threatening anyone with violence if he thinks they're ready to support the covenant."

Zevi shrugged. "Despite what you may think, I'm not Yavin's keeper."

Ihsan smiled. "See to it that you become so. Second, you will attend the council vote tomorrow. Not only will you vote for the covenant, you will also make an impassioned speech, touting its many merits." He paused. "I hope you can see past the somewhat crude methods I'm employing, Zevi. You stand to benefit greatly from the covenant's passage. In a few short months, you will rule as a King along the Trough and beyond."

"Is there more?"

"Yes. You will leave me and my daughter alone. You will make no move against Shohreh. And you will call Nazanin off."

Zevi's look of angry sufferance faded. His mouth opened and closed. "I can agree to the first two, but I'm afraid the last is outside my purview."

"Come now, Zevi."

"I'm telling you the truth. Nazanin takes no orders from *me*."

Ihsan found himself flat-footed. He'd been so sure. "Are you saying you *didn't* send Nazanin to kill me?"

"Had she come to me after returning to the city, I might have. But she didn't. I haven't seen Nazanin in over a year."

Ihsan closed his eyes, cursed himself for a fool. *Mehmed* had sent Nazanin, not Zevi. He'd been bargaining with the wrong man. "Arrange a meeting with your cousin, then."

"That's going to be rather difficult. Mehmed has gone into hiding and likely won't resurface until the council vote."

"I heard," Ihsan said, "but do you really expect me to believe he didn't tell *you* where he was going?"

"I don't care if you believe me or not—"

A loud knock came at the door. "Lord Zevi? There's someone here. A messenger."

"When I'm done," Zevi called loudly.

"The message isn't for you, Lord Zevi, but the King."

Zevi turned to Ihsan with a questioning look.

A feeling of deep dread stole over Ihsan. He had no idea what the messenger had been sent to deliver, but he was sure he wasn't going to like it. "Send him in."

The door opened and a hook-nosed messenger in green livery stepped inside. Shohreh accepted the note, and the messenger exhaled a long breath, bowed, and left. Shohreh gave the scroll a cursory inspection, sniffed it, then handed it to Ihsan.

Ihsan broke the seal and unfurled the paper.

The sun dawns tomorrow on a monumental decision for Sharakhai. Conditions have changed. No longer are you required to leave the city. Instead, you will attend the coming council at the Sun Palace. You will vote to restore the houses that have stood from the beginning of your reign and beyond and thereby return Sharakhai to its former glory.

Only when this is done can negotiations for the safe return of your daughter begin.

Ihsan felt himself go cold. His breath came rapidly, but he couldn't get seem to get enough air. Shohreh shook her head, questioning him, and he handed her the note. Then, with all the calm he could muster, he said to Zevi, "Remember the tale I told you here today. Remember what I've asked you to do. Most of all, Zevi, remember the bounty on your bloody fucking head."

He left without another word, Shohreh trailing behind him. They ran to the stables. The stable boy stared at them as they mounted. Then they rode north as fast as their mounts would carry them, toward Tariq's estate.

Chapter Eight

They rode hard up the drive to Tariq's estate. Tariq emerged from the heavy doors of the manor to greet them, a bloody bandage covering his head.

"Where's Ransaneh?" Ihsan asked as he and Shohreh slipped down from their horses.

"Gone"—Tariq's gaze slid to Shohreh—"taken by Nazanin."

"Goezhen's pendulous balls! You said you'd have men watching her! What happened?"

Tariq looked like he was about to bark back a reply, but then he clamped his mouth shut, spun, and headed back inside. Ihsan and Shohreh shared confused looks, then followed Tariq into the manor, up the central stairs, and down the hallway toward the rooms Ihsan and Shohreh had been given. Halfway along it, two men lay sprawled on the fine tawny carpet. Their eyes were open, their lips blue. Neither was breathing.

"They were good men," Tariq said, staring down at them, "but also simple soldiers, ex-Spears. No match for a Kestrel." On the carpet beside the nearest of the two men lay a pair of tiny darts with downy red fletching. Tariq crouched and picked one of them up, held it out for Shohreh to see. "Look familiar?"

Shohreh nodded. "It would have been coated with poison."

"Is that so?" Tariq sneered. "I never would have guessed." He threw the dart back onto the carpet, then motioned to the open doorway on their right—Ihsan's room. "There's more."

Ihsan stepped inside, his dread deepening, and found Tariq's heavy-set cook pressing a damp cloth to Mala's forehead. The girl lay on the bed, her shirt off, bloody bandages around her arms, rib cage, waist, and legs.

"Bloody gods." Shohreh rushed to the bed, knelt beside it, and checked Mala's forehead. "She's burning up."

"I've only had time to bind her wounds," the cook said. "Most of them need stitching."

Shohreh hurried to the room across the hall and returned with her leather satchel. "My Lord King, I'm sorry, but I need to tend to Mala. I'll help you find your daughter once Mala is stabilized."

"Of course," Ihsan said. "Can I be of service in any way?"

Shohreh shook her head as she set the satchel onto the bed and began rummaging through it. "Two is enough."

Tariq stood in the doorway behind Ihsan. "I was downstairs when it happened. I heard a crash. I grabbed a sword and ran upstairs and found Mala going toe-to-toe with Nazanin. I rushed in"—he stared down at his hands—"traded a few blows with her, no more, and she smashed me in the side of the head with the pommel of her shamshir. When I woke, Mala was bleeding on the floor and Ransaneh was gone."

Ihsan blinked. Words escaped him.

Tariq's look was sympathetic, which was a fair bit more than Ihsan had expected from a man who'd done this out of loyalty to his mentor and former master. "Any idea where Nazanin would have taken her?"

"None," Ihsan said.

"I could ask around, if you'd like."

"Thank you," Ihsan said. "I would be in your debt."

Tariq nodded. "May the gods return her to you." He turned and left—to set wheels into motion, Ihsan supposed.

Tariq's network in Sharakhai was not inconsiderable, but Ihsan doubted it would provide any useful information on Nazanin or her whereabouts in time to make a difference. As he thought about where Nazanin might have taken Ransaneh, he was struck by the apparent ease with which the Kestrel had found him. Stealing into his palace was one thing. Finding him at the temple, and then at Tariq's estate, was quite another. It bordered on the arcane.

Slow down, Ihsan. Think. She's only a woman, not a blood mage.

The very notion made him think Davud might be involved, or one of the magi from the Enclave. But he discarded the idea immediately. Why would any of the city's blood magi be working against him when their nominal leader, Davud himself, had allied with Ihsan?

Nazanin must have had another source of information.

Ihsan gazed beyond Shoreh and the cook working on Mala, to the balcony doors. There, barely visible over the tops of the acacias, was Tauriyat and the House of Kings.

And suddenly Ihsan understood. He knew who'd betrayed him.

Chapter Nine

Late that night, Ihsan carried a brass lantern to Nayyan's laboratory. Much had changed since his last visit. The books on the floors had been returned to the shelves and stacked neatly. The vials, beakers, and other alchemycal equipment had been placed in an orderly manner along the worktables. The broken glass and stains on the floor were gone. There wasn't a sign of dust anywhere, not even on the high, stained-glass windows.

Ihsan worried that the toxin he'd come for would be missing, but when he rummaged through the large apothecary cabinet and found the drawers filled with various ingredients, he felt sure he'd find it eventually. It took him some time—there were several hundred to search through, and he had only the vaguest recollection of the particular ingredient's precise location—but finally, he found it: a drawer containing a lone vial. The vial contained the venom of the dancing butcher of Kundhun, the spider from the story Ihsan had told Zevi.

As he dropped the vial into the leather bag at his belt, his attention was drawn to a bright lantern approaching the entrance to the room. Tolovan stood in the doorway in his nightclothes and slippers. "My Lord King ... what are you doing here?"

"It *is* still my palace, Tolovan."

"Of course, my King"—Tolovan cast the lantern about the room, seemingly fearful they weren't alone—"but there's danger here. You said so yourself."

He wasn't wrong, but in truth, it was the path to the palace itself that had posed the greatest danger. The one he would normally have taken led through the House of Maidens and along King's Road. Mehmed would surely have learned of his passage had he taken it, which was why he'd taken a horse into the desert and entered the House of Kings through King's Harbor instead. With the harbor gates still broken and the harbor itself still controlled by the Mireans, entry hadn't been easy, precisely. But the Mirean commanders trusted him, at least far enough that they'd let him pass with only a handful of questions. So it was that Ihsan had made his way up to his palace, where he'd commanded the guards to send Tolovan to attend him in Nayyan's laboratory.

"I needed to gather a thing or two that I'd forgotten," Ihsan said. He moved to a stool and sat on it.

When he motioned to a second stool, an indication Tolovan should join him, Tolovan looked back at the empty doorway. "Wouldn't you be more comfortable beside a fire, my King? We could retire to your apartments—"

"Please"—Ihsan motioned to the stool again—"sit."

Tolovan slowly pulled the second stool over, still glancing at the hallway, and sat. He set the lantern on the table beside him, shivered when the handle clanked loudly against the glass shroud.

"Is something the matter, Tolovan?"

"It's only this business with your grandsons, with Nazanin. It has me on edge."

"Me as well," Ihsan said with a smile.

"Of course, my Lord King. When I received your message that Ransaneh had been taken ..." He grimaced, and Ihsan couldn't tell if it was genuine or not. "My heart breaks thinking of all she must be going through."

"Yes, well, we'll come back to that. When last we spoke, you said you were off to speak to the Widow. Did you?"

"I did." Tolovan's eyes darted around the room. "She told me she did indeed search far and wide for a curative for the black mould. She found little, sadly, and it's been decades since her husband's passing. The apothecary who was helping her now lives in Qaimir. She promised to send a message to him, to see if he knew more."

Ihsan was disappointed, but he could hardly spare a thought about the black mould. He was too focused on the revelation he'd had at Tariq's estate, the reason behind Nazanin's finding him with such frightening accuracy. "Sitting here," he said, casting his gaze over the room, "I can't help but think Nayyan is watching over me. It feels like she's already judged me and found me wanting. Not only did I fail to save *her*, thus far I've failed my pledge to provide our daughter a home she can grow up in without fear of being taken or slain because of her heritage. It's a heavy burden, Tolovan—"

"I'm certain it is, my Lord King."

"—made all the more burdensome when those for whom I care, those I trust, betray me."

Tolovan had opened his mouth to say more, but he closed it again. He seemed to calm a bit. He looked like a prisoner sentenced to hang who, only as the noose was slipping over his head and tightening around his neck, became accepting of his fate.

"Had it only been Nazanin's ambushing me at Naamdah's temple," Ihsan said, "I might have written it off as keen intuition, but to have her find me again so soon smacks of something more. Either we were followed or someone told her where we were. I ruled out the former as too coincidental. Shohreh and I were careful, both in approaching Tariq and while heading to his estate. Tariq himself might have fed the information to Mehmed, but he had no reason to. Nor did Shohreh. There's only one other person who had the information and access to Mehmed himself. You, Tolovan."

Tolovan's eyes reddened. Tears welled. *Tears!* In all their years together, Ihsan had never seen his stoic vizir cry. "I never meant for Ransaneh to be hurt."

"Horseshit, Tolovan. What did you *think* they were going to do with her?"

"Well, I didn't think Mehmed would take her from you."

"Then you're a bloody fool."

Tolovan blinked his tears away but said nothing.

"Of everyone," Ihsan went on, "the last person I thought would betray me was you. We've seen the worst the desert has to offer and lived to tell the tale. You helped me and Nayyan every step of the way. Why did you do it, Tolovan? What did Mehmed offer you? Wealth? A life of leisure? A position in his household?"

Tolovan's eyes narrowed as he met Ihsan's gaze. "All those years, I was fighting for what I thought *you* were fighting for." He waved to the patio doors, beyond which lay the slopes of Tauriyat. "You told me you wanted Eventide. You told me you wanted to rule Sharakhai. *I* wanted that as well, not for myself, but to see you stand at the top of the mountain, alone. I *admired* you. But then came the business with the gateway, with Ashael, with Nayyan. You let the dream wither and die. You bent the knee to *Davud*, a bread baker's son, for the gods' sake, a bloody *commoner*." He practically spat the word. "The moment you did that, you gave up on your dream and you gave up on mine as well. I don't know what happened to you, my Lord King. I don't know what could have influenced you so, but when I realized you'd truly given up, I grew blind with rage. Sharakhai is set to become a shadow of what it once was. You *must* see that by now."

Ihsan suddenly realized Tolovan had been wearing a mask of concern to hide his fury. Ihsan should have recognized the signs earlier, especially in Tolovan, a man he'd schemed with for decades. He'd just been so focused on Ransaneh and the covenant, he hadn't stopped to think of everything Tolovan would be forced to sacrifice should Ihsan's plans succeed.

Ihsan felt like he should be angry—and he was, to a degree—but he also regretted the path he'd chosen, regretted the missteps he'd made that had prompted Tolovan to betray him. He wasn't quite sure when he decided to tell Tolovan the truth, but the more he thought about it, the more it felt like the right course. The *only* course. He had to find his daughter, and to do that, he needed to regain Tolovan's trust.

"I'm dying, Tolovan."

Tolovan's head jerked back. "What?"

"The black mould. The cure from the Widow … It wasn't for Ransaneh. It was for me." He lifted the lantern, then pulled his lower lip down so Tolovan could see the brown spots. He stuck his tongue out so the ones at the back could be seen as well. Then he set the lantern down and waved to the room around them. "It was the elixir Nayyan created that caused it."

"I …" Tolovan shook his head and swallowed audibly. "I didn't know. I'm sorry."

"Do you see now? I made a vow to Nayyan, my queen, *your* queen. I promised her I would make this city safe for our daughter to grow up in. That vow is not yet fulfilled. We've reached an accord with Mirea, but if Mehmed has his way, the city will be plunged back into war. I can't let that happen. I won't." He allowed several seconds to pass so Tolovan could absorb all he'd told him. "Where is Ransaneh, Tolovan? Where did Nazanin take her?"

"I only told Mehmed where you were. As I said, I didn't know he was going to order Nazanin to take Ransaneh."

"You must know something."

Tolovan's gaze traveled beyond the stained-glass windows, where the twin moons hung low in the star-filled sky. "When I met with Mehmed and Nazanin, I had them brought to your audience chamber. I watched them through your peephole, listened to them from behind the walls. Mehmed feared you'd find him and use your power on him, which was surely why he went into hiding. He asked Nazanin if everything had been prepared. She said yes, but that she had to dig up her winter clothing. She said it was cold in that place."

"Cold in *what* place?"

"I'm not certain, but Mehmed asked her if she felt anything strange. 'A touch of the dead,' is how he put it."

"A touch of the dead?"

"Just so. A boneyard, perhaps?"

"If it was a boneyard, she wouldn't have had to dig up her winter clothing."

"A crypt, then, or a dungeon."

A touch of the dead, Ihsan mused. And then he had it. He knew where Nazanin was hiding. "They're in the cavern, Tolovan. The cavern below the mountain."

Chapter Ten

As Ihsan walked along the tunnels deep below the Sun Palace, he was reminded of other visits to this place. Then, he *had* felt a touch of the dead, and it had gone well beyond the cold that pervaded the tunnels and caverns. It was to do with the gateway, the doorway between worlds. That doorway had since been closed, which was why he felt nothing beyond a bone-deep chill. But it made sense why Mehmed would have asked—until a week ago, one *would* have felt the touch of the dead, especially here.

Ihsan carried a small bullseye lantern to light the way, but on seeing a soft light ahead, he blew it out and set it down on the tunnel's rocky floor. The sound of dripping water was everywhere. Even so, he was careful not to make a noise as he padded forward. The tunnel had once been covered with the creeping roots of the adichara trees, which muffled the echo of sounds. Those were gone as well. Queen Alansal's soldiers had cleared them away so she and her people had unobstructed access to the cavern that lay ahead, which only heightened his fear of being discovered.

His heart pounded as he neared the mouth of the tunnel. He wondered what state Ransaneh would be in. Was she being fed? Cared for in any way beyond what was needed to keep her alive? He was terrified that the moment he showed his face, Nazanin would slay Ransaneh.

Ahead, the massive cavern opened up, its heights and depths lost to darkness. To his left was a small but lively fire. Near it was a pile of what looked to be roots, the ones Ihsan had thought had all been cleared away. It made some sense that some would still be found nearby—they couldn't *all* have been cleared, Ihsan supposed.

Ihsan approached the fire warily. Beyond it, a bedroll was laid out on the cavern floor. Farther into the darkness, he saw a canvas bag and a large wicker basket.

"Nazanin?" Ihsan called into the darkness. "Nazanin, I only wish to talk."

When his calls were met by silence, he approached the fire carefully, peering into the darkness beyond it as he went. He felt the warmth of the fire as he passed it by, felt it fade as he neared the basket. He was still trying to determine whether there was anything in it when a voice called from the darkness to his right.

"Ihsan, watch out!"

It was Shohreh.

He dove instinctively to his right. Even so, the arrow that came whistling out of the darkness scraped across his left thigh. Blue powder burst into the air. It smelled like white lilies. He clamped his mouth shut and tried not to breathe, but in his surprise, he'd sucked some of it in. He was already feeling lightheaded. The arrow had been a powderhead, a payload in place of an arrowhead. The powder had been intended to disorient at the very least. More likely it had been to knock him out, possibly to kill him.

Shohreh's warning had allowed him to escape the worst of the cloud, but it was spreading around the basket. He staggered toward the basket, dragged it away from the fire. Only when he was clear of the powder did he spare a moment to look inside. There, lying in a pile of blankets, was Ransaneh. Her eyes were open, but they were heavy, almost languid. It was likely because of the powder, but it could also be from Nazanin having drugged her. Both possibilities enraged him.

From the darkness came the sounds of ringing steel. When Ihsan had told Shohreh of Ransaneh's location, she had insisted on joining him. She'd plotted an alternate approach to the cavern in hopes of catching Nazanin unawares, but in this, she'd clearly failed.

Ihsan took several deep breaths, and some of the powder's dizzying effects faded. He touched Ransaneh's cheek. "Daddy will be back shortly."

He ran to the fire and took up a thick length of burning root. He rushed toward the clanging metal and found the two women fighting in a large alcove deeper into the cavern. Their ebon blades clashed. Their red turbans and battle dresses were reduced to shades of black in the inky darkness.

Ihsan summoned the power of his voice. He'd been worried on the way here that it would fail him, but anger helped, and he was burning with rage.

"Nazanin, you will stop!" he called.

He felt his power flow, yet the women continued to trade blows. "Nazanin, stop!" he called again and tossed the burning root into the alcove. "Lower your sword!"

The flaming root twirled through the air. Landed on the stone floor near them.

And still, the women fought on.

Nazanin struck low, slicing Shohreh's leg, then high. Shohreh parried the blow, but she was wounded and off-balance. Nazanin struck a two-handed blow that sent Shohreh reeling, but Shohreh twisted and grabbed Nazanin's turban. She pulled hard, falling away, unfurling the headdress. With it came a white bandage that had been wrapped around Nazanin's ears.

"Now, Ihsan!" Shohreh called. She staggered backward and fell.

The bandage, Ihsan understood, had muffled the sound of Ihsan's voice, perhaps blocked it entirely. As Nazanin charged forward, her sword raised high, he roared, "Nazanin, stop!"

How his mouth ached. How it burned from the power flowing through it.

Though Nazanin's momentum carried her forward, her footsteps faltered, then stopped altogether. She lowered her shamshir and stared into the darkness.

"Sheathe your blade," Ihsan commanded.

Nazanin fumbled awkwardly with the weapon but managed to slide it into its scabbard.

Ihsan glanced toward the fire and saw that the cloud had dissipated. "Go to the fire," he said to Nazanin, "then kneel."

As she moved to obey, Ihsan lifted Shohreh from the floor and helped her over to the fire, retrieving Ransaneh's basket along the way. After setting the basket behind him, far from Nazanin, he took his place around the fire so that the three of them formed a rough triangle—Ihsan and Shohreh standing, Nazanin kneeling.

In the light of the fire, Shohreh was able to read Ihsan's lips. "Are you well?" he asked her.

Though bleeding from several cuts, she nodded. "Well enough."

Ihsan turned toward Nazanin. Her face was calm, but her chin was quivering as she fought Ihsan's command.

"Did you drug my daughter?" Ihsan asked her.

Nazanin nodded.

Ihsan's fury was so great he nearly drew his knife, ready to slit her throat. "What did you use?"

"A distillation of peony and motherwort."

Ihsan glanced at Shohreh.

"It's a mild soporific. Ransaneh shouldn't be in any danger unless the dose was very heavy."

"Was it?" Ihsan asked the Kestrel.

"No," replied Nazanin.

Content that Ransaneh was safe, he moved on to the business at hand. "Where is Mehmed hiding?"

At this Nazanin shook harder. Her face turned beet red.

"I asked you where Mehmed is hiding." Ihsan allowed more power to leech into his voice. Having used it so recently, the pain it brought on was terrible.

"He's hiding in the boatyard," Nazanin said.

One of Mehmed's side businesses was a boatyard that rented flat-bottomed riverboats to tourists in the rainy season, gave tours on horse-drawn sleighs at other times.

Ihsan retrieved the small glass vial from the leather pouch at his belt. "I'd planned on saving this for Mehmed, but given all you've done to my daughter, I think it more appropriate for you." He held the vial out. "Take it."

Nazanin grasped the little flask in her trembling hand, but her shivering had grown worse. Ihsan's power wasn't what it once was, but it was enough for this—she was still spellbound. As she held the vial before her, her gaze flicked between the clear liquid and Ihsan.

"Go ahead," Ihsan said. "I'll allow the question."

"What is it?"

"Venom from a particular spider in Kundhun known as the dancing butcher. Do you know it?"

Nazanin shook her head.

"It earned that name from the way it dances about after biting its prey and injecting it with poison. The poison causes paralysis, which allows the spider to drag its victims back to its burrow, where it feasts. Interestingly, it isn't the paralysis that kills those who drink it."

Nazanin stared at the vial, refusing to ask the obvious question.

He crouched beside her, close enough to kiss her cheek. "What kills them is their own saliva, which the venom causes them to produce in rather surprising amounts. With their choking and coughing reflexes numbed by the paralytic, they drown in their own spit." He let the words sink in before saying, "Drink it, Nazanin, the entire vial."

The pain inside his mouth was worse than ever. Tears blurred his vision. He let the pain flow, let the tears fall. Nazanin was fighting him harder than ever.

Her hands quivered as she pulled the cork stopper. She let out a long groan, lifted the vial, and poured the liquid onto her waiting tongue, into her mouth.

Each drop looked like a fire opal, the stream a spill of gemstones. Her breath, jackal quick earlier, began to slow. The fierce determination in her eyes faded. Her eyelids went heavy. When Ihsan pressed her gently backward, she simply fell over, onto the cold cavern floor, and stared up into the inky darkness. Her breath grew raspy. Then it sounded as if she were choking. Then she went silent and perfectly still.

Shohreh stared at her, perhaps regretting all that had happened, but soon enough she was staring intensely at Ihsan. "So, what now?"

"May I ask a favor of you? Can you take Ransaneh to Tariq's?"

"Of course, but …" She stared at the basket, then Nazanin. "You don't want help with Mehmed?"

Ihsan shook his head and picked up a flaming brand from the fire. "I'll return to the estate as soon as I'm able."

He got up and returned to the dark tunnel, lighting the way with the burning root. He might have accepted Shohreh's offer had it not felt as if Nayyan were watching over him, watching over Ransaneh as well, and that she was helping him from the land beyond. The power of his voice would remain with him for a while yet, he was certain, at least long enough to deal with the likes of Mehmed.

Chapter Eleven

On the day of the council vote, Mehmed woke in the early morning darkness. He sat up in his cot, then tried, unsuccessfully, to work out the kinks that sleeping on a length of canvas for days had produced. The accommodations were inconvenient—he'd been holed up in the back room of the boathouse for days—but they were necessary, and a small enough price to pay. He'd gone to the vacant business to prevent King Ihsan from using his power on him, and now the danger had all but passed.

"Azhdan?" He rose, walked to the window, and took up the pitcher of water from the table below it. "Prepare some tea, won't you?"

After pouring water into the ceramic basin, he opened the shutters and stared at the dry banks of the canal, the sandstone buildings beyond. Above them loomed Tauriyat, tall and imposing. Near its peak, lit golden by the rising sun, was Eventide, a palace that, more than any of the others on the mountain, represented honor, birthright, and, most of all, *authority* in Sharakhai. It had been so for centuries and would be so again, despite the Mireans having defiled it these past many months.

Mehmed wetted a rag in the basin, scrubbed his face vigorously, then ran the cool cloth over his neck. When he was done, he folded the rag, laid it across the edge of the basin, and took his turban from its hook and began winding it around his head. "Azhdan," he called, louder this time, "tea!"

Again, he received no answer, which was odd—the servant's muttering and scraping about had awoken Mehmed only moments ago. Perhaps he'd gone to fetch water or food.

He finished the final wrap of his turban and stared at the slopes of Tauriyat. In a few hours, the council of lords would vote on whether to ratify Davud Mahzun'ava's covenant. Mehmed had spoken to a dozen lords who'd been on the fence. He'd spoken to Zevi as well about their grandfather's infantile attempt to turn him.

In a way, it was too bad Zevi was still alive and breathing. Part of the reason Mehmed had hidden himself away was so that all the focus would be on his cousin. He'd secretly hoped Ihsan would kill him, which would forge the path for *Mehmed* to take Ihsan's throne when his grandfather was either killed or run out of the city. But the winds of fate were fickle in the desert, and Ihsan had done what he'd done.

Zevi had been nervous long into Mehmed's talk with him. Harivam, the moneylender with whom Ihsan had apparently worked out an arrangement to pay Zevi's seamstresses and enforcers, was no one to fool around with. But when Mehmed assured him he'd personally help negotiate a new arrangement with Harivam, Zevi had agreed to vote the way Mehmed wanted him to. Many of the other lords Mehmed had spoken with appeared ready to align with him as well.

Ihsan had been the most immediate threat, but with his daughter safe with Nazanin, Mehmed was sure he'd be kept in check. He might even do as Mehmed had commanded in his note and campaign *for* the covenant. Though Mehmed recognized the next few weeks would be a sandstorm of change, he was certain that, when the dunes had shifted for good, Eventide would be his.

He made a few final adjustments to his turban in front of the brass mirror by the window, then walked to the front room, where fares had formerly been sold for tours. The business, all but deserted for years, had become dusty and cluttered with disuse.

"Azhdan!"

The front door had been left ajar. From beyond it came a voice. "Azhdan is indisposed, I'm afraid."

By Bakhi's bright hammer, the voice was King Ihsan's. Mehmed's heart began to gallop. It came on so suddenly he coughed.

He stepped carefully toward the front of the room, swung the creaking door wide. There, in the dusty yard beyond the porch, Ihsan stood among the racks of flat-bottomed boats. Seeing the kenshar at Ihsan's belt, Mehmed suddenly wished he hadn't left his own in the back room. It was only a broad-bladed jambiya, a rather dull, ceremonial piece, but it would have been *something*.

"Don't be shy, Mehmed." King Ihsan spread his arms wide. His smile was even broader. "It's a new day, and the possibilities are *endless*."

Mehmed stepped to the edge of the porch but couldn't find it in himself to go farther. "What are you doing here?"

"Why, I've come to tell you a story."

"A story?"

Ihsan headed toward the boat launch, beyond which lay the dry bed of the canal. "Walk with me, Mehmed."

Mehmed thought about denying his request. He thought about going back inside and getting his knife. He thought about picking up the oar leaning against the boathouse wall and smashing in the back of Ihsan's head. But the simple truth was, he was terrified of his grandfather. To have his will taken from him would be like dying a little death. It was half the reason he'd hidden himself away until he was sure Ihsan could be controlled.

His thoughts still warring, he followed Ihsan toward the canal. As he strode across the dry dirt, a mule brayed, the telltale sign of the miller farther down the canal having begun his workday. As the two of them reached the canal's flat, rocky bed, Mehmed found himself wondering whether Ihsan actually *had* used his power on him. He'd never experienced it. Perhaps, to the person commanded, it didn't *feel* like a compulsion, more like his own thoughts leading him to what seemed like a perfectly reasonable course of action.

He shivered as Ihsan suddenly spoke.

"From time to time," he said in a singsong manner, "there are bodies found face down in the Haddah."

Mehmed said nothing. A short distance ahead, a stone bridge spanned the top of the canal. Two Silver Spears rode over it on horseback. Mehmed nearly called out to them. But what would he say? And why by the Great

Mother would they listen to *him* over their King? Soon the Spears were gone, the sounds of their horses' clopping hooves lost behind a clutch of mudbrick homes.

"Mostly it's the drug lords who kill them," Ihsan continued, "sending a message, as it were. Sometimes it's the leader of a flock of gutter wrens, *acting* like a lord. The custom came from the desert tribes, though." Ihsan glanced over at him. "Did you know that?"

Mehmed shook his head. The stones crunched beneath their feet as they paced along the canal bed.

"The shaikhs, on finding that they could no longer abide the presence of a thief, murderer, or adulterer, would knife them, thereby cutting them from the tribe like a cancer. The shaikh would then place them face down in the sand, and the tribe would sail on. Any idea as to why it was always face down, Mehmed?"

"So they would be blinded?" Mehmed said. "So they couldn't find their way to the farther fields?"

"That's what most people think, but in truth, it's the exact opposite. You see, the shaikhs of old were always careful to give offenders opportunities to atone for their sins. Those who chose not to were slain and placed face down in the sand so they would lie in eternal darkness. For darkness, it was believed, would allow them to see their failures that much more clearly. It was believed that those in the next life would see them as well, which would lead to atonement, redemption."

The light of dawn dimmed somewhat as they headed beneath the stone bridge the Spears had passed over. When they came to the center of it, Ihsan stopped and turned.

Mehmed stopped as well, several paces from Ihsan. "If you kill me, you'll never get what you want."

Ihsan drew his kenshar. The curved blade shone dully in the early morning light. "Won't I?"

Mehmed shook his head. "It will turn more of them against you. Against Davud. Against the *covenant*."

"Your reasoning?"

"It will show the covenant can't stand on its own. It will show that what you're offering is a mirage and that the only real path forward is the way the city has been run for generations, for centuries. It's precisely why Davud told everyone in his camp to step carefully. No coercion. No threats. Because they'd have the opposite effect of what he's looking for."

"He told me much the same. But Davud …" Ihsan's gaze wandered overhead—to the bridge's supports, perhaps, or the cobwebs in between. "How can I say this politely? Davud has been holding the reins of power for months. I've been holding them for *centuries*. He's idealistic, and I admire that about him, but he doesn't understand how the lords and ladies of this city think. In the coming hours, when they learn of your death, they will understand that they, too, are threatened. They'll understand, just as Zevi does, that the vote they're about to take places their own lives on the betting line."

"A house built on coercion will surely crumble."

"That's where you're wrong, Mehmed. The covenant is sound. Your supposed allies haven't given it its due. They will eventually, and by then it will be too late to stop the change that's coming. Davud can have his principled approach tomorrow, when it has a real chance at succeeding. Today is a day for other, more pragmatic means."

Mehmed raised his hands. "King Ihsan, Grandfather, *please*. It's not too late for the two of us to make an arrangement!"

At this, Ihsan rushed forward, grabbed Mehmed's thawb, and drove the knife deep into his gut. Pain seared the left side of his chest, just below his heart. He fell backward onto the parched earth, and Ihsan fell with him, driving the knife deeper. Mehmed groaned. He clutched Ihsan's knife and tried to push it from his midsection, but he was already too weak.

King Ihsan was a handsome man, but just then his face was ugly, animalistic. "I hope the shaikhs were right, Mehmed. I hope when I place you face down on the riverbed, you *will* see the wrongs you've committed. I hope those in the land beyond see it as well, because if so, Nayyan will be there, waiting for you—"he drew the knife from Mehmed's gut and plunged it deep again"—and she'll be *much* less merciful than I've been."

Mehmed wanted to say more. He wanted to plead for his life, even though he knew it was ending. He wanted to laugh in Ihsan's face, tell him his actions had doomed no one but himself and his daughter. He wanted to say he'd once looked up to his grandfather, but that Ihsan become a frail, laughable shadow of his former self.

But he couldn't. It was too painful.

And then the glorious morning that was dawning over Sharakhai went dark.

Chapter Twelve

Four days later, Ihsan sat on the roof of a three-story tea house. On the rickety table before him were two empty teacups and a pot of jasmine tea. Ransaneh, having downed a considerable amount of mashed berries and goat's milk, was napping in a shaded basket on the chair beside him. The deck, with its mishmash of tables and chairs, was normally busy this time of day, but Ihsan had paid the proprietor handsomely to give him a bit of privacy as he took an important meeting. The rooftop served an additional purpose as well. It overlooked a particular manor that hugged the banks of the River Haddah.

Ihsan peered through his spyglass and spotted an old woman in black clothes sitting on a veranda. She was the Widow, the drug lord Ihsan had bid Tolovan speak to about a cure for the black mould. While he watched, a servant approached with a tall, older gentleman wearing dark clothes. Even from this distance, it was easy to recognize him as Tolovan.

On hearing a newcomer climbing the steps leading to the roof, Ihsan lowered the spyglass. Mala rose gingerly from the stairwell, which was more than a little surprising—he'd been expecting Shohreh, not her apprentice.

"The Crone sends her regrets," Mala said, lowering herself into the bent metal chair across from him. "She was detained in the House of Kings."

Ihsan was certain there was more to it than that. Shohreh had suffered Ihsan's presence—and, to her credit, mostly without complaint—but only because of her strong sense of duty to the city. Now that she was working closely with Davud at Ihsan's request, she was only too glad to be free of his company. Mala, meanwhile, was an intriguing young woman. She was powerful, skilled in bladecraft and more. She seemed fiercely loyal to Shohreh.

Mala sat straighter in her chair. "Stop staring."

"Forgive me," Ihsan replied with a smile, "you remind me of someone, is all, another young woman from the Shallows who went on to do great things." He raised the pot of jasmine tea and held the spout near her cup.

She immediately raised a hand. "I can't stay long."

He set the pot back down. "To business, then?"

Mala nodded. "It was a near thing, but the vote went in our favor."

Relief flooded through Ihsan. The vote on the covenant had been delayed after Mehmed's body was found. Ihsan had heard rumors of the uproar. Some of the lords blamed Davud for it, claiming he'd ordered Mehmed's murder to secure passage of the covenant. Others blamed Ihsan. The sheer number of voices raised against them had eroded Ihsan's confidence to the point that he felt he'd taken a grave misstep in killing Mehmed. In the days since, however, much of that early uproar had faded. Ihsan had seen evidence of more lords siding with the covenant, a change due in no small part to Zevi, who had quietly campaigned for its passage.

Now that the covenant had been approved, Ihsan wasn't sure how to feel. He was relieved, of course—he'd worked so hard for its passage— but the vote also marked a turning of the page for old Sharakhai. He was the last of the Sharakhani Kings. And while he might still return to his palace and hold power for a time, he knew his presence would only impede Davud's progress.

Of course, there was also the not inconsiderable threat to his life. "Has Shohreh found who put a bounty on my head?"

Mala nodded. "As you suspected, it was Yavin."

Unlike Zevi, Yavin had been calling for the burning of the covenant, the ouster of Queen Alansal and the Mireans, and the return of the House of Kings. He'd been so full-throated about it, and so dismissive of the obvious consequences, Ihsan suspected his bluster had actually *helped* Davud's cause, not impeded it.

Mala took a deep breath. "As a show of gratitude for putting the needs of the city and its people before your own, Shohreh has authorized me to present you with three offers. The first is to deal with Yavin."

"In what way?"

"In any way you deem appropriate."

Ihsan suddenly realized he'd underestimated the girl. She might be young, but she was well on her way to acquiring the cold disposition required of all Kestrels.

"No," Ihsan said finally, "better that the Crone not be perceived as linked to me."

"We'd ensure that nothing would be traced back to the Kestrels."

"We shouldn't press things," Ihsan said. "Mehmed's death is enough."

"Very well. With regards to the second offer"—she gazed to her left, toward the manor Ihsan had been spying earlier—"the Crone recognizes how difficult it might be for you to deal with your vizir in the manner he deserves. She wonders if you'd rather the Silver Spears hang him for treason."

Ihsan could just make out Tolovan sitting with the Widow. He and the Widow were taking a trip to Qaimir together to speak to the Widow's apothecary. Tolovan had offered to take the trip to learn what he could of the black mould in person. Ihsan had agreed with the understanding that, when Tolovan returned to Sharakhai, he would be a free man. Ihsan had made arrangements with Harivam, the moneylender. Tolovan would want for nothing the rest of his life.

Ihsan had of course been angry with Tolovan at first, but the blame for his betrayal couldn't be laid entirely at his feet. Ihsan should have known how his vizir would react. He should have told Tolovan more, sooner. He should have helped him see that the future was bright, not grim.

"Thank you," he said to Mala, "but I'll decline that offer as well." He paused, smiling wryly. "Is the third offer as bloody as the other two?"

"Not at all." Mala's gaze slid to Ransaneh, who'd just drawn in a sudden, sharp breath. "With regards to her final offer"—Mala drew her gaze back to Ihsan, seeming a bit melancholy—"Shohreh wishes you to know that we're aware of your disease."

Ihsan felt blood rush to his face. Without meaning to, he glanced toward the manor.

"It wasn't Tolovan," Mala said quickly.

"Then how did she learn of it?"

"Shohreh saw the lesions on your tongue. Given what happened to your queen, it wasn't difficult to guess the sort of affliction you were suffering from. We're well aware of how hungry the black mould is. We know your days are numbered. We will raise Ransaneh if you like. We'll tend to her, see she has a good home."

Ihsan's eyebrows rose. "*Shohreh* made this offer?"

Mala shrugged. "I may have had something to do with it."

For a time, Ihsan merely listened to the muffled sounds of a storyteller spinning a tale in the nearby square. He wasn't sure how to respond. Mala had certainly doted on Ransaneh, and she apparently had experience from taking care of her younger sister. Even so, Mala was destined to become a Kestrel. She'd be sent on progressively more dangerous missions, some of which would take her out of the city. And Shohreh herself, though dutiful, might grow to resent Ransaneh. She might not give her the sort of care she needed. And Ihsan couldn't ignore the distinct possibility that others would learn of Ransaneh's heritage. If that happened, people would come for her, whether it was Yavin, Zevi, or someone else who wanted to settle their scores with Ihsan via his daughter.

He couldn't do it, he decided. He had to find another home for her. "It's a kind and generous offer, truly," Ihsan said, "but I must decline."

Mala looked like she wanted to argue, but then she nodded. "As you wish." She stood. "I suppose this is farewell, King Ihsan."

"I suppose it is. Thank you for all you've done, Mala."

She bowed, deeper than Ihsan would have guessed, then walked tenderly to the stairs and took them down, into the belly of the tea house.

For a time, Ihsan remained on the rooftop. He watched Tolovan and the Widow stand and head inside the manor. A coach with a pair of horses was waiting outside. Servants were busy around it, preparing to bring Tolovan and the Widow to the southern harbor and their sandship bound for Qaimir. He wondered what would become of them, whether things would progress beyond a simple business arrangement.

"I hope so," he whispered.

To a round of applause and whistles for the end of the storyteller's tale, Ihsan stood and picked up Ransaneh's basket. Ransaneh stared up at him with her mismatched eyes.

"Well look who's awake," Ihsan said.

Ransaneh burbled.

"Come, Ransaneh." Ihsan picked up the basket and headed for the stairs. "Time to lose ourselves in the city."

POSTSCRIPT

ADRIAN COLLINS

The house I grew up in had bookshelves full of history books, and some of my earliest memories are of poring over them. When you read a great deal of history books, you'll find plenty of stories about kings, queens, dictators, Caesars, generals, lords and ladies, gang bosses, and other leaders being brought down by either their foes, or those they trusted.

When Bradley P. Beaulieu approached me to produce an anthology with *The King Must Fall* as a theme, I knew I'd found our next major project. This was definitely in my wheelhouse. Since we published *Evil is a Matter of Perspective* in 2017 our team and network has grown significantly, and I was so excited to see such an amazing line-up of authors come together over the following months in the lead up to the Kickstarter launch.

This project has not been without its challenges. We changed editors mid-project. The global pandemic has wreaked absolute havoc on print publishing and shipping. The same global upheaval has caused chaos in the lives of our team members, contributors, and backers.

Despite the challenges, I am so proud to have this book in your hands, and so thankful that through this prolonged production period you, the backer community, continued to trust us to deliver this book to you.

Thank you.

I hope the wait was worth it.

Adrian Collins
Editor in Chief
January 2022

ACKNOWLEDGEMENTS

None of this could have happened without 818 amazing fantasy fans raiding their treasuries, giving the project a shout out to their mates, and joining our Kickstarter or purchasing through BackerKit. As your currently un-overthrown liege, I wave my hand at you graciously.

KNIFE IN THE DARK

Robert Moulden, Tracy Kaplan, Duncan Bain, Jeremy Kear, Geoff Squire, Peter Gee, Michael Skolnik, Philip Overby, anonymous1453, D Kelly, Simon Dick, Brian Abrams, justwes,

Irrevenant, Mike Myers, Rich Riddle, Jessica Enfante, Bruce Villas, Nati, Rolf Laun, Jacob Magnusson, Lukasz Przywoski, Levi Ergott, Michael Blevins, Berni Dunne, Craig Hackl, GhostBob, KatiFelix, Ulrika, Rex Wilburn, Jonathan Terrington, Tim, Ian Radford, Hurley, Benjamin Widmer, Rick Galli, Elizabeth Tabler, Al Burke, Pierre Gauthier, Christopher Horn, Michael, James Lucas, Elliot Harper, Jessica, Massimiliano, Curmudgeon of Phoenix Rising, Chuck Dee, Joseph Hoopman, Marie Blanchet, Marian Goldeen, Joe Martin, Robert, Chani, Seth Lindberg, Chris Hawks, Luke Padgett, Sean Tadsen, Eddie Chew, Alan Baxter, Chris Haught, myshade1973, Serena Zaccagnini, john brennan, Jan Katins, Belisarius, Sam Courtney, Max Lamers, Matt Dickinson, Joanne Burrows, Clio Thielemans, sam, Dann Todd, John Coombs, JKB, Braude, Wolfgang Goetz, Y. K. Lee, MARIA PILAR SAN ROMAN, Lauren Maillet, Cory Cepelak, Jed Herne, Zachary West, William Clark, Dylan, Sebastian H., Claire Rosser, Benjamin Busseniers, Ernesto, Miguel Domingo, Carsten Skansen, Cédric Jeanneret, Gary Phillips, Ross Williams, Mayhem, Debbie Leonard, Jen Clark, Katie O'Brien, Joe Cannon, Calvin, Airsaber, Matt Knepper, Sean Mead, David Benson, Jon Paul Anthony Hart, Monique Park-Smith.

CROSSBOW BOLT FROM THE ALLEY

Darren Fry, Joshua King, Joey Shepherd, John Gabriel, Aaron van Dorn, Kenneth Bragg, Michał Kabza, Aitor, Kim Stoker, Kevin Mealey, Justin James, Steven McKinnon, Dharmendra Kapadia, Pamela Hamlet, James Gotaas, Si2Au, stuart hall, Psybernary, David T List, olivier74, Arun Andhavarapu, Richmond Camero, Esko Lakso, Aaron Markworth, Jonathan Strugnell, Caleb Indenbaum, Darren Fuller, Chris Lira, Chris Chapman, Tiffany Marcheterre, Daniel, Goran Zadravec, Giuseppe, GMark C, Rob Holland,

Nathan Edwards, Dan Tang, Patrick P., Christopher Meadows, Troy, James McLauchlan, Andre, Dave Versace, Stefan M Nardi, Saren Roberts, Steven Peiper, Eddie Coulter, Nicholas Passalacqua, Ben Galley, Jonathan K. Crisler, Brian Becker, John Hardey, Benjamin Hayes, Joshua Barratt, ana rubio, Marnilo C, Vitaly Gann, Peggy Kimbell, Pedro Alfaro, Wolfgang Klövekorn, naso.003, Jeff Granger, Matthew Braymiller, James Morton, Elliott Hill, James McStravick, Richard, Tim, Barbara Butler Long, Dmitrii Nechaev, Simon Rees, Ken Hoover, Lance, Raphael, Chris, David Souch, Mike Jones, Gary, J Eric Dennis, Paul Burrow, Christopher Gates, George Pusins, Patrick Kansa, CWeber, oishisushi911, Stephen Dowling, Dan Holland, Kerry Smith, David Mortman, Robert c Flipse, Dipin Nayee, Brian D Lambert, Strella, nama0011, Harry Giovanopoulos, Michael Brooker, David Brideau, Dylan Clements, techxplorer, BvB, Steven Roman, john ferrick, Jo Beere, Paul Gardiner, Geoffrey Jacoby, Piet Wenings, Michael Sterling, Cavscott, Hello, Kyleigh Grove, Louiz, Liza Williams, Jay Dalziel, Nikolas Eibich, Jeffrey Hamblen, Laramie Martinez, Jarrod Lewis, Michael Papa-Adams, Borja, Martín de Zavala, Alexander Rodriguez, Emily, Cody, Mark Reynolds, Jeffrey Estabrooks, Shannon Roe, Peter Burke, lastgreypoet, Leland Hulbert, Juan Hamers, Simeon Gavalas, John Drake Pennick, Kris Davidson, Jan Birch, Sam Coombs, incandescens, Rich Davis, Keyon Hejazi-Far, chuck gilpin, Shreyas Kulkarni, ML, Georg Wille, Chawin Narkraksa, Anas Abusalih, Tasos Markides, Michael Spredemann - 2 Old Guys Games, Ke Sizemore, Ainsley, Jonathon Whitington, John M. Portley, A, Rory J. Somers, Danny Whittaker, Rackshaw, Taylor Moe, Ky Fajardo, Lindsinho, Andy Munn, BB, Hope Terrell, Peter Engelbrektsson, Patrik, Richard Whipkey, George Mann, Brandon, Nick Canzoneri, James Cleaveley, Pablo Sancho, Wilfred Berkhof, Ivan, Beau Rowland, Amanda Nixon, FredH, Emery Shier, Constanza Mestre,

John Scritchfield, Marc S, Holly Dingwall, Lewis Davies,
Roger Mortimer, Steve Banks, Peter Thew, Kelly Hoolihan,
Richard Smeeton, Adawia, Jennifer Beltrame, Steve D. Howarth,
David Darby, Rohan Scammell, NicolasD, Marc De Vos,
Elliott Malone, Rob Stewart, Isaac 'Will It Work' Dansicker,
Nicklas Andersson, estrus, John Spainhour, Lisa Herrick,
Amy Schriever, Everette, Chris Robinson, Ronald, Kiwi Tokoeka,
João Beraldo, Sarah Simpson, David Zurek, Kieran, Tim,
Angela Misner, Matthew Cleverdon, Jess Turner, Denis Berthelsen,
John Miyasato, A, Eron Wyngarde, Fionn, John Thomas,
Jasmin Babaie Kermanshahi, Emy, Jonathan, Chandler.

TRAITOR AMONGST THE COURT

Callum, Martin Key, Sebastiaan, Charlotte Wyatt, Jedidiah Blake II,
Aaron S. Jones, Daniel Moore, Paul Grindrod, Anders M. Ytterdahl,
Arne Radtke, Alexander Denley, Michael Brewer, Paul English, Dawn
McQueen, Millie, Adam Kelly, David W, patrick boyle,
Henry Lopez, Margaret St. John, Jon Adams, Joe Sokol,
Martin Jackson, Michael Shearer, Justine Bergman, brandon,
Joel Norden, Courtney, Wes Spence, Melissa Shumake, Jeff Scifert,
Jon Auerbach, Felix Ortiz, Paulie Wenger, Jonathan Deighton, Katrin,
Pamela Wickert, Eric, Wegner, Tina, Anthony Acosta,
Quentin Clauwaert, Josh Uitvlugt, Keith West, Andrew Zavitsanos,
Jackson Robertson, Thomas L Walcher, Douglas Lumsden,
Scott Frederick, Sean M, Olli La, Tenille, Glenn Curry, Dale Russell,
Joseph Harley, Evan Miller, Anna Smith-Spark, Matthew Hoffman,
Jeremy Berg, Larry Couch, Christian Xavier, Robyn, Janaki J,
Tom Maloney, Erik Henriksen, Ryan Neely, Scott Maynard,
James Alexander Tivendale, Andie Frogley, Alyssa, Tom Smith,
Trendane, Dan Peck, Christopher Michael Fisher, Logan,
Richard Kvale, Andy Holcombe, Ariane, Bryan Jones,

William Leitzke, Joel Rosen, John, Dorothy, Raniere,
Emperor Surly, Bradley Harris, Yutaka Ohshima, Jackie McKenzie,
ROMAN YEREMENKO, Tim Hargreaves, Sarah Weston,
Mitch Kable, bill hall, Rhel ná DecVandé, Thomas Legg,
Peter Philpott, Michael, Charlie, Alexander Ourique,
Sebastian Zeh, Matt Johnson, Liam Simmons, Benjamin Brinkley,
Phillip Wood, Randy Arnold, Alicia Mckenzie, Jim Bassett,
Joe McCann, Major Havoc, N. Scott Pearson, Benjamin D. Sparrow,
Action City Comics & Toys, Thomas Booker, Mrinal, Corbin,
Ann Holland, Steve Pickering, Lisa Greiner Maughan,
Amy Zimlinghaus, Lynne Everett, Ras Mitmug, Ryan, Gary Chappell,
Bruce Fenton, Ray Barker, Stelios Koutrakis, Ryan Reasor,
Nate Aubin, Chris Slottee, Joshua McGinnis, Jeffery Heileson,
Seb Fabre, Grimgravy, Will Hunt, Renae Stephens,
Geoffrey Englebach, Michael Byrd, Bequie Oyler, William Stark,
Scott Buck, Austin Appleby, Sondra Fielder, Andrew Weir,
Edwin Betar, Matthew Carpenter, Karl Ansell, Kenneth Skaldebø,
Todd Sansing, Jake, Ben Losasso, Aaron Turko, Zac Welch,
William M Cornette, Hoot, Ben Edwards, Stephen Boucher, Miriam,
Andrew Preece, Edgar Middel, Kurt Woods, Brenda J Hand,
Michael Mesina, Allen W. Sharpe, Thomas Kramer, Dyrk Ashton,
Joshua, Jose Ramirez, Cameron Rush, Thomas Dimmick, Neil Kellie,
Julian Koslow, Christina Bentley, Cathy Green, Raven Oak, Thomas,
Christophor Rick & Magnetic Spaghetti, Cheri Kannarr, Joie Broin,
Robert Belus, Niklas Krampe, Gary O'Brien, Kata Szász,
Richard Larsen, S Naomi Scott, Chris Antony, Elizabeth Crissey,
Tabby W, April, Joshua Carlson, Hayley Coniam, Dylan Ingram,
Mark Hardy, somcpier, Adam Colclough, Jessica Meade,
Jared Ferguson, Mark Pickard, Sarah Rains, Hayden Meyer,
Andrew Morrow, Stephen Wroth, Richard, Olivia Smith,
Ivan Torres, Franc cassar, Elaewin, Gavin Gonya, John Winkelman,
Dan Frederick, Sue Armitage, Kevin Perez, echs Incognito,

John O'Hare, Fredrik Karén, Louise Löwenspets, Shivang Naik,
Ricciardi Luc, Marie Caswell, Joan Digney, Darren Lay, Joao Silva,
Simon Elmslie, Zaq, David LS, Christopher Kanagy, David Ruddick,
Kai Rasmussen Charlton, Fotios Zemenides, Steve L.,
Lucas Papadopoulos, Cameron Breslow, Justin A Rosenbaum, Tsutako,
Susan, Monika Samul, Darius Zimmermann, Dom Reseigh-Lincoln,
Rhys, Tony Weston, Dan DeLano, Isobel Case-Punter, Rob,
Kyle Yawn, Ryan Hacala, Kelly Jensen, Robert Krieg, Valentin Gelb,
Jennifer Jarvis-Schroeder, Dean Whirley, Curtis Moore, david green,
chay, Colten Spivey, Nathan, Travis LaVanway, Randy Lawson, joebar,
Malinda Cracknell, Jan Michal Balo, Brandon, RoriJ, Jake Lawler,
Kaylee Rae Reed, Ryteck, Steve, Turfa Auliarachman, Tyler,
Leland Eaves, Ross O'Dell, Cathy Atela, Michael Voss, Gabby,
Ben H, Dave, Edgar, Noel Rivera, Rich Velez, Daniel M, Jeremy Brett,
Nathaniel Lanza, Michael A Biggs, Djerri Nuijen, Maximiliaan Canik,
Cory Russell Miller, todd, Kevin Co, Jon Terry, Tim Jordan,
Shawn Polka, AdrianFL, David Decero, Jack van Beynen,
Tomás Benjamín González Zarzar, Deryk Noonkester, BookReader,
Andrew, Jesse Bullington, James Joyce, Steven Nicoll, Trevor Maskell,
Jay K, Caleb Parker, Louise Martin, Heather Allen, Darjush, MG,
Andromeda Taylor, Pearski, Bret Charles, Christine Tate,
Emily McCutcheon, J Goldsmith, Andrew Sember,
Wilfredo Quiles Jr, C-Em, Ericc Whetstone, Mathew, Mike Connell,
Deborah A Wolf, Jonathan Seiglie, David Griffiths, Libriomancer,
David Raposa, Alyssa Cooper, V.L., Andrew Lindsay.

TUCKERIZATIONS

Adam, stef, Marc Rasp, Edward Potter, Kyle Anderson, KaiserKai,
Chuck, Macra Bill, Tony, DiMatteo, Shaun Rosel, Dan Andrews,
Ethan Pollard, Luke Walker, Tony, Pieter Willems,
Nicholas Passalacqua, Karl Ansell, Adam Holliday, Wilfred Berkhof.

DUEL IN THE COURTYARD

Gauthier, Thomas Bull, Vidur Paliwal, Tony Muzi, Arthur Dixon, Marc, Don Forster, Holly Bowers, Sean Pruitt, Todd Roark, Clay Cannon, Tynyssen, Andrew Carter, Christopher, Scott Casey, Daniel, Scott Sizemore, Kasper Grøftehauge, peter crooks, Pablo Salas Mercado, Jerry Øzell Poteet, Bobby Lee, Sorkin Lidor, Gerald P. McDaniel, Erik, Robert Thompson, John Nicholson, Shoni Pampling, Stephen Vercoe, bryan, Jonathan Williams, Mark Timmony, Robin Hill, Iain Brabant, Evotrev@gmail.com, Adam Patterson, Sean Lynch, Kevin Kastelic, Dave Baughman, Luke Tyler, Sean Meichle, Adrianne Cavaioli, Mason White, Chris Corke, Mike KItchell, Giulio Torlai, Robert Parks, Dan Barnes, Steven Nadel, Chris meson, Terry Adams, Christopher Thomson, David Salchow, Aaron | Wizard Fire Digital, Mat Meillier, Michael Delaney, John Sabia, Patrick High, Brian Kerber, Henrik Sörensen, Pat Grogan, Jack McGuire, Jamey Owens, Doni Savvides, David Roth, Zoe, Dirk Berger, DJP, hellantoys, Paul, Erik Dyrelius, Judykins, Jaden Fullerton, Joe Rivers, Jonathan Lee, Kris S, Modern Art, Gabriel Hernandez, Carrie, Michael DeCuypere, Shannon Tusler, Steffan P. Arndt, Dhalkar, Jairred Lambert, oliver, Phil Wallace, Karl Olsen, Pat Spanfelner, Douglas Cline, Jamie Ayers, Adam Holliday, Nick Scharenberg, Dean McBride, ThePapaTee, Charlotte Jacobson, Sean McElligott, Jamie Mynott, Andrew, Richard Mandolfo, Jae.

ASSUALT ON THE THRONE ROOM

Adrian, Graham Dauncey, Pierce Erickson, Pieter Willems, Doug Thomson, Dr. Charles Elbert Norton III, Stuart March, Rod Cressey, Esper Wadih, Maxime Gregoire, Valyndimir, Steven Renner, snail, Joey Hendrickson, Tony Farana,

Summer Applebaum, Chris Reason, Michael McNamara,
Corbin Talley, Sue DeNies, John Idlor, Shawnhuffman, Kyle Spencer,
Curtiss Talley, roger, Alberto Martinez.

NON-LEVEL BACKERS

MangoMaraudr, Judy Lunsford, The Creative Fund by BackerKit,
Atthis Arts, LLC, Jennifer, Founders House Publishing,
Logan Westerlind, Outland Publications.

PRE-ORDERS FROM BACKERKIT

Daniel, Bianca Hoppe, Adrian, Justin Travis Call, inkshoe,
Jon A Shelky, youko, rce, Alan Gelder, Mark Amen, Steve Drew,
tyrexs, bobby, Aaron Charlesworth, Mark Nolan, Daniel, astrid,
Robert Armstrong, rob.

9 780648 178484